HENRY FIELDING

Joseph Andrews and *Shamela*

THE CROWELL CRITICAL LIBRARY

Henry James, *Washington Square*
edited by Gerald Willen

William Shakespeare, *King Lear*
edited by Edward G. Quinn

Daniel Defoe, *Moll Flanders*
edited by J. Paul Hunter

Fyodor Dostoevsky, *Notes from Underground*
edited by Robert G. Durgy, in
a new translation by Serge Shishkoff

Charles Dickens, *Bleak House*
edited by Duane DeVries

Henry James, *The American*
edited by Gerald Willen

Henry Fielding, *Joseph Andrews* and *Shamela*
edited by Sheridan Baker

HENRY FIELDING

Joseph Andrews and *Shamela*

Edited by

SHERIDAN BAKER

University of Michigan

THE CROWELL CRITICAL LIBRARY

Thomas Y. Crowell Company, New York, Established 1834

 Published simultaneously in Canada by Fitzhenry & Whiteside Ltd., Toronto.

L. C. Card 75-165373

ISBN 0-690-46545-9

to SALLY

PREFACE

IN a way, this present volume really began some fifty years ago with the explorations of Aurélien Digeon, a Frenchman, a warm admirer of Fielding, virtually his first real modern critic. My aims here are Digeon's (I translate from the Preface to his little textual analysis of 1923, *Le Texte des Romans de Fielding*):

> I hope the reader will feel something of the pleasure I myself have often felt in seeing a phrase take shape, a thought sharpen or modify itself. One thus receives an author's involuntary confidences; one knows the places where his pen has hesitated, and tries to guess why; one sees him erase a word, weigh the poise of a sentence: one has the impression, in brief moments, of living at his side. One cannot but profit by thus assisting closely in the artistic labors of a Fielding.

Digeon had compared editions. He had discovered that our modern reprints of Joseph Andrews had all been (and still are, so far as our textbooks go) based on the somewhat inaccurate and slightly doctored edition of Arthur Murphy—*l'insouciant Murphy*, as Digeon calls him—the first collected *Works* of Fielding (1762). Digeon also discovered that Fielding had carefully corrected and amplified the text of the second edition, and had continued to make small changes each time he again looked over his novel for a new printing. The Wesleyan Edition of Fielding's *Works,* beginning with Martin Battestin's impeccable editing of *Joseph Andrews,* is now correcting our erroneous two centuries of Murphy. This present edition is the first textbook to be based on Fielding's first edition and to include Fielding's changes, presenting a text as near to its author's creative intentions as modern print can bring it.

But even such an accurate text denies the reader the creative, editorial enjoyment of arriving at it, the immediate pleasures of comparison, to which Digeon alludes—that feeling of watching a master at work. Consequently, I have marked on the text of the first edition, directly before the reader's eyes, as it were, those changes we can accept as Fielding's in the next three editions he successively touched up for the press. Fortunately, Fielding's changes do not come so thick and fast as to clutter any one page beyond easy legibility. One may read straight on, disregarding the unobtrusive brackets (explained on pages xxxi–xxxv), or one may pause to enjoy the artistic labors of the man whom Digeon called "a master writer, one of the most careful artists of style that has written in English." I have used the same system for *Shamela,* though Fielding's changes here are fewer and less interesting.

But I aim for a further advantage: I begin the present volume with *Shamela* to increase the illumination on Fielding as creative writer. The Introduction provides the necessary background to Fielding's finding himself as novelist by writing *Shamela,* and then, riding the crest of discovery, by transforming its wicked hilarity into the comic riches of *Joseph Andrews.* To read *Shamela* first is to recapture something of Fielding's exhilarating voyage into the first true comic novel in English. The footnotes will fill in the details of Fielding's highly allusive art, and a chronological outline of Fielding's life will help the reader place *Shamela* and *Joseph Andrews* in his busy career. A selection of critical essays follows to amplify the reading—then a selected bibliography for further study.

CONTENTS

INTRODUCTION

HENRY Fielding (1707–1754) was a struggling writer. He belonged to the lower branch of a noble family, and indeed was thought to be—and doubtless thought himself to be—descended from the great Austrian house of Hapsburg. Although genealogists have denied this supposition, the only picture of Fielding, William Hogarth's drawing of him from a recollection prompted by a silhouette snipped by a lady as she looked at his profile, shows the short upper lip and the protruding lower one that is known as the Hapsburg lip. Whatever his genealogical roots, he had a gentle patrician air. His mother came from an eminent landed family in Somersetshire, in the southwest of England. The elegant estate in Somersetshire he gives Squire Allworthy in *Tom Jones* certainly draws some of its features from that of Fielding's grandfather, who was also a distinguished judge. But Fielding's father, a retired colonel, was impecunious. Young Fielding found himself at twenty-two a gentleman without means. He must write himself back uphill to fame and fortune.

So his struggles begin. He was to achieve his fame, even in his own lifetime, but the fortune was sadly intermittent. After a thorough classical education at Eton, and some youthful attempts at poetry, and a year or two of gentlemanly frivolity (during which he and his valet attempted to run off with a fifteen-year-old heiress named Sarah Andrews), he came up to London in the fall of 1727, at the age of twenty. In January, 1728, he published his first work, *The Masquerade*, a satire in couplets on the London scene, signing himself "Lemuel Gulliver, Poet Laureat [sic] to the King of Lilliput," signaling his Swiftian aspirations. In February, his first play was produced. His noble cousin, Lady Mary Wortley Montagu, helped him to get it staged and published. Thus *Love in Several Masque*s (1728), a triple-plotted piece of ingenuity in the Restoration manner, becomes Fielding's first complete mimetic and comic work. He was not yet twenty-one. He then left for the University of Leyden (The Netherlands), perhaps to study law, with something of both fame and fortune in his pocket.

But his father's fortune ran out. In 1730, he is back in London, down on his uppers, working in earnest at playwrighting, his career in college abruptly over. He probably also tried to study some law—his second play, *The Temple Beau* (1730), is about law students—but another early play is more significant. At Leyden, he had written some scenes for *Don Quixote in England*, a play no one would produce until, four years later (1734), his reputation now firm, he could doll it up as a ballad-opera. But *Don Quixote in England* tells us how early young Fielding was caught by Cervantes's great comic powers, and how long he was in trying to naturalize those powers to England and himself, and in finding the form and manner that was at last to bloom overnight in *Joseph Andrews*.

Out of the early rejections of *Don Quixote in England*, and, presumably, *The Temple Beau*, his satiric urge bursts on the stage. He turns from comedy to write his first farce, signing himself "Scriblerus Secundus," again reaching toward Swift, and Pope, as heir to their Martin Scriblerus of their ludicrous *Scriblerus Papers*, and their Scriblerus Club (he was to use the signature in three more plays, adding his own initial to become "H. Scriblerus Secundus" of *The Tragedy of Tragedies* [1731], the complete version of *Tom Thumb*). This new kind of piece is *The Author's Farce* (1730), a wild little satire about a young playwright who cannot sell his plays. As the playwright reads a sample or two of his inflated couplets, we understand why, but the satire lays most of its spirited blame on the frivolous taste of "the Town," and the corrupt publishers and theatrical managers who serve it. The satire remains good-natured. Fielding openly includes himself in the laughter, though he certainly never wrote his plays in couplets, inflated or otherwise, except in burlesque. In his hero, Harry Luckless, young Harry Fielding is drawing a comic self-portrait in public: he himself would actually be there in the audience, and even at this early date the audience would know him and know of his presence. When the play's realistic, satirical comedy changes into a puppet show, which Harry Luckless stages, we can see Fielding's first step toward having an author, a dramatized version of himself, comment on the action he himself is unfolding—a first step toward finding that commentative voice that conveys so much of the comic irony in *Joseph Andrews* and *Tom Jones.* And when that comically autobiographical author merges with the zany fantasy of his own puppet show, and is discovered to be the lost heir of a Javanese kingdom, we see for the first time Fielding's fancifully comic personal involvement in the old story of romance, the world's basic success-story, identity lost then gloriously rediscovered, as he simultaneously mocks and fulfills his own aristocratic dreams—the story on which he was to build first *Joseph Andrews* then *Tom Jones.*

The Author's Farce also contains Fielding's first step toward the political farces that were to expel him from the stage when Sir Robert Walpole's government passed the Licensing Act seven years later (1737), specifically to get rid of Fielding's satirical attacks. Harry Luckless mentions "Mr. Keyber," which was the name the anti-Walpole satirists had tacked on Colley Cibber, the manager of Drury Lane Theater, whom Walpole had named Poet Laureate in what was taken to be a political payoff. Cibber was also the man who would turn down aspiring playwrights like Harry Luckless-Fielding. Cibber, as "Mr. Marplay," turns down Harry Luckless's play after appropriating the good parts for himself. *The Author's Farce* socks Cibber twice again: first, as "Sir Farcical Comic," who continually repeats a line of Cibber's in one of his famous and favorite roles as the comical, effeminate Restoration fop; and second, by turning his puppet "Poet" into "Poet Laureate" at the play's end. In this grand finale, even Mr. Marplay from the play's first part comes unaccountably in, so Harry Luckless has three Cibbers on stage at once, all of whom he genially gives offices in his newfound kingdom.[1] In *Shamela,* Fielding's unfair but hilarious fun at Cibber's expense comes full force, since Cibber's new autobiography had just called Fielding a failure and a slanderer; and *Joseph Andrews* carries over the fun from *Shamela* with irresistible wit.

The Author's Farce briefly opens still another major interest to be elaborated in *Shamela* and developed still more fully in *Joseph Andrews, Tom Jones,* and *Amelia:* Fielding's lasting concern for religion and the abuses of the clergy. At the end of the play, a Parson Murder-text—a Presbyterian, since the Methodists had not yet come to the fore—succumbs to a pretty girl's pleas to let everybody dance:

> Verily, I am conquer'd . . . the Flesh hath subdued the Spirit —I feel a motion in me, and whether it be of Grace or no I am not certain . . . I will abide the performing of a Dance, . . . being thereto mov'd by an inward working. . . .

In *Shamela,* Tickletext repeats both the ecclesiastical rhetoric and the comic mistaking of sexual stirrings for spiritual grace. In *The Grub-Street Opera* (1731), the year following *The Author's Farce,* Fielding evolves Murder-text into Puzzletext (see note 9, p. 9), who speaks the same language, but who is also the tobacco-and-ale man, the poacher, time-server, politician, and Latinist, the very kind of country parson we are to find in *Shamela* as Parson Williams.

Denied the stage for political reasons, after being far and away England's most productive playwright of the 1730s—perhaps, with his twenty-six plays, the most productive between Shakespeare and Shaw—Fielding became editor and leading essayist for *The Champion,* a newspaper sponsored by the lords of the

[1] See my "Political Satire in Fielding's *Author's Farce, Mock Doctor,* and *Tumble-Down Dick,*" PMLA 77 (1962): 226, n.21; and Charles B. Woods, "Cibber in Fielding's *Author's Farce:* Three Notes," *Philological Quarterly* 44 (1965): 149–51.

Opposition. The elegant Earl of Chesterfield, whom Fielding compliments in *Joseph Andrews* (III.i.242), was one; Lord Lyttelton, to whom he dedicated *Tom Jones* and on whom he partially patterned Squire Allworthy, was another. He also began reading law in earnest, in what hours he could spare. In spite of his passing the bar in record time (two and a half years), his success as a lawyer was meager as he followed the circuit court, looking for fees, along the very road Adams and Andrews were to travel.

But writing almost thrice weekly for *The Champion* was making Fielding a moral essayist, strengthening that commentative role he was to adapt to the novel. His religious convictions take shape in the very midst of his political-satirical concerns. We can almost see *Shamela* accumulating. In the spring of 1740, he wrote a series of four thoughtful essays about the abuses of the clergy, and about the spiritual virtues clergymen generally lacked—those with which he was to endow Parson Adams in *Joseph Andrews*. His first essay, on Saturday, March 29, is untitled. On the following Tuesday (April Fool's Day, by luck or design), he ridicules grammatical mistakes in a new book, none other than *An Apology for the Life of Mr. Colley Cibber, Comedian, Written by Himself*. His next clerical essay, on Saturday (April 5), appears under the title: THE APOLOGY FOR THE CLERGY,—*continued*. Here we can trace the movement of Fielding's thought; an essay on religion, a satire against Cibber, an essay on religion, but entitled, seriously, after Cibber's own ridiculed title. Religion and politics, personal and social satire, are mixing in Fielding's mind. Religion has, in a sense, bracketed and absorbed Cibber, who now seems to have added further egotistical pretentiousness and comic blindness—his name in the title, a life for which one must apologize, "Written by Himself"—to his political and literary sins. He stands ready to coalesce with Samuel Richardson's Pamela, when she arrives, to support Fielding's symbolizing of hypocritical vanity and dishonesty.

But Fielding's religious essays have even more to do with *Shamela*. In them, Fielding twice cautions himself against "being righteous over-much," and he once reprimands George Whitefield, a prominent young Methodist, for being "righteous overmuch" (April 5 and May 24). Fielding's essays, in short, are part of a controversy directed against Whitefield and Methodism, in which that phrase had become a slogan (see note 25, p. 29). *A Short Account of God's Dealings with the Reverend Mr. George Whitefield* (1740), recently published, had also, like Cibber's book, been "written by himself." That Whitefield should present himself as one so important as to demand God's personal attention must have looked to Fielding very much like Cibberian conceit in its religious aspect. Shamela's mother sends her a copy of Whitefield's book (p. 21), which she later packs with her belongings (p. 40), as Fielding mocks Pamela's self-satisfied piety; and Parson Williams is to preach a sermon on the text *"Be not Righteous over-much,"* as Fielding ridicules what he takes as the Methodists' chief hypocrisy—the popular anti-Methodist view—about faith and good works being sufficient to a religion that carried one to enthusiasms both religious and sexual. Parson Tickletext's titillations of Grace are part of the anti-Methodist satire Fielding was to amalgamate with his earlier criticisms of a lazy and selfish clergy. In *Shamela's* three parsons—two as satirical caricatures, one as a moral and spiritual mentor—Fielding has turned his religious thought into literary creation.

When Samuel Richardson published his *Pamela: or, Virtue Rewarded* on November 6, 1740, Fielding took no notice of it. Richardson had prefixed to his first edition two flattering letters from friends who had read the manuscript (Tickletext's "Little book, charming *Pamela*" comes from the first of these). To the second edition (February 14, 1741), Richardson added twenty-four more pages of flattering letters, including a poem, sent in by enthusiastic readers. Fielding evidently did not see the first edition: he naturally assumes that *all* of the letters had appeared for the first time in the second edition. Oliver refers to "those remarkable Epistles, which the Author, or Editor, hath prefix'd to the second Edition which you send me of his Book" (p. 12). In *Joseph Andrews* (I.i.75), Fielding again refers erroneously to "the excellent essays or letters prefixed to the second and subsequent editions" of *Pamela*. In other words, after two months, the popular enthusiasm over *Pamela,* and the early second edition it produced, finally caught Fielding's attention. Everything about *Pamela* seems to have irritated his amusement. One senses that he must have read the book through and then written his parody right off the top of his response. His slips in detail—confusing Mrs. Jervis and Mrs. Jewkes, for instance (p. 14)—clearly indicate his haste. Indeed, he probably did not begin to write until sometime after Thursday, March 12, 1741, the date of Richardson's third edition, since Tickletext, in his opening letter, says that Oliver must wait for the *fourth* edition to supply the neighboring pulpits, clearly indicating that the third not only had arrived but was selling out fast. In other words, Fielding picked up a copy of the second edition sometime between February 14 and March 12; and just three weeks later —on Thursday, April 2, 1741 [2]—*Shamela* was in print. Allowing a weekend and a few days for Richardson's third edition to reach a clamor of sales, and allowing at least a week for printing and binding, we may loosely guess that Fielding wrote *Shamela* at some time between March 18 and March 25, Wednesday to Wednesday, with March 18 the stronger locus.

Richardson claimed that his novel consisted of the actual letters of a girl whom he called Pamela Andrews to conceal her true identity, a real serving-girl, whose unbreakable virtue had withstood Squire B.'s assaults until, humbled, he was proud to claim her as his bride and Lady. The novel was immensely popular, the first best-seller. The clergy commended its morality. But Fielding saw things otherwise. To him, Pamela was a moral sham. No serving-girl ever bore such a romantic name (borrowed, it seems, from one of the princesses in Sir Philip Sidney's *Arcadia,* the great Elizabethan romance). No serving-girl wrote such genteel prose, if she could write at all. To him, virtue was not Pamela's feminine and self-seeking chastity but a selfless Christian benevolence, supported by masculine courage and honesty. In Pamela's self-satisfied story, and Richardson's self-satisfaction in it, Fielding saw only the vanity he was to name

[2] See "A Note on the Texts," p. xxxi.

in *Joseph Andrews* as one of the two essential roots of man's comic pretenses. In Pamela's claim about wanting to leave Mr. B.'s house, yet staying on, and in Richardson's somewhat similar claims that he was merely the editor, not the author, of a true and truly moral story, and then using this claim to prefix his letters of praise and to conclude with some praise of his own—in all this Fielding saw the hypocrisy he was to name as the other comic root.

He inverted Richardson's Pamela Andrews into Shamela Andrews, a calculating guttersnippet who knows her highest price, making *Pamela* a total sham by the deviltry of presenting his parodic letters as the real ones. And Richardson's Mr. B. is really, says Fielding, one Squire Booby. Fielding no doubt also saw the chance to make some desperately needed money himself. He now had a wife and two children. He had fallen into debt in March, 1741, at almost precisely the time he was writing *Shamela*. But *An Apology for the Life of Mrs. Shamela Andrews* suddenly pulled together for him a vast and active array of interests and with astonishing zest. A glance at the title page of *Shamela* tells us that we are suddenly in the presence of something new in English fiction, which, with the exception of Daniel Defoe's uneven genius two decades earlier, had produced little more than short entertainments—somewhat like the pulp thrillers of today—until Richardson and then Fielding came along. With *Shamela*, English fiction becomes literate. Here, suddenly, is a book that—like Joyce's *Ulysses*, let us say—generates its being, and its meaning, from other literature as it gets its hold on life.

Shamela gathers its satiric energy parodically and allusively from other books. Here on the title page of *Shamela*, we see Richardson's *Pamela* done up in the very typography of Cibber's *Apology*. By calling the supposed author "Conny Keyber," and by calling Pamela "that young Politician," Fielding thrusts out a political needle that also knits Conyers Middleton and his recent *Life of Cicero* (February, 1741—less than two months before *Shamela*) into the Cibber-Pamela satire: Middleton had slighted Lord Lyttelton's *Observations on the Life of Cicero* and had dedicated his book to one of Lyttelton's and Fielding's political opponents. And Fielding soon pulls Whitefield's *God's Dealings* into the satire too.

The name "Conny Keyber" is the very nub of Fielding's political-sexual-religious satire. "Conny" blends Cibber's "Colley" and Middleton's "Conyers" into an obscene word for the female pudendum (as Ian Watt and Eric Rothstein have pointed out), and allies them precisely with what Fielding takes as Pamela's hypocritical whoredom. "Keyber" identifies Cibber and politics as part of the meretricity. And then Fielding goes on, in his mock dedication, to parody Middleton's dedication of his *Life of Cicero* to Lord Hervey, one of the chief figures of what the Opposition took to be Walpole's meretricious government. "Miss *Fanny, &c.*" identifies Hervey (see Rothstein, p. 455) and continues the sexual joke and satirical point. To cap it all, Middleton is a clergyman, who, in Fielding's eyes, is toadying corruptly to one of the chief corrupters of Walpole's corrupt regime. Pamela, Cibber, and Middleton, with Hervey and Walpole in the background, are all hypocritically whoring in their several ways. Fielding condenses and parodies Middleton's dedication with devilish proximity: one may surmise how closely by comparing Fielding's opening sentence with Middleton's:

> The public will naturally expect, that in chusing a Patron for *the Life of* CICERO, I should address myself to some person of illustrious rank, distinguished by his parts and eloquence, and bearing a principal share in the great affairs of the Nation; who, according to the usual stile of Dedications, might be the proper subject of a comparison with the Hero of my piece.

Fielding's parody of *Pamela* is even more brilliant. He again condenses drastically, thus throwing Richardson's two spicy bedroom scenes into impudent prominence. Richardson's title page had claimed that his book was "intirely divested of all those Images, which, in too many Pieces calculated for Amusement only, tend to *inflame* the Minds they should *instruct.*" And Fielding hardly alters Richardson's most explicit details as he upsets his self-righteous claim, one that Oliver returns to again as he enumerates the defects of *Pamela* in a list that parallels the one in which Richardson, as "editor," sums up the virtues of his book as he concludes it. Fielding's "Hussy, Slut, Saucebox, Boldface" merely ridiculously concentrates Mr. B.'s angry terms. Pamela's pious exclamations, her swoons, her reading of good books, her dressing as a farmer's daughter, her feigned suicide, her meeting secretly with Parson Williams to seek help, her generous charities after marriage—all serve Fielding's parodic subversion. Pamela's somewhat egotistical virtue becomes Shamela's sham "Vartue," in which she nevertheless takes an amusingly Pamela-like pride. And Richardson's phrases and details—"my poor but honest Parents," Mrs. Jewkes and Shamela supping on "hot buttered Apple-Pie," Mrs. Jewkes's change of tune as the heroine's victory nears—all kinds of details from here and there in Richardson's book flow easily into Fielding's mimicry, as they suit his momentary purpose. But in his fifty-some pages he reproduces, exactly and precisely, the structural outlines of Richardson's two thick volumes, his beginning, his two bedroom climaxes, and the final triumph, together with the "editor's" enumerated moral, as if Richardson's book were only the distended shadow of this pert and authentic midget.

The fun of closely parodying *Pamela* occasionally releases Fielding's inventiveness in the direction it was to soar in *Joseph Andrews*. On the eve of Pamela's wedding, Richardson perturbs her spirits by having Mr. B. come home with some whip-snapping drinking companions, with whom he has been celebrating. Fielding imitates this scene by recreating from the political satirics of such of his plays as *Don Quixote in England* or *Pasquin* the scene in which Williams sits down to drink with the mayor and aldermen, thus robbing Shamela of his company. Or again, Mr. B., Pamela, and her father, out for a ride, see the banished Mr. Williams walking in a meadow, book in hand: Mr. B. stops the carriage, apologizes, and insists:

> Pray, Mr. *Williams,* oblige *Pamela* with your Hand; and step in yourself. He bow'd, and took my Hand, and my Master made him step in, and sit next me, all that ever could do. . . . (II. 123)

Fielding turns this into the breezy country scene where Shamela and Booby find Williams poaching with horse and hound, and Williams rides off in the coach with Shamela, leaving the frustrated Booby outside on horseback. The whole parodic extemporization that produces Fielding's Parson Williams is part of the elated impulse that is to produce *Joseph Andrews* and, indeed, Parson Adams.

Richardson, writing to one of his correspondents toward the end of 1749, after *Tom Jones* had appeared, still piqued, nevertheless rather accurately sums up Fielding's debt to him:

> So long as the world will receive, Mr. Fielding will write. . . . The Pamela, which he abused in his Shamela, taught him how to write to please, tho' his manners are so different. Before his Joseph Andrews (hints and names taken from that story, with a lewd and ungenerous engraftment) the poor man wrote without being read, except when his Pasquins, &c. roused party attention and the legislature at the same time. . . .[3]

Pamela, under the scrutiny of *Shamela*, gave Fielding not only the structural frame and the cast for his great *Joseph Andrews*, and not only his central focus on vanity and hypocrisy, but also the essential insight into the comedy of sex that he had previously lacked. The lusty ladies of his plays are perfectly candid with themselves. He had not yet seen that both the conscious and unconscious hypocrisies of sex in civilized life provide a most potent symbol for all of mankind's comic self-deceptions. Pamela's unconscious attraction to the cruel Mr. B., staying on when she intends to leave, opened Fielding's eyes to those comically unconscious and half-conscious disguises that passion puts upon the Lady Boobys, the Slipslops, and even the Joneses of us all.

Shamela also sharpened Fielding's belief, to be formulated in his Preface to *Joseph Andrews*, that comedy can be both realistic and morally instructive at once. The realistic idiom of Shamela and the housekeepers, and even their calculating morality, amusingly point up the falsity in Richardson's idea of virtue. Perhaps no flirtation was ever more accurately caught than in the close parody in Letter VI, where Fielding replaces Richardson's elegance with language that still rings true: ". . . come hither

[3] Anna Laetitia Barbauld, ed., *The Correspondence of Samuel Richardson* (London, 1804), IV. 285–86.

—Yes to be sure, says I; why don't you come, says he; what should I come for, says I; if you don't come to me, I'll come to you, says he; I shan't come to you I assure you, says I." And all the fun has a wholly serious intent. Charles B. Woods has shown how Fielding has repeated some essential points from his religious essays first in Parson Oliver's closing remarks in *Shamela* and again in *Joseph Andrews*.[4]

Indeed, here in this apparent bagatelle, this bawdy trifle, Parson Oliver is already propounding, and in much the same language, what were to become the two central lessons of *Tom Jones:* (1) that prudence must learn to control passion, and (2) that the inner satisfaction of selfless benevolence is its own reward. Oliver says that *Pamela* encourages young gentlemen into hasty marriages that will "sacrifice all the solid Comforts of their Lives, to a very transcient Satisfaction of a Passion . . . ." He commends "the secure Satisfaction of a good Conscience" and "the extatick Pleasure of contemplating" God's acceptance. He says that "worldly Honours" are often gained by "Force and Fraud." Both Adams (I.xvii.135) and Joseph Andrews (III.vi. 285–286) address themselves to this theme, and Tom Jones, facing the question of fraud—after Fielding himself has spoken in his Preface of "that solid inward Comfort of Mind, which is the sure Companion of Innocence and Virtue"— will sum up his book's central lesson almost in Parson Oliver's words:

> I had rather enjoy my own Mind than the Fortune of another Man. What is the poor Pride arising from a magnificent House, a numerous Equipage, a splendid Table, and from all the other Advantages or Appearances of Fortune, compared to the warm, solid Content, the swelling Satisfaction, the thrilling Transports, and the exulting Triumphs, which a good Mind enjoys, in the Contemplation of a generous, virtuous, noble, benevolent Action? (XII.x)

Shamela is a wonder. Fielding's deepest ideas, his satirical animus, his farcical verve, and his parodic inclination were all waiting for the touch of *Pamela* to bring them together.

[4] "Fielding and the Authorship of *Shamela*," *Philological Quarterly* 25 (1948): 257–60.

But *Joseph Andrews* is more wonderful still, bringing in even farther ranges of literature and life. Fielding finds at last how to naturalize the Cervantic comedy that had engaged him from the first. Again his imagination soars in a kind of parodic imitation of other books, although now he imitates chiefly those books that have caught life truly for him, and for which he sees further examples in the life around him. Again, we find an essentially literary mind, which has found in literature those brilliant epitomes that call attention to things otherwise unnoticed on the streets, and has fitted them into an understanding of life. *Shamela* sprang from negative examples. Now *Joseph Andrews* jumps off from the negatives to encompass the great positives of Cervantes and Scarron, and, to a lesser degree, of Marivaux and Lesage, with the recently translated *Arabian Nights* demonstrating how the sheer charm of story-telling can soothe our barbarities. These are the works Fielding praises in III.i, which, obviously written before his Preface, is his first and monumental summary of the truth of fiction.

One of the wonders of *Joseph Andrews* is how the force of literary discovery, beginning in *Shamela*, carries Fielding through a most desperate period and into the most lighthearted, amusing, and confident book in the English language. The evils are everywhere and comically there, but the good will prevail. Fielding's debt in March, 1741, was only the first register of trouble. His father died in June, and, toward the end of the same month, he quit *The Champion.* Quitting his only source of income, in the face of his monetary needs, must certainly have cost and caused considerable moral anguish. The Opposition, which he was serving better than any, was winning. Apparently, as Battestin has pointed out,[5] the lords of the Opposition were showing the very tendencies to line their nests of which they had long accused Walpole, and they were not paying Fielding's considerable labors even enough to keep him out of debt. The summer would have taken him off to tour the Western Circuit as a lawyer, providing a convenient time to break with *The Champion* and to hope for better things from his law

[5] "Fielding's Changing Politics and *Joseph Andrews*," *Philological Quarterly* 39 (1960): 39–55.

practice. He seems to have returned from the Somerset road, and to have been writing *Joseph Andrews* during the very months in which he imagines it to occur along that road, September and October of 1741, as Martin Battestin points out: the deposition against Joseph and Fanny identifies the day after their return to Lady Booby's as a Sunday in October, about twelve days after Joseph had started from London (Wesleyan Edition, p. xxvi). Battestin locates the writing of *Joseph Andrews* in the last four months of 1741, September through December. Fielding took a little time out in October to correct *Shamela* for its second and last edition of October 31, 1741. On December 15, he published *The Opposition: A Vision*, indicating his disaffection from his former political allegiance and his seeking help from his old adversary, Walpole. Chesterfield and Ralph Allen, both of whom he compliments in *Joseph Andrews*, may also have helped him out. But his description of the winter of 1741–1742, during which he wrote *Joseph Andrews*, and then went desperately on to bring out his two volumes of *Miscellanies*, leaves little doubt, as he says in the Preface thereto, as to "the Distresses I have waded through": "I was last Winter laid up in the Gout, with a favourite Child dying on one Bed, and my Wife in a Condition very little better on another, attended with Circumstances which served as very proper Decorations to such a Scene. . . ." *Joseph Andrews* was published on February 22, 1742. His elder daughter, Charlotte, her mother's namesake, died in March, a month before her sixth birthday.

The writing of *Joseph Andrews* must have sustained him as he sustained it. He no doubt first saw a way to extend his success with *Shamela* in the next inevitable rendition of the joke: transposing the sexes for the more ludicrous effect. Pamela Andrews, who had become Shamela Andrews, would now become Joseph Andrews, Pamela's equally virtuous, and hence more comically prudish, brother. The social counterparts of Richardson's cast would fall comically into place. Fielding even would dare, as his book evolved, to name his heroine after the obscene "Miss Fanny" of *Shamela*, rinsing the name clean without losing all of its comic potential, as if to demonstrate his absolute power over language. In fact, his Beau Didapper, as Battestin has pointed out,[6] is none other than Lord Hervey again (his first "Miss Fanny"), as if everything of *Shamela* must be converted to new uses, as the lewd Didapper now pursues the purified "Fanny." The very framework of Fielding's book would again be Richardson's, acquired through *Shamela:* two great bedroom episodes, followed by social elevation, marriage, and happiness. It is almost as if Fielding took Richardson's two volumes as bookends for his imitation of Cervantes, or, better, as if he cut *Shamela* down the middle, pulled the halves apart to accommodate his Cervantic roadway, and again elaborated, in a fresh allusive parody, Richardson's two scenes as the comic structural peaks of Books I and IV and the chief structural pillars of the novel itself.[7]

Fielding's allusive parody of Richardson is surprisingly pervasive in the first and last books of *Joseph Andrews,* at beginning and end. Book I, Chapter I, introduces Pamela Andrews with ironically sober encomiums of "authentic papers and records" (together with echoes of Colley Cibber, from *Shamela*) and of Richardson's self-laudatory letters: Fielding's "authentic history" will now present the "character of male chastity" in Pamela's brother, Joseph. In I.ii, we find Joey brought vis-à-vis *his* pursuer, the female counterpart of Mr. B. and Squire Booby, and we meet her parish priest, Parson Adams, who takes the place of Parson Williams. Then we meet the housekeeper, Mrs. Slipslop, the counterpart of Richardson's Mrs. Jewkes.

And now, with I.iv and Lady Booby's "innocent freedoms" in London with her footman, we are ready for the parodic bedroom scene of I.v, and its parodic sequels: Slipslop's version below stairs, Joseph's parodic letter to Pamela, Lady Booby's

[6] "Hervey's Role in *Joseph Andrews,*" *Philological Quarterly* 42 (1963): 226–41.

[7] See my "Fielding and the Irony of Form," *Eighteenth-Century Studies* 2 (1969): 138–54, from which I adopt these points, and some of what follows. Robert Alan Donovan argues, a little unconvincingly, that the *whole* book parodies Richardson (*The Shaping Vision* [Ithaca: Cornell University Press, 1966], pp. 68–88); Martin Battestin distinguishes *Joseph Andrews* as satirically allusive rather than parodically imitative, like *Shamela* (*The Moral Basis of Fielding's Art* [Middletown: Wesleyan University Press, 1959], pp. 6–10).

second attempt ("Madam," says Joseph, "that boy is the brother of Pamela. . ."), Joseph's second letter to Pamela, and his departure for the country, all interleaved with Slipslop's and Lady Booby's self-protective sparrings, which make clear that the parody is aimed not at Richardson but at the universal human turmoils and hypocrisies of sex, which Richardson depicted but could not see. Joseph's departure concludes the first bedroom episode, and, probably, the most hilariously comic scenes in the English novel. And this whole episode strongly though broadly parodies the trials of Richardson's chaste heroine.

As Joseph sets out for Somersetshire, in the middle of Book I, the story does indeed change—as many, from Lawrence onward, have observed—from its buoyant satiric and parodic comedy of sex. Joseph does not, says Fielding, head for his mother's and father's house (as Pamela longs to do), nor for "his dear beloved sister Pamela," but for the dwelling of a young girl whom he "(though the best of sons and brothers) longed more impatiently to see than his parents or his sister" (I.xi). And Fielding's genius is nowhere more blithely evident than in his ability to change the lighting on his hero, so to speak, and reveal the man within the parodic abstraction—this very funny male-Pamela—without losing his hero, or his readers. He aids the transition, and ends Book I with formal neatness, by echoing the book's big bedroom episode.

Now *Joseph* is in bed. Like our letter-writing Pamela (perhaps even the Shamela whom Fielding has writing in bed), he calls for paper and pen, but, too sick to write, he soliloquizes, merging his two roles to perfection, opening as parody of Pamela and ending as sighing lover: "O most adorable Pamela! most virtuous sister! whose example could alone enable me to withstand all the temptations of riches and beauty, and to preserve my virtue pure and chaste for the arms of my dear Fanny . . ." (I.xiii). And then Betty Chambermaid reenacts the comedy of Lady Booby's and Slipslop's fruitless passions; Joseph acts more realistically but still comically; and the scene and the Book end with a crescendo of beds and Tow-wouses, putting the major parodic bedroom episode firmly in place.

But Joseph is now almost completely the romantic hero. The parody has faded, except as an echo, even at the end, as Pamela herself enters and briefly plays the parodic prude. For now Fielding amuses us at Richardson's expense not by exaggeration but by presenting Richardson's characters as they really might be (the tack he had used with a vengeance in *Shamela*). Pamela and Mr. Booby are, for the most part, just decent young country gentlefolk, and Gaffar and Gammar Andrews (not the romanticized *Mr.* and *Mrs.* of Richardson) are amusingly realistic peasants, shrewd and noncommittal.

But the parodic context becomes vivid again in the novel's second great bedroom episode, for which we have been inadvertently waiting since the structural expectation established by the first, and here Fielding mocks and surpasses Richardson for the last time. Naturally, Richardson's second scene is more intense than his first, as any such seconding must be. But Fielding's hilarious tumble about the beds at Lady B.'s country estate surpasses all expectation. He transplants, into the place Richardson had prepared for him, a version of an old comic bedroom fabliau that simultaneously parallels two versions from Cervantes's *Don Quixote* (I.iii; II.xlvii) and three from Scarron's *The Comical Romance* (I.iv; I.xi; III.iv), and that nevertheless, as Mark Spilka has well explained (p. 403), still underlines Fielding's central point (at which even Lady Booby must laugh, in momentary realization)—the universal scrambling of sex, to which intrinsic virtue is impervious. But Richardson is present in more than structural coincidence. Pamela has just been particularly self-righteous with Joseph (and she has also just exchanged a smile of sexual understanding with her husband, parodying Richardson in reverse), and, more important, Fielding's romp takes place primarily in the bed of Mrs. Slipslop, that caricature of Richardson's Mrs. Jewkes, in whose bed, in B.'s country estate, Richardson's second great scene is laid, if one may use the term. In short, this parodic scene powerfully structures the novel at its end by balancing its mate at the beginning in the very act of emphasizing the novel's theme: the selfless virtue of Adams is impervious to the selfish lusts of the world, especially the sexual when it is not properly subsumed in marriage. The picture of tobaccoed old Adams obliviously in bed with the fragrant Fanny, obliviously stretching himself along the edge-board, a station his wife "had always assigned him" (after we have been well assured that Adams has been a good husband to his wife), provides a perfect transition from the comedy of sex to the paradox of sexual fulfillment in virtuous marriage with which the story ends. The structure Fielding has twice borrowed from Richardson in parody has again furnished Fielding's thematic emphasis.

This final episode illustrates beautifully how literature—or perhaps we should say, thinking about literature, remembering it as one looks at life around him and writes—stimulates Fielding's creative imagination. What starts in parody reaches out to a kind of extended paradiorthosis, as the Greeks would say—to an emulative borrowing and bending of a master's words for one's own purpose—except that Fielding finds a certain creative joy in allusively reapplying whole characterizations, episodes, and dramatic arrangements. It is a form of wit, really, a dramatized pun. Mrs. Slipslop is an excellent example, and Parson Adams an absolute triumph.

Fielding creates Mrs. Slipslop from Richardson's Mrs. Jewkes, happily adding coinciding details from Cervantes's grotesque chambermaid, Maritornes,[8] a libidinous little dwarf, with shoulders somewhat humped and a breath with "a stronger *Hogoe* than stale Venison" (I.iii.2). Mrs. Jewkes's salacious lesbianism, already caught in *Shamela*, now becomes Mrs. Slipslop's passion for Joseph, Pamela's counterpart. Mrs. Slipslop repeats the "sect" for "sex" of *Shamela's* Mrs. Jewkes, expanding the general malapropistic tendencies of the *Shamela* crowd into Mrs. Slipslop's distinctive comic pride in "hard words," as if Mrs. Slipslop's whole tendency to discuss religion with Par-

[8] Ronald Paulson, *Satire and the English Novel in Eighteenth-Century England* (New Haven: Yale University Press, 1967), pp. 103–104; Douglas Brooks, "Richardson's *Pamela* and Fielding's *Joseph Andrews*," *Essays in Criticism* 17 (1967): 161; my "Fielding and the Irony of Form," *op. cit.*, pp. 142–43; Homer Goldberg, *The Art of Joseph Andrews* (Chicago: University of Chicago Press, 1969), pp. 146–47, 232–33.

son Adams springs from that single comic capsule, *sect,* which contains Fielding's anti-Methodist point of the mutual excesses and hypocrisies of religion and sex.

Fielding's multiplex literary pleasure arises principally from his finding *English* equivalents for his general paradiorthosis on Cervantes (and Scarron and Marivaux). Mrs. Slipslop is English to the core—and superbly realistic, in spite of her cartooned physique—in her uppity talk to her mistress and one and all. Adams is even more so—an English country parson drawn from the very life—in fact, from Fielding's friend Parson William Young of East Stour, Fielding's childhood home.[9] Fielding fits a fictionalized version of his absent-minded, benevolent, learned friend, whose head is wonderfully turned by the New Testament and the classics alike, into the skinny outline of Cervantes's magnificently book-mad Spaniard, decrepit horse and all. Adams has Young's wife, six children, and meager salary (Fielding reduces Young's thirty pounds per annum to Adams's twenty-three), but he has Don Quixote's sixty years (Young was forty), his comically noble idealism (now realistically converted to the parson's essential Christianity), and pugnacity (now realistically applied by fist and crabstick to the hazards of travel in eighteenth-century England).

When Quixote rides off from an inn, disdaining to pay the bill because knights in books never pay for anything, expecting Sancho to follow but unwittingly leaving him to be tossed in a blanket and then charitably cared for by the chambermaid, Fielding introduces the old English custom of riding and tying to allow *his* innkeeper to detain Joseph-Sancho and horse for unpaid oats. Betty has already played the charitable chambermaid to Joseph, but Fielding gives the episode another more comic variation. He has literally Anglicized Don Quixote's decrepit steed, Rosinante, into Parson Adams's most clerical horse, which belongs to his ministerial clerk and frequently stumbles to its knees. The parson's kneeling horse now falls on Joseph's leg, an innkeeper's wife again gives succor, and Adams again sprints off horseless. Similarly, Fielding copies his

[9] J. Paul de Castro, "Fielding's 'Parson Adams,'" *Notes and Queries,* 12th ser., 1 (March 18, 1916): 224–25.

"roasting" squire (III.vii) after an actual English practical joker, as Battestin notes (Wesleyan Edition, p. xxiv), creating an English equivalent, structurally and thematically, for Cervantes's Duke and Duchess who pretend hospitality only to torment the good Don Quixote. Spanish roads become English, complete with an actual innkeeper who once played wonderfully on the French horn. And the two traveling lovers from Scarron's France overlap with Cervantes's Spanish pair as Fielding creates his very English version of Scarron's *The Comical Romance* and Cervantes's *Don Quixote* all in one. Again and again, Fielding finds a kind of creative pleasure in these and other parallels, as he discovers examples of literary universals in the English life he knew and loved.

And thus the parodic impulse of *Shamela* swept on to include a new world of fiction: a comic, realistic world, presented as a serious moral lesson, upon the old mythic and wishful framework of romance, in which Fielding and we can amusedly accept our desire for recognition and fortune and love as we tacitly acknowledge the grimmer realities surrounding us—the critically sick wife and dying child. In his Preface, and in III.i, Fielding declares the independence of fiction. No longer must it disguise itself as authentic letters or autobiography; now it is "a true History," a nice irony, which we know to be untrue as we accept its absolute truth. Fielding in his wide reading, in his literate mind's eye, saw that literature could reveal essential typicalities, essential truths about human nature that endure through ages and societies. And his joy in discovering this, and in creating—in his new comic romance, his new "Species of writing"—fresh English parallels that would strike harmonics both comic and emulative from other great books, accounts for the wonderfully happy energy of *Joseph Andrews,* never to be equalled before or since, by him or anyone else.

A NOTE on the TEXTS

THE text of *Shamela* follows the first edition (April 2, 1741), corrected to indicate those changes presumed to be Fielding's in the second, and last, edition (October 31, 1741). Wilbur L. Cross's dates (April 4 and November 3) are apparently in error (*The History of Henry Fielding*. New Haven, 1918. Vol I, p. 303; Vol III, p. 303–304). *The Daily Post* advertised *Shamela* as "*This Day is publish'd*" on Thursday, April 2, 1741, repeating the ad on Friday and Saturday. Other papers followed on Saturday, April 4. *The Norwich Gazette*, a weekly issued on Saturdays, advertised *Shamela* (presumably the second edition) on Saturday, October 31, 1741, repeating the ad the next two Saturdays. The only other ad I have found is the one Cross uses, that in *The Champion*, Fielding's former paper (issued Tuesdays, Thursdays, and Saturdays), on Tuesday, November 3, 1741.

In the present text, brackets and a subscript "2" indicate the changes carried in the second edition, thus: "at all [like]$_2$ the matchless *Shamela*" (p. 4). The canceled reading from the first edition appears in the margin, thus: "[alike]$_1$." I have corrected substantive slips carried over from the first to the second edition, adding a small "c" to the bracket to indicate this present Crowell edition, as on page 11: "[W]$_{c}$," with the marginal note reading "[w]$_{1-2}$." This correction matches Fielding's own correction on page 33. I indicate the few *additions* (as distinguished from changes) by a pointed bracket, as on page 48: "⟨,⟩ $_{c}$" and "⟨;⟩ $_{2}$." I have silently corrected other obvious typographical slips—about thirty missing commas, five doublings of words ("are are"), three misspellings, and the like—some corrected in the second edition, some not, and have also silently accepted the second edition's occasional changes in punctuation, when these seemed consistent with Fielding's practice. But punctuational changes demanded by meaning are bracketed as substantive changes.

Since the whole text of *Shamela* comprises the supposed epistles of eighteenth-century people, I have kept the characteristic capitalization and italicizing throughout.

Fielding polished his grammar on the title page, changing "different from what" to "different from that which," although he missed the typographical error of "MISREPRSENTAIONS." But "FALSHOODS" was standard spelling until about 1790.

"Necessary to be had in all Families" was a popular phrase to advertise books, and the first of the letters introducing *Pamela* claims: "it will be found worthy a Place, . . . in all Families."

Fielding's title, as well as the typographical layout of his title page, mimics *An Apology for the Life of Mr. Colley Cibber* (April, 1740), by Colley Cibber himself (see Introduction, pp. xiii–xv, and xviii–xix).

The text of *Joseph Andrews* follows that of the first edition (February 22, 1742), marking those changes that seem to be Fielding's in the second, third, and fourth editions (June 10, 1742; March 24 [?], 1743; October 29, 1748). The fifth edition, published simultaneously with Fielding's *Amelia* on December 19, 1751, and the last to appear before Fielding's death three years later, contains no authorial changes. These dates, and

Fielding's changes to his book, are established by Martin Battestin in his meticulous textual edition of *Joseph Andrews* (Wesleyan Edition, 1967), to whose notes I also am heavily indebted.

I have modernized and normalized spelling (*show* for *shew*, *kitchen* for *kitchin*, for instance), and I have similarly modernized the typography—except in quoted letters, where I thought we might afford the added amusement of eighteenth-century styling on dramatic grounds. In other words, common nouns lose their capitals and proper nouns their italics, thus: "turning to *Adams* with a Gravity of Countenance" becomes "turning to Adams with a gravity of countenance" (III.vii.302). But when nouns like "Gravity," "Vanity," and "Reason" approach personification, or when ascriptions like "Poet" and "Philosopher" attain heightened emphasis, ironic or otherwise, I leave them capitalized, as in the original. I have also retained Fielding's italicizing of quotations, and occasionally of dialogue, and his italicizing for emphasis. But I print Fielding's Preface, originally all in italics, according to eighteenth-century custom, in regular roman type.

I have not modernized Fielding's punctuation, except to omit those quotation marks that run down the margin, line by line, in long quotations in eighteenth-century texts, and to normalize such inconsistencies as failure to close a quotation, or Fielding's occasional use of both quotation marks and parentheses in dialogue. Thus "Harkee," (says the Justice, taking aside the Squire) "I should not . . ." becomes "Harkee, (says the justice, taking aside the squire) I should not . . ." (IX.v.342).

I have added the table of contents from the second edition, where it appeared for the first time, as the publisher (I presume) merely collected for the reader's convenience "the contents prefixed to every chapter," to borrow Fielding's words from II.i.143. The contents for Books III and IV, of course, appeared separately, in the second of Fielding's two little volumes, which contained Books III and IV.

My system for indicating changes is the same as in *Shamela*, except that I also indicate a word canceled and not replaced, thus: "~~Indeed~~$_2$" (here indicating a cancellation made for the second edition). Again, brackets with a small subscript number indicate a change and the edition for which Fielding made it, and a bracketed note in the margin indicates the original reading. Again, pointed brackets indicate *additions* as distinct from replacements. Here is a passage (now on page 249), which Fielding changed for the second edition:

> "And indeed"⟨, continued he,⟩ $_2$ "what Cicero says of a complete orator, may well be applied to a great poet; [*He*]$_2$ *ought to comprehend all perfections*. Indeed $_2$ Homer did this . . . ."

A bracketed note in the right margin contains the only *displaced* word, an unitalicized "[who]$_1$." The first edition read:

> "And indeed what Cicero says of a complete orator, may well be applied to a great poet; who *ought to comprehend all perfections*. Indeed Homer did this . . . ."

Another example will help elucidate the system as well as Fielding's care with punctuation (p. 308):

> The poet⟨,⟩ $_3$ who was the nimblest⟨,⟩ $_3$ entering the [chamber first,]$_2$ searched . . . .

The bracketed note reads "[chamber, first]$_1$." The first edition read:

> The poet who was the nimblest entering the chamber, first searched . . . .

And the second:

> The poet who was the nimblest entering the chamber first, searched . . . .

Fielding straightened his meaning and punctuation in the third edition. Lengthy additions, like the long new paragraph on pages 201–202, are marked at beginning and end thus: ⌈ ⌋ —to keep them sufficiently distinct.

Modern texts continue to print Murphy's emendations: "Ay" for "Aye" (Fielding used both, making no distinction, and this text retains both, as he used them), "God" for "G——" (pp. 112, 187, 193), "incapable myself of delivering" for "incapable of my self delivering" (p. 182), and "how Sophocles falls short" for "how short Sophocles falls" (p. 250). But the most interesting, however disappointing, is Murphy's having Joseph write that Lady Booby "was naked in bed," whereas Fielding has him write (throughout all authoritative editions) "was in naked Bed" (p. 86), a phrase meaning merely that she was undressed for bed, in her nightgown, in dishabille, or the like (see *Oxford English Dictionary*). I have replaced all such emendations with their originals.

AN

APOLOGY

FOR THE

LIFE

OF

Mrs. SHAMELA ANDREWS.

In which, the many notorious FALSHOODS and MISREPRSENTATIONS of a Book called

PAMELA,

Are exposed and refuted; and all the matchless ARTS of that young Politician, set in a true and just Light.

Together with

A full Account of all that passed between her and Parson *Arthur Williams;* whose Character is represented in a manner something different from what he bears in *PAMELA*. The whole being exact Copies of authentick Papers delivered to the Editor.

Necessary to be had in all FAMILIES.

By Mr. *CONNY KEYBER.*

LONDON:

Printed for A. DODD, at the *Peacock,* without *Temple-bar.*

M. DCC. XLI.

To Miss *Fanny, &c.*[1]

MADAM,

IT will be naturally expected, that when I write the Life of *Shamela,* I should dedicate it to some young Lady, whose Wit and Beauty might be the proper Subject of a Comparison with the Heroine of my Piece. This, those, who see I have done

[1] John, Lord Hervey, whom Pope had labeled "Lord Fanny" (*First Satire of the Second Book of Horace,* 1733, line 6), to match Horace's enemy Fannius and hit Hervey's effeminate appearance and reputed bisexuality (see Eric Rothstein's "The Framework of *Shamela,*" p. 455). See Rothstein also (pp. 457, 461) for the sexual implications of "Fanny," "&c.," and "Conny." Hervey was an able supporter and agent of Robert Walpole's government through his friendship with the queen. Fielding, active in the Opposition to Walpole's government, here parodies, almost word for word, the dedicatory letter to Lord Hervey in the Reverend Conyers Middleton's *Life of Cicero,* published less than two months earlier (February, 1741). "Conyers" supplies Fielding with "Conny," which he then attaches to "Keyber" to get at Colley Cibber both sexually and politically. Cibber was also in Walpole's camp: his appointment as Poet Laureate in 1730 was widely considered a political payoff. Journalists of the Opposition had frequently knocked Cibber as "Mr. Keyber." He was of Danish descent, but they pretended to think his name was

it in prefixing your Name to my Work, will much more confirmedly expect me to do; and, indeed, your Character would enable me to run some Length into a Parallel, tho' you, nor any
[alike]$_1$ one else, are at all [like]$_2$ the matchless *Shamela*.

You see, Madam, I have some Value for your Good-nature, when in a Dedication, which is properly a Panegyrick, I speak against, not for you; but I remember it is a Life which I am presenting you, and why should I expose my Veracity to any Hazard in the Front of the Work, considering what I have done in the Body. Indeed, I wish it was possible to write a Dedication, and get any thing by it, without one Word of Flattery; but since it is not, come on, and I hope to shew my Delicacy at least in the Compliments I intend to pay you.

First, then, Madam, I must tell the World, that you have tickled up and brightned many Strokes in this Work by your Pencil.

Secondly, You have intimately conversed with me, one of the greatest Wits and Scholars of my Age.

Thirdly, You keep very good Hours, and frequently spend an useful Day before others begin to enjoy it. This I will take my Oath on; for I am admitted to your Presence in a Morning before other People's Servants are up; when I have constantly found you reading in good Books; and if ever I have drawn you upon me, I have always felt you very heavy.

Fourthly, You have a Virtue which enables you to rise early and study hard, and that is, forbearing to over-eat yourself, and this in spite of all the luscious Temptations of Puddings and Custards, exciting the Brute (as Dr. *Woodward*[2] calls it) to

German (presumably to associate him with the Hanoverian court, of which Walpole was Prime Minister), thus telling us how they pronounced it: ". . . the German turn which is given to the Name, for we know well That Nation turns *Caesar* into KEYSAR . . ." (*The Weekly Journal,* March 22, 1722, as quoted by Charles B. Woods, "Cibber in Fielding's *Author's Farce:* Three Notes," *Philological Quarterly,* 44 (1965), 145–46).

[2] Dr. John Woodward, in his *The State of Physic and of Diseases* (1718), had attributed all the evils of modern society, including stupidity, atheism, and rebelliousness, to the rich pastries and sauces of "the New Cookery" (i.e., French). Woodward was considered homosexual (see Rothstein, p. 458).

rebel. This is a Virtue which I can greatly admire, though I much question whether I could imitate it.

Fifthly, A Circumstance greatly to your Honour, that by means of your extraordinary Merit and Beauty; you was carried into the Ball-Room at the *Bath,* by the discerning Mr. *Nash;*[3] before the Age that other young Ladies generally arrived at that Honour, and while your Mamma herself existed in her perfect Bloom. Here you was observed in Dancing to balance your Body exactly, and to weigh every Motion with the exact and equal Measure of Time and Tune; and though you sometimes made a false Step, by leaning too much to one Side;[4] yet every body said you would one Time or other, dance perfectly well, and uprightly.

Sixthly, I cannot forbear mentioning those pretty little Sonnets, and sprightly Compositions, which though they came from you with so much Ease, might be mentioned to the Praise of a great or grave Character.

And now, Madam, I have done with you; it only remains to pay my Acknowledgments to an Author, whose Stile I have exactly followed in this Life, it being the properest for Biography. The Reader, I believe, easily guesses, I mean *Euclid's Elements;*[5] it was *Euclid* who taught me to write. It is you, Madam, who pay me for Writing. Therefore I am to both,

A most Obedient, and

obliged humble Servant,

Conny Keyber.

[3] Richard "Beau" Nash, the Master of Ceremonies at Bath, whose rules of conduct had made the resort famous.

[4] That is, Hervey's political leaning toward Walpole. Middleton had commended Hervey for following his father (not mother) in the House of Commons (not the ballroom at Bath) and for observing an "equal balance of the laws."

[5] Euclid's *Elements* would produce a rather geometrical style of writing: Middleton had attributed his own stylistic achievement to the example of Cicero, whose *Life* he was writing.

LETTERS TO THE EDITOR.

The EDITOR to *Himself*.

Dear SIR,

HOWEVER you came by the excellent *Shamela*, out with it, without Fear or [Favour]$_2$, Dedication and all; [Honour]$_1$ believe me, it will go through many Editions, be translated into all Languages, read in all Nations and Ages, and to say a bold Word, it will do more good than the *C——y* [6] have done harm in the World.

I am, Sir,

Sincerely your Well-wisher,

Yourself.

[6] *C*[*lerg*]*y;* Pope had apparently said that *Pamela* "will do more good than many volumes of sermons" (Alan D. McKillop, *Samuel Richardson, Printer and Novelist* [Chapel Hill: The University of North Carolina Press, 1936], p. 74).

JOHN PUFF,[7] *Esq; to the* EDITOR.

SIR,

I HAVE read your *Shamela* through and through, and a most inimitable Performance it is. Who is he, what is he that could write so excellent a Book? he must be doubtless most agreeable to the Age, and to *his Honour* himself; [8] for he is able to draw every thing to Perfection but Virtue. Whoever the Author be, he hath one of the worst and most fashionable Hearts in the World, and I would recommend to him, in his next Performance, to undertake the Life of *his Honour.* For he who drew the Character of Parson *Williams,* is equal to the Task; nay he seems to have little more to do than to pull off the Parson's Gown, and *that* which makes him so agreeable to *Shamela,* and the Cap will fit.

I am, Sir,

Your humble Servant,

JOHN PUFF.

Note, Reader, several other COMMENDATORY LETTERS and COPIES OF VERSES will be prepared against the NEXT EDITION.

[7] To "puff" was to advertise. This letter and the one preceding closely parody and subvert the twenty-eight pages of laudatory letters that Richardson printed as an introduction to the second edition of *Pamela.* Fielding pretends (or thought) that Richardson wrote most of them himself, but they were actually sent in by admirers.

[8] The Prime Minister, Sir Robert Walpole, patron of Hervey and Cibber, and political target for Fielding. Walpole was a Member of Parliament, First Lord of the Treasury, and effective head of the government. In the nineteenth century, the term "prime minister," became attached to this position, here evolving.

AN APOLOGY For the LIFE of Mrs. SHAMELA ANDREWS.

Parson TICKLETEXT *to Parson* OLIVER.[9]

Rev. SIR,

HEREWITH I transmit you a Copy of sweet, dear, pretty *Pamela*, a little Book which this Winter hath produced; of which, I make no Doubt, you have already heard mention from some of your Neighbouring Clergy;

[9] In *The Author's Farce*, Fielding had briefly presented his first version of Tickletext as a parson named Murder-text. Parson Oliver, I once thought, went back to the Parson Oliver who was Fielding's boyhood tutor—the man to whom Arthur Murphy, who knew Fielding, traced Trulliber of *Joseph Andrews*, "Trulliber" being a comically condensed pronunciation of "Mister Oliver" (Wilbur L. Cross, *The History of Henry Fielding* [New Haven: Yale University Press, 1918], I. 22–23; see also my edition of *Shamela* [Berkeley: University of California Press, 1953], p. xviii). Eric Rothstein's identification of William Oliver, a benevolent physician of Bath, seems better (see p. 468). Both names may ultimately derive from Shakespeare's Parson Oliver Martext (*As You Like It*). Christopher Bullock's *Woman's Revenge: or, a Match in Newgate* (revived in 1728 and acted twenty times during Fielding's theatrical career) contains a malapropist, somewhat like Fielding's Mrs. Jewkes and Mrs. Slipslop, who mentions a Parson Tickletext. Immediately after *The Author's Farce* (1730), Fielding presented an extended version of his ecclesiastical hypocrite as Parson Puzzletext. Fielding's accumulative imagination is well suggested in the progression: Oliver Martext—Murder-text

for we have made it our common Business here, not only to cry it up, but to preach it up likewise: The Pulpit, as well as the Coffee-house, hath resounded with its Praise, and it is expected shortly, that his L——p will recommend it in a —— Letter to our whole Body.[10]

And this Example, I am confident, will be imitated by all our Cloth in the Country: For besides speaking well of a Brother, in the Character of the Reverend Mr. *Williams*, the useful and truly religious Doctrine of *Grace* is every where inculcated.

This Book is the "SOUL *of Religion,* Good-Breeding, Discretion, Good-Nature, Wit, Fancy, Fine Thought, and Morality. There is an Ease, a natural Air, a dignified Simplicity and MEASURED FULLNESS in it, that RESEMBLING LIFE, OUT-GLOWS IT. The Author hath reconciled the *pleasing* to the *proper;* the Thought is every where exactly cloathed by the Expression; and becomes its Dress as *roundly* and as close as *Pamela* her Country Habit; or *as she doth her no Habit,* when modest Beauty seeks to hide itself, by casting off the Pride of Ornament, and displays itself without any Covering;"[11] which it frequently doth in this admirable Work, and presents Images to the Reader, which the coldest Zealot cannot read without Emotion.

For my own Part (and, I believe, I may say the same of all the Clergy of my Acquaintance) "I have done nothing but read it to others, and hear others again read it to me, ever since it came into my Hands; and I find I am like to do nothing else, for I know not how long yet to come: because if I lay the Book

and Marplay, of *The Author's Farce*—Puzzletext—Tickletext and Oliver, with "Oliver" hitting both literature and life at a stroke.

[10] "His L[ordshi]p will recommend it in a [pastoral] Letter to our whole Body" (i.e., to all of us clergymen). "His Lordship" is the Bishop of London, Edmund Gibson, frequent writer of pastoral letters, in one of which he attacked John Whitefield, the Methodist, some of whose alleged characteristics Fielding gives to Parson Williams in *Shamela,* especially what Parson Tickletext calls "the useful and truly religious Doctrine of *Grace.*"

[11] This quoted passage and the three that follow come directly from the introductory letters in *Pamela,* with a few sly alterations by Fielding, as when he changes "(a poor Girl's little, innocent, Story)" to "(a poor Girl's little, *&* *c.*)."

down *it comes after me*. When it has dwelt all Day long upon the Ear, it takes Possession all Night of the Fancy. It hath Witchcraft in every Page of it."—Oh! I feel an Emotion even while I am relating this: Methinks I see *Pamela* at this Instant, with all the Pride of Ornament cast off.

"Little Book, charming *Pamela*, get thee gone; face the World, in which thou wilt find nothing like thy self." Happy would it be for Mankind, if all other Books were burnt, that we might do nothing but read thee all Day, and Dream of thee all Night. Thou alone art sufficient to teach us as much Morality as we want. Dost thou not teach us to pray, to sing Psalms, and to honour the Clergy? Are not these the [W]$_{c}$hole Duty of [w]$_{1\text{-}2}$
Man? [12] Forgive me, O Author of *Pamela*, mentioning the Name of a Book so unequal to thine: But, now I think of it, who is the Author, where is he, what is he, that hath hitherto been able to hide such an encircling, all-mastering Spirit, "he possesses every Quality that Art could have charm'd by: yet hath lent it to and concealed it in Nature. The Comprehensiveness of his Imagination must be truly prodigious! It has stretched out this diminutive mere Grain of Mustard-seed (a poor Girl's little, *&c.*) into a Resemblance of that Heaven, which the best of good Books has compared it to."

To be short, this Book will live to the Age of the Patriarchs,[13] and like them will carry on the good Work many hundreds of Years hence, among our Posterity, who will not HESITATE their Esteem with Restraint. If the *Romans* granted Exemptions to Men who begat a *few* Children for the Republick, what Distinction (if Policy and we should ever be reconciled) should we find to reward this Father of Millions, which are to owe Formation to the future Effect of his Influence.—I feel another Emotion.

As soon as you have read this your self five or six Times over (which may possibly happen within a Week) I desire you would

[12] *The Whole Duty of Man*, anonymously published in 1658, continued to be a tremendously popular handbook of religion and morality.

[13] The Patriarchs are those early Biblical figures, from Adam onward, famed for longevity—especially Methuselah, said to have lived 969 years (Gen. 5:27). This paragraph also closely mimics the introductory letters in *Pamela*.

give it to my little God-Daughter, as a Present from me. This being the only Education we intend henceforth to give our Daughters. And pray let your Servant-Maids read it over, or read it to them. Both your self and the neighbouring Clergy, will supply yourselves for the Pulpit from the Booksellers, as soon as the fourth Edition is published. I am,

Sir,

Your most humble Servant,

THO. TICKLETEXT.

Parson OLIVER *to Parson* TICKLETEXT.

Rev. SIR,

I Received the Favour of yours with the inclosed Book, and really must own myself sorry to see the Report I have heard of an epidemical Phrenzy now raging in Town, confirmed in the Person of my Friend.

If I had not known your Hand, I should, from the Sentiments and Stile of the Letter, have imagined it to have come from the Author of the famous Apology, which was sent me last Summer; and on my reading the remarkable Paragraph of *measured Fulness, that resembling Life out-glows it*, to a young Baronet, he cry'd out, *C——ly C——b——r* by G——.[14] But I have since observed, that this, as well as many other Expressions in your Letter, was borrowed from those remarkable Epistles, which the Author, or the Editor hath prefix'd to the second Edition which you send me of his Book.

Is it possible that you or any of your Function can be in earnest, or think the Cause of Religion, or Morality, can want such slender Support? God forbid they should. As for Honour to the Clergy, I am sorry to see them so solicitous about it; for if worldly Honour be meant, it is what their Predecessors in the pure and primitive Age, never had or sought. Indeed the secure

[14] *C*[*ol*]*ly C*[*ib*]*b*[*e*]*r* by G[od].

Satisfaction of a good Conscience, the Approbation of the Wise and Good, (which never were or will be the Generality of Mankind) and the extatick Pleasure of contemplating, that their Ways are acceptable to the Great Creator of the Universe, will always attend those, who really deserve these Blessings: But for worldly Honours, they are often the Purchase of Force and Fraud, we sometimes see them in an eminent Degree possessed by Men, who are notorious for Luxury, Pride, Cruelty, Treachery, and the most abandoned Prostitution; Wretches who are ready to invent and maintain Schemes repugnant to the Interest, the Liberty, and the Happiness of Mankind, not to supply their Necessities, or even Conveniencies, but to pamper their Avarice and Ambition. And if this be the Road to worldly Honours, God forbid the Clergy should be even suspected of walking in it.

The History of *Pamela* I was acquainted with long before I received it from you, from my Neighbourhood to the Scene of Action. Indeed I was in hopes that young Woman would have contented herself with the Good-fortune she hath attained; and rather suffered her little Arts to have been forgotten than have revived their Remembrance, and endeavoured by perverting and misrepresenting Facts to be thought to deserve what she now enjoys: for though we do not imagine her the Author of the Narrative itself, yet we must suppose the Instructions were given by her, as well as the Reward, to the Composer. Who that is, though you so earnestly require of me, I shall leave you to guess from that *Ciceronian* Eloquence,[15] with which the Work abounds; and that excellent Knack of making every Character amiable, which he lays his hands on.

But before I send you some Papers relating to this Matter, which will set *Pamela* and some others in a very different Light, than that in which they appear in the printed Book, I must beg leave to make some few Remarks on the Book itself, and its Tendency, (admitting it to be a true Relation,) towards improving Morality, or doing any good, either to the present Age, or Posterity: which when I have done, I shall, I flatter myself,

15 "*Ciceronian* Eloquence" seems to refer to Middleton and his *Life of Cicero*.

stand excused from delivering it, either into the hands of my Daughter, or my Servant-Maid.

The Instruction which it conveys to Servant-Maids, is, I think, very plainly this, To look out for their Masters as sharp as they can. The Consequences of which will be, besides Neglect of their Business, and the using all manner of Means to come at Ornaments of their Persons, that if the Master is not a Fool, they will be debauched by him; and if he is a Fool, they will marry him. Neither of which, I apprehend, my good Friend, we desire should be the Case of our Sons.

And notwithstanding our Author's Professions of Modesty,[16] which in my Youth I have heard at the Beginning of an Epilogue, I cannot agree that my Daughter should entertain herself with some of his Pictures; which I do not expect to be contemplated without Emotion, unless by one of my Age and Temper, who can see the Girl lie on her Back, with one Arm round Mrs.
[*Jervis*]$_1$ [*Jewkes*]$_2$ and the other round the Squire, naked in Bed, with his Hand on her Breasts, *&c.* with as much Indifference as I read any other Page in the whole Novel. But surely this, and some other Descriptions, will not be put in the hands of his Daughter by any wise Man, though I believe it will be difficult for him to keep them from her; especially if the Clergy in Town have cried and preached it up as you say.

But, my Friend, the whole Narrative is such a Misrepresentation of Facts, such a Perversion of Truth, as you will, I am perswaded, agree, as soon as you have perused the Papers I now inclose to you, that I hope you or some other well-disposed Person, will communicate these Papers to the Publick, that this little Jade may not impose on the World, as she hath on her Master.

The true name of this Wench was SHAMELA, and not *Pamela*, as she stiles herself. Her Father had in his Youth the
[*Baily*]$_1$ Misfortune to appear in no good Light at the *Old*-[*Bailey*]$_2$; [17]

[16] Richardson's title page claimed that *Pamela* was "intirely divested of all those Images, which, in too many Pieces calculated for Amusement only, tend to *inflame* the Minds they should *instruct*." An epilogue (spoken by an actress in tights) frequently claimed a moral lesson for a bawdy play.

[17] London's criminal court.

he afterwards served in the Capacity of a Drummer in one of the *Scotch* Regiments in the *Dutch* Service; [18] where being drummed out, he came over to *England*, and turned Informer against several Persons on the late Gin-Act; [19] and becoming acquainted with an Hostler at an Inn, where a *Scotch* Gentleman's Horses stood, he hath at last by his Interest obtain'd a pretty snug Place in the *Custom-house*. Her Mother sold Oranges in the Play-House; and whether she was married to her Father or no, I never could learn.

After this short Introduction, the rest of her History will appear in the following Letters, which I assure you are authentick.

[18] Scotch regiments served Holland under an oath of allegiance originally directed against England.

[19] The Gin Act (1736), aimed at curbing widespread drunkenness by raising the price of gin, was extremely unpopular. Becoming a tax-collector in the custom house would not improve one's popularity.

LETTER I.

SHAMELA ANDREWS *to Mrs.* HENRIETTA MARIA HONORA ANDREWS *at her Lodgings at the* Fan *and* Pepper-Box *in* Drury-Lane.

Dear Mamma,

THIS comes to acquaint you, that I shall set out in the Waggon on *Monday,* desiring you to commodate me with a Ludgin, as near you as possible, in *Coulstin's-Court,* or *Wild-Street,* or somewhere thereabouts; pray let it be handsome, and not above two Stories high; For Parson *Williams* hath promised to visit me when he comes to Town, and I have got a good many fine Cloaths of the Old Put my Mistress's, who died a wil ago; and I beleve Mrs. *Jervis* will come along with me, for she says she would like to keep a House somewhere about *Short's-Gardens,* or towards *Queen-Street;* and if there was convenience for a *Bannio,* she should like it the better; but that she will settle herself when she comes to Town.—*O! How I long to be in the Balconey at the Old House* [20]—so no more at present from

Your affectionate Daughter,

SHAMELA.

[20] The Old House is the Drury Lane Playhouse (where Shamela's mother sold oranges), antedating the Covent Garden theater by a century.

LETTER II.

SHAMELA ANDREWS *to* HENRIETTA MARIA HONORA ANDREWS.

Dear Mamma,

O WHAT News, since I writ my last! the young Squire hath been here, and as sure as a Gun he hath taken a Fancy to me; *Pamela,* says he, (for so I am called here) you was a great Favourite of your late Mistress's; yes, an't please your Honour, says I; and I believe you deserved it, says he; thank your Honour for your good Opinion, says I; and then he took me by the Hand, and I pretended to be shy: Laud, says I, Sir, I hope you don't intend to be rude; no, says he, my Dear, and then he kissed me, 'till he took away my Breath—and I pretended to be Angry, and to get away, and then he kissed me again, and breathed very short, and looked very silly; and by Ill-Luck Mrs. *Jervis* came in, and had like to have spoiled Sport. —*How troublesome is such Interruption!* You shall hear now soon, for I shall not come away yet, so I rest,

Your affectionate Daughter,

SHAMELA.

LETTER III.

HENRIETTA MARIA HONORA ANDREWS *to* SHAMELA ANDREWS.

Dear Sham,

YOUR last Letter hath put me into a great hurry of Spirits, for you have a very difficult Part to act. I hope you will remember your Slip with Parson *Williams,* and not be guilty of any more such Folly. Truly, a Girl who hath once known what is what, is in the highest Degree inexcusable if she respects her *Digressions;* [21] but a Hint of this is sufficient. When Mrs. *Jervis* thinks of coming to Town, I believe I can procure her a good House, and fit for the Business, so I am,

Your affectionate Mother,

HENRIETTA MARIA HONORA ANDREWS.

LETTER IV.

SHAMELA ANDREWS *to* HENRIETTA MARIA HONORA ANDREWS.

MARRY come up, good Madam, the Mother had never looked into the Oven for her Daughter, if she had not been there herself. I shall never have done if you upbraid me with having had a small One by *Arthur Williams,* when you yourself—but I say no more. *O! What fine Times when the Kettle calls the Pot.* Let me do what I will, I say my Prayers as often as another, and I read in good Books, as often as I have Leisure; and Parson *William⟨s⟩* [e] says, that will make amends.—So no more, but I rest

Your afflicted Daughter,

S——.

[21] "Respects her *Digressions*" seems to be Mrs. Andrews's attempt at "repeats her transgressions," language a bit beyond her reach. This is Fielding's first touch of the malapropistic comedy, as with Shamela's "*Statue of Lamentations*" (for "statute of limitations," p. 32) and Mrs. Jewkes's "*Sect*" (for "sex," p. 35), which Fielding was to develop more fully with Mrs. Slipslop in *Joseph Andrews.*

LETTER V.

HENRIETTA MARIA HONORA ANDREWS *to* SHAMELA ANDREWS.

Dear Child,

WHY will you give such way to your Passion? How could you imagine I should be such a Simpleton, as to upbraid thee with being thy Mother's own Daughter! When I advised you not to be guilty of Folly, I meant no more than that you should take care to be well paid before-hand, and not trust to Promises, which a Man seldom keeps, after he hath had his wicked Will. And seeing you have a rich Fool to deal with, your not making a good Market will be the more inexcusable; indeed, with such Gentlemen as Parson *Williams*, there is more to be said; for they have nothing to give, and are commonly otherwise the best Sort of Men. I am glad to hear you read good Books, pray continue so to do. I have inclosed you one of Mr. *Whitefield*'s Sermons, and also the Dealings with him,[22] and am

Your affectionate Mother,

HENRIETTA MARIA, *&c.*

[22] *A Short Account of God's Dealings with the Reverend Mr. George Whitefield*, a popular book of Methodism, appearing in 1740, as did *Pamela* and Cibber's *Apology*. Whitefield tells how God's grace saved him from a wayward life.

LETTER VI.

SHAMELA ANDREWS *to* HENRIETTA MARIA HONORA ANDREWS.

O Madam, I have strange Things to tell you! As I was reading in that charming Book about the Dealings, in comes my Master—to be sure he is a precious One. *Pamela,* says he, what Book is that, I warrant you *Rochester*'s Poems.[23]—No, forsooth, says I, as pertly as I could; why how now Saucy Chops, Boldface, says he—Mighty pretty Words, says I, pert again.—Yes (says he) you are a d——d, impudent, stinking, cursed, confounded Jade, and I have a great Mind to kick your A——. You, kiss —— says I. A-gad, says he, and so I will; with that he caught me in his Arms; and kissed me till he made my Face all over Fire. Now this served purely you know, to put upon the Fool for Anger. O! What precious Fools Men are! And so I flung from him in a mighty Rage, and pretended as how I would go out at the Door; but when I came to the End of the Room, I stood still, and my Master cryed out, Hussy, Slut, Saucebox, Boldface, come hither—Yes, to be sure, says I; why don't you come, says he; what should I come for, says I; if you don't come to me, I'll come to you, says he; I shan't, come to you I assure you, says I. Upon which he run up, caught me in his Arms, and flung me upon a Chair, and began to offer to touch my Under-Petticoat. Sir, says I, you had better not offer to be rude; well, says he, no more I won't then; and away he went out of the Room. I was so mad to be sure I could have cry'd.

Oh what a prodigious Vexation it is to a Woman to be made a Fool of.

Mrs. *Jervis,* who had been without, harkening, now came to me. She burst into a violent Laugh the Moment she came in. Well, says she, as soon as she could speak, I have reason to bless

[23] Rochester's poems were eminently obscene.

myself that I am an Old Woman. Ah Child! if you had known the Jolly Blades of my Age, you would not have been left in the Lurch in this manner. Dear Mrs. *Jervis,* says I, don't laugh at one; and to be sure I was a little angry with her.—Come, says she, my dear Honeysuckle, I have one Game to play for you; he shall see you in Bed; he shall, my little Rosebud, he shall see those pretty, little, white, round, panting——and offer'd to pull off my Handkerchief.—Fie, Mrs. *Jervis,* says I, you make me blush, and upon my Fackins, I believe she did: She went on thus. I know the Squire likes you, and notwithstanding the Aukwardness of his Proceeding, I am convinced hath some hot Blood in his Veins, which will not let him rest, 'till he hath communicated some of his Warmth to thee, my little Angel; I heard him last Night at our Door, trying if it was open, now to-Night I will take care it shall be so; I warrant that he makes the second Trial; which if he doth, he shall find us ready to receive him. I will at first counterfeit Sleep, and after a Swoon; so that he will have you naked in his Possession: and then if you are disappointed, a Plague of all young Squires, say I.—And so, Mrs. *Jervis,* says I, you would have me yield my self to him, would you; you would have me be a second Time a Fool for nothing. Thank you for that, Mrs. *Jervis.* For nothing! marry forbid, says she, you know he hath large Sums of Money, besides abundance of fine Things; and do you think, when you have inflamed him, by giving his Hand a Liberty, with that charming Person; and that you know he may easily think he obtains against your Will, he will not give any thing to come at all—. This will not do, Mrs. *Jervis,* answered I. I have heard my Mamma say, (and so you know, Madam, I have) that in her Youth, Fellows have often taken away in the Morning, what they gave over Night. No, Mrs. *Jervis,* nothing under a regular taking into Keeping, a settled Settlement, for me, and all my Heirs, all my whole Lifetime, shall do the Business—or else cross-legged, is the Word, faith, with *Sham;* and then I snapt my Fingers.

Thursday Night, Twelve o'Clock.

Mrs. *Jervis* and I are just in Bed, and the Door unlocked; if my Master should come—Odsbobs! I hear him just coming in at the Door. You see I write in the present Tense, as Parson *Williams* says. Well, he is in Bed between us, we both shamming a Sleep, he steals his Hand into my Bosom, which I, as if in my Sleep, press close to me with mine, and then pretend to awake.—I no sooner see him, but I scream out to Mrs. *Jervis,* she feigns likewise but just to come to herself; we both begin, she to becall, and I to bescratch very liberally. After having made a pretty free Use of my Fingers, without any great Regard to the Parts I attack'd, I counterfeit a Swoon. Mrs. *Jervis* then cries out, O, Sir, what have you done, you have murthered poor *Pamela*: she is gone, she is gone.—

O what a Difficulty it is to keep one's Countenance, when a violent Laugh desires to burst forth.

The poor Booby frightned out of his Wits, jumped out of Bed, and, in his Shirt, sat down by my Bed-Side, pale and trembling, for the Moon shone, and I kept my Eyes wide open, and pretended to fix them in my Head. Mrs. *Jervis* apply'd Lavender Water, and Hartshorn, and this, for a full half Hour; when thinking I had carried it on long enough, and being likewise unable to continue the Sport any longer, I began by Degrees to come to my self.

The Squire who had sat all this while speechless, and was almost really in that Condition, which I feigned, the Moment he saw me give Symptoms of recovering my Senses, fell down on his Knees; and O *Pamela,* cryed he, can you forgive me, my injured Maid? by Heaven, I know not whether you are a Man or a Woman, unless by your swelling Breasts. Will you promise to forgive me: I forgive you! D——n you (says I) and d——n you, says he, if you come to that. I wish I had never seen your bold Face, saucy Sow, and so went out of the Room.

O what a silly Fellow is a bashful young Lover!

He was no sooner out of hearing, as we thought, than we both burst into a violent Laugh. Well, says Mrs. *Jervis,* I never saw any thing better acted than your Part: But I wish you may not have discouraged him from any future Attempt; especially since his Passions are so cool, that you could prevent his Hands going further than your Bosom. Hang him, answer'd I, he is not quite so cold as that I assure you; our Hands, on neither Side, were idle in the Scuffle, nor have left us any Doubt of each other as to that matter.

Friday Morning.

My Master sent for Mrs. *Jervis,* as soon as he was up, and bid her give an Account of the Plate and Linnen in her Care; and told her, he was resolved that both she and the little Gipsy (I'll assure him) should set out together. Mrs. *Jervis* made him a saucy Answer; which any Servant of Spirit, you know, would, tho' it should be one's Ruin; and came immediately in Tears to me, crying, she had lost her Place on my Account, and that she should be forced to take to a House, as I mentioned before; and, that she hoped I would, at least, make her all the amends in my power, for her Loss on my Account, and come to her House whenever I was sent for. Never fear, says I, I'll warrant we are not so near being turned away, as you imagine; and, i'cod, now it comes into my Head, I have a Fetch for him, and you shall assist me in it. But it being now late, and my Letter pretty long, no more at present from

Your Dutiful Daughter,

SHAMELA.

LETTER VII.

Mrs. LUCRETIA JERVIS *to* HENRIETTA MARIA HONORA ANDREWS.

Madam,

MISS *Sham* being set out in a Hurry for my Master's House in *Lincolnshire,* desired me to acquaint you with the Success of her Stratagem, which was to dress herself in the plain Neatness of a Farmer's Daughter, for she before wore the Cloaths of my late Mistress, and to be introduced by me as a Stranger to her Master. To say the Truth, she became the Dress extremely, and if I was to keep a House a thousand Years, I would never desire a prettier Wench in it.

As soon as my Master saw her, he immediately threw his Arms round her Neck, and smothered her with Kisses (for indeed he hath but very little to say for himself to a Woman.) He swore that *Pamela* was an ugly Slut (pardon, dear Madam, the Courseness of the Expression) compared to such divine Excellence. He added, he would turn *Pamela* away immediately, and take this new Girl, whom he thought to be one of his Tenants' Daughters, in her room.

Miss *Sham* smiled at these Words, and so did your humble Servant, which he perceiving, looked very earnestly at your fair Daughter, and discovered the Cheat.

How, *Pamela*, says he, is it you? I thought, Sir, said Miss, after what had happened, you would have known me in any Dress. No, Hussy, says he, but after what hath happened, I should know thee out of any Dress from all thy Sex. He then was what we Women call rude, when done in the Presence of others; but it seems it is not the first time, and Miss defended herself with great Strength and Spirit.

The Squire, who thinks her a pure Virgin, and who knows nothing of my Character, resolved to send her into *Lincolnshire*, on Pretence of conveying her home; where our old Friend *Nanny Jewkes* is Housekeeper, and where Miss had her small one by Parson *Williams* about a Year ago. This is a Piece of News communicated to us by *Robin* Coachman, who is intrusted by his Master to carry on this Affair privately for him: But we hang together, I believe, as well as any Family of Servants in the Nation.

You will, I believe, Madam, wonder that the Squire, who doth not want Generosity, should never have mentioned a Settlement all this while, I believe it slips his Memory: But it will not be long first, no Doubt: For, as I am convinced the young Lady will do nothing unbecoming your Daughter, nor ever admit him to taste her Charms, without something sure and handsome before-hand; so, I am certain, the Squire will never rest till they have danced *Adam* and *Eve*'s kissing Dance together. Your Daughter set out yesterday Morning, and told me, as soon as she arrived, you might depend on hearing from her.

Be pleased to make my Compliments acceptable to Mrs. *Davis* and Mrs. *Silvester*, and Mrs. *Jolly*, and all Friends, and permit me the Honour, Madam, to be with the utmost Sincerity,

Your most Obedient,

Humble Servant,

LUCRETIA JERVIS.

If the Squire should continue his Displeasure against me, so as to insist on the Warning he hath given me, you will see me soon, and I will lodge in the same House with you, if you have room, till I can provide for my self to my Liking.

LETTER VIII.

HENRIETTA MARIA HONORA ANDREWS *to* LUCRETIA JERVIS.

Madam,

I Received the Favour of your Letter, and I find you have not forgot your usual Poluteness, which you learned when you was in keeping with a Lord.

I am very much obliged to you for your Care of my Daughter, am glad to hear she hath taken such good Resolutions, and hope she will have sufficient Grace to maintain them.

All Friends are well, and remember to you. You will excuse the Shortness of this Scroll; for I have sprained my right Hand, with boxing three new made Officers.—Tho' to my Comfort, I beat them all. I rest,

Your Friend and Servant,

HENRIETTA, *&c.*

LETTER IX.

SHAMELA ANDREWS *to* HENRIETTA MARIA HONORA ANDREWS.

Dear Mamma,

I Suppose Mrs. *Jervis* acquainted you with what past 'till I left *Bedfordshire;* whence I am after a very pleasant Journey arrived in *Lincolnshire,* with your old Acquaintance Mrs. *Jewkes,* who formerly helped Parson *Williams* to me; and now designs I see, to sell me to my Master; thank her for that; she will find two Words go to that Bargain.

The Day after my Arrival here, I received a Letter from Mr. *Williams,* and as you have often desired to see one from him, I have inclosed it to you; it is, I think, the finest I ever received from that charming Man, and full of a great deal of Learning.

O! What a brave Thing it is to be a Scholard, and to be able to talk Latin.

Parson WILLIAMS *to* PAMELA ANDREWS.

Mrs. Pamela,

HAVING learnt by means of my Clerk, who Yesternight visited the Rev[d]. Mr. *Peters* with my Commands, that you are returned into this County, I purposed to have saluted your fair Hands this Day towards Even: But am obliged to sojourn this Night at a neighbouring Clergyman's; where we are to pierce a Virgin Barrel of Ale, in a Cup of which I shall not be unmindful to celebrate your Health.

I hope you have remembered your Promise, to bring me a Leaden Canister of Tobacco (the Saffron Cut) for in Troth, this Country at present affords nothing worthy the replenishing a Tube with. —Some I tasted the other Day at an Alehouse, gave me the Heart-Burn, tho' I filled no oftner than five Times.

I was greatly concerned to learn, that your late Lady left you nothing, tho' I cannot say the Tidings much surprized me: For I am too intimately acquainted with the Family; (myself, Father, and Grandfather having been successive Incumbents on the same Cure, which you know is in their Gift) I say, I am too well acquainted with them to expect much from their Generosity. They are in Verity, as worthless a Family as any other whatever. The young Gentleman I am informed, is a perfect Reprobate; that he hath an *Ingenium Versatile*[24] to every Species of Vice, which, indeed, no one can much wonder at, who animadverts on that want of Respect to the Clergy, which was observvable in him when a Child. I remember when he was at the Age of Eleven only, he met my Father without either pulling off his Hat, or riding out of the way. Indeed, a Contempt of the Clergy is the fashionable Vice of the Times; but let such Wretches know, they cannot hate, detest, and despise us, half so much as we do them.

However, I have prevailed on myself to write a civil Letter to your Master, as there is a Probability of his being shortly in a Capacity of rendring me a Piece of Service; my good Friend and Neighbour the Rev^d^. Mr. *Squeeze-Tithe* being, as I am informed by one whom I have employed to attend for that Purpose, very near his Dissolution.

You see, sweet Mrs. *Pamela,* the Confidence with which I dictate these Things to you; whom after those Endearments which have passed between us, I must in some Respects estimate as my Wife: For tho' the Omission of the Service was a Sin; yet, as I have told you, it was a Venial One, of which I have truly repented, as I hope you have; and also that you have continued the wholesome Office of reading good Books, and are improved in your Psalmody, of which I shall have a speedy Trial: For I purpose to give you a Sermon next *Sunday*, and shall spend the Evening with you, in Pleasures which tho' not strictly

24 "Versatile genius"; Battestin has found the source in Livy (see Rothstein, p. 472).

innocent, are however to be purged away by frequent and sincere Repentance. I am,

Sweet Mrs. Pamela,

Your faithful Servant,

ARTHUR WILLIAMS.

You find, Mamma, what a charming way he hath of Writing, and yet I assure you, that is not the most charming Thing belonging to him: For, tho' he doth not put any Dears, and Sweets, and Loves into his Letters, yet he says a thousand of them: For he can be as fond of a Woman, as any Man living.

Sure Women are great Fools, when they prefer a laced Coat to the Clergy, whom it is our Duty to honour and respect.

Well, on *Sunday* Parson *Williams* came, according to his Promise, and an excellent Sermon he preached; his Text was, *Be not Righteous over-much;* [25] and, indeed, he handled it in a very fine way; he shewed us that the Bible doth not require too much Goodness of us, and that People very often call things Goodness that are not so. That to go to Church, and to pray, and to sing Psalms, and to honour the Clergy, and to repent, is true Religion; and 'tis not doing good to one another, for that is one of the greatest Sins we can commit, when we don't do it for the sake of Religion. That those People who talk of Vartue and Morality, are the wickedest of all Persons. That 'tis not what we do, but what we believe, that must save us, and a great many other good Things; I wish I could remember them all.

As soon as Church was over, he came to the Squire's House, and drank Tea with Mrs. *Jewkes* and me; after which Mrs.

[25] *Be not Righteous over-much* (Eccl. 7:16) was the text for four sermons preached in April and May, 1739, by Joseph Trapp against the Methodist George Whitefield, himself present in the congregation during the first sermon. Rebuttals and reassertions were still in progress when *Shamela* appeared two years later. In *The Champion* (April 5 and May 24, 1740), just a year before *Shamela,* Fielding had used the phrase three times in his religious essays. Parson Williams uses the text to uphold the very excesses Trapp was opposing. The hypocritical Parson Thwackum of *Tom Jones* similarly upholds the doctrine of Grace and accuses Allworthy of "being righteous over-much" (XVIII. iv).

Jewkes went out and left us together for an Hour and half—Oh! he is a charming Man.

After Supper he went Home, and then Mrs. *Jewkes* began to catechize me, about my Familiarity with him. I see she wants him herself. Then she proceeded to tell me what an Honour my Master did me in liking me, and that it was both an inexcusable Folly and Pride in me, to pretend to refuse him any Favour. Pray, Madam, says I, consider I am a poor Girl, and have nothing but my Modesty to trust to. If I part with that, what will become of me. Methinks, says she, you are not so mighty modest when you are with Parson *Williams;* I have observed you gloat at one another, in a Manner that hath made me blush. I assure you, I shall let the Squire know what sort of Man he is;
[say]1-2 you may do your Will, [says]c I, as long as he hath a Vote for Pallamant-Men, the Squire dares do nothing to offend him; and you will only shew that you are jealous of him, and that's all. How now, Mynx, says she; Mynx! No more Mynx than yourself, says I; with that she hit me a Slap on the Shoulder, and I flew at her and scratched her Face, i'cod, 'till she went crying out of the Room; so no more at Present, from

Your Dutiful Daughter,

SHAMELA.

LETTER X.

SHAMELA ANDREWS *to* HENRIETTA MARIA HONORA ANDREWS.

O Mamma! Rare News! As soon as I was up this Morning, a Letter was brought me from the Squire, of which I send you a Copy.

Squire BOOBY *to* PAMELA.

Dear Creature,

I HOPE you are not angry with me for the Deceit put upon you, in conveying you to *Lincolnshire*, when you imagined yourself going to *London*. Indeed, my dear *Pamela*, I cannot live without you; and will very shortly come down and convince you, that my Designs are better than you imagine, and such as you may with Honour comply with. I am,

My Dear Creature,

Your doting Lover,

BOOBY.

Now, Mamma, what think you?—For my own Part, I am convinced he will marry me, and faith so he shall. O! Bless me! I shall be Mrs. *Booby*, and be Mistress of a great Estate, and have a dozen Coaches and Six, and a fine House at *London*, and another at *Bath*, and Servants, and Jewels, and Plate, and go to Plays, and Opera's, and Court; and do what I will, and spend what I will. But, poor Parson *Williams!* Well; and can't I see Parson *Williams*, as well after Marriage as before: For I shall never care a Farthing for my Husband. No, I hate and despise him of all Things.

Well, as soon as I had read my Letter, in came Mrs. *Jewkes*. You see, Madam, says she, I carry the Marks of your Passion about me; but I have received Order from my Master to be civil to you, and I must obey him: For he is the best Man in the World, notwithstanding your Treatment of him. My Treatment of him; Madam, says I? Yes, says she, your Insensibility to the Honour he intends you, of making you his Mistress. I would have you to know, Madam, I would not be Mistress to the greatest King, no nor Lord in the Universe. I value my Vartue more than I do any thing my Master can give me; and so we talked a full Hour and a half, about my Vartue; and I was afraid at first, she had heard something about the Bantling, but I find she hath not; tho' she is as jealous, and suspicious, as old Scratch.[26]

In the Afternoon, I stole into the Garden to meet Mr. *Williams;* I found him at the Place of his Appointment, and we staid in a kind of Arbour, till it was quite dark. He was very angry when I told him what Mrs. *Jewkes* had threatned—Let him refuse me the Living, says he, if he dares, I will vote for the other Party; and not only so, but will expose him all over the Country. I owe him 150*l.* indeed, but I don't care for that; by that Time the Election is past, I shall be able to plead the *Statue* of *Lamentations.*[27]

I could have stayed with the dear Man for ever, but when it grew dark, he told me, he was to meet the neighbouring Clergy, to finish the Barrel of Ale they had tapped the other Day, and believed they should not part till three or four in the Morning —So he left me, and I promised to be penitent, and go on with my reading in good Books.

As soon as he was gone, I bethought myself, what Excuse I should make to Mrs. *Jewkes,* and it came into my Head to pretend as how I intended to drown myself; so I stript off one of my Petticoats, and threw it into the Canal; and then I went and hid myself in the Coal-hole, where I lay all Night; and comforted myself with repeating over some Psalms, and other good things, which I had got by heart.

In the Morning Mrs. *Jewkes* and all the Servants were frighted out of their Wits, thinking I had run away; and not devising how they should answer it to their Master. They searched all the likeliest Places they could think of for me, and at last saw my Petticoat floating in the Pond. Then they got a Drag-Net, imagining I was drowned, and intending to drag me out; but at last *Moll* Cook coming for some Coals, discovered me lying all along in no very good Pickle. Bless me! Mrs. *Pamela,* says she, what can be the Meaning of this? I don't know, says I, help me up, and I will go in to Breakfast, for in-

[26] The Devil.

[27] The Statute of Limitations invalidated suits for debts after six years. See also p. 19, note 21.

deed I am very hungry. Mrs. *Jewkes* came in immediately, and was so rejoyced to find me alive, that she asked with great [good-Humour]$_2$, where I had been? and how my Petticoat came into the Pond. I answered, I believed the Devil had put it into my Head to drown my self; but it was a Fib; for I never saw the Devil in my Life, nor I don't believe he hath any thing to do with me.

[good Humour]$_1$

So much for this Matter. As soon as I had breakfasted, a Coach and Six came to the Door, and who should be in it but my Master.

I immediately run up into my Room, and stript, and washed, and drest my self as well as I could, and put on my prettiest round-ear'd Cap, and pulled down my Stays, to shew as much as I could of my Bosom, (for Parson *Williams* says, that is the most beautiful part of a Woman) and then I practised over all my Airs before the Glass, and then I sat down and read a Chapter in the [W]$_2$hole Duty of Man.

[w]$_1$

Then Mrs. *Jewkes* came to me and told me, my Master wanted me below, and says she, Don't behave like a Fool; No, thinks I to my self, I believe I shall find Wit enough for my Master and you too.

So down goes me I [28] into the Parlour to him. *Pamela,* says he, the Moment I came in, you see I cannot stay long from you, which I think is a sufficient Proof of the Violence of my Passion. Yes, Sir, says I, I see your Honour intends to ruin me, that nothing but the Destruction of my Vartue will content you.

O what a charming Word that is, rest his Soul who first invented it.

How can you say I would ruin you, answered the Squire, when you shall not ask any thing which I will not grant you. If that be true, says I, good your Honour, let me go Home to my poor but honest Parents; that is all I have to ask, and do not ruin a poor Maiden, who is resolved to carry her Vartue to the Grave with her.

Hussy, says he, don't provoke me, don't provoke me, I say. You are absolutely in my power, and if you won't let me lie

[28] A bolder colloquial version of the colloquial "I goes me down."

with you by fair Means, I will by Force. O La, Sir, says I, I don't understand your paw Words.[29]—Very pretty Treatment indeed, says he, to say I use paw Words; Hussy, Gipsie, Hypocrite, Saucebox, Boldface, get out of my Sight, or I will lend you such a Kick in the ———. I don't care to repeat the Word, but he meant my hinder part. I was offering to go away, for I was half afraid, when he called me back, and took me round the Neck and kissed me, and then bid me go about my Business.

I went directly into my Room, where Mrs. *Jewkes* came to me soon afterwards. So Madam, says she, you have left my Master below in a fine Pet, he hath threshed two or three of his Men already: It is mighty pretty that all his Servants are to be punished for your Impertinence.

Harkee, Madam, says I, don't you affront me, for if you do, d——n me (I am sure I have repented for using such a Word) if I am not revenged.

How sweet is Revenge: Sure the Sermon Book is in the Right, in calling it the sweetest Morsel the Devil ever dropped into the Mouth of a Sinner.[30]

Mrs. *Jewkes* remembered the Smart of my Nails too well to go farther, and so we sat down and talked about my Vartue till Dinner-time, and then I was sent for to wait on my Master. I took care to be often caught looking at him, and then I always turn'd away my Eyes, and pretended to be ashamed. As soon as the Cloth was removed, he put a Bumper of Champagne into my Hand, and bid me drink———O la I can't name the Health. Parson *Williams* may well say he is a wicked Man.

Mrs. *Jewkes* took a Glass and drank the dear *Monysyllable;* I don't understand that Word, but I believe it is baudy. I then drank towards his Honour's good Pleasure. Ay, Hussy, says he,

[29] Naughty words.

[30] Shamela refers to one of Fielding's favorite passages from the sermons of Robert South (1633–1716): "Revenge is certainly the most luscious morsel that the devil can put into the sinner's mouth." Fielding had already paraphrased this passage in *The Mock Doctor* (vi. 173) and in *The Champion* (February 2, 1740), and he later praised South for sermons having "perhaps more wit than in the comedies of Congreve," and "many strokes of the most exquisite drollery" (*The Covent-Garden Journal,* March 3, 1752).

you can give me Pleasure if you will; Sir, says I, I shall be always glad to do what is in my power, and so I pretended not to know what he meant. Then he took me into his Lap.—O Mamma, I could tell you something if I would—and he kissed me—and I said I won't be slobber'd about so, so I won't, and he bid me get out of the Room for a saucy Baggage, and said he had a good mind to spit in my Face.

Sure no Man ever took such a Method to gain a Woman's Heart.

I had not been long in my Chamber before Mrs. *Jewkes* came to me, and told me, my Master would not see me any more that Evening, that is, if he can help it; for, added she, I easily perceive the great Ascendant you have over him; and to confess the Truth, I don't doubt but you will shortly be my Mistress.

What⟨,⟩[2] says I, dear Mrs. *Jewkes*, what do you say? Don't flatter a poor Girl, it is impossible his Honour can have any honourable Design upon me. And so we talked of honourable Designs till Supper-time. And Mrs. *Jewkes* and I supped together upon a hot buttered Apple-Pie; and about ten o' Clock we went to Bed.

We had not been a Bed half an Hour, when my Master came pit a pat into the Room in his Shirt as before, I pretended not to hear him, and Mrs. *Jewkes* laid hold of one Arm, and he pulled down the Bed-cloaths and came into Bed on the other Side, and took my other Arm and laid it under him, and fell a kissing one of my Breasts as if he would have devoured it; I was then forced to awake, and began to struggle with him, Mrs. *Jewkes* crying why don't you do it? I have one Arm secure, if you can't deal with the rest I am sorry for you. He was as rude as possible to me; but I remembered, Mamma, the Instructions you gave me to avoid being ravished, and followed them, which soon brought him to Terms, and he promised me, on quitting my hold, that he would leave the Bed.

O Parson Williams, *how little are all the Men in the World compared to thee.*

My Master was as good as his Word; upon which Mrs. *Jewkes* said, O Sir, I see you know very little of our *Sect*, by parting so easily from the Blessing when you was so near it. No, Mrs *Jewkes*, answered he, I am very glad no more hath happened, I would not have injured *Pamela* for the World. And to-morrow Morning perhaps she may hear of something to her Advantage. This she may be certain of, that I will never take her by Force, and then he left the Room.

What think you now, Mrs. *Pamela*, says Mrs. *Jewkes*, Are you not yet persuaded my Master hath honourable Designs? I think he hath given no great Proof of them to-night, said I. Your Experience I find is not great, says she, but I am convinced you will shortly be my Mistress, and then what will become of poor me.

With such Sort of Discourse we both fell asleep. Next Morning early my Master sent for me, and after kissing me, gave a Paper into my Hand which he bid me read; I did so, and found it to be a Proposal for settling 250*l.* a Year on me, besides several other advantagious Offers, as Presents of Money and other Things. Well, *Pamela*, said he, what Answer do you make me to this. Sir, said I, I value my Vartue more than all the World, and I had rather be the poorest Man's Wife, than the richest Man's Whore. You are a Simpleton, said he; That may be, and yet I may have as much Wit as some Folks, cry'd I; meaning me, I suppose, said he; every Man knows himself best, says I. Hussy, says he, get out of the Room, and let me see your saucy Face no more, for I find I am in more Danger than you are, and therefore it shall be my Business to avoid you as much as I can; and it shall be mine, thinks I, at every turn to throw my self in your Way. So I went out, and as I parted, I heard him sigh and say he was bewitched.

Mrs. *Jewkes* hath been with me since, and she assures me she is convinced I shall shortly be Mistress of the Family, and she really behaves to me, as if she already thought me so. I am resolved now to aim at it. I thought once of making a little Fortune by my Person. I now intend to make a great one by my Vartue. So asking Pardon for this long Scroll, I am,

Your dutiful Daughter,

SHAMELA.

LETTER XI.

HENRIETTA MARIA HONORA ANDREWS *to* SHAMELA ANDREWS.

Dear Sham,

I RECEIVED your last Letter with infinite Pleasure, and am convinced it will be your own Fault if you are not married to your Master, and I would advise you now to take no less Terms. But, my dear Child, I am afraid of one Rock only, That Parson *Williams,* I wish he was out of the Way. A Woman never commits Folly but with such Sort of Men, as by many Hints in the Letters I collect him to be: but, consider, my dear Child, you will hereafter have Opportunities sufficient to indulge yourself with Parson *Williams,* or any other you like. My Advice therefore to you is, that you would avoid seeing him any more till the Knot is tied. Remember the first Lesson I taught you, that a Married Woman injures only her Husband, but a Single Woman herself. I am, in hopes of seeing you a great Lady,

Your affectionate Mother,

HENRIETTA MARIA, *&c.*

The following Letter seems to have been written before *Shamela* received the last from her Mother.

LETTER XII.

SHAMELA ANDREWS *to* HENRIETTA MARIA HONORA ANDREWS.

Dear Mamma,

I LITTLE feared when I sent away my last, that all my Hopes would be so soon frustrated; but I am certain you will blame Fortune and not me. To proceed then. About two Hours after I had left the Squire, he sent for me into the Parlour. *Pamela,* said he, and takes me gently by the Hand, will you walk with me in the Garden; yes, Sir, says I, and pretended to tremble; but I hope your Honour will not be rude. Indeed, says he, you have nothing to fear from me, and I have something to tell you, which if it doth not please you, cannot offend. We walked out together, and he began thus, *Pamela,* will you tell me Truth? Doth the Resistance you make to my Attempts proceed from Vartue only, or have I some Rival in thy dear Bosom who might be more successful? Sir, says I, I do assure you I never had a thought of any Man in the World. How, says he, not of Parson *Williams!* Parson *Williams,* says I, is the last Man upon Earth; and if I was a Dutchess, and your Honour was to make your Addresses to me, you would have no Reason to be jealous of any Rival, especially such a Fellow as Parson *Williams.* If ever I had a Liking, I am sure—but I am not worthy of you one Way, and no Riches should ever bribe me the other. My Dear, says he, you are worthy of every Thing, and suppose I should lay aside all Considerations of Fortune, and disregard the Censure of the World, and marry you. O Sir, says I, I am sure you can have no such Thoughts,

you cannot demean your self so low. Upon my Soul, I am in earnest, says he,—O Pardon me, Sir, says I, you can't persuade me of this. How [Mistress,]$_2$ says he, in a violent Rage, do you [Mrs.]$_1$
give me the Lie? Hussy, I have a great mind to box your saucy Ears, but I am resolved I will never put it in your power to affront me again, and therefore I desire you to prepare your self for your Journey this Instant. You deserve no better Vehicle than a Cart; however, for once you shall have a Chariot, and it shall be ready for you within this half Hour; and so he flung from me in a Fury.

What a foolish Thing it is for a Woman to dally too long with her Lover's Desires; how many have owed their being old Maids to their holding out too long.

Mrs. *Jewkes* came to me presently, and told me, I must make ready with all the Expedition imaginable, for that my Master had ordered the Chariot, and that if I was not prepared to go in it, I should be turned out of Doors, and left to find my way Home on Foot. This startled me a little, yet I resolved, whether in the right or wrong, not to submit nor ask Pardon: For that you know, Mamma, you never could your self bring me to from my Childhood: Besides, I thought he would be no more able to master his Passion for me now, than he had been hitherto; and if he sent two Horses away with me, I concluded he would send four to fetch me back. So, truly, I resolved to brazen it out, and with all the Spirit I could muster up, I told Mrs. *Jewkes* I was vastly pleased with the News she brought me; that no one ever went more readily than I should, from a Place where my Vartue had been in continual Danger. That as for my Master, he might easily get those who were fit for his Purpose; but, for my Part, I preferred my Vartue to all Rakes whatever—And for his Promises, and his Offers to me, I don't value them of a Fig—Not of a Fig, Mrs. *Jewkes;* and then I snapt my Fingers.

Mrs. *Jewkes* went in with me, and helped me to pack up my little All, which was soon done; being no more than two Day-Caps, two Night-Caps, five Shifts, one Sham,[31] a Hoop, a Quilted-Petticoat, two Flannel-Petticoats, two pair of Stockings,

[31] A false shirt-front.

one odd one, a pair of lac'd Shoes, a short flowered Apron, a lac'd Neck-Handkerchief, one Clog, and almost another, and
[*a*]1-2 some few Books: as, [*A*]c *full Answer to a plain and true Account,* &c.[32] *The Whole Duty of Man,* with only the Duty to one's Neighbour, torn out. The Third Volume of the *Atalantis. Venus in the Cloyster: Or, the Nun in her Smock. God's Dealings with Mr. Whitefield. Orfus and Eurydice.*[33] Some Sermon-Books; and two or three Plays, with their Titles, and Part of the first Act torn off.

So as soon as we had put all this into a Bundle, the Chariot was ready, and I took leave of all the Servants, and particularly Mrs. *Jewkes,* who pretended, I believe, to be more sorry to part with me than she was; and then crying out with an Air of Indifference, my Service to my Master, when he condescends to enquire after me, I flung my self into the Chariot, and bid *Robin* drive on.

We had not gone far, before a Man on Horseback, riding full Speed, overtook us, and coming up to the Side of the Chariot, threw a Letter into the Window, and then departed without uttering a single Syllable.

I immediately knew the Hand of my dear *Williams,* and was somewhat surprized, tho' I did not apprehend the Contents to be so terrible, as by the following exact Copy you will find them.

[32] *A full Answer to a plain and true Account, &c.* disputes Bishop Benjamin Hoadley's rationalistic *A Plain Account of the Nature and End of the Sacrament of the Lord's Supper* (1735), which Fielding admired, and which Parson Adams praises (*JA* I.xvii.136).

[33] The *Atalantis,* by Mary Manley (1709)—a collection of current scandals disguised as incidents on a newly discovered island of "Atalantis" in the Mediterranean (*Secret Memoirs and Manners of Several Persons of Quality of Both Sexes. From the New Atalantis*); Fielding mentions it again with scorn in *Joseph Andrews* (III.i.240).

Venus in the Cloyster: Or, the Nun in her Smock (1724), a translation of French pornography, which brought publisher Edmund Curll to trial.

Orpheus and Eurydice (1740), a musical pantomime by Lewis Theobald, at which Fielding scoffs in his periodical, *The Champion* (February 21 and May 24, 1740).

Parson WILLIAMS *to* PAMELA.

Dear Mrs. PAMELA,

THAT Disrespect for the Clergy, which I have formerly noted to you in that Villain your Master, hath now broke forth in a manifest Fact. I was proceeding to my Neighbour *Spruce's* Church, where I purposed to preach a Funeral Sermon, on the Death of Mr. *John Gage,* the Exciseman; when I was met by two Persons who are, it seems, Sheriffs Officers, and arrested for the 150*l.* which your Master had lent me; and unless I can find Bail within these few Days, of which I see no likelihood, I shall be carried to Goal.[34] This accounts for my not having visited you these two Days; which you might assure your self, I should not have fail'd, if the *Potestas* had not been wanting. If you can by any means prevail on your Master to release me, I beseech you so to do, not scrupling any thing for Righteousness sake. I hear he is just arrived in this Country, I have herewith sent him a Letter, of which I transmit you a Copy. So with Prayers for your Success, I subscribe my self

Your affectionate Friend,

ARTHUR WILLIAMS.

Parson WILLIAMS *to Squire* BOOBY.

Honoured Sir,

I Am justly surprized to feel so heavy a Weight of your Displeasure, without being conscious of the least Demerit towards so good and generous a Patron, as I have ever found you: For my own Part, I can truly say,

[34] A widespread eighteenth-century misspelling of *gaol,* the standard British spelling of *jail.*

Nil conscire sibi nullæ pallescere culpæ.[35]

And therefore, as this Proceeding is so contrary to your usual Goodness, which I have often experienced, and more especially in the Loan of this Money for which I am now arrested; I cannot avoid thinking some malicious Persons have insinuated false Suggestions against me; intending thereby, to eradicate those Seeds of Affection which I have hardly travailed to sowe in your Heart, and which promised to produce such excellent Fruit. If I have any ways offended you, Sir, be graciously pleased to let me know it, and likewise to point out to me, the Means whereby I may reinstate myself in your Favour: For next to him whom the great themselves must bow down before, I know none to whom I shall bend with more Lowliness than your Honour. Permit me to subscribe my self,

Honoured Sir,

Your most obedient, and most obliged,

And most dutiful humble Servant,

ARTHUR WILLIAMS.

The Fate of poor Mr. *Williams* shocked me more than my own: For, as the *Beggar's Opera* says, *Nothing moves one so much as a great Man in Distress.*[36] And to see a Man of his Learning forced to submit so low, to one whom I have often heard him say, he despises, is, I think, a most affecting Circumstance. I write all this to you, Dear Mamma, at the Inn where I lie this first Night, and as I shall send it immediately, by the Post, it will be in Town a little before me.—Don't let my coming away vex you: For, as my Master will be in Town in a few Days, I shall have an Opportunity of seeing him; and let the

[35] "To feel oneself guilty of nothing, to have no fault to turn one pale" (Horace, *Epistles* I.i.61). Fielding (or Williams) mistakes his grammar as he quotes from memory: *nullæ culpæ* should read *nulla culpa* (ablative, "by no fault").

[36] John Gay's *Beggar's Opera* (1728) makes fun of "great Men," particularly Prime Minister Robert Walpole, through its highwayman-hero.

worst come to the worst, I shall be sure of my Settlement at last. Which is all, from

Your Dutiful Daughter,

SHAMELA.

P. S. Just as I was going to send this away a Letter is come from my Master, desiring me to return, with a large Number of Promises.—I have him now as sure as a Gun, as you will perceive by the Letter itself, which I have inclosed to you.

This Letter is unhappily lost, as well as the next which *Shamela* wrote, and which contained an Account of all the Proceedings previous to her Marriage. The only remaining one which I could preserve, seems to have been written about a Week after the Ceremony was perform'd, and is as follows:

SHAMELA BOOBY *to* HENRIETTA MARIA HONORA ANDREWS.

Madam,

IN my last I left off at our sitting down to Supper on our Wedding Night,* where I behaved with as much Bashfulness as the purest Virgin in the World could have done. The most difficult Task for me was to blush; however, by holding my Breath, and squeezing my Cheeks with my Handkerchief, I did pretty well. My Husband was extreamly eager and impatient to have Supper removed, after which he gave me leave to retire into my Closet for a Quarter of an Hour, which was very agreeable to me; for I employed that time in writing to Mr. *Williams,* who, as I informed you in my last, is released, and presented to the Living, upon the Death of the last Parson.

* This was the Letter which is lost. [Fielding's note]

Well, at last I went to Bed, and my Husband soon leapt in after me; where I shall only assure you, I acted my Part in such a manner, that no Bridegroom was ever better satisfied with his Bride's Virginity. And to confess the Truth, I might have been well enough satisfied too, if I had never been acquainted with Parson *Williams*.

O what regard Men who marry Widows should have to the Qualifications of their former Husbands.

We did not rise the next Morning till eleven, and then we sat down to Breakfast; I eat two Slices of Bread and Butter, and drank three Dishes of Tea, with a good deal of Sugar, and we both look'd very silly. After Breakfast we drest our selves, he in a blue Camblet Coat, very richly lac'd, and Breeches of the same; with a Paduasoy [Waistcoat]$_2$ [Waste-coat]$_1$, laced with Silver; and I, in one of my Mistress's Gowns. I will have finer when I come to Town. We then took a Walk in the Garden, and he kissed me several Times, and made me a Present of 100 Guineas, which I gave away before Night to the Servants, twenty to one, and ten to another, and so on.

We eat a very hearty Dinner, and about eight in the Evening went to Bed again. He is prodigiously fond of me; but I don't like him half so well as my dear *Williams*. The next Morning we rose earlier, and I asked him for another hundred Guineas, and he gave them me. I sent fifty to Parson *Williams*, and the rest I gave away, two Guineas to a Beggar, and three to a Man riding along the Road, and the rest to other People. I long to be in *London* that I may have an Opportunity of laying some out, as well as giving away. I believe I shall buy every Thing I see. What signifies having Money if one doth not spend it.

The next Day, as soon as I was up, I asked him for another Hundred. Why, my Dear, says he, I don't grudge you any thing, but how was it possible for you to lay out the other two Hundred here. La! Sir, says I, I hope I am not obliged to give you an Account of every Shilling; Troth, that will be being your Servant still. I assure you, I married you with no such view, besides did not you tell me I should be Mistress of your Estate? And I will be too. For tho' I brought no Fortune, I am as much your Wife as if I had brought a Million—yes, but, my Dear, says he, if you had brought a Million, you would spend it all at

this rate; besides, what will your Expences be in *London,* if they are so great here. Truly, says I, Sir, I shall live like other Ladies of my Fashion; and if you think, because I was a Servant, that I shall be contented to be governed as you please, I will shew you, you are mistaken. If you had not cared to marry me, you might have let it alone. I did not ask you, nor I did not court you. Madam, says he, I don't value a Hundred Guineas to oblige you; but this is a Spirit which I did not expect in you, nor did I ever see any Symptoms of it before. O but Times are altered now, I am your Lady, Sir; yes to my Sorrow, says he, I am afraid—and I am afraid to my Sorrow too: For if you begin to use me in this manner already, I reckon you will beat me before a Month's at an End. I am sure if you did, it would injure me less than this barbarous Treatment; upon which I burst into Tears, and pretended to fall into a Fit. This frighted him out of his wits, and he called up the Servants. Mrs. *Jewkes* immediately came in, and she and another of the Maids fell heartily to rubbing my Temples, and holding Smelling-Bottles to my Nose. Mrs. *Jewkes* told him she fear'd I should never recover, upon which he began to beat his Breasts, and cried out, O my dearest Angel, curse on my passionate Temper, I have destroy'd her, I have destroy'd her[!]$_{2}$—would she had spent [,]$_{1}$
my whole Estate rather than this had happened. Speak to me, my Love, I will melt my self into Gold for thy Pleasure. At last having pretty well tired my self with counterfeiting, and imagining I had continu'd long enough for my purpose in the sham Fit, I began to move my Eyes, to loosen my Teeth, and to open my Hands, which Mr. *Booby* no sooner perceived then he embraced and kissed me with the eagerest Extacy, asked my Pardon on his Knees for what I had suffered through his Folly and Perverseness, and without more Questions fetched me the Money. I fancy I have effectually prevented any farther Refusals or Inquiry into my Expences. It would be hard indeed, that a Woman who marries a Man only for his Money, should be debarred from spending it.

Well, after all Things were quiet, we sat down to Breakfast, yet I resolved not to smile once, nor to say one good-natured, or good-humoured Word on any Account.

Nothing can be more prudent in a Wife, than a sullen Back-

wardness to Reconciliation; it makes a Husband fearful of offending by the Length of his Punishment.

When we were drest, the Coach was by my Desire ordered for an Airing, which we took in it. A long Silence prevailed on both Sides, tho' he constantly squeezed my Hand, and kissed me, and used other Familiarities, which I peevishly permitted. At last, I opened my Mouth first.—And so, says I, you are sorry you are married?—Pray, my Dear, says he, forget what I said in a Passion. Passion, says I, is apter to discover our Thoughts than to teach us to counterfeit. Well, says he, whether you will believe me or no, I solemnly vow, I would not change thee for the richest Woman in the Universe. No, I warrant you, says I; and yet you could refuse me a nasty hundred Pound. At these very Words, I saw Mr. *Williams* riding as fast as he could across a Field; and I looked out, and saw a Lease[37] of Greyhounds coursing a Hare, which they presently killed, and I saw him alight, and take it from them.

My Husband ordered *Robin* to drive towards him, and looked horribly out of Humour, which I presently imputed to Jealousy. So I began with him first; for that is the wisest way. La, Sir, says I; what makes you look so Angry and Grim? Doth the Sight of Mr. *Williams* give you all this Uneasiness? I am sure, I would never have married a Woman of whom I had so bad an Opinion, that I must be uneasy at every Fellow she looks at. My Dear, answered he, you injure me extremely, you was not in my Thoughts, nor, indeed, could be, while they were covered by so morose a Countenance; I am justly angry with that Parson, whose Family hath been raised from the Dunghill by ours; and who hath received from me twenty Kindnesses, and yet is not contented to destroy the Game in all other Places, which I freely give him leave to do; but hath the Impudence to pursue a few Hares, which I am desirous to preserve, round about this little Coppice. Look, my Dear, pray look, says he; I believe he is going to turn Higler. To confess the Truth, he had no less than three ty'd up behind his Horse, and a fourth he held in his Hand.

Pshaw, says I, I wish all the Hares in the Country were

[37] A "leash," or three hounds.

d——d (the Parson himself chid me afterwards for using the Word, tho' it was in his Service.) Here's a Fuss, indeed, about a nasty little pitiful Creature, that is not half so useful as a Cat. You shall not persuade me, that a Man of your Understanding, would quarrel with a Clergyman for such a Trifle. No, no, I am the Hare, for whom poor Parson *Williams* is persecuted; and Jealousy is the Motive. If you had married one of your Quality Ladies, she would have had Lovers by dozens, she would so; but because you have taken a Servant-Maid, forsooth! you are jealous if she but looks (and then I began to Water) at a poor P——a——a——rson in his Pu——u——u——lpit, and then out burst a Flood of Tears.

My Dear, said he, for Heaven's sake dry your Eyes, and don't let him be a Witness of your Tears, which I should be sorry to think might be imputed to my Unkindness; I have already given you some Proofs that I am not jealous of this Parson; I will now give you a very strong One: For I will mount my Horse, and you shall take *Williams* into the Coach. You may be sure, this Motion pleased me, yet I pretended to make as light of it as possible, and told him, I was sorry his Behaviour had made some such glaring Instance, necessary to the perfect clearing my Character.

He soon came up to Mr. *Williams,* who had attempted to ride off, but was prevented by one of our Horsemen, whom my Husband sent to stop him. When we met, my Husband asked him how he did with a very [good-humoured]$_2$ Air, and told him he perceived he had found good Sport that Morning. He answered pretty moderate, Sir; for that he had found the three Hares tied on to the Saddle dead in a Ditch (winking on me at the same Time) and added he was sorry there was such a Rot among them.

[good humoured]$_1$

Well, says Mr. *Booby,* if you please, Mr. *Williams,* you shall come in and ride with my Wife. For my own part, I will mount on Horseback; for it is fine Weather, and besides it doth not become me to loll in a Chariot, whilst a Clergyman rides on Horseback.

At which Words, Mr. *Booby* leapt out, and Mr. *Williams* leapt in, in an instant, telling my Husband as he mounted, he was glad to see such a Reformation, and that if he continued his Respect to the Clergy, he might assure himself of Blessings from above.

It was now that the Airing began to grow pleasant to me. Mr. *Williams,* who never had but one Fault, *viz.* that he generally smells of Tobacco, was now perfectly sweet; for he had for two Days together enjoined himself as a Penance, not to smoke till he had kissed my Lips. I will loosen you from that Obligation, says I, and observing my Husband looking another way, I gave him a charming Kiss, and then he asked me Questions concerning my Wedding-night; this actually made me blush: I vow I did not think it had been in him.

As he went along, he began to discourse very learnedly, and
[too]$_{1\text{-}2}$ told me the Flesh and the Spirit were [two]$_{c}$ distinct Matters, which had not the least relation to each other. That all immaterial Substances (those were his very Words) such as Love, Desire, and so forth, were guided by the Spirit: But fine Houses, large Estates, Coaches, and dainty Entertainments were the Product of the Flesh. Therefore, says he, my Dear, you have two Husbands, one the Object of your Love, and to satisfy your Desire; the other the Object of your Necessity, and to furnish you with those other Conveniencies. (I am sure I remember every Word, for he repeated it three Times; O he is very good whenever I desire him to repeat a thing to me three times he always doth it!) as then the Spirit is preferable to the Flesh, so am I preferable to your other Husband, to whom I am antecedent in Time likewise. I say these things, my Dear, (said he) to satisfie your Conscience. A Fig for my Conscience, said I, when shall I meet you again in the Garden?

My Husband now rode up to the Chariot, and asked us how we did—I hate the Sight of him. Mr. *Williams* answered⟨,⟩$_{c}$ very well, at your Service. They then talked of the Weather, and other things, I wished him gone again, every Minute; but all in vain⟨,⟩$_{c}$ I had no more Opportunity of conversing with Mr. *Williams.*

Well; at Dinner Mr. *Booby* was very civil to Mr. *Williams,* and told him he was sorry for what had happened, and would make him sufficient Amends, if in his power, and desired him to

accept of a Note for fifty Pounds; which he was so *good* to receive,
notwithstanding all that had past[;]$_2$ and told Mr. *Booby*, he [,]$_1$
hop'd he would be forgiven, and that he would pray for him.

We make a charming Fool of him, i'fackins⟨;⟩$_2$ Times are finely altered, I have entirely got the better of him, and am resolved never to give him his Humour.

O how foolish it is in a Woman, who hath once got the Reins into her own Hand, ever to quit them again.

After Dinner Mr. *Williams* drank the Church *et cætera;* and smiled on me; when my Husband's Turn came, he drank *et cætera* and the Church; for which he was very severely rebuked by Mr. *Williams;* it being a high Crime, it seems, to name any thing before the Church. I do not know what *Et cetera* is, but I believe it is something concerning chusing Pallament Men; for I asked if it was not a Health to Mr. *Booby*'s Borough, and Mr. *Williams* with a hearty Laugh answered, Yes, Yes, it is his Borough we mean.

I slipt out as soon as I could, hoping Mr. *Williams* would
finish the Squire, as I have heard him say he could easily do,
and come to me; but it happened quite otherwise, for in about
half an Hour, *Booby* came to me, and told me he had left
Mr. *Williams,* the Mayor of his Borough, and two or three
[Aldermen]$_2$ heartily at it, and asked me if I would go hear [Alderman]$_1$
Williams sing a Catch, which, added he, he doth to a Miracle.

Every Opportunity of seeing my dear *Williams,* was agreeable to me, which indeed I scarce had at this Time; for when we returned, the whole Corporation were got together, and the Room was in a Cloud of Tobacco; Parson *Williams* was at the upper End of the Table, and he hath pure round cherry Cheeks, and his Face look'd all the World to nothing like the Sun in a Fog. If the Sun had a Pipe in his Mouth, there would be no Difference.

I began now to grow uneasy, apprehending I should have no more of Mr. *Williams*'s Company that Evening, and not at all caring for my Husband, I advised him to sit down and drink for his Country with the rest of the Company; but he refused, and desired me to give him some Tea; swearing nothing made him so sick, as to hear a Parcel of Scoundrels, roaring forth the

Principles of honest Men over their Cups, when, says he, I know most of them are such empty Blockheads, that they don't know their right Hand from their left; and that Fellow there, who hath talked so much of *Shipping*,[38] at the left Side of the Parson, in whom they all place a Confidence, if I don't take care, will sell them to my Adversary.

I don't know why I mention this Stuff to you; for I am sure I know nothing about *Pollitricks*, more than Parson *Williams* tells me; who says that the Court-side are in the right on't, and that every Christian ought to be on the same with the Bishops.

When we had finished our Tea, we walked in the Garden till it was dark, and then my Husband proposed, instead of returning to the Company, (which I desired, that I might see Parson *Williams* again,) to sup in another Room by our selves, which, for fear of making him jealous, and considering too, that Parson *Williams* would be pretty far gone, I was obliged to consent to.

O! what a devilish Thing it is, for a Woman to be obliged to go to Bed to a spindle-shanked young Squire, she doth not like, when there is a jolly Parson in the same House she is fond of.

In the Morning I grew very peevish, and in the Dumps, notwithstanding all he could say or do to please me. I exclaimed against the Priviledge of Husbands, and vowed I would not be pulled and tumbled about. At last he hit on the only Method, which could have brought me into Humour, and proposed to me a Journey to *London*, within a few Days. This you may easily guess pleased me; for besides the Desire which I have of shewing my self forth, of buying fine Cloaths, Jewels, Coaches, Houses, and ten thousand other fine Things, Parson *Williams* is, it seems, going thither too, to be *instuted*.[39]

[38] In his copy of *Shamela*, Horace Walpole, Fielding's contemporary, wrote here, in the margin, "W. Shippen." William Shippen was a Member of Parliament, respected for his honesty by all (including Sir Robert Walpole, whom he opposed), even though he was an acknowledged Jacobite (one who wished to return the Stuarts to the English throne). Walpole's copy (a second edition) is now in Mr. Wilmarth Lewis's Walpole collection at Farmington, Connecticut.

[39] Parson Williams will be *instituted* by the bishop into the spiritual charge of the new living Mr. Booby has given him.

O! what a charming Journey I shall have; for I hope to keep the dear Man in the Chariot with me all the way; and that foolish Booby (*for that is the Name Mr.* Williams *hath set him*) *will ride on Horseback.*

So as I shall have an Opportunity of seeing you so shortly, I think I will mention no more Matters to you now. O I had like to have forgot one very material Thing; which is that it will look horribly, for a Lady of my Quality and Fashion, to own such a Woman as you for my Mother. Therefore we must meet in private only, and if you will never claim me, nor mention me to any one, I will always allow you what is very handsome. Parson *Williams* hath greatly advised me in this; and says, he thinks I should do very well to lay out twenty Pounds, and set you up in a little Chandler's Shop: but you must remember all my Favours to you will depend on your Secrecy; for I am positively resolved, I will not be known to be your Daughter; and if you tell any one so, I shall deny it with all my Might, which Parson *Williams* says, I may do with a safe Conscience, being now a married Woman. So I rest

Your humble Servant,

SHAMELA.

P. S. The strangest Fancy hath enter'd into my Booby's Head, that can be imagined. He is resolved to have a Book made about him and me; he proposed it to Mr. *Williams,* and offered him a Reward for his Pains; but he says he never writ any thing of that kind, but will recommend my Husband, when he comes to Town, to a Parson *who does that Sort of Business for Folks,* one who can make my Husband, and me, and Parson *Williams,* to be all great People; for he *can make black white,* it seems. Well, but they say my Name is to be altered, Mr. *Williams,* says the first Syllabub hath too comical a Sound, so it is to be changed into *Pamela;* I own I can't imagine what can be said; for to be sure I shan't confess any of my Secrets to them, and so I whispered Parson *Williams* about that, who answered me, I need not give my self any Trouble: for the Gentleman *who writes Lives,*[40] never asked more than a few Names of his Customers, and that he made all the rest out of his own Head; you mistake, Child, said he, if you apprehend any Truths are to be delivered. So far on the contrary, if you had not been acquainted with the Name, you would not have known it to be your own History. I have seen a *Piece of his Performance,* where the Person, whose Life was written, could he have risen from the Dead again, would not have even suspected he had been aimed at, unless by the Title of the Book, which was superscribed with his Name. Well, all these Matters are strange to me, yet I can't help laughing, to think I shall see my self in a printed Book.

So much for Mrs. *Shamela,* or *Pamela,* which I have taken Pains to transcribe from the Originals, sent down by her Mother in a Rage, at the Proposal in her last Letter. The Originals themselves are in my Hands, and shall be communicated to you, if you think proper to make them publick; and certainly they will have their Use. The Character of *Shamela,* will make young Gentlemen wary how they take the most fatal Step both to themselves and Families, by youthful, hasty and improper Matches; indeed, they may assure themselves, that all such Prospects of Happiness are vain and delusive, and that they sacrifice all the solid Comforts of their Lives, to a very transient Satisfaction of a Passion, which how hot so ever it be, will be soon cooled; and when cooled, will afford them nothing but Repentance.

Can any thing be more miserable, than to be despised by the whole World, and that must certainly be the Consequence; to be despised by the Person obliged, which it is more than probable will be the Consequence, and of which, we see an Instance in *Shamela;* and lastly to despise one's self, which must

[40] A parson "*who writes Lives*" seems to be Conyers Middleton, with Cicero rising from the dead to see his name on the *Life of Cicero*. In the margin, opposite "a Parson *who does that Sort of Business for Folks,*" Walpole wrote: "Dr Middleton."

be the Result of any Reflection on so weak and unworthy a Choice.

As to the Character of Parson *Williams,* I am sorry it is a true one. Indeed those who do not know him, will hardly believe it so; but what Scandal doth it throw on the Order to have one bad Member, unless they endeavour to screen and protect him? In him you see a Picture of almost every Vice exposed in nauseous and odious Colours; and if a Clergyman would ask me by what Pattern he should form himself, I would say, Be the reverse of *Williams:* So far therefore he may be of use to the Clergy themselves, and though God forbid there should be many *Williams*'s amongst them, you and I are too honest to pretend, that the Body wants no Reformation.

To say the Truth, I think no greater Instance of the contrary can be given than that which appears in your Letter. The confederating to cry up a nonsensical ridiculous Book, (I believe the most extensively so of any ever yet published,) and to be so weak and so wicked as to pretend to make it a Matter of Religion; whereas so far from having any moral Tendency, the Book is by no means innocent: For,

First, There are many lascivious Images in it, very improper to be laid before the Youth of either Sex.

2dly, Young Gentlemen are here taught, that to marry their Mother's Chambermaids, and to indulge the Passion of Lust, at the Expence of Reason and Common Sense, is an Act of Religion, Virtue, and Honour; and, indeed the surest Road to Happiness.

3dly, All Chambermaids are strictly enjoyned to look out after their Masters; they are taught to use little Arts to that purpose: And lastly, are countenanced in Impertinence to their Superiours, and in betraying the Secrets of Families.

4thly, In the Character of Mrs. *Jewkes* Vice is rewarded; whence every Housekeeper may learn the Usefulness of pimping and bawding for her Master.

5thly, In Parson *Williams,* who is represented as a faultless Character, we see a busy Fellow, intermeddling with the private Affairs of his Patron, whom he is very ungratefully forward to expose and condemn on every Occasion.

Many more Objections might, if I had Time or Inclination, be made to this Book; but I apprehend, what hath been said is sufficient to perswade you of the use which may arise from publishing an Antidote to this Poison. I have therefore sent you the Copies of these Papers, and if you have Leisure to communicate them to the Press, I will transmit you the Originals, tho' I assure you, the Copies are exact.

I shall only add, that there is not the least Foundation for any thing which is said of Lady *Davers*, or any of the other Ladies; all that is merely to be imputed to the Invention of the Biographer. I have particularly enquired after Lady *Davers*, and don't hear Mr. *Booby* hath such a Relation, or that there is indeed any such Person existing. I am,

Dear Sir,

Most faithfully and respectfully,

Your humble Servant,

J. OLIVER.

Parson TICKLETEXT *to Parson* OLIVER.

Dear SIR,

I Have read over the History of *Shamela*, as it appears in
[favour]$_1$ those authentick Copies you [favour'd]$_2$ me with, and am very much ashamed of the Character, which I was hastily prevailed on to give that Book. I am equally angry with the pert Jade herself, and with the Author of her Life: For I scarce know yet to whom I chiefly owe an Imposition, which hath been so general, that if Numbers could defend me from Shame, I should have no Reason to apprehend it.

As I have your implied Leave to publish, what you so kindly sent me, I shall not wait for the Originals, as you assure me the Copies are exact, and as I am really impatient to do what I think a serviceable Act of Justice to the World.

Finding by the End of her last Letter, that the little Hussy was in Town, I made it pretty much my Business to enquire after her, but with no effect hitherto: As soon as I succeed in this Enquiry, you shall hear what Discoveries I can learn. You will pardon the Shortness of this Letter, as you shall be troubled with a much longer very soon: And believe me,

Dear Sir,

Your most faithful Servant,

THO. TICKLETEXT.

P. S. Since I writ, I have a certain Account, that Mr. *Booby* hath caught his Wife in bed with *Williams;* hath turned her off, and is prosecuting him in the spiritual Court.[41]

[41] The spiritual court, having charge of all religious infractions, tried all marital cases.

FINIS.

THE
HISTORY
OF THE
ADVENTURES
OF
JOSEPH ANDREWS,

And of his FRIEND

Mr. *ABRAHAM ADAMS*.

Written in Imitation of

The *Manner* of CERVANTES,

Author of *Don Quixote*.

IN TWO VOLUMES.

VOL. I.

LONDON:

Printed for A. MILLAR, over-against *St. Clement's Church*, in the *Strand*.

M.DCC.XLII.

PREFACE

As it is possible the mere English reader may have a different idea of Romance with the author of these little volumes; [1] and may consequently expect a kind of entertainment, not to be found, nor which was even intended, in the following pages; it may not be improper to premise a few words concerning this kind of writing, which I do not remember to have seen hitherto attempted in our language.

The EPIC as well as the DRAMA is divided into Tragedy and Comedy. Homer, who was the father of this species of poetry, gave us a pattern of both these, though that of the latter kind is entirely lost; which Aristotle tells us, bore the same relation to Comedy which his *Iliad* bears to Tragedy. And perhaps, that we have no more instances of it among the writers of antiquity, is owing to the loss of this great pattern, which, had it survived, would have found its imitators equally with the other poems of this great original.

And farther, as this poetry may be tragic or comic, I will not scruple to say it may be likewise either in verse or prose: for

[1] The two small volumes (about 4 x 6¼ inches) in which *Joseph Andrews* first appeared, as compared to the huge romances of La Calprenède and Mlle. de Scudéry (*Clelia, Cleopatra,* etc., named below), about a foot wide and a foot and a half tall and thick as a telephone book.

though it wants one particular, which the critic enumerates in the constituent parts of an epic poem, namely metre; yet, when any kind of writing contains all its other parts, such as fable, action, characters, sentiments, and diction, and is deficient in metre only; it seems, I think, reasonable to refer it to the Epic; at least, as no critic hath thought proper to range it under any other head, nor to assign it a particular name to itself.

Thus the *Telemachus* of the Archbishop of Cambray appears to me of the Epic kind, as well as the *Odyssey* of Homer; indeed, it is much fairer and more reasonable to give it a name common with that species from which it differs only in a single instance, than to confound it with those which it resembles in no other. Such are those voluminous works commonly called Romances, namely, *Clelia, Cleopatra, Astræa, Cassandra,* the *Grand Cyrus,* and innumerable others, which contain, as I apprehend, very little instruction or entertainment.

Now a comic Romance is a comic Epic-Poem in prose; differing from Comedy, as the serious Epic from Tragedy: its action being more extended and comprehensive; containing a much larger circle of incidents, and introducing a greater variety of characters. It differs from the serious Romance in its fable and action, in this; that as in the one these are grave and solemn, so in the other they are light and ridiculous: it differs in its characters by introducing persons of inferior rank, and consequently, of inferior manners, whereas the grave Romance, sets the highest before us; lastly in its sentiments and diction, by preserving the ludicrous instead of the sublime. In the diction I think, Burlesque itself may be sometimes admitted; of which many instances will occur in this work, as in the descriptions of the battles, and some other places, not necessary to be pointed out to the classical reader; for whose entertainment those parodies or burlesque imitations are chiefly calculated.

But though we have sometimes admitted this in our diction, we have carefully excluded it from our sentiments and characters: for there it is never properly introduced, unless in writings of the Burlesque kind, which this is not intended to be. Indeed, no two species of writing can differ more widely than the Comic and the Burlesque: for as the latter is ever the exhibition of what is monstrous and unnatural, and where our delight, if we examine it, arises from the surprising absurdity, as in appropriating the manners of the highest to the lowest, or *è converso;* so in the former, we should ever confine ourselves strictly to Nature from the just imitation of which, will flow all the pleasure we can this way convey to a sensible reader. And perhaps, there is one reason, why a Comic writer should of all others be the least excused for deviating from Nature, since it may not be always so easy for a serious poet to meet with the great and the admirable; but life everywhere furnishes an accurate observer with the Ridiculous.

I have hinted this little, concerning Burlesque; because, I have often heard that name given to performances, which have been truly of the Comic kind, from the author's having sometimes admitted it in his diction only; which as it is the dress of poetry, doth like the dress of men establish characters, (the one of the whole poem, and the other of the whole man,) in vulgar opinion, beyond any of their greater excellencies: but surely, a certain drollery in style, where the characters and sentiments are perfectly natural, no more constitutes the Burlesque, than an empty pomp and dignity of words, where everything else is mean and low, can entitle any performance to the appellation of the true Sublime.

And I apprehend, my Lord Shaftesbury's opinion of mere Burlesque agrees with mine, when he asserts, "There is no such thing to be found in the writings of the ancients." But perhaps I have less abhorrence than he professes for it: and that, not because I have had some little success on the stage this way; but rather, as it contributes more to exquisite mirth and laughter than any other; and these are probably more wholesome physic for the mind, and conduce better to purge away spleen, melancholy and ill affections, than is generally imagined. Nay, I will appeal to common observation, whether the same companies are not found more full of good-humour and benevolence, after they have been sweetened for two or three hours with entertainments of this kind, than when soured by a tragedy or a grave lecture.

But to illustrate all this by another science, in which, perhaps, we shall see the distinction more clearly and plainly: let us examine the works of a comic history-painter, with those performances which the Italians call *Caricatura;* where we shall find the true [copy]1-2 excellence of the former, to consist in the exactest [copying]3 of nature; insomuch, that a judicious eye instantly rejects anything *outré;* any liberty which the painter hath taken with the features of that *Alma Mater.*——Whereas in the *Caricatura* we allow all licence. Its aim is to exhibit monsters, not men; and all distortions and exaggerations whatever are within its proper province.

Now what *Caricatura* is in painting, Burlesque is in writing; and in the same manner the comic writer and painter correlate to each other. And here I shall observe, that as in the former, the painter seems to have the advantage; so it is in the latter infinitely on the side of the writer: for the *Monstrous* is much easier to paint than describe, and the *Ridiculous* to describe than paint.

And though perhaps this latter species doth not in either science so strongly affect and agitate the muscles as the other; yet it will be owned, I believe, that a more rational and useful pleasure arises to us from it. He who should call the ingenious Hogarth a burlesque painter, would, in my opinion, do him very little honour; for sure it is much easier, much less the subject of admiration, to paint a man with a nose, or any other feature of a preposterous size, or to expose him in some absurd or monstrous attitude, than to express the affections of men on canvas. It hath been thought a vast commendation of a painter, to say his figures *seem to breathe;* but surely, it is a much greater and nobler applause, *that they appear to think.*

But to return — The Ridiculous only, as I have before said, falls within my province in the present work. — Nor will some explanation of this word be thought impertinent by the reader, if he considers how wonderfully it hath been mistaken, even by writers who have professed it: for to what but such a mistake, can we attribute the many attempts to ridicule the blackest villainies; and what is yet worse, the most dreadful calamities? What could exceed the absurdity of an author, who should write *the Comedy of Nero, with the merry Incident of ripping up his Mother's Belly;* or what would give a greater shock to humanity, than an attempt to expose the miseries of poverty and distress to ridicule? And yet, the reader will not want much learning to suggest such instances to himself.

Besides, it may seem remarkable, that Aristotle, who is so fond and free of definitions, hath not thought proper to define the Ridiculous. Indeed, where he tells us it is proper to Comedy, he hath remarked that villainy is not its object: but he hath not, as I remember, positively asserted what is. Nor doth the Abbé Bellegarde, who hath writ a treatise on this subject, though he shows us many species of it, once trace it to its fountain.

The only source of the true Ridiculous (as it appears to me) is affectation. But though it arises from one spring only, when we consider the infinite streams into which this one branches, we shall presently cease to admire at the copious field it affords to an observer. Now affectation proceeds from one of these two causes, vanity or hypocrisy: for as vanity puts us on affecting false characters, in order to purchase applause; so hypocrisy sets us on an endeavour to avoid censure by concealing our vices under an appearance of their opposite virtues. And though these two causes are often confounded [(for there is some difficulty in distinguishing them)]₃, yet, as they proceed from very different motives, so they are as clearly distinct in their operations: for indeed, the affectation which arises from vanity is nearer to truth than the other; as it hath not that violent repugnancy of nature to struggle with, which that of the hypocrite hath. It may be likewise noted, that affectation doth not imply an absolute negation of those qualities which are affected; and therefore, though, when it proceeds from hypocrisy, it be nearly allied to deceit; yet when it comes from vanity only, it partakes of the nature of ostentation: for instance, the affectation of liberality in a vain man, differs visibly from the same affection in the avaricious; for though the vain man is not what he would appear, or hath not the virtue he affects, to the degree he would be thought to have it; yet it sits less awkwardly on him than on the avaricious man, who *is* the very reverse of what he would *seem* to be.

[(for they require some difficulty in distinguishing)]1-2

From the discovery of this affectation arises the Ridiculous — which always strikes the reader with surprise and pleasure; and that in a higher and stronger degree when the affectation arises from hypocrisy, than when from vanity: for to discover anyone to be the exact reverse of what he affects, is more surprising, and consequently more ridiculous, than to find him a little deficient in the quality he desires the reputation of. I might observe that our Ben Jonson, who of all men understood the Ridiculous the best, hath chiefly used the hypocritical affectation.

Now from affectation only, the misfortunes and calamities of life, or the imperfections of nature, may become the objects of ridicule. Surely he hath a very ill-framed mind, who can look on ugliness, infirmity, or poverty, as ridiculous in themselves: nor do I believe any man living, who meets a dirty fellow riding through the streets in a cart, is struck with an idea of the Ridiculous from it; but if he should see the same figure descend from his coach and six, or bolt from his chair with his hat under his arm, he would then begin to laugh, and with justice. In the same manner, were we to enter a poor house, and behold a wretched family shivering with cold and languishing with hunger, it would not incline us to laughter, (at least we must have very diabolical natures, if it would;) but should we discover there a grate, instead of coals, adorned with flowers, empty plate or china dishes on the sideboard, or any other affectation of riches and finery either on their persons or in their furniture; we might then indeed be excused for ridiculing so fantastical an appearance. Much less are natural imperfections the object of derision: but when ugliness aims at the applause of beauty, or lameness endeavours to display agility; it is then that these unfortunate circumstances, which at first moved our compassion, tend only to raise our mirth.

The poet [2] carries this very far;

> *None are for being what they are in fault,*
> *But for not being what they would be thought.*

Where if the metre would suffer the word *Ridiculous* to close the first line, the thought would be rather more proper. Great vices are the proper objects of our detestation, smaller faults of our pity: but affectation appears to me the only true source of the Ridiculous.

But perhaps it may be objected to me, that I have against

[2] Playwright, William Congreve, from his poem, "Of Pleasing" (ll. 63–64).

my own rules introduced vices, and of a very black kind into this work. To which I shall answer: first, that it is very difficult to pursue a series of human actions and keep clear from them. Secondly, that the vices to be found here, are rather the accidental consequences of some human frailty, or foible, than causes habitually existing in the mind. Thirdly, that they are never set forth as the objects of ridicule, but detestation. Fourthly, that they are never the principal figure at that time on the scene; and lastly, they never produce the intended evil.

Having thus distinguished *Joseph Andrews* from the productions of Romance writers on the one hand, and Burlesque writers on the other, and given some few very short hints (for I intended no more) of this species of writing, which I have affirmed to be hitherto unattempted in our language; I shall leave to my good-natured reader to apply my piece to my observations, and will detain him no longer than with a word concerning the characters in this work.

And here I solemnly protest, I have no intention to vilify or asperse anyone: for though everything is copied from the book of Nature, and scarce a character or action produced which I have not taken from my own observations and experience, yet I have used the utmost care to obscure the persons by such different circumstances, degrees, and colours, that it will be impossible to guess at them with any degree of certainty; and if it ever happens otherwise, it is only where the failure characterized is so minute, that it is a foible only which the party himself may laugh at as well as any other.

As to the character of Adams, as it is the most glaring in the whole, so I conceive it is not to be found in any book now extant. It is designed a character of perfect simplicity; and as the goodness of his heart will recommend him to the good-natured; so I hope it will excuse me to the gentlemen of his cloth; for whom, while they are worthy of their sacred order, no man can possibly have a greater respect. They will therefore excuse me, notwithstanding the low adventures in which he is engaged, that I have made him a clergyman; since no other office could have given him so many opportunities of displaying his worthy inclinations.

CONTENTS

BOOK I

BOOK II

BOOK III

BOOK IV

THE HISTORY OF THE ADVENTURES OF *Joseph Andrews*, and of his Friend Mr. *Abraham Adams*

BOOK I.

CHAP. I.

Of writing lives in general, and particularly of Pamela; *with a word by the bye of Colley Cibber and others.*

IT is a trite but true observation, that examples work more forcibly on the mind than precepts: and if this be just in what is odious and blameable, it is more strongly so in what is amiable and praiseworthy. Here emulation most effectually operates upon us, and inspires our imitation in an irresistible manner. A good man therefore is a standing lesson to all his acquaintance, and of far greater use in that narrow circle than a good book.

But as it often happens that the best men are but little known, and consequently cannot extend the usefulness of their examples a great way; the writer may be called in aid to spread their history farther, ⟨and⟩$_3$ to present the amiable pictures to those who have not the happiness of knowing the originals; and ⟨so,⟩$_3$ by communicating such valuable patterns to the world, ⟨he⟩$_3$ may perhaps do a more extensive service to mankind than the person whose life originally afforded the pattern.

In this light I have always regarded those biographers who have recorded the actions of great and worthy persons of both sexes. Not to mention those ancient writers which of late days are little read, being written in obsolete, and as they are generally thought, unintelligible languages; such as Plutarch, Nepos, and others which I heard of in my youth; our own language affords many of excellent use and instruction, finely calculated to sow the seeds of virtue in youth, and very easy to be comprehended by persons of moderate capacity. Such are the history of John the Great, who, by his brave and heroic actions against men of large and athletic bodies, obtained the glorious appellation of the Giant-killer; that of an Earl of Warwick, whose Christian name was Guy; the lives of Argalus and Parthenia, and above all, the history of those seven worthy personages, the Champions of Christendom. In all these, delight is mixed with instruction, and the reader is almost as much improved as entertained.

But I pass by these and many others, to mention two books lately published, which represent an admirable pattern of the amiable in either sex. The former of these which deals in male virtue, was written by the great person himself, who lived the life he hath recorded, and is by many thought to have lived such a life only in order to write it. The other is communicated to us by an historian who borrows his lights, as the common method is, from authentic papers and records. The reader, I believe, already conjectures, I mean, the lives of Mr. Colley Cibber, and of Mrs. Pamela Andrews.[3] How artfully doth the

[3] "*Mrs.*" denotes Pamela's *unmarried* state, as with "*Mrs.* Slipslop." "Mrs." is merely an abbreviation for "Mistress" (as in "Mistress Mary, quite contrary"), a term for unmarried ladies, particularly domestic servants.

former, by insinuating that he *escaped* being promoted to the highest stations in Church and State, teach us a contempt of worldly grandeur! how strongly doth he inculcate an absolute submission to our superiors! Lastly, how completely doth he arm us against so uneasy, so wretched a passion as the fear of shame; how clearly doth he expose the emptiness and vanity of that phantom, reputation!

What the female readers are taught by the memoirs of Mrs. Andrews, is so well set forth in the excellent essays or letters prefixed to the second and subsequent editions of that work, that it would be here a needless repetition. The authentic history with which I now present the public, is an instance of the great good that book is likely to do, and of the prevalence of example which I have just observed: since it will appear that it was by keeping the excellent pattern of his sister's virtues before his eyes, that Mr. Joseph Andrews was chiefly enabled to preserve his purity in the midst of such great temptations; I shall only add, that this character of male chastity, though doubtless as desirable [and]₃ becoming in one part of the human species as [as]₁₋₂ in the other, is almost the only virtue which the great Apologist hath not given himself for the sake of giving the example to his readers.

CHAP. II.

Of Mr. Joseph Andrews his birth, parentage, education, and great endowments, with a word or two concerning ancestors.

MR. Joseph Andrews, the hero of our ensuing history, was esteemed to be the only son of Gaffar and Gammar Andrews, and brother to the illustrious Pamela, whose virtue is at present so famous. As to his ancestors, we have searched with great diligence, but little success: being unable to trace them farther than his great-grandfather, who, as an elderly person in the parish remembers to have heard his father say, was an excellent cudgel-player. Whether he had any ancestors before this, we must leave to the opinion of our curious reader, finding nothing of sufficient certainty to rely on. However, we cannot omit inserting an epitaph which an ingenious friend of ours hath communicated.

Stay Traveller, for underneath this Pew
Lies fast asleep that merry Man Andrew;
When the last Day's great Sun shall gild the Skies,
Then he shall from his Tomb get up and rise.
Be merry while thou can'st: for surely thou
Shalt shortly be as sad as he is now.

The words are almost out of the stone with antiquity. But it is needless to observe that *Andrew* here is writ without an *s*, and is besides a Christian name. My friend moreover conjectures this to have been the founder of that sect of laughing philosophers, since called *Merry Andrews.*

To waive therefore a circumstance, which, though mentioned in conformity to the exact rules of biography, is not greatly material; I proceed to things of more consequence. Indeed it is sufficiently certain, that he had as many ancestors, as the best man living; and perhaps, if we look five or six hundred years backwards, might be related to some persons of very great figure at present, whose ancestors within half the last century are buried in as great obscurity. But suppose for argument's sake we should admit that he had no ancestors at all, but had sprung up, according to the modern phrase, out of a dunghill, as the Athenians pretended they themselves did from the earth, would not this **Autokopros* have been justly entitled to all the praise arising from his own virtues? Would it not be hard, that a man who hath no ancestors should therefore be rendered incapable of acquiring honour, when we see so many who have no virtues enjoying the honour of their forefathers? At ten years old (by which time his education was advanced to writing and reading) he was bound an apprentice, according to the statute, to Sir Thomas Booby, an uncle of Mr. Booby's by the father's side. Sir Thomas having then an estate in his own hands, the young Andrews was at first employed in what in the country they call

* In English, sprung from a dunghill [Fielding's note].

keeping birds. His office was to perform the part the ancients assigned to the god *Priapus*,[4] which deity the moderns call by the name of *Jack-o'-Lent*: but his voice being so extremely musical, that it rather allured the birds than terrified them, he was soon transplanted from the fields into the dog-kennel, where he was placed under the huntsman, and made what sportsmen term a *whipper-in*. For this place likewise the sweetness of his voice disqualified him: the dogs preferring the melody of his chiding to all the alluring notes of the huntsman, who soon became so incensed at it, that he desired Sir Thomas to provide otherwise for him; and constantly laid every fault the dogs were at, to the account of the poor boy, who was now transplanted to the stable. Here he soon gave proofs of strength and agility, beyond his years, and constantly rode the most spirited and vicious horses to water with an intrepidity which surprised everyone. While he was in this station, he rode several races for Sir Thomas, and this with such expertness and success, that the neighbouring gentlemen frequently solicited the knight, to permit little Joey (for so he was called) to ride their matches. The best gamesters, before they laid their money, always inquired which horse little Joey was to ride, and the bets were rather proportioned by the rider than by the horse himself; especially after he had scornfully refused a considerable bribe to play booty on such an occasion. This extremely raised his character, and so pleased the Lady Booby, that she desired to have him (being now seventeen years of age) for her own footboy.

Joey was now preferred from the stable to attend on his lady; to go on her errands, stand behind her chair, wait at her tea-table, and carry her prayer-book to church; at which place, his voice gave him an opportunity of distinguishing himself by singing psalms: he behaved likewise in every other respect so well at divine service, that it recommended him to the notice of Mr. Abraham Adams the curate; who took an opportunity one day, as he was drinking a cup of ale in Sir Thomas's kitchen, to ask the young man several questions concerning religion; with his answers to which he was wonderfully pleased.

[4] Priapus, the god of fertility, was also the god of gardens, where his image served as scarecrow.

CHAP. III.

Of Mr. Abraham Adams the curate, Mrs. Slipslop the chambermaid, and others.

MR. Abraham Adams was an excellent scholar. He was a perfect master of the Greek and Latin languages; to which he added a great share of knowledge in the Oriental tongues, and could read and translate French, Italian and Spanish. He had applied many years to the most severe study, and had treasured up a fund of learning rarely to be met with in a university. He was besides a man of good sense, good parts, and good nature; but was at the same time as entirely ignorant of the ways of this world, as an infant just entered into it could possibly be. As he had never any intention to deceive, so he never suspected such a design in others. He was generous, friendly and brave to an excess; but simplicity was his characteristic: he did, no more than Mr. Colley Cibber, apprehend any such passions as malice and envy to exist in mankind, which was indeed less remarkable in a country parson than in a gentleman who hath passed his life behind the scenes, a place which hath been seldom thought the school of innocence; and where a very little observation would have convinced the great Apologist, that those passions have a real existence in the human mind.

His virtue and his other qualifications, as they rendered him equal to his office, so they made him an agreeable and valuable companion, and had so much endeared and well recommended him to a bishop, that at the age of fifty, he was provided with a handsome income of twenty-three pounds a year; which however, he could not make any great figure with: because he lived in a dear country, and was a little encumbered with a wife and six children.

It was this gentleman, who, having, as I have said, observed the singular devotion of young Andrews, had found means to question him, concerning several particulars; as how many books there were in the New Testament? which were they? how many chapters they contained? and such like; to all which Mr. Adams ⟨privately⟩$_4$ said, he answered much better than Sir Thomas, or two other neighbouring justices of the peace could probably have done.

Mr. Adams was wonderfully solicitous to know at what time, and by what opportunity the youth became acquainted with these matters: [Joey]$_2$ told him, that he had very early learnt to read and write by the goodness of his father, who, though he had not interest enough to get him into a charity school, because a cousin of his father's landlord did not vote on the right side for a churchwarden in a borough-town, yet had been himself at the expense of sixpence a week for his learning. [He told him likewise, that ever since he was in Sir Thomas's family, he had employed]$_2$ all his hours of leisure in reading good books; that he had read the Bible, the *Whole Duty of Man,* and Thomas à Kempis; and that as often as he could, without being perceived, he had studied a great good book which lay open in the hall window, where he had read, *as how the Devil carried away half a church in sermon-time, without hurting one of the congregation;* and *as how a field of corn ran away down a hill with all the trees upon it, and covered another man's meadow.* This sufficiently assured Mr. Adams, that the good book meant could be no other than Baker's *Chronicle.*[5]

[who]$_1$

[That he had ever since he was in Sir Thomas's family, employed]$_1$

The curate, surprised to find such instances of industry and application in a young man, who had never met with the least encouragement, asked him, if he did not extremely regret the want of a liberal education, and the not having been born of parents, who might have indulged his talents and desire of knowledge? To which he answered, "he hoped he had profited somewhat better from the books he had read, than to lament his condition in this world. That for his part, he was perfectly content with the state to which he was called, that he should endeavour to improve his Talent, which was all required of him,. but not repine at his own lot, nor envy those of his betters."

[5] Sir Richard Baker's *A Chronicle of the Kings of England, From the time of the Romans Government Unto the Death of King James* (1643) records these incidents under the reigns of Henry IV and Elizabeth.

"Well said, my lad," replied the curate, "and I wish some who have read many [more good books, nay and some who have written good books themselves, had profited]$_2$ so much by them."

[more books, had profited]$_1$

Adams had no nearer access to Sir Thomas, or my lady, than [through]$_2$ the waiting-gentlewoman: for Sir Thomas was too apt to estimate men merely by their dress, or fortune; and my lady was a woman of gaiety, who had been blest with a town-education, and never spoke of any of her country neighbours, by any other appellation than that of ⟨*The*⟩$_2$ *Brutes.* They both regarded the curate as a kind of domestic only, belonging to the parson of the parish, who was at this time at variance [with the knight; for the parson had for many years lived in a constant state of civil war, or, which is perhaps as bad, of civil law, with Sir Thomas himself and the tenants of his manor. The foundation of this quarrel was a modus, by setting which aside, an advantage of several shillings *per annum* would have accrued to the rector: but he had not yet been able to accomplish his purpose; and had reaped hitherto nothing better from the suits than the pleasure (which he used indeed frequently to say was no small one) of reflecting that he had utterly undone many of the poor tenants, though he had at the same time greatly impoverished himself.]$_2$

[by]$_1$

[with the knight on suits, which he then had for tithes with seven tenants of his manor, in order to set aside a modus, by which the parson proposed an advantage of several shillings *per annum*, and by these suits had greatly impoverished himself, and utterly undone the poor tenants.]$_1$

Mrs. Slipslop the waiting-gentlewoman, being herself the daughter of a curate, preserved some respect for Adams; she professed great regard for his learning, and would frequently dispute with him on points of theology; but always insisted on a deference to be paid to her understanding, as she had been frequently at London, and knew more of the world than a country parson could pretend to.

She had in these disputes a particular advantage over Adams: for she was a mighty affecter of hard words, which she used in such a manner, that the parson, who durst not offend her, by calling her words in question, was frequently at some loss to guess her meaning, and would have been much less puzzled by an Arabian manuscript.

[Adams therefore took an opportunity one day, after a pretty long discourse with her on the *essence*, (or, as she pleased to term it, the *incense*) of matter, to mention the case of young

Andrews; desiring]$_2$ her to recommend him to her lady as a youth very susceptible of learning, and one whose instruction in Latin he would himself undertake; by which means he might be qualified for a higher station than that of a footman: and added, she knew it was in his master's power easily to provide for him in a better manner. He therefore desired, that the boy might be left behind under his care.

[To her therefore, Adams mentioned the case of young Andrews, and desired]$_1$

"La! Mr. Adams," said Mrs. Slipslop, "do you think my lady will suffer any *preambles* about [any such]$_2$ matter? She is going to London very *concisely*, and I am *confidous* would not leave Joey behind her on any account; for he is one of the genteelest young fellows you may see in a summer's day, and I am *confidous* she would as soon think of parting with a pair of her grey mares: for she values herself as much on one as the other." Adams would have interrupted, but she proceeded: "And why is Latin more *necessitous* for a footman than a gentleman? It is very proper that you clargymen must learn it, because you can't preach without it: but I have heard gentlemen say in London, that it is fit for nobody else. I am *confidous* my lady would be angry with me for mentioning it, and I shall draw myself into no such *delemy*." At which words her lady's bell rung, and Mr. Adams was forced to retire; nor could he gain a second opportunity with her before their London journey, which happened a few days afterwards. However, Andrews behaved very thankfully and gratefully to him for his intended kindness, which he told him he never would forget, and at the same time received from the good man many admonitions concerning the regulation of his future conduct, and his perseverance in innocence and industry.

[such a]$_1$

CHAP. IV.

What happened after their journey to London.

No sooner was young Andrews arrived at London, than he began to scrape an acquaintance with his party-coloured brethren, who endeavoured to make him despise his former course of life. His hair was cut after the newest fashion, and became his chief care. He went abroad with it all the morning in papers, and drest it out in the afternoon; they could not however teach him to game, swear, drink, nor any other genteel vice the town abounded with. He applied most of his leisure hours to music, in which he greatly improved himself, and became so perfect a connoisseur in that art, that he led the opinion of all the other footmen at an opera, and they never condemned or applauded a single song contrary to his approbation or dislike. He was a little too forward in riots at the play-houses and assemblies; and when he attended his lady at church (which was but seldom) he behaved with less seeming devotion than formerly: however, if he was outwardly a pretty fellow, his morals remained entirely uncorrupted, though he was at the same time smarter and genteeler, than any of the beaus in town, either in or out of livery.

His lady, who had often said of him that Joey was the handsomest and genteelest footman in the kingdom, but that it was pity he wanted spirit, began now to find that fault no longer; on the contrary, she was frequently heard to cry out, *Ay, there is some life in this fellow.* She plainly saw the effects which town-air hath on the soberest constitutions. She would now walk out with him into Hyde Park in a morning, and when tired, which happened almost every minute, would lean on his arm, and converse with him in great familiarity. Whenever she stept out of her coach she would take him by the hand, and sometimes, for fear of stumbling, press it very hard; she admitted him to deliver messages at her bedside in a morning, leered at him at table, and indulged him in all those innocent freedoms which women of figure may permit without the least sully of their virtue.

But though their virtue remains unsullied, yet now and then
[at]1 some small arrows will glance [on]2 the shadow of it, their reputation; and so it fell out to Lady Booby, who happened to be walking arm-in-arm with Joey one morning in Hyde Park, when Lady Tittle and Lady Tattle came accidently by in their coach. *Bless me,* says Lady Tittle, *can I believe my eyes? Is that Lady Booby? Surely,* says Tattle. *But what makes you surprised?*

Why is not that her footman? replied Tittle. At which Tattle laughed and cried, *An old business, I assure you, is it possible you should not have heard it? The whole town hath known it this half year.* The consequence of this interview was a whisper through a hundred visits, which were separately performed by the two ladies * the same afternoon, and might have had a mischievous effect, had it not been stopt by two fresh reputations which were published the day afterwards, and engrossed the whole talk of the town.

But whatever opinion or suspicion the scandalous inclination of defamers might entertain of Lady Booby's innocent freedoms, it is certain they made no impression on young Andrews, who never offered to encroach beyond the liberties which his lady allowed him, a behaviour which she imputed to the violent respect he preserved for her, and which served only to heighten a something she began to conceive, and which the next chapter will open a little farther.

CHAP. V.

The death of Sir Thomas Booby, with the affectionate and mournful behaviour of his widow, and the great purity of Joseph Andrews.

AT this time, an accident happened which put a stop to those agreeable walks, which probably would have soon puffed up the cheeks of Fame, and caused her to blow her brazen trumpet through the town, and this was no other than the death of Sir Thomas Booby, who departing this life, left his disconsolate lady confined to her house as closely as if she herself had been attacked by some violent disease. During the first six days the poor lady admitted none but Mrs. Slipslop and three female friends, who made a party at cards: but on the seventh she

* It may seem an absurdity that Tattle should visit, as she actually did, to spread a known scandal: but the reader may reconcile this, by supposing, with me, that, notwithstanding what she says, this was her first acquaintance with it [Fielding's note].

ordered Joey, whom for a good reason we shall hereafter call JOSEPH, to bring up her tea-kettle. The lady being in bed, called Joseph to her, bade him sit down, and having accidentally laid her hand on his, she asked him, *if he had never been in love?* Joseph answered, with some confusion, "it was time enough for one so young as himself to think on such things." "As young as you are," replied the lady, "I am convinced you are no stranger to that passion; Come, Joey," says she, "tell me truly, who is the happy girl whose eyes have made a conquest of you?" Joseph returned, "that all women he had ever seen were equally indifferent to him." "O then," said the lady, "you are a general lover. Indeed you handsome fellows, like handsome women, are very long and difficult in fixing; but yet you shall never persuade me that your heart is so insusceptible of affection; I rather impute what you say to your secrecy, a very commendable quality, and what I am far from being angry with you for. Nothing can be more unworthy in a young man than to betray any intimacies with the ladies." *Ladies! Madam,* said Joseph, *I am sure I never had the impudence to think of any that deserve that name.* "Don't pretend to too much modesty," said she, "for that sometimes may be impertinent: but pray, answer me this question, Suppose a lady should happen to like you, suppose she should prefer you to all your sex, and admit you to the same familiarities as you might have hoped for, if you had been born her equal, are you certain that no vanity could tempt you to discover her? Answer me honestly, Joseph, Have you so much more sense and so much more virtue than you handsome young fellows generally have, who make no scruple of sacrificing our dear reputation to your pride, without considering the great obligation we lay on you, by our condescension and confidence? Can you keep a secret, my Joey?" "Madam," says he, "I hope your ladyship can't tax me with ever betraying the secrets of the family, and I hope, if you was to turn me away, I might have that character of you." "I don't intend to turn you away, Joey," said she, and sighed, "I am afraid it is not in my power." She then raised herself a little in her bed, and discovered one of the whitest necks that ever was seen; at which Joseph blushed. "La!" says she, in an affected surprise, "what am I doing? I

have trusted myself with a man alone, naked in bed; suppose you should have any wicked intentions upon my honour, how should I defend myself?" Joseph protested that he never had the least evil design against her. "No," says she, "perhaps you may not call your designs wicked, and perhaps they are not so." —He swore they were not. "You misunderstand me," says she, "I mean if they were against my honour, they may not be wicked, but the world calls them so. But then, say you, the world will never know anything of the matter, yet would not that be trusting to your secrecy? Must not my reputation be then in your power? Would you not then be my master?" Joseph begged her ladyship to be comforted, for that he would never imagine the least wicked thing against her, and that he had rather die a thousand deaths than give her any reason to suspect him. "Yes," said she, "I must have reason to suspect you. Are you not a man? and without vanity I may pretend to some charms. But perhaps you may fear I should prosecute you; indeed I hope you do, and yet Heaven knows I should never have the confidence to appear before a court of justice, and you know, Joey, I am of a forgiving temper. Tell me Joey, don't you think I should forgive you?" "Indeed madam," says Joseph, "I will never do anything to disoblige your ladyship." "How," says she, "do you think it would not disoblige me then? Do you think I would willingly suffer you?" "I don't understand you, madam," says Joseph. "Don't you?" said she, "then you either are a fool or pretend to be so, I find I was mistaken in you, so get you down stairs, and never let me see your face again: your pretended innocence cannot impose on me." "Madam," said Joseph, "I would not have your ladyship think any evil of me. I have always endeavoured to be a dutiful servant both to you and my master." "O thou villain," answered my lady, "Why didst thou mention the name of that dear man, unless to torment me, to bring his precious memory to my mind, (*and then she burst into a fit of tears.*) Get thee from my sight, I shall never endure thee more." At which words she turned away from him, and Joseph retreated from the room in a most disconsolate condition, and writ [that]$_2$ letter which the reader [the]$_1$
will find in the next chapter.

CHAP. VI.

How Joseph Andrews writ a letter to his sister Pamela.

To Mrs. Pamela Andrews, living with Squire Booby.

"*Dear Sister,*

"Since I received your Letter of your good Lady's Death, we have had a Misfortune of the same kind in our Family. My worthy Master, Sir *Thomas,* died about four Days ago, and what is worse, my poor Lady is certainly gone distracted. None of the Servants expected her to take it so to heart, because they quarrelled almost every day of their Lives: but no more of that, because you know, *Pamela,* I never loved to tell the Secrets of my Master's Family; but to be sure you must have known they never loved one another, and I have heard her Ladyship wish his Honour dead above a thousand times: but no body knows what it is to lose a Friend till they have lost him.

"Don't tell any body what I write, because I should not care to have Folks say I discover what passes in our Family: but if it had not been so great a Lady, I should have thought she had had a mind to me. Dear *Pamela,* don't tell any body: but she ordered me to sit down by her Bed-side, when she was in naked Bed; and she held my Hand, and talked exactly as a Lady does to her Sweetheart in a Stage-Play, which I have seen in *Covent-Garden,* while she wanted him to be no better than he should be.

"If Madam be mad, I shall not care for staying long in the Family; so I heartily wish you could get me a Place either at the Squire's, or some other neighbouring Gentleman's, unless it be true that you are going to be married to Parson *Williams,* as Folks talk, and then I should be very willing to be his Clerk: for which you know I am qualified, being able to read, and to set a Psalm.

"I fancy, I shall be discharged very soon; and the Moment I am, unless I hear from you, I shall return to my old Master's

Country Seat, if it be only to see Parson *Adams*, who is the best Man in the World. *London* is a bad Place, and there is so little good Fellowship, that next-door Neighbours don't know one another. Pray give my Service to all Friends that enquire for me; so I rest

Your Loving Brother,
Joseph Andrews."

As soon as Joseph had sealed and directed this letter, he walked down stairs, where he met Mrs. Slipslop, with whom we shall take this opportunity to bring the reader a little better acquainted. She was [a maiden]$_{3}$ gentlewoman of about forty-five years of age, who, having made a small slip in her youth, [an ancient maiden]$_{1\text{-}2}$ had continued a good maid ever since. She was not at this time remarkably handsome; being very short, and rather too corpulent in body, and somewhat red, with the addition of pimples in the face. Her nose was likewise rather too large, and her eyes too little; nor did she resemble a cow so much in her breath, as in two brown globes which she carried before her; one of her legs was also a little shorter than the other, which occasioned her to limp as she walked. This fair creature had long cast the eyes of affection on Joseph, in which she had not met with quite so good success as she probably wished, though besides the allurements of her native charms, she had given him tea, sweetmeats, wine, and many other delicacies, of which, by keeping the keys, she had the absolute command. Joseph however, had not returned the least gratitude to all these favours, not even so much as a kiss; though I would not insinuate she was so easily to be satisfied: for surely then he would have been highly blameable. The truth is, she was arrived at an age when she thought she might indulge herself in any liberties with a man, without the danger of bringing a third person into the world to betray them. She imagined, that by so long a self-denial, she had not only made amends for the small slip of her youth above hinted at: but had likewise laid up a quantity of merit to excuse any future failings. In a word, she resolved to give a loose to her amorous inclinations, and pay off the debt of pleasure which she found she owed herself, as fast as possible.

With these charms of person, and in this disposition of mind, she encountered poor Joseph at the bottom of the stairs, and asked him if he would drink a glass of something good this morning. Joseph, whose spirits were not a little cast down, very readily and thankfully accepted the offer; and together they went into a closet, where having delivered him a full glass of ratifia, and desired him to sit down, Mrs. Slipslop thus began:

"Sure nothing can be a more simple *contract* in a woman, than to place her affections on a boy. If I had ever thought it would have been my fate, I should have wished to die a thousand deaths rather than live to see that day. If we like a man, the lightest hint *sophisticates*. Whereas a boy *proposes* upon us to break through all the *regulations* of modesty, before we can make any *oppression* upon him." Joseph, who did not understand a word she said, answered, "*Yes madam;* — " "Yes, madam!" replied Mrs. Slipslop with some warmth, "Do you intend to *result* my passion? Is it not enough, ungrateful as you are, to make no return to all the favours I have done you: but you must treat me with *ironing?* Barbarous monster! how have I deserved that my passion should be *resulted* and treated with *ironing?*" "Madam," answered Joseph, "I don't understand your hard words: but I am certain, you have no occasion to call me ungrateful: for so far from intending you any wrong, I have always loved you as well as if you had been my own mother." "How, sirrah!" says Mrs. Slipslop in a rage: "Your own mother! Do you *assinuate* that I am old enough to be your mother? I don't know what a stripling may think: but I believe a man would *refer* me to any green-sickness silly girl *whatsomdever:* but I ought to despise you rather than be angry with you, for *referring* the conversation of girls to that of a woman of sense." "Madam," says Joseph, "I am sure I have always valued the honour you did me by your conversation; for I know you are a woman of learning." "Yes but, Joesph," said she a little softened by the compliment to her learning, "If you had a value for me, you certainly would have found some method of showing it me; for I am *convicted* you must see the value I have for you. Yes, Joseph, my eyes whether I would or no, must have declared a passion I cannot conquer. — Oh! Joseph! — "

As when a hungry tigress, who long has traversed the woods in fruitless search, sees within the reach of her claws a lamb, she prepares to leap on her prey; or as a voracious pike, of immense size, surveys through the liquid element a roach or gudgeon which cannot escape her jaws, opens them wide to swallow the little fish: so did Mrs. Slipslop prepare to lay her violent amorous hands on the poor Joseph, when luckily her mistress's bell rung, and delivered the intended martyr from her clutches. She was obliged to [leave him]$_3$ abruptly, and to defer the execution of her purpose [till]$_4$ some other time. We shall therefore return to the Lady Booby, and give our reader some account of her behaviour, after she was left by Joseph in a temper of mind not greatly different from that of the inflamed Slipslop.

[break off]$_{1\text{-}2}$
[to]$_{1\text{-}3}$

CHAP. VII.

Sayings of wise men. A dialogue between the lady and her maid, and a panegyric or rather satire on the passion of love, in the sublime style.

IT is the observation of some ancient sage, whose name I have forgot, that passions operate differently on the human mind, as diseases on the body, in proportion to the strength or weakness, soundness or rottenness of the one and the other.

We hope therefore, a judicious reader will give himself some pains to observe, what we have so greatly laboured to describe, the different operations of this passion of love in the gentle and cultivated mind of the Lady Booby, from those which it effected in the less polished and coarser disposition of Mrs. Slipslop.

[Another]$_3$ philosopher, whose name also at present escapes my memory, hath somewhere said, that resolutions taken in the absence of the beloved object are very apt to vanish in its presence; on both which wise sayings the following chapter may serve as a comment.

[One other]$_{1\text{-}2}$

No sooner had Joseph left the room in the manner we have before related, than the lady, enraged at her disappointment, began to reflect with severity on her conduct. Her love was now changed to disdain, which pride assisted to torment her. She despised herself for the meanness of her passion, and Joseph for its ill success. However, she had now got the better of it in her own opinion, and determined immediately to dismiss the object. After much tossing and turning in her bed, and many soliloquies, which, if we had no better matter for our reader, we would give him; she at last rung the bell as above-mentioned, and was presently attended by Mrs. Slipslop, who was not much better pleased with Joseph, than the lady herself.

Slipslop, said Lady Booby, *when did you see Joseph?* The poor woman was so surprised at the unexpected sound of his name, at so critical a time, that she had the greatest difficulty to conceal the confusion she was under from her mistress, whom she answered nevertheless, with pretty good confidence, though not entirely void of fear of suspicion, that she had not seen him that morning. "I am afraid," said Lady Booby, "he is a wild young fellow." "That he is," said Slipslop, "and a wicked one too. To my knowledge he games, drinks, swears and fights eternally: besides he is horribly *indicted* to wenching." "Ay!" said the lady, "I never heard that of him." "O madam," answered the other, "he is so lewd a rascal that if your ladyship keeps him much longer, you will not have one virgin in your house except myself. And yet I can't conceive what the wenches see in him, to be so foolishly fond as they are; in my eyes he is as ugly a scarecrow as I ever *upheld*." "Nay," said the lady, "the boy is well enough." — "La ma'am," cries Slipslop, "I think him the *ragmaticallest* fellow in the family." "Sure, Slipslop," says she, "you are mistaken: but which of the women do you most suspect?" "Madam," says Slipslop, "there is Betty the chambermaid, I am almost *convicted*, is with child by him." "Ay!" says the lady, "then pray pay her her wages instantly. I will keep no such sluts in my family. And as for Joseph, you may discard him too." "Would your ladyship have him paid off immediately?" cries Slipslop, "for perhaps, when Betty is gone, he may mend; and really the boy is a good servant, and a strong healthy *luscious* boy enough." "This morning," answered the lady with some vehemence. "I wish madam," cries Slipslop, "your ladyship would be so good as to try him a little longer." "I will not have my commands disputed," said the lady, "sure you are not fond of him yourself." "I madam?" cries Slipslop, reddening, if not blushing, "I should be sorry to think your ladyship had any reason to *respect* me of fondness for a fellow; and if it be your pleasure, I shall fulfill it with as much *reluctance* as possible." "As little, I suppose you mean," said the lady; "and so about it instantly." Mrs. Slipslop went out, and the lady had scarce taken two turns before she fell to knocking and ringing with great violence. Slipslop, who did not travel post-haste, soon returned, and was countermanded as to Joseph, but ordered to send Betty about her business without delay. She went out a second time with much greater alacrity than before; when the lady began immediately to accuse herself of want of resolution, and to apprehend the return of her affection with its pernicious consequences: she therefore applied herself again to the bell, and resummoned Mrs. Slipslop into her presence; who again returned, and was told by her mistress, that she had considered better of the matter, and was absolutely resolved to turn away Joseph; which she ordered her to do immediately. Slipslop, who knew the violence of her lady's temper, and would not venture her place for any Adonis or Hercules in the universe, left her a third time; which she had no sooner done, than the little god Cupid, fearing he had not yet done the lady's business, took a fresh arrow with the sharpest point out of his quiver, and shot it directly into her heart: in other and plainer language, the lady's passion got the better of her reason. She called back Slipslop once more, and told her she had resolved to see the boy, and examine him herself; therefore bid her send him up. This wavering in her mistress's temper probably put something into the waiting-gentlewoman's head, not necessary to mention to the sagacious reader.

Lady Booby was going to call her back again, but could not prevail with herself. The next consideration therefore was, how she should behave to Joseph when he came in. She resolved to preserve all the dignity of the woman of fashion to her servant, and to indulge herself in this last view of Joseph (for that she was most certainly resolved it should be) at his own expense, by first insulting, and then discarding him.

O Love, what monstrous tricks dost thou play with thy

votaries of both sexes! How dost thou deceive them, and make them deceive themselves! Their follies are thy delight! Their sighs make thee laugh, and their pangs are thy merriment!

Not the great Rich,[6] who turns men into monkeys, wheelbarrows, and whatever else best humours his fancy, hath so strangely metamorphosed the human shape; nor the great Cibber, who confounds all number, gender, and breaks through every rule of grammar at his will, hath so distorted the English language, as thou dost metamorphose and distort the human senses.

Thou puttest out our eyes, stoppest up our ears, and takest away the power of our nostrils; so that we can neither see the largest object, hear the loudest noise, nor smell the most poignant perfume. Again, when thou pleasest, thou canst make a molehill appear as a mountain; a Jew's-harp sound like a trumpet; and a daisy smell like a violet. Thou canst make cowardice brave, avarice generous, pride humble, and cruelty tenderhearted. In short, thou turnest the heart of man inside out, as a juggler doth a petticoat, and bringest whatsoever pleaseth thee out from it. If there be anyone who doubts all this, let him read the next chapter.

CHAP. VIII.

In which, after some very fine writing, the history goes on, and relates the interview between the lady and Joseph; where the latter hath set an example, which we despair of seeing followed by his sex, in this vicious age.

NOW the rake Hesperus had called for his breeches, and having well rubbed his drowsy eyes, prepared to dress himself for all night; by whose example his brother rakes on earth likewise leave those beds, in which they had slept away the day. Now Thetis the good housewife began to put on the pot in order to regale the good man Phoebus, after his daily labours were over.

[6] John Rich, dressed as a magical Harlequin, was a master of pantomime and theatrical illusions.

In vulgar language, it was in the evening when Joseph attended his lady's orders.

But as it becomes us to preserve the character of this lady, who is the heroine of our tale; and as we have naturally a wonderful tenderness for that beautiful part of the human species called, the fair sex; before we discover too much of her frailty to our reader, it will be proper to give him a lively idea of that vast temptation, which overcame all the efforts of a modest and virtuous mind; and then we humbly hope his good-nature will rather pity than condemn the imperfection of human virtue.

Nay, the ladies themselves will, we hope, be induced, by considering the uncommon variety of charms, which united in this young man's person, to bridle their rampant passion for chastity, and be at least, as mild as their violent modesty and virtue will permit them, in censuring the conduct of a woman, who, perhaps, was in her own disposition as chaste as those pure and sanctified virgins, who, after a life innocently spent in the gaieties of the town, begin about fifty to attend twice *per diem*, at the polite churches and chapels, to return thanks for the grace which preserved them formerly amongst beaus from temptations, perhaps less powerful than what now attacked the Lady Booby.

Mr. Joseph Andrews was now in the one and twentieth year of his age. He was of the highest degree of middle stature. His limbs were put together with great elegance and no less strength. His legs and thighs were formed in the exactest proportion. His shoulders were broad and brawny, but yet his arms hung so easily, that he had all the symptoms of strength without the least clumsiness. His hair was of a nut-brown colour, and was displayed in wanton ringlets down his back. His forehead was high, his eyes dark, and as full of sweetness as of fire. His nose a little inclined to the Roman. His teeth white and even. His lips [full, red]$_2$, and soft. His beard was only rough on his [full red]$_1$
chin and upper lip; but his cheeks, in which his blood glowed, were overspread with a thick down. His countenance had a tenderness joined with a sensibility inexpressible. Add to this the most perfect neatness in his dress, and an air, which to those who have not seen many noblemen, would give an idea of nobility.

Such was the person who now appeared before the lady. She

viewed him some time in silence, and twice or thrice before she spake, changed her mind as to the manner in which she should begin. At length, she said to him, "Joseph, I am sorry to hear such complaints against you; I am told you behave so rudely to the maids, that they cannot do their business in quiet; I mean those who are not wicked enough to hearken to your solicitations. As to others, they may not, perhaps, call you rude: for there are wicked sluts who make one ashamed of one's own sex; and are as ready to admit any nauseous familiarity as fellows to offer it; nay, there are such in my family: but they shall not stay in it; that impudent trollop, who is with child by you, is discharged by this time."

As a person who is struck through the heart with a thunder-bolt, looks extremely surprised, nay, and perhaps is so too.—Thus the poor Joseph received the false accusation of his mistress; he blushed and looked confounded, which she misinterpreted to be symptoms of his guilt, and thus went on.

"Come hither, Joseph: another mistress might discard you for
these offences; but I have a compassion for your youth, ⟨and⟩$_2$ if
[guilty. And I could be certain you would be no more [guilty — Consider]$_2$,
consider]$_1$ child, (*laying her hand carelessly upon his*) you are a handsome young fellow, and might do better; you might make
your fortune—." "Madam," said Joseph, "I do assure your ladyship, I don't know whether any maid in the house is man or
woman—." "Oh fie! Joseph," answered the lady, "don't commit
another crime in denying the truth. I could pardon the first;
but I hate a liar." "Madam," cries Joseph, "I hope your lady-
[and]$_{1-2}$ ship will not be offended at my asserting my innocence: [for]$_3$
by all that is sacred, I have never offered more than kissing."
"Kissing!" said the lady, ⟨with great discomposure of countenance, and more redness in her cheeks, than anger in her eyes,⟩$_2$
[but]$_{1-2}$ "do you call that no crime? Kissing, Joseph, is [as]$_3$ a prologue
to a play. Can I believe a young fellow of your age and complexion will be content with kissing? No, Joseph, there is no
woman who grants that but will grant more, and I am deceived
greatly in you, if you would not put her closely to it. What
would you think, Joseph, if I admitted you to kiss me?" Joseph
replied, "he would sooner die than have any such thought."

"And yet, Joseph," returned she, "ladies have admitted their footmen to such familiarities; and footmen, I confess to you, much less deserving them; fellows without half your charms: for such might almost excuse the crime. Tell me, therefore, Joseph, if I should admit you to such freedom, what would you think of me? — tell me freely." "Madam," said Joseph, "I should think your ladyship condescended a great deal below yourself." "Pugh!" said she, "that I am to answer to myself: but would not you insist on more? Would you be contented with a kiss? Would not your inclinations be all on fire rather by such a favour?" "Madam," said Joseph, "if they were, I hope I should be able to control them, without suffering them to get the better of my virtue." — You have heard, reader, poets talk of the *Statue of Surprise;* [7] you have heard likewise, or else you have heard very little, how Surprise made one of the sons of Crœsus speak though he was dumb. You have seen the faces, in the eighteen-penny gallery, when through the trap-door, to soft or no music, Mr. Bridgewater, Mr. William Mills, or some other of ghostly appearance, hath ascended with a face all pale with powder, and a shirt all bloody with ribbons; but from none of these, nor from Phidias, or Praxiteles, if they should return to life — no, not from the inimitable pencil of my friend Hogarth, could you receive such an idea of Surprise, as would have entered in at your eyes, had they beheld the Lady Booby, when those last words issued out from the lips of Joseph. — "Your virtue! (said the lady recovering after a silence of two minutes) I shall never survive it. Your virtue! Intolerable confidence! Have you the assurance to pretend, that when a lady demeans herself to throw aside the rules of decency, in order to honour you with the highest favour in her power, your virtue should resist her inclination? That when she had conquered her own virtue, she should find an obstruction in yours?" "Madam," said Joseph, "I can't see why her having no virtue should be a reason against my having any. Or why, because I am a man, or

[7] No specific "Statue of Surprise" has yet been discovered, though Professor Battestin has found several approximate references to people who stand "like statues" from confusion, despair, and similar amazements. Fielding is probably misquoting one of these passages from memory.

because I am poor, my virtue must be subservient to her pleasures." "I am out of patience," cries the lady: "Did ever mortal hear of a man's virtue! Did ever the greatest, or the gravest men pretend to any of this kind! Will magistrates who punish lewdness, or parsons, who preach against it, make any scruple of committing it? And can a boy, a stripling, have the confidence to talk of his virtue?" "Madam," says Joseph, "that boy is the brother of Pamela, and would be ashamed that the chastity of his family, which is preserved in her, should be stained in him. If there are such men as your ladyship mentions, I am sorry for it, and I wish they had an opportunity of reading over those letters, which my father hath sent me of my sister Pamela's, nor do I doubt but such an example would amend them." "You impudent villain," cries the lady in a rage, "Do you insult me with the follies of my relation, who hath exposed himself all over the country upon your sister's account? a little vixen, whom I have always wondered my late Lady John Booby ever kept in her house. Sirrah! get out of my sight, and prepare to set out this night, for I will order you your wages immediately, and you shall be stripped and turned away. — " "Madam," says Joseph, "I am sorry I have offended your ladyship, I am sure I never intended it." "Yes, sirrah," cries she, "you have had the vanity to misconstrue the little innocent freedom I took in order to try, whether what I had heard was true. O' my conscience, you have had the assurance to imagine, I was fond of you myself." Joseph [answered, he had only spoke out of tenderness for his virtue; at which words she flew into a violent passion, and refusing to hear more, ordered]$_2$ him instantly to leave the room.

[was going to speak, when she refused to hear him, and ordered]$_1$

He was no sooner gone, than she burst forth into the following exclamation: "Whither doth this violent passion hurry us? What meannesses do we submit to from its impulse? Wisely we resist its first and least approaches; for it is then only we can assure ourselves the victory. No woman could ever safely say, *so far only will I go*. Have I not exposed myself to the refusal of my footman? I cannot bear the reflection." Upon which she applied herself to the bell, and rung it with infinite more violence than was necessary; the faithful Slipslop attending near at hand: To say the truth, she had conceived a suspicion at her last interview with her mistress; and had waited ever since in the antechamber, having carefully applied her ears to the keyhole during the whole time, that the preceding conversation passed between Joseph and the lady.

CHAP. IX.

What passed between the lady and Mrs. Slipslop, in which we prophesy there are some strokes which everyone will not truly comprehend at the first reading.

"SLIPSLOP," said the lady, "I find too much reason to believe all thou hast told me of this wicked Joseph; I have determined to part with him instantly; so go you to the steward, and bid him pay him his wages." Slipslop, who had preserved hitherto a distance to her lady, rather out of necessity than inclination, and who thought the knowledge of this secret had thrown down all distinction between them, answered her mistress very pertly, "she wished she knew her own mind; and that she was certain she would call her back again before she was got half way down stairs." The lady replied, "she had taken a resolution, and was resolved to keep it." "I am sorry for it," cries Slipslop; "and if I had known you would have punished the poor lad so severely, you should never have heard a *particle* of the matter. Here's a fuss indeed,.about nothing." "Nothing!" returned my lady; "Do you think I will countenance lewdness in my house?" "If you will turn away every footman," said Slipslop, "that is a lover of the sport, you must soon open the coach door yourself, or get a set of *mophrodites* to wait upon you; and I am sure I hated the sight of them even singing in an opera." "Do as I bid you," says my lady, "and don't shock my ears with your beastly language." "Marry-come-up," cries Slipslop, "People's ears are sometimes the nicest part about them."

The lady, who began to admire the new style in which her waiting-gentlewoman delivered herself, and by the conclusion of her speech, suspected somewhat of the truth, called her back, and desired to know what she meant by the extraordinary degree of freedom ⟨in⟩ $_2$ which she thought proper to indulge ~~to~~ $_2$ her tongue. "Freedom!" says Slipslop, "I don't know what you call freedom, madam; servants have tongues as well as their mistresses." "Yes, and saucy ones too," answered the lady: "but I assure you I shall bear no such impertinence." "Impertinence! I don't know that I am impertinent," says Slipslop. "Yes indeed you are," cries my lady; "and unless you mend your manners, this house is no place for you." "Manners!" cries Slipslop, "I never was thought to want manners *nor modesty neither;* and for places, there are more places than one; and I know what I know." "What do you know, mistress?" answered the lady. "I am not obliged to tell that to everybody," says Slipslop, "any more than I am obliged to keep it a secret." "I desire you would provide yourself," answered the lady. "With all my heart," replied the waiting-gentlewoman; and so departed in a passion, and slapped the door after her.

The lady too plainly perceived that her waiting-gentlewoman knew more than she would willingly have had her acquainted with; and this she imputed to Joseph's having discovered to her what passed at the first interview. This therefore blew up her rage against him, and confirmed her in a resolution of parting with him.

But the dismissing Mrs. Slipslop was a point not so easily to be resolved upon: she had the utmost tenderness for her reputation, as she knew on that depended many of the most valuable blessings of life; particularly cards, making curtsies in public places, and above all, the pleasure of demolishing the reputations of others, in which innocent amusement she had an extraordinary delight. She therefore determined to submit to any insult from a servant, rather than run a risk of losing the title to so many great privileges.

She therefore sent for her steward, Mr. Peter Pounce; and ordered him to pay Joseph his wages, to strip off his livery and to turn him out of the house that evening.

She then called Slipslop up, and after refreshing her spirits with a small cordial which she kept in her closet, she began in the following manner:

"Slipslop, why will you, who know my passionate temper,

attempt to provoke me by your answers? I am convinced you are an honest servant, and should be very unwilling to part with you. I believe likewise, you have found me an indulgent mistress on many occasions, and have as little reason on your side to desire a change. I can't help being surprised therefore, that you will take the surest method to offend me. I mean repeating my words, which you know I have always detested."

The prudent waiting-gentlewoman had duly weighed the whole matter, and found on mature deliberation, that a good place in possession was better than one in expectation; as she found her mistress therefore inclined to relent, she thought proper also to put on some small condescension; which was as readily accepted: and so the affair was reconciled, all offences forgiven, and a present of a gown and petticoat made her as an instance of her lady's future favour.

She offered once or twice to speak in favour of Joseph; but found her lady's heart so obdurate, that she prudently dropt all such efforts. She considered there were more footmen in the house, and some as stout fellows, though not quite so handsome as Joseph: besides, the reader hath already seen her tender advances had not met with the encouragement she might have reasonably expected. She thought she had thrown away a great deal of sack and sweetmeats on an ungrateful rascal; and being a little inclined to the opinion of that female sect, who hold one lusty young fellow to be near as good as another lusty young fellow, she at last gave up Joseph and his cause, and with a triumph over her passion highly commendable, walked off with her present, and with great tranquillity paid a visit to a stone-bottle, which is of sovereign use to a philosophical temper.

She left not her mistress so easy. The poor lady could not reflect, without agony, that her dear reputation was in the power of her servants. All her comfort, as to [Joseph]$_2$ was, that she [Joey]$_1$
hoped he did not understand her meaning; at least, she could say for herself, she had not plainly expressed anything to him; and as to Mrs. Slipslop, she imagined she could bribe her to secrecy.

But what hurt her most was, that in reality she had not so entirely conquered her passion; the little god lay lurking in her heart, though Anger and Disdain so hoodwinked her, that she could not see him. She was a thousand times on the very brink of revoking the sentence she had passed against the poor youth. Love became his advocate, and whispered many things in his favour. Honour likewise endeavoured to vindicate his crime, and Pity to mitigate his punishment; on the other side, Pride and Revenge spoke as loudly against him: and thus the poor lady was tortured with perplexity; opposite passions distracting and tearing her mind different ways.

So have I seen, in the hall of Westminster; where Serjeant Bramble hath been retained on the right side, and Serjeant Puzle on the left; the balance of opinion (so equal were their fees) alternately incline to either scale.[8] Now Bramble throws in an argument, and Puzzle's scale strikes the beam; again, Bramble shares the like fate, overpowered by the weight of Puzzle. Here Bramble hits, there Puzzle strikes; here one has you, there t'other has you; 'till at last all becomes one scene of confusion in the tortured minds of the hearers; equal wagers are laid on the success, and neither judge nor jury can possibly make anything of the matter; all things are so enveloped by the careful serjeants in doubt and obscurity.

Or as it happens in the conscience, where honour and honesty pull one way, and a bribe and necessity another. — If it was only our present business to make similes, we could produce many more to this purpose: but a simile (as well as a word) to the wise. We shall therefore see a little after our hero, for whom the reader is doubtless in some pain.

CHAP. X.

Joseph writes another letter: His transactions with Mr. Peter Pounce, &c. with his departure from Lady Booby.

THE disconsolate Joseph, would not have had an understanding sufficient for the principal subject of such a book as this, if he had

[8] The "Serjeants" are serjeants-at-law, the highest rank of barristers, or trial lawyers—a title equivalent to "Doctor."

any longer misunderstood the drift of his mistress; and indeed that he did not discern it sooner, the reader will be pleased to apply to an unwillingness in him to discover what he must condemn in her as a fault. Having therefore quitted her presence, he retired into his own garret, and entered himself into an ejaculation on the numberless calamities which attended beauty, and the misfortune it was to be handsomer than one's neighbours.

He then sat down and addressed himself to his sister Pamela in the following words:

"*Dear Sister* Pamela,

"Hoping you are well, what News have I to tell you! O *Pamela,* my Mistress is fallen in love with me — That is, what great Folks call falling in love, she has a mind to ruin me; but I hope, I shall have more Resolution and more Grace than to part with my Virtue to any Lady upon Earth.

"Mr. *Adams* [hath]$_2$ often told me, that Chastity is as great a [has]$_1$ Virtue in a Man as in a Woman. He says he never knew any more than his Wife, and I shall endeavour to follow his Example. Indeed, it is owing entirely to his excellent Sermons and Advice, together with your Letters, that I have been able to resist a Temptation, which he says no Man complies with, but he repents in this World, or is damned for it in the next; and why should I trust to Repentance on my Death-bed, since I may die in my sleep? What fine things are good Advice and good Examples! But I am glad she turned me out of the Chamber as she did: for I had once almost forgotten every word Parson *Adams* had ever said to me.

"I don't doubt, dear Sister, but you will have Grace to preserve your Virtue against all Trials; and I beg you earnestly to pray, I may be enabled to preserve mine: for truly, it is very severely attacked by more than one: but, I hope I shall copy your Example, and that of *Joseph,* my Name's-sake; and maintain my Virtue against all temptations."

Joseph had not finished his letter, when he was summoned down stairs by Mr. Peter Pounce, to receive his wages: for, besides that out of eight pounds a year he allowed his father and mother four, he had been obliged, in order to furnish himself with musical instruments, to apply to the generosity of the aforesaid Peter, who, on urgent occasions, used to advance the servants their wages: not before they were due, but before they were payable; that is, perhaps, half a year after they were due, and this at the moderate *premiums* of fifty *per cent.* or a little more; by which charitable methods, together with lending money to other people, and even to his own master and mistress, the honest man had, from nothing, in a few years amassed a small sum of twenty thousand pounds or thereabouts.

Joseph having received his little remainder of wages, and having stript off his livery, was forced to borrow a frock and breeches of one of the servants: (for he was so beloved in the family, that they would all have lent him anything), and being told by Peter, that he must not stay a moment longer in the house, than was necessary to pack up his linen, which he easily did in a very narrow compass; he took a melancholy leave of his fellow-servants, and set out at seven in the evening.

He had proceeded the length of two or three streets, before he absolutely determined with himself, whether he should leave
[this]$_1$ the town [that]$_2$ night, or, procuring a lodging, wait 'till the morning. At last, the moon, shining very bright, helped him to come to a resolution of beginning his journey immediately, to which likewise he had some other inducements which the reader, without being a conjurer, cannot possibly guess; 'till we have given him those hints, which it may be now proper to open.

CHAP. XI.

Of several new matters not expected.

It is an observation sometimes made, ⟨that⟩$_3$ to indicate our
[*That he*]$_{1\text{-}2}$ idea of a simple fellow, [we say, *He*]$_3$ *is easily to be seen through:* Nor do I believe it a more improper denotation of a simple book. Instead of applying this to any particular performance, we choose rather to remark the contrary in this

history, where the scene opens itself by small degrees, and he is a sagacious reader who can see two chapters before him.

For this reason, we have not hitherto hinted a matter which now seems necessary to be explained; since it may be wondered at, first, that Joseph made such extraordinary haste out of town, which hath been already shown; and secondly, which will be now shown, that instead of proceeding to the habitation of his father and mother, or to his beloved sister Pamela, he chose rather to set out full speed to the Lady Booby's country seat, which he had left on his journey to London.

Be it known then, that in the same parish where this seat stood, there lived a young girl whom Joseph (though the best of sons and brothers) longed more impatiently to see than his parents or his sister. She was a poor girl, who had been formerly bred up in Sir John's family; [9] whence a little before the journey to London, she had been discarded by Mrs. Slipslop on account of her extraordinary beauty: for I never could find any other reason.

This young creature (who now lived with a farmer in the parish) had been always beloved by Joseph, and returned his affection. She was two years only younger than our hero. They had been acquainted from their infancy, and had conceived a very early liking for each other, which had grown to such a degree of affection, that Mr. Adams had with much ado prevented them from marrying, and persuaded them to wait, 'till a few years' service and thrift had a little improved their experience, and enabled them to live comfortably together.

They followed this good man's advice; as indeed his word was little less than a law in his parish: for as he had shown his parishioners by a uniform behaviour of thirty-five years duration, that he had their good entirely at heart; so they consulted him on every occasion, and very seldom acted contrary to his opinion.

Nothing can be imagined more tender than was the parting between these two lovers. A thousand sighs heaved the bosom of Joseph; a thousand tears distilled from the lovely eyes of Fanny (for that was her name.) Though her modesty would only suffer

[9] Fielding forgets he had named him Sir Thomas.

her to admit his eager kisses, her violent love made her more than passive in his embraces; and she often pulled him to her breast with a soft pressure, which, though perhaps it would not have squeezed an insect to death, caused more emotion in the heart of Joseph, than the closest Cornish hug [10] could have done.

The reader may perhaps wonder, that so fond a pair should during a twelvemonth's absence never converse with one another; indeed there was but one reason which did, or could have
[that]$_1$ prevented them; and [this]$_2$ was, that poor Fanny could neither write nor read, nor could she be prevailed upon to transmit the delicacies of her tender and chaste passion, by the hands of an amanuensis.

They contented themselves therefore with frequent inquiries after each other's health, with a mutual confidence in each other's fidelity, and the prospect of their future happiness.

Having explained these matters to our reader, and, as far as possible, satisfied all his doubts, we return to honest Joseph, whom we left just set out on his travels by the light of the moon.

Those who have read any romance or poetry ancient or modern, must have been informed, that Love hath wings; by which they are not to understand, as some young ladies by mistake have done, that a lover can fly: the writers, by this ingenious allegory, intending to insinuate no more, than that lovers do not march like Horse-Guards; in short, that they put the best leg foremost, which our lusty youth, who could walk with any man, did so heartily on this occasion, that within four hours, he
[the]$_1$ reached [a]$_2$ famous house of hospitality well known to the western traveller. It presents you a lion on the sign-post: and the master, who was christened *Timotheus*, is commonly called plain *Tim*. Some have conceived that he hath particularly chosen the lion for his sign, as he doth in countenance greatly resemble that magnanimous beast, though his disposition savours more of the sweetness of the lamb. He is a person well received among all sorts of men, being qualified to render himself agreeable to any; as he is well versed in history and politics, hath a smattering in law and divinity, cracks a good jest, and plays wonderfully well on the French horn.

[10] Cornwall was noted for its wrestlers.

A violent storm of hail forced Joseph to take shelter in this inn, where he remembered Sir [Thomas]$_2$ had dined in his way [John]$_1$ to town. Joseph had no sooner seated himself by the kitchen fire than Timotheus, observing his livery, began to condole the loss of his late master; who was, he said, his very particular and intimate acquaintance, with whom he had cracked many a merry bottle, aye many a dozen in his time. He then remarked that all those things were over now, all past, and just as if they had never been; and concluded with an excellent observation on the certainty of death, which his wife said was indeed very true. A fellow now arrived at the same inn with two horses, one of which he was leading farther down into the country to meet his master; these he put into the stable, and came and took his place by Joseph's side, who immediately knew him to be the servant of a neighbouring gentleman, who used to visit at their house.

This fellow was likewise forced in by the storm; for he had orders to go twenty miles farther that evening, and luckily on the same road which Joseph himself intended to take. He therefore embraced this opportunity of complimenting his friend with his master's [horse]$_c$, [horses]$_{1\text{-}5}$ (notwithstanding he had received express commands to the contrary) which was readily accepted: and so after they had drank a loving pot, and the storm was over, they set out together.

CHAP. XII.

Containing many surprising adventures, which Joseph Andrews met with on the road, scarce credible [*to*]$_3$ [*by*]$_{1\text{-}2}$ *those who have never travelled in a stage-coach.*

NOTHING remarkable happened on the road, 'till their arrival at the inn [to which the horses were ordered; whither]$_3$ [whither . . . where]$_{1\text{-}2}$ they came about two in the morning. The moon then shone very bright, and Joseph making his friend a present of a pint of wine, and thanking him for the favour of his horse, notwithstanding all entreaties to the contrary, proceeded on his journey on foot.

He had not gone above two miles, charmed with the hopes of shortly seeing his beloved Fanny, when he was met by two fellows in a narrow lane, and ordered to stand and deliver. He readily gave them all the money he had, which was somewhat less than two pounds; and told them he hoped they would be so generous as to return him a few shillings, to defray his charges on his way home.

One of the ruffians answered with an oath, *Yes, we'll give you something presently: but first strip and be d—n'd to you.—Strip,* cried the other, *or I'll blow your brains to the Devil.* Joseph, remembering that he had borrowed his coat and breeches of a friend; and that he should be ashamed of making any excuse for not returning them, replied, he hoped they would not insist on his clothes, which were not worth much; but consider the coldness of the night. *You are cold, are you, you rascal!* says one of the robbers, *I'll warm you with a vengeance;* and damning his eyes, snapt a pistol at his head: which he had no sooner done, than the other levelled a blow at him with his stick, which Joseph, who was expert at cudgel-playing, caught with his, and returned the favour so successfully on his adversary, that he laid him sprawling at his feet, and at the same instant received a blow from behind, with the butt-end of a pistol from the other villain, which felled him to the ground, and totally deprived him of his senses.

The thief, who had been knocked down, had now recovered himself; and both together fell to be-labouring poor Joseph with their sticks, till they were convinced they had put an end to his miserable being: They then stript him entirely naked, threw him into a ditch, and departed with their booty.

The poor wretch, who lay motionless a long time, just began to recover his senses as a stage-coach came by. The postilion hearing a man's groans, stopt his horses, and told the coachman, "he was certain there was a *dead* man lying in the ditch, for he heard him groan." "Go on, sirrah," says the coachman, "we are confounded late, and have no time to look after dead men." A lady, who heard what the postilion said, and likewise heard the groan, called eagerly to the coachman, "to stop and see what was the matter." Upon which he bid the postilion "alight, and look into the ditch." He did so, and returned, "that there was a man sitting upright as naked as ever he was born." — "O J—sus," cried the lady, "A naked man! Dear coachman, drive on and leave him." Upon this the gentlemen got out of the coach; and Joseph begged them, "to have mercy upon him: For that he had been robbed, and almost beaten to death." "Robbed," cries an old gentleman; "Let us make all the haste imaginable, or we shall be robbed too." A young man, who belonged to the law answered, "he wished they had passed by without taking any notice: But that now they might be proved to have been *last in his company;* if he should die, they might be called to some account for his murder. He therefore thought it advisable to save the poor creature's life, for their own sakes, if possible; at least, if he died, to prevent the jury's finding *that they fled for it.* He was therefore *of opinion,* to take the man into the coach, and carry him to the next inn." The lady insisted, "that he should not come into the coach. That if they lifted him in, she would herself alight: for she had rather stay in that place to all eternity, than ride with a naked man." The coachman objected, "that he could not suffer him to be taken in, unless somebody would pay a shilling for his carriage the four miles." Which the two gentlemen refused to do; but the lawyer, who was afraid of some mischief happening to himself if the wretch was left behind in that condition, saying, "no man could be too cautious in these matters, and that he remembered very extraordinary cases in the books," threatened the coachman, and bid him deny taking him up at his peril; "for that if he died, he should be indicted for his murder, and if he lived, and brought an action against him, he would willingly take a brief in it." These words had a sensible effect on the coachman, who was well acquainted with the person who spoke them; and the old gentleman abovementioned, thinking the naked man would afford him frequent opportunities of showing his wit to the lady, offered to join with the company in giving a mug of beer for his fare; till partly alarmed by the threats of the one, and partly by the promises of the other, and being perhaps *a little* moved with compassion at the poor creature's condition, who stood bleeding and shivering with the cold, he at length agreed; and Joseph was now advancing to the coach, where seeing the lady, who held the sticks of her fan before her eyes, he absolutely refused, miserable as he was, to enter, unless he was furnished with sufficient covering, to prevent giving the least offence to decency. So perfectly modest was this young man; such mighty effects had the spotless example of the amiable Pamela, and the excellent sermons of Mr. Adams wrought upon him.

Though there were several greatcoats about the coach, it was not easy to get over this difficulty which Joseph had started. The two gentlemen complained they were cold, and could not spare a rag; the man of wit saying, with a laugh, *that charity began at home;* and the coachman, who had two ⟨greatcoats⟩ 2 spread under him, refused to lend either, lest they should be made bloody; the lady's footman desired to be excused for the same reason, which the lady herself, notwithstanding her abhorrence of a naked man, approved: and it is more than probable, poor Joseph, who obstinately adhered to his modest resolution, must have perished, unless the postilion, (a lad who hath been since transported for robbing a hen-roost) had voluntarily stript off a greatcoat, his only garment, at the same time swearing a great oath, (for which he was rebuked by the passengers) "that he would rather ride in his shirt all his life, than suffer a fellow-creature to lie in so miserable a condition."

Joseph, having put on the greatcoat, was lifted into the coach, which now proceeded on its journey. He declared himself almost dead with the cold, which gave the man of wit an occasion to ask the lady, if she could not accommodate him with a dram. She answered with some resentment, "she wondered at his asking her such a question;" but assured him, "she never tasted any such thing."

The lawyer was inquiring into the circumstances of the robbery, when the coach stopt, and one of the ruffians, putting a pistol in, demanded their money of the passengers; who readily gave it them; and the lady, in her fright, delivered up a little silver bottle, of about a half-pint size, which, the rogue, clapping it to his mouth, and drinking her health, declared held some of the best *Nantes* he had ever tasted: this the lady afterwards assured the company was the mistake of her maid, for that she had ordered her to fill the bottle with *Hungary* water.[11]

As soon as the fellows were departed, the lawyer, who had, it seems, a case of pistols in the seat of the coach, informed the company, that if it had been daylight, and he could have come at his pistols, he would not have submitted to the robbery; he likewise set forth, that he had often met highwaymen when he travelled on horseback, but none ever durst attack him; concluding, that if he had not been more afraid for the lady than for himself, he should not have now parted with his money so easily.

As wit is generally observed to love to reside in empty pockets; so the gentleman, whose ingenuity we have above remarked, as soon as he had parted with his money, began to grow wonderfully facetious. He made frequent allusions to Adam and Eve, and said many excellent things on figs and fig-leaves; which perhaps gave more offence to Joseph than to any other in the company.

The lawyer likewise made several very pretty jests, without departing from his profession. He said, "if Joseph and the lady were alone, he would be the more capable of making a *conveyance* to her, as his *affairs* were not *fettered* with any *incumbrance;* he'd warrant, he soon suffered a *recovery* by a writ of *entry*, which was the proper way to create *heirs in tail;* that, for his own part, he would engage to make so *firm a settlement* in a coach, that there should be no danger of an *ejectment;*" with an inundation of the like gibberish, which he continued to vent till the coach arrived at an inn, where one servant-maid only was up in readiness to attend the coachman, and furnish him with cold meat and a dram. Joseph desired to alight, and that he might have a bed prepared for him, which the maid readily promised to perform; and being a good-natured wench, and not so squeamish as the lady had been, she clapt a large fagot on the fire, and furnishing Joseph with a greatcoat belonging to one of the hostlers, desired him to sit down and warm himself, whilst she made his bed. The coachman, in the meantime, took

[11] Nantes is brandy; Hungary-water, a toilet-water made of oil of rosemary and alcohol.

an opportunity to call up a surgeon, who lived within a few doors: after which, he reminded his passengers how late they were, and after they had taken leave of Joseph, hurried them off as fast as he could.

The wench soon got Joseph to bed, and promised to use her interest to borrow him a shirt; but imagined, as she afterwards said, by his being so bloody, that he must be a dead man: she ran with all speed to hasten the surgeon, who was more than half drest, apprehending that the coach had been overturned and some gentleman or lady hurt. As soon as the wench had informed him at his window, that it was a poor foot passenger who had been stripped of all he had, and almost murdered; he chid her for disturbing him so early, slipped off his clothes again, and very quietly returned to bed and to sleep.

Aurora now began to show her blooming cheeks over the hills, whilst ten millions of feathered songsters, in jocund chorus, repeat⟨ed⟩$_2$ odes a thousand times sweeter than those of our
[sing]$_1$ *Laureate,*[12] and [sung]$_2$ both *the Day and the Song;* when the master of the inn, Mr. Tow-wouse, arose, and learning from his maid an account of the robbery, and the situation of his poor naked guest, he shook his head, and cried, *Good-lack-a-day!* and then ordered the girl to carry him one of his own shirts.

Mrs. Tow-wouse was just awake, and had stretched out her arms in vain to fold her departed husband, when the maid en-
[,]$_{1\text{-}2}$ tered the room. "Who's there[?]$_3$ Betty?" "Yes madam." "Where's your master?" "He's without, madam; he hath sent me for a shirt to lend ~~to~~$_2$ a poor naked man, who hath been robbed and murdered." "Touch one, if you dare, you slut," said Mrs. Tow-wouse, "your master is a pretty sort of a man to take in

[12] The Laureate is Cibber, famous for his poor official odes each New Year's Day and each birthday of the king. Fielding had parodied Cibber's odes in his farce, *The Historical Register* (1737), like this:

Then sing the Day,
And sing the Song;
And thus be merry
All Day long.

And Cibber, in his *Apology,* refers back to Fielding, in turn, as he describes his first boyhood poem: "I cannot say it was much above the merry Style of *Sing! Sing the Day, and sing the Song,* in the Farce . . ." (Battestin, pp. 55–56).

naked vagabonds, and clothe them with his own clothes. I shall have no such doings.—If you offer to touch anything, I will throw the chamber-pot at your head. Go, send your master to me." "Yes madam," answered Betty. As soon as he came in, she thus began: "What the devil do you mean by this, Mr. Tow-wouse? Am I to buy shirts to lend to a set of scabby rascals?" "My dear," said Mr. Tow-wouse, "this is a poor wretch." "Yes," says she, "I know it is a poor wretch, but what the devil have we to do with poor wretches? The law makes us provide for too many already. We shall have thirty or forty poor wretches in red coats shortly."[13] "My dear," cries Tow-wouse, "this man
hath been robbed of all he [hath]$_2$." "Well then," said she, [has]$_1$
"where's his money to pay his reckoning? Why [doth]$_2$ not such [does]$_1$
a fellow go to an ale-house? I shall send him packing as soon as I am up, I assure you." "My dear," said he, "common charity won't suffer you to do that." "Common charity, a f—t!" says she, "Common charity teaches us to provide for ourselves, and our families; and I and mine won't be ruined by your charity, I assure you." "Well," says he, "my dear, do as you will when you are up, you know I never contradict you." "No," says she, "if the Devil was to contradict me, I would make the house too hot to hold him."

With such like discourses they consumed near half an hour, whilst Betty provided a shirt from the hostler, who was one of her sweethearts, and put it on poor Joseph. The surgeon had likewise at last visited him, and washed and drest his wounds, and was now come to acquaint Mr. Tow-wouse, that his guest was in such extreme danger of his life, that he scarce saw any hopes of his recovery. — "Here's a pretty kettle of fish," cries Mrs. Tow-wouse, "you have brought upon us! We are like to have a funeral at our own expense." Tow-wouse, (who, notwithstanding his charity, would have given his vote as freely as he ever did at an election, that any other house in the kingdom, should have quiet possession of his guest) answered, "My dear, I am not to blame: he was brought hither by the stage-coach; and Betty had put him to bed before I was stirring."

[13] Innkeepers were required to house soldiers, and to provide them food and beer at the daily rate of four pence a man.

"I'll Betty her," says she — At which, with half her garments on, the other half under her arm, she sallied out in quest of the unfortunate Betty, whilst Tow-wouse and the surgeon went to pay a visit to poor Joseph, and inquire into the circumstance of this melancholy affair.

CHAP. XIII.

What happened to Joseph during his sickness at the inn, with the curious discourse between him and Mr. Barnabas the parson of the parish.

As soon as Joseph had communicated a particular history of the robbery, together with a short account of himself, and his intended journey, he asked the surgeon "if he apprehended him to be in any danger:" To which the surgeon very honestly answered, "he feared he was; for that his pulse was very exalted and feverish, and if his fever should prove more than *symptomatic*, it would be impossible to save him." Joseph, fetching a deep sigh, cried, "*Poor Fanny, I would I could have lived to see thee! but G—'s Will be done.*"

The surgeon then advised him, "if he had any worldly affairs to settle, that he would do it as soon as possible; for though he hoped he might recover, yet he thought himself obliged to acquaint him he was in great danger, and if the malign concoction of his humours should cause a suscitation of his fever, he might soon grow delirious, and incapable to make his will." Joseph answered, "that it was impossible for any creature in the universe to be in a poorer condition than himself: for since the robbery he had not one thing of any kind whatever, which he could call his own." *I had* ⟨, said he,⟩$_2$ *a poor little piece of*
[*be*]$_1$ *gold which they took away, that would* [*have been*]$_2$ *a comfort to me in all my afflictions; but surely, Fanny, I want nothing to remind me of thee. I have thy dear image in my heart, and no villain can ever tear it thence.*

Joseph desired paper and pens to write a letter, but they

were refused him; and he was advised to use all his endeavours to compose himself. They then left him; and Mr. Tow-wouse sent to a clergyman to come and administer his good offices to the soul of poor Joseph, since the surgeon despaired of making any successful applications to his body.

Mr. Barnabas (for that was the clergyman's name) came as soon as sent for, and having first drank a dish of tea with the landlady, and afterwards a bowl of punch with the landlord, he walked up to the room where Joseph lay: but, finding him asleep, returned to take the other sneaker, which when he had finished, he again crept softly up to the chamber-door, and, having opened it, heard the sick man talking to himself in the following manner:

"O most adorable Pamela! most virtuous sister, whose example could alone enable me to withstand all the temptations of riches and beauty, and to preserve my virtue pure and chaste, for the arms of my dear Fanny, if it had pleased Heaven that I should ever have come unto them. What riches, or honours, or pleasures can make us amends for the loss of innocence? Doth not that alone afford us more consolation, than all worldly acquisitions? What but innocence and virtue could give any comfort to such a miserable wretch as I am? Yet these can make me prefer this sick and painful bed to all the pleasures I should have found in my lady's. These can make me face death without fear; and though I love my Fanny more than ever man loved a woman; these can teach me to resign myself to the Divine Will without repining. O thou delightful charming creature, [if Heaven had]$_3$ indulged thee to my arms, the poorest, humblest state would have been a paradise; I could have lived with thee in the lowest cottage, without envying the palaces, the dainties, or the riches of any man breathing. But I must leave thee, leave thee for ever, my dearest angel, I must think of another world, and I heartily pray thou may'st meet comfort in this." — Barnabas thought he had heard enough; so down stairs he went, and told Tow-wouse he could do his guest no service: for that he was very light-headed, and had uttered nothing but a rhapsody of nonsense all the time he stayed in the room.

[would Heaven have]$_{1-2}$

The surgeon returned in the afternoon, and found his patient in a higher fever ⟨, as he said,⟩ 2 than when he left him, though not delirious: for notwithstanding Mr. Barnabas's opinion, he had not been once out of his senses since his arrival at the inn.

Mr. Barnabas was again sent for, and with much difficulty prevailed on to make another visit. As soon as he entered the room, he told Joseph, "he was come to pray by him, and to prepare him for another world: In the first place therefore, he hoped he had repented of all his sins?" Joseph answered, "he hoped he had: but there was one thing which he knew not whether he should call a sin; if it was, he feared he should die in the commission of it, and that was the regret of parting with a young woman, whom he loved as tenderly as he did his heart-
[bid] 1 strings?" Barnabas [bade] 2 him be assured, "that any repining at the Divine Will, was one of the greatest sins he could commit; that he ought to forget all carnal affections, and think of better things." Joseph said, "that neither in this world nor the next, he could forget his Fanny, and that the thought, however grievous, of parting from her for ever, was not half so tormenting, as the fear of what she would suffer when she knew his misfortune." Barnabas said, "that such fears argued a diffidence and despondence very criminal; that he must divest himself of all human passion, and fix his heart above." Joseph answered, "that was what he desired to do, and should be obliged to him, if he would enable him to accomplish it." Barnabas replied, "That must be done by Grace." Joseph besought him to discover how he might attain it. Barnabas answered, "By prayer and faith." He then questioned him concerning his forgiveness of the thieves. Joseph answered, "he feared, that was more than he could do: for nothing would give him more pleasure than to hear they were taken." "That," cries Barnabas, "is for the sake of justice." "Yes," said Joseph, "but if I was to meet them again, I am afraid I should attack them, and kill them too, if I could." "Doubtless," answered Barnabas, "it is lawful to kill a thief: but can you say, you forgive them as a Christian ought?" Joseph desired to know what that forgiveness was. "That is," answered Barnabas, "to forgive them as — as — it is to forgive them as — in short, it is to forgive them as a Christian." Joseph replied, "he forgave them as much as he could." "Well, well," said Barnabas,

"that will do." He then demanded of him, "if he remembered any more sins unrepented of; and if he did, he desired him to make haste and repent of them as fast as he could: that they might repeat over a few prayers together." Joseph answered, "he could not recollect any great crimes he had been guilty of, and that those he had committed, he was sincerely sorry for." Barnabas ⟨said that was enough, and⟩ $_2$ then proceeded to prayer with all the expedition he was master of: Some company then waiting for him below in the parlour, where the ingredients for punch were all in readiness; but no one would squeeze‸ the oranges till he came.

Joseph complained he was dry, and desired a little tea; which Barnabas reported to Mrs. Tow-wouse, who answered, "she had just done drinking it, and could not be slopping all day;" but ordered Betty to carry him up some small beer.

Betty obeyed her mistress's commands; but Joseph, as soon as he had tasted it, said, he feared it would increase his fever, and that he longed very much for tea: To which the good-natured Betty answered, he should have tea, if there was any in the land; she accordingly went and bought him some herself, and attended him with it; where we will leave her and Joseph together for some time, to entertain the reader with other matters.

CHAP. XIV.

Bring very full of adventures, which succeeded each other at the inn.

IT was now the dusk of the evening, when a grave person rode into the inn, and committing his horse to the hostler, went directly into the kitchen, and having called for a pipe of tobacco, ~~he~~ $_2$ took his place by the fireside; where several other persons were likewise assembled.

The discourse ran altogether on the robbery which was committed the night before, and on the poor wretch, who lay above in the dreadful condition, in which we have already seen him.

Mrs. Tow-wouse said, "she wondered what the devil Tom Whipwell meant by bringing such guests to her house, when there were so many ale-houses on the road proper for their reception? But she assured him, if he died, the parish should be at the expense of the funeral." She added, "nothing would serve the fellow's turn but tea, she would assure him." Betty, who was just returned from her charitable office, answered, she believed he was a gentleman: for she never saw a finer skin in her life. "Pox on his skin," replied Mrs. Tow-wouse, "I suppose, that is all we are like to have for the reckoning. I desire no such gentlemen should ever call at the Dragon;" (which it seems was the sign of the inn).

The gentleman lately arrived discovered a great deal of emotion at the distress of this poor creature, whom he observed not to be fallen into the most compassionate hands. And indeed, if Mrs. Tow-wouse had given no utterance to the sweetness of her temper, nature had taken such pains in her countenance, that Hogarth himself never gave more expression to a picture.

Her person was short, thin, and crooked. Her forehead projected in the middle, and thence descended in a declivity to the top of her nose, which was sharp and red, and would have hung over her lips, had not nature turned up the end of it. Her lips were two bits of skin, which, whenever she spoke, she drew together in a purse. Her chin was [peeked]$_{5}$, and at the upper end of that skin, which composed her cheeks, stood two bones, that almost hid a pair of small red eyes. Add to this, a voice most wonderfully adapted to the sentiments it was to convey, being both loud and hoarse.

[pecked $_{1\text{-}2}$; picked $_{3\text{-}4}$][14]

It is not easy to say, whether the gentleman had conceived a greater dislike for his landlady, or compassion for her unhappy guest. He inquired very earnestly of the surgeon, who was now come into the kitchen, "whether he had any hopes of his recovery?" he begged him to use all possible means towards it, telling him, "it was the duty of men of all professions, to apply their skill *gratis* for the relief of the poor and necessitous." The surgeon answered, "he should take proper care: but he defied all

[14] Fielding missed this typographical error in all four of the editions he corrected; someone caught it for the fifth, with which Fielding seems not to have bothered.

the surgeons in London to do him any good." "Pray, sir," said the gentleman, "What are his wounds?" — "Why, do you know anything of wounds?" says the surgeon, (winking upon Mrs. Tow-wouse.) "Sir, I have a small smattering in surgery," answered the gentleman. "A smattering,— ho, ho, ho!" said the surgeon, "I believe it is a smattering indeed."

The company were all attentive, expecting to hear the doctor, who was what they call a dry fellow, expose the gentleman.

He began therefore with an air of triumph: "I suppose, sir, you have travelled." "No really, sir," said the gentleman. "Ho! then you have practised in the hospitals, perhaps." — "No, sir." "Hum! not that neither? Whence, sir, then, if I may be so bold to inquire, have you got your knowledge in surgery?" "Sir," answered the gentleman, "I do not pretend to much; but, the little I know I have from books." "Books!" cries the doctor.— "What, I suppose you have read Galen and Hippocrates!" "No, sir," said the gentleman. "How! you understand surgery," answers the doctor, "and not read Galen and Hippocrates!" "Sir," cries the other, "I believe there are many surgeons who ⟨have⟩ $_2$ never read these authors." "I believe so too," says the doctor, "more shame for them: but thanks to my education: I have them by heart, and very seldom go without them both in my pocket." "They are pretty large books," said the gentleman. "Aye," said the doctor, "I believe I know how large they are better than you," (at which he fell a winking, and the whole company burst into a laugh.)

The doctor pursuing his triumph, asked the gentleman, "if he did not understand physic as well as surgery." "Rather better," answered the gentleman. "Aye, like enough," cries the doctor, with a wink. "Why, I know a little of physic too." "I wish I knew half so much," said Tow-wouse, "I'd never wear an apron again." "Why, I believe, landlord," cries the doctor, "there are few men, though I say it, within twelve miles of the place, that handle a fever better. — *Veniente* [*accurrite*]$_2$ *morbo:* That is my method. — I suppose, brother you understand Latin?" "A

[*occurrite*]$_1$ [15]

[15] Fielding seems here to have corrupted the correct Latin of the first edition to reflect the doctor's ignorance. This favorite commonplace of Fielding's means "When disease approaches, run to attack it" (Persius, *Satires*, iii. 64).

little," says the gentleman. "Aye, and Greek now I'll warrant you: *Ton dapomibominos poluflosboio thalasses.*[16] But I have almost forgot these things, I could have repeated Homer by
[got]$_1$ heart once." — "Efags! the gentleman has [caught]$_2$ a *traitor,*"
says Mrs. Tow-wouse; at which they all fell a laughing.

The gentleman, who had not the least affection for joking, very contentedly suffered the doctor to enjoy his victory; which he did with no small satisfaction: and having sufficiently sounded his depth, ~~he~~$_2$ told him, "he was thoroughly convinced of his great learning and abilities; and that he would be obliged to him if he would let him know his opinion of his patient's case above stairs." "Sir," says the doctor, "his case is that of a dead man. — The contusion on his head has *perforated* the *internal membrane* of the *occiput,* and *divellicated* that *radical* small *minute* invisible *nerve,* which *coheres* to the *pericranium;* and this was attended with a fever at first *symptomatic,* then *pneumatic,* and ⟨he⟩$_2$ is at length *grown deliruus,* or delirious, as the vulgar express it."

He was proceeding in this learned manner, when a mighty noise interrupted him. Some young fellows in the neighbourhood had taken one of the thieves, and were bringing him into the inn. Betty ran up stairs with this news to Joseph; who begged they might search for a little piece of broken gold,
[on]$_{1-2}$ which had a ribband tied [to]$_3$ it, and which he could swear to
[man]$_{1-2}$ amongst all the hoards of the richest [men]$_3$ in the universe.

Notwithstanding the fellow's persisting in his innocence, the mob were very busy in searching him, and presently, among other things, pulled out the piece of gold just mentioned; which Betty no sooner saw, than she laid violent hands on it, and conveyed it up to Joseph, who received it with raptures of joy, and hugging it in his bosom declared, *he could now die contented.*

Within a few minutes afterwards, came in some other fellows, with a bundle which they had found in a ditch; and which was indeed the clothes which had been stripped off from Joseph, and the other things they had taken from him.

The gentleman no sooner saw the coat, than he declared he

[16] *Ton dapomibominos* ("answering him") and *poluflosboio thalasses* ("of the loud-sounding sea") are unconnected scraps from the *Iliad.*

knew the livery; and ~~that~~ $_2$ if it had been taken from the poor creature above stairs, ~~he~~ $_2$ desired he might see him: for that he was very well acquainted with the family to whom that livery belonged.

He was accordingly conducted up by Betty: but what, reader, was the surprise on both sides, when he saw Joseph was the person in bed; and when Joseph discovered the face of his good friend Mr. Abraham Adams.

It would be impertinent to insert a discourse which chiefly turned on the relation of matters already well known to the reader: for as soon as the curate had satisfied Joseph concerning the perfect health of his Fanny, he was on his side very inquisitive into all the particulars which had produced this unfortunate accident.

To return therefore to the kitchen, where a great variety of company were now assembled from all the rooms of the house, as well as the neighbourhood: so much delight do men take in contemplating the countenance of a thief:

Mr. Tow-wouse began to rub his hands with pleasure, at seeing so large an assembly; who would, he hoped, shortly adjourn into several apartments, in order to discourse over the robbery; and drink a health to all honest men: but Mrs. Tow-wouse, whose misfortune it was commonly to see things a little perversely, began to rail at those who brought the fellow into her house; telling her husband, "they were very likely to thrive, who kept a house of entertainment for beggars and thieves."

The mob had now finished their search; and could find nothing about the captive likely to prove any evidence: for as to the clothes, though the mob were very well satisfied with that proof; yet, as the surgeon observed, they could not convict him, because they were not found in his custody; to which Barnabas agreed: and added, that these were *bona waviata*, and belonged to the lord of the manor.[17]

"How," says the surgeon, "do you say these goods belong to the lord of the manor?" "I do," cried Barnabas. "Then I deny

[17] *bona waviata:* goods abandoned by a fleeing thief, forfeited to the king or the lord of the manor as punishment to the owner for not pressing his pursuit.

it," says the surgeon. "What can the lord of the manor have to do in the case? Will anyone attempt to persuade me that what a man finds is not his own?" "I have heard, (says an old fellow in the corner) Justice Wise-one say, that if every man had his right, whatever is found belongs to the king of London." "That may be true," says Barnabas, "in some sense: for the law makes a difference between things stolen, and things found: for a thing may be stolen that never is found; and a thing may be found that never was stolen. Now goods that are both stolen and found are *waviata;* and they belong to the lord of the manor." "So the lord of the manor is the receiver of stolen goods:" (says the doctor) at which there was a universal laugh, being first begun by himself.

While the prisoner, by persisting in his innocence, had almost (as there was no evidence against him) brought over Barnabas, the surgeon, Tow-wouse, and several others to his side; Betty informed them, that they had overlooked a little piece of gold, which she had carried up to the man in bed; and which he offered to swear to amongst a million, aye, amongst ten thousand. This immediately turned the scale against the prisoner; and everyone now concluded him guilty. It was resolved therefore, to keep him secured that night, and early in the morning to carry him before a justice.

CHAP. XV.

Showing how Mrs. Tow-wouse was a little mollified; and how officious Mr. Barnabas and the surgeon were to prosecute the thief: With a dissertation accounting for their zeal; and that of many other persons not mentioned in this history.

BETTY told her mistress, she believed the man in bed was a greater man than they took him for: for besides the extreme whiteness of his skin, and the softness of his hands; she observed a very great familiarity between the gentleman and him; and added, she was certain they were intimate acquaintance, if not relations.

This somewhat abated the severity of Mrs. Tow-wouse's countenance. She said, "God forbid she should not discharge the duty of a Christian, since the poor gentleman was brought to her house. She had a natural antipathy to vagabonds: but could pity the misfortunes of a Christian as soon as another." Tow-wouse said, "If the traveller be a gentleman, though he hath no money about him now, we shall most likely be paid hereafter; so you may begin to score whenever you will." ⟨Mrs. Tow-wouse answered, "Hold your simple tongue, and don't instruct me in my business. I am sure I am sorry for the gentleman's misfortune with all my heart, and I hope the villain who hath used him so barbarously will be hanged. Betty, go, see what he wants. G— forbid he should want anything in my house."⟩ $_2$

Barnabas, and the surgeon went up to Joseph, to satisfy themselves concerning the piece of gold. Joseph was with difficulty prevailed upon to show it them; but would by no entreaties be brought to deliver it out of his own possession. He, however, attested this to be the same which had been taken from him; and Betty was ready to swear to the finding it on the thief.

The only difficulty that remained, was how to produce this gold before the justice: for as to carrying Joseph himself, it seemed impossible; nor was there any greater likelihood of obtaining it from him: for he had fastened it with a ribband to his arm, and solemnly vowed, that nothing but irresistible force should ever separate them; ⟨in⟩ $_2$ which resolution, Mr. Adams, ~~in~~ $_2$ clenching a fist rather less than the knuckle of an ox, declared he would support him.

A dispute arose on this occasion concerning evidence, not very necessary to be related here; after which the surgeon dressed Mr. Joseph's head; still persisting in the imminent danger in which his patient lay: but concluding with a very important look, "that he began to have some hopes; that he should send him a *Sanative soporiferous* draught, and would see him in the morning." After which Barnabas and he departed, and left Mr. Joseph and Mr. Adams together.

Adams informed Joseph of the occasion of this journey which he was making to London, namely to publish three volumes of sermons; being encouraged, he said, by an advertisement lately set forth by a Society of Booksellers, who proposed to purchase any copies offered to them at a price to be settled by two persons:[18] but though he imagined he should get a considerable sum of money on this occasion, which his family were in urgent need of; he protested, "he would not leave Joseph in his present condition:" finally, he told him, "he had nine shillings and three-pence-halfpenny in his pocket, which he was welcome to use as he pleased."

This goodness of Parson Adams brought tears into Joseph's eyes; he declared "he had now a second reason to desire life, that he might show his gratitude to such a friend." Adams
[bid]$_1$ [bade]$_2$ him "be cheerful, for that he plainly saw the surgeon, besides his ignorance, desired to make a merit of curing him, though the wounds in his head, he perceived, were by no means dangerous; that he was convinced he had no fever, and doubted not but he would be able to travel in a day or two."

These words infused a spirit into Joseph; he said, "he found himself very sore from the bruises, but had no reason to think any of his bones injured, or that he had received any harm in his inside; unless that he felt something very odd in his stomach: but ⟨he⟩$_2$ knew not whether that might not arise from not having eaten one morsel for above twenty-four hours." Being then asked, if he had any inclination to eat, he answered in the affirmative; then Parson Adams desired him to name what he had the greatest fancy for; whether a poached egg, or chicken-broth: he answered, "he could eat both very well; but that he seemed to have the greatest appetite for a piece of boiled beef and cabbage."

Adams was pleased with so perfect a confirmation that he had not the least fever: but advised him to a lighter diet, for that evening. He accordingly eat either a rabbit or a fowl, I never could with any tolerable certainty discover which; ⟨after this

[18] The Society of Booksellers for Promoting Learning had actually placed such an ad in the newspapers, including Fielding's *Champion*, from March 4 to August 8, 1741—at about which time Fielding was beginning to write *Joseph Andrews:* thus Fielding dates the travels of Adams and Joseph (Battestin, p. xxv). Adams's three volumes have become nine by the time he looks in his saddlebags for them (II.ii.145); Fielding corrected the "three" to "nine" in I.xvi.130, but missed the reference in Book II.

he⟩ 4 was by Mrs. Tow-wouse's order conveyed into a better bed, and equipped with one of her husband's shirts.

In the morning early, Barnabas and the surgeon came to the inn, in order to see the thief conveyed before the justice. They had consumed the whole night in debating what measures they should take to produce the piece of gold in evidence against him: for they were both extremely zealous in the business, though neither of them were in the least interested in the prosecution; neither of them had ever received any private injury from the fellow, nor had either of them ever been suspected of loving the public well enough, to give them a sermon or a dose of physic for nothing.

To help our reader therefore as much as possible to account for this zeal, we must inform him, that as this parish was so unfortunate ⟨as⟩ 2 to have no lawyer in it; there had been a constant contention between the two doctors, spiritual and physical, concerning their abilities in a science, in which, as neither of them professed it, they had equal pretensions to dispute each other's opinions. These disputes were carried on with great contempt on both sides, and had almost divided the parish; Mr. Tow-wouse and one half of the neighbours inclining to the surgeon, and Mrs. Tow-wouse with the other half to the parson. The surgeon drew his knowledge from those inestimable fountains, called the *Attorney's Pocket-Companion*, and Mr. Jacob's *Law-Tables;* Barnabas trusted entirely to Wood's *Institutes.* It happened on this occasion, as was pretty frequently the case, that these two learned men differed about the sufficiency of evidence: the doctor being of opinion, that the maid's oath would convict the prisoner without producing the gold; the parson, *è contra, totis viribus.*[19] To display their parts therefore before the justice and the parish was the sole motive, which we can discover, to this zeal, which both of them pretended to be for public justice.

O Vanity! How little is thy force acknowledged, or thy operations discerned? How wantonly dost thou deceive mankind under different disguises? Sometimes thou dost wear the face of Pity, sometimes of Generosity: nay, thou hast the assurance even to put on those glorious ornaments which belong only to heroic

[19] "On the opposite side, with all his might."

Virtue. Thou odious, deformed monster! whom priests have railed at, philosophers despised, and poets ridiculed: Is there a wretch so abandoned as to own thee for an acquaintance in public? yet, how few will refuse to enjoy thee in private? nay, thou art the pursuit of most men through their lives. The greatest villainies are daily practised to please thee: nor is the meanest thief below, or the greatest hero above thy notice. Thy embraces are often the sole aim and sole reward of the private robbery, and the plundered province. It is, to pamper up thee, thou Harlot, that we attempt to withdraw from others what we do not want, or to with-hold from them what they do. All our passions are thy slaves. Avarice itself is often no more than thy handmaid, and even Lust thy pimp. The bully Fear like a coward, flies before thee, and Joy and Grief hide their heads in thy presence.

I know thou wilt think, that whilst I abuse thee, I court thee; and that thy love hath inspired me to write this sarcastical panegyric on thee: but thou art deceived, I value thee not of a farthing; nor will it give me any pain, if thou shouldst prevail on the reader to censure this digression as arrant nonsense: for know to thy confusion, that I have introduced thee for no other purpose than to lengthen out a short chapter; and so I return to my history.

CHAP. XVI.

The escape of the thief. Mr. Adams's disappointment. The arrival of two very extraordinary personages, and the introduction of Parson Adams to Parson Barnabas.

BARNABAS and the surgeon being returned, as we have said, to the inn, in order to convey the thief before the justice, were greatly concerned to find a small accident had happened which somewhat disconcerted them; and this was no other than the thief's escape, who had modestly withdrawn himself by night, declining all ostentation, and not choosing, in imitation of some great men, to distinguish himself at the expense of being pointed at.

When the company had retired the evening before, the thief was detained in a room where the constable, and one of the young fellows who took him, were planted as his guard. About the second watch, a general complaint of drought was made both by the prisoner and his keepers. Among whom it was at last agreed, that the constable should remain on duty, and the young fellow [call]$_3$ up the tapster; in which disposition the [latter]$_2$ apprehended not the least danger, as the constable was well armed, and could besides easily summon him back to his assistance, if the prisoner made the least attempt to gain his liberty.

[should call]$_{1\text{-}2}$ [young fellow]$_1$

The young fellow had not long left the room, before it came into the constable's head, that the prisoner might leap on him by surprise, and thereby, preventing him of the use of his weapons, especially the long staff in which he chiefly confided, might reduce the success of a struggle to an equal chance. He wisely therefore, to prevent this inconvenience, slipt out of the room himself and locked the door, waiting without with his staff in his hand, ready lifted to fell the unhappy prisoner, if by ill fortune he should attempt to break out.

[But human life, as]$_2$ hath been discovered by some great man or other, (for I would by no means be understood to affect the honour of making any such discovery) ~~human life~~$_2$ very much resembles a game at chess: for, as in the latter, while a gamester is too attentive to secure himself very strongly on one side the board, he is apt to leave an unguarded opening on the other; so doth it often happen in life; and so did it happen on this occasion: for whilst the cautious constable with such wonderful sagacity had possessed himself of the door, he most unhappily forgot the window.

[But as it]$_1$

The thief who played on the other side, no sooner perceived this opening, than he began to move that way; and finding the passage easy, he took with him the young fellow's hat; and without any ceremony, stepped into the street, and made the best of his way.

The young fellow returning with a double mug of strong beer

was a little surprised to find the constable at the door: but much more so, when, the door being opened, he perceived the prisoner had made his escape, and which way: he threw down the beer, and without uttering anything to the constable, except a hearty curse or two, he nimbly leapt out at the window, and went again in pursuit of his prey: being very unwilling to lose the reward which he had assured himself of.

The constable hath not been discharged of suspicion on this account: It hath been said, that not being concerned in the taking the thief, he could not have been entitled to any part of the reward, if he had been convicted. That the thief had several guineas in his pocket; that it was very unlikely he should have been guilty of such an oversight. That his pretence for leaving the room was absurd: that it was his constant maxim, that a wise man never refused money on any conditions: That at every election, he always had sold his vote to both parties, *&c.*

But notwithstanding these and many other such allegations, I am sufficiently convinced of his innocence; having been positively assured of it, by those who received their informations from his own mouth ⟨;which, in the opinion of some moderns, is the best and indeed only evidence⟩ [2].

All the family were now up, and with many others assembled in the kitchen, where Mr. Tow-wouse was in some tribulation; the surgeon having declared, that by law, he was liable to be indicted for the thief's escape, as it was out of his house: He was a little comforted however by Mr. Barnabas's opinion, that as the escape was by night, the indictment would not lie.

Mrs. Tow-wouse delivered herself in the following words: "Sure never was such a fool as my husband! would any other person living have left a man in the custody of such a drunken, drowsy blockhead as Tom Suckbribe?" (which was the constable's name) "and if he could be indicted without any harm to his wife and children, I should be glad of it." (Then the bell rung in Joseph's room.) "Why Betty, John Chamberlain, where the devil are you all? Have you no ears, or no conscience, not to tend the sick better? — See what the gentleman wants; why don't you go yourself, Mr. Tow-wouse? but anyone may die for you; you have no more feeling than a deal-board. If a man lived a fortnight in your house without spending a penny, you would never put him in mind of it. See whether he drinks tea or coffee for breakfast." "Yes, my dear," cried Tow-wouse. She then asked the doctor and Mr. Barnabas what morning's draught they chose, who answered, they had a pot of *Cider-and,* at the fire; which we will leave them merry over, and return to Joseph.

He had rose pretty early this morning: but though his wounds were far from threatening any danger, he was so sore with the bruises, that it was impossible for him to think of undertaking a journey yet; Mr. Adams therefore, whose stock was visibly decreased with the expenses of supper and breakfast, and which could not survive that day's scoring, began to consider how it was possible to recruit it. At last he cried, "he had luckily hit on a sure method, and though it would oblige him to return himself ⟨home⟩$_2$ together with Joseph, it mattered not much." He then sent for Tow-wouse, and taking him into another room, told him, "he wanted to borrow three guineas, for which he would put ample security in⟨to⟩$_2$ his hands." Tow-wouse who expected a watch, or ring, or something of double the value, answered, "he believed he could furnish him." Upon which Adams pointing to his saddle-bag told him with a face and voice full of solemnity, "that there were in that bag no less than nine volumes of manuscript sermons, as well worth a hundred pound as a shilling was worth twelve pence, and that he would deposit one of the volumes in his hands by way of pledge; not doubting but that he would have the honesty to return it on his repayment of the money: for otherwise he must be a very great loser, seeing that every volume would at least bring him ten pounds, as he had been informed by a neighbouring clergyman in the country: "for, (said he) as to my own part, having never yet dealt in printing, I do not pretend to ascertain the exact value of such things."

Tow-wouse, who was a little surprised at the pawn, said (and not without some truth) "that he was no judge of the price of such kind of goods; and as for money, he really was very short." Adams answered, "certainly he would not scruple to lend him three guineas, on what was [undoubtedly]$_2$ worth at least ten." [certainly]$_1$
The landlord replied, "he did not believe he had so much money

in the house, and besides he was to make up a sum. He was very confident the books were of much higher value, and heartily sorry it did not suit him." He then cried out, *Coming Sir!* though nobody called, and ran down stairs without any fear of breaking his neck.

Poor Adams was extremely dejected at this disappointment, nor knew he what farther stratagem to try. He immediately applied to his pipe, his constant friend and comfort in his afflictions; and leaning over the rails, he devoted himself to meditation, assisted by the inspiring fumes of tobacco.

He had on a night-cap drawn over his wig, and a short great-coat, which half covered his cassock; a dress, which added to something comical enough in his countenance, composed a figure likely to attract the eyes of those who were not over-given to observation.

Whilst he was smoking his pipe in this posture, a coach and six, with a numerous attendance, drove into the inn. There alighted from the coach a young fellow, and a brace of pointers, after which another young fellow leapt from the box, and shook the former by the hand, and both together with the dogs were instantly conducted by Mr. Tow-wouse into an apartment; whither as they passed, they entertained themselves with the following short facetious dialogue.

"You are a pretty fellow for a coachman, Jack!" says he from the coach, "you had almost overturned us just now." "Pox take you," says the coachman, "if I had only broke your neck, it would have been saving somebody else the trouble: but I should have been sorry for the pointers." "Why, you son of a b—," answered the other, "if nobody could shoot better than you, the pointers would be of no use." "D—n me," says the coachman, "I will shoot with you, five guineas a shot." "You be hanged," says the other, "for five guineas you shall shoot at my a—." "Done," says the coachman, "I'll pepper you better than ever you was peppered by Jenny Bouncer." "Pepper your grand-mother," says the other, "here's Tow-wouse will let you shoot at him for a shilling a time." "I know his honour better," cries Tow-wouse, "I never saw a surer shot at a partridge. Every man misses now and then; but if I could shoot half as well as his honour, I would desire no better livelihood than I could get by my gun." "Pox on you," said the coachman, "you demolish more game now than your head's worth. There's a bitch, Tow-wouse, by G— she never *blinked** a bird in her life." "I have a puppy, not a year old, shall hunt with her for a hundred," cries the other gentleman. "Done," says the coachman, "but you will be pox'd before you make the bet. If you have a mind for a bet," cries the coachman, "I will match my spotted dog with your white bitch for a hundred, play or pay." "Done," says the other, "and I'll run Baldface against Slouch with you for another." "No," cries he from the box, "but I'll venture Miss Jenny against Baldface, or Hannibal either." "Go to the Devil," cries he from the coach, "I will make every bet your own way, to be sure! I will match Hannibal with Slouch for a thousand, if you dare, and I say done first."

They were now arrived, and the reader will be very contented to leave them, and repair to the kitchen, where Barnabas, the surgeon, and an exciseman were smoking their pipes over some *Cider-and*, [and where]$_3$ the servants, who attended the two noble gentlemen we have just seen alight, were now arrived. [whither]$_{1-2}$

"Tom," cries one of the footmen, "there's Parson Adams smoking his pipe in the gallery." "Yes," says Tom, "I pulled off my hat to him, and the parson spoke to me."

"Is the gentleman a clergyman then?" says Barnabas, (for his cassock had been tied up when first he arrived.) "Yes, sir," answered the footman, "and one there be but few like." "Ay," said Barnabas, "if I had known it sooner, I should have desired his company; ⟨I would always show a proper respect for the cloth;⟩$_2$ but what say you, doctor, shall we adjourn into a room, and invite him to take part of a bowl of punch?"

This proposal was immediately agreed to, and executed; and Parson Adams accepting the invitation; much civility passed between the two clergymen, who both declared the great honour they had for the cloth. They had not been long together before they entered into a discourse on small tithes, which continued a full hour, without the doctor or the exciseman's having one opportunity to offer a word.

It was then proposed to begin a general conversation, and the

* To *blink* is a term used [to signify the dog's passing by a bird without pointing at it].$_2$ [Fielding's note.] [in setting]$_1$

exciseman opened on foreign affairs: but a word unluckily dropping from one of them introduced a dissertation on the hardships suffered by the inferior clergy; which, after a long duration, [three]$_{1\text{-}3}$ concluded with bringing the [nine]$_{4}$ volumes of sermons on the carpet.

Barnabas greatly discouraged poor Adams; he said, "The age was so wicked, that nobody read sermons: Would you think it, Mr. Adams, (said he) I once intended to print a volume of sermons myself, and they had the approbation of two or three bishops: but what do you think a bookseller offered me?" "Twelve guineas perhaps (cried Adams.)" "Not twelve pence, I assure you," answered Barnabas, "nay the dog refused me a Concordance in exchange. — At last, I offered to give him the printing them, for the sake of dedicating them to that very gentleman who just now drove his own coach into the inn, and I assure you, he had the impudence to refuse my offer: by which means I lost a good living, that was afterwards given away in exchange for a pointer, to one who — but I will not say anything against the cloth. So you may guess, Mr. Adams, what you are to expect; for if sermons would have gone down, I believe — I will not be vain: but to be concise with you, three bishops said, they were the best that ever were writ: but indeed there are a pretty moderate number printed already, and not all sold yet." [says]$_{1}$ — "Pray, sir," [said]$_{2}$ Adams, "to what do you think the numbers may amount?" "Sir," answered Barnabas, "a bookseller told me he believed five thousand volumes at least." "Five thousand!" quoth the surgeon, "what can they be writ upon? I remember, when I was a boy, I used to read one Tillotson's sermons; and I am sure, if a man practised half so much as is in one of those sermons, he will go to Heaven." "Doctor," cried Barnabas, "you have a profane way of talking, for which I must reprove you. A man can never have his duty too frequently inculcated into him. And as for Tillotson, to be sure he was a good writer, and said things very well: but comparisons are odious, another man may write as well as he — I believe there are some of my sermons," — and then he applied the candle to his pipe. — "And I believe there are some of my discourses," cries Adams, "which the bishops would not think totally unworthy of being

printed; and I have been informed, I might procure a very large sum (indeed an immense one) on them." "I doubt that;" answered Barnabas: "however, if you desire to make some money of them, perhaps you may sell them by advertising *the Manuscript Sermons of a Clergyman lately deceased, all warranted Originals, and never printed.* And now I think of it, I should be obliged to you, if there be ever a funeral one among them, to lend it me: for I am this very day to preach a funeral sermon, for which I have not penned a line, though I am to have a double price." Adams answered, "he had but one, which he feared would not serve his purpose, being sacred to the memory of a magistrate, who had exerted himself very singularly in the preservation of the morality of his neighbours, insomuch, that he had neither ale-house, nor lewd [woman]$_2$ in the parish where [women]$_1$
he lived." — "No," replied Barnabas, "that will not do quite so well; for the deceased, upon whose virtues I am to harangue, was a little too much addicted to liquor, and publicly kept a mistress. — I believe I must take a common sermon, and trust to my memory to introduce something handsome on him." — "To your invention rather, (said the doctor) your memory will be apter to put you out: for no man living remembers anything good of him."

With such kind of spiritual discourse, they emptied the bowl of punch, paid their reckoning, and separated: Adams and the doctor went up to Joseph; Parson Barnabas departed to celebrate the aforesaid deceased, and the exciseman descended into the cellar to gauge the vessels.

Joseph was now ready to sit down to a loin of mutton, and waited for Mr. Adams, when he and the doctor came in. The doctor having felt his pulse, and examined his wounds, declared him much better, which he imputed to that *Sanative soporiferous Draught,* a medicine, "whose virtues," he said, "were never to be sufficiently extolled:" And great indeed they must be, if Joseph was so much indebted to them as the doctor imagined, since nothing more than those effluvia, which escaped the cork, could have contributed to his recovery: for the medicine had stood untouched in the window ever since its arrival.

Joseph passed that day and the three following with his friend

Adams, in which nothing so remarkable happened as the swift progress of his recovery. As he had an excellent habit of body, his wounds were now almost healed, and his bruises gave him so little uneasiness, that he pressed Mr. Adams to let him depart, told him he should never be able to return sufficient thanks for all his favours; but begged that he might no longer delay his journey to London.

Adams, notwithstanding the ignorance, as he conceived it, of Mr. Tow-wouse, and the envy (for such he thought it) of Mr. Barnabas, had great expectations from his sermons: seeing therefore Joseph in so good a way, he told him he would agree to his setting out the next morning in the stage-coach, that he believed he should have sufficient after the reckoning paid, to procure him one day's conveyance in it, and afterwards he would be able to get on, on foot, or might be favoured with a lift in some neighbour's wagon, especially as there was then to be a fair in the town whither the coach would carry him, to which numbers from his parish resorted. — And as to himself, he agreed to proceed to the great city.

They were now walking in the inn yard, when a fat, fair, short person rode in, and alighting from his horse went directly up to Barnabas, who was smoking his pipe on a bench. The parson and the stranger shook one another very lovingly by the hand, and went into a room together.

The evening now coming on, Joseph retired to his chamber, whither the good Adams accompanied him; and took this opportunity to expatiate on the great mercies God had lately shown him, of which he ought not only to have the deepest inward sense; but likewise to express outward thankfulness for them. They therefore fell both on their knees, and spent a considerable time in prayer and thanksgiving.

They had just finished, when Betty came in and told Mr. Adams, Mr. Barnabas desired to speak to him on some business of consequence below stairs. Joseph desired, if it was likely to detain him long, he would let him know it, that he might go to bed, which Adams promised, and in that case, they wished one another good night.

CHAP. XVII.

A pleasant discourse between the two parsons and the bookseller, which was broke off by an unlucky accident happening in the inn, which produced a dialogue between Mrs. Tow-wouse and her maid of no gentle kind.

As soon as Adams came into the room, Mr. Barnabas introduced him to the stranger, who was, he told him, a bookseller, and would be as likely to deal with him for his sermons as any man whatever. Adams, saluting the stranger, answered Barnabas, that he was very much obliged to him, that nothing could be more convenient, for he had no other business to the great city, and was heartily desirous of returning with the young man who was just recovered of his misfortune. He then snapt his fingers (as was usual with him) and took two or three turns about the room in an ecstasy. — And to induce the bookseller to be as expeditious as possible, as likewise to offer him a better price for his commodity, he assured him, their meeting was extremely lucky to himself: for that he had the most pressing occasion for money at that time, his own being almost spent, and having a friend then in the same inn who was just recovered from some wounds he had received from robbers, and was in a most indigent condition. ⟨"So that nothing," says he, "could be so opportune, for the supplying both our necessities, as my making an immediate bargain with you."⟩ ₂

As soon as he had seated himself, the stranger began in these words, "Sir, I do not care absolutely to deny engaging in what my friend Mr. Barnabas recommends: but sermons are mere drugs. The trade is so vastly stocked with them, that really unless they come out with the name of Whitefield or Wesley, or some other such great man, as a bishop, or those sort of people, I don't care to touch, unless now it was a sermon preached on the *30th of January*,[20] or we could say in the title page, published at

[20] Sermons preached on the anniversary of Charles I's decapitation (1649).

the *earnest Request* of the congregation, or the inhabitants: but truly for a dry piece of sermons, I had rather be excused; especially as my hands are so full at present. However, sir, as Mr. Barnabas mentioned them to me, I will, if you please, take the manuscript with me to town, and send you my opinion of it in a very short time."

"O," said Adams, "if you desire it, I will read two or three discourses as a specimen." This Barnabas, who loved sermons no better than a grocer doth figs, immediately objected to, and advised Adams to let the bookseller have his sermons; telling him, if he gave him a direction, he might be certain of a speedy answer: Adding, he need not scruple trusting them in his possession. "No," said the bookseller, "if it was a play that had been acted twenty nights together, I believe it would be safe."

Adams did not at all relish the last expression; he said, he was sorry to hear sermons compared to plays. "Not by me, I assure you," cried the bookseller, "though I don't know whether the licensing act [21] may not shortly bring them to the same footing: but I have formerly known a hundred guineas given for a play—." "More shame for those who gave it," cried Barnabas. "Why so?" said the bookseller, "for they got hundreds by it." "But is there no difference between conveying good or ill instructions to mankind?" said Adams; "would not an honest mind rather lose money by the one, than gain it by the other?" "If you can find any such, I will not be their hindrance," answered the bookseller, "but I think those persons who get by preaching sermons, are the properest to lose by printing them: for my part, the copy that sells best, will be always the best copy in my opinion; I am no enemy to sermons but because they don't sell: for I would as soon print one of Whitefield's, as any farce whatever."

"Whoever prints such heterodox stuff, ought to be hanged," says Barnabas. "Sir," said he, turning to Adams, "this fellow's writings (I know not whether you have seen them) are levelled

[21] Passed June 21, 1737, three years before *Joseph Andrews,* this act of Robert Walpole's closed all unlicensed theaters, like Fielding's Little Theatre in the Haymarket, which had strongly satirized Walpole's government, requiring the Lord Chamberlain's approval of all new plays.

at the clergy. He would reduce us to the example of the primitive ages forsooth! and would insinuate to the people, that a clergyman ought to be always preaching and praying. He pretends to understand the Scripture literally, and would make mankind believe, that the poverty and low estate, which was recommended to the Church in its infancy, and was only temporary doctrine adapted to her under persecution, was to be preserved in her flourishing and established state. Sir, the principles of Toland, Woolston, and all the free-thinkers, are not calculated to do half the mischief, as those professed by this fellow and his followers."

"Sir," answered Adams, "if Mr. Whitefield had carried his doctrine no farther than you mention, I should have remained, as I once was, his well-wisher. I am myself as great an enemy to the luxury and splendour of the clergy as he can be. I do not, more than he, by the flourishing estate of the Church, understand the palaces, equipages, dress, furniture, rich dainties, and vast fortunes of her ministers. Surely those ⟨things⟩[3], which savour so strongly of this world, become not the servants of one who professed his kingdom was not of it: but when he began to call nonsense and enthusiasm ~~in~~[2] to his aid, and to set up the detestable doctrine of faith against good works, I was his friend no longer; for surely, that doctrine was coined in Hell, and one would think none but the Devil himself could have the confidence to preach it. For can anything be more derogatory to the honour of God, than for men to imagine that the All-wise Being will hereafter say to the good and virtuous, *Notwithstanding the purity of thy life, notwithstanding that constant rule of virtue and goodness in which you walked upon earth, still as thou did'st not believe everything in the true orthodox manner, thy want of faith shall condemn thee?* Or on the other side, can any doctrine have a more pernicious influence on society than a persuasion, that it will be a good plea for the villain at the last day; *Lord, it is true I never obeyed one of thy Commandments, yet punish me not, for I believe them all?*" "I suppose, sir," said the bookseller, "your sermons are of a different kind." "Ay, sir," said Adams, "the contrary, I thank Heaven, is inculcated in almost every page, or I should belie my own opinion, which hath always been, that a virtuous and good Turk, or heathen, are more acceptable in the sight of their Creator, than a vicious and wicked Christian, though his faith was as perfectly orthodox as St. Paul's himself." — "I wish you success," says the bookseller, "but must beg to be excused, as my hands are so very full at present; and indeed I am afraid, you will find a backwardness in the trade, to engage in a book which the clergy would be certain to cry down." "God forbid," says Adams, "any books should be propagated which the clergy would cry down: but if you mean by the clergy, some few designing factious men, who have it at heart to establish some favourite schemes at the price of the liberty of mankind, and the very essence of religion, it is not in the power of such persons to decry any book they please; witness that excellent book called, *A Plain Account of the Nature and End of the Sacrament;* a book written (if I may venture on the expression) with the pen of an angel, and calculated to restore the true use of Christianity, and of that Sacred Institution: for what could tend more to the noble purposes of religion, than frequent cheerful meetings among the members of a society, in which they should in the presence of one another, and in the service of the supreme Being, make promises of being good, friendly and benevolent to each other? Now this excellent book was attacked by a party, but unsuccessfully." At these words Barnabas fell a ringing with all the violence imaginable, upon which a servant attending, he bid him "bring a bill immediately: for that he was in company, for aught he knew, with the Devil himself; and he expected to hear the Alcoran, the *Leviathan*, or Woolston commended, if he stayed a few minutes longer." Adams desired, "as he was so much moved at his mentioning a book, which he did without apprehending any possibility of offence, that he would be so kind to propose any objections he had to it, which he would endeavour to answer." "I propose objections!" said Barnabas, "I never read a syllable in any such wicked book; I never saw it in my life, I assure you." — Adams was going to answer, when a most hideous uproar began in the inn. Mrs. Tow-wouse, Mr. Tow-wouse, and Betty, all lifting up their voices together: but Mrs. Tow-wouse's voice, like a bass viol in a concert, was clearly and distinctly distinguished among the rest, and was heard to articulate the following sounds. — "O you damn'd villain, is this the return to all the care I have taken of your family? This the reward of my virtue? Is this the manner in which you behave to one who brought you a fortune, and preferred you to so many matches, all your betters? To abuse my bed, my own bed, with my own servant: but I'll maul the slut, I'll tear her nasty eyes out; was ever such a pitiful dog, to take up with such a mean trollop? If she had been a gentlewoman like myself, it had been some excuse, but a beggarly saucy dirty servant-maid. Get you out of my house, you whore." To which, she added another name, which we do not care to stain our paper with. — It was a monosyllable beginning with a b—, and indeed was the same, as if she had pronounced the words, *she-dog*. Which term, we shall, to avoid offence, use on this occasion ⟨, though indeed both the mistress and maid uttered the above-mentioned b—, a word extremely disgustful to females of the lower sort⟩ $_2$. Betty had borne all hitherto with patience, and had uttered only lamentations: but the last appellation stung her to the quick, "I am a woman as well as yourself," she roared out, "and no she-dog, and if I have been a little naughty, I am not the first; if I have been no better than I should be," cries she sobbing, "that's no reason you should call me out of my name ⟨; my be—betters are wo—worse than me⟩ $_2$." "Huzzy, huzzy," says Mrs. Tow-wouse, "have you the impudence to answer me? Did I not catch you, you saucy — " and then again repeated the terrible word so odious to female ears. "I can't bear that name," answered Betty, "if I have been wicked, I am to answer for it myself in the other world, but I have done nothing that's unnatural, and I will go out of your house this moment: for I will never be called *she-dog*, by any mistress in England." Mrs. Tow-wouse then armed herself with the spit: but was prevented from executing any dreadful purpose by Mr. Adams, who confined her arms with the strength of a wrist, which Hercules would not have been ashamed of. Mr. Tow-wouse being caught, as our lawyers express it, with the manner, and having no defence to make, very prudently withdrew himself, and Betty committed

herself to the protection of the hostler, who, though [she could
[he was not]$_{1}$ not conceive him]$_{2}$ pleased with what had happened, was in her
opinion rather a gentler beast than her mistress.

Mrs. Tow-wouse, at the intercession of Mr. Adams, and find-
[We will ing the enemy vanished, began to compose herself [, and at
therefore leave length recovered the usual serenity of her temper, in which we
her in this will leave her]$_{2}$ to open to the reader the steps which led to a
temper]$_{1}$ catastrophe, common enough, and comical enough too, perhaps
in modern history, yet often fatal to the repose and well-being
of families, and the subject of many tragedies, both in life and
on the stage.

CHAP. XVIII.

The history of Betty the chambermaid, and an account of what occasioned the violent scene in the preceding chapter.

BETTY, who was the occasion of all this hurry, had some good
qualities. She had good-nature, generosity and compassion, but
[unhappily]$_{1}$ [unfortunately], $_{2}$ her constitution was composed of those warm
ingredients, which, though the purity of courts or nunneries
might have happily controlled ⟨them⟩ $_{2}$, were by no means able
to endure the ticklish situation of a chambermaid at an inn, who
is daily liable to the solicitations of lovers of all complexions, to
the dangerous addresses of fine gentlemen of the army, who
sometimes are obliged to reside with them a whole year together,
and above all are exposed to the caresses of footmen, stage-
[drawers, and coachmen, [and drawers; all of whom]$_{2}$ employ the whole artil-
others, all of lery of kissing, flattering, bribing, and every other weapon which
which]$_{1}$ is to be found in the whole Armory of Love, against them.

[about]$_{1\text{-}2}$ Betty, who was [but]$_{3}$ one and twenty, had now lived three
years in this dangerous situation, during which she had escaped
pretty well. An ensign of foot was the first person who made an
impression on her heart; he did indeed raise a flame in her,
which required the care of a surgeon to cool.

While she burnt for him, several others burnt for her. Officers of the army, young gentlemen travelling the western circuit,[22] inoffensive squires, and some of graver character were set afire by her charms!

At length, having perfectly recovered the effects of her first unhappy passion, she seemed to have vowed a state of perpetual chastity. She was long deaf to all the sufferings of her lovers, till one day at a neighbouring fair, the rhetoric of John the hostler, with a new straw hat, and a pint of wine, made a second conquest over her.

She did not however feel any of those flames on this occasion, which had been the consequence of her former amour; nor indeed those other ill effects, which prudent young women very justly apprehend from too absolute an indulgence to the pressing endearments of their lovers. This latter, perhaps, was a little owing to her not being entirely constant to John, with whom she permitted Tom Whipwell the stage-coachman, and now and then a handsome young traveller, to share her favours.

Mr. Tow-wouse had for some time cast the languishing eyes of affection on this young maiden. He had laid hold on every opportunity of saying tender things to her, squeezing her by the hand, and sometimes kissing her lips: for as the violence of his passion had considerably abated to Mrs. Tow-wouse; so like water, which is stopt from its usual current in one place, it naturally sought a vent in another. Mrs. Tow-wouse is thought to have perceived this abatement, and probably it added very little to the natural sweetness of her temper: for though she was as true to her husband, as the dial to the sun, she was rather more desirous of being shone on, as being more capable of feeling his warmth.

Ever since Joseph's arrival, Betty had conceived an extraordinary liking to him, which discovered itself more and more, as he grew better and better; till that fatal evening, when⟨, as⟩ $_2$ she was warming his bed, her passion grew to such a height, and so perfectly mastered both her modesty and her reason, that after

[22] Fielding refers to young lawyers, like himself, who followed the travels of the circuit-judge, on one of the eight "circuits" throughout England, hearing each quarter of the year the cases waiting trial. Fielding himself followed the western circuit, along the road Adams and Andrews are taking.

many fruitless hints, and sly insinuations, she at last threw down the warming-pan, and embracing him with great eagerness, swore he was the handsomest creature she had ever seen.

Joseph in great confusion leapt from her, and told her, he was sorry to see a young woman cast off all regard to modesty: but she had gone too far to recede, and grew so very indecent, that Joseph was obliged, contrary to his inclination, to use some violence to her, and taking her in his arms, he shut her out of the room, and locked the door.

How ought man to rejoice, that his chastity is always in his own power, that if he hath sufficient strength of mind, he hath always a competent strength of body to defend himself: and cannot, like a poor weak woman, be ravished against his will.

Betty was in the most violent agitation at this disappointment. Rage and Lust pulled her heart, as with two strings, two different ways; one moment she thought of stabbing Joseph, the next, of taking him in her arms, and devouring him with kisses; but the latter passion was far more prevalent. Then she thought of revenging his refusal on herself: but whilst she was engaged in this meditation, happily Death presented himself to her in so many shapes of drowning, hanging, poisoning, *&c.* that her distracted mind could resolve on none. In this perturbation of spirit, it accidentally occurred to her memory, that her master's bed was not made, she therefore went directly to his room; where he happened at that time to be engaged at his bureau. As soon as she saw him, she attempted to retire: but he called her
[it]$_1$ back, and taking her by the hand, squeezed [her]$_2$ so tenderly,
at the same time whispering so many soft things into her ears, and, then pressed her so closely with his kisses, that the vanquished fair-one, whose passions were already raised, and which were not so whimsically capricious that one man only could lay them, though perhaps, she would have rather preferred that one: The vanquished fair-one quietly submitted, I say, to her master's will, who had just attained the accomplishment of his bliss, when Mrs. Tow-wouse unexpectedly entered the room, and caused all that confusion which we have before seen, and
[of. ¶As which it is not necessary at present to take any farther notice [of:
every]$_1$ Since without the assistance of a single hint from us, every]$_2$

reader of any speculation, or experience, though not married himself, may easily conjecture, that it concluded with the discharge of Betty, the submission of Mr. Tow-wouse, with some things to be performed on his side by way of gratitude for his wife's goodness in being reconciled to him, with many hearty promises never to offend any more in the like manner: and lastly, his quietly and contentedly bearing to be reminded of his transgressions, as a kind of penance, once or twice a day, during the residue of his life.

THE HISTORY OF THE ADVENTURES OF *Joseph Andrews*, and of his Friend Mr. *Abraham Adams*

BOOK II.

CHAP. I.

Of divisions in authors.

THERE are certain mysteries or secrets in all trades from the highest to the lowest, from that of *Prime Ministering* to this of *Authoring*, which are seldom discovered, unless to members of the same calling. Among those used by us gentlemen of the latter occupation, I take this of dividing our works into books and chapters to be none of the least considerable. Now for want of being truly acquainted with this secret, common readers imagine, that by this art of dividing, we mean only to swell our works to a much larger bulk than they would otherwise be extended to. These several places therefore in our paper, which are filled with our books and chapters, are understood as so much buckram, stays, and stay-tape in a tailor's bill, serving only to make up the sum total, commonly found at the bottom of our first page, and of his last.

But in reality the case is otherwise, and in this, as well as all other instances, we consult the advantage of our reader, ~~and~~ [2] not our own; and indeed many notable uses arise to him from this method: for first, those little spaces between our chapters may be looked upon as an inn or resting-place, where he may stop and take a glass, or any other refreshment, as it pleases him. Nay, our fine readers will, perhaps, be scarce able to travel farther than through one of them in a day. As to those vacant pages which are placed between our books, they are to be regarded as those stages, where, in long journeys, the traveller stays some time to repose himself, and consider of what he hath seen in the parts he hath already passed through; a consideration which I take the liberty to recommend a little to the reader: for however swift his capacity may be, I would not advise him to travel through these pages too fast: for if he doth, he may probably miss the seeing some curious productions of Nature which will be observed by the slower and more accurate reader. A volume without any such places of rest resembles the opening of wilds or seas, which tires the eye and fatigues the spirit when entered upon.

Secondly, What are the contents prefixed to every chapter, but so many inscriptions over the gates of inns (to continue the same metaphor,) informing the reader what entertainment he is to expect, which if he likes not, he may travel on to the next: for in Biography, as we are not tied down to an exact concatenation equally with other historians; so a chapter or two (for instance this I am now writing) may be often passed over without any injury to the whole. And in these inscriptions I have been as faithful as possible, not imitating the celebrated Montaigne, who promises you one thing and gives you another; nor some title-page authors, who promise a great deal, and produce nothing at all.

There are, besides these more obvious benefits, several others which our readers enjoy from this art of dividing; though perhaps most of them too mysterious to be presently understood, by any who are not initiated into the Science of *Authoring*. [To mention therefore but one which is most obvious, it prevents spoiling the beauty of a book by turning down its leaves, a method otherwise necessary to those readers, who, (though they read with great improvement and advantage) are apt, when they return to their study, after half an hour's absence, to forget where they left off.

[These]₁ These divisions]₂ have the sanction of great Antiquity. Homer not only divided his great work into twenty-four books, (in compliment perhaps to the twenty-four letters to which he had very particular obligations) but ⟨, according to the opinion of some very sagacious critics,⟩ ₂ hawked them all separately, delivering only one book at a time, (probably by subscription). He [so long lay]₁ was the first inventor of the art which [hath so long lain]₂ dormant, of publishing by numbers, an art now brought to such perfection, that even dictionaries are divided and exhibited piecemeal to the public; nay, one bookseller hath (*to encourage Learning and ease the Public*) contrived to give them a dictionary in this divided manner for only fifteen shillings more than it would have cost entire.

Virgil hath given us his poem in twelve books, an argument of his modesty; for by that doubtless he would insinuate that he pretends to no more than half the merit of the Greek: for the same reason, our Milton went originally no farther than ten; 'till being puffed up by the praise of his friends, he put himself on the same footing with the Roman poet.

I shall not however enter so deep into this matter as some very learned critics have done; who have with infinite labour and acute discernment discovered what books are proper for embellishment, and what require simplicity only, particularly with regard to similes, which I think are now generally agreed to become any book but the first.

I will dismiss this chapter with the following observation: That it becomes an author generally to divide a book, as it does a butcher to joint his meat, for such assistance is of great help to both the reader and the carver. And now having indulged myself a little, I will endeavour to indulge the curiosity of my reader, who is no doubt impatient to know what he will find in the subsequent chapters of this book.

CHAP. II.

A surprising instance of Mr. Adams's short memory, with the unfortunate consequences which it brought on Joseph.

MR. ADAMS and Joseph were now ready to depart ⟨different ways⟩ 2, when an accident determined the former to return ⟨with his friend⟩ 2, which Tow-wouse, Barnabas, and the bookseller had not been able to do. This accident was [, that those sermons, which the parson was travelling to London to publish, were, O my good reader,]2 left behind; what he had mistaken for them in the saddle-bags being no other than three shirts, a pair of shoes, and some other necessaries, which Mrs. Adams, who thought her husband would want shirts more than sermons on his journey, had carefully provided him.

[no other than the forgetting to put up the sermons, which were indeed]1

⌈This discovery was now luckily owing to the presence of Joseph at the opening the saddle-bags; who having heard his friend say, he carried with him nine volumes of sermons, and not being of that sect of philosophers, who can reduce all the matter of the world into a nut-shell, seeing there was no room for them in the bags, where the parson had said they were deposited, had the curiosity to cry out, "Bless me, sir, where are your sermons?" The parson answered, "There, there, child, there they are, under my shirts." Now it happened that he had taken forth his last shirt, and the vehicle remained visibly empty. "Sure, sir," says Joseph, "there is nothing in the bags." Upon which Adams starting, and testifying some surprise, cried, "Hey! fie, fie, upon it; they are not here sure enough. Ay, they are certainly left behind."

Joseph was greatly concerned at the uneasiness which he apprehended his friend must feel from this disappointment: he begged him to pursue his journey, and promised he would himself return with the books to him, with the utmost expedition. "No, thank you, child," answered Adams, "it shall not be so. What would it avail me, to tarry in the Great City, unless I had my discourses with me, which are, *ut ita dicam,* the sole cause, the *Aitia monotate* of my peregrination.[1] No, child, as this accident hath happened, I am resolved to return back to my cure, together with you; which indeed my inclination sufficiently leads me to. This disappointment may, perhaps, be intended for my good." He concluded with a verse out of Theocritus, which signifies no more than, *that sometimes it rains and sometimes the sun shines.*

[the bill was now called for, and]1

Joseph bowed with obedience, and thankfulness for the inclination which the parson expressed of returning with him; and now the bill was called for, which,] 2 on examination, amounted within a shilling to the sum which 2 Mr. Adams had in his pocket. Perhaps the reader may wonder how he was able to produce a sufficient sum for so many days: that he may not be ~~too much~~ 2 surprised, therefore, it cannot be unnecessary to acquaint him, that he had borrowed a guinea of a servant belonging to the coach and six, who had been formerly one of his parishioners, and whose master, the owner of the coach, then lived within three miles of him: for so good was the credit of Mr. Adams, that even Mr. Peter the Lady Booby's steward, would have lent him a guinea with very little security.

Mr. Adams discharged the bill, and they were both setting out, having agreed *to ride and tie:* a method of travelling much used by ~~two~~ 2 persons who have but one horse between them, and is thus performed. The two travellers set out together, one on horseback, the other on foot: Now as it generally happens that he on horseback out-goes him on foot, the custom is, that when he arrives at the distance agreed on, he is to dismount, tie the horse to some gate, tree, post, or other thing, and then proceed on foot; when the other comes up to the horse, he unties him, mounts and gallops on, 'till having passed by his fellow-traveller, he likewise arrives at the place of tying. And this is that method of travelling so much in use among our prudent ancestors, who knew that horses had mouths as well as legs, and that they could

[1] "*Ut ita dicam*": "as I might say" (Latin). "*Aitia monotate*": Adams shifts to Greek—*aitia* (cause); *monotate* ("onliest").

not use the latter, without being at the expense of suffering the beasts themselves to use the former. This was the method in use in those days: when, instead of a coach and six, a Member of Parliament's lady used to mount a pillion behind her husband; and a grave Serjeant at Law condescended to amble to Westminster on an easy pad, with his clerk kicking his heels behind him.

Adams was now gone some minutes, having insisted on Joseph's beginning the journey on horseback, and Joseph had his foot in the stirrup, when the hostler presented him a bill for the horse's board during his residence at the inn. Joseph said Mr. Adams had paid all; but this matter being referred to Mr. Tow-wouse was by him decided in favour of the hostler, and indeed with truth and justice: for this was a fresh instance of that shortness of memory which did not arise from want of parts, but that continual hurry in which Parson Adams was always involved.

Joseph was now reduced to a dilemma which extremely puzzled him. The sum due for horse-meat was twelve shillings, (for Adams, who had borrowed the beast ⟨of his clerk⟩$_2$, had ordered him to be fed as well as they could feed him) and the cash in his pocket amounted to sixpence, (for Adams had divided the last shilling with him). Now, though there have been some ingenious persons who have contrived to pay twelve shillings with sixpence, Joseph was not one of them. He had never contracted a debt in his life, and was consequently the less ready at an expedient to extricate himself. Tow-wouse [was willing to give him credit 'till next time, to which Mrs. Tow-wouse would probably have consented (for such was Joseph's beauty, that it had made some impression even on that piece of flint which that good woman wore in her bosom by way of heart.) Joseph would have found therefore, very likely, the passage free, had he not, when he honestly]$_2$ discovered the nakedness of his pockets, pulled out that little piece of gold which we have mentioned before. This caused [Mrs. Tow-wouse's eyes to water; she told Joseph, she]$_2$ did not conceive a man could want money whilst he had gold in his pocket. Joseph answered, he had such a value for that little piece of gold, that he would not part with it for a hundred times the riches which the greatest Esquire in the

[would probably have been willing to give him credit 'till next time, had not Joseph, when he honestly]$_1$

[Mr. Tow-wouse's eyes to water; he told Joseph he]$_1$

[Mr.]$_1$ county was worth. "A pretty way indeed," said [Mrs.]$_2$ Tow-wouse, "to run in debt, and then refuse to part with your money, because you have a value for it. I never knew any piece of gold of more value than as many shillings as it would change for." "Not to preserve my life from starving, nor to redeem it from a robber, would I part with this dear piece," answered Joseph.
[Then I cannot part with the horse, replied]$_1$ ["What (says Mrs. Tow-wouse) I suppose, it was given you by some vile trollop, some miss or other; if it had been the present of a virtuous woman, you would not have had such a value for it. My husband is a fool if he parts with the horse, without being paid for him." "No, no, I can't part with the horse indeed, till I have the money," cried]$_2$ Tow-wouse. A resolution highly commended by a lawyer then in the yard, who declared Mr. Tow-wouse might justify the detainer.

As we cannot therefore at present get Mr. Joseph out of the inn, we shall leave him in it, and carry our reader on after Parson Adams, who, his mind being perfectly at ease, fell into a contemplation on a passage in Æschylus, which entertained him for three miles together, without suffering him once to reflect on his fellow-traveller.

At length having spun out his thread, and being now at the summit of a hill, he cast his eyes backwards, and wondered that he could not see any sign of Joseph. As he left him ready to mount the horse, he could not apprehend any mischief had happened, neither could he suspect that he missed his way, it being so broad and plain: the only reason which presented itself to him, was that he had met with an acquaintance who had prevailed with him to delay some time in discourse.

He therefore resolved to proceed slowly forwards, not doubting but that he should be shortly overtaken, and soon came to a large water, which filling the whole road, he saw no method of passing unless by wading through, which he accordingly did up to his middle; but was no sooner got to the other side, than he perceived, if he had looked over the hedge, he would have found a foot-path capable of conducting him without wetting his shoes.

His surprise at Joseph's not coming up grew now very troublesome: he began to fear he knew not what, and as he determined, to move no farther; and, if he did not shortly overtake him, to return back; he wished to find a house of public entertainment where he might [dry]$_2$ his clothes and refresh himself with a pint: but seeing no such (for no other reason than because he did not cast his eyes a hundred yards forwards) he sat himself down on a stile, and pulled out his Æschylus. [have dried]$_1$

A fellow passing presently by, Adams asked him, if he could direct him to an alehouse. The fellow who had just left it, and perceived the house and sign to be within sight, thinking he had jeered him, and being of a morose temper, [bade]$_2$ him *follow his nose and be d—n'd.* Adams told him he was a *saucy Jackanapes;* upon which the fellow turned about angrily: but perceiving Adams clench his fist he thought proper to go on without taking any farther notice. [bid]$_1$

A horseman following immediately after, and being asked the same question, answered, "Friend, there is one within a stone's-throw; I believe you may see it before you." Adams lifting up his eyes, cried, "I protest and so there is;" and thanking his informer proceeded directly to it.

CHAP. III.

The opinion of two lawyers concerning the same gentleman, with Mr. Adams's enquiry into the religion of his host.

HE had just entered the house, had called for his pint and seated himself, when two horsemen came to the door, and fastening their horses to the rails, alighted. They said there was a violent shower of rain coming on, which they intended to weather there, and went into a little room by themselves, not perceiving Mr. Adams.

One of these immediately asked the other, if he had seen a more comical adventure a great while? Upon which the other said, "he doubted whether by law, the landlord could justify detaining the horse for his corn and hay." But the [former]$_2$ answered, "Undoubtedly he can: it is an adjudged case, and I have known it tried." [first]$_1$

Adams, who though he was, as the reader may suspect, a little inclined to forgetfulness, never wanted more than a hint to remind him, overhearing their discourse, immediately suggested to himself that this was his own horse, and that he had forgot to pay for him, which upon inquiry, he was certified of by the gentlemen; who added, that the horse was likely to have more rest than food, unless he was paid for.

The poor parson resolved to return presently to the inn, though he knew no more than Joseph, how to procure his horse his liberty: he was however prevailed on to stay under covert, 'till the shower which was now very violent, was over.

[now]$_1$ The three travellers [then]$_2$ sat down together over a mug of good beer; when Adams, who had observed a gentleman's house as he passed along the road, inquired to whom it belonged: one of the horsemen had no sooner mentioned the owner's name, than the other began to revile him in the most opprobrious terms. The English language scarce affords a single reproachful word, which he did not vent on this occasion. He charged him likewise with many particular facts. He said, — "he no more regarded a field of wheat when he was hunting, than he did the high-way; that he had injured several poor farmers by trampling their corn under his horse's heels; and if any of them begged him with the utmost submission to refrain, his horse-whip was always ready to do them justice." He said, "that he was the greatest tyrant to the neighbours in every other instance, and would not suffer a farmer to keep a gun, though he might justify it by law; and in his own family so cruel a master, that he never kept a servant a twelve-month. In his capacity as a justice," continued he, "he behaves so partially, that he commits or acquits just as he is in the humour, without any regard to truth or evidence: The devil may carry anyone before him for me; I would rather be tried before some judges than be a prosecutor before him: If I had an estate in the neighbourhood, I would sell it for half the value, rather than live near him." Adams shook his head, and said, "he was sorry such men were suffered to proceed with impunity, and that riches could set any man above law." The reviler a little after retiring into the yard, the gentleman, who had first mentioned his name to Adams, began to assure him, "that his companion was a prejudiced person. It is

true," says he, "perhaps, that he may have sometimes pursued his game over a field of corn, but he hath always made the party ample satisfaction; that so far from tyrannizing over his neighbours, or taking away their guns, he himself knew several farmers not qualified, who not only kept guns, but killed game with them. That he was the best of masters to his servants, and several of them had grown old in his service. That he was the best Justice of Peace in the kingdom, and to his certain knowledge had decided many difficult points, which were referred to him, with the greatest equity, and the highest wisdom. And he verily believed, several persons would give a year's purchase more for an estate near him, than under the wings of any other great man." He had just finished his encomium, when his companion returned and acquainted him the storm was over. Upon which, they presently mounted their horses and departed.

Adams, who was in the utmost anxiety at those different characters of the same person, asked his host if he knew the gentleman: for he began to imagine they had by mistake been speaking of two several gentlemen. "No, no, master!" answered the host, a shrewd cunning fellow, "I know the gentleman very well of whom they have been speaking, as I do the gentlemen who spoke of him. As for riding over other men's corn, to my knowledge he hath not been on horseback these two years. I never heard he did any injury of that kind; and as to making reparation, he is not so free of his money as that comes to neither. Nor did I ever hear of his taking away any man's gun; nay, I know several who have guns in their houses: but as for killing game with them, no man is stricter; and I believe he would ruin any who did. You heard one of the gentlemen say, he was the worst master in the world, and the other that he is the best: but as for my own part, I know all his servants, and never heard from any of them that he was either one or the other. — " "Aye, aye," says Adams, "and how doth he behave as a justice, pray?" "Faith, friend," answered the host, "I question whether he is in the commission: the only cause I have heard he hath decided a great while, was one between those very two persons who just went out of this house; and I am sure he determined that justly, for I heard the whole matter." "Which did he decide it in favour of?" quoth Adams. "I think I need not answer that question," cried the host, "after the different characters you have heard of him. It is not my business to contradict gentlemen, while they are drinking in my house: but I knew neither of them spoke a syllable of truth." "God forbid! (said Adams,) that men should arrive at such a pitch of wickedness, to be-lie the character of their neighbour from a little private affection, or what is infinitely worse, a private spite. I rather believe we have mistaken them, and they mean two other persons: for there are many houses on the road." "Why prithee, friend," cries the host, "dost thou pretend never to have told a lie in thy life?" "Never a malicious one, I am certain," answered Adams; "nor with a design to injure the reputation of any man living." "Pugh, malicious! no, no," replied the host; "not malicious with a design to hang a man, or bring him into trouble: but surely out of love to one's self, one must speak better of a friend than an enemy." "Out of love to your self, you should confine yourself to truth," says Adams, "for by doing otherwise, you injure the noblest part of yourself, your immortal soul. I can hardly believe any man such an idiot to risk the loss of that by any trifling gain, and the greatest gain in this world is but dirt in comparison of what shall be revealed hereafter." Upon which the host taking up the cup, with a smile drank a health to Hereafter: adding, "he was for something present." "Why," says Adams very gravely, "Do not you believe another world?" To which the host answered, "yes, he was no atheist." "And you believe you have an immortal soul?" cries Adams: He answered, "God forbid he should not." "And Heaven and Hell?" said the parson. The host then bid him "not to profane: for those were things not to be mentioned nor thought of but in church." Adams asked him, "why he went to church, if what he learned there had no influence on his conduct in life?" "I go to church," answered the host, "to say my prayers and behave godly." "And dost not thou," cried Adams, "believe what thou hearest at church?" "Most part of it, master," returned the host. "And dost not thou then tremble," cries Adams, "at the thought of eternal punishment?" "As for that, master," said he, "I never once thought about it: but what signifies talking about matters so far off? the mug is out, shall I draw another?"

Whilst he was gone for that purpose, a stage-coach drove up to the door. The coachman coming into the house, was asked by the mistress, [what passengers]$_2$ he had in his coach? "A [whom]$_1$ parcel of *squinny-gut* b—s, (says he) I have a good mind to overturn them; you won't prevail upon them to drink anything I assure you." Adams asked him, if he had not seen a young man on horseback on the road, (describing Joseph). "Aye," said the coachman, "a gentlewoman in my coach that is his acquaintance redeemed him and his horse; he would have been here before this time, had not the storm driven him to shelter." "God bless her," said Adams in a rapture; nor could he delay walking out to satisfy himself who this charitable woman was; but what was his surprise, when he saw his old acquaintance, Madam Slipslop? Hers indeed was not so great, because she had been informed by Joseph, that he was on the road. Very civil were the salutations on both sides; and Mrs. Slipslop rebuked the hostess for denying the gentleman to be there when she asked for him: but indeed the poor woman had not erred designedly: for Mrs. Slipslop asked for a clergyman; and she had unhappily mistaken [Adams]$_2$ for a person travelling to a neighbour- [him]$_1$ ing fair with the thimble and button, or some other such operation: for he marched in a swinging great ⟨, but short,⟩$_2$ white coat with black buttons, a short wig, and a hat, which so far from having a black hatband, had nothing black about it.

Joseph was now come up, and Mrs. Slipslop would have had him quit his horse to the parson, and come himself into the coach: but he absolutely refused, saying he thanked Heaven he was well enough recovered to be very able to ride, and added, he hoped he knew his duty better than to ride in a coach while Mr. Adams was on horseback.

Mrs. Slipslop would have persisted longer, had not a lady in the coach put a short end to the dispute, by refusing to suffer a fellow in a livery to ride in the same coach with herself: so it was at length agreed that Adams should fill the vacant place in the coach, and Joseph should proceed on horseback.

They had not proceeded far before Mrs. Slipslop, addressing herself to the parson, spoke thus: "There hath been a strange alteration in our family, Mr. Adams, since Sir [Thomas's]$_2$ [John's]$_1$ death." "A strange alteration indeed!" says Adams, "as I gather

from some hints which have dropped from Joseph." "Aye," says
she, "I could never have believed it, but the longer one lives in
the world, the more one sees. So Joseph hath given you hints."
— "But of what nature, will always remain a perfect secret with
me," cries the parson; "he forced me to promise before he
would communicate anything. [I am indeed concerned to find
her Ladyship behave in so unbecoming a manner. I always
thought her in the main, a good lady, and should never have
suspected her of thoughts so unworthy a Christian, and with a
[They]$_1$ young lad her own servant." "These things]$_2$ are no secrets to
me, I assure you," cries Slipslop; "and I believe, they will be
[his]$_1$ none anywhere shortly: for ever since [the boy's]$_2$ departure she
hath behaved more like a mad woman than anything else."
"Truly, I am heartily concerned," says Adams, "for she was a
good sort of a lady; indeed I have often wished she had attended
a little more constantly at the service, but she hath done a great
deal of good in the parish." "O Mr. Adams!" says Slipslop,
"People that don't see all, often know nothing. Many things
have been given away in our family, I do assure you, without
her knowledge. I have heard you say in the pulpit, we ought not
to brag: but indeed I can't avoid saying, if she had kept the
keys herself, the poor would have wanted many a cordial which
I have let them have. As for my late master, he was as worthy
a man as ever lived, and would have done infinite good if he
had not been controlled: but he loved a quiet life, Heavens rest
his soul! I am confident he is there, and enjoys a quiet life,
which some folks would not allow him here." Adams answered,
"he had never heard this before, and was mistaken, if she her-
[master . . . self," (for he remembered she used to commend her [mistress
mistress]$_1$ and blame her master]$_2$,) "had not formerly been of another
opinion." "I don't know, (replied she,) what I might once think:
but now I am *confidous* matters are as I tell you: The world will
shortly see who hath been deceived; for my part I say nothing,
but that it is *wondersome* how some people can carry all things
with a grave face."

Thus Mr. Adams and she discoursed: 'till they came opposite to a great house which stood at some distance from the road; a lady in the coach spying it, cried, "Yonder lives the unfortunate Leonora, if one can ⟨justly⟩$_2$ call a woman ~~justly~~$_2$ unfortunate, whom we must own at the same time guilty, and the author of her own calamity." This was abundantly sufficient to awaken the curiosity of Mr. Adams, as indeed it did that of the whole company, who jointly solicited the lady to acquaint them with Leonora's history, since it seemed, by what she had said, to contain something remarkable.

The lady, who was perfectly well bred, did not require many entreaties, and having only wished [their]$_2$ entertainment might [this]$_1$ make amends for the company's attention, she began in the following manner.

CHAP. IV.

The History of Leonora, or the Unfortunate Jilt.

LEONORA was the daughter of a gentleman of fortune; she was tall and well-shaped, with a sprightliness in her countenance, which often attracts beyond ~~the~~$_2$ more regular features joined with an insipid air; nor is this kind of beauty less apt to deceive than ⟨allure;⟩$_2$ the good-humour which it indicates, being often mistaken for good-nature, and the vivacity for true understanding.

Leonora ⟨, who⟩$_2$ was now at the age of eighteen, lived with an aunt of hers in a town in the north of England. She was an extreme lover of gaiety, and very rarely missed a ball or any other public assembly; where she had frequent opportunities of satisfying a greedy appetite of vanity with the preference which was given her by the men to almost every other woman present.

Among many young fellows who were particular in their gallantries towards her, Horatio soon distinguished himself in her eyes beyond all his competitors; she danced with more than ordinary gaiety when he happened to be her partner; neither the fairness of the evening nor the music of the nightingale, could lengthen her walk like his company. She affected no longer to understand the civilities of others: whilst she inclined so attentive an ear to every compliment of Horatio, that she often smiled even when it was too delicate for her comprehension.

"Pray, madam," says Adams, "who was this Squire Horatio?"

Horatio, says the lady, was a young gentleman of a good family, bred to the law, and had been some few years called to the degree of a barrister. His face and person were such as the generality allowed handsome: but he had a dignity in his air very rarely to be seen. His temper was of the saturnine complexion, but without the least taint of moroseness. He had wit and humour with an inclination to satire, which he indulged rather too much.

This gentleman, who had contracted the most violent passion for Leonora, was the last person who perceived the probability of its success. The whole town had made the match for him, before he himself had drawn a confidence from her actions sufficient to mention his passion to her; for it was his opinion, (and perhaps he was there in the right) that it is highly impolitic to talk seriously of love to a woman before you have made such a progress in her affections, that she herself expects and desires to hear it.

But whatever diffidence the fears of a lover may create, which are apt to magnify every favour conferred on a rival, and to see the little advances towards themselves through the other end of the perspective; it was impossible that Horatio's passion should so blind his discernment, as to prevent his conceiving hopes from the behaviour of Leonora; whose fondness for him was now as visible to an indifferent person in their company, as his for her.

"I never knew any of these forward sluts come to good, (says the lady, who refused Joseph's entrance into the coach,) nor shall I wonder at anything she doth in the sequel."

The lady proceeded in her story thus: It was in the midst of a gay conversation in the walks one evening, when Horatio whispered Leonora, "that he was desirous to take a turn or two with her in private; for that he had something to communicate to her of great consequence." "Are you sure it is of consequence?" said she, smiling. — "I hope," answered he, "you will think so too, since the whole future happiness of my life must depend on the event."

Leonora, who very much suspected what was coming, would have deferred it 'till another time: but Horatio, who had more than half conquered the difficulty of speaking by the first motion, was so very importunate, that she at last yielded, and leaving the rest of the company, they turned aside into an unfrequented walk.

They had retired far out of the sight of the company, both maintaining a strict silence. At last Horatio made a full stop, and taking Leonora, who stood pale and trembling, gently by the hand, he fetched a deep sigh, and then looking on her eyes with all the tenderness imaginable, he cried out in a faltering accent; "O Leonora! [is it]$_2$ necessary for me to declare to you [it is]$_1$
on what the future happiness of my life must be founded! Must I say, there is something belonging to you which is a bar to my happiness, and which unless you will part with, I must be miserable?" "What can that be?" replied Leonora. — "No wonder," said he, "you are surprised, that I should make an objection to anything which is yours, yet sure you may guess, since it is the only one which the riches of the world, if they were mine, should purchase of me. — O it is that which you must part with, to bestow all the rest! Can Leonora, or rather will she doubt longer? — Let me then whisper it in her ears, — It is your name, madam. It is by parting with that, by your condescension to be for ever mine, which must at once prevent me from being the most miserable, and will render me the happiest of mankind."

Leonora, covered with blushes, and with as angry a look as she could possibly put on, told him, "that had she suspected what his declaration would have been, he should not have decoyed her from her company; that he had so surprised and frighted her, that she begged him to convey her back as quick as possible;" which he, trembling very near as much as herself, did.

"More fool he," cried Slipslop, "it is a sign he knew very little of our *sect*." "Truly, madam," said Adams, "I think you are in the right. I should have insisted to know a piece of her mind, when I had carried matters so far." But Mrs. Grave-airs desired the lady to omit all such fulsome stuff in her story: for that it made her sick.

Well then, madam, to be as concise as possible, said the lady, many weeks had not passed after this interview, before Horatio and Leonora were what they call on a good footing together. All ceremonies except the last were now over; the writings were now drawn, and everything was in the utmost forwardness preparative to the putting Horatio in possession of all his wishes. I will if you please repeat you a letter from each of them which I have got by heart, and which will give you no small idea of their passion on both sides.

Mrs. Grave-airs objected to hearing these letters: but being put to the vote, it was carried against her by all the rest in the coach; Parson Adams contending for it with the utmost vehemence.

HORATIO *to* LEONORA

HOW vain, most adorable creature, is the pursuit of pleasure in the absence of an object to which the mind is entirely devoted, unless it have some relation to that object! I was last night condemned to the society of men of wit and learning, which, however agreeable it might have formerly been to me, now only gave me a suspicion that they imputed my absence in conversation to the true cause. For which reason, when your engagements forbid me the ecstatic happiness of seeing you, I am always desirous to be alone; since my sentiments for Leonora are so delicate, that I cannot bear the apprehension of another's prying into those delightful endearments with which the warm imagination of a lover will sometimes indulge him, and which I suspect my eyes then betray. To fear this discovery of our thoughts, may perhaps appear too ridiculous a nicety to minds, not susceptible of all the tenderness of [this delicate passion. And surely we shall suspect there are few such, when we consider that it]$_2$ requires every human virtue to exert itself in its full extent. Since the beloved whose happiness it ultimately respects, may

[a passion which]$_1$

give us charming opportunities of being brave in her defence, generous to her wants, compassionate to her afflictions, grateful to her kindness, and, in the same manner, of exercising every other virtue, which he who would not do to any degree, and that with the utmost rapture, can never deserve the name of a lover: It is therefore with a view to the delicate modesty of your mind that I cultivate it so purely in my own, and it is that which will sufficiently suggest to you the uneasiness I bear from those liberties which men to whom the world allow politeness will sometimes give themselves on these occasions.

Can I tell you with what eagerness I expect the arrival of that blest day, when I shall experience the falsehood of a common assertion that the greatest human happiness consists in hope? A doctrine which no person had ever stronger reason to believe than myself at present, since none ever tasted such bliss as fires my bosom with the thoughts of spending my future days with such a companion, and that every action of my life will have the glorious satisfaction of conducing to your happiness.

⟨*⟩ 2 LEONORA *to* HORATIO

THE refinement of your mind has been so evidently proved, by every word and action ever since I had first the pleasure of knowing you, that I thought it impossible my good opinion of Horatio could have been heightened by any additional proof of merit. This very thought was my amusement when I received your last letter, which, when I opened, I confess I was surprised to find the delicate sentiments expressed there, so far exceeded what I thought could come even from you, (although I know all the generous principles human nature is capable of, are centred in your breast) that words cannot paint what I feel on the reflection, that my happiness shall be the ultimate end of all your actions.

Oh Horatio! what a life must that be, where the meanest domestic cares are sweetened by the pleasing consideration that

⟨* This letter was written by a young lady on reading the former.⟩ 2 [Fielding's note]

the man on earth who best deserves, and to whom you are most inclined to give your affections, is to reap either profit or pleasure from all you do! In such a case, toils must be turned into diversions, and nothing but the unavoidable inconveniences of life can make us remember that we are mortal.

If the solitary turn of your thoughts, and the desire of keeping them undiscovered, makes even the conversation of men of wit and learning tedious to you, what anxious hours must I spend who am condemned by custom to the conversation of women, whose natural curiosity leads them to pry into all my thoughts, and whose envy can never suffer Horatio's heart to be possessed by any one without forcing them into malicious designs, against the person who is so happy as to possess it: but indeed, if ever envy can possibly have any excuse, or even alleviation, it is in this case, where the good is so great, that it must be equally natural to all to wish it for themselves, nor am I ashamed to own it: and to your merit, Horatio, I am obliged, that prevents my being in that most uneasy of all the situations I can figure in my imagination, of being led by inclination to love the person whom my own judgment forces me to condemn.

Matters were in so great forwardness between this fond couple, that the day was fixed for their marriage, and was now within a fortnight, when the sessions chanced to be held for that county in a town about twenty miles distance from that which is the scene of our story. It seems, it is usual for the young gentlemen of the bar to repair to these sessions, not so much for the sake of profit, as to show their parts and learn the law of the Justices of Peace: for which purpose one of the wisest and gravest of all the justices is appointed Speaker or Chairman, as they modestly call it, and he reads them a lecture, and instructs them in the true knowledge of the law.

"You are here guilty of a little mistake," says Adams, "which, if you please I will correct; I have attended at one of these Quarter Sessions, where I observed the counsel taught the justices, instead of learning anything of them."

It is not very material, said the lady: hither repaired Horatio, who as he hoped by his profession to advance his fortune, which was not at present very large, for the sake of his dear Leonora, he resolved to spare no pains, nor lose any opportunity of improving or advancing himself in it.

The same afternoon in which he left the town, as Leonora stood at her window, a coach and six passed by: which she declared to be the completest, genteelest, prettiest equipage she ever saw; adding these remarkable words, *O I am in love with that equipage!* which, though her friend Florella at that time did not greatly regard, she hath since remembered.

In the evening an assembly was held, which Leonora honoured with her company: but intended to pay her dear Horatio the compliment of refusing to dance in his absence.

O Why have not women as good resolution to maintain their vows, as they have often good inclinations in making them!

The gentleman who owned the coach and six, came to the assembly. His clothes were as remarkably fine as his equipage could be. He soon attracted the eyes of the company; all the smarts, all the silk waistcoats with silver and gold edgings, were eclipsed in an instant.

"Madam," said Adams, "if it be not impertinent, I should be glad to know how this gentleman was drest."

Sir, answered the lady, I have been told, he had on a cut-velvet coat of a cinnamon colour, lined with a pink satin, embroidered all over with gold; his waistcoat, which was cloth of silver, was embroidered with gold likewise. I cannot be particular as to the rest of his dress: but it was all in the French fashion, for Bellarmine, (that was his name) was just arrived from Paris.

This fine figure did not more entirely engage the eyes of every lady in the assembly, than [Leonora]$_2$ did his. He had [her]$_1$ scarce beheld her, but he stood motionless and fixed as a statue, or at least would have done so, if good-breeding had permitted him. However, he carried it so far before he had power to correct himself, that every person in the room easily discovered where his admiration was settled. The other ladies began to single out their former partners, all perceiving who would be Bellarmine's choice; which they however endeavoured, by all possible means, to prevent: Many of them saying to Leonora,

"O madam, I suppose we shan't have the pleasure of seeing you dance tonight;" and then crying out in Bellarmine's hearing, "O Leonora will not dance, I assure you; her partner is not here." One maliciously attempted to prevent her, by sending a disagreeable fellow to ask her, that so she might be obliged either to dance with him, or sit down: but this scheme proved abortive.

Leonora saw herself admired by the fine stranger, and envied by every woman present. Her little heart began to flutter within her, and her head was agitated with a convulsive motion; she seemed as if she would speak to several of her acquaintance, but had nothing to say: for as she would not mention her present triumph, so she could not disengage her thoughts one moment from the contemplation of it: She had never tasted anything like this happiness. She had before known what it was to torment a single woman; but to be hated and secretly cursed by a whole assembly, was a joy reserved for this blessed moment. As this
[awaked]$_2$ vast profusion of ecstasy had [confounded]$_2$ her understanding, so there was nothing so foolish as her behaviour; she played a thousand childish tricks, distorted her person into several shapes, and her face into several laughs, without any reason. In a word, her carriage was as absurd as her desires, which were to affect an insensibility of the stranger's admiration, and at the same time a triumph from that admiration over every woman in the room.

In this temper of mind, Bellarmine, having inquired who she was, advanced to her, and with a low bow, begged the honour of dancing with her, which she with as low a curtsy immediately granted. She danced with him all night, and enjoyed perhaps the highest pleasure, which she was capable of feeling.

At these words, Adams fetched a deep groan, which frighted the ladies, who told him, "they hoped he was not ill." He answered, "he groaned only for the folly of Leonora."

Leonora retired, (continued the lady) about six in the morning, but not to rest. She tumbled and tossed in her bed, with very short intervals of sleep, and those entirely filled with dreams of the equipage and fine clothes she had seen, and the balls, operas and ridottos, which had been the subject of their conversation.

In the afternoon Bellarmine, in the dear coach and six, came to wait on her. He was indeed charmed with her person, and was, on inquiry, so well pleased with the circumstances of her father, (for he himself, notwithstanding all [his]$_2$ finery, was [this]$_1$ not quite so rich as a Crœsus or an Attălus.) "Attălus," says Mr. Adams, "but pray how came you acquainted with these names?" The lady smiled at the question, and proceeded — He was so pleased, I say, that he resolved to make his addresses to her directly. He did so accordingly, and that with so much warmth and briskness, that he quickly baffled her weak repulses, and obliged the lady to refer him to her father, who, she knew, would quickly declare in favour of a coach and six.

Thus, what Horatio had by sighs and tears, love and tenderness, been so long obtaining, the French-English Bellarmine with gaiety and gallantry possessed himself of in an instant. In other words, what Modesty had employed a full year in raising, Impudence demolished in twenty-four hours.

Here Adams groaned a second time, but the ladies, who began to smoke him, took no notice.

From the opening of the assembly 'till the end of Bellarmine's visit, Leonora had scarce once thought of Horatio: but he now began, though an unwelcome guest, to enter into her mind. She wished she had seen the charming Bellarmine and his charming equipage before matters had gone so far. "Yet, why (says she) should I wish to have seen him before, or what signifies it that I have seen him now? Is not Horatio my lover? almost my husband? Is he not as handsome, nay handsomer than Bellarmine? Aye, but Bellarmine is the genteeler and the finer man; yes, that he must be allowed. Yes, yes, he is that certainly. But did not I no longer ago than yesterday love Horatio more than all the world? aye, but yesterday I had not seen Bellarmine. But doth not Horatio doat on me, and may he not in despair break his heart if I abandon him? Well, and hath not Bellarmine a heart to break too? Yes, but I promised Horatio first; but that was poor Bellarmine's misfortune, if I had seen him first, I should certainly have preferred him. Did not the dear creature prefer me to every woman in the assembly, when every She was laying out for him? When was it in Horatio's power to give me such an instance of affection? Can he give me an equipage or any of those things which Bellarmine will make me mistress of? How vast is the difference between being the wife of a poor counsellor, and the wife of one of Bellarmine's fortune! ⟨If I marry Horatio, I shall triumph over no more than one rival: but by marrying Bellarmine, I shall be the envy of all my acquaintance. What happiness! —⟩ [2] But can I suffer Horatio to die? for he hath sworn he cannot survive my loss: but perhaps he may not die; if he should, can I prevent it? Must I sacrifice myself to him? besides, Bellarmine may be as miserable for me too." She was thus arguing with herself, when some young ladies called her to the walks, and a little relieved her anxiety for the present.

The next morning Bellarmine breakfasted with her in presence of her aunt, whom he sufficiently informed of his passion for Leonora; he was no sooner withdrawn, than the old lady began to advise her niece on this occasion. — "You see, child, (says she) what Fortune hath thrown in your way, and I hope you will not withstand your own preferments." Leonora sighing, "begged her not to mention any such thing, when she knew her engagements to Horatio." "Engagements to a fig," cried the aunt, "you should thank Heaven on your knees that you have it yet in your power to break them. Will any woman hesitate a moment, whether she shall ride in a coach or walk on foot all the days of her life? — But Bellarmine drives six, and Horatio not even a pair." "Yes, but, madam, what will the world say?" answered Leonora; "will not they condemn me?" "The world is always on the side of prudence," cries the aunt, "and would surely condemn you if you sacrificed your interest to any motive whatever. O, I know the world very well, and you show your ignorance, my dear, by your objection. O' my conscience the world is wiser. I have lived longer in it than you, and I assure you there is not anything worth our regard besides money: nor did I ever know one person who married from other considerations, who did not afterwards heartily repent it. Besides, if we examine the two men, can you prefer a sneaking fellow, who hath been bred at a university, to a fine gentleman just come from his travels? — All the world must allow Bellarmine to be a fine gentleman, positively a fine gentleman, and a handsome man. — " "Perhaps, madam, I should not doubt, if I knew how to be handsomely off with the other." "O leave that to me," says the aunt. "You know your father hath not been acquainted with the affair. Indeed, for my part, I thought it might do well enough, not dreaming of such an offer: but I'll disengage you, Leave me to give the fellow an answer. I warrant [you shall have]$_2$ no farther trouble."

[you, he shall give you]$_1$

Leonora was at length satisfied with her aunt's reasoning; and Bellarmine supping with her that evening, it was agreed he should the next morning go to her father and propose the match, which she consented should be consummated at his return.

The aunt retired soon after supper, and the lovers being left together, Bellarmine began in the following manner: "Yes, madam, this coat I assure you was made at Paris, and I defy the best English tailor even to imitate it. There is not one of them can cut, madam, they can't cut. If you observe how this skirt is turned, and this sleeve, a clumsy English rascal can do nothing like it. — Pray how do you like my liveries?" Leonora answered, "she thought them very pretty." "All French," says he, "I assure you, except [the]$_2$ greatcoats; I never trust anything more than a greatcoat to an Englishman; you know one must encourage our own people what one can, ⟨especially as, before I had a place, I was in the Country Interest,⟩$_2$ he, he, he! but for myself, I would see the dirty island at the bottom of the sea, rather than wear a single rag of English work about me, and I am sure after you have made one tour to Paris, you will be of the same opinion with regard to your own clothes. You can't conceive what an addition a French dress would be to your beauty; I positively assure you, at the first opera I saw since I came over, I mistook the English ladies for chambermaids, he, he, he!"

[their]$_1$

With such sort of polite discourse did the gay Bellarmine entertain his beloved Leonora, when the door opened on a sudden, and Horatio entered the [room. Here 'tis]$_2$ impossible to express the surprise of Leonora.

[room; 'tis]$_1$

"Poor woman," says Mrs. Slipslop, "what a terrible *quandary* she must be in!" "Not at all," says Miss Grave-airs, "such sluts can never be confounded." ⟨"She must have then more than Corinthian assurance," said Adams; "ay, more than Lais herself."⟩$_{2}$ [2]

A long silence, continued the lady, prevailed in the whole company: If the familiar entrance of Horatio struck the greatest astonishment into Bellarmine, the unexpected presence of Bellarmine no less surprised Horatio. At length Leonora collecting all the spirits she was mistress of, addressed herself to the latter, and pretended to wonder at the reason of so late a visit. "I should, indeed," answered he, "have made some apology for disturbing you at this hour, had not my finding you in company assured me I do not break in on your repose." Bellarmine rose from his chair, traversed the room in a minuet step, and hummed an opera tune, while Horatio advancing to Leonora asked her in a whisper, if that gentleman was not a relation of hers; to which she answered with a smile, or rather sneer, "No, he is no relation of mine yet;" adding, "she could not guess the meaning of his question." Horatio told her softly, "it did not arise from jealousy." "Jealousy!" cries she, "I assure you; — it would be very strange in a common acquaintance to give himself any of those airs." These words a little surprised Horatio, but before he had time to answer, Bellarmine danced up to the lady, and told her, "he feared he interrupted some business between her and the gentleman." "I can have no business," said she, "with the gentleman, nor any other, which need be any secret to you."

"You'll pardon me," said Horatio, "if I desire to know who this gentleman is, who is to be intrusted with all our secrets." "You'll know soon enough," cries Leonora, "but I can't guess what secrets can ever pass between us of such mighty consequence." "No madam!" cries Horatio, "I'm sure you would not
[It's]$_{1-2}$ have me understand you in earnest." "['Tis]$_{3}$ indifferent to me," says she, "how you understand me; but I think so unseasonable a visit is difficult to be understood at all, at least when people find one engaged, though one's servants do not deny one, one

[2] Corinth was famous for its wealthy materialism (especially for its *brass*, meaning both the actual metal and the Corinthians' impudence), and for the stoning to death of Lais, a wealthy lady of pleasure, by outraged wives (340 B.C.).

may expect a well-bred person should soon take the hint." "Madam," said Horatio, "I did not imagine any engagement with a stranger, as it seems this gentleman is, would have made my visit impertinent, or that any such ceremonies were to be preserved between persons in our situation." "Sure you are in a dream," says she, "or would persuade me that I am in one. I know no pretensions a common acquaintance can have to lay aside the ceremonies of good-breeding." "Sure," said he, "I am in a dream; for it is impossible I should be really esteemed a common acquaintance by Leonora, after what has passed between us!" "Passed between us! Do you intend to affront me before this gentleman?" "D—n me, affront the lady," says Bellarmine, cocking his hat and strutting up to Horatio, "does any man dare affront this lady before me, d—n me?" "Harkee, sir," says Horatio, "I would advise you to lay aside that fierce air; for I am mightily deceived, if this lady has not a violent desire to get your worship a good drubbing." "Sir," said Bellarmine, "I have the honour to be her protector, and d—n me, if I understand your meaning." "Sir," answered Horatio, "she is rather your protectress: but give yourself no more airs, for you see I am prepared for you," (shaking his whip at him.) "Oh! *Serviteur tres humble*," says Bellarmine, "*Je vous entend parfaitement bien.*" At which time the aunt, who had heard of Horatio's visit, entered the room and soon satisfied all his doubts. She convinced him that he was never more awake in his life, and that nothing more extraordinary had happened in his three days absence, than a small alteration in the affections of Leonora: who now burst into tears, and wondered what reason she had given him to use her in so barbarous a manner. Horatio desired Bellarmine to withdraw with him: but the ladies prevented it by laying violent hands on the latter; upon which, the former took his leave without any great ceremony, and departed, leaving the lady with his rival to consult for his safety, which Leonora feared her indiscretion might have endangered: but the aunt comforted her with assurances, that Horatio would not venture his person against so accomplished a cavalier as Bellarmine, and that being a lawyer, he would seek revenge in his own way, and the most they had to apprehend from him was an action.

They at length therefore agreed to permit Bellarmine to retire to his lodgings, having first settled all matters relating to the journey which he was to undertake in the morning, and their preparations for the nuptials at his return.

But alas! as wise men have observed, the seat of valour is not the countenance, and many a grave and plain man, will, on a just provocation, betake himself to that mischievous metal, cold iron; while men of a fiercer brow, and sometimes with that emblem of courage, a cockade, will more prudently decline it.

Leonora was waked in the morning, from a visionary coach and six, with the dismal account, that Bellarmine was run through the body by Horatio, that he lay languishing at an inn, and the surgeons had declared the wound mortal. She immediately leaped out of the bed, danced about the room in a frantic manner, tore her hair and beat her breast in all the agonies of despair; in which sad condition her aunt, who likewise arose at the news, found her. The good old lady applied her utmost art to comfort her niece. She told her, "while there was life, there was hope: but that if he should die, her affliction would be of no service to Bellarmine, and would only expose herself, which might probably keep her some time without any future offer; that as matters had happened, her wisest way would be to think
[reconcile no more of Bellarmine, but to endeavour to [regain the affec-
herself to]$_{1-2}$ tions of]$_3$ Horatio." "Speak not to me," cried the disconsolate Leonora, "is it not owing to me, that poor Bellarmine has lost his life? have not these cursed charms" (at which words she looked steadfastly in the glass,) "been the ruin of the most charming man of this age? Can I ever bear to contemplate my own face again?" (with her eyes still fixed on the glass.) "Am I not the murderess of the finest gentleman? ⟨No other woman in the town could have made any impression on him.⟩$_2$" "Never
[reconciling think of things past," cries the aunt, "think of [regaining the af-
yourself to]$_{1-2}$ fections of]$_3$ Horatio." "What reason," said the niece, "have I to hope he would forgive me? no, I have lost him as well as the other, and it was your wicked advice which was the occasion of all; you seduced me, contrary to my inclinations, to abandon poor Horatio," at which words she burst into tears; "you prevailed upon me, whether I would or no, to give up my affections

for him; had it not been for you, Bellarmine never would have entered into my thoughts; had not his addresses been backed by your persuasions, they never would have made any impression on me; I should have defied all the fortune and equipage in the world: but it was you, it was you, who got the better of my youth and simplicity, and forced me to lose my dear Horatio for ever."

The aunt was almost borne down with this torrent of words, she however rallied all the strength she could, and drawing her mouth up in a purse, began: "I am not surprised, niece, at this ingratitude. Those who advise young women for their interest, must always expect such a return: I am convinced my brother will thank me for breaking off your match with Horatio at any rate." "That may not be in your power yet," answered Leonora; "though it is very ungrateful in you to desire or attempt it, after the presents you have received from him." (For indeed true it is, that many presents, and some pretty valuable ones, had passed from Horatio to the old lady: but as true it is, that Bellarmine when he breakfasted with her and her niece, had complimented her with a brilliant from his finger, of much greater value than all she had touched of the other.)

The aunt's gall was on float to reply, when a servant brought a letter into the room; which Leonora hearing it came from Bellarmine, with great eagerness opened, and read as follows:

"*Most Divine Creature,*

The Wound which I fear you have heard I received from my Rival, is not like to be so fatal as those shot into my Heart, which have been fired from your Eyes, *tout-brilliant*. Those are the only Cannons by which I am to fall: for my Surgeon gives me Hopes of being soon able to attend your *Ruelle;* 'till when, unless you would do me an Honour which I have scarce the *Hardiesse* to think of, your Absence will be the greatest Anguish which can be felt by,

MADAM,

Avec tout le respecte *in the World,*

Your most Obedient, most Absolute

Devoté,

Bellarmine"

As soon as Leonora perceived such hopes of Bellarmine's recovery, and that the gossip Fame had, according to custom, so enlarged his danger, she presently abandoned all further thoughts of Horatio, and was soon reconciled to her aunt, who received her again into favour, with a more Christian forgiveness than we generally meet with. Indeed it is possible she might be a little alarmed at the hints which her niece had given her concerning the presents. She might apprehend such rumours, should they get abroad, might injure a reputation, which by frequenting church twice a day, and preserving the utmost rigour and strictness in her countenance and behaviour for many years, she had established.

Leonora's passion returned now for Bellarmine with greater force after its small relaxation than ever. She proposed to her aunt to make him a visit in his confinement, which the old lady, with great and commendable prudence advised her to decline: "For," says she, "should any accident intervene to prevent your intended match, too forward a behaviour with this lover may injure you in the eyes of others. Every woman 'till she is married ought to consider of and provide against the possibility of the affair's breaking off." Leonora said, "she should be indifferent to whatever might happen in such a case: for she had now so absolutely placed her affections on this dear man (so she called him) that, if it was her misfortune to lose him, she should for ever abandon all thoughts of mankind." She therefore resolved to visit him, notwithstanding all the prudent advice of her aunt to the contrary, and that very afternoon executed her resolution.

The lady was proceeding in her story, when the coach drove into the inn where the company were to dine, sorely to the dissatisfaction of Mr. Adams, whose ears were the most hungry part about him; he being, as the reader may perhaps guess, of an insatiable curiosity, and heartily desirous of hearing the end of this amour, though he professed he could scarce wish success to a lady of so inconstant a disposition.

CHAP. V.

A dreadful quarrel which happened at the inn where the company dined, with its bloody consequences to Mr. Adams.

As soon as the passengers had alighted from the coach, Mr. Adams, as was his custom, made directly to the kitchen, where he found Joseph sitting by the fire and the hostess anointing his leg; for the horse which Mr. Adams had borrowed of his clerk, had so violent a propensity to kneeling, that one would have thought it had [been his trade as well as his master's]2: nor would he always give any notice of such his intention; he was often found on his knees, when the rider least expected it. This foible however was of no great inconvenience to the parson, who was accustomed to it, and ⟨as his legs almost touched the ground when he bestrode the beast, had but a little way to fall, and⟩2 threw himself forward on such occasions with so much dexterity, that he never received any mischief; the horse and he frequently rolling many paces distance, and afterwards both getting up and meeting as good friends as ever.

[likewise been his trade]1

Poor Joseph, who had not been used to such kind of cattle, though an excellent horseman, did not so happily disengage himself: but falling with his leg under the beast, received a violent contusion, to which the woman was, as we have said, applying a warm hand with some camphorated spirits just at the time when the parson entered the kitchen.

He had scarce expressed his concern for Joseph's misfortune, before the host likewise entered. He was by no means of Mr. Tow-wouse's gentle disposition, and was indeed perfect master of his house and everything in it but his guests.

This surly fellow, who always proportioned his respect to the appearance of a traveller, from *God bless your honour,* down to plain *Coming presently,* observing his wife on her knees to a footman, cried out, without considering his circumstances, "What a pox is the woman about? why don't you mind the

company in the coach? Go and ask them what they will have for dinner?" "My dear," says she, "you know they can have nothing but what is at the fire, which will be ready presently; and really the poor young man's leg is very much bruised." At which words, she fell to chafing more violently than before: the bell then happening to ring, he damn'd his wife, and bid her go in to the company, and not stand rubbing there all day: for he did not believe the young fellow's leg was so bad as he pretended; and if it was, within twenty miles he would find a surgeon to cut it off. Upon these words, Adams fetched two strides across the room; and snapping his fingers over his head muttered aloud, "he would excommunicate such a wretch for a farthing: for he believed the Devil had more humanity." These words occasioned a dialogue between Adams and the host, in which there were two or three sharp replies, 'till Joseph bade the latter know how to behave himself to his betters. At which the host ⟨,(having first strictly surveyed Adams)⟩$_2$ scornfully repeating the word *Betters,* flew into a rage, and telling Joseph he was as able to walk out of his house as he had been to walk into it, offered to
[Adams perceiving,]$_1$ lay violent hands on him; which [perceiving, Adams]$_2$ dealt him so sound a compliment over his face with his fist, that the blood immediately gushed out of his nose in a stream. The host being unwilling to be outdone in courtesy, especially by a person of Adams's figure, returned the favour with so much gratitude, that the parson's nostrils likewise began to look a little redder than usual. Upon which he again assailed his antagonist, and with another stroke laid him sprawling on the floor.

The hostess, who was a better wife than so surly a husband deserved, seeing her husband all bloody and stretched along, hastened presently to his assistance, or rather to revenge the blow which to all appearance was the last he would ever receive; when, lo! a pan full of hog's-blood, which unluckily stood on the dresser, presented itself first to her hands. She seized it in her fury, and without any reflection discharged it into the parson's face, and with so good an aim, that much the greater
[saluting]$_{1\text{-}2}$ part first [saluted]$_3$ his countenance, ⟨and⟩$_3$ trickled thence in so large a current down to his beard, and over his garments, that a more horrible spectacle was hardly to be seen or even imagined.

All which was perceived by Mrs. Slipslop, who entered the kitchen at that instant. This good gentlewoman, not being of a temper so extremely cool and patient as perhaps was required to ask many questions on this occasion; flew with great impetuosity at the hostess's cap, which, together with some of her hair, she plucked from her head in a moment, giving her at the same time several hearty cuffs in the face, which by frequent practice on the inferior servants, she had learned an excellent knack of delivering with a good grace. Poor Joseph could hardly rise from his chair; the parson was employed in wiping the blood from his eyes, which had entirely blinded him, and the landlord was but just beginning to stir, whilst Mrs. Slipslop holding down the landlady's face with her left hand, made so dexterous a use of her right, that the poor woman began to roar in a key, which alarmed all the company in the inn.

There happened to be in the inn at this time, besides the ladies who arrived in the stage-coach, the two gentlemen who were present at Mr. Tow-wouse's when Joseph was detained for his horse's-meat, and whom we have before mentioned to have stopt at the alehouse with Adams. There was likewise a gentleman just returned from his travels ⟨to Italy⟩$_{2}$; all whom the horrid outcry of murder, presently brought into the kitchen, where the several combatants were found in the postures already described.

It was now no difficulty to put an end to the fray, the conquerors being satisfied with the vengeance they had taken, and the conquered having no appetite to renew the fight. The principal figure, and which engaged the eyes of all was Adams, who was all over covered with blood, which the whole company concluded to be his own; and consequently imagined him no longer for this world. But the host, who had now recovered from his blow, and was risen from the ground, soon delivered them from this apprehension, by damning his wife, for wasting the hog's puddings, and telling her all would have been very well if she had not intermeddled like a b— as she was; adding, he was very glad the gentlewoman had paid her, though not half what she deserved. The poor woman had indeed fared much the worst, having, besides the unmerciful cuffs received, lost a quantity of hair which Mrs. Slipslop in triumph held in her left hand.

The traveller, addressing himself to Miss Grave-airs, desired her not to be frightened: for here had been only a little boxing, which he said to their *disgracia* the English were *accustomata* to; adding, it must be however a sight somewhat strange to him, who was just come from Italy, the Italians not being addicted to the *cuffardo*, but *bastonza*, says he. He then went up to Adams, and telling him he looked like the ghost of Othello, bid him *not shake his gory locks at him, for he could not say he did it.* Adams very innocently answered, *Sir, I am far from accusing you.* He then returned to the lady, and cried, "I find the bloody gentleman is *uno insipido del nullo senso.* ⟨*Damnata di me*, if I have seen such a *spectaculo* in my way from Viterbo.⟩[2]"

One of the gentlemen having learnt from the host the occasion of this bustle, and being assured by him that Adams had struck the first blow, whispered in his ear: "he'd warrant he would *recover.*" "Recover! master," said the host, smiling: "Yes, yes, I am not afraid of dying with a blow or two neither; I am not such a chicken as that." "Pugh!" said the gentleman, "I mean you will recover damages, in that action which undoubtedly you intend to bring, as soon as a writ can be returned from London; for you look like a man of too much spirit and courage to suffer anyone to beat you without bringing your action against him: He must be a scandalous fellow indeed, who would put up with a drubbing whilst the law is open to revenge it; besides, he hath drawn blood from you and spoiled your coat, and the jury will give damages for that too. An excellent new coat upon my word, and now not worth a shilling!

"I don't care," continued he, "to intermeddle in these cases: but you have a right to my evidence; and if I am sworn, I must speak the truth. I saw you sprawling on the floor, and the blood gushing from your nostrils. You may take your own opinion; but was I in your circumstances, every drop of my blood should convey an ounce of gold into my pocket: remember I don't advise you to go to law, but if your jury were Christians, they must give swinging damages, that's all." "Master," cried the host, scratching his head, "I have no stomach to law, I thank you. I have seen enough of that in the parish, where two of my neighbours have been at law about a house, 'till they have both lawed themselves into a gaol." At which words he turned about, and began to inquire again after his hog's puddings, nor would it probably have been a sufficient excuse for his wife that she spilt them in his defence, had not some awe of the company, especially of the Italian traveller, ⟨who was a person of great dignity,⟩ $_2$ withheld his rage. Whilst one of the above-mentioned gentlemen was employed, as we have seen him, on the behalf of the landlord, the other was no less hearty on the side of Mr. Adams, whom he advised to bring his action immediately. He said the assault of the wife was in law the assault of the husband; for they were but one person; and he was liable to pay damages, which he said must be considerable, where so bloody a disposition appeared. Adams answered, if it was true that they were but one person he had assaulted the wife; for he was sorry to own he had struck the husband the first blow. "I am sorry you own it too," cries the gentleman; "for it could not possibly appear to the court: for here was no evidence present but the lame man in the chair, whom I [suppose]$_2$ to be your friend, and would consequently say nothing but what made for you." "How, sir," says Adams, "do you take me for a villain, who would prosecute revenge in cold blood, and use unjustifiable means to obtain it? If you knew me and my Order, I should think you affronted both." At the word Order, the gentleman stared, (for he was too bloody to be of any modern Order of Knights,) and turning hastily about, said, every man knew his own business.

[supposed]$_1$

Matters being now composed, the company retired to their several apartments, the two gentlemen congratulating each other on the success of their good offices, in procuring a perfect reconciliation between the contending parties; and the traveller went to his repast, [crying, as the Italian poet says,

> "*Je voi* very well, *que tutta e pace,*
> So send up Dinner, good Boniface."]$_2$[3]

[crying: *Tutta è Pace; so send in my Dinner, good* Boniface.]$_1$

The coachman began now to grow importunate with his passengers, whose entrance into the coach was retarded by Miss Grave-airs insisting, against the remonstrances of all the rest,

[3] Boniface is the innkeeper in Farquhar's *Beaux' Stratagem* (1707), a play whose popularity lasted throughout Fielding's lifetime.

that she would not admit a footman into the coach: for poor Joseph was too lame to mount a horse. A young lady, who was, as it seems, an earl's grand daughter, begged it with almost tears in her eyes; Mr. Adams prayed, and Mrs. Slipslop scolded, but all to no purpose. She said, "she would not demean herself to ride with a footman: that there were wagons on the road: that if the master of the coach desired it, she would pay for two places; but would suffer no such fellow to come in." "Madam," says Slipslop, "I am sure no one can refuse another coming into a stage-coach." "I don't know, madam," says the lady, "I am not much used to stage-coaches, I seldom travel in them." "That may be, madam," replied Slipslop, "very good people do, and some people's betters, for aught I know." Miss Grave-airs said, "some folks, might sometimes give their tongues a liberty, to some people that were their betters, which did not become them: for her part, she was not used to converse with servants." Slipslop returned, "some people kept no servants to converse with: for her part, she thanked Heaven, she lived in a family where there were a great many; and had more under her own command, than any paltry little gentlewoman in the kingdom." Miss Grave-airs cried, "she believed, her mistress would not encourage such sauciness to her betters." "My betters," says Slipslop, "who is my betters, pray?" "I am your betters," answered Miss Grave-airs, "and I'll acquaint your mistress."—At which Mrs. Slipslop laughed aloud, and told her, "her lady was one of the great gentry, and such little paltry gentlewomen, as some folks who travelled in stage-coaches, would not easily come at her."

This smart dialogue between some people, and some folks, was going on at the coach-door, when a solemn person riding into the inn, and seeing Miss Grave-airs, immediately accosted her with, "Dear child, how do you?" She presently answered, "O! Papa, I am glad you have overtaken me." "So am I," answered he: "for one of our coaches is just at hand; and there being room for you in it, you shall go no farther in the stage, unless you desire it." "How can you imagine I should desire it?" says she; so bidding Slipslop, "ride with her fellow, if she pleased;" she took her father by the hand, who was just alighted, and walked with him into a room.

Adams instantly asked the coachman in a whisper, if he knew who the gentleman was? The coachman answered, he was now a gentleman, and kept his horse and man: "but times are altered, master," said he, "I remember, when he was no better born than myself." "Aye, aye," says Adams. "My father drove the squire's coach," answered he, "when that very man rode postilion; but he is now his steward, and a great gentleman." Adams then snapped his fingers, and cried, he thought *she was some such trollop*.

Adams made haste to acquaint Mrs. Slipslop with this good news, as he imagined it; but it found a reception different from what he expected. The prudent gentlewoman, who despised the anger of Miss Grave-airs, whilst she conceived her the daughter of a gentleman of small fortune, now she heard her alliance with the upper servants of a great family in her neighbourhood, began to fear her interest with the mistress. She wished she had not carried the dispute so far, and began to think of endeavouring to reconcile herself to the young lady before she left the inn; when luckily, the scene at London, which the reader can scarce have forgotten, presented itself to her mind, and comforted her with such assurance, that she no longer apprehended any enemy with her mistress.

Everything being now adjusted, the company entered the coach, which was just on its departure, when one lady recollected she had left her fan, a second her gloves, a third a snuff-box, and a fourth a smelling-bottle behind her; to find all which, occasioned some delay, and much swearing of the coachman.

As soon as the coach had left the inn, the women all together fell to the character of Miss Grave-airs, whom one of them declared she had suspected to be some low creature from the beginning of their journey; and another affirmed had not even the looks of a gentlewoman; a third warranted she was no better than she should be, and turning to the lady who had related the story in the coach, said, "Did you ever hear, madam, anything so prudish as her remarks? Well, deliver me from the censoriousness of such a prude." The fourth added, "O madam! all these creatures are censorious: but for my part, I wonder where the wretch was bred; indeed I must own I have seldom conversed with these mean kind of people, so that it may appear stranger to me; but to refuse the general desire of a whole company, hath something in it so astonishing, that, for my part, I own I should hardly believe it, if my own ears had not been witnesses to it." "Yes, and so handsome a young fellow," cries Slipslop, "the woman must have no compassion in her, I believe she is more of a Turk than a Christian; I am certain if she had any Christian woman's blood in her veins, the sight of such a young fellow must have warmed it. Indeed there are some wretched, miserable old objects that turn one's stomach, I should not wonder if she had refused such a one; I am as nice as herself, and should have cared no more than herself for the company of *stinking* old fellows: but hold up thy head, Joseph, thou art none of those, and she who hath no *compulsion* for thee is a *Myhummetman*, and I will maintain it." This conversation made Joseph uneasy, as well as the ladies; who perceiving the spirits which Mrs. Slipslop was in, (for indeed she was not a cup too low) began to fear the consequence; one of them therefore desired the lady to conclude the story — "Ay madam," said Slipslop, "I beg your ladyship to give us that story you *commencated* in the morning," which request that well-bred woman immediately complied with.

CHAP. VI.

Conclusion of the Unfortunate Jilt.

LEONORA having once broke through the bounds which custom and modesty impose on her sex, soon gave an unbridled indulgence to her passion. Her visits to Bellarmine were more constant, as well as longer, than his surgeon's; in a word, she became absolutely his nurse, made his water-gruel, administered him his medicines, and, notwithstanding the prudent advice of her aunt to the contrary, almost entirely resided in her wounded lover's apartment.

The ladies of the town began to take her conduct under consideration; it was the chief topic of discourse at their tea-tables, and was very severely censured by the most part; especially by Lindamira, a lady whose discreet and starch carriage, together with a constant attendance at church three times a day, had utterly defeated many malicious attacks on her own reputation: for such was the envy that Lindamira's virtue had attracted, that notwithstanding her own strict behaviour and strict inquiry into the lives of others, she had not been able to escape being the mark of some arrows herself, which however did her no injury; a blessing perhaps owed by her to the clergy, who were her chief male companions, and with two or three of whom she had been barbarously and unjustly calumniated.

"Not so unjustly neither perhaps," says Slipslop, "for the clergy are men as well as other folks."

The extreme delicacy of Lindamira's virtue was cruelly hurt by those freedoms which Leonora allowed herself; she said, "it was an affront to her sex, that she did not imagine it consistent with any woman's honour to speak to the creature, or to be seen in her company; and that, for her part, she should always refuse to dance at an assembly with her, for fear of contamination, by taking her by the hand."

But to return to my story: As soon as Bellarmine was recovered, which was somewhat within a month from his receiving the wound, he set out, according to agreement, for Leonora's father's, in order to propose the match, and settle all matters with him touching settlements, and the like.

A little before his arrival, the old gentleman had received an intimation of the affair by the following letter; which I can repeat *verbatim*, and which they say was written neither by Leonora nor her aunt, though it was in a woman's hand. The letter was in these words:

"*Sir*,

I am sorry to acquaint you that your Daughter *Leonora* hath acted one of the basest, as well as most simple Parts with a young Gentleman to whom she had engaged herself, and whom she hath (pardon the Word) jilted for another of inferiour Fortune, notwithstanding his superiour Figure. You may take what

Measures you please on this Occasion; I have performed what I thought my Duty, as I have, tho' unknown to you, a very great Respect for your Family."

The old gentleman did not give himself the trouble to answer this kind epistle, nor did he take any notice of it after he had read it, 'till he saw Bellarmine. He was, to say the truth, one of those fathers who look on children as an unhappy consequence of their youthful pleasures; which as he would have been delighted not to have had attended them, so was he no less pleased with any opportunity to rid himself of the incumbrance. He passed in the world's language, as an exceeding good father, being not only so rapacious as to rob and plunder all mankind to the utmost of his power, but even to deny himself the conveniences and almost necessaries of life; which his neighbours attributed to a desire of raising immense fortunes for his children: but in fact it was not so, he heaped up money for its own sake only, and looked on his children as his rivals, who were to enjoy his beloved mistress, when he was incapable of possessing her, and which he would have been much more charmed with the power of carrying along with him: nor had his children any other security of being his heirs, than that the law would constitute them such without a will, and that he had not affection enough for anyone living to take the trouble of writing one.

To this gentleman came Bellarmine on the errand I have mentioned. His person, his equipage, his family and his estate seemed to the father to make him an advantageous match for his daughter; he therefore very readily accepted his proposals: but ⟨when⟩ $_3$ Bellarmine ~~when he~~ $_3$ imagined the principal affair concluded, and began to open the incidental matters of fortune; the old gentleman presently changed his countenance, saying, "he resolved never to marry his daughter on a Smithfield match;[4] that whoever had love for her to take her, would, when he died, find her share of his fortune in his coffers: but he had seen such examples of undutifulness happen from the too early generosity

[4] A marriage arranged for money; Smithfield is a district in London famed as a cattle and meat market.

of parents, that he had made a vow never to part with a shilling whilst he lived." He commended the saying of Solomon, *he that spareth the rod, spoileth the child:* but added, "he might have likewise asserted, that *he that spareth the purse, saveth the child.*" He then ran into a discourse on the extravagance of the youth of the age; whence he launched into a dissertation on horses, and came at length to commend those Bellarmine drove. That fine gentleman, who at another season would have been well enough pleased to dwell a little on that subject, was now very eager to resume the circumstance of fortune. He said, "he had a very high value for the young lady, and would receive her with less than he would any other whatever; but that even his love to her made some regard to worldly matters necessary; for it would be a most distracting sight for him to see her, when he had the honour to be her husband, in less than a coach and six." The old gentleman answered, "Four will do, four will do;" and then took a turn from horses to extravagance, and from extravagance to horses, till he came round to the equipage again, whither he was no sooner arrived, than Bellarmine brought him back to the point; but all to no purpose, he made his escape ⟨from that subject⟩$_2$ in a minute, till at last the lover declared, "that in the present situation of his affairs it was impossible for him, though he loved Leonora more than *tout le monde*, to marry her without any fortune." To which the father answered, "he was sorry then his daughter must lose so valuable a match; that if he had an inclination at present, it was not in his power to advance a shilling: that he had had great losses and been at great expenses on projects, which, though he had great expectation from them, had yet produced him nothing: that he did not know what might happen hereafter, as on the birth of a son, or such accident, but he would make no promise, or enter into any article: for he would not break his vow for all the daughters in the world."

In short, ladies, to keep you no longer in suspense, Bellarmine having tried every argument and persuasion which he could invent, and finding them all ineffectual, at length took his leave, but not in order to return to Leonora; he proceeded directly to his own seat, whence after a few days stay, he returned to Paris, to the great delight of the French, and the honour of the English nation.

But as soon as he arrived at his home, he presently dispatched a messenger, with the following epistle to Leonora.

"*Adorable* and *Charmante*,

I am sorry to have the Honour to tell you I am not the *heureux* Person destined for your divine Arms. Your Papa hath told me so with a *Politesse* not often seen on this side *Paris*. You may perhaps guess his manner of refusing me — *Ah mon Dieu!* You will certainly believe me, Madam, incapable of my self delivering this *triste* Message: Which I intend to try the *French* Air to cure the Consequences of — *Ah jamais! Cœur! Ange!* — *Ah Diable!* — If your Papa obliges you to a Marriage, I hope we shall see you at *Paris*, till when the Wind that flows from thence will be the warmest *dans le Monde:* for it will consist almost entirely of my Sighs. *Adieu, ma Princesse! Ah* ⟨*L'*⟩ 2 *Amour!*

Bellarmine"

I shall not attempt ladies, to describe Leonora's condition when she received this letter. It is a picture of horror, which I should have as little pleasure in drawing as you in beholding. She immediately left the place, where she was the subject of conversation and ridicule, and retired to that house I showed you when I began the story, where she hath ever since led a disconsolate life, and deserves perhaps pity for her misfortunes more than our censure, for a behaviour to which the artifices of her aunt very probably contributed, and to which very young women are often rendered too liable, by that blameable levity in the education of our sex.

"If I was inclined to pity her," said a young lady in the coach, "it would be for the loss of Horatio; for I cannot discern any misfortune in her missing such a husband as Bellarmine."

"Why, I must own," says Slipslop, "the gentleman was a little false-hearted: but *howsumever* it was hard to have two lovers, and get never a husband at all — But pray, madam, what became of *Ourasho?*"

He remains ⟨, said the lady,⟩$_2$ still unmarried, and hath applied himself so strictly to his business, that he hath raised I hear a very considerable fortune. And what is remarkable, they say, he never [hears]$_2$ the name of Leonora without a sigh, [heard]$_1$
⟨n⟩$_2$or hath ever uttered one syllable to charge her with her ill-conduct towards him.

CHAP. VII.

A very short chapter, in which Parson Adams went a great way.

THE lady having finished her story received the thanks of the company, and now Joseph putting his head out of the coach, cried out, "Never believe me, if yonder be not our Parson Adams walking along without his horse." "On my word, and so he is," says Slipslop; "and as sure as two-pence, he hath left him behind at the inn." Indeed, true it is, the parson had exhibited a fresh instance of his absence of mind: for he was so pleased with having got Joseph into the coach, that he never once thought of the beast in the stable; and finding his legs as nimble as he desired, he sallied out brandishing a crabstick, and had kept on before the coach, mending and slackening his pace occasionally, so that he had never been much more or less than a quarter of a mile distant from it.

Mrs. Slipslop desired the coachman to overtake him, which he attempted, but in vain: for the faster he drove, the faster ran the parson, often crying out, *Aye, aye, catch me if you can:* 'till at length the coachman swore he would as soon attempt to drive after a greyhound; and giving the parson two or three hearty curses, he cried, "Softly, softly boys," to his horses, which the civil beasts immediately obeyed.

But we will be more courteous to our reader than he was to Mrs. Slipslop, and leaving the coach and its company to pursue

their journey, we will carry our reader on after Parson Adams,
[on]$_1$ who stretched [forwards]$_2$ without once looking behind him, 'till having left the coach full three miles in his rear, he came to a place, where by keeping the extremest track to the right, it was just barely possible for a human creature to miss his way. This track however did he keep, as indeed he had a wonderful capacity at these kinds of bare possibilities; and travelling in it about three miles over the plain, he arrived at the summit of a hill, whence looking a great way backwards, and perceiving no coach in sight, he sat himself down on the turf, and pulling out his Æschylus, determined to wait here for its arrival.

He had not sat long here, before a gun going off very near, a little startled him; he looked up, and saw a gentleman within a hundred paces taking up a partridge, which he had just shot.

Adams stood up, and presented a figure to the gentleman which would have moved laughter in many: for his cassock had just again fallen down below his greatcoat, that is to say, it reached his knees; whereas the skirts of his greatcoat descended no lower than half way down his thighs: but the gentleman's mirth gave way to his surprise, at beholding such a personage in such a place.

Adams advancing to the gentleman told him he hoped he had good sport; to which the other answered, "Very little." "I see, sir," says Adams, "you have *smote* one partridge:" to which the sportsman made no reply, but proceeded to charge his piece.

Whilst the gun was charging, Adams remained in silence, which he at last broke, by observing that it was a delightful evening. The gentleman, who had at first sight conceived a very distasteful opinion of the parson, began, on perceiving a book in his hand, and smoking likewise the information of the cassock, to change his thoughts, and made a small advance to conversation on his side, by saying, *Sir, I suppose you are not one of these parts?*

Adams immediately told him, No; that he was a traveller, and invited by the beauty of the evening and the place to repose a little, and amuse himself with reading. "I may as well repose myself too," said the sportsman; "for I have been out this whole afternoon, and the devil a bird have I seen 'till I came hither."

"Perhaps then the game is not very plenty hereabouts," cries Adams. "No, sir," said the gentleman, "the soldiers, who are quartered in the neighbourhood, have killed it all." "It is very probable," cries Adams, "for shooting is their profession." "Ay, shooting the game," answered the other, "but I don't see they are so forward to shoot our enemies. I don't like that affair of Carthagena;[5] if I had been there, I believe I should have done other-guess things, d—n me; what's a man's life when his country demands it; a man who won't sacrifice his life for his country deserves to be hanged, d—n me." Which words he spoke with so violent a gesture, so loud a voice, so strong an accent, and so fierce a countenance, that he might have frightned a captain of Trained-Bands[6] at the head of his company; but Mr. Adams was not greatly subject to fear, he told him intrepidly that he very much approved his virtue, but disliked his swearing, and begged him not to addict himself to so bad a custom, without which he said he might fight as bravely as Achilles did. Indeed he was charmed with this discourse, he told the gentleman he would willingly have gone many miles to have met a man of his generous way of thinking; that if he pleased to sit down, he should be greatly delighted to commune with him: for though he was a clergyman, he would himself be ready, if thereto called, to lay down his life for his country.

The gentleman sat down and Adams by him, and then the latter began, as in the following chapter, a discourse which we have placed by itself, as it is not only the most curious in this, but perhaps in any other book.

[5] At the end of May, 1741, the British, under Admiral Edward Vernon, had attacked the Spaniards' fortified harbor at Cartegena on the Caribbean coast of South America (modern Colombia), and the inexperienced troops of General Thomas Wentworth had been badly beaten, owing to poor leadership and poor coordination between army and navy. Sir Robert Walpole took a somewhat equivalent beating in the newspapers for using green troops abroad and a large standing army at home to impress the people.

[6] A civilian army corps, a kind of National Guard.

CHAP. VIII.

A notable dissertation, by Mr. Abraham Adams; wherein that gentleman appears in a political light.

"I do assure you, sir," says he, taking the gentleman by the hand, "I am heartily glad to meet with a man of your kidney: for though I am a poor parson, I will be bold to say, I am an honest man, and would not do an ill thing to be made a bishop: Nay, though it hath not fallen in my way to offer so noble a sacrifice, I have not been without opportunities of suffering for the sake of my conscience, I thank Heaven for them: for I have had relations, though I say it, who made some figure in the world; particularly a nephew, who was a shopkeeper, and an alderman of a corporation.[7] He was a good lad, and was under
[bid]1 my care when a boy, and I believe would do what I [bade]2 him to his dying day. Indeed, it looks like extreme vanity in me, to affect being a man of such consequence, as to have so great an interest in an alderman; but others have thought so too, as manifestly appeared by the rector, whose curate I formerly was, sending for me on the approach of an election, and telling me if I expected to continue in his cure, that I must bring my nephew to vote for one Colonel Courtly, a gentleman whom I had never heard tidings of 'till that instant. I told the rector, I had no power over my nephew's vote, (God forgive me for such prevarication!) That I supposed he would give it according to his conscience, that I would by no means endeavour to influence him to give it otherwise. He told me it was in vain to equivocate: that he knew I had already spoke to him in favour of Esquire Fickle my neighbour, and indeed it was true I had: for it was at a season when the *Church was in danger*, and when all good men expected they knew not what would happen to us all. I then answered boldly, If he thought I had given my promise, he affronted me, in proposing any breach of it. Not to be ⟨too⟩ 2

[7] An alderman of an incorporated town, or a borough.

prolix: I persevered, and so did my nephew, in the esquire's interest, who was chose chiefly through his means, and so I lost my curacy. Well, sir, but do you think the esquire ever mentioned a word of the Church? *Ne verbum quidem, ut ita dicam;* [8] within two years he got a place, and hath ever since lived in London; where I have been informed, (but G— forbid I should believe that) that he never so much as goeth to church. I remained, sir, a considerable time without any cure, and lived a full month on one funeral sermon, which I preached on the indisposition of a clergyman: but this by the bye. At last, when Mr. Fickle got his place, Colonel Courtly stood again; and who should make interest for him, but Mr. Fickle himself: that very identical Mr. Fickle, who had formerly told me, the colonel was an enemy to both the Church and State, had the confidence to solicit my nephew for him, and the colonel himself offered me to make me chaplain to his regiment, which I refused in favour of Sir Oliver Hearty, who told us, he would sacrifice everything to his country; and I believe he would, except his hunting, which he stuck so close to, that in five years together, he went but twice up to Parliament; and one of those times, I have been told, never was within sight of the House. However, he was a worthy man, and the best friend I ever had: for by his interest with a bishop, he got me replaced into my curacy, and gave me eight pounds out of his own pocket to buy me a gown and cassock, and furnish my house. He had our interest while he lived, which was not many years. On his death, I had fresh applications made to me; for all the world knew the interest I had in my good nephew, who now was a leading man in the Corporation; and Sir Thomas Booby, buying the estate which had been Sir Oliver's, proposed himself a candidate. He was then a young gentleman just come from his travels; and it did me good to hear him discourse on affairs, which for my part I knew nothing of. If I had been master of a thousand votes, he should have had them all. I engaged my nephew in his interest, and he was elected, and a very fine Parliament-Man he was. They tell me he made speeches of an hour long; and I have been told very fine ones: but he could never persuade the

[8] "Not even a word, I might say."

Parliament to be of his opinion. — *Non omnia possumus omnes.*[9] He promised me a living, poor man; and I believe I should have had it, but an accident happened; which was, that my lady had promised it before unknown to him. This indeed I never heard 'till afterwards: for my nephew, who died about a month before the incumbent, always told me I might be assured of it. Since that time, Sir Thomas, poor man, had always so much business, that he never could find leisure to see me. I believe it was partly my lady's fault too: who did not think my dress good enough for the gentry at her table. However, I must do him the justice to say, he never was ungrateful; and I have always found his kitchen, and his cellar too, open to me; many a time after service on a Sunday, for I preach at four churches, have I recruited my spirits with a glass of his ale. Since my nephew's death, the Corporation is in other hands; and I am not a man of that consequence I was formerly. I have now no longer any Talents to lay out in the service of my country; and to whom nothing is given, of him can nothing be required. However, on all proper seasons, such as the approach of an election, I throw a suitable dash or two into my sermons; which I have the pleasure to hear is not disagreeable to Sir Thomas, and the other honest gentlemen my neighbours, who have all promised me these five years, to procure an ordination for a son of mine, who is now near thirty, hath an infinite stock of learning, and is, I thank Heaven, of an unexceptionable life; though, as he was never at an university, the bishop refuses to ordain him. Too much care cannot indeed be taken in admitting any to the sacred office; though I hope he will never act so as to be a disgrace to any Order: but will serve his God and his country to the utmost of his power, as I have endeavoured to do before him; nay, and will lay down his life whenever called to that purpose. I am sure I have educated him in those principles; so that I have acquitted my duty, and shall have nothing to answer for on that account: but I do not distrust him; for he is a good boy; and if Providence should throw it in his way, to be of ⟨as⟩ $_3$ much consequence in a public light, as his father once was, I can answer for him, he will use his Talents as honestly as I have done."

[9] "We all can't do all" (Virgil, *Eclogues* VIII.63).

CHAP. IX.

In which the gentleman descants on bravery and heroic virtue, 'till an unlucky accident puts an end to the discourse.

THE gentleman highly commended Mr. Adams for his good resolutions, and told him, "he hoped his son would tread in his steps;" adding, "that if he would not die for his country, he would not be worthy to live in it; I'd make no more of shooting a man that would not die for his country, than —

"Sir," said he, "I have disinherited a nephew who is in the army, because he would not exchange his commission, and go to the West-Indies. I believe the rascal is a coward, though he pretends to be in love forsooth. I would have all such fellows hanged, sir, I would have them hanged." Adams answered, "that would be too severe: That men did not make themselves; and if fear had too much ascendance in the mind, the man was rather to be pitied than abhorred: That reason and time might teach him to subdue it." He said, "a man might be a coward at one time, and brave at another. Homer," says he, "who so well understood and copied Nature, hath taught us this lesson: for Paris fights, and Hector runs away: nay, we have a mighty instance of this in the history of later ages, no longer ago than the 705th year of Rome, when the great Pompey, who had won so many battles, and been honoured with so many triumphs, and of whose valour, several authors, especially Cicero and Paterculus, have formed such elogiums; this very Pompey left the battle of Pharsalia before he had lost it, and retreated to his tent, where he sat like the most pusillanimous rascal in a fit of despair, and yielded a victory, which was to determine the empire of the world, to Cæsar. I am not much travelled in the history of modern times, that is to say, these last thousand years: but those who are, can, I make no question, furnish you with parallel instances." He concluded therefore, that had he taken any such hasty resolutions against his nephew, he hoped he would consider better and retract them. The gentleman answered with great warmth, and talked much of courage and his country, 'till perceiving it grew late, he asked Adams, "what place he intended for that night?" He told him, "he waited there for the stage-coach." "The stage-coach! Sir," said the gentleman, "they are all passed by long ago. You may see the last yourself, almost three miles before us." "I protest and so they are," cries Adams, "then I must make haste and follow them." The gentleman told him, "he would hardly be able to overtake them; and that if he did not know his way, he would be in danger of losing himself on the downs; for it would be presently dark; and he might ramble about all night, and perhaps, find himself farther from his journey's end in the morning than he was now. He advised him therefore to accompany him to his house, which was very little out of his way," assuring him, "that he would find some country-fellow in his parish, who would conduct him for six-pence to the city, where he was going." Adams accepted this proposal, and on they travelled, the gentleman renewing his discourse on courage, and the infamy of not being ready at all times to sacrifice our lives to our country. Night overtook them much about the same time as they arrived near some bushes: whence, on a sudden, they heard the most violent shrieks imaginable in a female voice. Adams offered to snatch the gun out of his companion's hand. "What are you doing?" said he. "Doing!" said Adams, "I am hastening to the assistance of the poor creature whom some villains are murdering." "You are not mad enough, I hope," says the gentleman, trembling: "Do you consider this gun is only charged with shot, and that the robbers are most probably furnished with pistols loaded with bullets? This is no business of ours; let us make as much haste as possible out of the way, or we may fall into their hands ourselves." The shrieks now increasing, Adams made no answer, but snapt his fingers, and brandishing his crabstick, made directly to the place whence the voice issued; and the man of courage made as much expedition towards his own home, whither he escaped in a very short time without once looking behind him: where we will leave him, to contemplate his own bravery, and to censure the want of it in others; and return to the good Adams, who, on coming up to the place whence the noise proceeded, found a woman struggling with a man, who had thrown her on the ground, and had almost overpowered her. The great abilities of Mr. Adams were not necessary to have formed a right judgment of this affair, on the first sight. He did not therefore want the entreaties of the poor wretch to assist her, but lifting up his crabstick, he immediately levelled a blow at that part of the ravisher's head, where, according to the opinion of the Ancients, the brains of some persons are deposited, and which he had undoubtedly let forth, had not Nature, (who, as wise men have observed, equips all creatures with what is most expedient for them;) taken a provident care, (as she always doth with those she intends for encounters) to make this part of the head three times as thick as those of ordinary men, who are designed to exercise talents which are vulgarly called rational, and for whom, as brains are necessary, she is obliged to leave some room for them in the cavity of the skull; whereas, those ingredients being entirely useless to persons of the heroic calling, she hath an opportunity of thickening the bone, so as to make it less subject to any impression or liable to be cracked or broken; and indeed, in some who are predestined to the command of armies and empires, she is supposed sometimes to make that part perfectly solid.

As a game-cock when engaged in amorous toying with a hen, if perchance he espies another cock at hand, immediately quits his female, and opposes himself to his rival; so did the ravisher, on the information of the crabstick, immediately leap from the woman, and [hasten]$_2$ to assail the man. He had no weapons but [hastened]$_1$ what Nature had furnished him with. However, he clenched his fist, and presently darted it at that part of Adams's breast where the heart is lodged. Adams staggered at the violence of the blow, when throwing away his staff, he likewise clenched that fist which we have before commemorated, and would have discharged it full in the breast of his antagonist, had he not dexterously caught it with his left hand, at the same time darting his head, (which some modern heroes, of the lower class, use like the battering-ram of the Ancients, for a weapon of offence; another reason to admire the cunningness of Nature, in composing it of those impenetrable materials) dashing his head, I say, into the stomach of Adams, he tumbled him on his back, and not having any regard to the laws of heroism, which would have restrained him from any farther attack on his enemy, 'till he was again on his legs, he threw himself upon him, and laying hold on the ground with his left hand, he with his right belaboured the body of Adams 'till he was weary, and indeed, 'till he concluded (to use the language of fighting) *that he had done his business;* or, in the language of poetry, *that he had sent him to the shades below;* in plain English, *that he was dead.*

But Adams, who was no chicken, and could bear a drubbing as well as any boxing champion in the universe, lay still only to watch his opportunity; and now perceiving his antagonist to pant with his labours, he exerted his utmost force at once, and with such success, that he overturned him and became his superior; when fixing one of his knees in his breast, he cried out in an exulting voice, *It is my turn now:* and after a few minutes constant application, he gave him so dexterous a blow just under his chin, that the fellow no longer retained any motion, and Adams began to fear he had struck him once too often; for he often asserted, "he should be concerned to have the blood of even the wicked upon him."

Adams got up, and called aloud to the young woman, — "Be of good cheer, damsel," said he, "you are no longer in danger of your ravisher, who, I am terribly afraid, lies dead at my feet; but G— forgive me what I have done in defence of innocence." The poor wretch, who had been some time in recovering strength enough to rise, and had afterwards, during the engagement, stood trembling, being disabled by fear, even from running away, hearing her champion was victorious, came up to him, but not without apprehensions, even of her deliverer; which, however, she was soon relieved from, by his courteous behaviour and gentle words. They were both standing by the body, which lay motionless on the ground, and which Adams wished to see stir much more than the woman did, when he earnestly begged her to tell him "by what misfortune she came, at such a time of night, into so lonely a place?" She acquainted him, "she was travelling towards London, and had accidentally met with the person from whom he had delivered her, who told her he was likewise on his journey to the same place, and would keep her company; an offer which, suspecting no harm, she had accepted; that he told her, they were at a small distance from an inn where she might take up her lodging that evening, and he would show her a nearer way to it than by following the road. That if she had suspected him, (which she did not, he spoke so kindly to her,) being alone on these downs in the dark, she had no human means to avoid him; that therefore she put her whole trust in Providence, and walked on, expecting every moment to arrive at the inn; when, on a sudden, being come to those bushes, he desired her to stop, and after some rude kisses, which she resisted, and some entreaties, which she rejected, he laid violent hands on her, and was attempting to execute his wicked will, when, she thanked G—, he timely came up and prevented him." Adams encouraged her for saying, she had put her whole trust in Providence, and told her "he doubted not but Providence had sent him to her deliverance, as a reward for that trust. He wished indeed he had not deprived the wicked wretch of life, but G—'s Will be done;" he said, "he hoped the goodness of his intention would excuse him in the next world, and he trusted in her evidence to acquit him in this." He was then silent, and began to consider with himself, whether it would be properer to make his escape, or to deliver himself into the hands of justice; which meditation ended, as the reader will see in the next chapter.

C H A P. X.

Giving an account of the strange catastrophe of the preceding adventure, which drew poor Adams into fresh calamities; and who the woman was who owed the preservation of her chastity to his victorious arm.

THE silence of Adams, added to the darkness of the night, and loneliness of the place, struck dreadful apprehensions into the poor woman's mind: She began to fear as great an enemy in her

deliverer, as he had delivered her from; and as she had not light
enough to discover the age of Adams, and the benevolence
visible in his countenance, she suspected he had used her as some
very honest men have used their country; and had rescued her
out of the hands of one rifler, in order to rifle her himself. Such
[WHILST were the suspicions she drew from his silence: but indeed they
Adams was]$_1$ were ill-grounded. He stood over his vanquished enemy,|$_2$
wisely weighing in his mind the objections which might be made
[these two to either of [the two methods of proceeding mentioned in the
methods of last chapter]$_2$, his judgment sometimes inclining to the one and
proceeding]$_1$ sometimes to the other; for both seemed to him so equally
advisable, and so equally dangerous, that probably he would
have ended his days, at least two or three of them, on that very
[; he]$_1$ spot, before he had taken any resolution [: At length he]$_2$ lifted
up his eyes, and spied a light at a distance, to which he instantly
addressed himself with *Heus tu, traveller, heus tu!* [10] He presently heard several voices, and perceived the light approaching
toward him. The persons who attended the light began some to
laugh, others to sing, and others to hollow, at which the woman
testified some fear, ⟨(for she had concealed her suspicions of the
parson himself,)⟩$_2$ but Adams said, "Be of good cheer, damsel,
and repose thy trust in the same Providence, which hath hitherto
protected thee, and never will forsake the innocent." These people who now approached were no other, reader, than a set of
young fellows, who came to these bushes in pursuit of a diversion which they call *bird-batting*. This, if thou art ignorant of it
(as perhaps if thou hast never travelled beyond Kensington,
Islington, Hackney, or the Borough, thou mayst be) I will inform thee, is performed by holding a large clap-net before a
lantern, and at the same time, beating the bushes: for the birds,
when they are disturbed from their places of rest, or roost, immediately make to the light, and so are enticed within the net.
Adams immediately told them, what had happened, and desired
them "to hold the lantern to the face of the man on the ground,
for he feared he had *smote* him fatally." But indeed his fears
were frivolous, for the fellow, though he had been stunned by
the last blow he received, had long since recovered his senses,

[10] "Hey, you."

and finding himself quit of Adams, had listened attentively to the discourse between him and the young woman; for whose departure he had patiently waited, that he might likewise withdraw himself, having no longer hopes of succeeding in his desires, which were moreover almost as well cooled by Mr. Adams, as they could have been by the young woman herself, had he obtained his utmost wish. This fellow, who had a readiness at improving any accident, thought he might now play a better part than that of a dead man; and accordingly, the moment the candle was held to his face, he leapt up, and laying hold on Adams, cried out, "No, villain, I am not dead, though you and your wicked whore might well think me so, after the barbarous cruelties you have exercised on me. Gentlemen," said he, "you are luckily come to the assistance of a poor traveller, who would otherwise have been robbed and murdered by this vile man and woman, who led me hither out of my way from the high-road, and both falling on me have used me as you see." Adams was going to answer, when one of the young fellows, cried, "D—n them, let's carry them both before the justice." The poor woman began to tremble, and Adams lifted up his voice, but in vain. Three or four of them laid hands on him, and one holding the lantern to his face, they all agreed, *he had the most villainous countenance* they ever beheld, and an attorney's clerk who was of the company declared, *he was sure he had remembered him at the bar*. As to the woman, her hair was dishevelled in the struggle, and her nose had bled, so that they could not perceive whether she was handsome or ugly: but they said her fright plainly discovered her guilt. And searching her pockets, as they did those of Adams for money, which the fellow said he had lost, they found in her pocket a purse with some gold in it, which abundantly convinced them, especially as the fellow offered to swear to it. Mr. Adams was found to have no more than one halfpenny about him. This the clerk said, "was a great presumption that he was an old offender, by cunningly giving all the booty to the woman." To which all the rest readily assented.

This accident promising them better sport, than what they had proposed, they quitted their intention of catching birds, and unanimously resolved to proceed to the justice with the offenders. Being informed what a desperate fellow Adams was, they tied his hands behind him, and having hid their nets among the bushes, and the lantern being carried before them, they placed the two prisoners in their front, and then began their march: Adams not only submitting patiently to his own fate, but comforting and encouraging his companion under her sufferings.

Whilst they were on their way, the clerk informed the rest, that this adventure would prove a very beneficial one: for that they would be all entitled to their proportions of 80 l. for apprehending the robbers. This occasioned a contention concerning the parts which they had severally borne in taking them; one insisting, "he ought to have the greatest share, for he had first laid his hands on Adams;" another claiming a superior part for having first held the lantern to the man's face, on the ground, by which, he said, "the whole was discovered." The clerk claimed four fifths of the reward, for having proposed to search the prisoners; and likewise the carrying them before the justice: he said indeed, "in strict justice he ought to have the whole." These claims however they at last consented to refer to a future decision, but seemed all to agree that the clerk was entitled to a moiety. They then debated what money should be allotted to the young fellow, who had been employed only in holding the nets. He very modestly said, "that he did not apprehend any large proportion would fall to his share; but hoped they would allow him something he desired them to consider, that they had assigned their nets to his care, which prevented him from being as forward as any in laying hold of the robbers, (for so these innocent people were called;) that if he had not occupied the nets, some other must; concluding however that he should be contented with the smallest share imaginable, and should think that rather their bounty than his merit." But they were all unanimous in excluding him from any part whatever, the clerk particularly swearing, "if they give him a shilling, they might do what they pleased with the rest; for he would not concern himself with the affair." This contention was so hot, and so totally engaged the attention of all the parties, that a dexterous nimble thief, had he been in Mr. Adams's situation, would have taken care to have given the justice no trouble that evening.

Indeed it required not the art of a Shepherd to escape,[11] especially as the darkness of the night would have so much befriended him: but Adams trusted rather to his innocence than his heels and, without thinking of flight, which was easy, or resistance (which was impossible, as there were six lusty young fellows, besides the villain himself, present) he walked with perfect resignation the way they thought proper to conduct him.

Adams frequently vented himself in ejaculations during their journey; at last poor Joseph Andrews occurring to his mind, he could not refrain sighing forth his name, which being heard by his companion in affliction, she cried, with some vehemence, "Sure I should know that voice, you cannot certainly, sir, be Mr. Abraham Adams?" "Indeed damsel," says he, "that is my name; there is something also in your voice, which persuades me I have heard it before." "La, sir," says she, "don't you remember poor Fanny?" "How Fanny!" answered Adams, "indeed I very well remember you; what can have brought you hither?" "I have told you sir," replied she, "I was travelling towards London; but I thought you mentioned Joseph Andrews, pray what is become of him?" "I left him, child, this afternoon," said Adams, "in the stage-coach, in his way towards our parish, whither he is going to see you." "To see me? La, sir," answered Fanny, "sure you jeer me; what should he be going to see me for?" "Can you ask that?" replied Adams. "I hope Fanny, you are not inconstant; I assure you he deserves much better of you." "La! Mr. Adams," said she, "what is Mr. Joseph to me? I am sure I never had anything to say to him, but as one fellow-servant might to another." "I am sorry to hear this," said Adams, "a virtuous passion for a young man, is what no woman need be ashamed of. You either do not tell me truth, or you are false to a very worthy man." Adams then told her what had happened at the inn, to which she listened very attentively; and a sigh often escaped from her, notwithstanding her utmost endeavours to the contrary, nor could she prevent herself from asking a thousand questions, which would have assured anyone but Adams, who never saw farther into people than they desired

[11] Jack Sheppard had escaped prison four times in five months before being hanged as a bandit at twenty-two, in 1724.

to let him, of the truth of a passion she endeavoured to conceal. Indeed the fact was, that this poor girl having heard of Joseph's [that]$_{1\text{-}2}$ misfortune by some of the servants belonging to [the]$_{3}$ coach, which we have formerly mentioned to have stopt at the inn while the poor youth was confined to his bed, that instant abandoned the cow she was milking, and taking with her a little bundle of clothes under her arm, and all the money she was worth in her own purse, without consulting anyone, immediately set forward, in pursuit of one, whom, notwithstanding her shyness to the parson, she loved with inexpressible violence, though with the purest and most delicate passion. This shyness therefore, as we trust it will recommend her character to all our female readers, and not greatly surprise such of our males as are well acquainted with the younger part of the other sex, we shall not give ourselves any trouble to vindicate.

CHAP. XI.

What happened to them while before the justice. A chapter very full of learning.

THEIR fellow-travellers were so engaged in the hot dispute concerning the division of the reward for apprehending these innocent people, that they attended very little to their discourse. They were now arrived at the justice's house, and sent one of his servants in to acquaint his worship, that they had taken two robbers, and brought them before him. The justice, who was just returned from a fox-chase, and had not yet finished his dinner, ordered them to carry the prisoners into the stable, whither they were attended by all the servants in the house, and all the people in the neighbourhood, who flocked together to see them with as much curiosity as if there was something uncommon to be seen, or that a rogue did not look like other people.

The justice now being in the height of his mirth and his cups, bethought himself of the prisoners, and telling his company he believed they should have good sport in their examination, he ordered them into his presence. They had no sooner entered the room, than he began to revile them, saying, "that robberies on the highway were now grown so frequent, that people could not sleep safely in their beds, and assured them they both should be made examples of at the ensuing Assizes." After he had gone on some time in this manner, he was reminded by his clerk, "that it would be proper to take the deposition of the witnesses against them." Which he bid him do, and he would light his pipe in the meantime. Whilst the clerk was employed in writing down the depositions of the fellow who had pretended to be robbed, the justice employed himself in cracking jests on poor Fanny, in which he was seconded by all the company at table. One asked, "whether she was to be indicted for a *highwayman?*" Another whispered in her ear, "if she had not provided herself a great belly, he was at her service." A third said, "he warranted she was a relation of *Turpin*." To which one of the company, a great wit, shaking his head and then his sides, answered, "he believed she was nearer related to *Turpis*;" at which there was an universal laugh.[12] They were proceeding thus with the poor girl, when somebody smoking the cassock, peeping forth from under the greatcoat of Adams, cried out, "what have we here, a parson?" "How, sirrah," says the justice, "do you go a robbing in the dress of a clergyman? let me tell you, your habit will not entitle you to the *Benefit of the Clergy*." [13] "Yes," said the witty fellow, "he will have one benefit of clergy, he will be exalted above the heads of the people," at which there was a second laugh. And now the witty spark, seeing his jokes take, began to rise in spirits; and turning to Adams, challenged him to *cap*

[12] "Great belly": pregnant women usually escaped the death penalty. Dick Turpin (b. 1705) was hanged as a highwayman in 1739; *turpis* means "filthy" in Latin.

[13] For centuries in England, anyone who could read Latin (especially the opening words of the fifty-first psalm, hence known as the "neck verse") was presumed to be a clergyman and was exempt from trial in a secular court; he could be tried, if at all, by an ecclesiastical court, which could not exact the penalty of death. But by this time, the exemption had been increasingly removed, particularly for highwaymen.

verses,[14] and provoking him by giving the first blow, he repeated,

Molle meum levibus cord est vilebile Telis.[15]

Upon which Adams, with a look full of ineffable contempt, told him, he deserved scourging for his pronunciation. The witty fellow answered, "What do you deserve, doctor, for not being able to answer the first time? Why, I'll give you one, you blockhead — with an *S*?

Si licet, ut fulvum spectatur in igdibus haurum.[16]

"What canst not with an *M* neither? Thou art a pretty fellow for a parson —. Why didst not steal some of the parson's Latin as well as his gown?" Another at the table then answered, "If he had, you would have been too hard for him; I remember you at the college a very devil at this sport, I have seen you catch a fresh man: for nobody that knew you, would engage with you." "I have forgot those things now," cried the wit. "I believe I could have done pretty well formerly. — Let's see, what did I end with —an *M* again — ay ——

Mars, Bacchus, Apollo, virorum.[17]

I could have done it once." — "Ah! evil betide you, and so you can now," said the other, "nobody in this county will undertake

[14] To quote a line of Latin poetry beginning with the last letter of the line quoted by the opponent.

[15] The witty fellow misquotes "*molle meum levibusque cor est violabile telis*" ("my heart is soft, and vulnerable to the light spear"), from Ovid, *Heroides* XV.79.

[16] Another misquotation; it should be "*scilicet ut fulvum spectatur in ignibus aurum*" ("Indeed, as yellow gold is tested in flames"), from Ovid, *Tristia* I.v.25.

[17] This, with Adams's correction, is from one of the first lessons in William Lily's Latin grammar book (ca. 1527—actually in collaboration with John Colet and Erasmus), also known as the Eton Latin grammar, from which all the educated men of England, from Shakespeare through Fielding and onward through most of the nineteenth century, first learned their Latin. Lily wrote these grammatical rules and examples in dactylic hexameter verse, as an aid to memorizing. Adams's boy Dick is still working on the first lesson in IV.ix. The rule says that the names of gods (Mars, Bacchus, Apollo) and of men are masculine in nature.

you." Adams could hold no longer; "Friend," said he, "I have a boy not above eight years old, who would instruct thee, that the last verse runs thus:

Ut sunt Divorum, Mars, Bacchus, Apollo, virorum."

"I'll hold thee a guinea of that," said the wit, throwing the money on the table. — "And I'll go your halves," cried the other. "Done," answered Adams, but upon applying to his pocket, he was forced to retract, and own he had no money about him; which set them all a laughing, and confirmed the triumph of his adversary, which was not moderate, any more than the approbation he met with from the whole company, who told Adams he must go a little longer to school, before he attempted to attack that gentleman in Latin.

The clerk having finished the depositions, as well of the fellow himself, as of those who apprehended the prisoners, delivered them to the justice; having sworn the several witnesses, without reading a syllable, ordered his clerk to make the *Mittimus.*[18]

Adams then said, "he hoped he should not be condemned unheard." "No, no," cries the justice, "you will be asked what you have to say for yourself, when you come on your trial, we are not trying you now; I shall only commit you to gaol: if you can prove your innocence at *Size,* you will be found *Ignoramus,* and so no harm done." [19] "Is it no punishment, sir, for an innocent man to lie several months in gaol?" cries Adams: "I beg you would at least hear me before you sign the *Mittimus.*" "What signifies all you can say?" says the justice, "is it not here in black and white against you? I must tell you, you are a very impertinent fellow, to take up so much of my time. — So make haste with his *Mittimus.*"

The clerk now acquainted the justice, that among other suspicious things, as a penknife, *&c.* found in Adams's pocket, they had discovered a book written, as he apprehended, in ciphers: for no one could read a word in it. "Ay," says the justice, "this fellow may be more than a common robber, he may be

[18] The commitment to jail.

[19] If proved innocent at the *assize* (the session in court), you will be found *ignoramus* ("we are ignorant, we have insufficient evidence").

in a plot against the government. — Produce the book." Upon which the poor manuscript of Æschylus, which Adams had transcribed with his own hand, was brought forth; and the justice looking at it, shook his head, and turning to the prisoner, asked the meaning of those ciphers. "Ciphers!" answered Adams, "it is a manuscript of Æschylus." "Who? who?" said the justice. Adams repeated, "Æschylus." "That is an outlandish name," cried the clerk. "A fictitious name rather, I believe," said the justice. One of the company declared it looked very much like Greek. "Greek!" said the justice, "why 'tis all writing." "Nay," says the other, "I don't positively say it is so: for it is a very long time since I have seen any Greek. There's one," says he, turning to the parson of the parish, who was present, "will tell us immediately." The parson taking up the book, ⟨and⟩ [3] putting on his spectacles and gravity together, muttered some words to himself, and then pronounced aloud — "Ay indeed it is a Greek manuscript, a very fine piece of Antiquity. I make no doubt but it was stolen from the same clergyman from whom the rogue took the cassock." "What did the rascal mean by his Æschylus?" says the justice. "Pooh!" answered the doctor, with a contemptuous grin, "do you think that fellow knows anything of this book? Æschylus! ho! ho! ho! I see now what it is. — A manuscript of one of the fathers. I know a nobleman who would give a great deal of money for such a Piece of Antiquity. — Ay, ay, question and answer. The beginning is the cathechism in Greek. — Ay, — Ay, — *Pollaki toi* [20] — What's your name?" — "Ay, what's your name?" says the justice to Adams, who answered, "It is Æschylus, and I will maintain it." — "O it is," says the justice; "make Mr. Æschylus his *Mittimus.* I will teach you to banter me with a false name." 2

One of the company having looked steadfastly at Adams, asked him, "if he did not know Lady Booby?" Upon which Adams presently calling him to mind, answered in a rapture, "O squire, are you there? I believe you will inform his worship I am innocent." "I can indeed say," replied the squire, "that I am very much surprised to see you in this situation;" and then addressing himself to the justice, he said, "Sir, I assure you Mr.

[20] "Often," Aeschylus's *Seven Against Thebes,* line 227.

Adams is a clergyman as he appears, and a gentleman of a very good character. I wish you would inquire a little farther into this affair: for I am convinced of his innocence." "Nay," says the justice, "if he is a gentleman, and you are sure he is innocent, I don't desire to commit him, not I; I will commit the woman by herself, and take your bail for the gentleman; look into the book, clerk, and see how it is to take bail; come — and make the *Mittimus* for the woman as fast as you can." "Sir," cries Adams, "assure you she is as innocent as myself." "Perhaps," said the squire, "there may be some mistake; pray let us hear Mr. Adams's relation." "With all my heart," answered the justice, "and give the gentleman a glass to whet his whistle before he begins. I know how to behave myself to gentlemen as well as another. Nobody can say I have committed a gentleman since I have been in the commission." Adams then began the narrative, in which, though he was very prolix, he was uninterrupted ~~too~~ $_2$, unless by several *Hums* and *Ha's* of the justice, and his desire to repeat those parts which seemed to him most material. When he had finished; the justice, who, on what the squire had said, believed every syllable of his story on his bare affirmation, notwithstanding the depositions on oath to the contrary, began to let loose several *Rogues and Rascals* against the witness, whom he ordered to stand forth, but in vain: the said witness, long since finding what turn matters were like to take, had privily withdrawn, without attending the issue. The justice now flew into a violent passion, and was hardly prevailed with not to commit the innocent fellows, who had been imposed on as well as himself. He swore, "they had best find out the fellow who was guilty of perjury, and bring him before him within two days; or he would bind them all over to their good behaviour." They all promised to use their best endeavours to that purpose, and were dismissed. Then the justice insisted, that Mr. Adams should sit down and take a glass with him ⟨; and the parson of the parish delivered him back the manuscript without saying a word; nor would Adams, who plainly discerned his ignorance, expose it.⟩ $_2$ As for Fanny, she was, at her own request, recommended to the care of a maid-servant of the house, who helped her to new dress, and clean herself.

[they two only had been the competitors on whom]$_1$

The company in the parlour had not been long seated, before they were alarmed with a horrible uproar from without, where the persons who had apprehended Adams and Fanny, had been regaling, according to the custom of the house, with the justice's strong beer. These were all fallen together by the ears, and were cuffing each other without any mercy. The justice himself sallied out, and with the dignity of his presence, soon put an end to the fray. On his return into the parlour, he reported, "that the occasion of the quarrel, was no other than a dispute, to whom, if Adams had been convicted, the greater share of the reward for apprehending him had belonged." All the company laughed at this, except Adams, who taking his pipe from his mouth fetched a deep groan, and said, he was concerned to see so litigious a temper in men. That he remembered a story something like it in one of the parishes where his cure lay: "There was," continued he, "a competition between three young fellows, for the place of the clerk, which I disposed of, to the best of my abilities, according to merit: that is, I gave it to him who had the happiest knack at setting a psalm. The clerk was no sooner established in his place, than a contention began between the two disappointed candidates, concerning their excellence, each contending, [on whom, had they two been the only competitors,]$_2$ my election would have fallen. This dispute frequently disturbed the congregation, and introduced a discord into the psalmody, 'till I was forced to silence them both. But alas, the litigious spirit could not be stifled; and being no longer able to vent itself in singing, it now broke forth in fighting. It produced many battles, (for they were very near a match;) and, I believe, would have ended fatally, had not the death of the clerk given me an opportunity to promote one of them to his place; which presently put an end to the dispute, and entirely reconciled the contending parties." Adams then proceeded to make some philosophical observations on the folly of growing warm in disputes, in which neither party is interested. He then applied himself vigorously to smoking; and a long silence ensued, which was at length broken by the justice; who began to sing forth his own praises, and to value himself exceedingly on his nice discernment in the cause, which had lately been before him. He was quickly interrupted by Mr. Adams, between whom and his worship a dispute now arose, whether he ought not, in strictness of law, to have committed him, the said Adams; in which the latter maintained he ought to have been committed, and the justice as vehemently held he ought not. This had most probably produced a quarrel, (for both were very violent and positive in their opinions) had not Fanny accidentally heard, that a young fellow was going from the justice's house, to the very inn where the stage-coach in which Joseph was, put up. Upon this news, she immediately sent for the parson out of the parlour. Adams, when he found her resolute to go, (though she would not own the reason, but pretended she could not bear to see the faces of those who had suspected her of such a crime,) was as fully determined to go with her; he accordingly took leave of the justice and company, and so ended a dispute, in which the law seemed shamefully to intend to set a magistrate and a divine together by the ears.

CHAP. XII.

A very delightful adventure, as well to the persons concerned as to the good-natured reader.

ADAMS, Fanny, and the guide set out together, about one in the morning, the moon then just being risen. They had not gone above a mile, before a most violent storm of rain obliged them to take shelter in an inn, or rather alehouse; where Adams immediately procured himself a good fire, a toast and ale, and a pipe, and began to smoke with great content, utterly forgetting everything that had happened.

Fanny sat likewise down by the fire; but was much more impatient at the storm. She presently engaged the eyes of the host, his wife, the maid of the house, and the young fellow who was their guide; they all conceived they had never seen anything half so handsome: and indeed, reader, if thou art of an amorous hue, I advise thee to skip over the next paragraph; which to render our history perfect, we are obliged to set down, humbly hoping, that we may escape the fate of Pygmalion: for if it should happen to us or to thee to be struck with this picture, we should be perhaps in as helpless a condition as Narcissus; and might say to ourselves, *Quod petis est nusquam.*[21] Or if the finest features in it should set ~~a~~$_2$ Lady ——'s image before our eyes, we should be still in as bad situation, and might say to our desires, *Cœlum ipsum petimus stultitia.*[22]

Fanny was now in the nineteenth year of her age; she was tall and delicately shaped; but not one of those slender young women, who seem rather intended to hang up in the hall of an anatomist, than for any other purpose. On the contrary, she was so plump, that she seemed bursting through her tight stays, especially in the part which confined her swelling breasts. Nor did her hips want the assistance of a hoop to extend them. The exact shape of her arms, denoted the form of those limbs which she concealed; and though they were a little reddened by her labour, yet if her sleeve slipt above her elbow, or her handkerchief discovered any part of her neck, a whiteness appeared which the finest Italian paint would be unable to reach. Her hair was of a chestnut brown, and Nature had been extremely lavish to her of it, which she had cut, and on Sundays used to curl down her neck in the modern fashion. Her forehead was high, her eye-brows arched, and rather full than otherwise. Her eyes black and sparkling; her nose, just inclining to the Roman; her lips red and moist, and her under-lip, according to the opinion of the ladies, too pouting. Her teeth were white, but not exactly even. The small-pox had left one only mark on her chin, which was so large, it might have been mistaken for a dimple, had not her left cheek produced one so near a neighbour to it, that the former served only for a foil to the latter. Her complexion was fair, a little injured by the sun, but overspread with such a bloom, that the finest ladies would have exchanged all their white for it: add to these, a countenance in which though she was extremely bashful, a sensibility appeared almost incredible; and a sweetness, whenever she smiled, beyond either imita-

[21] "What you seek is nowhere" (Ovid, *Metamorphoses* III.433).
[22] "We foolishly seek heaven itself" (Horace, *Odes* I.iii.38).

tion or description. To conclude all, she had a natural gentility, superior to the acquisition of art, and which surprised all who beheld her.

This lovely creature was sitting by the fire with Adams, when her attention was suddenly engaged by a voice from an inner room, which sung the following song:

The Song

Say, Chloe, where must the swain stray
Who is by thy beauties undone,
To wash their remembrance away,
To what distant Lethe must run?
The wretch who is sentenc'd to die,
May escape and leave Justice behind;
From his country perhaps he may fly,
But O can he fly from his mind!

O rapture! unthought of before,
To be thus of Chloe possest;
Nor she, nor no tyrant's hard power,
Her image can tear from my breast.
But felt not Narcissus more joy,
With his eyes he beheld his lov'd charms?
Yet what he beheld, the fond boy
More eagerly wish'd in his arms.

How can it thy dear image be,
Which fills thus my bosom with woe?
Can aught bear resemblance to thee,
Which grief and not joy can bestow?
This counterfeit snatch from my heart,
Ye pow'rs, tho' with torment I rave,
Tho' mortal will prove the fell smart,
I then shall find rest in my grave.

Ah! see, the dear nymph o'er the plain,
Comes smiling and tripping along,
A thousand Loves dance in her train,
The Graces around her all throng.
To meet her soft Zephyrus flies,
And wafts all the sweets from the flow'rs;

Ah rogue! whilst he kisses her eyes,
More sweets from her breath he devours.

My soul, whilst I gaze, is on fire,
But her looks were so tender and kind,
My hope almost reach'd my desire,
And left lame Despair far behind.
Transported with madness I flew,
And eagerly seiz'd on my bliss;
Her bosom but half she withdrew,
But half she refus'd my fond kiss.

Advances like these made me bold,
I whisper'd her, Love,—we're alone,
The rest let Immortals unfold,
No language can tell but their own.
Ah! Chloe, expiring, I cry'd,
How long I thy cruelty bore?
Ah! Strephon, she blushing reply'd,
You ne'er was so pressing before.

Adams had been ruminating all this time on a passage in Æschylus, without attending in the least to the voice, though one of the most melodious that ever was heard, when casting his eyes on Fanny, he cried out, "Bless us, you look extremely pale." "Pale! Mr. Adams," says she; "O Jesus!" and fell backwards in her chair. Adams jumped up, flung his Æschylus into the fire, and fell a roaring to the people of the house for help. He soon summoned everyone into the room, and the songster among the rest: But, O reader, when this nightingale, who was no other than Joseph Andrews himself, saw his beloved Fanny in the situation we have described her, canst thou conceive the agitations of his mind? If thou canst not, waive that meditation to behold his happiness, when clasping her in his arms, he found life and blood returning into her cheeks; when he saw her open her beloved eyes, and heard her with the softest accent whisper, "Are you Joseph Andrews?" "Art thou my Fanny?" he answered eagerly, and pulling her to his heart, he imprinted numberless kisses on her lips, without considering who were present.

If prudes are offended at the lusciousness of this picture, they may take their eyes off from it, and survey Parson Adams dancing about the room in a rapture of joy. Some philosophers may perhaps doubt, whether he was not the happiest of the three; for the goodness of his heart enjoyed the blessings which were exulting in the breasts of both the other two, together with his own. But we shall leave such disquisitions as too deep for us, to those who are building some favourite hypotheses, which they will refuse no metaphysical rubbish to erect, and support: for our part, we give it clearly on the side of Joseph, whose happiness was not only greater than the parson's, but of longer duration: for as soon as the first tumults of Adams's rapture were over, he cast his eyes towards the fire, where Æschylus lay expiring; and immediately rescued the poor remains, to wit, the sheepskin covering, of his dear friend, [which was the work of his own hands, and]$_2$ had been his inseparable companion for [who]$_1$ upwards of thirty years.

Fanny had no sooner perfectly recovered herself, than she began to restrain the impetuosity of her transports; and, reflecting on what she had done and suffered in the presence of so many, she was immediately covered with confusion; and pushing Joseph gently from her, she begged him to be quiet; nor would admit of either kiss or embrace any longer. Then seeing Mrs. Slipslop she curtsied, and offered to advance to her; but that high woman would not return her curtsies; but casting her eyes another way, ~~she~~ $_2$ immediately withdrew into another room, muttering as she went, she wondered *who the Creature was.*

CHAP. XIII.

A dissertation concerning high people and low people, with Mrs. Slipslop's departure in no very good temper of mind, and the evil plight in which she left Adams and his company.

It will doubtless seem extremely odd to many readers, that Mrs. Slipslop, who had lived several years in the same house with Fanny, should in a short separation utterly forget her. And indeed the truth is, that she remembered her very well. As we would not willingly therefore, that anything should appear unnatural in this our history, we will endeavour to explain the reasons of ~~this~~ [2] her conduct; nor do we doubt being able to satisfy the most curious reader, that Mrs. Slipslop did not in the least deviate from the common road in this behaviour; and indeed, had she done otherwise, she must have descended below herself, and would have very justly been liable to censure.

Be it known then, that the human species are divided into two sorts of people, to wit, *High* People and *Low* People. As by High People, I would not be understood to mean persons literally born higher in their dimensions than the rest of the species, nor metaphorically those of exalted characters or abilities; so by Low People I cannot be construed to intend the reverse. High People signify no other than People of Fashion, and Low People those of no Fashion. Now, this word *Fashion*, hath by long use lost its original meaning, from which at present it gives us a very different idea: for I am deceived, if by persons of Fashion, we do not generally include a conception of birth and accomplishments superior to the herd of mankind; whereas in reality, nothing more was originally meant by a Person of Fashion, than a person who drest himself in the fashion of the times; and the word really and truly signifies no more at this day. Now the world being thus divided into People of Fashion and People of no Fashion, a fierce contention arose between them, nor would those of one party, to avoid suspicion, be seen publicly to speak to those of the other; though they often held a very good correspondence in private. In this contention, it is difficult to say which party succeeded: for whilst the People of Fashion seized several places to their own use, such as courts, assemblies, operas, balls, *&c.* the People of no Fashion, besides one royal place called his Majesty's Bear-Garden, have been in constant possession of all hops, fairs, revels, *&c.* Two places have been agreed to be divided between them, namely the church and the play-house; where they segregate themselves from each other in a remarkable manner: for as the People of Fashion exalt themselves at church over the heads of the People of no

Fashion; so in the play-house they abase themselves in the same degree under their feet. This distinction I have never met with anyone able to account for; it is sufficient, that so far from looking on each other as brethren in the Christian language, they seem scarce to regard each other as of the same species. This the terms *strange Persons*, *People one does not know*, *the Creature*, *Wretches*, *Beasts*, *Brutes*, and many other appellations evidently demonstrate; which Mrs. Slipslop having often heard her mistress use, thought she had also a right to use in her turn: and perhaps she was not mistaken; for these two parties, especially those bordering nearly on each other, to wit the lowest of the High, and the highest of the Low, often change their parties according to place and time; for those who are People of Fashion in one place, are often People of no Fashion in another: And with regard to time, it may not be unpleasant to survey the picture of dependence like a kind of ladder; as for instance, early in the morning arises the postilion, or some other boy which great families no more than great ships are without, and falls to brushing the clothes, and cleaning the shoes of John the footman, who being drest himself, applies his hands to the same labours for Mr. Second-hand the squire's gentleman; the gentleman in the like manner, a little later in the day, attends the squire; the squire is no sooner equipped, than he attends the levee of my lord; which is no sooner over, than my lord himself is seen at the levee of the favourite, who after his hour of homage is at an end, appears himself to pay homage to the levee of his sovereign. Nor is there perhaps, in this whole Ladder of Dependence, any one step at a greater distance from the other, than the first from the second: so that to a philosopher the question might only seem whether you would choose to be a great man at six in the morning, or at [two in the afternoon]$_2$. And yet [twelve]$_1$
there are scarce two of these, who do not think the least familiarity with the persons below them a condescension, and if they were to go one step farther, a degradation.

And now, reader, I hope thou wilt pardon this long digression, which seemed to me necessary to vindicate the great character of Mrs. Slipslop, from what low people, who have never seen high people, might think an absurdity: but we who know them, must have daily found very high persons know us in one place and not in another, to-day, and not to-morrow; ~~for~~$_2$ all which, it is difficult to account for, otherwise than I have here endeavoured; and perhaps, if the gods, according to the opinion of some, made men only to laugh at them, there is no part of our behaviour which answers the end of our creation better than this.

But to return to our history: Adams, who knew no more of this than the cat which sat on the table, imagining Mrs. Slipslop's memory had been much worse than it really was, followed her into the next room, crying out, "Madam Slipslop, here is one of your old acquaintance: Do but see what a fine woman she is grown since she left Lady Booby's service." "I think I *reflect* something of her," answered she with great dignity, "but I can't remember all the inferior servants in our family." She then proceeded to satisfy Adams's curiosity, by telling him, "when she arrived at the inn, she found a chaise ready for her; that her lady being expected very shortly in the country, she was obliged to make the utmost haste, and in *commensuration* of Joseph's lameness, she had taken him with her;" and lastly, "that the
[violence]$_1$ excessive [*virulence*]$_2$ of the storm had driven them into the house where he found them." After which, she acquainted Adams with his having left his horse, and exprest some wonder at his having strayed so far out of his way, and at meeting him, as she said, "in the company of that wench, who she feared was no better than she should be."

The horse was no sooner put into Adams's head, but he was immediately driven out by this reflection on the character of Fanny. He protested, "he believed there was not a chaster damsel in the universe. I heartily wish, I heartily wish," cried he, (snapping his fingers) "that all her betters were as good." He then proceeded to inform her of the accident of their meeting; but when he came to mention the circumstance of delivering her from the rape, she said, "she thought him properer for the army than the clergy: that it did not become a clergyman to lay violent hands on anyone, that he should have rather prayed that she might be strengthened." Adams said, "he was very far from being ashamed of what he had done;" she replied, "want of shame was not the *currycuristic* of a clergyman." This dialogue might have probably grown warmer, had not Joseph opportunely entered the room, to ask leave of Madam Slipslop to introduce Fanny: but she positively refused to admit any such trollops; and told him, "she would have been burnt before she would have suffered him to get into a chaise with her; if she had once *respected* him of having his sluts way-laid on the road for him," adding, "that Mr. Adams acted a very pretty part, and she did not doubt but to see him a bishop." He made the best bow he could, and cried out, "I thank you, madam, for that Right Reverend appellation, which I shall take all honest means to deserve." "Very honest means," she returned with a sneer, "to bring good people together." At these words, Adams took two or three strides a-cross the room, when the coachman came to inform Mrs. Slipslop, "that the storm was over, and the moon shone very bright." She then sent for Joseph, who was sitting without with his Fanny; and would have had him gone with her: but he peremptorily refused to leave Fanny behind; which threw the good woman into a violent rage. She said, "she would inform her lady what doings were carrying on, and did not doubt, but she would rid the parish of all such people;" and concluded a long speech full of bitterness and very hard words, with some reflections on the clergy, not decent to repeat: at last finding Joseph unmoveable, she flung herself into the chaise, casting a look at Fanny as she went, not unlike that which Cleopatra gives Octavia in the play.[23] To say the truth, she was most disagreeably disappointed by the presence of Fanny; she had from her first seeing Joseph at the inn, conceived hopes of something which might have been accomplished at an alehouse as well as a palace; in-

[23] Fielding seems to have in mind some actress interpreting the following lines and stage direction from Dryden's *All For Love* (III.i.471–76), where Cleopatra, Antony's mistress, meets Octavia, Antony's wife and Octavius Caesar's sister, for the first time:

Cleo. Were she the sister of the Thunderer Jove,
And bore her brother's lightning in her eyes,
Thus would I face my rival.

[*Meets* OCTAVIA *with* VENTIDIUS. OCTAVIA *bears up to her. Their Trains come up on either side.*]

Octav. I need not ask if you are Cleopatra; your haughty carriage—

Cleo. Shows I am a queen. . . .

deed it is probable, Mr. Adams had rescued more than Fanny from the danger of a rape that evening.

When the chaise had carried off the enraged Slipslop; Adams, Joseph, and Fanny assembled over the fire; where they had a great deal of innocent chat, pretty enough; but as possibly, it would not be very entertaining to the reader, we shall hasten to the morning; only observing that none of them went to bed that night. Adams, when he had smoked three pipes, took a comfortable nap in a great chair, and left the lovers, whose eyes were too well employed to permit any desire of shutting them, to enjoy by themselves during some hours, an happiness which none of my readers, who have never been in love, are capable of the least conception of, though we had as many tongues as
[had]$_{1}$ Homer [desired],$_{2}$[24] to describe it with, and which all true lovers will represent to their own minds without the least assistance from us.

Let it suffice then to say, that Fanny after a thousand entreaties at last gave up her whole soul to Joseph, and almost fainting in his arms, with a sigh infinitely softer and sweeter too, than any Arabian breeze, she whispered to his lips, which were then close to hers, "O Joseph, you have won me; I will be yours for ever." Joseph, having thanked her on his knees, and embraced her with an eagerness, which she now almost returned, leapt up in a rapture, and awakened the parson, earnestly begging him "that he would that instant join their hands together." Adams rebuked him for his request, and told him, "he would by no means consent to anything contrary to the forms of the Church, that he had no license, nor indeed would he advise him to obtain one. That the Church had prescribed a form, namely the Publication of Banns, with which all good Christians ought to comply, and to the omission of which, he attributed the many miseries which befell great folks in marriage; concluding, *As many as are joined together otherwise than G—'s Word doth allow, are not joined together by G—, neither is their matrimony lawful.*" Fanny agreed with the parson, saying to Joseph with a blush, "she assured him she would not consent to any such thing, and that she wondered at his offering it." In which resolution she was comforted and commended by Adams; and

[24] Homer asked for ten tongues and ten mouths (*Iliad* II.489).

Joseph was obliged to wait patiently till after the third Publication of the Banns, which however, he obtained the consent of Fanny in the presence of Adams to put in at their arrival.

The sun had been now risen some hours, when Joseph finding his leg surprisingly recovered, proposed to walk forwards, but when they were all ready to set out, an accident a little retarded them. This was no other than the reckoning which amounted to seven shillings; no great sum, if we consider the immense quantity of ale which Mr. Adams poured in. Indeed they had no objection to the reasonableness of the bill, but many to the probability of paying it; for the fellow who had taken poor Fanny's purse, had unluckily forgot to return it. So that the account stood thus:

Mr. *Adams* and Company Dr. ————	0	7	0
In Mr. *Adams's* Pocket, ————	0	0	6½
In Mr. *Joseph's*, ————	0	0	0
In Mrs. *Fanny's*, ————	0	0	0
Balance ————	0	6	5½

They stood silent some few minutes, staring at each other, when Adams whipt out on his toes, and asked the hostess "if there was no clergyman in that parish?" She answered, "there was." "Is he wealthy?" replied he, to which she likewise answered in the affirmative. Adams then snapping his fingers returned overjoyed to his companions, crying out, "*Eureka, Eureka;*" which not being understood, he told them in plain English "they need give themselves no trouble; for he had a brother in the parish, who would defray the reckoning, and that he would just step to his house and fetch the money, and return to them instantly."

CHAP. XIV.

An interview between Parson Adams and Parson Trulliber.

PARSON Adams came to the house of Parson Trulliber, whom he found stript into his waistcoat, with an apron on, and a pail in his hand, just come from serving his hogs; for Mr. Trulliber was a parson on Sundays, but all the other six might more properly be called a farmer. He occupied a small piece of land of his own, besides which he rented a considerable deal more. His [waited in]$_1$ wife milked his cows, [managed]$_2$ his dairy, and followed the markets with butter and eggs. The hogs fell chiefly to his care, which he carefully waited on at home, and attended to fairs; on which occasion he was liable to many jokes, his own size being with much ale rendered little inferior to that of the beasts he sold. He was indeed one of the largest men you should see, and could have acted the part of Sir John Falstaff without stuffing. Add to this, that the rotundity of his belly was considerably increased by the shortness of his stature, his shadow ascending very near as far in height when he lay on his back, as when he stood on his legs. His voice was loud and hoarse, and his accents extremely broad; to complete the whole, he had a stateliness in his gait, when he walked, not unlike that of a goose, only ⟨he stalked⟩$_2$ slower.

Mr. Trulliber being informed that somebody wanted to speak with him, immediately slipt off his apron, and clothed himself in an old night-gown,[25] being the dress in which he always saw his company at home. His wife who informed him of Mr. Adams's arrival, had made a small mistake; for she had told her husband, "she believed he⟨re⟩$_2$ was a man come for some of his hogs." This supposition made Mr. Trulliber hasten with the utmost expedition to attend his guest; he no sooner saw Adams, than not in the least doubting the cause of his errand to be what his wife had imagined, he told him, "he was come in very good time; that he expected a dealer that very afternoon;" and added, "they were all pure and fat, and upwards of twenty score a piece." Adams answered, "he believed he did not know him." "Yes, yes," cried Trulliber, "I have seen you often at fair; why, we have dealt before now mun, I warrant you; yes, yes," cries he, "I remember thy face very well, but won't mention a word more till you have seen them, though I have never sold thee a flitch of such bacon as is now in the sty." Upon which he laid violent hands on Adams, and dragged him into the hogs-sty,

[25] A dressing gown, or bathrobe.

which was indeed but two steps from his parlour window. They were no sooner arrived there than he cried out, "Do but handle them, step in, friend, art welcome to handle them whether dost buy or no." At which words opening the gate, he pushed Adams into the pig-sty, insisting on it, that he should handle them, before he would talk one word with him. Adams, whose natural complacence was beyond any artificial, was obliged to comply before he was suffered to explain himself, and laying hold on one of their tails, the unruly beast gave such a sudden spring, that he threw poor Adams all along in the mire. Trulliber instead of assisting him to get up, burst into a laughter, and entering the sty, said to Adams with some contempt, *Why, dost not know how to handle a hog?*" and was going to lay hold of one himself; but Adams, who thought he had carried his complacence far enough, was no sooner on his legs, than he escaped out of the reach of the animals, and cried out, *nihil habeo cum porcis:* [26] I am a clergyman, sir, and am not come to buy hogs." Trulliber answered, "he was sorry for the mistake; but that he must blame his wife;" adding, "she was a fool, and always committed blunders." He then desired him to walk in and clean himself, that he would only fasten up the sty and follow him. Adams desired leave to dry his greatcoat, wig, and hat by the fire, which Trulliber granted. Mrs. Trulliber would have brought him a basin of water to wash his face, but her husband bid her be quiet like a fool as she was, or she would commit more blunders, and then directed Adams to the pump. While Adams was thus employed, Trulliber conceiving no great respect for the appearance of his guest, fastened the parlour-door, and now conducted him into the kitchen; telling him, he believed a cup of drink would do him no harm, and whispered his wife to draw a little
of the worst [ale]$_2$. After a short silence, Adams said, "I fancy, [cider]$_1$
sir, you already perceive me to be a clergyman." "Ay, ay," cries Trulliber grinning; "I perceive you have some cassock; I will
not venture to [*caale*]$_2$ it a whole one." Adams answered, "it was [call]$_1$
indeed none of the best; but he had the misfortune to tear it about ten years ago in passing over a stile." Mrs. Trulliber returning with the drink, told her husband "she fancied the gentle-

[26] "I have nothing to do with hogs."

man was a traveller, and that he would be glad to eat a bit." Trulliber bid her "hold her impertinent tongue;" and asked her "if parsons used to travel without horses?" adding, "he supposed the gentleman had none by his having no boots on." "Yes, sir, yes," says Adams, "I have a horse, but I have left him behind me." "I am glad to hear you have one," says Trulliber; "for I assure you, I don't love to see clergymen on foot; it is not seemly nor suiting the dignity of the cloth." Here Trulliber made a long oration on the dignity of the cloth (or rather gown) not much worth relating, till his wife had spread the table and set a mess of porridge on it for his breakfast. He then said to
[call]$_1$ Adams, "I don't know, friend, how you came to [*caale*]$_2$ on me; however, as you are here, if you think proper to eat a morsel, you may." Adams accepted the invitation, and the two parsons sat down together, Mrs. Trulliber waiting behind her husband's chair, as was, it seems, her custom. Trulliber eat heartily, but scarce put anything in his mouth without finding fault with his wife's cookery. All which the poor woman bore patiently. Indeed she was so absolute an admirer of her husband's greatness and importance, of which she had frequent hints from his own mouth, that she almost carried her adoration to an opinion of his infallibility. To say the truth, the parson had exercised her more ways than one; and the pious woman had so well edified by her husband's sermons, that she had resolved to receive the good things of this world together with the bad. She had indeed been at first a little contentious; but he had long since got the better, partly by her love for *this*, partly by her fear of *that*, partly by her religion, partly by the respect he paid himself, and partly by that which he received from the parish: She had, in short, absolutely submitted, and now worshipped her husband as Sarah did Abraham, calling him (not Lord but) Master. Whilst they were at table, her husband gave her a fresh example of his greatness; for as she had just delivered a cup of ale to Adams, he
[*called*]$_1$ snatched it out of his hand, and crying out, *I* [*caal'd*]$_2$ *vurst,* swallowed down the ale. Adams denied it, and it was referred to the wife, who though her conscience was on the side of Adams, durst not give it against her husband. Upon which he said, "No, sir, no, I should not have been so rude to have taken it from you

if you had [*caal'd*]$_2$ *vurst;* but I'd have you know I'm a better [*called*]$_1$
man than to suffer the best He in the kingdom to drink before
me in my own house, when I [*caale*]$_2$ *vurst.*" [*call*]$_1$

As soon as their breakfast was ended, Adams began in the following manner: "I think, sir, it is high time to inform you of the business of my embassy. I am a traveller, and am passing this way in company with two young people, a lad and a damsel, my parishioners, towards my own cure: we stopt at a house of hospitality in the parish, where they directed me to you as having the cure." — "Though I am but a curate," says Trulliber, "I believe I am as warm as the vicar himself, or perhaps the rector of the next parish too; I believe I could buy them both." "Sir," cries Adams, "I rejoice thereat. Now, sir, my business is, that we are by various accidents stript of our money, and are not able to pay our reckoning, being seven shillings. I therefore request you to assist me with the loan of those seven shillings, and also seven shillings more, which peradventure I shall return to you; but if not, I am convinced you will joyfully embrace such an opportunity of laying up a treasure in a better place than any this world affords."

Suppose a stranger, who entered the chambers of a lawyer, being imagined a client, when the lawyer was preparing his palm for the fee, should pull out a writ against him. Suppose an apothecary, at the door of a chariot containing some great doctor of eminent skill, should, instead of directions to a patient, present him with a potion for himself. Suppose a Minister should, instead of a good round sum, treat my Lord —— or Sir —— or Esq; —— with a good broomstick. Suppose a civil companion, or a led captain should, instead of virtue, and honour, and beauty, and parts, and admiration, thunder vice and infamy, and ugliness, and folly, and contempt, in his patron's ears. Suppose when a tradesman first carries in his bill, the man of fashion should pay it; or suppose, if he did so, the tradesman should abate what he had overcharged on the supposition of waiting. In short — suppose what you will, you never can nor will suppose anything equal to the astonishment which seized on Trulliber, as soon as Adams had ended his speech. A while he rolled his eyes in silence, sometimes surveying Adams, then his wife, then casting them on the ground, then lifting them to Heaven. At last, he burst forth in the following accents. "Sir, I believe I know where to lay up my little treasure as well as another; I thank G— if I am not so warm as some, I am content; that is a blessing greater than riches; and he to whom that is given need ask no more. To be content with a little is greater than to possess the world, which a man may possess without being so. Lay up my treasure! what matters where a man's treasure is, whose heart is in the Scriptures? there is the treasure of a Christian." At these words the water ran from Adams's eyes; and catching Trulliber by the hand, in a rapture, "Brother," says he, "Heavens bless the accident by which I came to see you; I would have walked many a mile to have communed with you, and, believe me, I will shortly pay you a second visit: but my friends, I fancy, by this time, wonder at my stay, so let me have the money immediately." Trulliber then put on a stern look, and cried out, "Thou dost not intend to rob me?" At which the wife, bursting into tears, fell on her knees and roared out, "O dear sir! for Heaven's sake don't rob my master, we are but poor people." "Get up for a fool as thou art, and go about thy business," said Trulliber, "dost think the man will venture his life? he is a beggar and no robber." "Very true indeed," answered Adams. "I wish, with all my heart, the tithing-man was here," cries Trulliber,[27] "I would have thee punished as a vagabond for thy impudence. Fourteen shillings indeed! I won't give thee a farthing. I believe thou are no more a clergyman than the woman there, (pointing to his wife) but if thou art, dost deserve to have thy gown stript over thy shoulders, for running about the country in such a manner." "I forgive your suspicions," says Adams, "but suppose I am not a clergyman, I am nevertheless thy brother, and thou, as a Christian, much more as a clergyman, art obliged to relieve my distress." "Dost preach to me," replied Trulliber, "dost pretend to instruct me in my duty?" "Ifacks, a good story," cries Mrs. Trulliber, "to preach to my master." "Silence, woman," cries Trulliber; "I would have thee know, friend, (addressing himself to Adams,) I shall not learn my duty from

[27] The constable of a "tithing," a small district in rural England, originally the holdings of ten men with families.

such as thee; I know what charity is, better than to give to vagabonds." "Besides, if we were inclined, the Poors Rate obliges us to give so much charity," (cries the wife.) "Pugh! thou art a fool. Poors Reate! hold they nonsense," answered Trulliber, and then turning to Adams, he told him, "he would give him nothing." "I am sorry," answered Adams, "that you do know what charity is, since you practise it no better; I must tell you, if you trust to your knowledge for your justification, you will find yourself deceived, though you should add faith to it without good works." "Fellow," cries Trulliber, "Dost thou speak against faith in my house? Get out of my doors, I will no longer remain under the same roof with a wretch who speaks wantonly of faith and the Scriptures." "Name not the Scriptures," says Adams. "How, not name the Scriptures! Do you disbelieve the Scriptures?" cries Trulliber. "No, but you do," answered Adams, "if I may reason from your practice: for their commands are so explicit, and their rewards and punishments so immense, that it is impossible a man should steadfastly believe without obeying. Now, there is no command more express, no duty more frequently enjoined than charity. Whoever therefore is void of charity, I make no scruple of pronouncing that he is no Christian." "I would not advise thee, (says Trulliber) to say that I am no Christian. I won't take it of you: for I believe I am as good a man as thyself;" (and indeed, though he was now rather too corpulent for athletic exercises, he had in his youth been one of the best boxers and cudgel-players in the county.) His wife seeing him clench his fist, interposed, and begged him not to fight, but show himself [a]$_{2}$ true Christian, and take the law of [the]$_{1}$
him. As nothing could provoke Adams to strike, but an absolute assault on himself or his friend; he smiled at the angry look and gestures of Trulliber; and telling him, he was sorry to see such men in orders, departed without farther ceremony.

CHAP. XV.

An adventure, the consequence of a new instance which Parson Adams gave of his forgetfulness.

WHEN he came back to the inn, he found Joseph and Fanny sitting together. They were so far from thinking his absence long, as he had feared they would, that they never once missed or thought of him. Indeed, I have been often assured by both, that they spent these hours in a most delightful conversation: but as I never could prevail on either to relate it, so I cannot communicate it to the reader.

Adams acquainted the lovers with the ill success of his enterprise. They were all greatly confounded, none being able to propose any method of departing, 'till Joseph at last advised calling in the hostess, and desiring her to trust them; which Fanny said she despaired of her doing, as she was one of the sourest-faced women she had ever beheld.

But she was agreeably disappointed; for the hostess was no sooner asked the question than she readily agreed; and with a curtsy and smile, wished them a good journey. However, lest Fanny's skill in physiognomy should be called in question, we will venture to assign one reason, which might probably incline her to this confidence and good-humour. When Adams said he was going to visit his brother, he had unwittingly imposed on Joseph and Fanny; who both believed he had meant his natural brother, and not his brother in divinity; and had so informed the hostess on her inquiry after him. Now Mr. Trulliber had by his ⟨professions of⟩$_{2}$ piety, ⟨by his⟩$_{2}$ gravity, austerity, reserve, and the opinion of his great wealth, so great an authority in his parish, that they all lived in the utmost fear and apprehension of him. It was therefore no wonder that the hostess, who knew it was in his option whether she should ever sell another mug of drink, did not dare ⟨to⟩$_{2}$ affront his supposed brother by denying him credit.

They were now just on their departure, when Adams recollected he had left his greatcoat and hat at Mr. Trulliber's. As he was not desirous of renewing his visit, the hostess herself, having no servant at home, offered to fetch it.

This was an unfortunate expedient: for the hostess was soon undeceived in the opinion she had entertained of Adams, whom Trulliber abused in the grossest terms, especially when he heard he had had the assurance to pretend to be his near relation.

At her return therefore, she entirely changed her note. She said, "Folks might be ashamed of travelling about and pretending to be what they were not. That taxes were high, and for her part, she was obliged to pay for what she had; she could not therefore possibly, nor [would she]$_3$ trust anybody, no not her own father. That money was never scarcer, and she wanted to make up a sum. That she expected therefore they should pay their reckoning before they left the house."

[she would not]$_{1-2}$

Adams was now greatly perplexed: but as he knew that he could easily have borrowed such a sum [in]$_2$ his own parish, and as he knew he would have lent it himself to any mortal in distress; so he took fresh courage, and sallied out all round the parish, but to no purpose; he returned as pennyless as he went, groaning and lamenting, that it was possible in a country professing Christianity, for a wretch to starve in the midst of his fellow-creatures who abounded.

[at]$_1$

Whilst he was gone, the hostess who stayed as a sort of guard with Joseph and Fanny entertained them with the goodness of Parson Trulliber; and indeed he had not only a very good character, as to other qualities, in the neighbourhood, but was reputed a man of great charity⟨: for though he never gave a farthing, he had always that word in his mouth⟩$_2$.

Adams was no sooner returned the second time, than the storm grew exceeding high, the hostess declaring among other things, that if they offered to stir without paying her, she would soon overtake them with a warrant.

Plato or Aristotle, or somebody else hath said, THAT WHEN THE MOST EXQUISITE CUNNING FAILS, CHANCE OFTEN HITS THE MARK, AND THAT BY MEANS THE LEAST EXPECTED. Virgil expresses this very boldly:

Turne quod optanti Divûm promittere nemo
Auderet, volvenda Dies en attulit ultro.[28]

I would quote more great men if I could: but my memory not permitting me, I will proceed to exemplify these observations by the following instance.

There chanced (for Adams had not cunning enough to contrive it) to be at that time in the alehouse, a fellow, who had been formerly a drummer in an Irish regiment, and now travelled the country as a pedlar. This man having attentively listened to the discourse of the hostess, at last took Adams aside, and asked him what the sum was for which they were detained. As soon as he was informed, he sighed and said, "he was sorry it was so much: for that he had no more than six shillings and sixpence in his pocket, which he would lend them with all his heart." Adams gave a caper, and cried out, "it would do: for that he had sixpence himself." And thus these poor people, who could not engage the compassion of riches and piety, were at length delivered out of their distress by the charity of a poor pedlar.

I shall refer it to my reader, to make what observations he pleases on this incident: it is sufficient for me to inform him, that after Adams and his companions had returned him a thousand thanks, and told him where he might call to be repaid, they all sallied out of the house without any compliments from their hostess, or indeed without paying her any; Adams declaring, he would take particular care never to call there again, and she on her side assuring them she wanted no such guests.

CHAP. XVI.

A very curious adventure, in which Mr. Adams gave a much greater instance of the honest simplicity of his heart than of his experience in the ways of this world.

OUR travellers had walked about two miles from that inn, which they had more reason to have mistaken for a castle, than

[28] "Turnus, what no god would have dared promise your wishes, look, the rolling day has more than brought" (*Aeneid* IX.6–7).

Don Quixote ever had any of those in which he sojourned; seeing they had met with such difficulty in escaping out if its walls; when they came to a parish, and beheld a sign of invitation hanging out. A gentleman sat smoking a pipe at the door; of whom Adams inquired the road, and received so courteous and obliging an answer, accompanied with so smiling a countenance, that the good parson, whose heart was naturally disposed to love and affection, began to ask several other questions; particularly the name of the parish, and who was the owner of a large house whose front they then had in prospect. The gentleman answered as obligingly as before; and as to the house, acquainted him it was his own. He then proceeded in the following manner: "Sir, I presume by your habit you are a clergyman: and as you are travelling on foot, I suppose a glass of good beer will not be disagreeable to you; and I can recommend my landlord's within, as some of the best in all this county. What say you, will you halt a little and let us take a pipe together: there is no better tobacco in the kingdom?" This proposal was not displeasing to Adams, who had allayed his thirst that day, with no better liquor than what Mrs. Trulliber's cellar had produced; and which was indeed little superior either in richness or flavour to that which distilled from those grains her generous husband bestowed on his hogs. Having therefore abundantly thanked the gentleman for his kind invitation, and bid Joseph and Fanny follow him, he entered the ale-house, where a large loaf and cheese and a pitcher of beer, which truly answered the character given of it, being set before them, the three travellers fell to eating with appetites infinitely more voracious than are to be found at the most exquisite eating-houses in the parish of St. James's.

The gentleman expressed great delight in the hearty and cheerful behaviour of Adams; and particularly in the familiarity with which he conversed with Joseph and Fanny, whom he often called his children, a term he explained to mean no more than his parishioners; saying, he looked on all those whom God had entrusted to his cure, to stand to him in that relation. The gentleman shaking him by the hand highly applauded those sentiments. "They are indeed," says he, "the true principles of a Christian divine; and I heartily wish they were universal: but on the contrary, I am sorry to say the parson of our parish instead of esteeming his poor parishioners as a part of his family, seems rather to consider them as not of the same species with himself. He seldom speaks to any unless some few of the richest of us; nay indeed, he will not move his hat to the others. I often laugh when I behold him on Sundays strutting along the churchyard like a turkey-cock, through rows of his parishioners; who bow to him with as much submission and are as unregarded as a set of servile courtiers by the proudest prince in Christendom. But if such temporal pride is ridiculous, surely the spiritual is odious and detestable: if such a puffed up empty human bladder strutting in princely robes, justly moves one's derision; surely in the habit of a priest it must raise our scorn."

"Doubtless," answered Adams, "your opinion is right; but I hope such examples are rare. The clergy whom I have the honour to know, maintain a different behaviour; and you will allow me, sir, that the readiness, which too many of the laity show to contemn the order, may be one reason of their avoiding too much humility." "Very true indeed," says the gentleman; "I find, sir, you are a man of excellent sense, and am happy in this opportunity of knowing you: perhaps, our accidental meeting may not be disadvantageous to you neither. At present, I shall only say to you, that the incumbent of this living is old and infirm; and that it is in my gift. Doctor, give me your hand; and assure yourself of it at his decease." Adams told him, "he was never more confounded in his life, than at his utter incapacity to make any return to such noble and unmerited generosity." "A mere trifle, sir," cries the gentleman, "scarce worth your acceptance; a little more than three hundred a year. I wish it was double the value for your sake." Adams bowed, and cried from the emotions of his gratitude; when the other asked him, "if he was married, or had any children, besides those in the spiritual sense he had mentioned." "Sir," replied the parson, "I have a wife and six at your service." "That is unlucky," says the gentleman; "for I would otherwise have taken you into my own house as my chaplain: however, I have another in the parish, (for the parsonage-house is not good enough) which I will furnish for you. Pray does your wife understand a dairy?" "I can't profess she does," says Adams. "I am sorry for it," quoth the gentleman; "I would have given you half a dozen cows, and

very good grounds to have maintained them." "Sir," said Adams, in an ecstasy, "you are too liberal; indeed you are." "Not at all," cries the gentleman, "I esteem riches only as they give me an opportunity of doing good; and I never saw one whom I had ⟨a⟩$_2$ greater inclination to serve." At which words he shook him heartily by the hand, and told him he had sufficient room in his house to entertain him and his friends. Adams begged he might give him no such trouble, that they could be very well accommodated in the house where they were; forgetting they had not a sixpenny piece among them. The gentleman would not be denied; and informing himself how far they were travelling, he said it was too long a journey to take on foot, and begged that they would favour him, by suffering him to lend them a servant and horses; adding withal, that if they would do him the pleasure of their company only two days, he would furnish them with his coach and six. Adams turning to Joseph, said, "How lucky is this gentleman's goodness to you, who I am afraid would be scarce able to hold out on your lame leg," and then addressing the person who made him these liberal promises, after much bowing, he cried out, "Blessed be the hour which first introduced me to a man of your charity: you are indeed a Christian of the true primitive kind, and an honour to the country wherein you live. I would willingly have taken a pilgrimage to the Holy Land to have beheld you: for the advantages which we draw from your goodness, give me little pleasure, in comparison of what I enjoy for your own sake; when I consider the treasures you are by these means laying up for yourself in a country that passeth not away. We will therefore, most generous sir, accept your goodness, as well the entertainment you have so kindly offered us at your house this evening, as the accommodation of your horses to-morrow morning." He then began to search for his hat, as did Joseph for his; and both they and Fanny were in order of departure, when the gentleman stopping short, and seeming to meditate by himself for the space of about a minute, exclaimed thus: "Sure never anything was so unlucky; I had forgot that my house-keeper was gone abroad, and [hath]$_2$ [has]$_1$ [29]
locked up all my rooms; indeed I would break them open for

[29] Fielding corrected this one, but apparently missed the *has* three lines below, which remained throughout the five editions in his lifetime.

you, but shall not be able to furnish you with a bed; for she has likewise put away all my linen. I am glad it entered into my head before I had given you the trouble of walking there; besides, I believe you will find better accommodations here than you expected. Landlord, you can provide good beds for these people, can't you?" "Yes and please your worship," cries the host, "and such as no Lord or Justice of the Peace in the kingdom need be ashamed to lie in." "I am heartily sorry," says the gentleman, "for this disappointment. I am resolved I will never suffer her to carry away the keys again." "Pray, sir, let it not make you uneasy," cries Adams, "we shall do very well here; and the loan of your horses is a favour, we shall be incapable of making any return to." "Ay!" said the squire, "the horses shall attend you here at what hour in the morning you please." And now after many civilities too tedious to enumerate, many squeezes by the hand, with most affectionate looks and smiles on each other, and after appointing the horses at seven the next morning, the gentleman took his leave of them, and departed to his own house. Adams and his companions returned to the table, where the parson smoked another pipe, and then they all retired to rest.

Mr. Adams rose very early and called Joseph out of his bed, between whom a very fierce dispute ensued, whether Fanny should ride behind Joseph, or behind the gentleman's servant; Joseph insisting on it, that he was perfectly recovered, and was as capable of taking care of Fanny, as any other person could be. But Adams would not agree to it, and declared he would not trust her behind him; for that he was weaker than he imagined himself to be.

This dispute continued a long time, and had begun to be very hot, when a servant arrived from their good friend, to acquaint them, that he was unfortunately prevented from lending them any horses; for that his groom had, unknown to him, put his whole stable under a course of physic.

This advice presently struck the two disputants dumb; Adams cried out, "Was ever anything so unlucky as this poor gentleman? I protest I am more sorry on his account, than my own. You see, Joseph, how this good-natured man is treated by his servants; one locks up his linen, another physics his horses; and I suppose by his being at this house last night, the butler had locked up his cellar. Bless us! how good-nature is used in this world! I protest I am more concerned on his account than my own." "So am not I," cries Joseph; "not that I am much troubled about walking on foot; all my concern is, how we shall get out of the house; unless God sends another pedlar to redeem us. But certainly, this gentleman has such an affection for you, that he would lend you a larger sum than we owe here; which is not above four or five shillings." "Very true, child," answered Adams; "I will write a letter to him, and will even venture to solicit him for three half-crowns; there will be no harm in having two or three shillings in our pockets: as we have full forty miles to travel, we may possibly have occasion for them."

Fanny being now risen, Joseph paid her a visit, and left Adams to write his letter; which having finished, he dispatched a boy with it to the gentleman, and then seated himself by the door, lighted his pipe, and betook himself to meditation.

The boy staying longer than seemed to be necessary, Joseph who with Fanny was now returned to the parson, expressed some apprehensions, that the gentleman's steward had locked up his purse too. To which Adams answered, "It might very possibly be; and he should wonder at no liberties which the Devil might put into the head of a wicked servant to take with so worthy a master:" but added, "that as the sum was so small, so noble a gentleman would be easily able to procure it in the parish; though he had it not in his own pocket. Indeed," says he, "if it was four or five guineas, or any such large quantity of money, it might be a different matter."

They were now sat down to breakfast over some toast and ale, when the boy returned; and informed them, that the gentleman was not at home. "Very well," cries Adams; "but why, child, did you not stay 'till his return? Go back again, my good boy, and wait for his coming home: he cannot be gone far, as his horses are all sick; and besides, he had no intention to go abroad; for he invited us to spend this day and to-morrow at his house. Therefore, go back, child, and tarry 'till his return home." The messenger departed, and was back again with great expedition;

bringing an account, that the gentleman was gone a long journey, and would not be at home again this month. At these words, Adams seemed greatly confounded, saying, "This must be a sudden accident, as the sickness or death of a relation, or some such unforeseen misfortune;" and then turning to Joseph cried, "I wish you had reminded me to have borrowed this money last night." Joseph smiling, answered, "he was very much deceived, if the gentleman would not have found some excuse to avoid lending it. I own," says he, "I was never much pleased with his professing so much kindness for you at first sight: for I have heard the gentlemen of our cloth in London tell many such stories of their masters. But when the boy brought the message back of his not being at home, I presently knew what would follow; for whenever a man of fashion doth not care to fulfil his promises, the custom is, to order his servants that he will never be at home to the person so promised. In London they call it *denying him*. I have myself denied Sir Thomas
[has]$_1$ Booby above a hundred times; and when the man [hath]$_2$ danced attendance for about a month, or sometimes longer, he is acquainted in the end, that the gentleman is gone out of town, and could do nothing in the business." "Good Lord!" says Adams; "What wickedness is there in the Christian world? I profess, almost equal to what I have read of the heathens. But surely, Joseph, your suspicions of this gentleman must be unjust; for, what a silly fellow must he be, who would do the Devil's work for nothing? and canst thou tell me any interest he could possibly propose to himself by deceiving us in his professions?" "It is not for me," answered Joseph, "to give reasons for what men do, to a gentleman of your learning." "You say right," quoth Adams; "Knowledge of men is only to be learnt from books, Plato and Seneca for that; and those are authors, I am afraid child, you never read." "Not I, sir, truly," answered Joseph; "all I know is, it is a maxim among the gentlemen of our cloth, that those masters who promise the most perform the least; and I have often heard them say, they have found the largest vails in those families, where they were not promised any. But, sir, instead of considering any farther these matters, it would be our wisest way to contrive some method of getting out

of this house: for the generous gentleman, instead of doing us any service, hath left us the whole reckoning to pay." Adams was going to answer, when their host came in; and with a kind of jeering-smile said, "Well, masters! the squire [hath]$_2$ not [has]$_1$ sent his horses for you yet. Laud help me! how easily some folks make promises!" "How!" says Adams, "have you ever known him do anything of this kind before?" "Aye marry have I," answered the host; "it is no business of mine, you know, sir, to say anything to a gentleman to his face: but now he is not here, I will assure you, he [hath]$_2$ not his fellow within the three [has]$_1$ next market-towns. I own, I could not help laughing, when I heard him offer you the living; for thereby hangs a good jest. I thought he would have offered you my house next; for one is no more his to dispose of than the other." At these words, Adams blessing himself, declared, "he had never read of such a monster; but what vexes me most," says he, "is, that he hath decoyed us into running up a long debt with you, which we are not able to pay; for we have no money about us; and what is worse, live at such a distance, that if you should trust us, I am afraid you would lose your money, for want of our finding any conveniency of sending it." "Trust you, master!" says the host, "that I will with all my heart; I honour the clergy too much to deny trusting one of them for such a trifle; besides, I like your fear of never paying me. I have lost many a debt in my lifetime; but was promised to be paid them all in a very short time. I will score this reckoning for the novelty of it. It is the first I do assure you of its kind. But what say you, master, shall we have t'other pot before we part? It will waste but a little chalk more; and if you never pay me a shilling, the loss will not ruin me." Adams liked the invitation very well; especially as it was delivered with so hearty an accent.—He shook his host by the hand, and thanking him, said, "he would tarry another pot, rather for the pleasure of such worthy company than for the liquor;" adding, "he was glad to find some Christians left in the kingdom; for that he almost began to suspect that he was sojourning in a country inhabited only by Jews and Turks."

The kind host produced the liquor, and Joseph with Fanny retired into the garden; where while they solaced themselves with amorous discourse, Adams sat down with his host; and both filling their glasses and lighting their pipes, they began that dialogue, which the reader will find in the next chapter.

CHAP. XVII.

A dialogue between Mr. Abraham Adams and his host, which, by the disagreement in their opinions seemed to threaten an unlucky catastrophe, had it not been timely prevented by the return of the lovers.

"'SIR,'' said the host, "I assure you, you are not the first to whom our squire hath promised more than he hath performed. He is so famous for this practice, that his word will not be taken for much by those who know him. I remember a young fellow whom he promised his parents to make an exciseman. The poor people, who could ill afford it, bred their son to writing and accounts, and other learning, to qualify him for the place; and the boy held up his head above his condition with these hopes; nor would he go to plough, nor to any other kind of work; and went constantly drest as fine as could be, with two clean Holland shirts a week, and this for several years; 'till at last he followed the squire up to London, thinking there to mind him of his promises: but he could never get sight of him. So that being out of money and business, he fell into evil company, and wicked courses; and in the end came to a sentence of transportation, the news of which broke the mother's heart. ⟨I will tell you another true story of him:⟩ 2 There was a neighbour of mine, a farmer, who had two sons whom he bred up to the business. Pretty lads they were; nothing would serve the squire, but that the youngest must be made a parson. Upon which, he persuaded the father to send him to school, promising, that he would afterwards maintain him at the university; and when he was of ⟨a⟩ 2 proper age, give him a living. But after the lad had been seven years at school, and his father brought him to the squire with a letter from his master, that he was fit for the university; the squire, instead of minding his promise, or sending him thither at his expense, only told his father, that the young man was a fine scholar; and it was pity he could not afford to keep him at Oxford for four or five years more, by which time, if he could get him a curacy, he might have him ordained. The farmer said, 'he was not a man sufficient to do any such thing.' 'Why then,' answered the squire; 'I am very sorry you have given him so much learning; for if he cannot get his living by that, it will rather spoil him for anything else; and your other son who can hardly write his name, will do more at ploughing and sowing, and is in a better condition than he': and indeed so it proved; for the poor lad not finding friends to maintain him in his learning, as he had expected; and being unwilling to work, fell to drinking, though he was a very sober lad before; and in a short time, partly with grief, and partly with good liquor, fell into a consumption and died. ⟨Nay, I can tell you more still:⟩ $_2$ There was another, a young woman, and the handsomest in all this neighbourhood, whom he enticed up to London, promising to make her a gentlewoman to one of your women of quality: but instead of keeping his word, we have since heard, after having a child by her himself, she became a common whore; then kept a coffee-house in Covent-Garden, and a little after died of the French distemper in a gaol. I could tell you many more stories: but how do you imagine he served me myself? You must know, sir, I was bred a sea-faring man, and have been many voyages; 'till at last I came to be master of a ship myself, and was in a fair way of making a fortune, when I was attacked by one of those cursed *guarda-costas,* who took our ships before the beginning of the war; [30] and after a fight wherein I lost the greater part of my crew, my rigging ⟨being⟩ $_2$ all demolished,

[30] Spanish coast guards in the Caribbean attacked British merchantmen, who were actually violating a treaty forbidding them to trade in Spanish waters. War with Spain was declared on October 19, 1739—known as the War of Jenkins's Ear, because a Spanish guarda-costa captain had cut off the ear of a British captain, Richard Jenkins, in 1731. After December 16, 1740, when Prussia invaded Silesia, the war branched out into the War of the Austrian Succession (England, Holland, Sardinia, and others, against Prussia, Austria, Spain, France, Bavaria, and others). The war was gathering force during 1741 at the time of Parson Adams's conversation. The war continued until 1748.

and two shots received between wind and water, I was forced to strike. The villains carried off my ship, a brigantine of 150 tons⟨, a pretty creature she was,⟩ [2] and put me, a man, and a boy, into a little bad pink, in which with much ado, we at last made Falmouth; though I believe the Spaniards did not imagine she could possibly live a day at sea. Upon my return hither, where my wife who was of this country then lived, the squire told me, he was so pleased with the defence I had made against the enemy, that he did not fear getting me promoted to a lieutenancy of a man of war, if I would accept of it, which I thankfully assured him I would. Well, sir, two or three years passed, during which I had many repeated promises, not only from the squire, but (as he told me) from the Lords of the Admiralty. He never returned from London, but I was assured I might be satisfied now, for I was certain of the first vacancy; and what surprises me still, when I reflect on it, these assurances were given me with no less confidence, after so many disappointments, than at first. At last, sir, growing weary and somewhat suspicious after so much delay, I wrote to a friend in London, who I knew had some acquaintance at the best house in the Admiralty; and desired him to back the squire's interest: for indeed, I feared he had solicited the affair with more coldness than he pretended.— And what answer do you think my friend sent me? — Truly, sir, he acquainted me, that the squire had never mentioned my name at the Admiralty in his life; and unless I had much faithfuller interest, advised me to give over my pretensions, which I immediately did; and with the concurrence of my wife, resolved to set up an alehouse, where you are heartily welcome: and so my service to you; and may the squire, and all such sneaking rascals go to the Devil together." "O fie!" says Adams; "O fie! He is indeed a wicked man; but G— will, I hope, turn his heart to repentance. Nay, if he could but once see the meanness of this detestable vice; would he but once reflect that he is one of the most scandalous as well as pernicious liars; sure he must despise himself to so intolerable a degree, that it would be impossible for him to continue a moment in such a course. And to confess the truth, notwithstanding the baseness of this character, which he hath too well deserved, he hath in his countenance sufficient symptoms of that *bona indoles*, that sweetness of disposition which furnishes out a good Christian." "Ah! master, master, (says the host,) if you had travelled as far as I have, and conversed with the many nations where I have traded, you would not give any credit to a man's countenance. Symptoms in his countenance, quotha! I would look there perhaps to see whether a man had had the small-pox, but for nothing else!" He spoke this with so little regard to the parson's observation, that it a good deal nettled him; and taking the pipe hastily from his mouth, he thus answered: — "Master of mine, perhaps I have travelled a great deal farther than you without the assistance of a ship. Do you imagine sailing by different cities or countries is travelling? No.

Cœlum non animum mutant qui trans mare currunt.[31]

I can go farther in an afternoon, than you in a twelve-month. What, I suppose you have seen the Pillars of Hercules, and perhaps the walls of Carthage. Nay, you may have heard Scylla, and seen Charybdis; you may have entered the closet where Archimedes was found at the taking Syracuse. I suppose you have sailed among the Cyclades, and passed the famous straits which take their name from the unfortunate Helle, whose fate is sweetly described by Apollonius Rhodius; you have passed the very spot, I conceive, where Dædalus fell into that sea, his waxen wings being melted by the sun; you have traversed the Euxine Sea, I make no doubt; nay, you may have been on the banks of the Caspian, and called at Colchis, to see if there is ever another Golden Fleece." — "Not I truly, master," answered the host, "I never touched at any of these places." "But I have been at all these," replied Adams. "Then I suppose," cries the host, "you have been at the East Indies, for there are no such, I will be sworn, either in the West or the Levant." "Pray where's the Levant?" quoth Adams, "that should be in the East Indies by right." — "O ho! you are a pretty traveller," cries the host, "and not know the Levant. My service to you, master; you must not talk of these things with me! you must not tip us the traveller;

31 "Those who sail across the sea change sky, not mind" (Horace, *Epistles* I.xi.27).

it won't go here." "Since thou art so dull to misunderstand me still," quoth Adams, "I will inform thee; the travelling I mean is in books, the only way of travelling by which any knowledge is to be acquired. From them I learn what I asserted just now, that Nature generally imprints such a portraiture of the mind in the countenance, that a skilful physiognomist will rarely be deceived. I presume you have never read the story of Socrates to this purpose, and therefore I will tell it you. A certain physiognomist asserted of Socrates, that he plainly discovered by his features that he was a rogue in his nature. A character so contrary to the tenour of all this great man's actions, and the generally received opinion concerning him, [incensed the boys of Athens so that they]$_2$ threw stones at the physiognomist, and would have demolished him for his ignorance, had not Socrates himself prevented them by confessing the truth of his observations, and acknowledging that though he corrected his disposition by philosophy, he was indeed naturally as inclined to vice as had been predicated of him. Now, pray resolve me, — How should a man know this story, if he had not read it?" "Well master," said the host, "and what signifies it whether a man knows it or no? He who goes abroad as I have done, will always have opportunities enough of knowing the world, without troubling his head with Socrates, or any such fellows." — "Friend," cries Adams, "if a man would sail round the world, and anchor in every harbour of it, without learning, he would return home as ignorant as he went out." "Lord help you," answered the host, "there was my boatswain, poor fellow! he could scarce either write or read, and yet he would navigate a ship with any master of a man of war; and a very pretty knowledge of trade he had too." "Trade," answered Adams, "as Aristotle proves in his first chapter of *Politics,* is below a philosopher, and unnatural as it is managed now." The host looked steadfastly at Adams, and after a minute's silence asked him "if he was one of the writers of the *Gazetteers?* for I have heard," says he, "they are writ by parsons." "*Gazetteers!*" answered Adams. "What is that?" "It is a dirty news-paper," replied the host, "which hath been given away all over the nation for these many years to abuse trade and honest men, which I would not suffer to lie on

[that the boys of Athens]$_1$

my table, though it hath been offered me for nothing."[32] "Not I truly," said Adams, "I never write anything but sermons, and I assure you I am no enemy to trade, whilst it is consistent with honesty; nay, I have always looked on the tradesman, as a very valuable member of society, and perhaps inferior to none but the man of learning." "No, I believe he is not, nor to him neither," answered the host. "Of what use would learning be in a country without trade? What would all you parsons do to clothe your backs and feed your bellies? Who fetches you your silks and your linens, and your wines, and all the other necessaries of life? I speak chiefly with regard to the sailors." "You should say the extravagancies of life," replied the parson, "but admit they were the necessaries, there is something more necessary than life itself, which is provided by learning; I mean the learning of the clergy. Who clothes you with Piety, Meekness, Humility, Charity, Patience, and all the other Christian Virtues? Who feeds your souls with the Milk of brotherly Love, and diets them with all the dainty Food of Holiness, which at once cleanses them of all impure carnal affections, and fattens them with the truly rich Spirit of Grace? — Who doth this?" "Ay, who indeed!" cries the host; "for I do not remember ever to have seen any such clothing or such feeding. And so in the mean time, master, my service to you." Adams was going to answer with some severity, when Joseph and Fanny returned, and pressed his departure so eagerly, that he would not refuse them; and so grasping his crabstick, he took leave of his host, (neither of them being so well pleased with each other as they had been at their first sitting down together) and with Joseph and Fanny, who both expressed much impatience, departed; and now all together renewed their journey.

[32] *The Daily Gazetteer* was subsidized by Prime Minister Robert Walpole and from time to time "given away all over the nation" by him. Several clergymen had written for it.

THE HISTORY OF THE ADVENTURES OF *Joseph Andrews*, and of his Friend Mr. *Abraham Adams*

BOOK III.

CHAP. I.

Matter prefatory in praise of Biography.

NOTWITHSTANDING the preference which may be vulgarly given to the authority of those Romance-writers, who entitle their books, the *History of England*, the *History of France*, of *Spain*, &c. it is most certain,
[their works]$_{1}$ that truth is only to be found in [the works of those]$_{2}$ who celebrate the lives of great men, and are commonly called biographers, as the others should indeed be termed topographers or chorographers: words which might well mark the distinction between them; it being the business of the latter chiefly to describe countries and cities, which, with the assistance of maps, they do

pretty justly, and may be depended upon: But as to the actions and characters of men, their writings are not quite so authentic, of which there needs no other proof than those eternal contradictions, occurring between two topographers who undertake the history of the same country: For instance, between my Lord Clarendon and Mr. Whitlock, between Mr. Echard and Rapin, and many others; where facts being set forth in a different light, every reader believes as he pleases, [and indeed the more judicious and suspicious very justly esteem the whole as no other than a Romance, in which the writer hath indulged a happy and fertile invention. But though these widely differ in the narrative of facts; some ascribing victory to the one, and others to the other party: Some representing the same man as a rogue, {to whom others give}$_{4}$ a great and honest character, yet]$_{2}$ all agree in the scene where [the fact]$_{3}$ is supposed to have happened ⟨; and where the person, who is both a rogue, and an honest man, lived⟩$_{2}$. Now with us biographers the case is different, the facts we deliver may be relied on, though we often mistake the age and country wherein they happened: For though it may be worth the examination of critics, whether the shepherd Chrysostom, who, as Cervantes informs us, died for love of the fair Marcella, who hated him, was ever in Spain, will anyone doubt but that such a silly fellow hath really existed? Is there in the world such a sceptic as to disbelieve the madness of Cardenio, the perfidy of Ferdinand, the impertinent curiosity of Anselmo, the weakness of Camilla, the irresolute friendship of Lothario; though perhaps as to the time and place where those several persons lived, that good historian may be deplorably deficient: But the most known instance of this kind is in the true history of Gil Blas, where the inimitable biographer hath made a notorious blunder in the country of Dr. Sangrado, who used his patients as a vintner doth his wine-vessels, by letting out their blood, and filling them up with water. ⟨Doth not everyone, who is the least versed in physical history, know that Spain was not the country in which this doctor lived?⟩$_{2}$ The same writer hath likewise erred in the country of his arch-bishop, as well as that of those great personages whose understandings were too sublime to taste anything but tragedy, and ~~perhaps~~$_{2}$ in many others.

{while others give him}$_{2\text{-}3}$
[but]$_{1}$
[it]$_{1}$

The same mistakes may likewise be observed in Scarron, the *Arabian Nights,* the history of *Marianne* and *Le Paisan Parvenu,* and perhaps some few other writers of this class, whom I have not read, or do not at present recollect; [1] for I would by no means be thought to comprehend those [persons of surprising genius]$_2$ [great geniuses]$_1$ the authors of immense Romances, or the modern novel and *Atalantis* writers; who without any assistance from Nature or History, record persons who never were, or will be, and facts which never did nor possibly can, happen: Whose heroes are of their own creation, and their brains the Chaos whence all their materials are collected. Not that such writers deserve no honour; so far otherwise, that perhaps they merit the highest: for what can be nobler than to be as an example of the wonderful extent of human genius. One may apply to them what Balzac says of Aristotle,[2] that they are *a second Nature;* for they have no communication with the first; by which authors of an inferior class, who cannot stand alone, are obliged to support themselves as with crutches; but these of whom I am now speaking, seem to be possessed of *those stilts,* which the excellent Voltaire tells us in his Letters *carry the genius far off, but with an irregular pace.* Indeed far out of the sight of the reader,

Beyond the Realm of Chaos and old Night.[3]

But, to return to the former class, who are contented to copy Nature, instead of forming originals from [the]$_2$ [their]$_1$ confused heap of matter in their own brains; is not such a book as that which records the achievements of the renowned Don Quixote more

[1] In addition to Cervantes's *Don Quixote* and the *Arabian Nights,* the books on Fielding's honor roll are Alain-René Le Sage's *Gil Blas* (1715–35), Paul Scarron's *Le Roman comique* (1651–57), Pierre Carlet de Chamblain de Marivaux' *La Vie de Marianne* (1731–41) and *Le Paisan Parvenu* (1735–36). Fielding had previously slurred Mrs. Manley's *New Atalantis* (1709) in *Shamela.*

[2] "Balzac" (unrelated to the nineteenth-century writer) is Jean-Louis Guez de Balzac (1594–1654), famous for his letters to prominent men, several times collected and published during his life, trite in subject but written in a clear, precise, and idiomatic style credited with establishing French prose.

[3] Fielding's inaccurate remembrance of *Paradise Lost* I.542–43: "A shout that tore Hell's concave, and beyond/Frighted the reign of Chaos and old Night."

worthy the name of a history than even Mariana's; [4] for whereas the latter is confined to a particular period of time, and to a particular nation; the former is the history of the world in general, at least that part which is polished by laws, arts and sciences; and of that from the time it was first polished to this day; nay and forwards, as long as it shall so remain.

I shall now proceed to apply these observations to the work before us; for indeed I have set them down principally to obviate some constructions, which the good-nature of mankind, who are always forward to see their friends virtues recorded, may put to particular parts. I question not but several of my readers will know the Lawyer in the stage-coach, the moment they hear his voice. It is likewise odds, but the Wit and the Prude meet with some of their acquaintance, as well as all the rest of my characters. To prevent therefore any such malicious applications, I declare here once for all, I describe not men, but manners; not an individual, but a species. Perhaps it will be answered, Are not the characters then taken from life? To which I answer in the affirmative; nay, I believe I might aver, that I have writ little more than I have seen. The Lawyer is not only alive, but hath been so these [4000]$_2$ years, and I hope G— will indulge his [5000]$_1$
life as many yet to come. He hath not indeed confined himself to one profession, one religion, or one country; but when the first mean selfish creature appeared on the human stage, who made self the centre of the whole creation; would give himself no pain, incur no danger, advance no money to assist, or preserve his fellow-creatures; then was our Lawyer born; and whilst such a person as I have described, exists on earth, so long shall he remain upon it. It is therefore doing him little honour, to imagine he endeavours to mimic some little obscure fellow, because he happens to resemble him in one particular feature, or perhaps in his profession; whereas his appearance in the world is calculated for much more general and noble purposes [; not]$_2$ to [, than]$_1$
expose one pitiful wretch, to the small ⟨and contemptible⟩$_2$ circle of his acquaintance; but to hold the glass to thousands in their closets, that they may contemplate their deformity, and endeav-

[4] Juan de Mariana's *Historia general de España* (1601); Fielding owned, and elsewhere uses, an English translation (Battestin, p. 188).

our to reduce it, and thus by suffering private mortification may avoid public shame. This places the boundary between, and distinguishes the satirist from the libeller; for the former privately corrects the fault for the benefit of the person, like a parent; the latter publicly exposes the person himself, as an example to others, like an executioner.

There are besides little circumstances to be considered, as the drapery of a picture, which though fashion varies at different times, the resemblance of the countenance is not by those means diminished. Thus, I believe, we may venture to say, Mrs. Towwouse is coeval with our Lawyer, and though perhaps during the changes, which so long an existence must have passed through, she may in her turn have stood behind the bar at an inn, I will not scruple to affirm, she hath likewise in the revolution of ages sat on a throne. In short where extreme turbulency of temper, avarice, and an insensibility of human misery, with a degree of hypocrisy, have united in a female composition, Mrs. Tow-wouse was that woman; and where a good inclination eclipsed by a poverty of spirit and understanding, hath glimmered forth in a man, that man hath been no other than her sneaking husband.

I shall detain my reader no longer than to give him one caution more of an opposite kind: For as in most of our particular
[that]$_1$ characters we mean not to lash individuals, but all of [the]$_2$ like sort; so in our general descriptions, we mean not universals, but would be understood with many exceptions: For instance, in our description of high people, we cannot be intended to include such, as whilst they are an honour to their high rank, by a well-guided condescension, make their superiority as easy as possible,
[hath to those whom fortune [chiefly hath]$_3$ placed below them. Of
chiefly]$_{1\text{-}2}$ this number I could name a Peer no less elevated by Nature than by Fortune, who whilst he wears the noblest ensigns of Honour on his person, bears the truest stamp of Dignity on his mind, adorned with Greatness, enriched with Knowledge, and embellished with Genius. I have seen this man relieve with generosity, while he hath conversed with freedom, and be to the same person a patron and a companion.[5] I could name a Com-

[5] Probably the Earl of Chesterfield.

moner raised higher above the multitude by superior talents, than is in the power of his Prince to exalt him; whose behaviour to those he hath obliged is more amiable than the obligation itself, and who is so great a master of affability, that if he could divest himself of an inherent greatness in his manner, would often make the lowest of his acquaintance forget who was the master of that palace, in which they are so courteously entertained.[6] These are pictures which must be, I believe, known: I declare they are taken from the life, [and not]$_3$ intended to exceed it. By those high people therefore whom I have described, I mean a set of wretches, who while they are a disgrace to their ancestors, whose honours and fortunes they inherit, (or perhaps a greater to their mother, for such degeneracy is scarce credible) have the insolence to treat those with disregard, who [are at least]$_3$ equal to the founders of their own splendor. It is, I fancy, impossible to conceive a spectacle more worthy of our indignation, than that of a fellow who is not only a blot in the escutcheon of a great family, but a scandal to the human species, maintaining a supercilious behaviour to men who are an honour to their nature, and a disgrace to their fortune.

[nor are]$_{1\text{-}2}$

[have been]$_{1\text{-}2}$

And now, reader, taking these hints along with you, you may, if you please, proceed to the sequel of this our true history.

CHAP. II.

A night-scene, wherein several wonderful adventures befell Adams and his fellow-travellers.

IT was so late when our travellers left the inn or ale-house, (for it might be called either) that they had not travelled many miles before night overtook them, or met them, which you please. The reader must excuse me if I am not particular as to

[6] Ralph Allen, one of the models for Squire Allworthy in *Tom Jones*, at whose elegant Palladian home on a hill near Bath, Fielding had recently been entertained with Alexander Pope. See Joseph's further praise on p. 286.

the way they took; for as we are now drawing near the seat of the Boobies; and as that is a ticklish name, which malicious persons may apply according to their evil inclinations to several worthy Country' Squires, a race of men whom we look upon as entirely inoffensive, and for whom we have an adequate regard, we shall lend no assistance to any such malicious purposes.

Darkness had now overspread the hemisphere, when Fanny whispered Joseph, "that she begged to rest herself a little, for that she was so tired, she could walk no farther." Joseph immediately prevailed with Parson Adams, who was as brisk as a bee, to stop. He had no sooner seated himself, than he lamented the loss of his dear Æschylus; but was a little comforted, when reminded, that if he had it in his possession, he could not see to read.

The sky was so clouded, that not a star appeared. It was indeed, according to Milton, darkness visible. This was a circumstance however very favourable to Joseph; for Fanny, not suspicious of being overseen by Adams, gave a loose to her passion, which she had never done before; and reclining her head on his bosom, threw her arm carelessly round him, and suffered him to lay his cheek close to hers. All this infused such happiness into Joseph, that he would not have changed his turf for the finest down in the finest palace in the universe.

Adams sat at some distance from the lovers, and being unwilling to disturb them, applied himself to meditation; in which he had not spent much time, before he discovered a light at some distance, that seemed approaching towards him. He immediately hailed it, but to his sorrow and surprise it stopped for a moment and then disappeared. He then called to Joseph, asking him, "if he had not seen the light." Joseph answered, "he had." "And did you not mark how it vanished? (returned he) though I am not afraid of ghosts, I do not absolutely disbelieve them."

He then entered into a meditation on those unsubstantial beings, which was soon interrupted, by several voices which he thought almost at his elbow, though in fact they were not so extremely near. However, he could distinctly hear them agree on the murder of anyone they met. And a little after heard one of them say, "he had killed a dozen since that day fortnight."

Adams now fell on his knees, and committed himself to the care of Providence; and poor Fanny, who likewise heard those terrible words, embraced Joseph so closely, that had not he, whose ears were also open, been apprehensive on her account, he would have thought no danger ⟨which threatened only himself⟩ $_2$ too dear a price for such embraces.

Joseph now drew forth his penknife, and Adams having finished his ejaculations, grasped his crabstick, his only weapon, and coming up to Joseph would have had him quit Fanny, and place her in their rear: but his advice was fruitless, she clung closer to him, not at all regarding the presence of Adams, and in a soothing voice declared, "she would die in his arms." Joseph clasping her with inexpressible eagerness, whispered her, "that he preferred death in hers, to life out of them." Adams brandishing his crabstick, said, "he despised death as much as any man," and then repeated aloud,

> *"Est hic, est animus lucis contemptor, et illum,*
> *Qui vita bene credat emi quo tendis, Honorem."* [7]

Upon this the voices ceased for a moment, and then one of them called out, "D—n you, who is there?" To which Adams was prudent enough to make no reply; and of a sudden he observed half a dozen lights, which seemed to rise all at once from the ground, and advance briskly towards him. This he immediately concluded to be an apparition, and now beginning to conceive that the voices were of the same kind, he called out, "In the name of the L—d what wouldst thou have?" He had no sooner spoke, than he heard one of the voices cry out, "D—n them, here they come;" and soon after heard several hearty blows, as if a number of men had been engaged at quarterstaff. He was just advancing towards the place of combat, when Joseph catching him by the skirts, begged him that they might take the opportunity of the dark, to convey away Fanny from the danger which threatened her. He presently complied, and Joseph lifting up Fanny, they all three made the best of their

[7] "Here it is, here is a spirit contemptuous of light, one who believes the honor you seek well bought with his life" (*Aeneid* IX.205–6).

way, and without looking behind them or being overtaken, they had travelled full two miles, poor Fanny not once complaining of being tired; when they saw far off several lights scattered at a small distance from each other, and at the same time found themselves on the descent of a very steep hill. Adams's foot slipping, he instantly disappeared, which greatly frightned both Joseph and Fanny; indeed, if the light had permitted them to see it, they would scarce have refrained laughing to see the parson rolling down the hill, which he did from top to bottom, without receiving any harm. He then hollowed as loud as he could, to inform them of his safety, and relieve them from the fears which they had conceived for him. Joseph and Fanny halted some time, considering what to do; at last they advanced a few paces, where the declivity seemed least steep; and then Joseph taking his Fanny in his arms, walked firmly down the hill, without making a false step, and at length landed her at the bottom, where Adams soon came to them.

Learn hence, my fair countrywomen, to consider your own weakness, and the many occasions on which the strength of a man may be useful to you; and duly weighing this, take care, that you match not yourselves with the spindle-shanked Beaus and Petit Maîtres of the age, who instead of being able like Joseph Andrews, to carry you in lusty arms through the rugged ways and downhill steeps of life, will rather want to support their feeble limbs with your strength and assistance.

Our travellers now moved forwards, whither the nearest light presented itself, and having crossed a common field, they came to a meadow, whence they seemed to be at a very little distance from the light, when, to their grief, they arrived at the banks of a river. Adams here made a full stop, and declared he could swim, but doubted how it was possible to get Fanny over; to which Joseph answered, "if they walked along its banks they might be certain of soon finding a bridge, especially as by the number of lights they might be assured a parish was near." "Odso, that's true indeed," said Adams, "I did not think of that." Accordingly Joseph's advice being taken, they passed over two meadows, and came to a little orchard, which led them to a house. Fanny begged of Joseph to knock at the door, assuring him, "she was so weary that she could hardly stand on her feet." Adams who was foremost performed this ceremony, and the door being immediately opened, a plain kind of man appeared at it: Adams acquainted him, "that they had a young woman with them, who was so tired with her journey, that he should be much obliged to him, if he would suffer her to come in and rest herself." The man, who saw Fanny by the light of the candle which he held in his hand, perceiving her innocent and modest look, and having no apprehensions from the civil behaviour of Adams, presently answered, ⟨that⟩ $_2$ the young woman was very welcome to rest herself in his house, and so were her company. He then ushered them into a very decent room, where his wife was sitting at a table; she immediately rose up, and assisted them in setting forth chairs, and desired them to sit down, which they had no sooner done, than the man of the house asked them if they would have anything to refresh themselves with? Adams thanked him, and answered, he should be obliged to him for a cup of his ale, which was likewise chosen by Joseph and Fanny. Whilst he was gone to fill a very large jug with this liquor, his wife told Fanny she seemed greatly fatigued, and desired her to take something stronger than ale; but she refused, with many thanks, saying it was true, she was very much tired, but a little rest she hoped would restore her. As soon as the company were all seated, Mr. Adams, who had filled himself with ale, and by public permission had lighted his pipe; turned to the master of the house, asking him, "if evil spirits did not use to walk in that neighbourhood?" To which receiving no answer, he began to inform him of the adventure which they met with on the downs; nor had he proceeded far in his story, when somebody knocked very hard at the door. The company expressed some amazement, and Fanny and the good woman turned pale: her husband went forth, and whilst he was absent, which was some time, they all remained silent, looking at one another, and heard several voices discoursing pretty loudly. Adams was fully persuaded that spirits were abroad, and began to meditate some exorcisms; Joseph a little inclined to the same opinion: Fanny was more afraid of men, and the good woman herself began to suspect her guests, and imagained those without were rogues belonging to their gang. At length the master of the house returned, and laughing, told Adams he had discovered his apparition; that the murderers were sheep-stealers, and the twelve persons murdered were no other than twelve sheep. Adding that the shepherds had got the better of them, had secured two, and were proceeding with them to a Justice of Peace. This account greatly relieved the fears of the whole company; but Adams muttered to himself, "he was convinced of the truth of apparitions for all that."

They now sat cheerfully round the fire, 'till the master of the house having surveyed his guests, and conceiving that the cassock, which having fallen down, appeared under Adams's great-coat, and the shabby livery on Joseph Andrews, did not well suit with the familiarity between them, began to entertain some suspicions, not much to their advantage: addressing himself therefore to Adams, he said, "he perceived he was a clergyman by his dress, and supposed that honest man was his footman." "Sir," answered Adams, "I am a clergyman at your service; but as to that young man, whom you have rightly termed honest, he is at present in nobody's service, he never lived in any other family than that of Lady Booby, from whence he was discharged, I assure you, for no crime." Joseph said, "he did not wonder the gentleman was surprised to see one of Mr. Adams's character condescend to so much goodness with a poor man." "Child," said Adams, "I should be ashamed of my cloth, if I thought a poor man, who is honest, below my notice or my familiarity. I know not how those who think otherwise, can profess themselves followers and servants of him who made no distinction, unless, peradventure, by preferring the poor to the rich. Sir," said he, addressing himself to the gentleman, "these two poor young people are my parishioners, and I look on them and love them as my children. There is something singular enough in their history, but I have not now time to recount it." The master of the house, notwithstanding the simplicity which discovered itself in Adams, knew too much of the world to give a hasty belief to professions. He was not yet quite certain that Adams had any more of the clergyman in him than his cassock. To try him therefore further, he asked him, "if Mr.

Pope had lately published anything new?" Adams answered, "he had heard great commendations of that poet, but that he had never read, nor knew any of his works." "Ho! ho!" says the gentleman to himself, "have I caught you?" "What," said he, "have you never seen his *Homer?*" Adams answered, "he had never read any translation of the classics." "Why truly," replied the gentleman, "there is a dignity in the Greek language which I think no modern tongue can reach." "Do you understand Greek, sir?" said Adams hastily. "A little, sir," answered the gentleman, "Do you know, sir," ⟨cried Adams,⟩ $_{2}$ "where I can buy an Æschylus? an unlucky misfortune lately happened to mine." Æschylus was beyond the gentleman, though he knew him very well by name; he therefore returning back to Homer, asked Adams, "what part of the *Iliad* he thought most excellent." Adams returned, "his question would be properer, what kind of beauty was the chief in poetry, for that Homer was equally excellent in them all.

"And indeed" ⟨, continued he,⟩ $_{2}$ "what Cicero says of a complete orator, may well be applied to a great poet; [*He*]$_{2}$ *ought* [who]$_{1}$
to comprehend all perfections. ~~Indeed~~ $_{2}$ Homer did this in the most excellent degree; it is not without reason therefore that the philosopher, in the 22d chapter of his Poetics, mentions him by no other appellation than that of *The Poet:* He was the father of the Drama, as well as the Epic: Not of Tragedy only, but of Comedy also; for his *Margites,* which is deplorably lost, bore, says Aristotle, the same analogy to Comedy as his *Odyssey* and *Iliad* to Tragedy. To him therefore we owe Aristophanes, as well as Euripides, Sophocles, and my poor Æschylus. But if you please we will confine ourselves (at least for the present) to the *Iliad,* his noblest work; though neither Aristotle, nor Horace give it the preference, as I remember, to the *Odyssey.* First then as to his Subject, can anything be more simple, and at the same time more noble? He is rightly praised by the first of those judicious critics, for not choosing the whole war, which, though he says, it hath a complete Beginning and End, would have been too great for the understanding to comprehend at one view. I have therefore often wondered why so correct a writer as Horace should in his epistle to Lollius call him the *Trojani Belli*

Scriptorem. Secondly, his Action, termed by Aristotle *Pragmaton Systasis;* is it possible for the mind of man to conceive an idea of such perfect unity, and at the same time so replete with greatness? And here I must observe what I do not remember to have seen noted by any, the *Harmotton,* that agreement of his Action to his Subject: For as the Subject is Anger, how agreeable is his Action, which is War? from which every incident arises, and to which every episode immediately relates. Thirdly, his Manners, which Aristotle places second in his description of the several Parts of Tragedy, and which he says are included in the Action; I am at a loss whether I should rather admire the exactness of his judgment in the nice distinction, or the immensity of his imagination in their variety. For, as to the former of these, how accurately is the sedate, injured resentment of Achilles distinguished from the hot insulting passion of Agamemnon? How widely doth the brutal courage of Ajax differ from the amiable bravery of Diomedes; and the wisdom of Nestor, which is the result of long reflection and experience, from the cunning of Ulysses, the effect of art and subtlety only? If we consider their variety, we may cry out with Aristotle in his 24th chapter, that no part of this divine poem is destitute of Manners. Indeed I might affirm, that there is scarce a character in human nature untouched in some part or other. And as there is no passion which he is not able to describe, so is there none in his reader which he cannot raise. If he hath any superior excellence to the rest, I have been inclined to fancy it is in the Pathetic. I am sure I never read with dry eyes, the two episodes, where Andromache is introduced, in the former lamenting the danger, and in the latter the death, of Hector. The images are so extremely tender in these, that I am convinced, the poet had the worthiest and best heart imaginable. ⟨Nor can I help observing how short Sophocles falls of the beauties of the original, in that imitation of the dissuasive speech of Andromache, which he hath put into the mouth of Tecmessa.[8] And yet Sophocles was the greatest genius who ever wrote tragedy, nor have any of his successors in that art, that is to say, neither Euripides nor Seneca the tragedian, been able to come near him.⟩ $_2$ As to his

[8] In his *Ajax*, ll. 485–524.

Sentiments and Diction, I need say nothing; the former are particularly remarkable for the utmost perfection on that head, namely, propriety; and as to the latter, Aristotle, whom doubtless you have read over and over, is very diffuse. I shall mention but one thing more, which that great critic in his division of Tragedy calls *Opsis*, or the scenery, and which is as proper to the Epic as to the Drama, with this difference, that in the former it falls to the share of the poet, and in the latter to that of the painter. But did ever painter imagine a scene like that in the 13th and 14th Iliads? where the reader sees at one view the prospect of Troy, with the army drawn up before it; the Grecian army, camp, and fleet, Jupiter sitting on Mount Ida, with his head wrapt in a cloud, and a thunderbolt in his hand, looking towards Thrace; Neptune driving through the sea, which divides on each side to permit his passage, and then seating himself on Mount Samos: The heavens opened, and the deities all seated on their thrones. This is sublime! This is poetry!" [Adams]$_2$ then rapt out a hundred Greek verses, [and with such a voice, emphasis and action, that he almost frightened the women; and as for the gentleman, he]$_2$ was so far from entertaining any further suspicion of Adams, that he now doubted whether he had not a bishop in his house. [He ran into the most extravagant encomiums on his learning, and the goodness of his heart began to dilate to all the strangers.]$_2$ He said he had great compassion for the poor young woman, who looked pale and faint with her journey; and in truth he conceived a much higher opinion of her quality than it deserved. He said, he was sorry he could not accommodate them all: But if they were contented with his fire-side, he would sit up with the men, and the young woman might, if she pleased, partake his wife's bed, which he advised her to; for that they must walk upwards of a mile to any house of entertainment, and that not very good neither. Adams, who liked his seat, his ale, his tobacco and his company, persuaded Fanny to accept this kind proposal, in which solicitation he was seconded by Joseph. Nor was she very difficultly prevailed on [; for she had slept little the last night, and not at all the preceding, so that love itself was]$_2$ scarce able to keep her eyes open any longer. The offer therefore being kindly accepted,

[He]$_1$

['till the gentleman]$_1$

[The goodness of his heart began therefore to dilate without any further restraint]$_1$

[, love itself being]$_1$

the good woman produced everything eatable in her house on
[while]1 the table, [and]2 the guests being heartily invited, as heartily regaled themselves, especially Parson Adams. As to the other two, they were examples of the truth of that physical observation, that love, like other sweet things, is no whetter of the stomach.

Supper was no sooner ended, than Fanny at her own request retired, and the good woman bore her company. The man of the house, Adams and Joseph, who would modestly have withdrawn, had not the gentleman insisted on the contrary, drew round the fire-side, where Adams, (to use his own words) replenished his pipe, and the gentleman produced a bottle of excellent beer, being the best liquor in his house.

The modest behaviour of Joseph, with the gracefulness of his person, the character which Adams gave of him, and the friendship he seemed to entertain for him, began to work on the gentleman's affections, and raised in him a curiosity to know the singularity which Adams had mentioned in his history. This curiosity Adams was no sooner informed of, than with Joseph's consent, he agreed to gratify it, and accordingly related all he knew, with as much tenderness as was possible for the character of Lady Booby; and concluded with the long, faithful and mutual passion between him and Fanny, not concealing the meanness of her birth and education. These latter circumstances entirely cured a jealousy which had lately risen in the gentleman's mind, that Fanny was the daughter of some person of fashion, and that Joseph had run away with her, and Adams was concerned in the plot. He was now enamoured of his guests, drank their healths with great cheerfulness, and returned many thanks to Adams, who had spent much breath; for he was a circumstantial teller of a story.

Adams told him it was now in his power to return that favour; for his extraordinary goodness, as well as that fund of literature he was master of, ⟨*⟩ 2 which he did not expect to find

⟨* The author hath by some been represented to have made a blunder here: For Adams had indeed shown some learning, (say they) perhaps all the author had; but the gentleman hath shown none, unless his approbation of Mr. Adams be such: But surely it would be preposterous in him to call it so. I have however, notwithstanding this criticism which I am told

under such a roof, had raised in him more curiosity than he had ever known. "Therefore," said he, "if it be not too troublesome, sir, your history, if you please."

The gentleman answered, he could not refuse him what he had so much right to insist on; and after some of the common apologies, which are the usual preface to a story, he thus began.

CHAP. III.

In which the gentleman relates the history of his life.

SIR, I am descended of a good family, and was born a gentleman. My education was liberal, and at a public school, in which I proceeded so far as to become master of the Latin, and to be tolerably versed in the Greek language. My father died when I was sixteen, and left me master of myself. He bequeathed me a moderate fortune, which he intended I should not receive till I attained the age of twenty-five: For he constantly asserted that was full early enough to give up any man entirely to the guidance of his own discretion. However, as this intention was so obscurely worded in his will, that the lawyers advised me to contest the point with my trustees, I own I paid so little regard to the inclinations of my dead father, which were sufficiently certain to me, that I followed their advice, and soon succeeded: For the trustees did not contest the matter very obstinately on their side. "Sir," said Adams, "May I crave the favour of your name?" The gentleman answered, "his name was Wilson," and then proceeded.

I stayed a very little while at school after his death; for

came from the mouth of a great Orator [probably "Orator" Henley himself, mentioned below, p. 287], in a public coffee-house, left this blunder as it stood in the first edition. I will not have the vanity to apply to anything in this work, the observation which M. Dacier makes in her Preface to her *Aristophanes: Je tiens pour une Maxime constante qu'une Beauté médiocre* [*plait*]3 *plus generalement qu'une Beauté sans défaut*. Mr. Congreve hath made such another blunder in his *Love for Love*, where Tattle tells Miss Prue, *She should admire him as much for the beauty he commends in her, as if he himself was possest of it.*〉2 [Fielding's note.] [*plaire*]2 being a forward youth, I was extremely impatient to be in the world: For which I thought my parts, knowledge, and manhood thoroughly qualified me. And to this early introduction into life, without a guide, I impute all my future misfortunes; for besides the obvious mischiefs which attend this, there is one which hath not been so generally observed. The first impression which mankind receives of you, will be very difficult to eradicate. How unhappy, therefore, must it be to fix your character in life, before you can possibly know its value, or weigh the consequences of those actions which are to establish your future reputation?

A little under seventeen I left my school and went to London, with no more than six pounds in my pocket. A great sum as I then conceived; and which I was afterwards surprised to find so soon consumed.

The character I was ambitious of attaining, was that of a fine gentleman; the first requisites to which, I apprehended were to be supplied by a tailor, a periwig-maker, and some few more tradesmen, who deal in furnishing out the human body. Notwithstanding the lowness of my purse, I found credit with them more easily than I expected, and was soon equipped to my wish. This I own then agreeably surprised me; but I have since [that]$_1$ learned, that it is a maxim among many tradesmen at [the]$_2$ polite end of the town to deal as largely as they can, reckon as high as they can, and arrest as soon as they can.

The next qualifications, namely dancing, fencing, riding the great horse,[9] and music, came into my head; but as they required expense and time, I comforted myself, with regard to dancing, that I had learned a little in my youth, and could walk a minuet genteelly enough; as to fencing, I thought my good-humour would preserve me from the danger of a quarrel; as to the horse, I hoped it would not be thought of; and for music, I imagined I could easily acquire the reputation of it; for I had heard some of my school-fellows pretend to knowledge in operas, without being able to sing or play on the fiddle.

Knowledge of the town seemed another ingredient; this I thought I should arrive at by frequenting public places. Accordingly I paid constant attendance to them all; by which means I

[9] A war horse.

was soon master of the fashionable phrases, learned to cry up the fashionable diversions, and knew the names and faces of the most fashionable men and women.

Nothing now seemed to remain but an intrigue, which I was resolved to have immediately; I mean the reputation of it; and indeed I was so successful, that in a very short time I had half a dozen with the finest women in town.

At these words Adams fetched a deep groan, and then blessing himself, cried out, *Good Lord! What wicked times these are?*

Not so wicked as you imagine, continued the gentleman; for I assure you, they were all Vestal Virgins for anything which I knew to the contrary. The reputation of intriguing with them was all I sought, and was what I arrived at: and perhaps I only flattered myself even in that; for very probably the persons to whom I showed their billets, knew as well as I, that they were counterfeits, and that I had written them to myself.

"*WRITE letters to yourself!*" said Adams staring!

O sir, answered the gentleman, *It is the ⟨very⟩ $_2$ error of the times.* Half our modern plays have one of these characters in them. It is incredible the pains I have taken, and the absurd methods I employed to traduce the character of women of distinction. When another had spoken in raptures of anyone, I have answered, "D—n her, she! We shall have her at H——d's very soon." [10] When he hath replied, "he thought her virtuous," I have answered, "Ay, thou wilt always think a woman virtuous, till she is in the streets, but you and I, Jack or Tom, (turning to another in company) know better." At which I have drawn a paper out of my pocket, perhaps a tailor's bill, and kissed it, crying at the same time, *By Gad I was once fond of her.*

"Proceed, if you please, but do not swear any more," said Adams.

Sir, said the gentleman, I ask your pardon. Well, sir, in this course of life I continued full three years,—"What course of life?" answered Adams; "I do not remember you have yet mentioned any."—Your remark is just, said the gentleman smiling; I should rather have said, in this course of doing nothing. I

[10] Mother Haywood's renowned brothel in Covent Garden.

remember some time afterwards I wrote the journal of one day, which would serve, I believe, as well for any other, during the whole time; I will endeavour to repeat it to you.

In the morning I arose, took my great stick, and walked out in my green frock with my hair in papers, (*a groan from Adams*) and sauntered about till ten.

Went to the auction; told Lady —— she had a dirty face; laughed heartily at something Captain —— said; I can't remember what, for I did not very well hear it; whispered Lord ——; bowed to the Duke of ——; and was going to bid for a snuff-box; but did not, for fear I should have had it.

From 2 to 4, drest myself. A groan.
4 to 6, dined. A groan.
6 to 8, Coffee-house.
8 to 9, *Drury-Lane* Play-house.
9 to 10, *Lincoln's-Inn-Fields*.[11]
10 to 12, Drawing-Room. ⟨A great groan.⟩ 2

At all which places nothing happened worth remark. At which Adams ~~having fetched a great groan~~ 2 said with some vehemence, "Sir, this is below the life of an animal, hardly above vegetation; and I am surprised what could lead a man of your sense into it." What leads us into more follies than you imagine, doctor, answered the gentleman; vanity: For as contemptible a creature as I was, and I assure you, yourself cannot have more contempt for such a wretch than I now have, I then admired myself, and should have despised a person of your present appearance (you will pardon me) with all your learning, and those excellent qualities which I have remarked in you. Adams bowed, and begged him to proceed. After I had continued two years in this course of life, said the gentleman, an accident happened which obliged me to change the scene. As I was one day at St. James's Coffee-house, making very free with the character of a young lady of quality, an officer of the Guards who was present, thought proper to give me the lie. I answered, I might possibly be mistaken; but I intended to tell no more

[11] Another theater.

than the truth. To which he made no reply, but by a scornful sneer. After this I observed a strange coldness in all my acquaintance; none of them spoke to me first, and very few returned me even the civility of a bow. The company I used to dine with, left me out, and within a week I found myself in as much solitude at St. James's, as if I had been in a desert. An honest elderly man ⟨, with a great hat and long sword,⟩ $_2$ at last told me, he had a compassion for my youth, and therefore advised me to show the world I was not such a rascal as they thought me to be. I did not at first understand him: But he explained himself, and ended with telling me, if I would write a challenge to the captain, he would out of pure charity go to him with it. "A very charitable person truly!" cried Adams. I desired till the next day, continued the gentleman, to consider on it, and retiring to my lodgings, I weighed the consequences on both sides as fairly as I could. On the one, I saw the risk of this alternative, either losing my own life, or having on my hands the blood of a man with whom I was not in the least angry. I soon determined that the good which appeared on the other, was not worth this hazard. I therefore resolved to quit the scene, and presently retired to the Temple, where I took chambers.[12] Here I soon got a fresh set of acquaintance, who knew nothing of what had happened to me. Indeed they were not greatly to my approbation; for the beaus of the Temple are only the shadows of the others. They are the affectation of affectation. The vanity of these is still more ridiculous, if possible, than of the others. Here I met with smart fellows who drank with lords they did not know, and intrigued with women they never saw. Covent-Garden was now the farthest stretch of my ambition, where I shone forth in the balconies at the play-houses, visited whores, made love to orange-wenches, and damned plays. This career was soon put a stop to by my surgeon, who convinced me of the necessity of confining myself to my room for a month. At the

[12] Formerly the property of the Knights Templar; in Fielding's day (and since the thirteenth century), the buildings of the several Inns of Court and Chancery, societies in which law students lived and studied near the courts of Westminster.

end of which, having had leisure to reflect, I resolved to quit [any further conversation with beaus and smarts of all kinds]$_1$ [all further conversation with beaus and smarts of every kind]$_2$, and to avoid, if possible, any occasion of returning to this place of confinement. "I think," said Adams, "the advice of a month's retirement and reflection was very proper; but I should rather have expected it from a divine than a surgeon." The gentleman smiled at Adams's simplicity, and without explaining himself farther on such an odious subject went on thus: I was no sooner perfectly restored to health, than I found my passion for women, which I was afraid to satisfy as I had done, made me very uneasy; I determined therefore to keep a mistress. Nor was I long before I fixed my choice on a young woman, who had before been kept by two gentlemen, and to whom I was recommended by a celebrated bawd. I took her home to my chambers, and made her a settlement, during cohabitation. This would perhaps have been very ill paid: However, she did not suffer me to be [this]$_1$ perplexed on [that]$_2$ account; for before quarter-day, I found her at my chambers in too familiar conversation with a young fellow who was drest like an officer, but was indeed a City apprentice.[13] Instead of excusing her inconstancy, she rapped out half a dozen oaths, and snapping her fingers at me, swore she scorned to confine herself to the best man in England. Upon this we parted, and the same bawd presently provided her another keeper. I was not so much concerned at our separation, as I found within a day or two I had reason to be for our meeting: For I was obliged to pay a second visit to my surgeon. I was [obliged]$_{1\text{-}2}$ now [forced]$_3$ to do penance for some weeks, during which time I contracted an acquaintance with a beautiful young girl, the daughter of a gentleman, who after having been forty years in the army, and in all the campaigns under the Duke of Marlborough, died a lieutenant on half-pay; and had left a widow with this only child, in very distrest circumstances: they had only a small pension from the government, with what little the daughter could add to it by her work; for she had great excellence at her needle. This girl was, at my first acquaintance with her, solicited in marriage by a young fellow in good cir-

[13] The "City," London's financial district, lies within the old walls of the city.

cumstances. He was apprentice to a linen-draper, and had a little fortune sufficient to set up his trade. The mother was greatly pleased with this match, as indeed she had sufficient reason. However, I soon prevented it. I represented him in so low a light to his mistress, and made so good an use of flattery, promises, and presents, that, not to dwell longer on this subject than is necessary, I prevailed with the poor girl, and conveyed her away from her mother! In a word, I debauched her. — (At which words, Adams started up, fetched three strides cross the room, and then replaced himself in his chair.) You are not more affected with this part of my story than myself: I assure you it will never be sufficiently repented of in my own opinion: But if you already detest it, how much more will your indignation be raised when you hear the fatal consequences of this barbarous, this villainous action? If you please therefore, I will here desist. — "By no means," cries Adams, "Go on, I beseech you, and Heaven grant you may sincerely repent of this and many other things you have related." — I was now, continued the gentleman, as happy as the possession of a fine young creature, who had a good education, and was endued with many agreeable qualities, could make me. We lived some months with vast fondness together, without any company or conversation more than we found in one another: But this could not continue always; and though I still preserved a great affection for her, I began more and more to want the relief of other company, and consequently to leave her by degrees, at last, whole days to herself. She failed not to testify some uneasiness on these occasions, and complained of the melancholy life she led; to remedy which, I introduced her into the acquaintance of some other kept mistresses, with whom she used to play at cards, and frequent plays and other diversions. She had not lived long in this intimacy, before I perceived a visible alteration in her behaviour; all her modesty and innocence vanished by degrees, till her mind became thoroughly tainted. She affected the company of rakes, gave herself all manner of airs, was never easy but abroad, or when she had a party at my chambers. She was rapacious of money, extravagant to excess, loose in her conversation; and if ever I demurred to any of her demands, oaths, tears, and fits, were the immediate consequences. As the first raptures of fondness were long since over, this behaviour soon estranged my affections from her; I began to reflect with pleasure that she was not my wife, and to conceive an intention of parting with her, of which having given her a hint, she took care to prevent me the pains of turning her out of doors, and accordingly departed herself, having first broken open my escrutore, and taken with her all she could find, to the amount of about 200 *l*. In the first heat of my resentment, I resolved to pursue her with all the vengeance of the law: But as she had the good luck to escape me during that ferment, my passion afterwards cooled, and having reflected that I had been the first aggressor, and had done her an injury for which I could make her no reparation, by robbing her of the innocence of her mind; and hearing at the same time that the poor old woman her mother had broke her heart, on her daughter's elopement from her, I, concluding myself her murderer ("As you very well might," cries Adams, with a groan;) I$_2$ was pleased that God Almighty had taken this method of punishing me, and resolved quietly to submit to the loss. Indeed I could wish I had never heard more of the poor creature, who became in the end an abandoned profligate; and after being some years a common prostitute, at last ended her miserable life in Newgate. — Here the gentleman fetched a deep sigh, which Mr. Adams echoed very loudly, and both continued silent looking on each other for some minutes. At last the gentleman proceeded thus: I had been perfectly constant to this girl, during the whole time I kept her: But she had scarce departed before I discovered more marks of her infidelity to me, than the loss of my money. In short, I was forced to make a third visit to my surgeon, out of whose hands I did not get a hasty discharge.

I now forswore all future dealings with the sex, complained loudly that the pleasure did not compensate the pain, and railed at the beautiful creatures, in as gross language as Juvenal himself formerly reviled them in. I looked on all the town-harlots with a detestation not easy to be conceived, their persons appeared to me as painted palaces inhabited by Disease and Death: Nor could their beauty make them more desirable objects in my eyes, than gilding could make me covet a pill, or golden plates a coffin. But though I was no longer the absolute slave, I found some reasons to own myself still the subject of Love. My hatred for women decreased daily; and I am not positive but time might have betrayed me again to some common harlot, had I not been secured by a passion for the charming Saphira; which having once entered upon, made a violent progress in my heart. Saphira was wife to a man of fashion and gallantry, and one who seemed, I own, every way worthy of her affections, which however he had not the reputation of having. She was indeed a *Coquette achevée.* "Pray sir," says Adams, "what is a Coquette? I have met with the word in French authors, but never could assign any idea to it. I believe it is the same with *une Sotte,* Anglicé *a Fool.*" Sir, answered the gentleman, perhaps you are not much mistaken: but as it is a particular kind of folly, I will endeavour to describe it. Were all creatures to be ranked in the Order of Creation, according to their usefulness, I know few animals that would not take place of a Coquette; nor indeed hath this creature much pretence to anything beyond instinct: for though sometimes we might imagine it was animated by the passion of vanity, yet far the greater part of its actions fall beneath even that low motive; For instance, several absurd gestures and tricks, infinitely more foolish than what can be observed in the most ridiculous birds and beasts, and which would persuade the beholder that the silly wretch was aiming at our contempt. Indeed its characteristic is affectation, and this led and governed by whim only: for as beauty, wisdom, wit, good-nature, politeness and health are sometimes affected by this creature; so are ugliness, folly, nonsense, ill-nature, ill-breeding and sickness likewise put on by it in their turn. Its life is one constant lie, and the only rule by which you can form any judgment of them is, that they are never what they seem. If it was possible for a Coquette to love (as it is not, for if ever it attains this passion, the Coquette ceases instantly) it would wear the face of indifference if not of hatred to the beloved object; you may therefore be assured, when they endeavour to persuade you of their liking, that they are indifferent to you at least. And indeed this was the case of my Saphira, who no sooner saw me in the number of her admirers, than she gave me what is commonly called encouragement; she would often look at me, and when she perceived me meet her eyes, would instantly take them off, discovering at the same time as much surprise and emotion as possible. These arts failed not of the success she intended; and as I grew more particular to her than the rest of her admirers, she advanced in proportion more directly to me than to the others. She affected the low voice, whisper, lisp, sigh, start, laugh, and many other indications of passion, which daily deceive thousands. When I played at whisk with her, she would look earnestly at me, and at the same time lose deal or revoke;[14] then burst into a ridiculous laugh, and cry, "[La! I can't imagine what I was thinking of].$_{2}$" To detain you no longer, after I had gone through a sufficient course of gallantry, as I thought, and was thoroughly convinced I had raised a violent passion in my mistress; I sought an opportunity of coming to an eclaircissement with her. She avoided this as much as possible, however great assiduity at length presented me one. I will not describe all the particulars of this interview; let it suffice, that [when]$_{4}$ she could no longer pretend not to see my drift, she first affected a violent surprise, and immediately after as violent a passion: She wondered what I had seen in her conduct, which could induce me to affront her in this manner: And breaking from me the first moment she could, told me, I had no other way to escape the consequence of her resentment, than by never seeing, or at least speaking to her more. I was not contented with this answer; I still pursued her, but to no purpose, and was at length convinced that her husband had the sole possession of her person, and that neither he nor any other had made any impression on her heart. I was taken off from following this *Ignis Fatuus* by some advances which were made me by the wife of a Citizen, who though neither very young nor handsome, was yet too agreeable to be rejected by my amorous constitution. I accordingly soon satisfied her, that she had not cast away her hints on a barren or cold soil; on the contrary, they instantly

[I would not have you guess what I was thinking of for the world]$_{1}$

[till]$_{1\text{-}3}$

[14] The original whist—from whisking up the tricks (Fielding calls it "whisk and swabbers" in *Jonathan Wild* I.iv), systematized and taught by Edmund Hoyle, who finally published his long-circulated rules for whist (his *Short Treatise*) in November, 1742—"according to Hoyle." To "revoke" is to "renege."

produced her an eager and desiring lover. Nor did she give me any reason to complain; she met the warmth she had raised with equal ardour. I had no longer a Coquette to deal with, but one who was wiser than to prostitute the noble passion of Love to the ridiculous lust of Vanity. We presently understood one another; and as the pleasures we sought lay in a mutual gratification, we soon found and enjoyed them. I thought myself at first greatly happy in the possession of this new mistress, whose fondness would have quickly surfeited a more sickly appetite, but it had a different effect on mine; she carried my passion higher by it than Youth or [Beauty]$_2$ had been able: But my happiness could not [Vanity]$_1$
long continue uninterrupted. The apprehensions we lay under from the jealousy of her husband, gave us great uneasiness. "Poor wretch! I pity him," cried Adams. He did indeed deserve it, said the gentleman, for he loved his wife with great tenderness, and I assure you it is a great satisfaction to me that I was not the man who first seduced her affections from him. These apprehensions appeared also too well grounded; for in the end he discovered us, and procured witnesses of our caresses. He then prosecuted me at law, and recovered 3000 *l.* damages, which much distressed my fortune to pay: and what was worse, his wife being divorced, came upon my hands. I led a very uneasy life with her; for besides that my passion was now much abated, her excessive jealousy was very troublesome. At length Death [delivered me from]$_4$ an inconvenience, which the con- [rid me of]$_{1\text{-}3}$
sideration of my having been the author of her misfortunes, would never suffer me to take any other method of discarding.

I now [bade]$_2$ adieu to Love, and resolved to pursue other [bid]$_1$
less dangerous and expensive pleasures. I fell into the acquaintance of a set of jolly companions, who slept all day and drank all night: fellows who might rather be said to consume time than to live. Their best conversation was nothing but noise: singing, hollowing, wrangling, drinking, toasting, sp—wing,[15] smoking, were the chief ingredients of our entertainment. And yet bad as these were, they were more tolerable than our graver scenes, which were either excessive tedious narratives of dull common matters of fact, or hot disputes about trifling matters,

[15] Spewing, vomiting.

which commonly ended in a wager. This way of life the first serious reflection put a period to, and I ~~now~~[2] became member of a club frequented by young men of great abilities. The bottle was now only called in to the assistance of our conversation, which rolled on the deepest points of philosophy. These gentlemen were engaged in a search after truth, in the pursuit of which they threw aside all the prejudices of education, and governed themselves only by the infallible guide of human reason. This great guide, after having shown them the falsehood of that very ancient but simple tenet, that there is such a being as a Deity in the universe, helped them to establish in his stead a certain *Rule of Right,* by adhering to which they all arrived at the utmost purity of morals. Reflection made me as much delighted with this society, as it had taught me to despise and detest the former. I began now to esteem myself a being of a higher order than I had ever before conceived, and was the more charmed with this Rule of Right, as I really found in my own nature nothing repugnant to it. I held in utter contempt all persons who wanted any other inducement to Virtue besides her intrinsic beauty and excellence; and had so high an opinion of my present companions, with regard to their morality, that I would have trusted them with whatever was nearest and dearest to me. Whilst I was engaged in this delightful dream, two or three accidents happened successively, which at first much surprised me. For, one of our greatest Philosophers, or *Rule of Right-men* withdrew himself from us, taking with him the wife of one of his most intimate friends. Secondly, another of the same society left the club without remembering to take leave of his bail. A third having borrowed a sum of money of me, for which I received no security, when I asked him to repay it, absolutely denied the loan. These several practices, so inconsistent with our golden Rule, made me begin to suspect its infallibility; but when I communicated my thoughts to one of the club, he said "there was nothing absolutely good or evil in itself; that actions were denominated good or bad by the circumstances of the agent. That possibly the man who ran away with his neighbour's wife might be one of very good inclinations, but over-prevailed on by the violence of an unruly passion, and in other particulars might be a very worthy member of society: That if the beauty of any woman created in him an uneasiness, he had a right from Nature to relieve himself;" with many other things, which I then detested so much, that I took leave of the society that very evening, and never returned to it again. Being now reduced to a state of solitude, which I did not like, I became a great frequenter of the play-houses, which indeed was always my favourite diversion, and most evenings passed away two or three hours behind the scenes, where I met with several poets, with whom I made engagements at the taverns. Some of the players were likewise of our parties. At these meetings we were generally entertained by the poets with reading their performances, and by the players with repeating their parts: Upon which occasions, I observed the gentleman who furnished our entertainment, was commonly the best pleased of the company; who, though they were pretty civil to him to his face, seldom failed to take the first opportunity of his absence to ridicule him. Now I made some remarks, which probably are too obvious to be worth relating. "Sir," says Adams, "your remarks if you please." First then, says he, I concluded that the general observation, that wits are most inclined to Vanity, is not true. Men are equally vain of riches, strength, beauty, honours, *&c.* But, these appear of themselves to the eyes of the beholders, whereas the poor wit is obliged to produce his performance to show you his perfection, and on his readiness to do this that vulgar opinion I have before mentioned is grounded: But doth not the person who expends vast sums in the furniture of his house, or in the ornaments of his person, who consumes much time, and employs great pains in dressing himself, or who thinks himself paid for self-denial, labour, or even villainy by a title or a ribbon, sacrifice as much to Vanity as the poor wit, who is desirous to read you his poem or his play? My second remark was, that Vanity is the worst of passions, and more apt to contaminate the mind than any other: For as selfishness is much more general than we please to allow it, so it is natural to hate and envy those who stand between us and the good we desire. Now in Lust and Ambition these are few; and even in Avarice we find many who are no obstacles to our pursuits; but the vain man seeks pre-eminence;

and everything which is excellent or praise-worthy in another, renders him the mark of his antipathy. Adams now began to fumble in his pockets, and soon cried out, "O la! I have it not about me." — Upon this the gentleman asking him what he was searching for, he said he searched after a sermon, which he thought his master-piece, against Vanity. "Fie upon it, fie upon it," cries he, "why do I ever leave that sermon out of my pocket? I wish it was within five miles, I would willingly fetch it, to read it to you." The gentleman answered, that there was no need, for he was cured of the passion. "And for that very reason," quoth Adams, "I would read it, for I am confident you would admire it: Indeed, I have never been a greater enemy to any passion
[simple]$_{1-2}$ than that [silly]$_{3}$ one of Vanity." The gentleman smiled, and proceeded — From this society I easily passed to that of the gamesters, where nothing remarkable happened, but the finishing my fortune, which those gentlemen soon helped me to the end of. This opened scenes of life hitherto unknown; Poverty and Distress with their horrid train of duns, attorneys, bailiffs, haunted me day and night. My clothes grew shabby, my credit bad, my friends and acquaintance of all kinds cold. In this situation the strangest thought imaginable came into my head; and what was this, but to write a play? for I had sufficient leisure; Fear of bailiffs confined me every day to my room; and having always had a little inclination and something of a genius that way, I set myself to work, and within few months produced a piece of five acts, which was accepted of at the theatre. I remembered to have formerly taken tickets of other poets for their benefits long before the appearance of their performances, and resolving to follow a precedent, which was so well suited to my present circumstances; I immediately provided myself with a large number of little papers. Happy indeed would be the state of poetry, would these tickets pass current at the bakehouse, the ale-house, and the chandler's-shop: But alas! far otherwise; no tailor will take them in payment for buckram, stays, stay-tape; nor no bailiff for civility-money.[16] They are indeed no more than a passport to beg with, a certificate that the owner wants five shillings, which induces well-disposed Christians to charity.

[16] A bribe to a jailer for favors.

I now experienced what is worse than poverty, or rather what is the worst consequence of poverty, I mean attendance and dependence on the great. Many a morning have I waited hours in the cold parlours of men of quality, where after seeing the lowest rascals in lace and embroidery, the pimps and buffoons in fashion admitted, I have been sometimes told on sending in my name, that my lord could not possibly see me this morning: A sufficient assurance that I should never more get entrance into that house. Sometimes I have been at last admitted, and the great man hath thought proper to excuse himself, by telling me he was *tied up*. "*Tied up*," says Adams, "pray what's that?" Sir, says the gentleman, the profit which booksellers allowed authors for the best works, was so very small, that certain men of birth and fortune some years ago, who were the patrons of wit and learning, thought fit to encourage them farther, by entering into voluntary subscriptions for their encouragement. Thus Prior, Rowe, Pope, and some other men of genius, received large sums for their labours from the public. This seemed so easy a method of getting money, that many of the lowest scribblers of the times ventured to publish their works in the same way; and many had ~~even~~ $_{3}$ the assurance to take in subscriptions for what was [not]$_{3}$ writ, nor ⟨ever⟩ $_{3}$ intended. Subscrip- [never]$_{1-2}$
tions in this manner growing infinite, and a kind of tax on the public; some persons finding it not so easy a task to discern good from bad authors, or to know what genius was worthy encouragement, and what was not, to prevent the expense of subscribing to so many, invented a method to excuse themselves from all subscriptions whatever; and this was to receive a small sum of money in consideration of giving a large one if ever they subscribed; which many have done, and many more have pretended to have done, in order to silence all solicitation. The same method was likewise taken with play-house tickets, which were no less a public grievance; and this is what they call being *tied up* from subscribing. "I can't say but the term is apt enough, and somewhat typical," said Adams; "for a man of large fortune, who ties himself up, as you call it, from the encouragement of men of merit, ought to be tied up in reality." Well, sir, says the gentleman, to return to my story. Sometimes I have received

a guinea from a man of quality, given with as ill a grace as alms are generally to the meanest beggar, and purchased too with as much time spent in attendance, as, if it had been spent in honest industry, might have brought me more profit with infinitely more satisfaction. After about two months spent in this disagreeable way with the utmost mortification, when I was pluming my hopes on the prospect of a plentiful harvest from my play, upon applying to the prompter to know when it came into rehearsal, he informed me he had received orders from the managers to return me the play again; for that they could not possibly act it that season; but if I would take it and revise it against the next, they would be glad to see it again. I snatched it from him with great indignation, and retired to my room, where I threw myself on the bed in a fit of despair — "You should rather have thrown yourself on your knees," says Adams; "for despair is sinful." As soon, continued the gentleman, as I had indulged the first tumult of my passion, I began to consider coolly what course I should take, in a situation without friends, money, credit or reputation of any kind. After revolving many things in my mind, I could see no other possibility of furnishing myself with the miserable necessaries of life than to retire to a garret near the Temple, and commence hackney-writer to the lawyers; for which I was well qualified, being an excellent penman. This purpose I resolved on, and immediately put it in execution. I had an acquaintance with an attorney who had formerly transacted affairs for me, and to him I applied; But instead of furnishing me with any business, he laughed at my undertaking, and told me, "he was afraid I should turn his deeds into plays, and he should expect to see them on the stage." Not to tire you with instances of this kind from others, I found that Plato himself did not hold poets in greater abhorrence than these men of business do. Whenever I durst venture to a coffee-house, which was on Sundays only,[17] a whisper ran round the room, which was constantly attended with a sneer — *That's Poet Wilson:* for I know not whether you have observed it, but there is a malignity in the nature of man, which when not weeded out, or at least covered by a good education and polite-

[17] When he was exempt from arrest.

ness, delights in making another uneasy or dissatisfied with himself. This abundantly appears in all assemblies, except those which are filled by people of fashion, and especially among the younger people of both sexes, whose birth and fortunes place them just without the polite circles; I mean the lower class of the gentry, and the higher of the mercantile world, who are in reality the worst bred part of mankind. Well, sir, whilst I continued in this miserable state, with scarce sufficient business to keep me from starving, the reputation of a poet being my bane, I accidentally became acquainted with a bookseller, who told me, "it was pity a man of my learning and genius should be obliged to such a method of getting his livelihood; that he had a compassion for me, and if I would engage with him, he would undertake to provide handsomely for me." A man in my circumstances, as he very well knew, had no choice. I accordingly accepted his proposal with his conditions, which were none of the most favourable, and fell to translating with all my might. I had no longer reason to lament the want of business; for he furnished me with so much, that in half a year I almost writ myself blind. I likewise contracted a distemper by my sedentary life, in which no part of my body was exercised but my right arm, which rendered me incapable of writing for a long time.
This unluckily happening to delay the publication of [a]$_2$ work, [the]$_1$
and my last performance not having sold well, the bookseller declined any further engagement, and aspersed me to his brethren as a careless, idle fellow. I had however, by having half-worked and half-starved myself to death during the time I was
in his service, [saved]$_3$ a few guineas, with which I bought a [amassed]$_{1-2}$
lottery-ticket, resolving to throw myself into Fortune's lap, and try if she would make me amends for the injuries she had done me at the gaming-table. This purchase being made left me almost pennyless; when, as if I had not been sufficiently miserable, a bailiff in woman's clothes got admittance to my chamber, whither he was directed by the bookseller. He arrested me at my tailor's suit, for thirty-five pounds; a sum for which I could not procure bail, and was therefore conveyed to his house, where I was locked up in an upper chamber. I had now neither health (for I was scarce recovered from my indisposition) liberty,

money, or friends; and had abandoned all hopes, and even the desire of life. "But this could not last long," said Adams, "for doubtless the tailor released you the moment he was truly acquainted with your affairs; and knew that your circumstances would not permit you to pay him." Oh, sir, answered the gentleman, he knew that before he arrested me; nay, he knew that nothing but incapacity could prevent me paying my debts; for I had been his customer many years, had spent vast sums of money with him, and had always paid most punctually in my prosperous days: But when I reminded him of this, with assurance⟨s⟩$_2$ that if he would not molest my endeavours, I would pay him all the money I could, by my utmost labour and industry, procure, reserving only what was sufficient to preserve me alive: He answered, His patience was worn out; that I had put him off from time to time; that he wanted the money; that he had put it into a lawyer's hands; and if I did not pay him immediately, or find security, I must lie in gaol and expect no mercy. "He may expect mercy," cries Adams starting from his chair, "where he will find none. How can such a wretch repeat the Lord's Prayer, where the word which is translated, I know not for what reason, *trespasses,* is in the original *debts?* And as surely as we do not forgive others their debts when they are unable to pay them; so surely shall we ourselves be unforgiven, when we are in no condition of paying." He ceased, and the gentleman proceeded. While I was in this deplorable situation a former acquaintance, to whom I had communicated my lottery-ticket, found me out, and making me a visit with great delight in his countenance, shook me heartily by the hand, and wished me joy of my good fortune: "For," says he, "your ticket is come up a prize of 3000 *l.*" Adams snapt his fingers at these words in an ecstasy of joy; which however did not continue long: For the
[the]$_1$ gentleman thus proceeded. Alas! sir, this was only [a]$_2$ trick of Fortune to sink me the deeper: For I had disposed of this lottery-ticket two days before to a relation, who refused lending me a shilling without it, in order to procure myself bread. As soon as my friend was acquainted with my unfortunate sale, he began to revile me, and to remind me of all the ill conduct and miscarriages of my life. He said, "I was one whom Fortune could

not save, if she would; that I was now ruined without any hopes of retrieval, nor must expect any pity from my friends; that it would be extreme weakness to compassionate the misfortunes of a man who ran headlong to his own destruction." He then painted to me in as lively colours as he was able, the happiness I should have now enjoyed, had I not foolishly disposed of my ticket. I urged the plea of necessity: But he made no answer to that, and began again to revile me, till I could bear it no longer, and desired him to finish his visit. I soon exchanged the bailiff's house for a prison; where, as I had not money sufficient to procure me a separate apartment, I was crowded in with a great number of miserable wretches, in common with whom I was destitute of every convenience of life, even that which all the brutes enjoy, wholesome air. In these dreadful circumstances I applied by letter to several of my old acquaintance, and such to whom I had formerly lent money without any great prospect of its being returned, for their assistance; but in vain. An excuse instead of a denial was the gentlest answer I received. — Whilst I languished in a condition too horrible to be described, and which in a land of humanity, and, what is much more Christianity, seems a strange punishment for a little inadvertency and indiscretion. Whilst I was in this condition, a fellow came ~~one day~~[3] into the prison, and inquiring me out delivered me the following letter:

Sir,

My Father, to whom you sold your Ticket in the last Lottery, died the same Day in which it came up a Prize, as you have possibly heard, and left me sole Heiress of all his Fortune. I am so much touched with your present Circumstances, and the Uneasiness you must feel at having been driven to dispose of what might have made you happy, that I must desire your Acceptance of the inclosed, and am

Your humble Servant,
Harriet Hearty

And what do you think was inclosed? "I don't know," cried Adams: "Not less than a guinea, I hope." — Sir, it was a bank-note for 200 *l.* — "200 *l.*!" says Adams, in a rapture. — No less, I assure you, answered the gentleman; a sum I was not half so delighted with, as with the dear name of the generous girl that sent it me; and who was not only the best, but the handsomest creature in the universe; and for whom I had long had a passion, which I never durst disclose to her. I kissed her name a thousand times, my eyes overflowing with tenderness and gratitude, I repeated — . But not to detain you with these raptures, I immediately acquired my liberty, and having paid all my debts, departed with upwards of fifty pounds in my pocket, to thank my kind deliverer. She happened to be then out of town, a circumstance which, upon reflection, pleased me; for by that means I had an opportunity to appear before her in a more decent dress. At her return to town within a day or two, I threw myself at her feet with the most ardent acknowledgments, which she rejected with an unfeigned greatness of mind, and told me, I could not oblige her more than by never mentioning, or if possible, thinking on a circumstance which must bring to my mind an accident that might be grievous to me to think on. She proceeded thus: "What I have done is in my own eyes a trifle, and perhaps infinitely less than would have become me to do. And if you think of engaging in any business, where a larger sum may be serviceable to you, I shall not be over-rigid, either as to the security or interest." I endeavoured to express all the gratitude in my power to this profusion of goodness, though perhaps it was my enemy, and began to afflict my mind with more agonies, than all the miseries I had underwent; ⟨it affected me with severer reflections⟩ [2] than poverty, distress, and prisons united had been able to make me feel: For, sir, these acts and professions of kindness, which were sufficient to have raised in a good heart the most violent passion of friendship to one of the same, or to age and ugliness in a different sex, came to me from a woman, a young and beautiful woman, one whose perfections I had long known; and for whom I had long conceived a violent passion, though with a despair, which made me endeavour rather to curb and conceal, than to nourish or acquaint her with it. In short, they came upon me united with beauty, softness, and tenderness, such bewitching smiles. — O

Mr. Adams, in that moment, I lost myself, and forgetting our different situations, nor considering what return I was making to her goodness, by desiring her who had given me so much, to bestow her all, I laid gently hold on her hand, and conveying it to my lips, I prest it with inconceivable ardour; then lifting up my swimming eyes, I saw her face and neck overspread with one blush; she offered to withdraw her hand, yet not so as to deliver it from mine, though I held it with the gentlest force. We both stood trembling, her eyes cast on the ground, and mine steadfastly fixed on her. Good G—, what was then the condition of my soul! burning with Love, Desire, Admiration, Gratitude, and every tender passion, all bent on one charming object. Passion at last got the better of both Reason and Respect, and softly letting go her hand, I offered madly to clasp her in my arms; when a little recovering herself, she started from me, asking me with some show of anger, "if she had any reason to expect this treatment from me." I then fell prostrate before her, and told her, "if I had offended, my life was absolutely in her power, which I would in any manner lose for her sake. Nay, madam, (said I) you shall not be so ready to punish me, as I to suffer. I own my guilt. I detest the reflection that I would have sacrificed your happiness to mine. Believe me, I sincerely repent my ingratitude, yet believe me too, it was my passion, my unbounded passion for you, which hurried me so far; I have loved you long and tenderly; and the goodness you have shown me, hath innocently weighed down a wretch undone before. Acquit me of all mean mercenary views, and before I take my leave of you for ever, which I am resolved instantly to do, believe me, that Fortune could have raised me to no height to which I could not have gladly lifted you. O curst be Fortune." — "Do not," says she, interrupting me with the sweetest voice, "Do not curse Fortune, since she hath made me happy, and if she hath put your happiness in my power, I have told you, you shall ask nothing in reason which I will refuse." "Madam," said I, "you mistake me if you imagine, as you seem, my happiness is in the power of Fortune now. You have obliged me too much already; if I have any wish, it is for some blest accident, by which I may contribute with my life to the least augmentation of your felicity. As for myself, the only happiness I can ever have, will be hearing of yours; and if Fortune will make that complete, I will forgive her all her wrongs to me." "You may, indeed," answered she, smiling, "For [it]$_1$ your own ⟨happiness⟩$_2$ must be included in [mine].$_2$ I have long known your worth; nay, I must confess," said she, blushing, "I have long discovered that passion for me you profess, notwithstanding those endeavours which I am convinced were unaffected, to conceal it; and if all I can give with reason will not suffice, — take reason away, — and now I believe you cannot ask me what I will deny." — She uttered these words with a sweetness not to be imagined. I immediately started, my blood which lay freezing at my heart, rushed tumultuously through every vein. I stood for a moment silent, then flying to her, I caught her in my arms, no longer resisting, — and softly told her, she must give me then herself. — O sir, — Can I describe her look? She remained silent and almost motionless several minutes. At last, recovering herself a little, she insisted on my leaving her, and in such a manner that I instantly obeyed: You may imagine, however, I soon saw her again. — But I ask pardon, I fear I have detained you too long in relating the particulars of the former interview. "So far otherwise," said Adams, licking his lips, "that I could willingly hear it over again." Well, sir, continued the gentleman, to be as concise as possible, within a week she consented to make me the happiest of mankind. We were married shortly after; and when I came to examine the circumstances of my wife's fortune; (which I do assure you I was not presently at leisure enough to do) I found it amounted to about six thousand pounds, most part of which lay in effects; for her father had been a wine-merchant, and she seemed willing, if I liked it, that I should carry on the same trade. I readily and too inconsiderately undertook it: For not having been bred up to the secrets of the business, and endeavouring to deal with the utmost honesty and uprightness, I soon found our fortune in a declining way, and my trade decreasing by little and little: For my wines, which I never adulterated after their importation, and were sold as neat as they came over, were universally decried by the vintners, to whom I could not allow them quite as cheap as those who gained double the profit by a less price. I soon began to despair of improving our fortune by these means; nor was I at all easy at the visits and familiarity of many who had been my acquaintance in my prosperity, but denied, and shunned me in my adversity, and now very forwardly renewed their acquaintance with me. In short, I had sufficiently seen, that the pleasures of the world are chiefly folly, and the business of it mostly knavery; and both, nothing better than vanity: The men of pleasure tearing one another to pieces, from the emulation of spending money, and the men of business from envy in getting it. My happiness consisted entirely in my wife, whom I loved with an inexpressible fondness, which was perfectly returned; and my prospects were no other than to provide for our growing family; for she was now big of her second child; I therefore took an opportunity to ask her opinion of entering into a retired life, which after hearing my reasons, and perceiving my affection for it, she readily embraced. We soon put our small fortune, now reduced under three thousand pounds, into money, with part of which we purchased this little place, whither we retired soon after her delivery, from a world full of Bustle, Noise, Hatred, Envy, and Ingratitude, to Ease, Quiet, and Love. We have here lived almost twenty years, with little other conversation than our own, most of the neighbourhood taking us for very strange people; the squire of the parish representing me as a madman, and the parson as a Presbyterian; because I will not hunt with the one, nor drink with the other. "Sir," says Adams, "Fortune hath I think paid you all her debts in this sweet retirement." Sir, replied the gentleman, I am thankful to the great Author of all Things for the blessings I here enjoy. I have the best of wives, and three pretty children, for whom I have the true tenderness of a parent; but no blessings are pure in this world. Within three years of my arrival here I lost my eldest son. (*Here he sighed bitterly.*) "Sir," says Adams, "we must submit to Providence, and consider death is common to all." We must submit, indeed, answered the gentleman; and if he had died, I could have borne the loss with patience: But alas! sir, he was stolen away from my door by some wicked travelling people whom they call *Gipsies;* nor

could I ever with the most diligent search recover him. Poor
[Jacky]1 [child]2! he had the sweetest look, the exact picture of his mother; at which some tears unwittingly dropt from his eyes, as did likewise from those of Adams, who always sympathized with his friends on those occasions. Thus, sir, said the gentleman, I have finished my story, in which if I have been too particular, I ask your pardon; and now, if you please, I will fetch you another bottle; which proposal the parson thankfully accepted.

CHAP. IV.

A description of Mr. Wilson's way of living. The tragical adventure of the dog, and other grave matters.

THE gentleman returned with the bottle, and Adams and he sat some time silent, when the former started up and cried, "*No, that won't do.*" The gentleman inquired into his meaning; he answered, "he had been considering that it was possible the late famous King Theodore might have been that very son whom he lost"; [18] but added, "that his age could not answer that imagination. However," says he, "G— disposes all things for the best, and very probably he may be some great man, or duke, and may one day or other revisit you in that capacity." The gentleman answered, he should know him amongst ten thousand, for he had a mark on his left breast, of a strawberry, which his mother had given him by longing for that fruit.

That beautiful young lady, the Morning, now rose from her bed, and with a countenance blooming with fresh youth and

[18] In March, 1736, Theodore Stephen, Baron Von Neuhof, a German soldier of fortune, had been crowned Theodore I of Corsica, at the head of a group of Corsicans rebelling against their Genoese overlords. He decamped in November, 1736, to seek foreign aid, and returned in 1738 and again in 1739. He was still very much alive in 1741, when Adams describes him as "the late," returning to Corsica once again in 1743 and ending his days in London, December 11, 1756 (two years after Fielding himself).

sprightliness, like Miss *——, with soft dews hanging on her pouting lips, began to take her early walk over the eastern hills; and presently after, that gallant person the Sun stole softly from his wife's chamber to pay his addresses to her; when the gentleman asked his guest if he would walk forth and survey his little garden, which he readily agreed to, and Joseph at the same time awaking from a sleep in which he had been two hours buried, went with them. No parterres, no fountains, no statues embellished this little garden. Its only ornament was a short walk, shaded on each side by a filbert hedge, with a small alcove at one end, whither in hot weather the gentleman and his wife used to retire and divert themselves with their children, who played in the walk before them: But though Vanity had no votary in this little spot, here was variety of fruit, and everything useful for the kitchen, which was abundantly sufficient to catch the admiration of Adams, who told the gentleman he had certainly a good gardener. Sir, answered he, that gardener is now before you: whatever you see here, is the work solely of my own hands. Whilst I am providing necessaries for my table, I likewise procure myself an appetite for them. In fair seasons I seldom pass less than six hours of the twenty-four in this place, where I am not idle, and by these means I have been able to preserve my health ever since my arrival here without assistance from physic. Hither I generally repair at the dawn, [and]$_3$ [where I]$_{1-2}$
exercise myself whilst my wife dresses her children, and prepares our breakfast, after which we are seldom asunder during the residue of the day; for when the weather will not permit them to accompany me here, I am usually within with them; for I am neither ashamed of conversing with my wife, nor of playing with my children: to say the truth, I do not perceive that inferiority of understanding which the levity of rakes, the dulness of men of business, or the austerity of the learned would persuade us of in women. As for my woman, I declare I have found none of my own sex capable of making juster observations on life, or of delivering them more agreeably; nor do I believe anyone possessed of a faithfuller or braver friend. And sure as this friendship is sweetened with more delicacy and ten-

* *Whoever the reader pleases.* [Fielding's note.]

derness, so is it confirmed by dearer pledges than can attend the closest male alliance: For what union can be so fast, as our common interest in the fruits of our embraces? Perhaps, sir, you are not yourself a father; if you are not, be assured you cannot conceive the delight I have in my little-ones. Would you not despise me, if you saw me stretched on the ground, and my children playing round me? "I should reverence the sight," quoth Adams, "~~and~~$_{2}$ I myself am now the father of six, and have been of eleven, and I can say I never scourged a child of my own, unless as his school-master, and then have felt every stroke on my own posteriors. And as to what you say concerning women, I have often lamented my own wife did not understand Greek." — The gentleman smiled, and answered, he would not be apprehended to insinuate that his own had an understanding above the care of her family, on the contrary, says he, my Har- [few gentlemen's house-keepers]$_{1\text{-}3}$ riet I assure you is a notable house-wife, and [the house-keepers of few gentlemen]$_{4}$ understand cookery or confectionery better; but these are arts which she hath no great occasion for now: however, the wine you commended so much last night at supper, was of her own making, as is indeed all the liquor in my house, except my beer, which falls to my province. ⟨("And I assure you it is as excellent," quoth Adams, "as ever I tasted.")⟩$_{2}$ We formerly kept a maid-servant, but since my girls have been growing up, she is unwilling to indulge them in idleness; for as the fortunes I shall give them will be very small, we intend not to breed them above the rank they are likely to fill hereafter, nor to teach them to despise or ruin a plain husband. Indeed I could wish a man of my own temper, and a retired life, might fall to their lot: for I have experienced that calm serene happiness which is seated in content, is inconsistent with the hurry and bustle of the world. He was proceeding thus, when the little things, being just risen, ran eagerly towards him, and asked him blessing: They were shy to the strangers, but the eldest acquainted her father that her mother and the young gentlewoman were up, and that breakfast was ready. They all went in, where the gentleman was surprised at the beauty of Fanny, who had now recovered herself from her fatigue, and was entirely clean drest; for the rogues who had taken away her purse, had left her her bundle. But if he was so much amazed at the beauty of this young creature, his guests were no less charmed at the tenderness which appeared in the behaviour of husband and wife to each other, and to their children, and ⟨at⟩ $_2$ the dutiful and affectionate behaviour of these to their parents. These instances pleased the well-disposed mind of Adams equally with the readiness which they exprest to oblige their guests, and their forwardness to offer them the best of everything in their house; and what delighted him still more, was an instance or two of their Charity: for whilst they were at breakfast, the good woman was called for to assist her sick neighbour, which she did with some cordials made for the public use; and the good man went into his garden at the same time, to supply another with something which he wanted thence, for they had nothing which those who wanted it were not welcome to. These good people were in the utmost cheerfulness, when they heard the report of a gun, and immediately afterwards a little dog, the favourite of the eldest daughter, came limping in all bloody, and laid himself at his mistress's feet: The poor girl, who was about eleven years old, burst into tears at the sight, and presently one of the neighbours came in and informed them, that the young squire, the son of the lord of the manor, had shot him as he passed by, swearing at the same time he would prosecute the master of him for keeping a spaniel; for that he had given notice he would not suffer one in the parish. The dog, whom his mistress had taken into her lap, died in a few minutes, licking her hand. She exprest great agony at loss, and the other children began to cry for their sister's misfortune, nor could Fanny herself refrain. Whilst the father and mother attempted to comfort her, Adams grasped his crabstick, and would have sallied out after the squire, had not Joseph with-held him. He could not however bridle his tongue — He pronounced the word *Rascal* with great emphasis, said he deserved to be hanged more than a highwayman, and wished he had the scourging him. The mother took her child, lamenting and carrying the dead favourite in her arms out of the room, when the gentleman said, this was the second time this squire had endeavoured to kill the little wretch, and had wounded him smartly once before, adding, he could have no motive but ill-nature; for the little thing, which was not near as big as one's fist, had never been twenty yards from the house in the six years his daughter had had it. He said he had done nothing to deserve this usage: but his father had too great a fortune to contend with. That he was as absolute as any tyrant in the universe, and had killed all the dogs, and taken away all the guns in the neighbourhood, and not only that, but he trampled down hedges, and rode over corn and gardens, with no more regard than if they were the highway. "I wish I could catch him in my garden," said Adams; "though I would rather forgive him riding through my house than such an ill-natured act as this."

The cheerfulness of their conversation being interrupted by this accident, in which the guests could be of no service to their kind entertainer, and as the mother was taken up in administering consolation to the poor girl, whose disposition was too good hastily to forget the sudden loss of her little favourite, which had been fondling with her a few minutes before; and as Joseph and Fanny were impatient to get home and begin those previous ceremonies to their happiness which Adams had insisted on, they now offered to take their leave. The gentleman importuned them much to stay dinner; but when he found their eagerness to depart, he summoned his wife, and accordingly having performed all the usual ceremonies of bows and curtsies, more pleasant to be seen than to be related, they took their leave, the gentleman and his wife heartily wishing them a good journey, and they as heartily thanking them for their kind entertainment. They then departed, Adams declaring that this was the manner in which the people had lived in the Golden Age.

CHAP. V.

A disputation on schools, held on the road between Mr. Abraham Adams and Joseph; and a discovery not unwelcome to them both.

OUR travellers having well refreshed themselves at the gentleman's house, Joseph and Fanny with sleep, and Mr. Abraham

Adams with ale and tobacco, renewed their journey with great alacrity; and, pursuing the road into which they were directed, travelled many miles before they met with any adventure worth relating. In this interval, we shall present our readers with a very curious discourse, as we apprehend it, concerning public schools, which passed between Mr. Joseph Andrews and Mr. Abraham Adams.

They had not gone far, before Adams calling to Joseph, asked him if he had attended to the gentleman's story; he answered, "to all the former [part]. 2" "And don't you think," says he, "he was a very unhappy man in his youth?" "A very unhappy man indeed," answered the other. "Joseph," cries Adams, screwing up his mouth, "I have found it; I have discovered the cause of all the misfortunes which befell him. A public school, Joseph, was the cause of all the calamities which he after⟨wards⟩ 2 suffered. Public schools are the nurseries of all vice and immorality. All the wicked fellows whom I remember at the university were bred at them. — Ah Lord! I can remember as well as if it was but yesterday, a knot of them; they called them King's Scholars, I forget why — very wicked fellows! [19] Joseph, you may thank the Lord you were not bred at a public school, you would never have preserved your virtue as you have. The first care I always take, is of a boy's morals, I had rather he should be a blockhead than an atheist or a Presbyterian. What is all the learning of the world compared to his immortal soul? What shall a man take in exchange for his soul? But the masters of great schools trouble themselves about no such thing. I have known a lad of eighteen at the university, who hath not been able to say his Catechism; but for my own part, I always scourged a lad sooner for missing that than any other lesson. Believe me, child, all that gentleman's misfortunes arose from his being educated at a public school."

[parts] 1

"It doth not become me," answered Joseph, "to dispute anything, sir, with you, especially a matter of this kind; for to be sure you must be allowed by all the world to be the best teacher of a school in all our county." "Yes, that," says Adams, "I be-

[19] Students on scholarship to Oxford (or Cambridge) from Westminster School, supported by the crown.

lieve, is granted me; that I may without much vanity pretend to—nay I believe I may go to the next county too—but *gloriari non est meum.*"[20]—"However, sir, as you are pleased to bid me speak," says Joseph, "you know, my late master, Sir Thomas Booby, was bred at a public school, and he was the finest gentleman in all the neighbourhood. And I have often heard him say, if he had a hundred boys he would breed them all at the same place. It was his opinion, and I have often heard him deliver it, that a boy taken from a public school, and carried into the world, will learn more in one year there, than one of a private education will in five. He used to say, the school itself initiated him a great way, (I remember that was his very expression) for great schools are little societies, where a boy of any observation may see in epitome what he will after⟨wards⟩ 2
find in the world at large." "*Hinc illæ lachrymæ;*[21] for that very reason," quoth Adams, "I prefer a private school, where boys may be kept in innocence and ignorance: for, according to that fine passage in the play of *Cato*, the only English tragedy I ever read,

> *If Knowledge of the World must make Men Villains,*
> *May* Juba *ever life in Ignorance.*[22]

Who would not rather preserve the purity of his child, than wish him to attain the whole circle of arts and sciences; which, by the bye, he may learn in the classes of a private school? for I would not be vain, but I esteem myself to be second to none, *nulli secundum*, in teaching these things; so that a lad may have as much learning in a private as in a public education." "And with submission," answered Joseph, "he may get as much vice, witness several country gentlemen, who were educated within five miles of their own houses, and are as wicked as if they had known the world from their infancy. I remember when I was in the stable, if a young horse was vicious in his nature, no correction would make him otherwise; I take it to be equally the same among men: if a boy be of a mischievous wicked inclina-

[20] "It is not my place to brag."

[21] "Hence those tears" (Horace, *Epistles* I.xix.41).

[22] After Joseph Addison's *Cato* II.v: "If Knowledge of the World makes Man perfidious,/May *Juba* ever live in Ignorance!"

tion, no school, though ever so private, will ever make him good; on the contrary, if he be of a righteous temper, you may trust him to London, or wherever else you please, he will be in no danger of being corrupted. Besides, I have often heard my master say, that the discipline practised in public schools was much better than that in private."—"You talk like a Jackanapes," says Adams, "and so did your master. Discipline indeed! because one man scourges twenty or thirty boys more in a morning than another, is he therefore a better disciplinarian? I do presume to confer in this point with all who have taught from Chiron's time to this day; and, if I was master of six boys only, I would preserve as good discipline amongst them as the master of the greatest school in the world. I say nothing, young man; remember, I say nothing; but if Sir Thomas himself had been educated nearer home, and under the tuition of somebody, remember, I name nobody, it might have been better for him—but his father must institute him in the knowledge of the world. *Nemo mortalium omnibus horis sapit.*"[23] Joseph seeing him run on in this manner asked pardon many times, assuring him he had no intention to offend. "I believe you had not, child," said he, "and I am not angry with you: but for maintaining good discipline in a school; for this,—" And then he ran on as before, named all the masters who are recorded in old books, and preferred himself to them all. Indeed if this good man had an enthusiasm, or what the vulgar call a blind-side, it was this: He thought a schoolmaster the greatest character in the world, and himself the greatest of all schoolmasters, neither of which points he would have given up to Alexander the Great at the head of his army.

Adams continued his subject till they came to one of the beautifullest spots of ground in the universe. It was a kind of natural amphitheatre, formed by the winding of a small rivulet, which was planted with thick woods, [and the]$_2$ trees rose gradually [whose]$_1$ above each other by the natural ascent of the ground they stood on; which ascent, as they hid with their boughs, they seemed to have been disposed by the [design of the most skilful]$_3$ planter. [most skillful design of the]$_{1\text{-}2}$

[23] "No mortal understands at all hours" (Pliny, *Natural History* VII.xl. 131).

The soil was spread with a verdure which no paint could imitate, and the whole place might have raised romantic ideas in elder minds than those of Joseph and Fanny, without the assistance of love.

Here they arrived about noon, and Joseph proposed to Adams that they should rest a while in this delightful place, and refresh themselves with some provisions which the good-nature of Mrs. Wilson had provided them with. Adams made no objection to the proposal, so down they sat, and pulling out a cold fowl, and a bottle of wine, they made a repast with a cheerfulness which might have attracted the envy of more splendid tables. I should not omit, that they found among their provision a little paper, containing a piece of gold, which Adams ~~it~~$_3$ imagining had been put there by mistake, would have returned [deliver them]$_{1-2}$ back, to [restore it]$_3$; but he was at last convinced by Joseph, that Mr. Wilson had taken this handsome way of furnishing them with a supply for their journey, on his having related the distress which they had been in, when they were relieved by the generosity of the pedlar. Adams said, he was glad to see such an instance of goodness, not so much for the conveniency which [but]$_{1-2}$ it brought ~~to~~$_2$ them, [as]$_3$ for the sake of the doer, whose reward would be great in heaven. He likewise comforted himself with a reflection, that he should shortly have an opportunity of returning it him; for the gentleman was within a week to make a journey into Somersetshire, to pass through Adams's parish, and had faithfully promised to call on him: A circumstance which we thought too immaterial to mention before; but which those who have as great an affection for that gentleman as ourselves will rejoice at, as it may give them hopes of seeing him again. Then Joseph made a speech on Charity, which the reader, if he is so disposed, may see in the next chapter; for we scorn to betray him into any such reading, without first giving him warning.

CHAP. VI.

Moral reflections by Joseph Andrews, with the hunting adventure, and Parson Adams's miraculous escape.

"I have often wondered, sir," said [Joseph]$_2$, "to observe so few instances of Charity among mankind; for though the goodness of a man's heart did not incline him to relieve the distresses of his fellow-creatures, methinks the desire of honour should move him to it. What inspires a man to build fine houses, to purchase fine furniture, pictures, clothes, and other things at a great expense, but an ambition to be respected more than other people? Now would not one great act of charity, one instance of redeeming a poor family from all the miseries of poverty, restoring an unfortunate tradesman by a sum of money to the means of procuring a livelihood by his industry, discharging an undone debtor from his debts or a gaol, or any such like example of goodness, create a man more honour and respect than he could acquire by the finest house, furniture, pictures or clothes that were ever beheld? For not only the object himself, who was thus relieved, but all who heard the name of such a person must, I imagine, reverence him infinitely more than the possessor of all those other things: which when we so admire, we rather praise the builder, the workman, the painter, the laceman, the tailor, and the rest, by whose ingenuity they are produced, than the person who by his money makes them his own. For my own part, when I have waited behind my lady in a room hung with fine pictures, while I have been looking at them I have never once thought of their owner, nor hath anyone else, as I ever observed; for when it hath been asked whose picture that was, it was never once answered, the master's of the house, but *Ammyconni*, *Paul Varnish*, *Hannibal* [*Scratchi*]$_2$, or *Hogarthi*, which I suppose were the names of the painters: [24] but if it was

[he]$_1$

[*Scarachi*]$_1$

[24] Jacopo Amigoni (1675–1752), who had visited England from 1730 to 1739, and who had painted the portrait of Queen Caroline; Paolo Veronese (1528–1588); Annibale Carracci (1560–1609); and William Hogarth (1697–1764).

asked, who redeemed such a one out of prison? who lent such a ruined tradesman money to set up? who clothed that family
[little]$_{1\text{-}2}$ of poor [small]$_3$ children? it is very plain, what must be the answer. And besides, these great folks are mistaken, if they imagine they get any honour at all by these means; for I do not
[have ever remember I [ever was]$_3$ with my lady at any house where she
been]$_3$ commended the house or furniture, but I have heard her at her return home make sport and jeer at whatever she had before commended: and I have been told by other gentlemen in livery, that it is the same in their families: but I defy the wisest man in the world to turn a true good action into ridicule. I defy him to do it. He who should endeavour it, would be laughed at himself, instead of making others laugh. Nobody scarce doth any good, yet they all agree in praising those who do. Indeed it is strange that all men should consent in commending goodness, and no man endeavour to deserve that commendation; whilst, on the contrary, all rail at wickedness, and all are as eager to be what they abuse. This I know not the reason of, but it is as plain as daylight to those who converse in the world, as I have done these three years." "Are all the great folks wicked then?" says Fanny. "To be sure there are some exceptions," answered Joseph. "Some gentlemen of our cloth report charitable actions done by their lords and masters, and I have heard 'Squire Pope, the great poet, at my lady's table, tell stories of a man that lived at a place called Ross,[25] and another at the Bath, one Al— Al— I forget his name,[26] but it is in the book of verses. This gentleman hath built up a stately house too, which the 'Squire likes very well; but his Charity is seen farther than his house, though it stands on a hill, ay, and brings him more honour ⟨too⟩$_3$. It
[upon]$_{1\text{-}2}$ was his Charity that put him [in]$_3$ the book, where the 'Squire says he puts all those who deserve it; and to be sure, as he lives among all the great people, if there were any such, he would know them." — This was all of Mr. Joseph Andrews's speech which I could get him to recollect, which I have delivered as

[25] John Kyrle; Pope's *Epistle to Bathurst* (ll. 250–90) praises his benevolence.

[26] Ralph Allen; his generosity is praised in Pope's *Epilogue to the Satires* I.135–36. See above, pp. 242–43.

near as was possible in his own words, with a very small embellishment. But I believe the reader hath not been a little surprised at the long silence of Parson Adams, especially as so many occasions offered themselves to exert his curiosity and observation. The truth is, he was fast asleep, and had so been from the beginning of the preceding narrative: and indeed if the reader considers that [so many hours]$_2$ had passed since he had closed his eyes, he will not wonder at his repose, though even Henley himself, or as great an orator (if any such be) had been in his *Rostrum* or Tub before him.[28]

[two nights]$_1$ [27]

Joseph, who, whilst he was speaking, had continued in one attitude, with his head reclining on one side, and his eyes cast on the ground, no sooner perceived, on looking up, the position of Adams, who was stretched on his back, and snored louder than the usual braying of the animal with long ears; than he turned towards Fanny, and taking her by the hand, began ⟨a⟩$_2$ dalliance, which, though consistent with the purest innocence and decency, neither he would have attempted, nor she permitted before any witness. Whilst they amused themselves in this harmless and delightful manner, they heard a pack of hounds approaching in full cry towards them, and presently

[27] In the first edition, Fielding had added a note on the otherwise blank page facing page one of his text and following his Preface: "Among other errors, the reader is desired to excuse this: that in the second volume, Mr. Adams is, by mistake, mentioned to have sat up two subsequent nights; when in reality, a night of rest intervened" (the one at the inn, II.xvi); noted by Battestin, p. 235.

[28] John Henley (1692–1759), an eccentric clergyman known as "Orator" Henley. In 1726, he resigned two appointments in the regular church to set up an independent church, which he called his "oratory," licensed by the government and opened in Newport Market, London. In 1729, he moved his chapel to Lincoln's Inn Fields, where he held forth for the rest of his (and Fielding's) life. His sermons were full of wild eloquence and gesture, wit and absurdity. He seems to have used an old style of pulpit commonly called a "tub" (from its tub-like construction), though, since it was covered with velvet embroidered with fleur-de-lis, the frequent references to his "Tub" may indicate a standing witticism. He wrote a "Primitive Liturgy" and celebrated a "Primitive Eucharist" (unleavened bread and mixed wine). He sold medals for a shilling as tickets of admission, and lectured on secular subjects on Wednesdays, with his usual facetious extravagance. He edited a weekly newspaper, *The Hyp-Doctor* (1730–41), supporting Sir Robert Walpole, from whom he soon received a pension of £100 a year.

afterwards saw a hare pop forth from the wood, and crossing
the water, land within a few yards of them in the meadows. The
hare was no sooner on shore, than it seated itself on its hinder
legs, and listened to the sound of the pursuers. Fanny was wonderfully pleased with the little wretch, and eagerly longed to
have it in her arms, that she might preserve it from the dangers
[sensible and which seemed to threaten it: but the [rational]$_3$ part of the crea-
human]$_{1\text{-}2}$ tion do not always aptly distinguish their friends from their
foes; what wonder then if this silly creature, the moment it
[, fled from beheld [her, fled from the friend]$_2$ who would have protected
her]$_1$ it, and traversing the meadows again, passed the little rivulet on
the opposite side. It was however so spent and weak, that it fell
down twice or thrice in its way. This affected the tender heart
of Fanny, who exclaimed with tears in her eyes against the bar-
barity of worrying a poor innocent defenceless animal out of its
life, and putting it to the extremest torture for diversion. She
had not much time to make reflections of this kind, for on a
sudden the hounds rushed through the wood, which resounded
[attendants with their throats, and the throats of their [*retinue,* who *at-*
who waited]$_1$ *tended*]$_2$ on them on horseback. The dogs now passed the rivulet, and pursued the footsteps of the hare; five horsemen attempted to leap over, three of whom succeeded, and two were
in the attempt thrown from their saddles into the water; their
companions and their own horses too proceeded after their sport,
and left their friends and riders to invoke the assistance of Fortune, or employ the more active means of strength and agility
for their deliverance. Joseph however was not so unconcerned
on this occasion; he left Fanny for a moment to herself, and ran
to the gentlemen, who were immediately on their legs, shaking
their ears, and easily with the help of his hand attained the bank,
(for the rivulet was not at all deep) and without staying to
thank their kind assister, ran dripping across the meadow, calling to their brother sportsmen to stop their horses: but they
heard them not.

The hounds were now very little behind their poor reeling, staggering prey, which fainting almost at every step, crawled through the wood, and had almost got round to the place where Fanny stood, when it was overtaken by its enemies; and being driven out of the covert was caught, and instantly tore to pieces before Fanny's face, who was unable to assist it with any aid more powerful than pity; nor could she prevail on Joseph, who had been himself a sportsman in his youth, to attempt anything contrary to the laws of hunting, in favour of the hare, which he said was killed fairly.

The hare was caught within a yard or two of Adams, who lay asleep at some distance from the lovers, and the hounds in devouring it, and pulling it backwards and forwards, had drawn it so close to him, that some of them (by mistake perhaps for the hare's skin) laid hold of the skirts of his cassock[;]$_{3}$ others [,]$_{1\text{-}2}$
at the same time applying their teeth to his wig, which he had with a handkerchief fastened to his head, they began to pull him about; and had not the motion of his body had more effect on him than seemed to be wrought by the noise, they must certainly have tasted his flesh, which delicious flavour might have been fatal to him: But being roused by these tuggings, he instantly awaked, and with a jerk delivering his head from his wig, he with most admirable dexterity recovered his legs, which now seemed the only members he could entrust his safety to. Having therefore escaped likewise from at least a third part of his cassock, which he willingly left as his *Exuviæ* or spoils to the enemy, he fled with the utmost speed he could summon to his assistance. Nor let this be any detraction from the bravery of his character; let the number of the enemies, and the surprise in which he was taken, be considered; and if there be any Modern so outrageously brave, that he cannot admit of flight in any circumstance whatever, I say (but I whisper that softly, and I solemnly declare, without any intention of giving offence to any brave man in the nation) I say, or rather I whisper that he is an ignorant fellow, and hath never read Homer nor Virgil, nor knows he anything of Hector or Turnus; nay, he is unacquainted with the history of some great men living, who, though as brave as lions, ay, as tigers, have run away the Lord knows how far, and the Lord knows why, to the surprise of their friends, and the entertainment of their enemies. But if persons of such heroic disposition are a little offended at the behaviour of Adams, we assure them they shall be as much

pleased with what we shall immediately relate of Joseph Andrews. The master of the pack was just arrived, or, as the sportsmen call it, *Come in,* when Adams set out, as we have before mentioned. This gentleman was generally said to be a great lover of humour; but not to mince the matter, especially as we are upon this subject, he was a great *Hunter of Men:* indeed he had hitherto followed the sport only with dogs of his own species; for he kept two or three couple of barking curs for that use only. However, as he thought he had now found a man nimble enough, he was willing to indulge himself with other sport, and accordingly crying out, *Stole away,* encouraged the hounds to pursue Mr. Adams, swearing it was the largest jack-hare he ever saw; at the same time hallooing and hooping as if a conquered foe was flying before him; in which he was imitated by these two or three couple of human, or rather two-legged curs on horseback which we have mentioned before.

Now thou, whoever thou art, whether a Muse, or by what other name soever thou choosest to be called, who presidest over Biography, and hast inspired all the writers of lives in these our times: Thou who didst infuse such wonderful humour into the pen of immortal Gulliver, who hast carefully guided the judgment, whilst thou hast exalted the nervous manly style of thy Mallet: [29] Thou who hadst no hand in that Dedication, and Preface, or the translations which thou wouldst willingly have struck out of the *Life of Cicero:* [30] Lastly, Thou who without the assistance of the least spice of literature, and even against his inclination, hast, in some pages of his book, forced Colley Cibber to write English; do thou assist me in what I find myself unequal to. Do thou introduce on the plain, the young, the gay, the brave Joseph Andrews, whilst men shall view him with admiration and envy; tender virgins with love and anxious concern for his safety.

[29] David Mallet (1705–65), an anti-Walpole writer; his recent *Life of Francis Bacon* (1740), was dedicated to the Earl of Chesterfield and published by Andrew Millar (Fielding's publisher) in an edition of Bacon's works.

[30] *The Life of Cicero* (1740) is Conyers Middleton's book, already lambasted in *Shamela* for its Dedication to Lord Hervey (Walpole's friend), who is soon to appear caricatured as Beau Didapper (IV.vii and ix ff.).

No sooner did Joseph Andrews perceive the distress of his friend, when first the quick-scenting dogs attacked him, than he grasped his cudgel in his right hand, a cudgel which his father had of his grandfather, to whom a mighty strong man of Kent had given it for a present in that day, when he broke three heads on the stage.[31] It was a cudgel of mighty strength and wonderful art, made by one of Mr. Deard's best workmen,[32] whom no other artificer can equal; and who hath made all those sticks which the beaus have lately walked with about the Park in a morning: But this was far his master-piece; on its head was engraved a nose and chin, which might have been mistaken for a pair of nut-crackers. The learned have imagined it designed to represent the Gorgon: but it was in fact copied from the face of a certain ⟨long⟩ $_2$ English baronet of infinite wit, humour, and gravity.[33] He did intend to have engraved here many histories: As the first night of Captain B——'s play, where you would have seen critics in embroidery transplanted from the boxes to the pit, whose ancient inhabitants were exalted to the galleries, where they played on catcalls.[34] He did intend to have painted an auction-room, where Mr. Cock would have appeared aloft in his pulpit, trumpeting forth the praises of a China basin; and with astonishment wondering that *Nobody bids more for that fine, that superb*——[35] He did intend to have engraved many other things, but was forced to leave all out for want of room.

No sooner had Joseph grasped this cudgel in his hands, than

[31] William Joy (d. 1734), known as "Samson, the strong man of Kent."

[32] William Deard (d. 1734), fashionable merchant of jewelry and accessories, here corresponds to Hephaestus, the smith-god and artificer, who made the shield of Achilles, in this mock-heroic parallel to the *Iliad* XVIII.478–613.

[33] "Long" Sir Thomas Robinson (1700?–77), Walpole's Commissioner of the Excise, noted for his height and his dullness, and his extravagant parties: he gave a ball for 300 that lasted until 6 A.M. at the begining of December, 1741, about the time Fielding would have been writing this passage (Battestin, p. 240).

[34] *The Modish Couple*, by Charles Bodens, Gentleman Usher to the King, was actually written by Lord Hervey and the Prince of Wales. The secret leaked, and the audience organized to boo it when it opened on January 10, 1732. Fielding had written the Epilogue to it, before the secret was out.

[35] Christopher Cock (d. 1748) ran a fashionable auction in Covent Garden.

lightning darted from his eyes; and the heroic youth, swift of foot, ran with the utmost speed to his friend's assistance. He overtook him just as Rockwood had laid hold of the skirt of his cassock, which being torn hung to the ground. Reader, we would make a simile on this occasion, but for two reasons: The first is, it would interrupt the description, which should be *rapid* in this part; but that doth not weigh much, many precedents occurring for such an interruption: The second, and much the greater reason is, that we could find no simile adequate to our purpose: For indeed, what instance could we bring to set before our reader's eyes at once the idea of Friendship, Courage, Youth, Beauty, Strength, and Swiftness; all which blazed in the person of Joseph Andrews. Let those therefore that describe lions and tigers, and heroes fiercer than both, raise their poems or plays with the simile of Joseph Andrews, who is himself above the reach of any simile.

Now Rockwood had laid fast hold on the parson's skirts, and stopt his flight; which Joseph no sooner perceived, than he levelled his cudgel at his head, and laid him sprawling. Jowler and Ringwood then fell on his greatcoat, and had undoubtedly brought him to the ground, had not Joseph, collecting all his force given Jowler such a rap on the back, that quitting his hold he ran howling over the plain: A harder fate remained for thee, O Ringwood. Ringwood the best hound that ever pursued a hare, who never threw his tongue but where the scent was undoubtedly true; good at *trailing;* and *sure in a highway,* no *Babler,* no *Over-runner,* respected by the whole pack[: For, whenever he opened, they]$_4$ knew the game was at hand. He fell by the stroke of Joseph. Thunder, and Plunder, and Wonder, and Blunder, were the next victims of his wrath, and measured their lengths on the ground. Then Fairmaid, a bitch which Mr. John Temple [36] had bred up in his house, and fed at his own table, and lately sent the squire fifty miles for a present, ran fiercely at Joseph, and bit him by the leg; no dog was ever fiercer than she, being descended from an Amazonian breed, and

[, who, whenever he opened,]$_{1-3}$

[36] Mr. John Temple (1680–1752) lived at Moor Park, Surrey—which he had acquired by marrying his cousin—the estate made famous by Jonathan Swift's residence there in his service to Sir William Temple.

had worried bulls in her own country, but now waged an unequal fight; and had shared the fate of [those]$_3$ we have mentioned before, had not Diana (the reader may believe it or not, as he pleases) in that instant interposed, and in the shape of the huntsman snatched her favourite up in her arms. [these]$_{1-2}$

The parson now faced about, and with his crabstick felled many to the earth, and scattered others, till he was attacked by Cæsar and pulled to the ground; then Joseph flew to his rescue, and with such might fell on the victor, that, O eternal blot to his name! Cæsar ran yelping away.

The battle now raged with the most dreadful violence, when lo the huntsman, a man of years and dignity, lifted his voice, and called his hounds from the fight; telling them, in a language they understood, that it was in vain to contend longer; for that Fate had decreed the victory to their enemies.

Thus far the Muse hath with her usual dignity related this prodigious battle, a battle we apprehend never equalled by any poet, romance or life-writer whatever, and having brought it to a conclusion she ceased; we shall therefore proceed in our ordinary style with the continuation of this history. The squire and his companions, whom the figure of Adams and the gallantry of Joseph had at first thrown into a violent fit of laughter, and who had hitherto beheld the engagement with more delight than any chase, shooting-match, race, cock-fighting, bull or bear-baiting had ever given them, began now to apprehend the danger of their hounds, many of which lay sprawling in the fields. The squire therefore having first called his friends about him, as guards for safety of his person, rode manfully up to the combatants, and summoning all the terror he was master of, into his countenance, demanded with an authoritative voice of Joseph, what he meant by assaulting his dogs in that manner. Joseph answered with great intrepidity, that they had first fallen on his friend; and if they had belonged to the greatest man in the kingdom, he would have treated them in the same way; for whilst his veins contained a single drop of blood, he would not stand idle by, and see that gentleman (*pointing to Adams*) abused either by man or beast; and having so said, both he and Adams brandished their wooden weapons, and put themselves into such a posture, that the squire and his company thought proper to preponderate, before they offered to revenge the cause of their four-footed allies.

At this instant Fanny, whom the apprehension of Joseph's danger had alarmed so much, that forgetting her own she had made the utmost expedition, came up. The squire and all the horsemen were so surprised with her beauty, that they immediately fixed both their eyes and thoughts solely on [her, everyone declaring]$_2$ he had never seen so charming a creature. Neither mirth nor anger engaged them a moment longer; but all sat in silent amaze. The huntsman only was free from her attraction, who was busy in cutting the ears of the dogs, and endeavouring to recover them to life; in which he succeeded so well, that only two of no great note remained slaughtered on the field of action. Upon this the huntsman declared, "'twas well it was no worse; for his part he could not blame the gentleman, and wondered his master would encourage the dogs to hunt *Christians;* that it was the surest way to spoil them, to make them follow *vermin* instead of sticking to a hare."

[her. Everyone declared]$_1$

The squire being informed of the little mischief that had been done; and perhaps having more mischief of another kind in his head, accosted Mr. Adams with a more favourable aspect than before: he told him he was sorry for what had happened; that he had endeavoured all he could to prevent it, the moment he was acquainted with his cloth, and greatly commended the courage of his servant; for so he imagined Joseph to be. He then invited Mr. Adams to dinner, and desired the young woman might come with him. Adams refused a long while; but the invitation was repeated with so much earnestness and courtesy, that at length he was forced to accept it. His wig and hat, and other spoils of the field, being gathered together by Joseph, (for otherwise probably they would have been forgotten;) he put himself into the best order he could; and then the horse and foot moved forward in the same pace towards the squire's house, which stood at a very little distance.

Whilst they were on the road, the lovely Fanny attracted the eyes of all; they endeavoured to outvie one another in encomiums on her beauty; which the reader will pardon my not relating, as they had not anything new or uncommon in them: So must he likewise my not setting down the many curious jests which were made on Adams, some of them declaring that parson-hunting was the best sport in the world: Others commending his standing at bay, which they said he had done as well as any badger; with such like merriment, which though it would ill become the dignity of this history, afforded much laughter and diversion to the squire, and his facetious companions.

CHAP. VII.

A scene of roasting very nicely adapted to the present taste and times.[37]

THEY arrived at the squire's house just as his dinner was ready. A little dispute arose on the account of Fanny, whom the squire who was a bachelor, was desirous to place at his own table; but she would not consent, nor would Mr. Adams permit her to be parted from Joseph: so that she was at length with him consigned over to the kitchen, where the servants were ordered to make him drunk; a favour which was likewise intended for Adams: which design being executed, the squire thought he should easily accomplish, what he had, when he first saw her, intended to perpetrate with Fanny.

It may not be improper, before we proceed farther, to open a little the character of this gentleman, and that of his friends. The master of this house then, was a man of a very considerable fortune; a bachelor, as we have said, and about forty years of age: He had been educated (if we may [here use that]$_4$ expres- [use the]$_{1\text{-}3}$
sion) in the country, and at his own home, under the care of his mother and a tutor, who had orders never to correct him nor to

[37] Based on the apparently not untypical amusements of an actual eighteenth-century squire, including the mock ceremony and tub of water (Digeon, *The Novels of Fielding* [London: George Routledge & Sons, Ltd., 1925], p. 65, n.2; Battestin, *Joseph Andrews,* Wesleyan Edition, p. xxiv, n.1).

compel him to learn more than he liked, which it seems was very little, and that only in his childhood; for from the age of fifteen he addicted himself entirely to hunting and other rural amusements, for which his mother took care to equip him with horses, hounds, and all other necessaries: and his tutor endeavouring to ingratiate himself with his young pupil, who would, he knew, be able handsomely to provide for him, became his companion, not only at these exercises, but likewise over a bottle, which the young squire had a very early relish for. At the age of twenty, his mother began to think she had not fulfilled the duty of a parent; she therefore resolved to persuade her son, if possible, to that which she imagined would well supply all that he might have learned at a public school or university. This is what they commonly call *Travelling;* which, with the help of the tutor who was fixed on to attend him, she easily succeeded in. He made in three years the Tour of Europe, as they term it, and returned home, well furnished with French clothes, phrases and servants, with a hearty contempt for his own country; especially what had any savour of the plain spirit and honesty of our ancestors. His mother greatly applauded herself at his return; and now being master of his own fortune, he soon procured himself a seat in Parliament, and was in the common opinion one of the finest gentlemen of his age: But what distinguished him chiefly, was a strange delight which he took in everything which is ridiculous, odious, and absurd in his own species; so that he never chose a companion without one or more of these ingredients, and those who were marked by Nature in the most eminent degree with them, were most his favourites: if he ever found a man who either had not or endeavoured to conceal these imperfections, he took great pleasure in inventing methods of forcing him into absurdities, which were not natural to him, or in drawing forth and exposing those that were; for which purpose he was always provided with a set of fellows whom we have before called curs; and who did indeed no great honour to the canine kind: Their business was to hunt out and display everything that had any savour of the above-mentioned qualities, and especially in the gravest and best characters: but if they failed in their search, they were to turn even Virtue and Wisdom themselves into ridicule for the diversion of their master and feeder. The gentlemen of curlike disposition, who were now at his house, and whom he had brought with him from London, were an old half-pay officer, a player, a dull poet, a quack doctor, a scraping fiddler, and a lame German dancing-master.

As soon as dinner was served, while Mr. Adams was saying grace, the captain conveyed his chair from behind him; so that when he endeavoured to seat himself, he fell down on the ground; and thus completed joke the first, to the great entertainment of the whole company. The second joke was performed by the poet, who sat next him on the other side, and took an opportunity, while poor Adams was respectfully drinking to the master of the house, to overturn a plate of soup into his breeches; which, with the many apologies he made, and the parson's gentle answers, caused much mirth in the company. Joke the third was [served up by one of the waiting-men]2, who had been ordered to convey a quantity of gin into Mr. Adams's ale, which he declaring to be the best liquor he ever drank, but rather too rich of the malt, contributed again to their laughter. Mr. Adams, from whom we had most of this relation, could not recollect all the jests of this kind practised on him, which the inoffensive disposition of his own heart made him slow in discovering; and indeed, had it not been for the information which we received from a servant of the family, this part of our history, which we take to be none of the least curious, must have been deplorably imperfect; though we must own it probable, that some more jokes were (as they call it) *cracked* during their dinner; but we have by no means been able to come at the knowledge of them. When dinner was removed, the poet began to repeat some verses, which he said were made *extempore*. The following is a copy of them, procured with the greatest difficulty.

[performed by one of the serving-men]1

An extempore *Poem on Parson Adams.*

Did ever Mortal such a Parson view;
His Cassock old, his Wig not over-new?
Well might the Hounds have him for Fox mistaken,
*In Smell more like to that, than rusty Bacon.**

* All hounds that will hunt fox or other vermin, will hunt a piece of rusty bacon trailed on the ground. [Fielding's note.]

But would it not make any Mortal stare,
To see this Parson taken for a Hare?
Could Phœbus *err thus grossly, even he*
For a good Player might have taken thee.

At which words the bard whipt off the player's wig, and received the approbation of the company, rather perhaps for the dexterity of his hand than his head. The player, instead of retorting the jest on the poet, began to display his talents on the same subject. He repeated many scraps of wit out of plays, reflecting on the whole body of the clergy, which were received with great acclamations by all present. It was now the dancing-master's turn to exhibit his talents; he therefore addressing himself to Adams in broken English, told him, "he was a man ver well made for de dance, and he suppose by his walk, dat he had learn of some great master. He said it was ver pretty quality in clergyman to dance;" and concluded with desiring him to dance a minuet, telling him, "his cassock would serve for petticoats; and that he would himself be his partner." At which words, without waiting for an answer, he pulled out his gloves, and the fiddler was preparing his fiddle. The company all offered the dancing-master wagers that the parson outdanced him, which he refused, saying, "he believed so too; for he had never seen any man in his life who looked de dance so well as de gentleman:" He then stepped forwards to take Adams by the hand, which
[he]$_1$ [the latter]$_2$ hastily withdrew, and at the same time clenching his fist, advised him not to carry the jest too far, for he would not endure being put upon. The dancing-master no sooner saw the fist than he prudently retired out of its reach, and stood aloof mimicking Adams, whose eyes were fixed on him, not guessing what he was at, but to avoid his laying hold on him, which he had once attempted. In the meanwhile, the captain perceiving an opportunity pinned a cracker or devil to the cassock, and then lighted it with their little smoking candle. Adams being a stranger to this sport, and believing he had been blown up in reality, started from his chair, and jumped about the room, to the infinite joy of the beholders, who declared he was the best dancer in the universe. As soon as the devil had done tormenting him,

and he had a little recovered his confusion, he returned to the table, ~~and~~$_3$ standing up in the posture of one who intended to make a [speech. They]$_3$ all cried out, *Hear him, Hear him;* and he then spoke in the following manner: "Sir, I am sorry to see one to whom Providence hath been so bountiful in bestowing his favours, make so ill and ungrateful a return for them; for though you have not insulted me yourself, it is visible you have delighted in those that do it, nor have once discouraged the many rudenesses which have been shown towards me; indeed towards yourself, if you rightly understood them; for I am your guest, and by the laws of hospitality entitled to your protection. One gentleman hath thought proper to produce some poetry upon me, of which I shall only say, that I had rather be the subject than the composer. He hath pleased to treat me with disrespect as a parson; I apprehend my order is not the object of scorn, nor that I can become so, unless by being a disgrace to it, which I hope poverty will never be called. Another gentleman indeed hath repeated some sentences, where the order itself is mentioned with contempt. He says they are taken from plays. I am sure such plays are a scandal to the Government which permits them, and cursed will be the Nation where they are represented. How others have treated me, I need not observe; they themselves, when they reflect, must allow the behaviour to be as improper to my years as to my cloth. You found me, sir, travelling with two of my parishioners, (I omit your hounds falling on me; for I have quite forgiven it, whether it proceeded from the wantonness or negligence of the huntsman,) my appearance might very well persuade you that your invitation was an act of charity, though in reality we were well provided; yes, sir, if we had had an hundred miles to travel, we had sufficient to bear our expenses in a noble manner." (At which words he produced the half guinea which was found in the basket.) "I do not show you this out of ostentation of riches, but to convince you I speak truth. Your seating me at your table was an honour which I did not ambitiously affect; when I was here, I endeavoured to behave towards you with the utmost respect; if I have failed, it was not with design, nor could I, certainly, so far be guilty as to deserve the insults I have suffered. If they were

[speech, they]$_{1-2}$

meant therefore either to my order or my poverty (and you see I am not ~~so~~$_{2}$ very poor) the shame doth not lie at my door, and I heartily pray, that the sin may be averted from yours." He thus finished, and received a general clap from the whole company. Then the gentleman of the house told him, "he was sorry for what had happened; that he could not accuse him of any share in it: That the verses were, as himself had well observed, so bad, that he might easily answer them; and for the serpent, it was undoubtedly a very great affront done him by the dancing-master, for which if he well thrashed him, as he deserved, ⟨(the gentleman said)⟩$_{4}$ he should be very much pleased to see it;" (in which probably he spoke truth.) Adams answered, "whoever had done it, it was not his profession to punish him that way; but for the person whom he had accused, I am a witness, (says he) of his innocence, for I had my eye on him all the while. Whoever he was, God forgive him, and bestow on him a little more sense as well as humanity." The captain answered with a surly look and accent, "that he hoped he did not mean to reflect on him; d—n him, he had as much *Imanity* as another, and if any man said he had not, he would convince him of his mistake by cutting his throat." Adams smiling, said, "he believed he had spoke right by accident." To which the captain returned, "what do you mean by my speaking right? if you was not a parson, I would not take these words; but your gown protects you. If any man who wears a sword had said so much, I had pulled him by the nose before this." Adams replied, "if he attempted any rudeness to his person, he would not find any protection for himself in his gown;" and clenching his fist, declared he had threshed many a stouter man. The gentleman did all he
[the]$_{1}$ could to encourage [this]$_{2}$ warlike disposition in Adams, and was in hopes to have produced a battle: But he was disappointed; for the captain made no other answer than, "It is very well you are a parson," and so drinking off a bumper to old Mother Church, ended the dispute.

Then the doctor, who had hitherto been silent, and who was the gravest, but most mischievous dog of all, in a very pompous speech highly applauded what Adams had said; and as much discommended the behaviour to him; he proceeded to encomiums on the Church and Poverty; and lastly recommended forgiveness of what had passed to Adams, who immediately answered, "that everything was forgiven;" and in the warmth of his goodness he filled a bumper of strong beer, (a liquor he preferred to wine) and drank a health to the whole company, shaking the captain and the poet heartily by the hand, and addressing himself with great respect to the doctor; who indeed had not laughed outwardly at anything that passed, as he had a perfect command of his muscles, and could laugh inwardly without betraying the least symptoms in his countenance. The doctor now began a second formal speech, in which he declaimed against all levity of conversation, and what is usually called mirth. He said, "there were amusements fitted for persons of all ages and degrees, from the rattle to the discussing a point of philosophy, and that men discovered themselves in nothing more than in the choice of their amusements; for," says he, "as it must greatly raise our expectation of the future conduct in life of boys, whom in their tender years we perceive instead of taw or balls, or other childish play-things, to choose, at their leisure-hours, to exercise their genius in contentions of wit, learning, and such like; so must it inspire one with equal contempt of a man, if we should discover him playing at taw or other childish play." Adams highly commended the doctor's opinion, and said, "he had often wondered at some passages in ancient authors, where Scipio, Lælius, and other great men were represented to have passed many hours in amusements of the most trifling kind." [38] The doctor replied, "he had by him an old Greek manuscript where a favourite diversion of Socrates was recorded." "Ay," says the parson eagerly, "I should be most infinitely obliged to you for the favour of perusing it." The doctor promised to send it him, and farther said, "that he believed he could describe it. I think," says he, "as near as I can remember, it was this. There was a throne erected, on one side of which sat a king, and on the other a queen, with their guards and attendants ranged on both sides; to them was introduced an ambassador, which part Socrates

[38] Scipio and his friend Laelius, both great warriors and statesmen, would take outings to the beach to gather mussels and shells (Cicero, *De Oratore* II.6).

always used to perform himself; and when he was led up to the footsteps of the throne, he addressed himself to the monarchs in some grave speech, full of Virtue and Goodness, and Morality, and such like. After which, he was seated between the king and queen, and royally entertained. This I think was the chief part. — Perhaps I may have forgot some particulars; for it is long since I read it." Adams said, "it was indeed a diversion worthy the relaxation of so great a man; and thought something resembling it should be instituted among our great men, instead of cards and other idle pass-time, in which he was informed they trifled away too much of their lives." He added, "the Christian Religion was a nobler subject for these speeches than any Socrates could have invented." The gentleman of the house approved what Mr. Adams said, and declared, "he was resolved to perform the ceremony this very evening." To which the doctor objected, as no one was prepared with a speech, "Unless," said he, (turning to Adams with a gavity of countenance which would have deceived a more knowing man) "you have a sermon about you, doctor." — "Sir," says Adams, "I never travel without one, for fear of what may happen." He was easily prevailed on by his worthy friend, as he now called the doctor, to undertake the part the ambassador; so that the gentleman sent immediate orders to have the throne erected; which was performed before they had drank two bottles: And perhaps the reader will hereafter have no great reason to admire the nimbleness of the servants. Indeed, to confess the truth, the throne was no more than this; there was a great tub of water provided, on each side of which were placed two stools raised higher than the surface of the tub, and over the whole was laid a blanket; on these stools were placed the king and queen, namely, the master of the house, and the captain. And now the ambassador was introduced, between the poet and the doctor, who having read his sermon to the great entertainment of all present, was led up to his place, and [seated between their majesties. They]3 immediately rose up, when the blanket wanting its supports at either end, gave way, and soused Adams over head and ears in the water; the captain made his escape, but unluckily the gentleman himself not being as nimble as he ought, Adams caught hold of him

[being seated between their majesties, they]1-2

before he descended from his throne, and pulled him in with him, to the entire secret satisfaction of all the company. Adams after ducking the squire twice or thrice leapt out of the tub, and looked sharp for the doctor, whom he would certainly have conveyed to the same place of honour; but he had wisely withdrawn: he then searched for his crabstick, and having found that, as well as his fellow-travellers, he declared he would not stay a moment longer in such a house. He then departed, without taking leave of his host, whom he had exacted a more severe revenge on than he intended: For as he did not use sufficient care to dry himself in time, he caught a cold by the accident, which threw him into a fever, that had like to have cost him his life.

CHAP. VIII.

Which some readers will think too short, and others too long.

ADAMS, and Joseph, who was no less enraged than his friend, at the treatment he met with, went out with their sticks in their hands; and carried off Fanny, notwithstanding the opposition of the servants, who did all, without proceeding to violence, in their power to detain them. They walked as fast as they could, not so much from any apprehension of being pursued, as that Mr. Adams might by exercise prevent any harm from the water. The gentleman who had given such orders to his servants concerning Fanny, that he did not in the least fear her getting away, no sooner heard that she was gone, than he began to rave, and immediately dispatched several with orders, either to bring her back, or never return. The poet, the player, and all but the dancing-master and doctor went on this errand.

The night was very dark, in which our friends began their journey; however they made such expedition, that they soon arrived at an inn, which was at seven miles distance. Here they unanimously consented to pass the evening, Mr. Adams being now as dry as he was before he had set out on his embassy.

This inn, which indeed we might call an ale-house, had not

the words, *The New Inn,* been writ on the sign, afforded them no better provision than bread and cheese, and ale; on which, however, they made a very comfortable meal; for hunger is better than a French cook.

They had no sooner supped, than Adams returning thanks to the Almighty for his food, declared he had eat his homely commons, with much greater satisfaction than his splendid dinner, and expressed great contempt for the folly of mankind, who sacrificed their hopes of Heaven to the acquisition of vast wealth, since so much comfort was to be found in the humblest state and the lowest provision. "Very true, sir," says a grave man who sat smoking his pipe by the fire, and who was a traveller as well as himself. "I have often been as much surprised as you are, when I consider the value which mankind in general set on riches, since every day's experience shows us how little is in their power; for what indeed truly desirable can they bestow on us? Can they give beauty to the deformed, strength to the weak, or health to the infirm? Surely if they could, we should not see so many ill-favoured faces haunting the assemblies of the great, nor would such numbers of feeble wretches languish in their coaches and palaces. No, not the wealth of a kingdom can purchase any paint, to dress pale Ugliness in the bloom of that young maiden, nor any drugs to equip Disease with the vigour of that young man. Do not riches bring us Solicitude instead of Rest, Envy instead of Affection, and Danger instead of Safety? Can they prolong their own possession, or lengthen his days who enjoys them? So far otherwise, that the sloth, the luxury, the care which attend them, shorten the lives of millions, and bring them with pain and misery, to an untimely grave. Where then is their value, if they can neither embellish, or strengthen our forms, sweeten or prolong our lives? Again—Can they adorn the mind more than the body? Do they not rather swell the heart with Vanity, puff up the cheeks with Pride, shut our ears to every call of Virtue, and our bowels to every motive of Compassion!" "Give me your hand, brother," said Adams in a rapture; "for I suppose you are a clergyman." "No truly," answered the other, (indeed he was a priest of the Church of Rome; but those who understand our laws will not wonder he was not over-ready to own it.) [39] "Whatever you are," cries Adams, "you have spoken my sentiments: I believe I have preached every syllable of your speech twenty times over: For it hath always appeared to me easier for a cable rope (which by the way is the true rendering of that word we have translated *camel*) [40] to go through the eye of a needle, than for a rich man to get into the Kingdom of Heaven." "That, sir," said the other, "will be easily granted you by divines, and is deplorably true: But as the prospect of our good at a distance doth not so forcibly affect us, it might be of some service to mankind to be made thoroughly sensible, which I think they might be with very little serious attention, that even the blessings of this world, are not to be purchased with riches. A doctrine in my opinion, not only metaphysically, but if I may so say, mathematically demonstrable; and which I have been always so perfectly convinced of, that I have a contempt for nothing so much as for gold." Adams now began a long discourse; but as most which he said occurs among many authors, who have treated this subject, I shall omit inserting it. During its continuance Joseph and Fanny retired to rest, and the host likewise left the room. When the English parson had concluded, the Romish resumed the discourse, which he continued with great bitterness and invective; and at last ended by desiring Adams to lend him eighteen pence to pay his reckoning; promising, if he never paid him, he might be assured of his prayers. The good man answered, that eighteen pence would be too little to carry him any very long journey; that he had half a guinea in his pocket, which he would divide with him. He then fell to searching his pockets, but could find no money: For indeed the company with whom he dined, had passed one jest upon him which we did not then enumerate, and had picked his pocket of all that treasure which he had so ostentatiously produced.

"Bless me," cried Adams, "I have certainly lost it, I can never have spent it. Sir, as I am a Christian I had a whole half

[39] A Catholic priest could be fined £200 and even executed for high treason for saying mass, and informers could collect a reward of £100. Catholicism was looked on as an international conspiracy.

[40] Adams's interpretation, not original with him, is still considered a possibility by some Biblical scholars.

guinea in my pocket this morning, and have not now a single halfpenny of it left. Sure the Devil must have taken it from me." "Sir," answered the priest smiling, "You need make no excuses; if you are not willing to lend me the money, I am contented." "Sir," cries Adams, "if I had the greatest sum in the world; ay, if I had ten pounds about me, I would bestow it all to rescue any Christian from distress. I am more vexed at my loss on your account than my own. Was ever anything so unlucky? because I have no money in my pocket, I shall be suspected to be no Christian." "I am more unlucky," quoth the other, "if you are as generous as you say: For really a crown would have made me happy, and conveyed me in plenty to the place I am going, which is not above twenty miles off, and where I can arrive by to-morrow night. I assure you I am not accustomed to travel
[: But am I]$_{1-2}$ pennyless[. I am but]$_3$ just arrived in England, and we were forced by a storm in our passage to throw all we had overboard. I don't suspect but this fellow will take my word for the trifle I owe him; but I hate to appear so mean as to confess myself without a shilling to such people: For these, and indeed too many others know little difference in their estimation between a beggar and a thief." However, he thought he should deal better with the host that evening than the next morning; he therefore resolved to set out immediately, notwithstanding the darkness; and accordingly as soon as the host returned he communicated to him the situation of his affairs; upon which the host scratching his head answered, "Why, I do not know, master, if it be so, and you have no money, I must trust I think, though I had rather always have ready money if I could; but, marry, you look like so honest a gentleman, that I don't fear your paying me, if it was twenty times as much." The priest made no reply, ⟨but⟩$_2$ taking leave of him and Adams, as fast as he could, not without confusion, and perhaps with some distrust of Adams's sincerity, departed.

He was no sooner gone than the host fell a shaking his head, and declared if he had suspected the fellow had no money, he would not have drawn him a single drop of drink; saying, he despaired of ever seeing his face again; for that he looked like a confounded rogue. "Rabbit the fellow," cries he, "I thought by his talking so much about riches, that he had a hundred pounds at least in his pocket." Adams chid him for his suspicions, which he said were not becoming a Christian; and then without reflecting on his loss, or considering how he himself should depart in the morning, he retired to a very homely bed, as his companions had before; however, health and fatigue gave them a sweeter repose than is often in the power of velvet and down to bestow.

CHAP. IX.

Containing as surprising and bloody adventures as can be found in this, or perhaps any other authentic history.

It was almost morning when Joseph Andrews, whose eyes the thoughts of his dear Fanny had opened, as he lay fondly meditating on that lovely creature, heard a violent knocking at the door over which he lay; he presently jumped out of bed, and opening the window, was asked if there were no travellers in the house; and presently by another voice, If two men and a young woman had not taken up their lodgings there that night. Though he knew not the voices, he began to entertain a suspicion of the truth; for indeed he had received some information from one of the servants of the squire's house, of his design; and answered in the negative. One of the servants who knew the host well, called out to him by his name, just as he had opened another window, and asked him the same question; to which he answered in the affirmative. "O ho!" said another; "Have we found you?" And ordered the host to come down and open his door. Fanny, who was as wakeful as Joseph, no sooner heard all this, than she leaped from her bed, and hastily putting on her gown and petticoats, ran as fast as possible to Joseph's room, who then was almost drest; he immediately let her in, and embracing her with the most passionate tenderness, bid her fear nothing: For he would die in her defence. "Is that a reason why I should not fear," says she, "when I should lose what is dearer to me than the whole world?" Joseph then kissing her hand, said he could almost thank the occasion which had extorted from her a tenderness she would never indulge him with before. He then ran and waked his bedfellow Adams, who was yet fast asleep, notwithstanding many calls from Joseph: But was no sooner made sensible of their danger than he leaped from his bed, without considering the presence of Fanny, who hastily turned her face from him, and enjoyed a double benefit from the dark, which as it would have prevented any offence to an innocence less pure, or a modesty less delicate, so it concealed even those blushes which were raised in her.

Adams had soon put on all his clothes but his breeches, which in the hurry he forgot; however, they were pretty well supplied
[the rest]$_1$ by the length of [his other garments]$_2$: And now the house-door being opened, the captain, the poet, the player, and three servants came in. The captain told the host, that ~~the~~ $_2$ two fellows who were in his house had run away with a young woman, and desired to know in which room she lay. The host, who presently believed the story, directed them, and instantly the captain and poet, jostling one another, ran up. The poet⟨,⟩$_3$ who was the
[chamber, nimblest⟨,⟩$_3$ entering the [chamber first,]$_2$ searched the bed and
first]$_1$ every other part, but to no purpose; the bird was flown, as the impatient reader, who might otherwise have been in pain for her, was before advertised. They then inquired where the men lay, and were approaching the chamber, when Joseph roared out in a loud voice, that he would shoot the first man who offered to attack the door. The captain inquired what fire-arms they had; to which the host answered, he believed they had none; nay, he was almost convinced of it: For he had heard one ask the other in the evening, what they should have done, if they had been overtaken when they had no arms; to which the other answered, they would have defended themselves with their sticks as long as they were able, and G—— would assist a just cause. This satisfied the captain, but not the poet, who prudently retreated down stairs, saying it was his business to record great actions, and not to do them. The captain was no sooner well satisfied that there were no fire-arms, than bidding defiance to gunpowder, and swearing he loved the smell of it,

he ordered the servants to follow him, and marching boldly up, immediately attempted to force the door, which the servants soon helped him to accomplish. When it was opened, they discovered the enemy drawn up three deep; Adams in the front, and Fanny in the rear. The captain told Adams, that if they would go all back to the house again, they should be civilly treated: but unless they consented, he had orders to carry the young lady with him, whom there was great reason to believe they had stolen from her parents; for notwithstanding her disguise, her air, which she could not conceal, sufficiently discovered her birth to be infinitely superior to theirs. Fanny bursting into tears, solemnly assured him he was mistaken; that she was a poor helpless foundling, and had no relation in the world which she knew of; and throwing herself on her knees, begged that he would not attempt to take her from her friends, who she was convinced would die before they would lose her, which Adams confirmed with words not far from amounting to an oath. The captain swore he had no leisure to talk, and bidding them thank themselves for what happened, he ordered the servants to fall on, at the same time endeavouring to pass by Adams in order to lay hold on Fanny; but the parson interrupting him, received a blow from one of them, which without considering whence it came, he returned to the captain, and gave him so dexterous a knock in that part of the stomach which is vulgarly called the pit, that he staggered some paces backwards. The captain, who was not accustomed to this kind of play, and who wisely apprehended the consequence of such another blow, two of them seeming to him equal to a thrust through the body, drew forth his hanger, as Adams approached him, and was levelling a blow at his head, which would probably have silenced the preacher for ever, had not Joseph in that instant lifted up a certain huge stone pot of the chamber with one hand, which six beaus could not have lifted with both, and discharged it, together with the contents, full in the captain's face. The uplifted hanger dropped from his hand, and he fell prostrate on the floor *with a lumpish Noise, and his Halfpence rattled in his Pocket;* [41] the red liquor

[41] Fielding's mock-heroic blend of *Aeneid* and *Iliad*. Turnus throws a stone at Aeneas (XII.896–902) which "scarce twice six chosen men could

which his veins contained, and the white liquor which the pot contained, ran in one stream down his face and his clothes. Nor had Adams quite escaped, some of the water having in its passage shed its honours on his head, and began to trickle down the wrinkles or rather furrows of his cheeks, when one of the servants snatching a mop out of a pail of water which had already done its duty in washing the house, pushed it in the parson's face; yet could not he bear him down; for the parson
[out of his hands]$_1$ wresting the mop [from the fellow with one hand]$_2$, with the other brought his enemy as low as the earth, having given him a stroke over that part of the face, where, in some men of pleasure, the natural and artificial noses are conjoined.[42]

Hitherto Fortune seemed to incline the victory on the travellers side, when, according to her custom, she began to show the fickleness of her disposition: for now the host entering the field, or rather chamber, of battle, flew directly at Joseph, and darting his head into his stomach (for he was a stout fellow, and an expert boxer) almost staggered him; but Joseph stepping one leg back, did with his left hand so chuck him under the chin that he reeled. The youth was pursuing his blow with his right hand, when he received from one of the servants such a stroke with a cudgel on his temples, that it instantly deprived him of sense, and he measured his length on the ground.

Fanny rent the air with her cries, and Adams was coming to the assistance of Joseph: but the two serving-men and the host now fell on him, and soon subdued him, though he fought like a madman, and looked so black with the impressions he had received from the mop, that Don Quixote would certainly have taken him for an enchanted Moor. But now follows the most
[being]$_1$ tragical part; for the captain [was]$_2$ risen again, and seeing Joseph on the floor, and Adams secured, he instantly laid hold on Fanny, and with the assistance of the poet and player, who hearing the battle was over, were now come up, dragged her, crying

uplift upon their shoulders, men of such frames as earth now begets" (trans. H. R. Fairclough, Loeb Classical Library); and one of the formal, recurring lines in the *Iliad* translates as "He fell with a thud, and his armor clanged upon him" (Battestin, p. 258).

[42] Syphilis frequently ate away the nose, and the victims wore false noses.

and tearing her hair, from the sight of her Joseph, and with a perfect deafness to all her entreaties, carried her down stairs by violence, and fastened her on the player's horse; and the captain mounting his own, and leading that on which this poor miserable wretch was, departed without any more consideration of her cries than a butcher hath of those of a lamb; for indeed his thoughts were only entertained with the degree of favour which he promised himself from the squire on the success of this adventure.

The servants who were ordered to secure Adams and Joseph as safe as possible, that the 'Squire might receive no interruption to his design on poor Fanny, immediately by the poet's advice tied Adams to one of the bed-posts, ~~with his hands behind him~~, 3
as they did Joseph on the other side, as soon as they could bring him to himself; and then leaving them together, back to back, and desiring the host not to set them at liberty, nor go near them till he had farther orders, they departed towards their master; but happened to take a different road from that which the captain had fallen into.

CHAP. X.

A discourse between the poet and player; of no other use in this history, but to divert the reader.

BEFORE we proceed any farther in this Tragedy, we shall leave Mr. Joseph and Mr. Adams to themselves, and imitate the wise conductors of the stage; who in the midst of a grave action entertain you with some excellent piece of satire or humour called a dance. Which piece indeed is therefore danced, and not spoke, as it is delivered to the audience by persons whose thinking faculty is by most people held to lie in their heels; and to whom, as well as heroes, who think with their hands, Nature hath only given heads for the sake of conformity, and as they are of use in dancing, to hang their hats on.

The poet addressing the player, proceeded thus: "As I was

saying" (for they had been at this discourse all the time of the engagement, above stairs) "the reason you have no good new plays is evident; it is from your discouragement of authors. Gentlemen will not write, sir, they will not write without the expectation of fame or profit, or perhaps both. Plays are like trees which will not grow without nourishment; but like mushrooms, they shoot up spontaneously, as it were, in a rich soil. The Muses, like vines, may be pruned, but not with a hatchet. The town, like a peevish child, knows not what it desires, and is always best pleased with a rattle. A farce-writer hath indeed some chance for success; but they have lost all taste for the Sublime. Though I believe one reason of their depravity is the badness of the actors. If a man writes like an angel, sir, those fellows know not how to give a sentiment utterance." "Not so fast," says the player, "the modern actors are as good at least as their authors, nay, they come nearer their illustrious predecessors, and I expect a Booth on the stage again, sooner than a Shakespear or an Otway; and indeed I may turn your observation against you, and with truth say, that the reason no authors are encouraged, is because we have no good new plays." "I have not affirmed the contrary," said the poet, "but I am surprised you grow so warm; you cannot imagine yourself interested in this dispute, I hope you have a better opinion of my taste, than to apprehend I squinted at yourself. No, sir, if we had six such actors as you, we should soon rival the Bettertons and Sandfords of former times; for, without a compliment to you, I think it impossible for anyone to have excelled you in most of your parts. Nay, it is solemn truth, and I have heard many, and all great judges, express as much; and you will pardon me if I tell you, I think every time I have seen you lately, you have constantly acquired some new excellence, like a snowball. You have deceived me in my estimation of perfection, and have outdone what I thought inimitable." "You are as little interested," answered the player, "in what I have said of other poets; for d—n me, if there are not manly strokes, ay whole scenes, in your last tragedy, which at least equal Shakespear. There is a delicacy of sentiment, a dignity of expression in it, which I will own many of our gentlemen did not do adequate justice to. To confess the truth, they are bad enough, and I pity an author who is present at the murder of his works." — "Nay, it is but seldom that it can happen," returned the poet, "the works of most modern authors, like dead-born children, cannot be murdered. It is such wretched half-begotten, half-wit, lifeless, spiritless, low, groveling stuff, that I almost pity the actor who is obliged to get it by heart, which must be almost as difficult to remember as words in a language you don't understand." "I am sure," said the player, "if the sentences have little meaning when they are writ, when they are spoken they have less. I know scarce one who ever lays an emphasis right, and much less adapts his action to his character. I have seen a tender lover in an attitude of fighting with his mistress, and a brave hero suing to his enemy with his sword in his hand — I don't care to abuse my profession, but rot me if in my heart I am not inclined to the poet's side." "It is rather generous in you than just," said the poet; "and though I hate to speak ill of any person's production, nay I never do it, nor will — but yet to do justice to the actors, what could Booth or Betterton have made of such horrible stuff as Fenton's *Mariamne,* Frowd's *Philotas,* or Mallet's *Eurydice,* or those low, dirty, last dying-speeches, which a fellow in the City or Wapping, your Dillo or Lillo, what was his name, called tragedies?" [43] — "Very well, sir," says the player, "and pray what do you think of such fellows as Quin and Delane, or that face-making puppy young Cibber, that ill-looked dog Macklin, or that saucy slut Mrs. Clive? What work would they make with your Shakespeares, Otways and Lees? How would those harmonious lines of the last come from their tongues?

——No more; for I disdain
All Pomp when thou art by—far be the Noise
Of Kings and Crowns from us, whose gentle Souls
Our kinder Fates have steer'd another way.
Free as the Forest Birds we'll pair together,

[43] George Lillo, a jeweler, wrote the influential *The London Merchant* (1731); Fielding befriended him; Fielding produced Lillo's *Fatal Curiosity* (1736) in his Little Theater in the Haymarket, and wrote the Prologue. Lillo probably serves as something of a model for Heartfree in Fielding's *Jonathan Wild.*

Without rememb'ring who our Fathers were:
Fly to the Arbors, Grots and flowry Meads,
There in soft Murmurs interchange our Souls,
Together drink the Crystal of the Stream,
Or taste the yellow Fruit which Autumn yields.
And when the golden Evening calls us home,
Wing to our downy Nests and sleep till Morn.[44]

"Or how would this disdain of Otway,

Who'd be that foolish, sordid thing, call'd Man?"

"Hold, hold, hold," said the poet, "Do repeat that tender speech in the third act of my play which you made such a figure in." — "I would willingly," said the player, "but I have forgot it." — "Ay, you was not quite perfect enough in it when you played it," cries the poet, "or you would have had such an applause as was never given on the stage; an applause I was extremely concerned for your losing." — "Sure," says the player, "if I remember, that was hissed more than any passage in the whole play." — "Ay your speaking it was hissed," said the poet. "My speaking it!" said the player. — "I mean your not speaking it," said the poet. "You was out, and then they hissed." — "They hissed, and then I was out, if I remember," answered the player; "and I must say this for myself, that the whole audience allowed I did your part justice, so don't lay the damnation of your play to my account." "I don't know what you mean by damnation," replied the poet. "Why you know it was acted but one night," cried the player. "No," said the poet, "you and the whole town know I had my enemies; the pit were all my enemies, fellows that would cut my throat, if the fear of hanging did not restrain them. All tailors, sir, all tailors." — "Why should the tailors be so angry with you?" cries the player. "I suppose you don't employ so many in making your clothes." "I admit your jest," answered the poet, "but you remember the affair as well as myself; you know there was a party in the pit and upper-gallery, would not suffer it to be given out again; though much,

[44] From Nathaniel Lee's *Theodosius* (1680); inaccuracies suggest that Fielding is quoting from memory. Similarly, the line from Otway's *The Orphan* (1680), below, reads: "Who'd be that sordid foolish thing call'd Man. . . ?"

ay infinitely, the majority, all the boxes in particular, were desirous of it; nay, most of the ladies swore they never would come to the house till it was acted again — Indeed I must own their policy was good, in not letting it be given out a second time; for the rascals knew if it had gone a second night, it would have run fifty: for if ever there was distress in a tragedy — I am not fond of my own performance; but if I should tell you what the best judges said of it — Nor was it entirely owing to my enemies neither, that it did not succeed on the stage as well as it hath since among the polite readers; for you can't say it had justice done it by the performers." — "I think," answered the player, "the performers did the distress of it justice: for I am sure we were in distress enough, who were pelted with oranges all the last act; we all imagined it would have been the last act of our lives."

The poet, whose fury was now raised, had just attempted to answer, when they were interrupted, and an end put to their discourse by an accident; which, if the reader is impatient to know, he must skip over the next chapter, which is a sort of counterpart to this, and contains some of the best and gravest matters in the whole book, being a discourse between Parson Abraham Adams and Mr. Joseph Andrews.

CHAP. XI.

Containing the exhortations of Parson Adams to his friend in affliction; calculated for the instruction and improvement of the reader.

JOSEPH no sooner came perfectly to himself, than perceiving his mistress gone, he bewailed her loss with groans, which would have pierced any heart but those which are possessed by some people, and are made of a certain composition not unlike flint in its hardness and other properties; for you may strike fire from them which will dart through the eyes, but they can never distil one drop of water the same way. His own, poor youth, was of a softer composition; and at those words, *O my dear Fanny! O my Love! shall I never, never see thee more?* his eyes overflowed with tears, which would have become any thing₄ but a hero. In a word, his despair was more easy to be conceived than related.—

Mr. Adams, after many groans, sitting with his back to Joseph, began thus in a sorrowful tone: "You cannot imagine, my good child, that I entirely blame these first agonies of your grief; for, when misfortunes attack us by surprise, it must require infinitely more learning than you are master of to resist them: but it is the business of a man and a Christian to summon Reason as quickly as he can to his aid; and she will presently teach him patience and submission. Be comforted, therefore, child, I say be comforted. It is true you have lost the prettiest, kindest, loveliest, sweetest young woman: One with whom you might have expected to have lived in Happiness, Virtue, and Innocence. By whom you might have promised yourself many little darlings, who would have been the delight of your youth, and the comfort of your age. You have not only lost her, but have reason to fear the utmost violence which Lust and Power can inflict upon her. Now indeed you may easily raise ideas of horror, which might drive you to Despair."—"O I shall run mad," cries Joseph, "O that I could but command my hands to tear my eyes out and my flesh off."—"If you would use them to such purposes, I am glad you can't," answered Adams. "I have stated your misfortune as strong as I possibly can; but on the other side, you are to consider you are a Christian, that no accident happens to us without the Divine Permission, and that
[and a]$_{1\text{-}3}$ it is the duty of a man[, much more of]$_4$ a Christian, to submit. We did not make ourselves; but the same Power which made us, rules over us, and we are absolutely at his disposal; he may do with us what he pleases, nor have we any right to complain. A second reason against our complaint is our ignorance; for as we know not future events, so neither can we tell to what purpose any accident tends; and that which at first threatens us with evil, may in the end produce our good. I should indeed have said our ignorance is twofold (but I have not at present time to divide properly) for as we know not to what purpose any event

is ultimately directed; so neither can we affirm from what cause it originally sprung. You are a man, and consequently a sinner; and this may be a punishment to you for your sins; indeed in this sense it may be esteemed as a good, yea as the greatest good, which satisfies the anger of Heaven, and averts that wrath which cannot continue without our destruction. Thirdly, our impotency of relieving ourselves, demonstrates the folly and absurdity of our complaints: for whom do we resist? or against whom do we complain, but a Power from whose shafts no armour can guard us, no speed can fly? A Power which leaves us no hope, but in submission." — "O sir," cried Joseph, "all this is very true, and very fine; and I could hear you all day, if I was not so grieved at heart as now I am." "Would you take physic," says Adams, "when you are well, and refuse it when you are sick? Is not comfort to be administered to the afflicted, and not to those who rejoice, or those who are at ease?" — "O you have not spoken one word of comfort to me yet," returned Joseph. "No!" cries Adams, "What am I then doing? what can I say to comfort you?" — "O tell me," cries Joseph, "that Fanny will escape back to my arms, that they shall again inclose that lovely creature, with all her sweetness, all her untainted innocence about her." — "Why perhaps you may," cries Adams; "but I can't promise you what's to come. [You must with perfect resignation wait the event; if she be restored to you again, it is your duty to be thankful, and so it is if she be not: Joseph, if you are wise, and truly know your own interest, you will peaceably and quietly submit to all the dispensations of Providence; being thoroughly assured, that all the misfortunes, how great soever, which happen to the righteous, happen to them for their own good. — Nay]$_2$ it is not your interest only, but your duty to abstain from immoderate grief; which if you indulge, you are not worthy the name of a Christian." — He spoke these last words with an accent a little severer than usual; upon which Joseph begged him not to be angry, saying he mistook him, if he thought he denied it was his duty; for he had known that long ago. "What signifies knowing your duty, if you do not perform it?" answered Adams. "Your knowledge increases your guilt — O Joseph, I never thought you had this stubbornness

[The doctrine I teach you is a certain security— nay]$_1$

in your mind." Joseph replied, "he fancied he misunderstood him, which I assure you, ⟨" says he, "⟩ $_2$ you do, if you imagine I endeavour to grieve; upon my soul I don't." Adams rebuked him for swearing, and then proceeded to enlarge on the folly of grief, telling him, all the wise men and philosophers, even among the heathens, had written against it, quoting several passages from Seneca, and the *Consolation*,[45] which though it was not Cicero's, was⟨, he said,⟩ $_2$ as good almost as any of his works,
[saying]$_1$ and concluded all by [hinting]$_2$, that immoderate grief in this case might incense that Power which alone could restore him his Fanny. This reason, or indeed rather the idea which it raised of the restoration of his mistress, had more effect than all which the parson had said before; and for a moment abated his agonies: but when his fears sufficiently set before his eyes the danger that poor creature was in, his grief returned again with repeated violence, nor could Adams in the least assuage it; though it may be doubted in his behalf, whether Socrates himself could have prevailed any better.

They remained some time in silence; and groans and sighs issued from them both, at length Joseph burst out into the following soliloquy:

Yes, I will bear my Sorrows like a Man,
But I must also feel them as a Man.
I cannot but remember such things were,
And were most dear to me [46] —

Adams asked him what stuff that was he repeated? — To which he answered, they were some lines he had gotten by heart out of a play. — "Ay, there is nothing but heathenism to be learned from plays," replied he — "I never heard of any plays fit for a Christian to read, but *Cato* and the *Conscious Lovers;* [47] and I must own in the latter there are some things almost solemn enough for a sermon." But we shall now leave them a little, and inquire after the subject of their conversation.

[45] A work purporting to be Cicero's, published in Venice about 1583; Fielding read it in times of sorrow (Battestin, p. 266).

[46] *Macbeth* IV.iii.258–62—again only an approximate quotation.

[47] *Cato* (1713), by Joseph Addison; *The Conscious Lovers* (1722), by Sir Richard Steele—the pair made famous by their *Spectator* papers.

CHAP. XII.

More adventures, which we hope will as much please as surprise the reader.

NEITHER the facetious dialogue which passed between the poet and the player, nor the grave and truly solemn discourse of Mr. Adams, will, we conceive, make the reader sufficient amends for the anxiety which he must have felt on the account of poor Fanny, whom we left in so deplorable a condition. We shall therefore now proceed to the relation of what happened to that beautiful and innocent virgin, after she fell into the wicked hands of the captain.

The man of war having conveyed his charming prize out of the inn a little before day, made the utmost expedition in his power towards the squire's house, where this delicate creature was to be offered up a sacrifice to the lust of a ravisher. He was not only deaf to all her bewailings and entreaties on the road, but accosted her ears with impurities, which, having been never before accustomed to them, she happily for herself very little understood. At last he changed his note, and attempted to soothe and mollify her, by setting forth the splendour and luxury which would be her fortune with a man who would have the inclination, and power too, to give her whatever her utmost wishes could desire; and told her he doubted not but she would soon look kinder on him, as the instrument of her happiness, and despise that pitiful fellow, whom her ignorance only could make her fond of. She answered, [She knew not whom he meant, she never was fond of any pitiful fellow. "Are you affronted, madam," says he, "at my calling him so? but what better can be said of one in a livery, notwithstanding your fondness for him?" She returned, That she did not understand him, that the man had been her fellow-servant, and she believed was as honest a creature as any alive; but as for fondness for men]2 — "I warrant ye," cries the captain, "we shall find means to

[the riches of the world could not make her amends for the loss of him; nor would she be persuaded to exchange him for the greatest prince on earth]1

persuade you ⟨to be fond⟩$_2$; and I advise you to yield to gentle ones; for you may be assured that it is not in your power by any struggles whatever to preserve your virginity two hours longer. It will be your interest to consent; for the 'Squire will be much kinder to you if he enjoys you willingly than by force." — At which words she began to call aloud for assistance (for it was now open day) but finding none, she lifted her eyes to Heaven, and supplicated the Divine Assistance to preserve her innocence. The captain told her, if she persisted in her vociferation, he would find a means of stopping her mouth. And now the poor wretch perceiving no hope of succour, abandoned herself to Despair, and sighing out the name of *Joseph, Joseph!* a river of tears ran down her lovely cheeks, and wet the handkerchief which covered her bosom. A horseman now appeared in the road, upon which the captain threatened her violently if she complained; however, the moment they approached each other, she begged him with the utmost earnestness to relieve a distressed creature, who was in the hands of a ravisher. The fellow stopt at those words; but the captain assured him it was his wife, and that he was carrying her home from her adulterer. Which so satisfied the fellow, who was an old one, (and perhaps a married one too) that he wished him a good journey, and rode on. He was no sooner past, than the captain abused her violently for breaking his commands, and threatened to gag her; when two more horsemen, armed with pistols, came into the road just before them. She again solicited their assistance; and the captain told the same story as before. Upon which one said to the other — "That's a charming wench, Jack; I wish I had been in the fellow's place whoever he is." But the other, instead of answering him, cried out eagerly, "Zounds, I know her:" and then turning to her said, "Sure you are not Fanny Goodwill?"
[Thomas]$_1$ — "Indeed, indeed I am," she cried — "O [John]$_2$, I know you now — Heaven hath sent you to my assistance, to deliver me from this wicked man, who is carrying me away for his vile purposes — O for G—'s sake rescue me from him." A fierce dialogue immediately ensued between the captain and these two men, who being both armed with pistols, and the chariot which they attended being now arrived, the captain saw both force and

stratagem were vain, and endeavoured to make his escape; in which however he could not succeed. The gentleman who rode in the chariot, ordered it to stop, and with an air of authority examined into the merits of the cause; of which being advertised by Fanny, whose credit was confirmed by the fellow who knew her, he ordered the captain, who was all bloody from his encounter at the inn, to be conveyed as a prisoner behind the chariot, and very gallantly took Fanny into it; for, to say the truth, this gentleman (who was no other than ⟨the celebrated⟩$_{2}$ Mr. Peter Pounce, and who preceded the Lady Booby only a few miles, by setting out earlier in the morning) was a very gallant person, and loved a pretty girl better than anything, besides his own money, or the money of other people.

The chariot now proceeded towards the inn, which as Fanny was informed lay in their way, and where it arrived at that very time while the poet and player were disputing below stairs, and Adams and Joseph were discoursing back to back above: just at that period to which we brought them both in the two preceding chapters, the chariot stopt at the door, and in an instant Fanny leaping from it, ran up to her Joseph. — O reader, conceive if thou canst, the joy which fired the breasts of these lovers on this meeting; and, if thy own heart doth not sympathetically assist thee in this conception, I pity thee sincerely from my own: for let the hard-hearted villain know this, that there is a pleasure in a tender sensation beyond any which he is capable of tasting.

Peter being informed by Fanny of the presence of Adams, stopt to see him, and receive his homage; for, as Peter was an hypocrite, a sort of people whom Mr. Adams never saw through, [the one paid that respect to his seeming goodness which the other believed to be paid to his riches;]$_{3}$ hence Mr. Adams was so much his favourite, that he once lent him four pounds thirteen shillings and sixpence, to prevent his going to gaol, on no greater security than a bond and judgment, which probably he would have made no use of, though the money had not been (as it was) paid exactly at the time.

[this paid that respect to his goodness which the other attributed to be paid to his riches; and]$_{1\text{-}2}$

It is not perhaps easy to describe the figure of Adams; he had risen in such a ⟨violent⟩$_{4}$ hurry, that he had on neither breeches, ~~garters~~,$_{4}$ nor stockings; nor had he taken from his head a red [*viz.* a piss-burnt beard, which]$_{1}$

spotted handkerchief, which by night bound his wig, ⟨that was⟩ $_{4}$ turned inside out, around his head. He had on his torn cassock, and his greatcoat; but as the remainder of his cassock hung down below his greatcoat; so did a small stripe of white, or rather whitish linen appear below that; to which we may add the several colours which appeared on his face, [where a long piss-burnt beard]$_{2}$ served to retain the liquor of the stone pot, and that of a blacker hue which distilled from the mop. — This figure, which Fanny had delivered from his captivity, was no sooner spied by Peter, than it disordered the composed gravity of his muscles; however he advised him immediately to make himself clean, nor would accept his homage in that pickle.

The poet and player no sooner saw the captain in captivity, than they began to consider of their own safety, of which flight presented itself as the only means; they therefore both of them mounted the poet's horse, and made the most expeditious retreat in their power.

The host, who well knew Mr. Pounce and the Lady Booby's livery, was not a little surprised at this change of the scene, nor was his confusion much helped by his wife, who was now just risen, and having heard ⟨from him⟩ $_{3}$ the account of what had passed ~~from him~~ $_{3}$, comforted him with a decent number of Fools and Blockheads, asked him why he did not consult her, and told him he would never leave following the nonsensical dictates of his own numskull, till she and her family were ruined.

Joseph being informed of the captain's arrival, and seeing his Fanny now in safety, quitted her a moment, and running down stairs, went directly to him, and stripping off his coat challenged him to fight; but the captain refused, saying he did not understand boxing. He then grasped a cudgel in one hand, and catching the captain by the collar with the other, ~~he~~ $_{3}$ gave him a most severe drubbing, and ended with telling him, he had now had some revenge for what his dear Fanny had suffered.

When Mr. Pounce had a little regaled himself with some provision which he had in his chariot, and Mr. Adams had put on the best appearance his clothes would allow him, Pounce ordered the captain into his presence; for he said he was guilty of felony, and the next Justice of Peace should commit him: but the servants (whose appetite for revenge is soon satisfied) [being]3 [were]1-2 sufficiently contented with the drubbing which Joseph had inflicted on him, and which was indeed of no very moderate kind, ~~and~~ 3 had suffered him to go off, which he did, threatening a severe revenge against Joseph, which I have never heard he thought proper to take.

The mistress of the house made her voluntary appearance before Mr. Pounce, and with a thousand curtsies told him, "she hoped his honour would pardon her husband, who was a very *nonsense* man, for the sake of his poor family; that indeed if he could be ruined alone, she should be very willing of it, *for because as why*, his worship very well knew he deserved it: but she had three poor small children, who were not capable to get their own living; and if her husband was sent to gaol, they must all come to the parish; for she was a poor weak woman, continually a breeding, and had no time to work for them. She therefore hoped his honour would take it into his worship's consideration, and forgive her husband this time; for she was sure he never intended any harm to man, woman, or child; and if it was not for that block-head of his own, the man in some things was well enough; for she had had three children by him in less than three years, and was almost ready to cry out the fourth time." She would have proceeded in this manner much longer, had not Peter stopt her tongue, by telling her he had nothing to say to her husband, nor her neither. So, as Adams and the rest had assured her of forgiveness, she cried and curtsied out of the room.

Mr. Pounce was desirous that Fanny should continue her journey with him in the chariot, ⌈but she absolutely refused, saying she would ride behind Joseph, on a horse which one of Lady Booby's servants had equipped him with. But alas! when the horse appeared, it was found to be no other than that identical beast which Mr. Adams had left behind him at the inn, and which these honest fellows who knew him had redeemed. Indeed whatever horse they had provided for Joseph, they would have prevailed with him to mount none, no not even to ride before his beloved Fanny, till the parson was supplied;

⌈and she absolutely refused, being determined to ride behind Joseph, on a horse which one of Lady Booby's servants had equipped him with. (This was indeed the same which Adams had left behind him at the inn, and was by these honest men who knew him, redeemed): if any means could be contrived of conveying Mr. Adams with them; whose company Pounce, when he found he had no longer hopes of satisfying his old appetite with Fanny, desired in his vehicle. So that all matters being settled to the content of everyone, Adams and Pounce mounting the chariot, and Fanny being

much less would he deprive his friend of the beast which belonged to him, and which he knew the moment he saw, though Adams did not: however, when he was reminded of the affair, and told that they had brought the horse with them which he left behind, he answered — *Bless me! and so I did.*

Adams was very desirous that Joseph and Fanny should mount this horse, and declared he could very easily walk home. "If I walked alone," says he, "I would wage a shilling, that the *pedestrian* out-stripped the *equestrian* travellers: but as I intend to take the company of a pipe, peradventure I may be an hour later." One of the servants whispered Joseph to take him at his word, and suffer the old put to walk if he would: This proposal was answered with an angry look and a peremptory refusal by Joseph, who catching Fanny up in his arms, averred he would rather carry her home in that manner, than take away Mr. Adams's horse, and permit him to walk on foot.

Perhaps, reader, thou hast seen a contest between two gentlemen, or two ladies quickly decided, though they have both asserted they would not eat such a nice morsel, and each insisted on the other's accepting it; but in reality both were very desirous to swallow it themselves. Do not therefore conclude hence, that this dispute would have come to a speedy decision: for here both parties were heartily in earnest, and it is very probable, they would have remained in the inn-yard to this day, had not the good Peter Pounce put a stop to it; for finding he had no longer hopes of satisfying his old appetite with Fanny, and being desirous of having some one to whom he might communicate his grandeur, he told the parson he would convey him home in his chariot. This favour was by Adams, with many bows and acknowledgments, accepted, though he afterwards said, "he ascended the chariot rather that he might not offend, than from any desire of riding in it, for that in his heart he preferred the *pedestrian* even to the *vehicular* expedition." All matters being now settled, the chariot in which rode Adams and Pounce moved forwards; and Joseph having borrowed a pillion from the host, Fanny had just seated herself thereon, and had laid hold on the girdle which her lover wore for that purpose, when the wise beast, who concluded that one at a time was sufficient, that two to one were odds, &c. discovered much uneasiness at his double load, and began to consider his hinder as his fore-legs, moving the direct contrary way to that which is called forwards. Nor could Joseph with all his horsemanship persuade him to advance: but without having any regard to the lovely part of the lovely girl which was on his back, he used such agitations, that had not one of the men come immediately to her assistance, she had in plain English tumbled backwards on the ground. This inconvenience was presently remedied by an exchange of horses, and then Fanny being again placed on her pillion, on a better-natured, and somewhat a better fed beast, the parson's horse finding he had no longer odds to contend with, agreed to march, and the whole procession| 2 set forwards for Booby-Hall, where they arrived in a few hours without anything remarkable happening on the road, unless it was a curious dialogue between the parson and the steward; which, to use the language of a late Apologist, a pattern to all biographers, *waits for the reader in the next chapter*.

placed on a pillion, which Joseph borrowed of the host, they all| 1

CHAP. XIII.

A curious dialogue which passed between Mr. Abraham Adams and Mr. Peter Pounce, better worth reading than all the works of Colley Cibber and many others.

THE chariot had not proceeded far, before Mr. Adams observed it was a very fine day. "Ay, and a very fine country too," answered Pounce. "I should think so more," returned Adams, "if I had not lately travelled over the Downs, which I take to exceed this and all other prospects in the universe." "A fig for prospects," answered Pounce, "one acre here is worth ten there; and for my own part, I have no delight in the prospect of any land but my own." "Sir," said Adams, "you can indulge yourself with many fine prospects of that kind." "I thank God I have a little," replied the other, "with which I am content, and envy no man: I have a little, Mr. Adams, with which I do as much good as I can." Adams answered, that riches without charity were nothing worth; for that they were only a blessing to him who made them a blessing to others. "You and I," said Peter, "have different notions of Charity. I own, as it is generally used, I do not like the word, nor do I think it becomes one of us gentlemen; it is a mean parson-like quality; though I would not infer many parsons have it neither." "Sir," said Adams, "my definition of Charity is a generous disposition to relieve the distressed." "There is something in that definition," answered Peter, "which I like well enough; it is, as you say, a disposition — and does not so much consist in the act as in the disposition to do it; but alas, Mr. Adams, Who are meant by the distressed? Believe me, the distresses of mankind are mostly imaginary, and it would be rather folly than goodness to relieve them." "Sure, sir," replied Adams, "hunger and thirst, cold and nakedness, and other distresses which attend the poor, can never be said to be imaginary evils." "How can any man complain of hunger," said Peter, "in a country where such excellent salads are to be gathered in almost every field? or of thirst, where every river and stream produce such delicious potations? And as for cold and nakedness, they are evils introduced by luxury and custom. A man naturally wants clothes no more than a horse or any other animal, and there are whole nations who go without them: but these are things perhaps which you, who do not know the world ——" "You will pardon me, sir," returned Adams; "I have read of the Gymnosophists." "A plague of your Jehosaphats," cried Peter; "the greatest fault in our constitution is the provision made for the poor, except that perhaps made for some others. Sir, I have not an estate which doth not contribute almost as much again to the poor as to the land-tax, and I do assure you I expect to come myself to the parish in the end." To which Adams giving a dissenting smile, Peter thus proceeded: "I fancy, Mr. Adams, you are one of those who imagine I am a lump of money; for there are many who I fancy believe that not only my pockets, but my whole clothes, are lined with bank-bills; but I assure you, you are all mistaken: I am not the man the world esteems me. If I can hold my head above water, it is all I can. I have injured myself by purchasing. I have been too

liberal of my money. Indeed I fear my heir will find my affairs in a worse situation than they are reputed to be. Ah! he will have reason to wish I had loved money more, and land less. Pray, my good neighbour, where should I have that quantity of riches the world is so liberal to bestow on me? Where could I possibly, without I had stole it, acquire such a treasure?" "Why truly," says Adams, "I have been always of your opinion; I have wondered as well as yourself with what confidence they could report such things of you, which have to me appeared as mere impossibilities; for you know, sir, and I have often heard you say it, that your wealth is ⟨of⟩ $_3$ your own acquisition, and can it be credible that in your short time you should have amassed such a heap of treasure as these people will have you worth? Indeed had you inherited an estate like Sir Thomas Booby, which had descended in your family for many generations, they might have had a colour for their assertations." "Why, what do they say I am worth?" cries Peter with a malicious sneer. "Sir," answered Adams, "I have heard some aver you are not worth less than twenty thousand pounds." At which Peter frowned. "Nay, sir," said Adams, "you ask me only the opinion of others, for my own part I have always denied it, nor did I ever believe you could possibly be worth half that sum." "However, Mr. Adams," said he, squeezing him by the hand, "I would not sell them all I am worth for double that sum; and as to what you believe, or they believe, I care not a fig, no not a fart. I am not poor because you think me so, nor because you attempt to undervalue me in the country. I know the envy of mankind very well, but I thank Heaven I am above them. It is true my wealth is of my own acquisition. I have not an estate like Sir Thomas Booby, that [hath]$_4$ descended in my family through many generations; but [has]$_{1\text{-}3}$
I know the heirs of such estates who are forced to travel about the country like some people in torn cassocks, and might be glad to accept of a pitiful curacy for what I know. Yes, sir, as shabby fellows as yourself, whom no man of my figure, without that vice of good-nature about him, would suffer to ride in a chariot with him." "Sir," said Adams, "I value not your chariot of a rush; and if I had known you had intended to affront me, I would have walked to the world's end on foot ere I would have

accepted a place in it. However, sir, I will soon rid you of that inconvenience," and so saying, he opened the chariot-door without calling to the coachman, and leapt out into the highway, forgetting to take his hat along with him; which however Mr. Pounce threw after him with great violence. Joseph and Fanny stopt to bear him company the rest of the way, which was not above a mile.

THE HISTORY OF THE ADVENTURES OF *Joseph Andrews*, and of his Friend Mr. *Abraham Adams*

BOOK IV.

CHAP. I.

The arrival of Lady Booby and the rest at Booby-Hall.

THE coach and six, in which Lady Booby rode, overtook the other travellers as they entered the parish. She no sooner saw Joseph, than her cheeks glowed with red, and immediately after became as totally pale. She had in her surprise almost stopt her coach; but recollected herself timely enough to prevent it. She entered the parish amidst the ringing of bells, and the acclamations of the poor, who were rejoiced to see their patroness returned after so long an absence, during which time all her rents had been drafted to London, without a shilling being spent among them, which tended not a little to their utter impoverishing; for if the court would be severely missed in such a city as London, how much more must the absence of a person of great fortune be felt in a little country village, for whose inhabitants such a family finds a constant employment and supply; and with the offals of whose table the infirm, aged, and infant poor are abundantly fed, with a generosity which hath scarce a visible effect on their benefactor's pockets?

But if their interest inspired so public a joy into every countenance, how much more forcibly did the affection which they bore Parson Adams operate upon all who beheld his return. They flocked about him like dutiful children round an indulgent parent, and vied with each other in demonstrations of duty and love. The parson on his side shook every one by the hand, [inquired]$_{1-3}$ [inquiring]$_4$ heartily after the healths of all that were absent, of their children and relations, and exprest a satisfaction in his face, which nothing but Benevolence made happy by its objects could infuse.

Nor did Joseph and Fanny want a hearty welcome from all who saw them. In short, no three persons could be more kindly received, as indeed none ever more deserved to be universally beloved.

Adams carried his fellow-travellers home to his house, where he insisted on their partaking whatever his wife, whom with his children he found in health and joy, could provide. Where we shall leave them, enjoying perfect happiness over a homely meal, to view scenes of greater splendour but infinitely less bliss.

Our more intelligent readers will doubtless suspect by this second appearance of Lady Booby on the stage, that all was not ended by the dismission of Joseph; and to be honest with them, they are in the right; the arrow had pierced deeper than she imagined; nor was the wound so easily to be cured. The removal of the object soon cooled her Rage, but it had a different effect on her Love; that departed with his person; but this remained lurking in her mind with his Image. Restless, interrupted slumbers, and confused horrible dreams were her portion the first night. In the morning, Fancy painted her a more delicious scene; but to delude, not delight her: for before she could reach the promised happiness, it vanished, and left her to curse, not bless the vision.

She started from her sleep, her Imagination being all on fire with the phantom, when her eyes accidentally glancing towards the spot where yesterday the real Joseph had stood, that little circumstance raised his Idea in the liveliest colours in her memory. Each look, each word, each gesture rushed back on her mind with charms which all his coldness could not abate. Nay, she imputed that to his Youth, his Folly, his Awe, his Religion, to everything, but what would instantly have produced contempt, want of passion for the sex; or, that which would have roused her hatred, want of liking to her.

Reflection then hurried her farther, and told her she must see this beautiful Youth no more, nay, suggested to her, that she herself had dismissed him for no other fault, than probably that of too violent an awe and respect for herself; and which she ought rather to have esteemed a merit, the effects of which were besides so easily and surely to have been removed; she then blamed, she cursed the hasty rashness of her temper; her fury was vented all on herself, and Joseph appeared innocent in her eyes. Her Passion at length grew so violent that it forced her on seeking relief, and now she thought of recalling him: But Pride forbade that, Pride which soon drove all softer Passions from her soul, and represented to her the meanness of him she was fond of. That thought soon began to obscure his beauties; Contempt succeeded next, and then Disdain, which presently introduced her Hatred of the creature who had given her so much uneasiness. These Enemies of Joseph had no sooner taken possession of her mind, than they insinuated to her a thousand things in his disfavour; everything but dislike of her person; a Thought, which as it would have been intolerable to her, she checked the moment it endeavoured to arise. Revenge came now to her assistance; and she considered her dismission of him stript, and without a character, with the utmost pleasure. She rioted in the several kinds of misery, which her Imagination suggested to her, might be his fate; and with a smile composed of Anger, Mirth, and Scorn, viewed him in the rags in which her Fancy had drest him.

Mrs. Slipslop being summoned, attended her mistress, who had now in her own opinion totally subdued this passion. Whilst she was dressing, she asked if that fellow had been turned away

according to her orders. Slipslop answered, she had told her ladyship so, (as indeed she had) — "And how did he behave?" replied the lady. "Truly madam," cries Slipslop, "in such a manner that *infected* every body who saw him. The poor lad had but little wages to receive: for he constantly allowed his father and mother half his income; so that when your ladyship's livery was stript off, he had not wherewithal to buy a coat, and must have gone naked, if one of the footmen had not *incommodated* him with one; and whilst he was standing in his shirt,
[a lovely]1 (and to say truth, he was [an *amorous*]2 figure) being told your ladyship would not give him a character, he sighed, and said he had done nothing willingly to offend; that for his part he should always give your ladyship a good character where-ever he went; and he prayed God to bless you; for you was the best of ladies, though his enemies had set you against him: I wish you had not turned him away; for I believe you have not a faithfuller servant in the house." — "How came you then," replied the lady, "to advise me to turn him away?" "I, madam," said Slipslop, "I am sure you will do me the justice to say, I did all in my power to prevent it; but I saw your ladyship was angry; and it is not the business of us upper servants to *hintorfear* on those occasions." — "And was it not you, audacious wretch," cried the lady, "who made me angry? Was it not your tittle-tattle, in which I believe you belied the poor fellow, which incensed me against him? He may thank you for all that hath happened; and so may I for the loss of a good servant, and one who probably had more merit than all of you. Poor fellow! I am charmed with his goodness to his parents. Why did not you tell me of that, but suffer me to dismiss so good a creature without a character? I see the reason of your whole behaviour now as well as your complaint; you was jealous of the wenches." "I jealous!" said Slipslop, "I assure you I look upon myself as his betters; I am not meat for a footman I hope." These words threw the lady into a violent passion, and she sent Slipslop from her presence, who departed tossing her nose and crying, "Marry come up! there are some people more jealous than I, I believe." Her lady affected not to hear the words, though in reality she did, and understood them too. Now ensued a second conflict, so

like the former, that it might savour of repetition to relate it minutely. It may suffice to say, that Lady Booby found good reason to doubt whether she had so absolutely conquered her passion, as she had flattered herself; and in order to accomplish it quite, took a resolution more common than wise, to retire immediately into the country. The reader hath long ago seen the arrival of Mrs. Slipslop, whom no pertness could make her mistress resolve to part with; lately, that of Mr. Pounce, her forerunners; and lastly, that of the lady herself.

The morning after her arrival being Sunday, she went to church, to the great surprise of everybody, who wondered to see her ladyship, being no very constant churchwoman, there so suddenly upon her journey. Joseph was likewise there; and I have heard it was remarked, that she fixed her eyes on him much more than on the parson; but this I believe to be only a malicious rumour. When the prayers were ended Mr. Adams stood up, and with a loud voice pronounced: *I publish the Banns of Marriage between Joseph Andrews and Frances Goodwill, both of this parish,* &c. Whether this had any effect on Lady Booby or no, who was then in her pew, which the congregation could not see into, I could never discover: But certain it is, that in about a quarter of an hour she stood up, and directed her eyes to that part of the church where the women sat, and persisted in looking that way during the remainder of the sermon, in so scrutinising a manner, and with so angry a countenance, that most of the women were afraid she was offended at them.

The moment she returned home, she sent for Slipslop into her chamber, and told her, she wondered what that impudent fellow Joseph did in that parish? Upon which Slipslop gave her an account of her meeting Adams with him on the road, and likewise the adventure with Fanny. At the relation of which, the lady often changed her countenance; and when she had heard all, she ordered Mr. Adams into her presence, to whom she behaved as the reader will see in the next chapter.

CHAP. II.

A dialogue between Mr. Abraham Adams and the Lady Booby.

MR. Adams was not far off; for he was drinking her ladyship's health below in a cup of her ale. He no sooner came before her, than she began in the following manner: "I wonder, sir, after the many great obligations you have had to this family," (with all which the reader hath, in the course of this history, been minutely acquainted) "that you will ungratefully show any respect to a fellow who hath been turned out of it for his misdeeds. Nor [doth it, I can tell you, sir, become]$_2$ a man of your character, to run about the country with an idle fellow and wench. Indeed, as for the girl, I know no harm of her. Slipslop tells me she was formerly bred up in my house, and behaved as she ought, till she hankered after this fellow, and he spoiled her. Nay, she may still perhaps do very well, if he will let her alone. You are therefore doing a monstrous thing, in endeavouring to procure a match between these two people, which will be to the ruin of them both."—"Madam," said Adams, "if your ladyship will but hear me speak, I protest I never heard any harm of Mr. Joseph Andrews; if I had, I should have corrected him for it: For I never have, nor will encourage the faults of those under my cure. As for the young woman, I assure your ladyship I have as good an opinion of her as your ladyship yourself, or any other can have. She is the sweetest-tempered, honestest, worthiest, young creature; indeed as to her beauty, I do not commend her on that account, though all men allow she is the handsomest woman, gentle or simple, that ever appeared in the parish." "You are very impertinent," says she, "to talk such fulsome stuff to me. It is mighty becoming truly in a clergyman to trouble himself about handsome women, and you are a delicate judge of beauty, no doubt. A man who hath lived all his life in such a parish as this, is a rare judge of beauty. Ridiculous! Beauty indeed,—a country wench a beauty.—I shall be sick

[is it, I can tell you, sir, becoming in]$_1$

whenever I hear beauty mentioned again. — And so this wench is to stock the parish with beauties, I hope. — But, sir, our poor is numerous enough already; I will have no more vagabonds settled here." "Madam," says Adams, "your ladyship is offended with me, I protest, without any reason. This couple were desirous to consummate long ago, and I dissuaded them from it; nay, I may venture to say, I believe, I was the sole cause of their delaying it." "Well," says she, "and you did very wisely and honestly too, notwithstanding she is the greatest beauty in the parish." — "And now, madam," continued he, "I only perform my office to Mr. Joseph." — "Pray don't Mister such fellows to me," cries the lady. "He," said the parson, "with the consent of Fanny, before my face, put in the banns." — "Yes," answered the lady, "I suppose the slut is forward enough; Slipslop tells me how her head runs on fellows; that is one of her beauties, I suppose. But if they have put in the banns, I desire you will publish them no more without my orders." "Madam," cries Adams, "if anyone puts in sufficient caution, and assigns a proper reason against them, I am willing to surcease." — "I tell you a reason," says she, "he is a vagabond, and he shall not settle here, and bring a nest of beggars into the parish; it will make us but little amends that they will be beauties." "Madam," answered Adams, "with the utmost submission to your ladyship, I have been informed by Lawyer Scout, that any person who serves a year, gains a settlement in the parish where he serves." "Lawyer Scout," replied the lady, "is an impudent coxcomb; I will have no Lawyer Scout interfere with me. I repeat to you again, I will have no more incumbrances brought on us; so I desire you will proceed no [farther]$_2$." "Madam," returned [further]$_1$ Adams, "I would obey your ladyship in everything that is lawful; but surely the parties being poor is no reason against their marrying. G—d forbid there should be any such law. The poor have little share enough of this world already; it would be barbarous indeed to deny them the common privileges, and innocent enjoyments which Nature indulges to the animal creation." "Since you understand yourself no better," cries the lady, "nor the respect due from such as you to a woman of my distinction, than to affront my ears by such loose discourse, I shall mention but one short word; It is my orders to you, that you publish these banns no more; and if you dare, I will recommend it to your master, the Doctor, to discard you from his service. I will, sir, notwithstanding your poor family; and then you and the greatest beauty in the parish may go and beg together." "Madam," answered Adams, "I know not what your ladyship means by the terms *master* and *service*. I am in the Service of a Master who will never discard me for doing my duty: And if the Doctor (for indeed I have never been able to pay for a licence) thinks proper to turn me ⟨out⟩ 4 from my cure, G— will provide me, I hope, another. At least, my family as well as myself have hands; and he will prosper, I doubt not, our endeavours to get our bread honestly with them. Whilst my conscience is pure, I shall never fear what man can do unto me." — "I condemn my humility," said the lady, "for demeaning myself to converse with you so long. I shall take other measures; for I see you are a confederate with them. But the sooner you leave me, the better; and I shall give orders that my doors may no longer be open to you⟨, I will suffer no parsons who run about the country with beauties to be entertained here⟩ 2." — "Madam," said Adams, "I shall enter into no person's doors against their will: But I am assured, when you have inquired farther into this matter, you will applaud, not blame my proceeding; and so I humbly take my leave;" which he did with many bows, or at least many attempts at a bow.

CHAP. III.

What passed between the lady and Lawyer Scout.

In the afternoon the lady sent for Mr. Scout, whom she attacked most violently for intermeddling with her servants, which he denied, and indeed with truth; for he had only asserted accidentally, and perhaps rightly, that a year's service gained a settlement; and so far he owned he might have formerly informed the parson, and believed it was Law. "I am resolved," said the lady, "to have no discarded servants of mine settled here; and so, if this be your Law, I shall send to another lawyer." Scout said, "if she sent to a hundred lawyers, not one or all of them could alter the Law. The utmost that was in the power of a lawyer, was to prevent the Law's taking effect; and that he himself could do for her ladyship as well as any other: And I believe," says he, "madam, your ladyship not being conversant in these matters hath mistaken a difference: For I asserted only, that a man who served a year was settled. Now there is a material difference between being settled in Law and settled in Fact; and as I affirmed generally he was settled, and Law is preferable to Fact, my settlement must be understood in Law, and not in Fact! And suppose, madam, we admit he was settled in Law, what use will they make of it, how doth that relate to Fact? He is not settled in Fact; and if he be not settled in Fact, he is not an Inhabitant; and if he is not an Inhabitant, he is not of this parish; and then undoubtedly he ought not to be published here; for Mr. Adams hath told me your ladyship's pleasure, and the reason, which is a very good one, to prevent burdening us with the poor, we have too many already; and I think we ought to have an Act to hang or transport half of them. [If we can prove in evidence, that he is not settled in Fact, it is another matter. What I said to Mr. Adams, was on a supposition that he was settled in Fact; and indeed if that was the case, I should doubt." — "Don't tell me your *Facts* and your *ifs*," said the lady, "I don't understand your gibberish: You take too much upon you, and are very impertinent in pretending to direct in this parish, and you shall be taught better, I assure you, you shall. But as to the wench, I am resolved she shall not settle here; I will not suffer]$_2$ such beauties as these ⟨to⟩ $_2$ produce children for us to keep." — "Beauties, indeed! your ladyship is pleased to be merry," — answered Scout. — "Mr. Adams described her so to me," said the lady. "— Pray what sort of dowdy is it, Mr. Scout?" — "The ugliest creature almost I ever beheld, a poor dirty drab, your ladyship never saw such a wretch." — "Well but, dear Mr. Scout, let her be what she will, — these ugly women will bring children you know; so that we must prevent the marriage." — "True, madam," replied Scout,

["Truly," said the lady, "they are a grievous load, and unless we had an employment for them, it would be charity to send them where they might have something to do. At least, I am sure we ought to prevent the farther growth of the evil, and not let]$_1$

"for the subsequent marriage co-operating with the Law, will carry Law into Fact. When a man is married, he is settled in Fact; and then he is not removable. I will see Mr. Adams, and I make no doubt of prevailing with him. His only objection is doubtless that he shall lose his fee: But that being once made easy, as it shall be, I am confident no farther objection will remain. No, no, it is impossible: but your ladyship can't discom-
[with]$_{1-2}$ mend his unwillingness to depart [from]$_3$ his fee. Every man ought to have a proper value for his fee. As to the matter in question, if your ladyship pleases to employ me in it, I will venture to promise you success. The laws of this land are not so vulgar, to permit a mean fellow to contend with one of your ladyship's fortune. We have one sure card, which is to carry him before Justice Frolick, who, upon hearing your ladyship's name, will commit him without any farther questions. ⟨As for the dirty slut, we shall have nothing to do with her: for if we get rid of the fellow, the ugly jade will——"⟩$_2$ "Take what measures you please, good Mr. Scout," answered the lady, "but I wish you could rid the parish of both; for Slipslop tells me such stories of this wench, that I abhor the thoughts of her; and though you say she is such an ugly slut, yet you know, dear Mr. Scout, these forward creatures who run after men, will always find some as forward as themselves: So that, to prevent the increase of beggars, we must get rid of her."—"Your ladyship is very much in the right," answered Scout; "but I am afraid the Law is a little deficient in giving us any such power of prevention; however the justice will stretch it as far as he is able, to oblige your ladyship. To say truth, it is a great blessing to the country that he is in the commission; for he hath taken several poor off our hands, that the Law would never lay hold on. I know some justices who make as much of committing a man to Bridewell as his lordship at *Size* would of hanging him:[1] But it would do a man good to see his worship our justice commit a fellow to Bridewell; he takes so much pleasure in it: And when once we ha' un there, we seldom hear any more o' un. He's either starved or eat up by vermin in a month's time."—

[1] Bridewell, London, a workhouse for minor offences, like vagabondage and prostitution.

Here the arrival of a visitor put an end to the conversation, and Mr. Scout having undertaken the cause, and promised it success, departed.

This Scout was one of those fellows, who without any knowledge of the law, or being bred to it, take upon them, in defiance of an Act of Parliament, to act as lawyers in the country, and are called so. They are the pests of society, and a scandal to a profession, to which indeed they do not belong; and which owes to such kind of rascallions the ill-will which weak persons bear towards it. With this fellow, to whom a little before she would not have condescended to have spoken, did a certain passion for Joseph, and the jealousy and the disdain of poor innocent Fanny, betray the Lady Booby, into a familiar discourse, in which she inadvertently confirmed many hints, with which Slipslop, whose gallant he was, had pre-acquainted him; and whence he had taken an opportunity to assert those severe falsehoods of little Fanny, which possibly the reader might not have been well able to account for, if we had not thought proper to give him this information.

CHAP. IV.

A short chapter, but very full of matter; particularly the arrival of Mr. Booby and his lady.

ALL that night and the next day, the Lady Booby passed with the utmost anxiety; her mind was distracted, and her soul tossed up and down by many turbulent and opposite passions. She loved, hated, pitied, scorned, admired, despised the same person by fits, which changed in a very short interval. On Tuesday morning, which happened to be a holiday, she went to church, where, to her surprise, Mr. Adams published the banns again with as audible a voice as before. It was lucky for her, that as there was no sermon, she had an immediate opportunity of returning home, to vent her rage, which she could not have concealed from the congregation five minutes; indeed it was not then very numerous, the assembly consisting of no more than Adams, his clerk, his wife, the lady, and one of her servants. At her return she met Slipslop, who accosted her in these words: — "O meam, what doth your ladyship think? To be sure Lawyer Scout hath carried Joseph and Fanny both before the justice. All the parish are in tears, and say they will certainly be hanged: For nobody knows what it is for." — "I suppose they deserve it," says the lady. "What dost thou mention such wretches to me?" — "O dear madam," answered Slipslop, "is it not a pity such a *graceless* young man should die a *virulent* death? I hope the judge will take *commensuration* on his youth. As for Fanny, I don't think it signifies much what becomes of her; and if poor Joseph hath done anything, I could venture to swear she *traduced* him to it: Few men ever come to *fragrant* punishment, but by those nasty creatures who are a scandal to our *sect*." The lady was no more pleased at this news, after a moment's reflection, than Slipslop herself: For though she wished Fanny far enough, she did not desire the removal of Joseph, especially with her. She was puzzled how to act, or what to say on this occasion, when a coach and six drove into the court, and a servant acquainted her with the arrival of her nephew Booby and his lady. She ordered them to be conducted into a drawing-room, whither she presently repaired, having composed her countenance as well as she could; and being a little satisfied that the wedding would by these means be at least interrupted; and that she should have an opportunity to execute any resolution she might take, for which she saw herself provided with an excellent instrument in Scout.

The Lady Booby apprehended her servant had made a mistake, when he had mentioned Mr. Booby's lady; for she had never heard of his marriage: but how great was her surprise, when at her entering the room, her nephew presented his wife to her, saying, "Madam, this is that charming Pamela, of whom I am convinced you have heard so much." The lady received her with more civility than he expected; indeed with the utmost: For she was perfectly polite, nor had any vice inconsistent with good-breeding. They passed some little time in ordinary discourse, when a servant came and whispered Mr. Booby, who presently told the ladies he must desert them a little on some business of consequence; and as their discourse during his absence would afford little improvement or entertainment to the reader, we will leave them for a while to attend Mr. Booby.

CHAP. V.

Containing justice business; curious precedents of depositions, and other matters necessary to be perused by all Justices of the Peace and their clerks.

THE young squire and his lady were no sooner alighted from their coach, than the servants began to inquire after Mr. Joseph, from whom they said their lady had not heard a word to her great surprise, since he had left Lady Booby's. Upon this they were instantly informed of what had lately happened, with which they hastily acquainted their master, who took an immediate resolution to go himself, and endeavour to restore his Pamela her brother, before she even knew she had lost him.

The justice, before whom the criminals were carried, and who lived within a short mile of the lady's house, was luckily Mr. Booby's acquaintance, by his having an estate in his neighbourhood. Ordering therefore his horses to his coach, he set out for the Judgment-Seat, and arrived when the justice had almost finished his business. He was conducted into a hall, where he was acquainted that his worship would wait on him in a moment; for he had only a man and ⟨a⟩ $_2$ woman to commit to Bridewell first. As he was now convinced he had not a minute to lose, he insisted on the servants introducing him directly ⟨in⟩$_2$to the room where the justice [was then]$_2$ executing his office, as he called it. [then was]$_1$
Being brought thither, and the first compliments being passed between the squire and his worship, the former asked the latter what crime those two young people had been guilty of. "No great crime," answered the justice. "I have only ordered them to Bridewell for a month." "But what is their crime?" repeated the squire. "Larceny, an't please your honour," said Scout.

"Ay," says the justice, "a kind of felonious larcenous thing. I believe I must order them a little correction too, a little stripping and whipping." (Poor Fanny, who had hitherto supported all with the thoughts of her Joseph's company, trembled at that sound; but indeed without reason, for none but the Devil himself would have executed such a sentence on her.) "Still," said the squire, "I am ignorant of the crime, the fact I mean." "Why, there it is in peaper," answered the justice, showing him a deposition, which in the absence of his clerk he had writ himself, of which we have with great difficulty procured an authentic copy; and here it follows *verbatim et literatim.*

The Depusition of James Scout, *Layer, and* Thomas Trotter, *Yeoman, taken befor mee, on of his Magesty's Justasses of the Piece for* Zumersetshire.

"These Deponants saith, and first *Thomas Trotter* for himself saith, that on the of this instant *October,* being Sabbath-Day, betwin the Ours of 2 and 4 in the afternoon, he zeed *Joseph Andrews* and *Francis Goodwill* walk akross a certane Felde belunging to Layer *Scout,* and out of the Path which ledes thru the said Felde, and there he zede *Joseph Andrews* with a Nife cut one Hassel-Twig, of the value, as he believes, of 3 half pence, or thereabouts; and he saith, that the said *Francis Goodwill* was likewise walking on the Grass out of the said Path in the said Felde, and did receive and karry in her Hand the said Twig, and so was cumfarting, eading and abatting to the said *Joseph* therein. And the said *James Scout* for himself says, that he verily believes the said Twig to be his own proper Twig, *&c.*"

"Jesu!" said the squire, "would you commit two persons to Bridewell for a twig?" "Yes," said the lawyer, "and with great lenity too; for if we had called it a young tree they would have been both hanged."—"Harkee, (says the justice, taking aside the squire) I should not have been so severe on this occasion, but Lady Booby desires to get them out of the parish; so Lawyer Scout will give the constable orders to let them run away, if they please; but it seems they intend to marry together, and the lady hath no other means, as they are legally settled there, to prevent their bringing an incumbrance on her own parish." "Well," said the squire, "I will take care my aunt shall be satisfied in this point; and likewise I promise you, Joseph here shall never be any incumbrance on her. I shall be obliged to you therefore, if, instead of Bridewell, you will commit them to my custody."—"O to be sure, sir, if you desire it," answered the justice; and without more ado, Joseph and Fanny were delivered over to Squire Booby, whom Joseph very well knew; but little guessed how nearly he was related to him. The justice burnt his *Mittimus*. The constable was sent about his business. The lawyer made no complaint for want of justice, and the prisoners, with exulting hearts, gave a thousand thanks to his honour Mr. Booby, who did not intend their obligations to him should cease here; for ordering his man to produce a cloakbag which he had caused to be brought from Lady Booby's on purpose, he desired the justice that he might have Joseph with him into a room; where ordering his servant to take out a suit of his own clothes, with linen and other necessaries, he left Joseph to dress himself, who not yet knowing the cause of all this civility, excused his accepting such a favour as long as decently he could. Whilst Joseph was dressing, the squire repaired to the justice, whom he found talking with Fanny; for during the examination she had lopped her hat over her eyes, which were also bathed in tears, and had by that means concealed from his worship what might perhaps have rendered the arrival of Mr. Booby unnecessary, at least for herself. The justice no sooner saw her countenance cleared up, and her bright eyes shining through her tears, than he secretly cursed himself for having once thought of Bridewell for her. He would willingly have sent his own wife thither, to have had Fanny in her place. And conceiving almost at the same instant desires and schemes to accomplish them, he employed the minutes whilst the squire was absent with Joseph, in assuring her how sorry he was for having treated her so roughly before he knew her merit; and told her, that since Lady Booby was unwilling that she should settle in her parish, she was heartily welcome to his, where he promised her his protection, adding, that he would take Joseph and her into his own family, if she liked it; which assurance he confirmed with a squeeze by the hand. She thanked him very kindly, and said, "she would acquaint Joseph with the offer, which he would certainly be glad to accept; for that Lady Booby was angry with them both; though she did not know either had done anything to offend her: but imputed it to Madam Slipslop, who had always been her enemy."

The squire now returned, and prevented any farther continuance of this conversation; and the justice out of a pretended respect to his guest, but in reality from an apprehension of a rival; (for he knew nothing of his marriage,) ordered Fanny into the kitchen, whither she gladly retired; nor did the squire, who declined the trouble of explaining the whole matter, oppose it.

It would be unnecessary, if I was able, which indeed I am not, to relate the conversation between these two gentlemen, which rolled, as I have been informed, entirely on the subject of horse-racing. Joseph was soon drest in the plainest dress he could find, which was a blue coat and breeches, with a gold edging, and a red waistcoat with the same; and as this suit, which was rather too large for the squire, exactly fitted him; so he became it so well, and looked so genteel, that no person would have doubted its being as well adapted to his quality as his shape; nor have suspected, as one might when my Lord ——, or Sir ——, or Mr. —— appear in lace or embroidery, that the tailor's man wore those clothes home on his back, which he should have carried under his arm.

The squire now took leave of the justice, and calling for Fanny, made her and Joseph, against their wills, get into the coach with him, which he then ordered to drive to Lady Booby's. — It had moved a few yards only, when the squire asked Joseph, if he knew who that man was crossing the field; for, added he, "I never saw one take such strides before." Joseph answered eagerly, "O sir, it is Parson Adams." — "O la, indeed, and so it is," said Fanny; "poor man he is coming to do what he could for us. Well, he is the worthiest best-natured creature." — "Ay," said Joseph, "God bless him; for there is not such another in the universe." — "The best creature living sure," cries Fanny. "Is he?" says the squire, "then I am resolved to have the best creature living in my coach," and so saying he ordered it to stop, whilst Joseph at his request hollowed to the parson, who well knowing his voice, made all the haste imaginable, and soon came up with them; he was desired by the master, who could scarce refrain from laughter at his figure, to mount into the coach, which he with many thanks refused, saying he could walk by its side, and he'd warrant he kept ⟨up⟩$_2$ with it; but he was at length over-prevailed on. The squire now acquainted Joseph with his marriage; but he might have spared himself that labour; for his servant, whilst Joseph was dressing, had performed that office before. He continued to express the vast happiness he enjoyed in his sister, and the value he had for all who belonged to her. Joseph made many bows, and exprest as many acknowledgments; and Parson Adams, who now first perceived Joseph's new apparel, burst into tears with joy, and fell to rubbing his hands and snapping his fingers, as if he had been mad.

They were now arrived at the Lady Booby's, and the squire desiring them to wait a moment in the court, walked in to his aunt, and calling her out from his wife, acquainted her with Joseph's arrival; saying, "Madam, as I have married a virtuous and worthy woman, I am resolved to [own her relations, and show them all a proper respect; I shall think myself therefore]$_2$ infinitely obliged to all mine, who will do the same. It is true, her brother hath been your servant; but he is now become my brother; and I have one happiness, that neither his character, his behaviour or appearance give me any reason to be ashamed of calling him so. In short, he is now below, dressed like a gentleman, in which light I intend he shall hereafter be seen; and you will oblige me beyond expression, if you will admit him to be of our party; for I know it will give great pleasure to my wife, though she will not mention it."

[show a proper respect, and own her relations, and I shall think myself]$_1$

This was a stroke of Fortune beyond the Lady Booby's hopes or expectation; she answered him eagerly, "Nephew, you know how easily I am prevailed on to do anything which Joseph Andrews desires — Phoo, I mean which you desire me, and as he is now your relation, I cannot refuse to entertain him as such." The squire told her, he knew his obligation to her for her compliance, and going three steps, returned and told her — he had one more favour, which he believed she would easily grant, as she had accorded him the former. "There is a young woman ——" "Nephew," says she, "don't let my good-nature make you desire, as is too commonly the case, to impose on me. Nor think, because I have with so much condescension agreed to suffer your brother-in-law to come to my table, that I will submit to the company of all my own servants, and all the dirty trollops in the country." "Madam," answered the squire, "I believe you never saw this young creature. I never beheld such Sweetness and Innocence joined with such Beauty, and withal so genteel." "Upon my soul, I won't admit her," replied the lady in a passion; "the whole world shan't prevail on me, I resent even the desire as an affront, and ——" The squire, who knew her inflexibility, interrupted her, by asking pardon, and promising not to mention it more. He then returned to Joseph, and she to Pamela. He took Joseph aside and told him, he would carry him to his sister; but could not prevail as yet for Fanny. Joseph begged that he might see his sister alone, and then be with his Fanny; but the squire knowing the pleasure his wife would have in her brother's company, would not admit it, telling Joseph there would be nothing in so short an absence from Fanny, whilst he was assured of her safety; adding, he hoped he could not so easily quit a sister whom he had not seen so long, and who so tenderly loved him —Joseph immediately complied; for indeed no brother could love a sister more; and recommending Fanny, who rejoiced that she was not to go before Lady Booby, to the care of Mr. Adams, he attended the squire up stairs, whilst Fanny repaired with the parson to his house, where she [thought herself secure]2 of a kind reception.

[was certain]1

CHAP. VI.

Of which you are desired to read no more than you like.

THE meeting between Joseph and Pamela was not without tears of joy on both sides; and their embraces were full of tenderness and affection. They were however regarded with much more pleasure by the nephew than by the aunt, to whose flame they were fuel only; and [this was increased]$_{4}$ by the addition [being assisted]$_{1\text{-}3}$ of dress, which was indeed not wanted to set off the lively colours in which Nature had drawn Health, Strength, Comeliness, and Youth. In the afternoon Joseph, at their request, entertained them with [the]$_{4}$ account of his adventures, nor could Lady [an]$_{1\text{-}3}$ Booby conceal her dissatisfaction at those parts in which Fanny was concerned, especially when Mr. Booby launched forth into such rapturous praises of her beauty. She said, applying to her niece, that she wondered her nephew, who had pretended to marry for love, should think such a subject proper to amuse his wife with: adding, that for her part, she should be jealous of a husband who spoke so warmly in praise of another woman. Pamela answered, indeed she thought she had cause; but it was an instance of Mr. Booby's aptness to see more beauty in women than they were mistresses of. At which words both the women fixed their eyes on two looking-glasses; and Lady Booby replied that men were in the general very ill judges of beauty; and then whilst both contemplated only their own faces, they paid a cross compliment to each other's charms. When the hour of rest approached, which the lady of the house deferred as long as decently she could, she informed Joseph (whom for the future we shall call Mr. Joseph, he having as good a title to that appellation as many others, I mean that incontested one of good clothes) that she had ordered a bed to be provided for him; he declined this favour to his utmost; for his heart had long been with his Fanny; but she insisted on his accepting it, alledging that the parish had no proper accommodation for such a person, as he was now to esteem himself. The squire and his lady both joining with her, Mr. Joseph was at last forced to give over his design of visiting Fanny that evening, who on her side as impatiently expected him till midnight, when in complacence to Mr. Adams's family, who had sat up two hours out of respect to her, she retired to bed, but not to sleep; the thoughts of her love kept her waking, and his not returning according to his promise, filled her with uneasiness; of which however she could not assign any other cause than merely that of being absent from him.

Mr. Joseph ~~however~~ $_2$ rose early in the morning, and visited her in whom his soul delighted. She no sooner heard his voice in the parson's parlour, than she leapt from her bed, and dressing herself in a few minutes, went down to him. They passed two hours with inexpressible happiness together, and then having appointed Monday, by Mr. Adams's permission, for their marriage, Mr. Joseph returned according to his promise, to breakfast at the Lady Booby's, with whose behaviour since the evening we shall now acquaint the reader.

She was no sooner retired to her chamber than she asked Slipslop what she thought of this wonderful creature her nephew had married. "Madam?" said Slipslop, not yet sufficiently understanding what answer she was to make. "I ask you," answered the lady, "what you think of the dowdy, my niece I think I am to call her?" Slipslop, wanting no further hint, began to pull her to pieces, and so miserably defaced her, that it would have been impossible for anyone to have known the person. The lady gave her all the assistance she could, and ended with saying — "I think, Slipslop, you have done her justice; but yet, bad as she is, she is an angel compared to this Fanny." Slipslop then fell on Fanny, whom she hacked and hewed in the like barbarous manner, concluding with an observation that there was always something in those low-life creatures which must eternally distinguish them from their betters. "Really," said the lady, "I think there
[must]$_1$ is one exception to your rule, I am certain you [may]$_2$ guess who I mean." — "Not I, upon my word, madam," said Slipslop. — "I mean a young fellow; sure you are the dullest wretch," said the lady. — "O la, I am indeed — Yes truly, madam, he is an *accession*," answered Slipslop. — "Ay, is he not, Slipslop?" returned the lady. "Is he not so genteel that a prince might without a blush acknowledge him for his son. His behaviour is such that would not shame the best education. He borrows from his station a condescension in everything to his superiors, yet unattended by that mean servility which is called good-behaviour in such persons. Everything he doth hath no mark of the base motive of fear, but visibly shows some respect and gratitude, and carries with it the persuasion of love — And then for his virtues; such piety to his parents, such tender affection to his

sister, such integrity in his friendship, such bravery, such goodness, that if he had been born a gentleman, his wife would have possessed the most invaluable blessing." — "To be sure, ma'am," says Slipslop. — "But as he is," answered the lady, "if he had a thousand more good qualities, it must render a woman of fashion contemptible even to be suspected of thinking of him, yes I should despise myself for such a thought." "To be sure, ma'am," said Slipslop. "And why to be sure?" replied the lady, "thou art always one's Echo. Is he not more worthy of affection than a dirty country clown, though ~~he's~~$_2$ born of a family as old as the flood, or an idle worthless rake, or little puisny beau of quality? And yet these we must condemn ourselves to, in order to avoid the censure of the world; to shun the contempt of others, we must ally ourselves to those we despise; we must prefer birth, title and fortune to real merit. It is a tyranny of custom, a tyranny we must comply with: For we people of fashion are the slaves of custom." — "Marry come up!" said Slipslop, who now well knew which party to take, "if I was a woman of your ladyship's fortune and quality, I would be a slave to nobody." — "Me," said the lady, "I am speaking, if a young woman of fashion who had seen nothing [of]$_2$ the world should happen to like such a fellow. — Me indeed; I [in]$_2$
hope thou dost not imagine——" "No, ma'am, to be sure," cries Slipslop. — "No! what no?" cried the lady. "Thou art always ready to answer, before thou hast heard one. So far I must allow he is a charming fellow. Me indeed! No, Slipslop, all thoughts of men are over with me. — I have lost a husband, who — but if I should reflect, I should run mad. — My future ease must depend upon forgetfulness. Slipslop, let me hear some of thy nonsense to turn my thoughts another way. What dost thou think of Mr. Andrews?" "Why I think," says Slipslop, "he is the handsomest most properest man I ever saw; and if I was a lady of the greatest degree, it would be well for some folks. Your ladyship may talk of custom if you please; but I am *confidous* there is no more comparison between young Mr. Andrews, and most of the young gentlemen who come to your ladyship's house in London; a parcel of *whipper-snapper* sparks: I would sooner marry our old Parson Adams. Never tell me what people say,

whilst I am happy in the arms of him I love. Some folks rail against other folks, because other folks have what some folks would be glad of." — "And so," answered the lady, "if you was a woman of condition, you would really marry Mr. Andrews?" — "Yes, I assure your ladyship," replied Slipslop, "if he would have me." — "Fool, idiot," cries the lady, "if he would have a woman of fashion! Is that a question?" "No truly, madam," said Slipslop, "I believe it would be none, if Fanny was out of the way; and I am *confidous* if I was in your ladyship's place, and liked Mr. Joseph Andrews, she should not stay in the parish a moment. I am sure Lawyer Scout would send her packing, if your ladyship would but say the word." This last speech of Slipslop raised a tempest in the mind of her mistress. She feared Scout had betrayed her, or rather that she had bertayed herself. After some silence and a double change of her complexion; first to pale and then to red, she thus spoke: "I am astonished at the liberty you give your tongue. Would you insinuate, that I employed Scout against this wench, on the account of the fellow?" "La ma'am," said Slipslop, frighted out of her wits. "I *assassinate* such a thing!" "I think you dare not," answered the lady, "I believe my conduct may defy malice itself to assert so cursed a slander. If I had ever discovered any wantonness, any lightness in my behaviour: If I had followed the example of some whom thou hast I believe seen, in allowing myself indecent liberties, even with a husband: But the dear man who is gone (*here she began to sob*) was he alive again, (*then she produced tears*) could not upbraid me with any one act of tenderness or passion. No, Slipslop, all the time I cohabited with him, he never obtained even a kiss from me, without my expressing reluctance in the granting it. I am sure he himself never suspected how much I loved him. — Since his death, thou knowest, though it is almost six weeks (it wants but a day) ago, I have not admitted one visitor, till this fool my nephew arrived. I have confined myself quite to one party of friends. — And can such a conduct as this fear to be arraigned? To be accused not only of a passion which I have always despised; but of fixing it on such an object, a creature so much beneath my notice." — "Upon my word, ma'am," says Slipslop, "I do not understand your ladyship, nor know I anything of the matter." — "I believe indeed thou dost not understand me. — Those are delicacies which exist only in superior minds; thy coarse ideas cannot comprehend them. Thou art a low creature, of the Andrews breed, a reptile of a lower order, a weed that grows in the common garden of the creation." — "I assure your ladyship," says Slipslop, whose passions were almost of as high an order as her lady's, "I have no more to do with *Common Garden* than other folks.[2] Really, your ladyship talks of servants as if they were not born of the Christian *specious*. Servants have flesh and blood as well as Quality; and Mr. Andrews himself is a proof that they have as good, if not better. And for my own part, I can't perceive my *dears* * are coarser than other people's; and I am sure, if Mr. Andrews was a *dear* of mine, I should not be ashamed of him in company with gentlemen; for whoever hath seen him in his new clothes, must confess he looks as much like a gentleman as anybody. Coarse, quotha! I can't bear to hear the poor young fellow run down neither; for I will say this, I never heard him say an ill word of anybody in his life. I am sure his coarseness doth not lie in his heart; for he is the best-natured man in the world; and as for his skin, it is no coarser than other people's, I am sure. His bosom when a boy was as white as driven snow; and where it is not covered with hairs, is so still. Ifaukins! if I was Mrs. Andrews, with a hundred a year, I should not envy the best She who wears a head. A woman that could not be happy with such a man, ought never to be so: For if he can't make a woman happy, I never yet beheld the man who could. I say again I wish I was a great lady for his sake, I believe when I had made a gentleman of him, he'd behave so, that nobody should [*deprecate*]$_2$ what I had done; and I fancy few would venture to tell him he was no gentleman to his face, nor to mine neither." At which words, taking up the candles, she asked her mistress, who had been some time in her bed, if she had any farther commands; who mildly answered she had none; and telling her, she was a comical creature, bid her good-night.

[dis-commend]$_1$

* Meaning perhaps ideas. [Fielding's note.]

[2] Familiar slang for Covent Garden; Mrs. Slipslop is thinking of its brothels.

CHAP. VII.

Philosophical reflections, the like not to be found in any light French Romance. Mr. Booby's grave advice to Joseph, and Fanny's encounter with a beau.

HABIT, my good reader, hath so vast a prevalence over the human mind, that there is scarce anything too strange or too strong to be asserted of it. The story of the miser, who from long accustoming to cheat others, came at last to cheat himself, and with great delight and triumph, picked his own pocket of a guinea, to convey to his hoard, is not impossible or improbable. In like manner, it fares with the practisers of deceit, who from having long deceived their acquaintance, gain at last a power of deceiving themselves, and acquire that very opinion (however false) of their own abilities, excellencies, and virtues, into which they have for years perhaps endeavoured to betray their neighbours. Now, reader, to apply this observation to my present purpose, thou must know, that as the passion generally called love, exercises most of the talents of the female or fair world; so in this they now and then discover a small inclination to deceit; for which thou wilt not be angry with the beautiful creatures, when thou hast considered, that at the age of seven or something earlier, Miss is instructed by her mother, that Master is a very monstrous kind of animal, who will, if she suffers him to come too near her, infallibly eat her up, and grind her to pieces. That so far from kissing or toying with him of her own accord, she must not admit him to kiss or toy with her. And lastly, that she must never have any affection towards him; for if she should, all her friends in petticoats would esteem her a traitress, point at her, and hunt her out of their society. These impressions being first received, are farther and deeper inculcated by their school-mistresses and companions; so that by the age of ten they have contracted such a dread ~~of~~ [3] and abhorrence of the above named monster, that whenever they see him, they fly from him as the innocent hare doth from the greyhound. Hence to the age of fourteen or fifteen, they entertain a mighty antipathy to Master; they resolve and frequently profess that they will never have any commerce with him, and entertain fond hopes of passing their lives out of his reach, of the possibility of which they have so visible an example in their good maiden aunt. But when they arrive at this period, and have now passed their second climacteric, when their wisdom grown riper, begins to see a little farther; and from almost daily falling in Master's way, to apprehend the great difficulty of keeping out of it; and when they observe him look often at them, and sometimes very eagerly and earnestly too, (for the monster seldom takes any notice of them till at this age) they then begin to think of their danger; and as they perceive they cannot easily avoid him, the wiser part bethink themselves of providing by other means for their security. They endeavour by all the methods they can invent to render themselves so amiable in his eyes, that he may have no inclination to hurt them; in which they generally succeed so well, that his eyes, by frequent languishing, soon lessen their idea of his fierceness, and so far abate their fears, that they venture to parley with him; and when they perceive him so different from what he hath been described, all Gentleness, Softness, Kindness, Tenderness, Fondness, their dreadful apprehensions vanish in a moment; and now (it being usual with the human mind to skip from one extreme to its opposite, as easily, and almost as suddenly, as a bird from one bough to another;) Love instantly succeeds to Fear: But as it happens to persons, who have in their infancy been thoroughly frightened with certain no persons called ghosts, that they retain their dread of those beings, after they are convinced that there are no such things; so these young ladies, though they no longer apprehend devouring, cannot so entirely shake off all that hath been instilled into them; they still entertain the idea of that censure which was so strongly imprinted on their tender minds, to which the declarations of abhorrence they every day hear from their companions greatly contribute. To avoid this censure therefore, is now their only care; for which purpose they still pretend the same aversion to the monster: And the more they love him, the more ardently they counterfeit the antipathy. By the continual and constant practice of which deceit on others, they at length impose on themselves, and really believe they hate what they love. Thus indeed it happened to Lady Booby, who loved Joseph long before she knew it; and now loved him much more than she suspected. She had indeed, from the time of his sister's arrival in the quality of her niece; and from the instant she viewed him in the dress and character of a gentleman, began to conceive secretly a design which Love had concealed from herself, 'till ⟨a⟩ [2] Dream betrayed it to her.

She had no sooner risen than she sent for her nephew; when he came to her, after many compliments on his choice, she told him, "he might perceive in her condescension to admit her own servant to her table, that she looked on the family of Andrews as his relations, and indeed hers; that as he had married into such a family, it became him to endeavour by all methods to raise it as much as possible; at length she advised him to use all his art to dissuade Joseph from his intended match, which would still enlarge their relation to meanness and poverty; concluding, that by a commission in the army, or some other genteel employment, he might soon put young Mr. Andrews on the foot of a gentleman; and that being once done, his accomplishments might quickly gain him an alliance, which would not be to their discredit."

Her nephew heartily embraced this proposal; and finding Mr. Joseph with his wife, at his return to her chamber, he immediately began thus: "My love to my dear Pamela, brother, will extend to all her relations; nor shall I show them less respect than if I had married into the family of a duke. I hope I have given you some early testimonies of this, and shall continue to give you daily more. You will excuse me therefore, brother, if my concern for your interest makes me mention what may be, perhaps, disagreeable to you to hear: But I must insist upon it, that if you have any value for my alliance or my friendship, you will decline any thoughts of engaging farther with a girl, who is, as you are a relation of mine, so much beneath you. I know there may be at first some difficulty in your compliance, but that will daily diminish; and you will in the end sincerely thank me for my advice. I own, indeed, the girl is handsome: But beauty alone is a poor ingredient, and will make but an uncomfortable marriage." "Sir," said Joseph, "I assure you her beauty is her least perfection; nor do I know a virtue which that young creature is not possest of." "As to her virtues," answered Mr. Booby, "you can be yet but a slender judge of them: But if she had never so many, you will find her equal in these among her superiors in birth and fortune, which now you are to esteem on a footing with yourself; at least I will take care they shall shortly be so, unless you prevent me by degrading yourself with such a match, a match I have hardly patience to think of; and which would break the hearts of your parents, who now rejoice in the expectation of seeing you make a figure in the world." "I know not," replied Joseph, "that my parents have any power over my inclinations; nor am I obliged to sacrifice my happiness to their whim or ambition: Besides, I shall be very sorry to see that the unexpected advancement of my sister, should so suddenly inspire them with this wicked pride, and make them despise their equals, I am resolved on no account to quit my dear Fanny, no, though I could raise her as high above her present station as you have raised my sister." "Your sister, as well as myself," said Booby, "are greatly obliged to you for the comparison: But, sir, she is not worthy to be compared in beauty to my Pamela; nor hath she half her merit. And besides, sir, as you civilly throw my marriage with your sister in my teeth, I must teach you the wide difference between us; my fortune enabled me to please myself; and it would have been as overgrown a folly in me to have omitted it, as in you to do it." "My fortune enables me to please myself likewise," said Joseph; "for all my pleasure is centered in Fanny, and whilst I have health, I shall be able to support her with my labour in that station to which she was born, and with which she is content." "Brother," said Pamela, "Mr. Booby advises you as a friend; and, no doubt, my Papa and Mamma will be of his opinion, and will have great reason to be angry with you for destroying what his goodness hath done, and throwing down our family again, after he hath raised it. It would become you better, brother, to pray for the assistance of Grace against such a passion, than to indulge ⟨it⟩ [3]." —

"Sure, sister, you are not in earnest; I am sure she is your equal at least." — "She was my equal," answered Pamela, "but I am [wife]$_{1-2}$ no longer Pamela Andrews, I am now this gentleman's [lady]$_{3}$, and as such am above her — I hope I shall never behave with an unbecoming pride; but at the same time I shall always endeavour to know myself, and question not the assistance of Grace to that purpose." They were now summoned to breakfast, and thus ended their discourse for the present, very little to the satisfaction of any of the parties.

Fanny was now walking in an avenue at some distance from the house, where Joseph had promised to take the first opportunity of coming to her. She had not a shilling in the world, and had subsisted ever since her return entirely on the charity of Parson Adams. A young gentleman attended by many servants, came up to her, and asked her if that was not the Lady Booby's house before him? This indeed he well knew; but had framed the question for no other reason than to make her look up and discover if her face was equal to the delicacy of her shape. He no sooner saw it, than he was struck with amazement. He stopt his horse, and swore she was the most beautiful creature he ever beheld. Then instantly alighting, and delivering his horse to his servant, he rapt out half a dozen oaths that he would kiss her; to which she at first submitted, begging he would not be rude: but he was not satisfied with the civility of a salute, nor even with the rudest attack he could make on her lips, but caught her in his arms and endeavoured to kiss her breasts, which with all her strength she resisted; and as our spark was not of the Herculean race, with some difficulty prevented. The young gentleman being soon out of breath in the struggle, quitted her, and remounting his horse called one of his servants to him, whom he ordered to stay behind with her, and make her any offers whatever, to prevail on her to return home with him in the evening; and to assure her he would take her into keeping. He then rode on with his other servants, and arrived at the lady's house, to whom he was a distant relation, and was come to pay a visit.

The trusty fellow, who was employed in an office he had been long accustomed to, discharged his part with all the fidelity and dexterity imaginable; but to no purpose. She was entirely deaf to his offers, and rejected them with the utmost disdain. At last the pimp, who had perhaps more warm blood about him than his master, began to solicit for himself; he told her, though he was a servant, he was a man of some fortune, which he would make her mistress of—and this without any insult to her virtue, for that he would marry her. She answered, if his master himself, or the greatest lord in the land would marry her, she would refuse him. At last being weary with persuasions, and on fire with charms which would have almost kindled a flame in the bosom of an ancient philosopher, or modern divine, he fastened his horse to the ground, and attacked her with much more force than the gentleman had exerted. Poor Fanny would ⟨not⟩$_3$ have been able to resist his rudeness [any long]$_4$ time, [but]$_3$ the deity who presides over chaste love sent her Joseph to her assistance. He no sooner came within sight, and perceived her struggling with a man, than like a cannon-ball, or like lightning, or anything that is swifter, if anything be, he ran towards her, and coming up just as the ravisher had torn her handkerchief from her breast, before his lips had touched that seat of innocence and bliss, he dealt him so lusty a blow in that part of his neck which a rope would have become with the utmost propriety, that the fellow staggered backwards, and perceiving he had to do with something rougher than the little, tender, trembling hand of Fanny, he quitted her, and turning about saw his rival, with fire flashing from his eyes, again ready to assail him; and indeed before he could well defend himself or return the first blow, he received a second, which had it fallen on that part of the stomach to which it was directed, would have been probably the last he would have had any occasion for; but the ravisher lifting up his hand, drove the blow upwards to his mouth, whence it dislodged three of his teeth; and now not conceiving any extraordinary affection for the beauty of Joseph's person, nor being extremely pleased with this method of salutation, he collected all his force, and aimed a blow at Joseph's breast, which he artfully parried with one fist, so that it lost its force entirely in air. And stepping one foot backward, he darted his fist so fiercely at his enemy, that had he not caught it in his hand (for he was a boxer of no inferior fame) it must have tumbled him on the

[a very short$_{1\text{-}2}$; a short$_3$]
[when]$_{1\text{-}2}$

ground. And now the ravisher meditated another blow, which he aimed at that part of the breast where the heart is lodged, [but]$_{1\text{-}2}$ Joseph did not catch it as before, [yet]$_3$ so prevented its aim, that it fell directly on his nose, but with abated force. Joseph then moving both fist and foot forwards at the same time, threw his head so dexterously into the stomach of the ravisher, that he fell a lifeless lump on the field, where he lay many minutes breathless and motionless.

When Fanny saw her Joseph receive a blow in his face, and blood running in a stream from him, she began to tear her hair, and invoke all human and divine power to his assistance. She was not, however, long under this affliction, before Joseph having conquered his enemy, ran to her, and assured her he was not hurt; she then instantly fell on her knees and thanked G—, that he had made Joseph the means of her rescue, and at the same time preserved him from being injured in attempting it. She offered with her handkerchief to wipe his blood from his face; but he seeing his rival attempting to recover his legs, turned to him and asked him if he had enough; to which the other answered he had; for he believed he had fought with the Devil, instead of a man, and loosening his horse, said he should not have attempted the wench if he had known she had been so well provided for.

Fanny now begged Joseph to return with her to Parson Adams, and to promise that he would leave her no more; these were propositions so agreeable to Joseph, that had he heard them he would have given an immediate assent: but indeed his eyes were now his only sense; for you may remember, reader, that the ravisher had tore her handkerchief from Fanny's neck, by which he had discovered such a sight; that Joseph hath declared all the statues he ever beheld were so much inferior to it in beauty, that it was more capable of converting a man into a statue, than of being imitated by the greatest master of that art. This modest creature, whom no warmth in summer could ever induce to expose her charms to the wanton sun, a modesty to which perhaps they owed their inconceivable whiteness, had stood many minutes bare-necked in the presence of Joseph, before her apprehension of his danger, and the horror of seeing his blood would suffer her once to reflect on what concerned herself; till at last, when the cause of her concern had vanished, an admiration at his silence, together with observing the fixed position of his eyes, produced an idea in the lovely maid, which brought more blood into her face than had flowed from Joseph's nostrils. The snowy hue of her bosom was likewise exchanged to vermilion at the instant when she clapped her handkerchief round her neck. Joseph saw the uneasiness she suffered, and immediately removed his eyes from an object, in surveying which he had felt the greatest delight which the organs of sight were capable of conveying to his soul. So great was his fear of offending her, and so truly did his passion for her deserve the noble name of love.

Fanny being recovered from her confusion, which was almost equalled by what Joseph had felt from observing it, again mentioned her request; this was instantly and gladly complied with, and together they crossed two or three fields, which brought them to ⟨the habitation of⟩ $_2$ Mr. Adams.

CHAP. VIII.

A discourse which happened between Mr. Adams, Mrs. Adams, Joseph and Fanny; with some behaviour of Mr. Adams, which will be called by some few readers very low, absurd, and unnatural.

THE parson and his wife had just ended a long dispute when the lovers came to the door. Indeed this young couple had been the subject of the dispute; for Mrs. Adams was one of those prudent people who never do anything to injure their families, or perhaps one of those good mothers who would even stretch their conscience to serve their children. She had long entertained hopes of seeing her eldest daughter succeed Mrs. Slipslop, and of making her second son an exciseman by Lady Booby's interest. These were expectations she could not endure the thoughts of quitting, and was therefore very uneasy to see her husband so resolute to oppose the lady's intention in Fanny's affair. She told him, "it behoved every man to take the first care of his family; that he had a wife and six children, the maintaining and providing for whom would be business enough for him without intermeddling in other folks affairs; that he had always preached up submission to superiors, and would do ill to give an example of the contrary behavior in his own conduct; that if Lady Booby did wrong, she must answer for it herself, and the sin would not lie at their door; that Fanny had been a servant, and bred up in the lady's own family, and consequently she must have known more of her than they did, and it was very improbable if she had behaved herself well, that the lady would have been so bitterly her enemy; that perhaps he was too much inclined to think well of her because she was handsome, but handsome women were often no better than they should be; that G— made ugly women as well as handsome ones, and that if a woman had virtue, it signified nothing whether she had beauty or no." For all which reasons she concluded, he should oblige the lady and stop the future publication of the banns: but all these excellent arguments had no effect on the parson, who persisted in doing his duty without regarding the consequence it might have on his worldly interest; he endeavoured to answer her as well as he could, to which she had just finished her reply, (for she had always the last word everywhere but at church) when Joseph and Fanny entered their kitchen, where the parson and his wife then sat at breakfast over some bacon and cabbage. There was a coldness in the civility of Mrs. Adams, which persons of accurate speculation might have observed, but escaped her present guests; indeed it was a good deal covered by the heartiness of Adams, who no sooner heard that Fanny had neither eat nor drank that morning, than he presented her a bone of bacon ~~which~~ [3] he had just been gnawing, being the only remains of his provision, and then ran nimbly to the tap, and produced a mug of small beer, which he called ale, however it was the best in his house. Joseph addressing himself to the parson, told him the discourse which had passed between Squire Booby, his sister, and himself, concerning Fanny: he then acquainted him with the dangers whence he had rescued her, and communicated some apprehensions on her account. He concluded, that he should never have an easy moment till Fanny was absolutely his, and begged that he might be suffered to fetch a licence, saying, he could easily borrow the money. The parson answered, that he had already given his sentiments concerning a licence, and that a very few days would make it unnecessary. "Joseph," says he, "I wish this haste doth not arise rather from your impatience than your fear: but as it certainly springs from one of these causes, I will examine both. Of each of these therefore in their turn; and first, for the first of these, namely, Impatience. Now, child, I must inform you, that if in your purposed marriage with this young woman, you have no intention but the indulgence of carnal appetites, you are guilty of a very heinous sin. Marriage was ordained for nobler purposes, as you will learn when you hear the service provided on that occasion read to you. ⟨Nay perhaps, if you are a good lad, I shall give you a sermon *gratis*, wherein I shall demonstrate how little regard ought to be had to the flesh on such occasions. The text will be, child, Matthew the 5th, and part of the 28th verse, *Whosoever looketh on a woman so as to lust after her.* The latter part I shall omit, as foreign to my purpose.⟩ $_2$[3] Indeed all such brutal lusts and affections are to be greatly subdued, if not totally eradicated, before the vessel can be said to be consecrated to honour. To marry with a view of gratifying those inclinations is a prostitution of that holy ceremony, and must entail a curse on all who so lightly undertake it. If, therefore, this haste arises from Impatience, you are to correct, and not give way to it. Now as to the second head which I propose to speak to, namely, Fear. It argues a diffidence highly criminal of that Power in which alone we should put our trust, seeing we may be well assured that he is able not only to defeat the designs of our enemies, but even to turn their hearts. Instead of taking therefore any unjustifiable or desperate means to rid ourselves of Fear, we should resort to prayer only on these occasions, and we may be then certain of obtaining what is best for us. When any accident threatens us, we are not to despair, nor when it

[3] Adams omits "hath committed adultery with her already in his heart."

[set our affections so much on nothing here that we cannot]$_{1-3}$

overtakes us, to grieve; we must submit in all things to the will of Providence, and [not set our affections so much on anything here, as not to be able to]$_{4}$ quit it without reluctance. You are a young man, and can know but little of this world; I am older, and have seen a great deal. All passions are criminal in their excess, and even love itself, if it is not subservient to our duty, may render us blind to it. Had Abraham so loved his son Isaac, as to refuse the sacrifice required, is there any of us who would not condemn him? Joseph, I know your many good qualities, and value you for them: but as I am to render an account of your soul, which is committed to my cure, I cannot see any fault without reminding you of it. You are too much inclined to passion, child, and have set your affections so absolutely on this young woman, that, if G— required her at your hands, I fear you would reluctantly part with her. Now believe me, no Christian ought so to set his heart on any person or thing in this world, but that whenever it shall be required or taken from him in any manner by Divine Providence, he may be able, peaceably, quietly, and contentedly to resign it." At which words one came hastily in and acquainted Mr. Adams that his youngest son was drowned. He stood silent a moment, and soon began to stamp about the room and deplore his loss with the bitterest agony. Joseph, who was overwhelmed with concern likewise, recovered himself sufficiently to endeavour to comfort the parson; in which attempt he used many arguments that he had at several times remembered out of his own discourses both in private and public, (for he was a great enemy to the passions, and preached nothing more than the conquest of them by Reason and Grace) but he was not at leisure now to hearken to his advice. "Child, child," said he, "do not go about impossibilities. Had it been any other of my children I could have borne it with patience; but my little prattler, the darling and comfort of my old age—the little wretch to be snatched out of life just at his entrance into it; the sweetest, best-tempered boy, who never did a thing to offend me. It was but this morning I gave him his first lesson in *Quæ Genus*.[4] This was the very book he learnt, poor child! it is

[4] Almost the first section in Lily's grammar. Fielding first names the boy "Jacky," below, then calls him "Dicky" thereafter.

of no further use to thee now. He would have made the best scholar, and have been an ornament to the Church — such parts and such goodness never met in one so young." "And the handsomest lad too," says Mrs. Adams, recovering from a swoon in Fanny's arms. — "My poor Jacky, shall I never see thee more?" cries the parson. — "Yes, surely," says Joseph, "and in a better place, you will meet again, never to part more." — I believe the parson did not hear these words, for he paid little regard to them, but went on lamenting whilst the tears trickled down into his bosom. At last he cried out, "Where is my little darling?" and was sallying out, when to his great surprise and joy, in which I hope the reader will sympathize, he met his son in a wet condition indeed, but alive, and running towards him. The person who brought the news of his misfortune, had been a little too eager, as people sometimes are, from I believe no very good principle, to relate ill news; and seeing him fall into the river, instead of running to his assistance, directly ran to acquaint his father of a fate which he had concluded to be inevitable, but whence the child was relieved by the same poor pedlar who had relieved his father before from a less distress. The parson's joy was now as extravagant as his grief had been before; he kissed and embraced his son a thousand times, and danced about the room like one frantic; but as soon as he discovered the face of his old friend the pedlar, and heard the fresh obligation he had to him, what were his sensations? not those which two courtiers feel in one another's embraces; not those with which a great man receives the vile, treacherous engines of his wicked purposes; not those with which a worthless younger brother wishes his elder joy of a son, or a man congratulates his rival on his obtaining a mistress, a place, or an honour. — No, reader, he felt the ebullition, the overflowings of a full, honest, open heart towards the person who had conferred a real obligation, and of which if thou canst not conceive an idea within, I will not vainly endeavour to assist thee.

When these tumults were over, the parson taking Joseph aside, proceeded thus — "No, Joseph, do not give too much way to thy passions, if thou dost expect happiness." — The patience of Joseph, nor perhaps of Job, could bear no longer; he interrupted the parson, saying, "it was easier to give advice than take it, nor did he perceive he could so entirely conquer himself, when he apprehended he had lost his son, or when he found him recovered." — "Boy," replied Adams, raising his voice, "it doth not become green heads to advise grey hairs — Thou art ignorant of the tenderness of fatherly affection; when thou art a father thou wilt be capable then only of knowing what a father can feel. No man is obliged to impossibilities, and the loss of a child is one of those great trials where our grief may be allowed to become immoderate." "Well, sir," cries Joseph, "and if I love a mistress as well as you your child, surely her loss would grieve me equally." "Yes, but such love is foolishness, and wrong in itself, and ought to be conquered," answered Adams, "it savours too much of the flesh." "Sure, sir," says Joseph, "it is not sinful to love my wife, no not even to doat on her to distraction!" "Indeed but it is," says Adams. "Every man ought to love his wife, no doubt; we are commanded so to do; but we ought to [them]$_1$ love [her]$_2$ with moderation and discretion." — "I am afraid I shall be guilty of some sin, in spite of all my endeavours," says Joseph; "for I shall love without any moderation, I am sure." — "You talk foolishly and childishly," cries Adams. "Indeed," says Mrs. Adams, who had listened to the latter part of their conversation, "you talk more foolishly yourself. I hope, my dear, you will never preach any such doctrine as that husbands can love their wives too well. If I knew you had such a sermon in the house, I am sure I would burn it; and I declare if I had not been convinced you had loved me as well as you could, I can answer for myself I should have hated and despised you. Marry come up! Fine doctrine indeed! A wife hath a right to insist on her husband's loving her as much as ever he can: And he is a sinful villain who doth not. Doth he not promise to love her, and to comfort her, and to cherish her, and all that? I am sure I remember it all, as well as if I had repeated it over but yesterday, and shall never forget it. Besides, I am certain you do not preach as you practise; for you have been a loving and a cherishing husband to me, that's the truth on't; and why you should endeavour to put such wicked nonsense into this young man's head, I cannot devise. Don't hearken to him, Mr. Joseph, be as good a husband as you are able, and love your wife with all your body and soul too." Here a violent rap at the door put an end to their discourse, and produced a scene which the reader will find in the next chapter.

CHAP. IX.

A visit which the good Lady Booby and her polite friend paid to the parson.

THE Lady Booby had no sooner had an account from the gentleman of his meeting a wonderful beauty near her house, and perceived the raptures with which he spoke of her, than immediately concluding it must be Fanny, she began to meditate a design of bringing them better acquainted; and to entertain hopes that the fine clothes, presents and promises of this youth, would prevail on her to abandon Joseph: She therefore proposed to her company a walk in the fields before dinner, when she led them towards Mr. Adams's house; and as she approached it, told them, if they pleased she would divert them with one of the most ridiculous sights they had ever seen, which was an old foolish parson, who, she said laughing, kept a wife and six brats on a salary of about twenty pounds a year; adding, that there was not such another ragged family in the parish. They all readily agreed to this visit, and arrived whilst Mrs. Adams was declaiming, as in the last chapter. Beau Didapper, which was the name of the young gentleman we have seen riding towards Lady Booby's, with his cane mimicked the rap of a London footman at the door. The people within; namely, Adams, his wife, and three children, Joseph, Fanny, and the pedlar, were all thrown into confusion by this knock; but Adams went directly to the door, which being opened, the Lady Booby and her company walked in, and were received by the parson with about two hundred bows; and by his wife with as many curtsies; the latter telling the lady, "she was ashamed to be seen in such a pickle, and that her house was in such a litter: But that if she had expected such an honour from her Ladyship, she should have found her in a better manner." The parson made no apologies, though he was in his half-cassock and a flannel night-cap. He said, "they were heartily welcome to his poor cottage," and turning to Mr. Didapper, cried out, *Non mea renidet in domo lacunar:* [5] The beau answered, "he did not understand *Welsh;*" at which the parson stared, and made no reply.

Mr. Didapper, or Beau Didapper, was a young gentleman of about four foot five inches in height. He wore his own hair, though the scarcity of it might have given him sufficient excuse for a periwig. His face was thin and pale: The shape of his body and legs none of the best; for he had very narrow shoulders, and no calf; and his gait might more properly be called hopping than walking. The qualifications of his mind were well adapted to his person. We shall handle them first negatively. He was not entirely ignorant: For he could talk a little French, and sing two or three Italian songs: He had lived too much in the world to be bashful, and too much at court to be proud: He seemed not much inclined to avarice; for he was profuse in his expenses: Nor had he all the features of prodigality; for he never gave a shilling: — No hater of women; for he always dangled after them; yet so little subject to lust, that he had, among those who knew him best, the character of great moderation in his pleasures. No drinker of wine; nor so addicted to passion, but that a hot word or two from an adversary made him immediately cool.

Now, to give him only a dash or two on the affirmative side: "Though he was born to an immense fortune, he chose, for the pitiful and dirty consideration of a place of little consequence, to depend entirely on the will of a fellow, whom they call a Great-Man; who treated him with the utmost disrespect, and exacted of him a plenary obedience to his commands; which he implicitly submitted to, at the expense of his conscience, his honour, and ⟨of⟩ $_2$ his country; in which he had himself so very large a share." And to finish his character, "As he was entirely

[5] "The ceiling in my house doesn't sparkle." Adams is abbreviating Horace (*Odes* II.xviii.1–2): *Non ebur neque aureum/ mea renidet in domo lacunar* ("Neither ivory nor a golden ceiling sparkles in my house").

well satisfied with his own person and parts, so he was very apt to ridicule and laugh at any imperfection in another." [6] Such was the little person or rather thing that hopped after Lady Booby into Mr. Adams's kitchen.

The parson and his company retreated from the chimney-side, where they had been seated, to give room to the lady and hers. Instead of returning any of the curtsies or extraordinary civility of Mrs. Adams, the lady turning to Mr. Booby, cried out, "*Quelle Bête! Quel Animal!*" And presently after discovering Fanny (for she did not need the circumstance of her standing by Joseph to assure the identity of her person) she asked the beau, "whether he did not think her a pretty girl?" — "Begad, madam," answered he, " 'tis the very same I met." "I did not imagine," replied the lady, "you had so good a taste." "Because I never liked you, I warrant," cries the beau. "Ridiculous!" said she, "you know you was always my aversion." "I would never mention aversion," answered the beau, "with that face * ; dear Lady Booby, wash your face before you mention aversion, I beseech you." He then laughed and turned about to coquet it with Fanny.

Mrs. Adams had been all this time begging and praying the ladies to sit down, a favour which she ~~had~~ [3] at last obtained. The little boy to whom the accident had happened, still keeping his place by the fire, was chid by his mother for not being more mannerly: But Lady Booby took his part, and commending his beauty, told the parson he was his very picture. She then seeing a book in his hand, asked, "if he could read?" "Yes," cried

* Lest this should appear unnatural to some readers, we think proper to acquaint them, that it is taken verbatim from very polite conversation. [Fielding's note.]

[6] These two quoted passages identify Didapper as a caricature of Lord Hervey, whom Fielding first satirized in *Shamela* by mimicking Middleton's dedication to Hervey in *The Life of Cicero*. In the first passage, Fielding again adapts phrases from this dedication to Hervey. The second quoted passage is adapted from Alexander Pope's reply to an attack by Hervey (Battestin, p. 313). But Didapper's height of four feet five, his baldness, his lack of a wig, his thin and pale face, and his meager legs are actually (and illogically) more suggestive of Pope than of Hervey, who, though effeminate and pale, was well shaped. Fielding's satirical exaggeration seems inadvertently to have included some characteristics of Pope, whom he was presumably defending.

Adams, "a little Latin, madam, he is just got into *Quæ Genus.*" — "A fig for *quere genius,*" answered she, "let me hear him read a little English." — "*Lege,* Dick, *lege,*" said Adams: But the boy made no answer, till he saw the parson knit his brows; and then cried, "I don't understand you, father." "How, boy," says Adams, "What doth *lego* make in the imperative mood? *Legito,* doth it not?" "Yes," answered Dick. — "And what besides?" says the father. "*Lege,*" quoth the son, after some hesitation. "A good boy," says the father: "And now, child, What is the English of *lego?*" — To which the boy, after long puzzling, answered, he could not tell. "How," cries Adams in a passion, — "What hath the water washed away your learning? Why, what is Latin for the English verb *read?* Consider before you speak." — The child considered some time, and then the parson cried twice or thrice, "*Le* —, *Le* —." —Dick answered, "*Lego.*" — "Very well; — and then, what is the English," says the parson, "of the verb *lego?*" — "*To read,*" cried Dick. — "Very well," said the parson, "a good boy, you can do well, if you will take pains. — I assure your Ladyship he is not much above eight years old, and is out of his *Propria quæ Maribus* already.[7] — Come, Dick, read to her ladyship;" — which she again desiring, in order to give the beau time and opportunity with Fanny, Dick began as in the following chapter.

CHAP. X.

The History of two Friends, which may afford an useful lesson to all those persons, who happen to take up their residence in married families.

"LEONARD and Paul were two friends." — "Pronounce it *Lennard,* child," cried the parson. — "Pray, Mr. Adams," says Lady Booby, "let your son read without interruption." Dick

[7] *Propria quae Maribus* ("proper names which to men [are attributed]") is the opening phrase of the lesson on gender that Adams has already quoted, as he mentioned his boy, in II.xi.201.

then proceeded. "Lennard and Paul were two friends, who, having been educated together at the same school, commenced a friendship which they preserved a long time for each other. It was so deeply fixed in both their minds, that a long absence, during which they had maintained no correspondence, did not eradicate nor lessen it: But it revived in all its force at their first meeting, which was not till after fifteen years absence, most of which time Lennard had spent in the East-Indi-es." — "Pronounce it short *Indies,*" says Adams. — "Pray, sir, be quiet," says the lady. — The boy repeated — "in the East-Indies, whilst Paul had served his king and country in the army. In which different services, they had found such different success, that Lennard was now married, and retired with a fortune of thirty thousand pound; and Paul was arrived to the degree of a lieutenant of foot; and was not worth a single shilling.

"The regiment in which Paul was stationed, happened to be ordered into quarters, within a small distance from the estate which Lennard had purchased; and where he was settled. This latter, who was now become a country gentleman, and a Justice of Peace, came to attend the quarter-sessions, in the town where his old friend was quartered, soon after his arrival. Some affair in which a soldier was concerned, occasioned Paul to attend the justices. Manhood, and time, and the change of climate had so much altered Lennard, that Paul did not immediately recollect the features of his old acquaintance: But it was otherwise with Lennard. He knew Paul the moment he saw him; nor could he contain himself from quitting the bench, and running hastily to embrace him. Paul stood at first a little surprised; but had soon sufficient information from his friend, whom he no sooner remembered, than he returned his embrace with a passion which made many of the spectators laugh, and gave to some few a much higher and more agreeable sensation.

"Not to detain the reader with minute circumstances, Lennard insisted on his friend's returning with him to his house that evening; which request was complied with, and leave for a month's absence for Paul, obtained of the commanding officer.

"If it was possible for any circumstance to give any addition to the happiness which Paul proposed in this visit, he received that additional pleasure, by finding on his arrival at his friend's house, that his lady was an old acquaintance which he had formerly contracted at his quarters; and who had always appeared to be of a most agreeable temper. A character she had ever maintained among her intimates, being of that number, every individual of which is called quite the best sort of woman in the world.

"But good as this lady was, she was still a woman; that is to say, an angel and not an angel—" "You must mistake, child," cries the parson, "for you read nonsense." "It is so in the book," answered the son. Mr. Adams was then silenced by authority, and Dick proceeded—"For though her person was of that kind to which men attribute the name of angel, yet in
[passions]$_1$ her [mind]$_2$ she was perfectly woman. Of which a great degree
[was]$_1$ of obstinacy [gave]$_2$ the most remarkable, and perhaps most pernicious ⟨instance⟩.$_2$

"A day or two passed after Paul's arrival before any instances of this appeared; but it was impossible to conceal it long. Both she and her husband soon lost all apprehension from their friend's presence, and fell to their disputes with as much vigour as ever. These were still pursued with the utmost ardour and eagerness, however trifling the causes were whence they first arose. Nay, however incredible it may seem, the little consequence of the matter in debate was frequently given as a reason for the fierceness of the contention, as thus: *If you loved me, sure you would never dispute with me such a trifle as this.* The answer to which is very obvious; for the argument would hold equally on both sides, and was constantly retorted with some addition, as—*I am sure I have much more reason to say so, who am in the right.* During all these disputes, Paul always kept strict silence, and preserved an even countenance without showing the least visible inclination to either party. One day, however, when madam had left the room in a violent fury, Lennard could not refrain from referring his cause to his friend. Was ever anything so unreasonable, says he, as this woman? What shall I do with her? I doat on her to distraction; nor have I any cause to complain of more than this obstinacy in her temper; whatever she asserts she will maintain against all the reason and conviction in the world. Pray give me your advice. — First, says Paul, I will give my opinion, which is flatly that you are in the wrong; for supposing she is in the wrong, was the subject of your contention anywise material? What signified it whether you was married in a red or a yellow waistcoat? for that was your dispute. Now suppose she was mistaken, as you love her you say so tenderly, and I believe she deserves it, would it not have been wiser to have yielded, though you certainly knew yourself in the right, than to give either her or yourself any uneasiness? For my own part, if ever I marry, I am resolved to enter into an agreement with my wife, that in all disputes (especially about trifles) that party who is most convinced they are right, shall always surrender the victory; by which means we shall both be forward to give up the cause. I own, said Lennard, my dear friend, shaking him by the hand, there is great truth and reason in what you say; and I will for the future endeavour to follow your advice. They soon after broke up the conversation, and Lennard going to his wife, asked her pardon, and told her his friend had convinced him he had been in the wrong. She immediately began a vast encomium on Paul, in which he seconded her, and both agreed he was the worthiest and wisest man upon earth. When next they met, which was at supper, though she had promised not to mention what her husband told her, she could not forbear casting the kindest and most affectionate looks on Paul, and asked him with the sweetest voice, whether she should help him to some potted woodcock? — Potted partridge, my dear, you mean, says the husband. My dear, says she, I ask your friend if he will eat any potted woodcock; and I am sure I must know, who potted it. I think I should know too, who shot them, replied the husband, and I am convinced I have not seen a woodcock this year; however, though I know I am in the right I submit, and the potted partridge is potted woodcock, if you desire to have it so. It is equal to me, says she, whether it is one or the other; but you would persuade one out of one's senses; to be sure you are always in the right in your own opinion; but your friend I believe knows which he is eating. Paul answered nothing, and the dispute continued as usual the greatest part of the evening. The next morning the lady accidentally meeting Paul, and being convinced he was her friend, and of her side, accosted him thus: — I am certain, sir, you have long since wondered at the unreasonableness of my husband. He is indeed in other respects a good sort of man; but so positive, that no woman but one of my complying temper could possibly live with him. Why last night now, was ever any creature so unreasonable? — I am certain you must condemn him — Pray answer me, was he not in the wrong? Paul, after a short silence, spoke as follows: I am sorry, madam, that as good-manners obliges me to answer against my will, so an adherence to truth forces me to declare myself of a different opinion. To be plain and honest, you was entirely in the wrong; the cause I own not worth disputing, but the bird was undoubtedly a partridge. O sir, replied the lady, I cannot possibly help your taste. — Madam, returned Paul, that is very little material; for had it been otherwise, a husband might have expected submission. — Indeed! sir, says she, I assure you! — Yes, madam, cried he, he might from a person of your excellent understanding; and pardon me for saying such a condescension would have shown a superiority of sense even to your husband himself. — But, dear sir, said she, why should I submit when I am in the right? — For that very reason, answered he, it would be the greatest instance of affection imaginable: for can anything be a greater object of our compassion than a person we love, in the wrong? Ay, but I should endeavour, said she, to set him right. Pardon me, madam, answered Paul, I will apply to your own experience, if you ever found your arguments had that effect. The more our judgments err, the less we are willing to own it: for my own part, I have always observed the persons who maintain the worst side in any contest are the warmest. Why, says she, I must confess there is truth in what you say, and I will endeavour to practise it. The husband then coming in, Paul departed. And Lennard approaching his wife with an air of good-humour, told her he was sorry for their foolish dispute the last night: but he was now convinced of his error. She answered smiling, she believed she owed his condescension to his complacence; that she was ashamed to think a word had passed on so silly an occasion, especially as she was satisfied she had been mistaken. A little contention followed, but with the utmost good-will to each other, and was concluded by her asserting that Paul had thoroughly convinced her she had been in the wrong. Upon which they both united in the praises of their common friend.

"Paul now passed his time with great satisfaction; these disputes being much less frequent as well as shorter than usual: but the Devil, or some unlucky accident in which perhaps the Devil had no hand, shortly put an end to his happiness. He was now eternally the private referee of every difference; in which after having perfectly as he thought established the doctrine of submission, he never scrupled to assure both privately that they were in the right in every argument, as before he had followed the contrary method. One day a violent litigation happened in his absence, and both parties agreed to refer it to his decision. The husband professing himself sure the decision would be in his favour, the wife answered, he might be mistaken; for she believed his friend was convinced how seldom she was to blame — and that if he knew all. —— The husband replied — My dear, I have no desire of any retrospect, but I believe if you knew all too, you would not imagine my friend so entirely on your side. Nay, says she, since you provoke me, I will mention one instance. You may remember our dispute about sending Jacky to school in cold weather, which point I gave up to you from mere compassion, knowing myself to be in the right, and Paul himself told me afterwards, he thought me so. My dear, replied the husband, I will not scruple your veracity; but I assure you solemnly, on my applying to him, he gave it absolutely on my side, and said he would have acted in the same manner. They then proceeded to produce numberless other instances, in all which Paul had, on vows of secrecy, given his opinion on both sides. In the conclusion, both believing each other, they fell severely on the treachery of Paul, and agreed that he had been the occasion of almost every dispute which had fallen out between them. They then became extremely loving, and so full of condescension on both sides, that they vied with each other in censuring their own conduct, and jointly vented their indignation on Paul, whom the wife, fearing a bloody consequence, earnestly entreated her husband to suffer quietly to depart the next day, which was the time fixed for his return to quarters, and then drop his acquaintance.

"However ungenerous this behaviour in Lennard may be esteemed, his wife obtained a promise from him (though with difficulty) to follow her advice; but they both expressed such unusual coldness that day to Paul, that he, who was quick of apprehension, taking Lennard aside, pressed him so home, that he at last discovered the secret. Paul acknowledged the truth, but told him the design with which he had done it — To which the other answered, he would have acted more friendly to have let him into the whole design; for that he might have assured himself of his secrecy. Paul replied, with some indignation, he had given him a sufficient proof how capable he was of concealing a secret from his wife. Lennard returned with some warmth — He had more reason to upbraid him, for that he had caused most of the quarrels between them by his strange conduct, and might (if they had not discovered the affair to each other) have been the occasion of their separation. Paul then said ——" But something now happened, which put a stop to Dick's reading, and of which we shall treat in the next chapter.

CHAP. XI.

In which the history is continued.

JOSEPH ANDREWS had borne with great uneasiness the impertinence of Beau Didapper to Fanny, who had been talking pretty freely to her, and offering her settlements; but the respect to the company had restrained him from interfering whilst the beau confined himself to the use of his tongue only; but the said beau watching an opportunity whilst the ladies eyes were disposed another way, offered a rudeness to her with his hands; which Joseph no sooner perceived than he presented him with so sound a box on the ear, that it conveyed him several paces from where he stood. The ladies immediately screamed out, rose from their chairs, and the beau, as soon as he recovered himself, drew his hanger, which Adams observing, snatched up the lid of a pot in his left hand, and covering himself with it as with a shield, without any weapon of offence in his other hand, stept in before Joseph, and exposed himself to the enraged beau, who threatened such perdition and destruction, that it frighted the women, who were all got in a huddle together, out of their wits; even to hear his denunciations of vengeance. Joseph was of a different complexion, and begged Adams to let his rival come on; for he had a good cudgel in his hand, and did not fear him. Fanny now fainted into Mrs. Adams's arms, and the whole room was in confusion, when Mr. Booby passing by Adams, who lay snug under the pot-lid, came up to Didapper, and insisted on his sheathing his hanger, promising he should have satisfaction; which Joseph declared he would give him, and fight him at any weapon whatever. The beau now sheathed his hanger, and taking out a pocket-glass, and vowing vengeance all the time, ~~he~~[3] re-adjusted his hair; the parson deposited his shield, and Joseph running to Fanny, soon brought her back to life. Lady Booby chid Joseph for his insult on Didapper; but he answered he would have attacked an army in the same cause. "What cause?" said the lady. "Madam," answered Joseph, "he was rude to that young woman." — "What," says the lady, "I suppose he would have kissed the wench; and is a gentleman to be struck for such an offer? I must tell you, Joseph, these airs do not become you." — "Madam," said Mr. Booby, "I saw the whole affair, and I do not commend my brother; for I cannot perceive why he should take upon him to be this girl's champion." — "I can commend him," says Adams, "he is a brave lad; and it becomes any man to be the champion of the innocent; and he must be the basest coward, who would not vindicate a woman with whom he is on the brink of marriage." — "Sir," says Mr. Booby, "my brother is not a proper match for such a young woman as this." — "No," says Lady Booby, "nor do you, Mr. Adams, act in your proper character, by encouraging any such doings; and I am very much surprised you should concern yourself in it. I think your wife and family your properer care." — "Indeed, madam, your ladyship says very true," answered Mrs. Adams, "he talks a pack of nonsense, that the whole parish are his children. I am sure I don't understand what he means by it; it would make some women suspect he had gone astray: but I acquit him of that; I can read Scripture as well as he; and I never found that the parson was obliged to provide for other folks children; and besides he is but a poor curate, and hath little enough, as your ladyship knows, for me and mine."—"You say very well, Mrs. Adams," quoth the Lady Booby, who had not spoke a word to her before, "you seem to be a very sensible woman; and I assure you, your husband is acting a very foolish part, and opposing his own interest; seeing my nephew is violently set against this match: and indeed I can't blame him; it is by no means one suitable to our family." In this manner the lady proceeded with Mrs. Adams, whilst the beau hopped about the room, shaking his head; partly from pain, and partly from anger; and Pamela was chiding Fanny for her assurance, in aiming at such a match as her brother.—Poor Fanny answered only with her tears, which had long since begun to wet her handkerchief; which Joseph perceiving, took her by the arm, and wrapping it in his, carried her off, swearing he would own no relation to anyone who was an enemy to her he loved more than all the world. He went out with Fanny under his left arm, brandishing a cudgel in his right, and neither Mr. Booby nor the beau thought proper to oppose him. Lady Booby and her company made a very short stay behind him; for the lady's bell now summoned them to dress; for which they had just time before dinner.

Adams seemed now very much dejected, which his wife perceiving, began to apply some matrimonial balsam. She told him he had reason to be concerned; for that he had ~~most~~$_{3}$ probably ruined his family with his ⟨foolish⟩$_{4}$ tricks ~~almost~~$_{4}$: But perhaps he was grieved for the loss of his two children, Joseph and Fanny. His eldest daughter went on:—"Indeed father, it is very hard to bring strangers here to eat your children's bread out of their mouths.—You have kept them ever since they came home; and for anything I see to the contrary may keep them a month longer: Are you obliged to give her meat, tho'f she was never so handsome? But I don't see she is so much handsomer than other people. If people were to be kept for their beauty, she would scarce fare better than her neighbours, I believe. — As for Mr. Joseph, I have nothing to say, he is a young man of honest principles, and will pay some time or other for what he hath: But for the girl, — Why doth she not return to her place she ran away from? I would not give such a vagabond slut a halfpenny, though I had a million of money; no, though she was starving." "Indeed but I would," cries little Dick; "and father, rather than poor Fanny shall be starved, I will give her all this bread and cheese." — (*offering what he held in his hand.*) — Adams smiled on the boy, and told him he rejoiced to see he was a Christian; and that if he had a halfpenny in his pocket he would have given it him; telling him, it was his duty to look upon all his neighbours as his brothers and sisters, and love them accordingly. "Yes, papa," says he, "I love her better than my sisters; for she is handsomer than any of them." "Is she so, saucebox?" says the sister, giving him a box on the ear, which the father would probably have resented, had not Joseph, Fanny, and the pedlar, at that instant, returned together. — Adams bid his wife prepare some food for their dinner; she said, "truly she could not, she had something else to do." Adams rebuked her for disputing his commands, and quoted many texts of Scripture to prove, *that the husband is the head of the wife, and she is to submit and obey*. The wife answered, "it was blasphemy to talk Scripture out of church; that such things were very proper to be said in the pulpit: but that it was profane to talk them in common discourse." Joseph told Mr. Adams "he was not come with any design to give him or Mrs. Adams any trouble; but to desire the favour of all their company to the George (an alehouse in the parish,) where he had bespoke a piece of bacon and greens for their dinner." Mrs. Adams, who was a very good sort of woman, only rather too strict in œconomics, readily accepted this invitation, as did the parson himself by her example; and away they all walked together, not omitting little Dick, to whom Joseph gave a shilling, when he heard of his intended liberality to Fanny.

CHAP. XII.

Where the good-natured reader will see something which will give him no great pleasure.

THE pedlar had been very inquisitive from the time he had first heard that the great house in this parish belonged to the Lady Booby; and had learnt that she was the widow of Sir Thomas, and that Sir Thomas had bought Fanny, at about the age of three or four years, of a travelling woman; and now their homely but hearty meal was ended, he told Fanny, he believed he could acquaint her with her parents. The whole company, especially she herself, started at this offer of the pedlar's. — He then proceeded thus, while they all lent their strictest attention: "Though I am now contented with this humble way of getting my livelihood, I was formerly a gentleman; for so all those of my profession are called. In a word, I was a drummer in an Irish regiment of foot. Whilst I was in this honourable station, I attended an officer of our regiment into England a recruiting. In our march from Bristol of Froome (for since the decay of the woolen trade, the clothing towns have furnished the army with a great number of recruits) we overtook on the road a woman who seemed to be about thirty years old or thereabouts, not very handsome; but well enough for a soldier. As we came up to her, she mended her pace, and falling into discourse with our ladies (for every man of the party, namely, a serjeant, two private men, and a drum, were provided with their woman, except myself) she continued to travel on with us. I perceiving she must fall to my lot, advanced presently to her, made love to her in our military way, and quickly succeeded to my wishes. We struck a bargain within a mile, and lived together as man and wife to her dying day." — "I suppose," says Adams interrupting him, "you were married with a licence: For I don't see how you could contrive to have the banns published while you were marching from place to place." — "No, sir," said the pedlar, "we took a licence to go to bed together, without any banns."—"Ay, ay," said the parson, "*ex necessitate*, a licence may be allowable enough; but surely, surely, the other is the more regular and eligible way."—The pedlar proceeded thus, "She returned with me to our regiment, and removed with us from quarters to quarters, till at last, whilst we lay at Galloway, she fell ill of a fever, and died. When she was on her death-bed she called me to her, and crying bitterly, declared she could not depart this world without discovering a secret to me, which she said was the only sin which sat heavy on her heart. She said she had formerly travelled in a company of gipsies, who had made a practice of stealing away children; that for her own part, she had been only once guilty of the crime; which she said she lamented more than all the rest of her sins, since probably it might have occasioned the death of the parents: For, added she, it is almost impossible to describe the beauty of the young creature, which was about a year and a half old when I kidnapped it. We kept her (for she was a girl) above two years in our company, when I sold her myself for three guineas to Sir Thomas Booby in Somersetshire. Now, you know whether there are any more of that name in this county."—"Yes," says Adams, "there are several Boobys who are squires; but I believe no baronet now alive, besides it answers so exactly in every point there is no room for doubt; but you have forgot to tell us the parents from whom the child was stolen."—"Their name," answered the pedlar, "was Andrews. They lived about thirty miles from the squire; and she told me, that I might be sure to find them out by one circumstance; for that they had a daughter of a very strange name, *Paměla* or *Pamēla;* some pronounced it one way, and some the other." Fanny, who had changed colour at the first mention of the name, now fainted away, Joseph turned pale, and poor Dicky began to roar; the parson fell on his knees and ejaculated many thanksgivings that this discovery had been made before the dreadful sin of incest was committed; and the pedlar was struck with amazement, not being able to account for all this confusion, the cause of which was presently opened by the parson's daughter, who was the only unconcerned person; (for the mother was chafing Fanny's temples, and taking the utmost care of her) and indeed Fanny was the only creature whom the daughter would not have pitied in her situation; wherein, though we compassionate her ourselves, we shall leave her for a little while, and pay a short visit to Lady Booby.

CHAP. XIII.

The history returning to the Lady Booby, gives some account of the terrible conflict in her breast between Love and Pride; with what happened on the present discovery.

THE lady sat down with her company to dinner: but eat nothing. As soon as her cloth was removed, she whispered Pamela, that she was taken a little ill, and desired her to entertain her husband and Beau Didapper. She then went up into her chamber, sent for Slipslop, threw herself on the bed, in the agonies of love, rage, and despair; nor could she conceal these boiling passions longer, without bursting. Slipslop now approached her bed, and asked how her ladyship did; but instead of revealing her disorder, as she intended, she entered into a long encomium on the beauty and virtues of Joseph Andrews; ending at last with expressing her concern, that so much tenderness should be thrown away on so despicable an object as Fanny. Slipslop well knowing how to humour her mistress's frenzy, proceeded to repeat, with exaggeration if possible, all her mistress had said, and concluded with a wish, that Joseph had been a gentleman, and that she could see her lady in the arms of such a husband. The lady then started from the bed, and taking a turn or two cross the room, cried out with a deep sigh, — *Sure he would make any woman happy.* — "Your ladyship," says she, "would be the happiest woman in the world with him. — A fig for custom and nonsense. What *vails* what people say? Shall I be afraid of eating sweetmeats, because people may say I have a sweet tooth? If I had a mind to marry a man, all the world should not hinder me. Your ladyship hath no parents to *tutelar* your *infections;* besides he is of your ladyship's family now, and as good a gentleman as any in the country; and why should not a woman follow her mind as well as man? Why should not your ladyship marry the brother, as well as your nephew the sister? I am sure, if it was a *fragrant* crime I would not persuade your ladyship to it." — "But, dear Slipslop," answered the lady, "if I could prevail on myself to commit such a weakness, there is that cursed Fanny in the way, whom the idiot, O how I hate and despise him —" "She, a little ugly minx," cries Slipslop, "leave her to me. — I suppose your ladyship hath heard of Joseph's *fitting* with one of Mr. Didapper's servants about her; and his master hath ordered them to carry her away by force this evening. I'll take care they shall not want assistance. I was talking with this gentleman, who was below just when your ladyship sent for me." — "Go back," says the Lady Booby, "this instant; for I expect Mr. Didapper will soon be going. Do all you can; for I am resolved this wench shall not be in our family; I will endeavour to return to the company; but let me know as soon as she is carried off." Slipslop went away, and her mistress began to arraign her ⟨own⟩ $_3$ conduct in the following manner:

"What am I doing? How do I suffer this passion to creep imperceptibly upon me! How many days are passed since I could have submitted to ask myself the question? — Marry a footman! Distraction! Can I afterwards bear the eyes of my acquaintance? But I can retire from them; retire with one in whom I propose more happiness than the world without him can give me! Retire — to feed continually on beauties, which my inflamed imagination sickens with eagerly gazing on; to satisfy every appetite, every desire, with their utmost wish. — Ha! and do I doat thus on a footman! I despise, I detest my passion. — Yet why? Is he not generous, gentle, kind? — Kind to whom? to the meanest wretch, a creature below my consideration. Doth he not? — Yes, he doth prefer her; curse his beauties, and the little low heart that possesses them; which can basely descend to this despicable wench, and be ungratefully deaf to all the honours I do him. — And can I then love this monster? No, I will tear his image from my bosom, tread on him, spurn him. I will have those pitiful charms which now I despise, mangled in my sight; for I will not suffer the little jade I hate to riot in the beauties I contemn. No, though I despise him myself; though I would spurn him from my feet, was he to languish at them, no other should taste the happiness I scorn. Why do I say happiness? To me it would be misery. — To sacrifice my reputation, my character, my rank in life, to the indulgence of a mean and a vile appetite. — How I detest the thought! How much more exquisite is the pleasure resulting from the reflection of virtue and prudence, than the faint relish of what flows from vice and folly! Whither did I suffer this improper, this mad passion to hurry me, only by neglecting to summon the aids of reason to my assistance? Reason, which hath now set before me my desires in their proper colours, and immediately helped me to expel them. Yes, I thank Heaven and my pride, I have now perfectly conquered this unworthy passion; and if there was no obstacle in its way, my pride would disdain any pleasures which could be the consequence of so base, so mean, so vulgar——" Slipslop returned at this instant in a violent hurry, and with the utmost eagerness, cried out, — "O, madam, I have strange news. Tom the footman is just come from the George; where it seems Joseph and the rest of them are a *jinketting;* and he says, there is a strange man who hath discovered that Fanny and Joseph are brother and sister." — "How, Slipslop," cries the lady in a surprise. — "I had not time, madam," cries Slipslop, "to inquire about *particles,* but Tom says, it is most certainly true."

This unexpected account entirely obliterated all those admirable reflections which the supreme power of reason had so wisely made just before. In short, when Despair, which had more share in producing the resolutions of hatred we have seen taken, began to retreat, the lady hesitated a moment, and then forgetting all the purport of her soliloquy, dismissed her woman again, with orders to bid Tom attend her in the parlour, whither she now hastened to acquaint Pamela with the news. Pamela said, she could not believe it: For she had never heard that her mother had lost any child, or that she had ever had ⟨any⟩[3] more than Joseph and herself. The lady flew into a violent rage with her, and talked of upstarts and disowning relations, who had so lately been on a level with her. Pamela made no answer:

But her husband, taking up her cause, severely reprimanded his aunt for her behaviour to his wife; he told her, if it had been earlier in the evening, she should not have stayed a moment longer in her house; that he was convinced, if this young woman could be proved her sister, she would readily embrace her as such; and he himself would do the same: He then desired the fellow might be sent for, and the young woman with him; which Lady Booby immediately ordered, and thinking proper to make some apology to Pamela for what she had said, it was readily accepted, and all things reconciled.

The pedlar now attended, as did Fanny, and Joseph who would not quit her; the parson likewise was induced, not only by curiosity, of which he had no small portion, but ⟨by⟩$_{4}$ his duty, as he apprehended ~~it~~$_{4}$, to follow them: for he continued all the way to exhort them, who were now breaking their hearts, to offer up thanksgivings, and be joyful for so miraculous an escape.

When they arrived at Booby-Hall, they were presently called into the parlour, where the pedlar repeated the same story he had told before, and insisted on the truth of every circumstance; so that all who heard him were extremely well satisfied of the truth, except Pamela, who imagined, as she had never heard either of her parents mention such an accident, that it must be certainly false; and except the Lady Booby, who suspected the falsehood of the story, from her ardent desire that it should be true; and Joseph who feared its truth, from his earnest wishes that it might prove false.

Mr. Booby now desired them all to suspend their curiosity and absolute belief or disbelief, till the next morning, when he expected old Mr. Andrews and his wife to fetch himself and Pamela home in his coach, and then they might be certain of
[perfectly]$_{4}$ knowing the truth or falsehood of this relation; in [certainly]$_{1\text{-}3}$
which he said, as there were many strong circumstances to induce their credit, so he could not perceive any interest the pedlar could have in inventing it, or in endeavouring to impose such a falsehood on them.

The Lady Booby, who was very little used to such company, entertained them all, *viz.* Her nephew, his wife, her brother and sister, the beau, and the parson, with great good-humour at her own table. As to the pedlar, she ordered him to be made as welcome as possible, by her servants. All the company in the parlour, except the disappointed lovers, who sat sullen and silent, were full of mirth: For Mr. Booby had prevailed on Joseph to ask Mr. Didapper's pardon; with which he was perfectly satisfied. Many jokes passed between the beau and the parson, chiefly on each other's dress; these afforded much diversion to the company. Pamela chid her brother Joseph for the concern which he exprest at discovering a new sister. She said, if he loved Fanny as he ought, with a pure affection, he had no reason to lament being related to her. — Upon which Adams began to discourse on Platonic love; whence he made a quick transition to the joys in the next world, and concluded with strongly asserting that there was no such thing as pleasure in this. At which Pamela and her husband smiled on one another.

This happy pair proposing to retire (for no other person gave the least symptom of desiring rest) they all repaired to several beds provided for them in the same house; nor was Adams himself suffered to go home, it being a stormy night. Fanny indeed often begged she might go home with the parson; but her stay was so strongly insisted on, that she at last, by Joseph's advice, consented.

CHAP. XIV.

Containing several curious night-adventures, in which Mr. Adams fell into many hair-breadth 'scapes, partly owing to his goodness, and partly to his inadvertency.

ABOUT an hour after they had all separated (it being now past three in the morning) Beau Didapper, whose passion for Fanny permitted him not to close his eyes, but had employed his imagination in contrivances how to satisfy his desires, at last hit on a method by which he hoped to effect it. He had ordered his servant to bring him word where Fanny lay, and had received his information; he therefore arose, put on his breeches and nightgown, and stole softly along the gallery which led to her apartment; and being come to the door, as he imagined it, he opened it with the least noise possible, and entered the chamber. A savour now invaded his nostrils which he did not expect in the room of so sweet a young creature, and which might have probably had no good effect on a cooler lover. However, he groped out the bed with difficulty; for there was not a glimpse of light, and opening the curtains, he whispered in Joseph's voice (for he was an excellent mimic) "Fanny, my angel, I am come to inform thee that I have discovered the falsehood of the story we last night heard. I am no longer thy brother, but thy lover; nor will I be delayed the enjoyment of thee one moment longer. You have sufficient assurances of my constancy not to doubt my marrying you, and it would be want of love to deny me the possession of thy charms." — So saying, he disencumbered himself from the little clothes he had on, and leaping into bed, embraced his angel, as he conceived her, with great rapture. If he was surprised at receiving no answer, he was no less pleased to find his hug returned with equal ardour. He remained not long in this sweet confusion; for both he and his paramour presently discovered their [error]$_{3}$ [mutual deceit]$_{1-2}$. Indeed it was no other than the accomplished Slipslop whom he had engaged; but though she immediately knew the person whom she had mistaken for Joseph, he was at a loss to guess at the representative of Fanny. He had so little seen or taken notice of this gentlewoman, that light itself would have afforded him no assistance in his conjecture. Beau Didapper no sooner had perceived his mistake, than he attempted to escape from the bed with much greater haste than he had made to it; but the watchful Slipslop prevented him. For that prudent woman being disappointed of those delicious offerings which her fancy had promised her pleasure, resolved to make an immediate sacrifice to her virtue. Indeed she wanted an opportunity to heal some wounds which her late conduct had, she feared, given her reputation; and as she had a wonderful presence of mind, she conceived the person of the unfortunate beau to be luckily thrown in her way to restore her lady's opinion of her impregnable chastity. At that instant therefore, when he offered to leap from the bed, she caught fast hold of his shirt, at the same time roaring out, "O thou villain! who hast attacked my chastity, and I believe ruined me in my sleep; I will swear a rape against thee, I will prosecute thee with the utmost vengeance." The beau attempted to get loose, but she held him fast, and when he struggled, she cried out, "Murther! Murther! Rape! Robbery! Ruin!" At which words Parson Adams, who lay in the next chamber, wakeful and meditating on the pedlar's discovery, jumped out of bed, and without staying to put a rag of clothes on, hastened into the apartment whence the cries proceeded. He made directly to the bed in the dark, where laying hold of the beau's skin (for Slipslop had torn his shirt almost off) and finding his skin extremely soft, and hearing him in a low voice begging Slipslop to let him go, he no longer doubted but this was the young woman in danger of ravishing, and immediately falling on the bed, and laying hold on Slipslop's chin, where he found a rough beard, his belief was confirmed; he therefore rescued the beau, who presently made his escape, and then turning towards Slipslop, received such a cuff on his chops, that his wrath kindling instantly, he offered to return the favour so stoutly, that had poor Slipslop received the fist, which in the dark passed by her and fell on the pillow, she would most probably have given up the ghost. — Adams missing his blow, fell directly on Slipslop, who cuffed and scratched as well as she could; nor was he behind-hand with her, in his endeavours, but happily the darkness of the night befriended her — She then cried she was a woman; but Adams answered she was rather the Devil, and if she was, he would grapple with him; and being again irritated by another stroke on his chops, he gave her such a remembrance in the guts, that she began to roar loud enough to be heard all over the house. Adams then seizing her by the hair (for her double-clout had fallen off in the scuffle) pinned her head down to the bolster, and then both called for lights together. The Lady Booby, who was as wakeful as any of her guests, had been alarmed from the beginning; and, being a woman of a bold spirit, she slipt on a nightgown, petticoat and slippers, and taking a candle, which always burnt in her chamber, in her hand, she walked undauntedly to Slipslop's room; where she entered just at the instant as Adams had discovered, by the two mountains which Slipslop carried before her, that he was concerned with a female. He then concluded her to be a witch, and said he fancied those breasts gave suck to a legion of devils. Slipslop seeing Lady Booby enter the room, cried, *Help! or I am ravished,* with a most audible voice, and Adams perceiving the light, turned hastily and saw the lady (as she did him) just as she came to the feet of the bed, nor did her modesty, when she found the naked condition of Adams, suffer her to approach farther. — She then began to revile the parson as the wickedest of all men, and particularly railed at his impudence in choosing her house for the scene of his debaucheries, and her own woman for the object of his bestiality. Poor Adams had before discovered the countenance of his bedfellow, and now first recollecting he was naked, he was no less confounded than Lady Booby herself, and immediately whipt under the bed-clothes, whence the chaste Slipslop endeavoured in vain to shut him out. Then putting forth his head, on which, by way of ornament, he wore a flannel nightcap, he protested his innocence, and asked ten thousand pardons of Mrs. Slipslop for the blows he had struck her, vowing he had mistaken her for a witch. Lady Booby then, casting her eyes on the ground, observed something sparkle with great lustre, which, when she had taken it up, appeared to be a very fine pair of diamond buttons for the sleeves. A little farther she saw lie the sleeve itself of a shirt with laced ruffles. "Heyday!" says she, "what is the meaning of this?" — "O madam," says Slipslop, "I don't know what hath happened, I have been so terrified. Here may have been a dozen men in the room." "To whom belongs this laced shirt and jewels?" says the lady. — "Undoubtedly," cries the parson, "to the young gentleman whom I mistook for a woman on coming into the room, whence proceeded all the subsequent mistakes; for if I had suspected him for a man, I would have seized him had he been another Hercules, though indeed he seems rather to resemble Hylas." [8] He then gave an account of the reason of his rising from bed, and the rest, till the lady came into the room; at which, and the figures of Slipslop and her gallant, whose heads only were vis-

[8] Hylas was a beautiful boy, the favorite of Hercules.

ible at the opposite corners of the bed, she could not refrain from laughter, nor did Slipslop persist in accusing the parson of any motions towards a rape. The lady therefore desired him to return to his bed as soon as she was departed, and then ordering Slipslop to rise and attend her in her own room, she returned herself thither. When she was gone, Adams renewed his petitions for pardon to Mrs. Slipslop, who with a most Christian temper not only forgave, but began to move with much courtesy towards him, which he taking as a hint to be gone, immediately quitted the bed, and made the best of his way towards his own; but unluckily instead of turning to the right, he turned to the left, and went to the apartment where Fanny ⟨lay⟩ $_3$, who (as the reader may remember) had not slept a wink the preceding night, and who was so hagged out with what had happened to her in the day, that notwithstanding all thoughts of her Joseph, she was fallen into so profound a sleep, that all the noise in the adjoining room had not been able to disturb her. Adams groped out the bed, and turning the clothes down softly, a custom Mrs. Adams had long accustomed him to, crept in, and deposited his carcase on the bedpost, a place which that good woman had always assigned him.

As the cat or lapdog of some lovely nymph for whom ten thousand lovers languish, lies quietly by the side of the charming maid, and ignorant of the scene of delight on which they repose, meditates the future capture of a mouse, or surprisal of a plate of bread and butter: so Adams, lay by the side of Fanny, ignorant of the paradise to which he was so near, nor could the emanation of sweets which flowed from her breath, overpower the fumes of tobacco which played in the parson's nostrils. And now sleep had not overtaken the good man, when Joseph, who had secretly appointed Fanny to come to her at the break of day, rapped softly at the chamber-door, which when he had repeated twice, Adams cried, *Come in, whoever you are*. Joseph thought he had mistaken the door, though she had given him the most exact directions; however, knowing his friend's voice, he opened it, and saw some female vestments lying on a chair. Fanny waking at the same instant, and stretching out her hand on Adams's beard, she cried out, — "O Heavens! where am I?"

"Bless me! where am I?" said the parson. Then Fanny screamed, Adams leapt out of bed, and Joseph stood, as the [tragedians call]$_3$ it, like the *statue of Surprise. "How came she into my room?"* cried Adams. *"How came you into hers?"* cried Joseph, in an astonishment. "I know nothing of the matter," answered Adams, "but that she is a vestal for me. As I am a Christian, I know not whether she is a man or woman. He is an infidel who doth not believe in witchcraft. They as surely exist now as in the days of Saul. My clothes are bewitched away too, and Fanny's brought into their place." For he still insisted he was in his own apartment; but Fanny denied it vehemently, and said his attempting to persuade Joseph of such a falsehood, convinced her of his wicked designs. "How!" said Joseph, in a rage, "hath he offered any rudeness to you?" — She answered, she could not accuse him of ⟨any⟩$_3$ more than villainously stealing to bed to her, which she thought rudeness sufficient, and what no man would do without a wicked intention. Joseph's great opinion of Adams was not easily to be staggered, and when he heard from Fanny that no harm had happened, he grew a little cooler; yet still he was confounded, and as he knew the house, and that the women's apartments were on this side Mrs. Slipslop's room, and the men's on the other, he was convinced that he was in Fanny's chamber. Assuring Adams, therefore, of this truth, he begged him to give some account how he came there. Adams then, standing in his shirt, which did not offend Fanny as the curtains of the bed were drawn, related all that had happened, and when he had ended, Joseph told him, it was plain he had mistaken, by turning to the right instead of the left.[9] "Odso!" cries Adams, "that's true, as sure as sixpence, you have hit on the very thing." He then traversed the room, rubbing his hands, and begged Fanny's pardon, assuring her he did not know whether she was man or woman. That innocent creature firmly believing all he said, told him, she was no longer angry, and begged Joseph to conduct him into his own apartment, where he should stay himself, till she had put her clothes

[tragedian calls]$_{1\text{-}2}$

[9] Fielding slips. When Adams mistakenly turns to Fanny's room: ". . . instead of turning to the right, he turned to the left . . ." (p. 388).

on. Joseph and Adams accordingly departed, and the latter soon was convinced of the mistake he had committed; however, whilst he was dressing himself, he often asserted he believed in the power of witchcraft notwithstanding, and did not see how a Christian could deny it.

CHAP. XV.

The arrival of Gaffar and Gammar Andrews, with another person, not much expected; and a perfect solution of the difficulties raised by the pedlar.

As soon as Fanny was drest, Joseph returned to her, and they had a long conversation together, the conclusion of which was, that if they found themselves to be really brother and sister, they vowed a perpetual celibacy, and to live together all their days, and indulge a Platonic friendship for each other.

The company were all very merry at breakfast, and Joseph and Fanny rather more cheerful than the preceding night. The Lady Booby produced the diamond button, which the beau most readily owned, and alleged that he was very subject to walk in his sleep. Indeed he was far from being ashamed of his amour, and rather endeavoured to insinuate that more than was really true had passed between him and the fair Slipslop.

Their tea was scarce over, when news came of the arrival of old Mr. Andrews and his wife. They were immediately introduced and kindly received by the Lady Booby, whose heart went now pit-a-pat, as did those of Joseph and Fanny. They felt perhaps little less anxiety in this interval than Œdipus himself whilst his fate was revealing.

Mr. Booby first opened the cause, by informing the old gentleman that he had a child in the company more than he knew of, and taking Fanny by the hand, told him, this was that daughter of his who had been stolen away by gipsies in her infancy. Mr. Andrews, after expressing some astonishment, assured his honour that he had never lost a daughter by gipsies, nor ever had any other children than Joseph and Pamela. These words were a cordial to the two lovers; but had a different effect on Lady Booby. She ordered the pedlar to be called, who recounted his story as he had done before. — At the end of which, old Mrs. Andrews running to Fanny, embraced her, crying out, *She is, she is my child*. The company were all amazed at this disagreement between the man and his wife; and the blood had now forsaken the cheeks of the lovers, when the old woman turning to her husband, who was more surprised than all the rest, and having a little recovered her own spirits, delivered herself as follows. "You may remember, my dear, when you went a serjeant to Gibraltar you left me big with child, you stayed abroad you know upwards of three years. In your absence I was brought to bed, I verily believe of this daughter, whom I am sure I have reason to remember, for I suckled her at this very breast till the day she was stolen from me. One afternoon, when the child was about a year, or a year and a half old, or thereabouts, two gipsy women came to the door, and offered to tell my fortune. One of them had a child in her lap; I showed them my hand, and desired to know if you was ever to come home again, which I remember as well as if it was but yesterday, they faithfully promised me you should — I left the girl in the cradle, and went to draw them a cup of liquor, the best I had; when I returned with the pot (I am sure I was not absent longer than whilst I am telling it to you) the women were gone. I was afraid they had stolen something, and looked and looked, but to no purpose, and Heaven knows I had very little for them to steal. At last hearing the child cry in the cradle, I went to take it up — but *O the living!* how was I surprised to find, instead of my own girl that I had put into the cradle, who was as fine a fat thriving child as you shall see in a summer's day, a poor sickly boy, that did not seem to have an hour to live. I ran out, pulling my hair off, and crying like any mad after the women, but never could hear a word of them from that day to this. When I came back, the poor infant (which is our Joseph there, as stout as he now stands) lifted up its eyes upon me so piteously, that to be sure, notwithstanding my passion, I could not find in my heart to do it any mischief. A neighbour of mine happening to come in at the same time, and hearing the case, advised me to take care of this poor child, and G— would perhaps one day restore me my own. Upon which I took the child up, and suckled it to be sure, all the world as if it had been born of my own natural body. And as true as I am alive, in a little time I loved the boy all to nothing as if it had been my own girl. — Well, as I was saying, times growing very hard, I having two children, and nothing but my own work, which was little enough, G— knows, to maintain them, was obliged to ask relief of the parish; but instead of giving it me, they removed me, by justices warrants, fifteen miles to the place where I now live, where I had not been long settled before you came home. Joseph (for that was the name I gave him myself — the Lord knows whether he was baptized or no, or by what name) Joseph, I say, seemed to me to be about five years old when you returned; for I believe he is two or three years older than our daughter here; (for I am thoroughly convinced she is the same) and when you saw him you said he was a chopping boy, without ever minding his age; and so I seeing you did not suspect anything of the matter, thought I might e'en as well keep it to myself, for fear you should not love him as well as I did. And all this is veritably true, and I will take my oath of it before any justice in the kingdom."

The pedlar, who had been summoned by the order of Lady Booby, listened with the utmost attention to Gammar Andrews's story, and when she had finished, asked her if the supposititious child had no mark on its breast? To which she answered, "Yes, he had as fine a strawberry as ever grew in a garden." This Joseph acknowledged, and unbuttoning his coat, at the intercession of the company, showed to them. "Well," says Gaffar Andrews, who was a comical sly old fellow, and very likely desired to have no more children than he could keep, "you have proved, I think, very plainly that this boy doth not belong to us; but how are you certain that the girl is ours?" The parson then brought the pedlar forward, and desired him to repeat the story which he had communicated to him the preceding day at the alehouse; which he complied with, and related what the reader, as well as Mr. Adams, hath seen before. He then confirmed, from his wife's report, all the circumstances of the exchange, and of the strawberry on Joseph's breast. At the repetition of the word *strawberry*, Adams, who had seen it without any emotion, started, and cried, *Bless me! something comes into my head.* But before he had time to bring anything out, a servant called him forth. When he was gone, the pedlar assured Joseph, that his parents were persons of much greater circumstances than those he had hitherto mistaken for such; for that he had been stolen from a gentleman's house, by those whom they call gipsies, and had been kept by them during a whole year, when looking on him as in a dying condition, they had exchanged him for the other healthier child, in the manner before related. He said, as to the name of his father, his wife had either never known or forgot it; but that she had acquainted him he lived about forty miles from the place where the exchange had been made, and which way, promising to spare no pains in endeavouring with him to discover the place.

But Fortune, which seldom doth good or ill, or makes men happy or miserable by halves, resolved to spare him this labour. The reader may please to recollect, that Mr. Wilson had intended a journey to the west, in which he was to pass through Mr. Adams's parish, and had promised to call on him. He was now arrived at the Lady Booby's gates for that purpose, being directed thither from the parson's house, and had sent in the servant whom we have above seen call Mr. Adams forth. This had no sooner mentioned the discovery of a stolen child, and had uttered the word *strawberry*, than Mr. Wilson, with wildness in his looks, and the utmost eagerness in his words, begged to be showed into the room, where he entered without the least regard to any of the company but Joseph, and embracing him with a complexion all pale and trembling, desired to see the mark on his breast; the parson followed him capering, rubbing his hands, and crying out, *Hic est quem quæris, inventus est, &c.*[10] Joseph complied with the request of Mr. Wilson, who no sooner saw the mark, than abandoning himself to the most extravagant rapture

[10] "Here is the one you seek, he is found, etc." Adams is mixing together phrases from the resurrection of Christ and the return of the Prodigal Son, whose father speaks of him as if he were resurrected.

of passion, he embraced Joseph with inexpressible ecstasy, and cried out in tears of joy, *I have discovered my son, I have him again in my arms.* Joseph, was not sufficiently apprised yet, to taste the same delight with his father, (for so in reality he was;) however, he returned some warmth to his embraces: But he no sooner perceived from his father's account, the agreement of every circumstance, of person, time, and place, than he threw himself at his feet, and embracing his knees, with tears begged his blessing, which was given with much affection, and received with such respect, mixed with such tenderness on both sides, that it affected all present: But none so much as Lady Booby, who left the room in an agony, which was but too much perceived, and not very charitably accounted for by some of the company.

CHAP. XVI.

Being the last. In which this true history is brought to a happy conclusion.

FANNY was very little behind her Joseph, in the duty she exprest towards her parents; and the joy she evidenced in discovering them. Gammar Andrews kissed her, and said she was heartily glad to see her: But for her part she could never love anyone better than Joseph. Gaffar Andrews testified no remarkable emotion, he blessed and kissed her, but complained bitterly, that he wanted his pipe, not having had a whiff that morning.

Mr. Booby, who knew nothing of his aunt's fondness, imputed her abrupt departure to her pride, and disdain of the family into which he was married; he was therefore desirous to be gone with the utmost celerity: And now, having congratulated Mr. Wilson and Joseph on the discovery, he saluted Fanny, called her sister, and introduced her as such to Pamela, who behaved with great decency on the occasion.

He now sent a message to his aunt, who returned, that she wished him a good journey; but was too disordered to see any company: He therefore prepared to set out, having invited Mr.

Wilson to his house, and Pamela and Joseph both so insisted on his complying, that he at last consented, having first obtained a messenger from Mr. Booby, to acquaint his wife with the news; which, as he knew it would render her completely happy, he could not prevail on himself to delay a moment in acquainting her with.

The company were ranged in this manner. The two old people with their two daughters rode in the coach, the squire, Mr. Wilson, Joseph, Parson Adams, and the pedlar proceeded on horseback.

In their way Joseph informed his father of his intended match with Fanny; to which, though he expressed some reluctance at first, on the eagerness of his son's instances he consented, saying if she was so good a creature as she appeared, and he described her, he thought the disadvantages of birth and fortune might be compensated. He however insisted on the match being deferred till he had seen his mother; in which Joseph perceiving him positive, with great duty obeyed him, to the great delight of Parson Adams, who by these means saw an opportunity of fulfilling the Church forms, and marrying his parishioners without a licence.

Mr. Adams greatly exulting on this occasion, (for such ceremonies were matters of no small moment with him) accidentally gave spurs to his horse, which the generous beast disdaining, for he was high of mettle, and had been used to more expert riders than the gentleman who at present bestrode him: for whose horsemanship he had perhaps some contempt, immediately ran away full speed, and played so many antic tricks, that he tumbled the parson from his back; which Joseph perceiving, came to his relief. This accident afforded infinite merriment to the servants, and no less frighted poor Fanny, who beheld him as he passed by the coach; but the mirth of the one, and terror of the other were soon determined, when the parson declared he had received no damage.

The horse having freed himself from his unworthy rider, as he probably thought him, proceeded to make the best of his way: but was stopped by a gentleman and his servants, who were travelling the opposite way; and were now at a little distance from the coach. They soon met; and as one of the servants delivered Adams his horse, his master hailed him, and Adams looking up, presently recollected he was the Justice of Peace before whom he and Fanny had made their appearance. The parson presently saluted him very kindly; and the justice informed him, that he had found the fellow who attempted to swear against him and the young woman the very next day, and had committed him to Salisbury gaol, where he was charged with many robberies.

Many compliments having passed between the parson and ⟨the⟩ ₂ justice, the latter proceeded on his journey, and the former having with some disdain refused Joseph's offer of changing horses; and declared he was as able a horseman as any in the kingdom, re-mounted his beast; and now the company again proceeded, and happily arrived at their journey's end, Mr. Adams by good luck, rather than by good riding, escaping a second fall.

The company arriving at Mr. Booby's house, were all received by him in the most courteous, and entertained in the most splendid manner, after the custom of the old English hospitality, which is still preserved in some very few families in the remote parts of England. They all passed that day with the utmost satisfaction; it being perhaps impossible to find any set of people more solidly and sincerely happy. Joseph and Fanny found means to be alone upwards of two hours, which were the shortest but the sweetest imaginable.

In the morning, Mr. Wilson proposed to his son to make a visit with him to his mother; which, notwithstanding his dutiful inclinations, and a longing desire he had to see her, a little concerned him as he must be obliged to leave his Fanny: But the goodness of Mr. Booby relieved him; for he proposed to send his own coach and six for Mrs. Wilson, whom Pamela so very earnestly invited, that Mr. Wilson at length agreed with the entreaties of Mr. Booby and Joseph, and suffered the coach to go empty for his wife.

On Saturday night the coach returned with Mrs. Wilson, who added one more to this happy assembly. The reader may imagine much better and quicker too than I can describe, the many embraces and tears of joy which succeeded her arrival. It is sufficient to say, she was easily prevailed with to follow her husband's example, in consenting to the match.

On Sunday Mr. Adams performed the service at the squire's parish church, the curate of which very kindly exchanged duty, and rode twenty miles to the Lady Booby's parish, so to do; being particularly charged not to omit publishing the banns, being the third and last time.

At length the happy day arrived, which was to put Joseph in the possession of all his wishes. He arose and drest himself in a neat, but plain suit of Mr. Booby's, which exactly fitted him; for he refused all finery; as did Fanny likewise, who could be prevailed on by Pamela to attire herself in nothing richer than a white dimity night-gown. Her shift indeed, which Pamela presented her, was of the finest kind, and had an edging of lace round the bosom; she likewise equipped her with a pair of fine white thread stockings, which were all she would accept; for she wore one of her own short round-eared caps, and over it a little straw hat, lined with cherry-coloured silk, and tied with a cherry-coloured ribbon. In this dress she came forth from her chamber, blushing, and breathing sweets; and was by Joseph, whose eyes sparkled fire, led to church, the whole family attending, where Mr. Adams performed the ceremony; at which nothing was so remarkable, as the extraordinary and unaffected modesty of Fanny, unless the true Christian piety of Adams, who publicly rebuked Mr. Booby and Pamela for laughing in so sacred a place, and so solemn an occasion. Our parson would have done no less to the highest prince on earth: For though he paid all submission and deference to his superiors in other matters, where the least spice of religion intervened, he immediately lost all respect of persons. It was his maxim, That he was a servant of the Highest, and could not, without departing from his duty, give up the least article of his honour, or of his cause, to the greatest earthly potentate. Indeed he always asserted, that Mr. Adams at church with his surplice on, and Mr. Adams without that ornament, in any other place, were two very different persons.

When the church rites were over, Joseph led his blooming

bride back to Mr. Booby's (for the distance was so very little, they did not think proper to use a coach) the whole company attended them likewise on foot; and now a most magnificent entertainment was provided, at which Parson Adams demonstrated an appetite surprising, as well as surpassing everyone present. Indeed the only persons who betrayed any deficiency on this occasion, were those on whose account the feast was provided. They pampered their imaginations with the much more exquisite repast which the approach of night promised them; the thoughts of which filled both their minds, though with different sensations; the one all desire, while the other had her wishes tempered with fears.

At length, after a day passed with the utmost merriment, corrected by the strictest decency; in which, however, Parson Adams, being well filled with ale and pudding, had given a loose to more facetiousness than was usual to him: The happy, the blest moment arrived, when Fanny retired with her mother, her mother-in-law, and her sister. She was soon undrest; for she had no jewels to deposit in their caskets, nor fine laces to fold with the nicest exactness. Undressing to her was properly discovering, not putting off ornaments: For as all her charms were the gifts of Nature, she could divest herself of none. How, reader, shall I give thee an adequate idea of this lovely young creature! the bloom of roses and lilies might a little illustrate her complexion, or their smell her sweetness: but to comprehend her entirely, conceive Youth, Health, Bloom, Beauty, Neatness, and Innocence in her bridal-bed; conceive all these in their utmost perfection, and you may place the charming Fanny's picture before your eyes.

Joseph no sooner heard she was in bed, than he fled with the utmost eagerness to her. A minute carried him into her arms, where we shall leave this happy couple to enjoy the private rewards of their constancy; rewards so great and sweet, that I apprehend Joseph neither envied the noblest duke, nor Fanny the finest duchess that night.

The third day, Mr. Wilson and his wife, with their son and daughter, returned home; where they now live together in a state of bliss scarce ever equalled. Mr. Booby hath with unprecedented generosity given Fanny a fortune of two thousand pound, which Joseph hath laid out in a little estate in the same parish with his father, which he now occupies, (his father having stocked it for him;) and Fanny presides, with most excellent management in his dairy; where, however, she is not at present very able to bustle much, being, as Mr. Wilson informs me in his last letter, extremely big with her first child.

Mr. Booby hath presented Mr. Adams with a living of one hundred and thirty pounds a year. He at first refused it, resolving not to quit his parishioners, with whom he hath lived so long: But on recollecting he might keep a curate at this living, he hath been lately inducted into it.

The pedlar, besides several handsome presents both from Mr. Wilson and Mr. Booby, is, by the latter's interest, made an excise-man; a trust which he discharges with such justice, that he is greatly beloved in his neighbourhood.

As for the Lady Booby, she returned to London in a few days, where a young captain of dragoons, together with eternal parties at cards, soon obliterated the memory of Joseph.

Joseph remains blest with his Fanny, whom he doats on with the utmost tenderness, which is all returned on her side. The happiness of this couple is a perpetual fountain of pleasure to their fond parents; and what is particularly remarkable, he declares he will imitate them in their retirement; nor will be prevailed on by any booksellers, or their authors, to make his appearance in *High-Life*.[11]

[11] In May 1741, a group of publishers capitalized on Richardson's anonymous success by producing a sequel: *Pamela's Conduct in High Life*. A second volume appeared in September, along with another serialized sequel, *Pamela in High Life: Or, Virtue Rewarded*. Richardson denounced the "*High-Life Men*" in the newspapers, and published his own two-volume continuation on December 7, 1741, presenting Pamela "*In her EXALTED CONDITION . . . In* GENTEEL LIFE."

ESSAYS
IN
CRITICISM

In the essays that follow, bracketed figures indicate the end of a page in the selection as it appears in the original source. Whenever necessary, footnotes have been renumbered, but there has been no attempt to make page references to the novel correspond to this edition, or quotations from other editions conform to the wording of this edition.

COMIC RESOLUTION in FIELDING'S *JOSEPH ANDREWS*

Mark Spilka

I

THOUGH the night adventures at Booby Hall are among the most memorable scenes in *Joseph Andrews*, many scholars tend to ignore them or to minimize their importance. Generally speaking, they pluck the adventures out of context and file them away—out of sight, out of mind—among even more colorful bedroom antics within the picaresque tradition. Thus J. B. Priestley writes: [11]

> Such chapters of accidents are very familiar to students of the *picaresque*, and all that need be said of this one is that there is some slight relation to character in it . . . but that it is not enough to make the episode anything more than a piece of comic business of a very familiar type. Smollett could bustle through such rough-and-tumble business just as well, if not better. . . .[1]

Source: "Comic Resolution in Fielding's *Joseph Andrews*," *College English* 15 (1953), pp. 11–19.

[1] *The English Comic Characters* (New York: Dodd, Mead, 1931), p. 113.

Priestley is right as far as he goes, but he forgets that *Joseph Andrews* is more novel than picaresque tale and that the novel requires special handling. In the picaresque tale there is little or no dramatic connection between one episode and the next, and the critic can lift things out of context to his heart's content. But with the more fully developed novel form he must show how an episode—lifted *from* a tradition—has been fitted *into* the scheme of a given book. Certainly this is the proper approach to the escapades at Booby Hall, the last major comic scenes in *Joseph Andrews*—scenes which involve all the major characters in the book and both aspects of the central theme, the lust-chastity theme.

Yet with all this in mind it may still be argued that the Booby Hall affair is a simple comic interlude, or diversion, which Fielding inserted at the most crucial point in the novel to increase suspense and at the same time to vary the fare. On the surface there is some truth to this assertion: the night adventures are sandwiched between the all-important chapters in which the incest problem is first introduced then happily solved. But the argument breaks down before a simple comparison: in the famous knocking-at-the-gate scene in *Macbeth*, the commonplace is used (according to De Quincey) to offset and heighten the essential strangeness and horror of murder; if the "diversion" argument holds true, the same function should be performed by the bedroom scenes in *Joseph Andrews;* but as any honest reader will admit, these scenes perform precisely the opposite function—that is, they neither increase nor heighten the dramatic intensity of the incest plot; rather, they lessen its seriousness and achieve a special importance of their own. In the next chapter, for example, the company are "all very merry at breakfast, and Joseph and Fanny rather more cheerful than the preceding night"; it becomes obvious that some sort of emotional purgation has occurred and that the resolution of the main plot will be anticlimactic.

All this seems normal enough for a comedy based on character rather than on situation. As Aurelien Digeon points out, "The ending is necessarily the weak point in works of this kind. It is almost always engineered from without; for passions never stop working nor come to an 'end.'"[2] Unfortunately, Digeon fails to add here that if passions never stop working, they are sometimes resolved, and that it is the business of a good comic writer to resolve them. In the night adventures at Booby Hall, Fielding has done just that; with the aid of condensed, violent action, he has stood his book on its head, shaken out all the themes and passions, and resolved them through warmhearted laughter. If this interpretation seems far-fetched, its essential soundness may become evident as we pay more attention to the lust-chastity theme, to Fielding's theory of humor, to the role of nakedness in the novel, and, finally, to two of the most comic figures in the book, Parson Adams and Mrs. Slipslop. As for the other relevant characters—Joseph Andrews, Fanny Goodwill, Lady Booby, and Beau Didapper—[12] we need only note here that the first two embody all the natural health, goodness, and beauty which Fielding admired, while the last two embody much of the vice and artificiality he deplored.

II

IN order to parody Richardson's *Pamela,* Fielding built *Joseph Andrews* around a central moral problem: the preservation of (and the assault upon) chastity. On the one hand, Joseph Andrews must protect his virtue from such lustful creatures as Lady Booby, Mrs. Slipslop, and Betty the chambermaid; on the other, Fanny Goodwill must withstand the attacks of a beau, a squire, a rogue, and a servant. But as most writers have observed, the scope of the novel is much broader than this. Fielding saw affection in two of its forms, vanity and hypocrisy, as the "only source of the true Ridiculous," and he hoped to expose these qualities wherever he found them. Accordingly, he also designed his novel along more general lines: three virtuous, good-natured persons—Joseph, Fanny, and Adams—must be thrust through every level of society as exemplars or as touchstones and instruments for exposing vanity and hypocrisy, and, just as important, goodness and kindness, in whomever they meet. Adams will be the foremost touchstone, since his religious position and his per-

[2] *The Novels of Fielding* (London: Routledge, 1925), p. 60.

sonal traits—innocence, simplicity, bravery, compassion, haste, pedantry, forgetfulness—will always pitch him into a good deal of trouble; yet, once in trouble, his virtues will make him stand out in complete contrast to those who take advantage to him. Finally, in his perfect innocence he will always be the main instrument for exposing his own mild affectations.

But, as these remarks indicate, Adams' position is somewhat ambiguous with regard to Fielding's formula for the ridiculous in humor. Like his predecessor, Don Quixote, he cuts a bizarre figure outwardly, but, at the same time, his inner dignity remains unassailable: as Joseph Andrews tells us, true virtue can never be ridiculed, and we know that Adams, however outlandish, is truly virtuous—so that he stands half within Fielding's theory of humor and half without.[3] But this theory is, after all, static and reductive rather than organic. Through shrewd analysis Fielding has called attention to the affectations, the *particular* qualities which make men appear in a ridiculous light. But through his admiration for Cervantes he has unconsciously seized on the principle of the *comic figure*—the whole man who is at once lovable and ridiculous, whose entire character is involved in each of his humorous actions, and whose character must be established through time and incident, in the reader's mind, before he becomes "wholly" laughable. To put it in different terms, when someone we know and like is involved in a ridiculous action, then the humor of the situation broadens and quickens to include our identification with and sympathy for that person. A sudden or prolonged juxtaposition of his inner dignity with his outer "awkwardness" produces a state of mixed emotions in us—love, sympathy, and identification, as well as condescension—and this state is released or resolved, in turn, through laughter.[4] The point can be [13] made clearer perhaps through a modern analogy: the amorphous Keystone Cops amuse us (at least they used to) in accord with Fielding's theory

[3] In Book III, chap. vi., Joseph says, "I defy the wisest man in the world to turn a good action into ridicule. . . . He, who should endeavour it, would be laughed at himself, instead of making others laugh."

[4] Fielding's (and Hobbes's) theory of humor depends upon the reader's feeling of superiority toward the person ridiculed. But in practice Fielding tapped a second psychological source by working upon our sympathies: all

of the ridiculous—that is to say, they lose their false outer dignity in falls and madcap fights; yet when Charlie Chaplin puts up a magnificent bluff in the boxing ring (as in *City Lights*), our laughter becomes much warmer and far more sympathetic in quality—Chaplin's bluff may be ridiculous, but the man who bluffs is brave, and we have learned something of this through time, situation, and the development of character; we are prepared, that is, for his simultaneous display of inner dignity and outer vanity in the boxing ring, and our laughter is accordingly that much richer. One Keystone Cop is much like the next, but Chaplin has become a unique and appealing figure in our eyes—and in a similar manner so has Parson Adams. Our respect, love, and admiration for Adams continue to grow through the length of *Joseph Andrews*. And only when his character has been firmly established in our minds (and in the same vein, only when the lust-chastity theme has been worked for all it is worth) can the night scenes at Booby Hall occur. Place these scenes earlier in the book and they will strike us as meaningless horseplay; but at the end of the book we are prepared for them—Parson Adams is now familiar to us as a well-developed comic figure, and his nakedness strikes us with symbolic force.

As a matter of fact the spectacle of nakedness is significantly common (though not always symbolic) in *Joseph Andrews*. Fanny, Joseph, Adams, Lady Booby, Mrs. Slipslop, Beau Didapper, Betty the chambermaid, Mr. Tow-wouse—all appear at one time or another and for various reasons, in a state of partial or complete undress. In the early chapters, for example, Joseph is beaten and stripped by robbers and left on the road to die; when a carriage passes, Fielding "tests" each of the passengers by his willingness to accept Joseph *as he is*, for what he is—a de-

of us know how it feels to be misunderstood or defeated, and such feelings help us to maintain a close identification with likable comic figures—Adams, Quixote, Chaplin. If, as Maynard Mack insists (in *Joseph Andrews*, ed. Maynard Mack [New York: Rinehart, 1948]), we view comedy from the outside, as a spectacle, this is only our conscious point of view; at the deeper emotional level we are actively engaged in the spectacle. Of course, all art demands some form of audience participation at this level, but the point deserves re-emphasis, since, in our current (and much-needed) passion for analysis, we have partially deadened our sense of the unity of aesthetic experience.

fenseless human being. And late in the book, when Adams appears in a nightshirt (the usual eighteenth-century equivalent for nakedness), Fielding tests, in effect, *our* willingness, as good-natured readers, to take Adams for what he is. It should not surprise us, therefore, that a definite symbolic equation between nakedness, on the one hand, and innocence and worth, on the other, occurs in other portions of Fielding's work: Squire Allworthy also appears in his nightshirt, for example, in the opening pages of *Tom Jones;* and in *The Champion* for January 24, 1740, Fielding even cites Plato to the effect that men would love virtue if they could see her naked. This platitude is put to good use in *Joseph Andrews,* though the problem there is to "expose" or "lay bare" both virtue and affectation, often in the same man.

With regard to affectation, Fielding's theory of the ridiculous fits in well with our "nakedness" theme. Affectations are "put on," and it is the humorist's job (or more properly the satirist's) to "strip them off." This much Fielding knew by rote from his earliest published work, a poem against masquerades, to his attack on masquerades in his last novel, *Amelia:* [14] take off the mask, remove the outer pretense, and expose the "bare facts" which lie beneath—vanity, hypocrisy, smugness. But his chief accomplishment, as well as his chief delight, was to distinguish between a man's defects and his essential goodness; and we think in this respect of Adams, Tom Jones, Captain Booth, and dozens of the minor creations. If a man is good-natured "at bottom," then the problem for the novelist is how to get to the bottom. Fielding usually arrives there by playing off the man's faults against his virtues, as when Adams first cautions Joseph against immoderate grief, then grieves immoderately, like any compassionate man, at the news of his son's supposed drowning. But a more pertinent example occurs in one of the inn scenes in *Joseph Andrews,* when Fanny faints and Adams, in his haste to rescue her, tosses his precious copy of Aeschylus into the fire. Here Adams has literally stripped off an affectation while revealing his natural goodness—the book is a symbol, that is, of his pedantry, of his excessive reliance upon literature as a guide to life, and this is what is tossed aside during the emergency. Later on, when the book is fished out of the fire, it has been reduced to its simple sheepskin covering—which is Fielding's way of reminding us that the contents of the book are superficial, at least in the face of harsh experience. Thus the whole incident underscores the fact that Adams' faults, like his torn, disordered clothes, are only the outward, superficial aspects of his character and that the essential Adams, a brave, good man, lies somewhere underneath; his heart—not his Aeschylus, not his harmless vanity—is his true guide in all things of consequence.[5]

Mrs. Slipslop is another matter. She is usually praised by critics as the well-rounded comic foil to Lady Booby. But she is something more than this, since her lust for Joseph, and for all manner of men, is more natural and appealing than Lady Booby's hot-and-cold passion. To begin with, Mrs. Slipslop is an unbelievably ugly maidservant who, after an early slip, has remained virtuous for many years. Now, at forty-five, she has resolved to pay off "the debt of pleasure" which she feels she owes to herself. Though Fielding heavily ridicules her vanity and hypocrisy throughout the book, he also brings out the pathetic strain in her makeup, and at times he even reveals an author's fondness for a favorite creation. Mrs. Slipslop may rail at Joseph, for example, but unlike Lady Booby she will never turn him out into the street; in fact, she saves or aids him on several important occasions; but, more than all this, there is something almost touching, as well as ridiculous, about her faulty speech, her grotesque body, and her foolish dream of becoming "Mrs. Andrews, with a hundred a-year." All in all, she is a comic figure in her own right, as well as a comic foil, and if Fielding deals her a sound drubbing in the night scenes at Booby Hall, he also "deals" her a last warm laugh.

III

FIELDING beds down his entire cast at Booby Hall in preparation for the night adventures. Then, when the household is asleep, he sends Beau Didapper off to ravish Fanny through

[5] Consider in this respect what a poor showing Partridge makes as a comic figure in *Tom Jones;* like Adams he is vain, pedantic, and superstitious, but he lacks the nobility of heart which great comic figures—at least in the quixotic tradition—must possess.

trickery, and the round of fun begins. By mistake, Didapper enters Mrs. Slipslop's pitch-dark room and, posing as Joseph, tells her that [15] the incest report was false, and that he can delay the enjoyment of her charms no longer; then he climbs into bed with her. She receives him willingly enough—her dream come true—but the two of them soon discover their mutual error. Ever-prudent, Mrs. Slipslop now sees her chance to win back her reputation for chastity, which she had damaged through recent conduct with Lawyer Scout; so she hugs Didapper even more firmly, calls out for help, and Parson Adams comes running to her rescue from the next chamber. But in his haste Adams has forgot to put on any clothes, and this action is far more characteristic of him than any we have yet seen in the novel. For Adams has now become his own true symbol: he stands there as God made him, all courage and kindness, with his affectations, his clothes, left in a heap behind him. He is now the naked truth, quite literally and lovably, and he is never more himself than at this moment, not even while throwing his Aeschylus into the fire to save Fanny. He is brave, true virtue on the march now, stripped clean of all encumbrance and far beyond the reach of ridicule—for true virtue, as we have already seen, can never be ridiculed. Of course, Adams is laughable because he is naked and imprudent and we are not; but mainly he arouses those feelings to which we have been conditioned, with regard to him, from the beginning of the novel. For as Fielding and Plato have told us, men will love virtue if they see her—or in this case him—naked. We see him naked now, and we laugh, to a great extent, out of love. But let us return for a moment to the goings-on in Mrs. Slipslop's bedroom.

Obeying, of all things, the dictates of common sense, Adams now passes over the small, whimpering body—obviously the woman—and proceeds to grapple with the large bearded one—obviously the man. Here Fielding ridicules, in Slipslop and Didapper, that vanity by which one poses as a seducible woman and the other as a virile man. For the small body (Beau Didapper) escapes, and Slipslop receives an almost fatal beating. But Lady Booby, attracted by all the noise, enters the room in the nick of time with lighted candle in hand. At which point Adams discovers both his error and his nakedness and leaps under the covers with Mrs. Slipslop. We have then, in one corner of the bed, Vice posing as Virtue, which is hypocrisy; and in the other corner, Virtue hiding its "lovable" nakedness and apparently acting as Vice—which is false, foolish modesty at the very least. And we also have, as Lady Justice with the Lighted Candle, Lady Booby, the far from blinded villainess of the novel.

Shall we stop a moment to straighten things out? We have already seen that vanity has been exposed to ridicule—a normal enough procedure. But now we can see that virtue itself has been exposed to some sort of laughter; moreover, it has been exposed in a worthless cause—until Adams arrived and began pummeling Mrs. Slipslop, no one was in any real danger. This reminds us at once of Don Quixote, and the comparison enables us to see that virtue has been confounded rather than ridiculed and that we laugh once more, in the main, out of sympathy for a brave man in an awkward fix.[6]

There is more to it than this, however. [16] We have been neglecting Mrs. Slipslop, who at long last has had not one but two men in her bed (simultaneously!), but who has been forced by circumstance to reject them both. The sex-starved maiden, with her mountainous breasts and her spur-of-the-moment virtue, has been soundly trounced. In a very real sense this is Waterloo for the prudent gentlewoman, and for the lust half of the lust-chastity theme as well. All, all is resolved through a burst of laughter, though again through laughter of a special kind. In a parody on *Pamela*, one of two lusting ladies (both foils for Richardson's clumsy Mr. B) was bound to receive a severe comeuppance. Fielding, the sure comic artist, chose the more comic figure; but the very condition which makes Slipslop appear so ridiculous in our eyes—the extreme distance between her desires and her qualifications—also makes her appeal to the

[6] This is also Adams' first "real" windmill and therefore the most quixotic moment in the book. Until now Adams' rescues have been much to the point and more or less successful, since Fielding always attempted to show that virtue can be a successful way of life—hence Adams' vigor, his robust strength, his eventual muddling through. As a knight-errant, he is generally far more effective than the gallant Quixote.

warm side of our (and Fielding's) sense of humor. She is a far less harsh figure than Lady Booby and therefore the more proper bed companion for the equally harmless, "sexless," but virtuous Parson Adams.

Nevertheless, we must return to Lady Booby, at the scene of the alleged rape, for the key to all these resolutions and reversals. After berating Adams as a wicked cleric, the stern hostess spies Didapper's telltale cuff links on the floor. Then, when she hears Adams' story, when she takes in "the figures of Slipslop and her gallant, whose heads only were visible at the opposite corners of the bed," she is unable to "refrain from laughter." For once, then, Lady Booby appears in a good light: until now she has behaved in a completely selfish manner, but the kind of laughter which we cannot withhold, *in spite of ourselves*, stems more from the heart than the ego. Even the opinionated Mrs. Slipslop now checks her tongue, and it becomes apparent that evil itself has been dissolved by some strange power. We can say, of course, that Lady Booby laughs at a maid and a parson who are far too old and ridiculous for zealous modesty; but, more to the point, she laughs at Adams' lovable innocence, and perhaps she laughs at herself as well, at her own defeat; for, as we have observed, Mrs. Slipslop is in part her comic foil, and Parson Adams now lies in the place where Joseph Andrews might have lain, if her own hopes had been fulfilled.

At any rate, a general absolution has obviously just occurred: through elaborate contrivance (the creation of Beau Didapper as catalytic agent, the convenient rainstorm, the crisis in the main plot, Slipslop's affair with Lawyer Scout, and so on) Fielding has brought Adams before us in all his nakedness. The good parson has never seemed so ridiculous, nor has he ever been burdened so heavily with the guilt which rightfully belongs to those around him—to Slipslop, to Didapper, to Lady Booby, and even to you and me, as we stand behind the bold hostess in judgment of the scene and see our own sins revealed by flickering candlelight—yet Adams emerges untarnished from under this double burden of guilt and ridicule, and, like the true comic hero, he absolves us all with his naïve triumph over circumstance: for good and bad men alike have a common stake in that perfect, naked innocence which can force a Lady Booby, or even a Peter Pounce, to grin or laugh from some buried store of benevolence.[7] All this is nicely under[17]scored, I think, when the lady retires once more and the scene at hand, which opens with naked Adams running characteristically to the rescue, now closes with naked Slipslop sliding lustfully, pathetically, characteristically, and as Fielding puts it, "with much courtesy," across the bed toward Parson Adams, who takes the hint and quickly leaves the room. One can't help thinking that at long last, among all those thorns, Fielding has placed a rose for Mrs. Slipslop—for the last warm laugh is hers, in a madcap world where virtue is masked as vice, and vice as virtue, while, in the unmasking, warmheartedness prevails over all morality.

In the next half of the chapter things begin to settle down. Adams, in his haste, inadvertently takes the wrong turn; he climbs quietly into what he thinks is his own bed and prepares for sleep. But in reality the poor man has moved directly from the bed of the ugliest, most indiscriminately lustful woman in the book to that of the loveliest and most chaste. On the other side of him lies Fanny "Goodwill" Andrews (not yet Joseph's wife but his supposed sister) in profound, peaceful, naked slumber; and Fielding promptly reminds us that Adams has done what every red-blooded man in the novel has been trying to do, unsuccessfully, since Book II, chapter ix: he has climbed into bed with Fanny:

> As the cat or lap-dog of some lovely nymph, for whom ten thousand lovers languish, lies quietly by the side of the charming maid, and, ignorant of the scene of delight on which they repose, meditates the future capture of a mouse, or surprisal of a plate of bread and butter, so Adams lay by the side of Fanny [writes Fielding], ignorant of the paradise to which he was so near.

The book has now come full circle, for not only Fanny's incomparable charms but her priceless chastity as well are treated

[7] In Book III, chap, xii, the normally severe Peter Pounce is also forced to grin at the sight of Adams' bedraggled figure. In the same manner, a misanthrope might grin at a mud-spattered child: the outer ridiculousness is reinforced by inward innocence in both Adams and the child, and the responsive grin or laugh is basically sympathetic.

with the utmost indifference by the one man who has succeeded, so far, in sharing her bed; nor is she in any real danger, for this man, this cat or lap dog, neither knows nor cares, nor would care if he knew, about the "paradise" beside him; he simply wants to go to sleep. We can safely say, then, that the lust-chastity theme has been fully and ironically resolved or, if you will, stood on both its ears.

But it is daybreak now, and Joseph Andrews has come for an innocent rendezvous with Fanny. When he raps at the door, the good-natured, hospitable parson calls out, "Come in, whoever you are." Consternation follows, and for the first time in the novel the three paragons of virtue, the three touchstones, are at complete odds with one another. Adams is again burdened with undeserved guilt and can only blame the affair on witchcraft; but, once he recounts his story, Joseph explains to him that he must have taken the wrong turn on leaving Slipslop's room. Then Fielding makes a significant emendation: he has already told his readers that the naked Adams is wearing a nightcap; now he reminds them that he is also wearing the traditional knee-length nightshirt—all this in deference, perhaps, to Fanny's modesty but nevertheless a sign that things are back to normal once more and that the naked truth no longer roams through the halls of night. Fanny and Joseph forgive the parson with the indulgence one shows to an innocent child, and again the scene ends on a benevolent note.

What are we to make of night adventures which serve as a kind of parody on the whole novel; which apparently involve no real problems but in which lust and self-love appear, momentarily, in an almost friendly light; in which chastity is [18] ignored, brave virtue confounded, and a whole comic method thrown thereby into reverse? One solution seems obvious: by sending his beloved parson from bed to bed, Fielding has put a kind of comic blessing upon the novel; he has resolved the major themes and passions through benevolent humor. Or to push on to a more inclusive theory, the comic resolution in *Joseph Andrews* depends for its warmth upon the flow of sympathy which Fielding creates between his readers and his comic figures; for its bite, upon his ridicule and deflation of those figures; and for its meaning, upon the long-range development of character and theme, as well as the local situation at Booby Hall. Apparently Fielding, like Parson Adams, did not always practice the simple theories he preached. But as Adams insists at the close of the night adventures, there is such a thing as witchcraft, and perhaps this is what Fielding practiced upon Adams and upon his readers, and with a good deal of awareness of what he was doing. [19]

JOSEPH AS HERO in *JOSEPH ANDREWS*

Dick Taylor, Jr.

COMMENTATORS have generally recognized that Fielding's Tom Jones develops maturity of character and depth of insight through his experiences and that Booth at the end of *Amelia*, albeit a trifle suddenly, attains a deeper vision of life. But they have not bestowed on Joseph Andrews his due meed of honor for his considerable increase in dignity and stature in the progress of the novel; [1] and consequently they have failed to assess prop-

Source: Dick Taylor, Jr., "Joseph as Hero in *Joseph Andrews*," *Tulane Studies in English* 7 (1957), pp. 91–109.

[1] Austin Dobson, in the series of English Men of Letters, does not treat Joseph at all in his chapter on *Joseph Andrews*. Wilbur L. Cross, *The History of Henry Fielding* (New Haven, 1918), I, 314–59 hardly mentions Joseph. F. Holmes Dudden, *Henry Fielding* (Oxford: Clarendon, 1952), I, 367, finds that "not much need be said" about "Joseph and Fanny, the nominal hero and heroine." They are to Dudden "pleasing but not humorous or particularly striking figures," and Joseph is a "manly and sensible fellow." Aurélien Digeon, *Les Romans de Fielding* (Paris, 1923), esp. p. 76, spends more time on Joseph than other commentators, considering that "Il annonce déjà, par son humanité, le grand héros fieldingesque," but nevertheless thinks that "il [Joseph] reste la plupart du temps une figure amusante de jeune amoureux simple et franc, vigoreux au physique comme au moral." He also notes that Joseph comes to "tenir tête au pasteur Adams." Oliver Elton, *A Survey of English Literature* (New York, 1928), I, 192, is briefly favorable to Joseph, noting that he "is not ridicu-

erly his real significance in Fielding's design. Probably the burlesque of *Pamela* and the forceful presence of Parson Adams have been mainly responsible for deflecting attention from Joseph's serious role. Possibly, too, Fielding's quiet method of portraying his hero set him in disadvantageous balance with Adams. However, Joseph was clearly intended by Fielding to occupy a significant place in the total design. He is certainly as important as Adams and well justifies his name as title of the novel.

In the early part of *Joseph Andrews* it is true that Fielding has contrived to make Joseph somewhat of a joke in the frame of the burlesque of *Pamela*. There is, however, a clearly discernible point [91] at which Joseph manifests a decided change in appearance on the stage and begins to show a noticeable elevation in character, personality and general status in the thought and action of the novel. This turning point occurs in the scene at the inn in Book II, chapter 12, which is focused on a song that he sings in one room, while unknown to him, Fanny and Adams sit in the next and listen to the unknown singer. This scene, amusing and adroitly done within itself, is one of the best bits of light ironic writing in the novel and can stand independently as such; but Fielding uses it in addition as the basis for further irony and further fun in the plot and for important thematic development and character portrayal. At first glance it appears that the song serves merely as a musical interlude used as a means of recognition, but actually Fielding initiates threads which are woven out until the end of the novel, as he lays the basis for following scenes which parody the song in action and language. The broad context of this current of action is the burlesque of *Pamela*, particularly as the wholesome, natural, headlong affections of Joseph and Fanny which become evident after the song contrast so markedly with the calculated scheming of Pamela in her love life. The threads of plot and theme which Fielding develops out of this scene are also re-

lous" and that he is "approved by the author, and . . . at last made happy with his Fanny." He also makes the point that Joseph, unlike Pamela, is not "calculated in his virtue." In his recent illuminating study, *The Early Masters of English Fiction* (Lawrence, 1956), Professor A. D. McKillop does not take the occasion to say much about Joseph as a character.

lated to the jocular side of his treatment of Adams, for Adams figures prominently in the later scenes which parody the song and its enveloping action. Most important, however is Joseph's emergence from the episode in II, 12 no longer a male Pamela but the hero of *Joseph Andrews,* who becomes increasingly the Master of the Event. Since this scene is so important for the currents of action and theme which it initiates—and is so good in itself—it seems best here to analyze it in some detail as a basis for further discussion.

I

ON their journey back down to the country, Parson Adams is separated from Joseph who must travel by coach with Slipslop because of an injury to his leg. As Adams goes along, he rescues a young lady in distress, who turns out to be Joseph's sweetheart Fanny (II, 10). Temporarily detained in a justice's court by circumstances arising from this rescue (II, 11), Adams and Fanny are soon freed and continuing on their way are driven into a handy alehouse by a sudden shower of rain. Adams immediately finds a [92] place by the fire, orders a toast and ale and a pipe, and devotes himself to his Aeschylean meditations, while Fanny also takes a place by the fire, possibly to dream of Joseph, who she thinks is far, far away. Fielding, then, after advising readers "of an amorous hue" to skip the forthcoming paragraph, gives a long, full and lusciously detailed portrait of Fanny and her beauties, which might indeed affect readers of an amorous hue. At this point Fanny's attention is suddenly engaged by a song which begins in the next room. The lyric of this song is a smooth sliding pastoral, telling of the love of the shepherd Strephon and the nymph Chloe.

As Fanny listens perhaps she is too intent upon identifying the strangely familiar voice of the singer, or perhaps she lacks the polish of the town ladies to interpret the various puns as the song trills on to its exciting climax, or perhaps she has never been to the plays, whose gay songs so delighted the sophisticated. However, a close inspection of its lines reveals that this is a very, very naughty little piece, in the manner of Dryden's "Whilst Alexis lay pressed," from *Marriage à la Mode,* or "After the pangs of a desperate lover," from *An Evening's Love,* or many other similar plaints which gayly toy with amorous innuendos, such as the word "die," and the like. Pamela might well have noticed that something was wrong and commented primly; and Shamela could always spot a "paw word." But Fanny is intent on the singer.

The song begins innocuously enough as it movingly describes Strephon's distraction because of Chloe. But the second and third stanzas produce suspicion of what is to come by their prominently placed use of several dangerous words, which had developed quite specific double meanings in the poetry of witty ribaldry of the stage or in the drolleries, or the amorous fiction of Mrs. Manley. "Rapture," "possest," "joy," "torment," and "smart" in such a context bode ill. In the fourth stanza the absent Chloe herself is brought on the scene by a bevy of Loves and Graces, with Zephyrus speeding to greet her and lead her to Strephon:

> A thousand Loves dance in her train
> And Graces around her all throng.
> To meet her soft Zephyrus flies,
> And wafts all the sweets from the flowers. [93]

The last two stanzas bring about a remarkable reversal in Strephon's frustrated situation:

> My *soul,* whilst I gaze, is on *fire:*
> But her looks were so tender and kind
> My hope almost reach'd my *desire,*
> And left lame Despair far behind.
> *Transported* with madness, I flew,
> And eagerly seiz'd on my *bliss;*
> Her bosom but half she withdrew,
> But half she refus'd my fond kiss.
>
> Advances like this made me bold,
> I whisper'd her,—Love, we're alone—
> The rest let immortals unfold:
> No language can tell but their own.
> Ah, Chloe, *expiring,* I cried

How long I thy *cruelty* bore!
Ah, Strephon, she blushing replied,
You n'er was so pressing before.

The song thus concludes with a high flown version of the common innuendo, *expiring* for *dying*, to describe Strephon's triumph, but this conclusion has been cleverly led up to by the prominent and bountiful use of key words in the previous stanzas, "Rapture," "joy," "on fire," the apparently harmless but deceptive word "soul," "transported," and "bliss," all related to the same innuendo—Fielding has sprinkled his song liberally with these *outré* words not only for the ironic effect of the present scene but to leave them in the reader's attention in preparation for effects he intends to achieve later. Thus we must conclude that here is a very wicked and wanton song, whose lyrical narrative plays an adroitly arranged crescendo to a lamentable incident, which is a violation of all that Pamela Andrews risked her virtue to uphold, or Shamela her "vartue."

But, lo! when the identity of the hitherto anonymous singer of such a song is discovered, he is none other than Joseph Andrews, that same Pamela's brother, who so far has distinguished himself by his Pamelian conduct in his firm repulse of three pressing females. The incident of recogniton thus constitutes an ironic reversal. But Fielding is to develop the irony further almost in a double reversal. As soon as Fanny has recovered from her swoon, while Adams, subsuming the roles of the Loves and the Graces and Zephyrus, capers vigorously around the room (wafting the strong [94] whiff of pipe and ale instead of "all the sweets from the flowers"), Joseph and she enact an ecstatic amorous scene of fervent kisses and embraces, which comes near to matching that of Strephon and Chloe. Fanny, however, recovers herself and restraining "the impetuosity of her *transports*," pushes him decorously from her and refuses any further kisses or embraces for the time. In this scene Joseph has demonstrated himself to be as fiery and pressing as Strephon, and Fanny has been momentarily yielding but properly coy as Chloe had remained for a long time. Fielding has previously noted their warm affection in I, 11, but has given only the slightest hint of Joseph's fiery impetuosity. A second more definite hint of Joseph's high natural spirits occurs in the second letter to Pamela, reporting Lady Booby's second attempt, as he remarks that "I am glad she turned me out of the chamber as she did, for I had almost forgotten every word parson Adams had ever said to me" (I, 10). Both of these hints, however, Fielding has carefully submerged in the context of the burlesque of Pamela.

Coming as it does between the luscious and warming description of Fanny and the luscious and warming love scene of Joseph and Fanny, the song is adroitly and amusingly ironic in its sly reflection of their own situation, feelings, and actions. Joseph's impetuous rush upon Fanny reveals that he has more than a touch of Strephon's smarting pain and more than a little of Strephon's fiery nature. Joseph has sung his song of longing even as Strephon the thwarted shepherd, and just as Chloe suddenly appears to Strephon so does Fanny suddenly reappear into Joseph's life led, of course, by Adams. Further, the scene at the inn, song and all, sets the pattern for the amorous behavior between Joseph and Fanny in the rest of the novel; and in the numerous love scenes which ensue, to the amusement of readers and at times to the discomfiture of Adams, they reenact, up to a critical point, the drama and the emotions of the song, the critical boundary being rigorously set by the convention of matrimony. Fielding casts the love scenes very much in the manner of the song, in Joseph's Strephon-like impetuosity, and in Fanny's coy but compulsive response; and his language describing these scenes echoes the language of the song in the romantic highly pitched emotion, in the mock pastoral manner, and in the sly use of some of the dangerous words applied to their innocent situation. Their love affair follows closely, then, the pattern of the song and the mood of the song, up to the critical point. [95] Our Strephon will not press his Chloe as far as the shepherd in the song did beyond the convention of marriage, but he is very pressing to get this convention out of his way.

In effect, the first parody of the witty song comes in the love scene which immediately follows the lovers' recognition through the song. The second parody follows shortly. With eager warmth Joseph is so pressing with Fanny that only a few hours after their re-union, he has persuaded her, under the nose of the slumbering Adams to a marriage right then and there on the spot (II, 13), and the passage describing this action echoes the song, sometimes in very specific words:

> Let it suffice then to say, that Fanny, after a thousand entreaties, at last *gave up her whole soul to Joseph;* and almost fainting in his arms, wth a sigh infinitely softer and sweeter too than any Arabian breeze, she whispered to his lips, which were then close to hers, 'O, Joseph, you have won me; I will be yours forever.' Joseph having thanked her on his knees, and embraced her with an eagerness which she now almost returned, *leapt up in a rapture,* and awakened the parson, earnestly begging him that he would that instant join their hands together.

Adams, however, less tolerant than the Loves, the Graces and Zephyrus, is scandalized by such impetuosity and such disregard for the forms of the Church. He rebukes Joseph strongly, lectures him characteristically on the serious aspects of matrimony, and insists, with Fanny's complete agreement, that they must observe the ceremony of the publication of the banns. Rapture is near for our Strephon, but it must await the third bann.

Various other love scenes between Joseph and Fanny then follow, some of which Fielding coyly hints at, suggesting to the reader, from the background of the song and the previous descriptions, the full warmth generated, as in II, 15, when he comments on their passing the time while Adams is visiting Trulliber, and then in II, 16, as "they solaced themselves with amorous discourse," while Adams is arguing with the kindly host. These scenes are innocently reminiscent of "I whisper'd her,—Love we're alone—" Then when they are travelling along after leaving this hospitable inn, they must stop for rest as nightfall overtakes them (III, 2); and as they tarry, Adams sits apart lost in his meditations, so they are "alone" again:

> This was a circumstance, however, very favorable to Joseph; for Fanny, not suspicious of being overseen by Adams, gave a loose [96] to her passion which she had never done before, and, reclining her head on his bosom, threw her arm carelessly round him, and suffered him to lay his cheek close to hers. All this infused such happiness into Joseph, that he would not have changed his turf for the finest down in the finest palace in the universe.

After they reach Somersetshire, Joseph and Fanny do not have much time together, and so the love scenes cease.

At the end of the novel the story of Joseph and Fanny just as that of Strephon and Chloe at the end of the song finally culminates in joy and rapture, as they are married with much merry making at which Adams, now a genially approving amalgam of the Loves, the Graces, and Zephyrus, whose spirits have been borne aloft by the happiness of the occasion and by an abundance of ale and pudding, gives "a loose to more facetiousness than was usual to him." The final note of the song is echoed as Fanny in the bloom of beauty is taken to bed, and Joseph rushes "with the utmost eagerness to her," and a "minute carried him to her arms." So Strephon finally wins his Chloe—and the rest let immortals unfold.

II

THE scene of the song at the inn not only establishes the pattern for one line of action which parodies the song in such a way as to allow for further strokes in the enrichment of the portrayal of Adams, to develop the contrasts with Pamela, and to afford the emergence of Joseph's amorous fire and impetuosity; more importantly it also marks the point of change in the appearance of Joseph in the thought and action so that he is treated on more serious levels of meaning, and it initiates a line of action which is to carry him to a dignity and a stature and an elevation of personality far beyond the original limitations imposed by the burlesque mode. After the scene at the inn, Joseph begins to appear with a poise, dignity, shrewdness and wisdom, and a courteous independence, which show up more and more in the novel leading to the conclusion when he settles down to run his estate, happily married to Fanny but without the false notions about himself that his erstwhile sister Pamela has developed upon her rise in the social scale. Still deferential to Adams, he nevertheless comes to maintain his own views against him in the discussion of ideas and in the making of arrangements, and he is used by Fielding to comment upon Adams' foibles. [97] Since he is not selfish, acquisitive, or hypocritical himself, but displays much of the innocence of the good-natured man, he is a good agent to comment upon Adams' unworldliness, an unworldliness which in most people would be fatal.

Fielding at times also uses Joseph to express his own views, as he could not have used Adams. In his actions Parson Adams exemplifies much of the view of life that Fielding is expounding, but he could not remain in character and be a mouthpiece. But in his later appearances Joseph is an excellent agent and is so used to some extent. Fielding's portrayal of the good-natured man was to change considerably in his later novels, so that he laid less emphasis on innocence, naiveté, or eccentricity and more on the wisdom and realism that should accompany goodness. Squire Allworthy is a wiser man than Parson Adams, and Dr. Harrison a wiser man than both. In the latter part of *Joseph Andrews,* Joseph shows a measure of the realistic, practical wisdom and social balance that Fielding must have come to consider necessary before he created Allworthy and Harrison.

Joseph's new appearance is no sudden inartistic trick of the author's, for Fielding has actually laid down several quiet hints and clues along in the early chapters. But these hints are not immediately striking, and it is only by reading back and disregarding the burlesque of *Pamela* that the reader sees their full import. Further, Joseph's increase in dignity and stature always remains within the frame of the mock heroic manner and in the ironic context of the satire. He is so inextricably enmeshed in the activities of Adams and in the rollicking treatment of this great character that he is unavoidably touched or colored by the episodes, mock heroic or picaresque, as in the mock epic Battle of the Canines. Thus as Fielding raises Joseph in stature, he nevertheless still has some fun at his expense; his treatment is not so serious as to deaden the fun.

In Book I and the early chapters of Book II, Joseph, either from the situation, action, or Fielding's comments, always appears in a laughable light, which, however, is not pejorative, as is true in the case of Shamela, or Pamela in her later appearance in this novel. Whatever one thinks of Joseph as a paragon of male chastity (and I suspect that the usual explanation that his affections are [98] already fixed on Fanny is not a good one), he is not portrayed as a hypocrite like Shamela or Pamela,[2] and his change into a young man of high physical spirits is an amusing but wholesome natural phenomenon. After all Parson Adams has six children, and Mrs. Adams openly avers that she has never had any complaints about his affection for her (IV, 8). At the first of the novel, Joey, because of the sweetness of his voice, fails as birdkeeper and kennel whipper-in, and is translated to stable boy, where he is so successful that upon becoming seventeen he is made footboy to Lady Booby and entrusted with such manly duties as standing behind her chair, carrying her prayerbook to church and singing psalms with the beautiful voice that had charmed the birds and the dogs into ruining the hunt. The description of Joseph's singing here has some function and articulation in the plot, too, as a preparation for his song later by the inn fireside, so that his beautiful singing should be no surprise, nor Fanny's recognition, since she has heard it so often before; and although jocularly treated here this gift could be one of the graces of a gentleman.

Joseph has attracted the interest of Parson Adams in the course of his instruction by the parson, and in the early part of the novel he is so deferential to Adams as to be subservient. Later it will be one of the signs of his growth that, still deferential except for one instance of extreme provocation, he will nevertheless dare to support his own opinions against this forceful and venerable man. Fielding gives a hint of his future plans for Joseph amid the early irony and jocularity at his expense in I, 3, when Joseph gives Adams an account of his independent and self-directed reading, amusing at the time in its inclusion of the *Whole Duty of Man* (which we recall was a favorite of Shamela) but still giving a hint of Joseph's independence of mind and of his search for a wider view of things and laying the basis for his sense and balance on later occasions. Next, in London Joseph is amusingly presented as he attends so closely yet so innocently upon Lady Booby with the scandalous whispers of Ladies Tittle and Tattle hissing in the background. However, he has been getting experience in his town sojourn, which later will help him to interpret action and character, as in the

[2] As Elton has pointed out; cf. note 3.

case of the generous gentleman—and he has had enough sparkishness to learn the popular wittily naughty songs of the day. And then after the death of Sir Thomas Booby, Joseph appears in [99] an even more laughable light as he resists Lady Booby's first advances and immediately writes Pamela a horrified letter, of whose tone she might well have been proud, and soon after he is nearly so rudely forced by Slipslop. Then Lady Booby returns to the game in I, 8, when Joseph in desperation—and to her shock and amazement—proclaims his "virtue," as he reports in another horrified letter to Pamela, in which he admits, however, his awareness of Lady Booby's charms; and it seems to be not his faithfulness to Fanny as much as his loyalty to Pamela and fear of Adams that has stood him in stead here.

Joseph, then, through the wrath of Lady Booby is started on his journey from London to the country, a mildly and comically allegorical journey, which is to result in his triumph. There is still left some of the phase wherein he is an object of laughter. The ironic satire still includes him in its fun, and he still carries on as a male Pamela. On the road he is beaten and left for dead, naked beside the road—later he will give a much better account of himself in fights, but here it is necessary that he lose. There follows some amusing action, the horror of the young lady at the sight of a naked man, the activity about getting him clothed, the remarks of the wit which embarrass Joseph more than they do any of the other occupants of the coach, his inhospitable reception at the Dragon (I, 12), his affirmation of male chastity and of his loyalty to his sister's ideals in a monologue which leads Parson Barnabas to think that he is out of his mind (I, 13), and finally the assault by Betty which so vigorously threatens his virtue (I, 18). The burlesque of *Pamela* is still evident in this last scene not only in the assault but in the device of lofty moral statement which accompanies it. After Joseph has successfully repulsed Betty and locked her out of his room, Fielding interpolates the remark, "How ought a man to rejoice, that his chastity is always in his own power; that if he hath sufficient strength of mind, he hath always a competent strength of body to defend himself, and cannot like a poor weak woman, be ravished against his will." This interpolation is a parody of the occasional moralistic pronouncements or sayings of Pamela about the ways of the world in Richardson's novel. After one of Squire B—'s attempts at her virtue has failed, Pamela (Letter XI) writes, "O how poor and mean must those actions be, and how little must they make the best of gentlemen look when they offer such things as are unworthy of themselves, and put it into the [100] power of their inferiors to be greater than they." In *Shamela* Fielding parodies these sayings by putting some of Shamela's best remarks into this form. With the incident of Betty, the parody of Joseph as a male Pamela ceases, and the ridiculous tone treating his actions almost disappears. He is caught with the bill for the horse's feed, which Adams has forgotten to pay, and he has a clumsy fall from a horse, which injures his leg. Although the fall from the horse is a comic episode, this injury is mainly a plot device to keep him separated from Adams for a time and thus to motivate the surprise meeting later in the inn. One small incident in their departure from the Dragon, however, is of some significance. It is Joseph who discovers that Adams does not have his sermons with him. This incident gives the first hint of Joseph's later change of status in relation to Adams.

Joseph begins to show a markedly different appearance soon after they leave the inn where he sang the song, and this is illustrated in the next incident. At the next stop they meet an apparently generous gentleman who offers Adams a three hundred pound living, lodgings for them all in his house for a couple of days, and the use of his coach and horses for a part of their journey (II, 16). In a burst of enthusiasm for such rare Christian charity, Adams accepts these offers, but in a series of events the gentleman eases out of every promise and in addition, it turns out, leaves them a score to pay for drinks. Adams is completely deceived, but Joseph soon realizes that they are being duped; and generally throughout this episode he displays good sense, good humor, and even wit.

The gentleman suddenly recollects first, just as he is leaving for home, that he cannot lodge them because his housekeeper has locked up all of his rooms and all of the linen, but he promises them his horses the next morning. When the travelers arise early to await the horses, Joseph has a difference of opinion with Adams as to whether Fanny should ride behind himself (II, 16), or as Adams demands, behind the gentleman's servant, since he says that Joseph is not to be trusted, "being weaker than he imagined himself to be"—Adams has not forgotten Joseph's fiery haste to have the marriage ceremony performed on the spot without benefit of banns. Although Adams is firm, Joseph is equally firm with his old preceptor that Fanny should be his riding partner. The dispute, which becomes more and more fierce, is saved from catastrophic developments by the arrival of a message from the gentleman [101] that his groom unknown to himself had put his whole stable under a course of physic, so that he could not furnish the horses. Whereupon Adams, bursting into expressions of sympathy for this good-natured man who is so badly treated by his servants, further wonders if in addition his butler had not locked up his cellar the night before and thus forced him to visit the inn. But Joseph realistically is concerned as to how they can depart from the inn without any money to pay their bill. Taking one more chance on the gentleman, he advises Adams to write him for a loan. The messenger's long delay in returning leads Joseph ironically to venture that the gentleman's steward may have locked up his purse; but Adams does not notice the irony. When the news comes that the gentleman has gone away for a month and Adams bemoans his failure to borrow the money the night before, Joseph "smiling" answers that he was very much deceived "if the gentleman would not have found some excuse to avoid lending it." Joseph then explains some of the tricks that gentlemen use to forestall suitors and callers whom they wish to avoid. Adams, horrified by such chicanery, begins against these dishonest practices a lecture which might have detained their party for an untold time if Joseph had not realistically called him back to the problem of getting out of the inn. On this occasion the innkeeper kindly helps them, and eventually they set on their way. Throughout this whole episode Joseph's new bearing is noteworthy.

In the next incident at Mr. Wilson's Joseph is inconspicuous, presumably because Fielding did not want to connect Joseph and Wilson at this time in any fashion which might tip off the surprise ending. His sleeping through Wilson's story and missing the clue of the strawberry birthmark is necessary for the plot, and as a matter of verisimilitude, he is normally weary and in need of sleep and further is lacking the incentive to stay awake since Fanny is asleep in the bedroom with Mrs. Wilson. When they get back on the road the next morning, Adams produces a tirade against the public schools for their breeding of wickedness and proclaims that Wilson's troubles all came from his having a public school education rather than the morally straightening private schooling (III, 5). Joseph, although deferential, disagrees with him by defending the public schools, cites the example of his own good master, Sir Thomas Booby, as a fine type of public school man, and, on the other hand, recalls several privately taught country gentlemen who [102] were nevertheless "as wicked as if they had known the world from their infancy." Joseph is probably thinking of some of the prototypes of the squire in Gay's *Birth of the Squire*. Adams is in forceful talking fettle; consequently, Joseph retires, but on the plane of reasonable argument and truth to society and nature, he has made an excellent case, impervious as Adams may be. That Fielding is siding with Joseph here is confirmed by the immediately following episode,[3] for he introduces in close juxtaposition the story of the merry squire, who plays nasty jokes on Adams (still nasty even if Adams maintains his dignity) and later tries to kidnap Fanny in order to seduce her, or rape her, if persuasion fails (III, 6,7,9). Fielding makes a special point in III, 7 of giving a detailed character sketch of the squire in which he explicitly describes his private education "at his own home under the care of his mother and a tutor," and he follows the character sketch with the lengthy account of the squire's irresponsible and at times evil actions against Adams and Fanny. Thus it is clear that he intends Joseph's arguments with Adams to have a serious significance in the thought of the novel, and that Joseph's intellectual stature is growing. It is also clear that Joseph is gradually taking over the guidance and direction of the

[3] Cross, *History of Henry Fielding*, I, 42ff. has described Fielding's life at Eton, his happiness there and its lasting effect upon himself and his views of education which are pertinent here.

expedition, for it is he who brings them to a stop for eating, and after Adams has found the gold piece which Wilson had quietly slipped into their basket of provisions, he convinces him that it was not a mistake but an intentional gift to help them and thus persuades him not to make a trip back to return it.

As they sit after their refreshment, so generously supplied by Wilson, Joseph, with an assurance not previously displayed in Adams' presence, is fittingly led to deliver a discourse on charity (III, 6). His discourse, although at times somewhat illiterately expressed (as his calling Veronese "Varnish," Carraci "Scratchi," and Hogarth "Hogarthi," and his referring to "Squire Pope"), is nevertheless intended by Fielding to be read on a serious level. With feeling and good sense, Joseph expounds Fielding's own views about charity and its manifestation in charitable acts. He touches briefly upon the expressed subject of the novel, as he exclaims "I defy the wisest man in the world to turn a good action into ridicule. [103] I defy him to do it." But Joseph's discussion of charity as it includes also reaches beyond Affectation and the Ridiculous as they were defined in the author's preface. He defines charity, gives instances of it, criticises its lack in rich people and their misuse of their wealth in false taste and bad spirit. The theme of *charity* is a dominant one in *Joseph Andrews*, which Fielding develops throughout with considerable complexity, in numerous aspects and gradations, usually in the actions or statements, charitable or uncharitable, of the characters. Although, in accordance with the preface, Affectation, Hypocrisy, or the Ridiculous, are important springs of action and appearance in the novel, Fielding has developed the concept of charity in its own independent entity, even if often he treats it in relation to these other traits. He has developed his theme of charity in many strands both positively, by the postillion, by Betty, by the friendly innkeeper, by Wilson, by the pedlar, and of course, by Adams, and antithetically by various of the riders in the first coach, by Mrs. Towwouse, Trulliber, Slipslop, the merry squire, and others. Thus he is making Joseph the explicit spokesman for an important theme which elsewhere he has been presenting in action and has generally been rendering rather than expounding. The seriousness and depth of Joseph's discourse are further revealed as Fielding puts into his mouth praise of people whom he himself considered examples of the noblest practice of charity. When Fanny asks whether all the great folks are wicked (we are beginning to wonder if they are not), Joseph answers:

> Some gentlemen of our cloth report charitable notions done by their lords and masters; and I have heard Squire Pope, the great poet, at my lady's table, tell stories of a man that lived at a place called Ross, and another at Bath, one Al-Al- I forget his name, but it is in the book of verses. The gentleman hath built up a house, too, which the squire likes very well; but his charity is seen farther than his house, though it stands on a hill,—, ay, and brings him more honour too. It was his charity that put him in the book, where the squire says he puts all those who deserve it. . . .

The two examples of charity are, of course, John Kyrle, the Man of Ross and Ralph Allen, whom Pope praised for their charity, respectively, in *Moral Essays,* III, 250–90, and *Epilogue to the Satires,* Dial. I, 135–36. Fielding, who had good reason to know of Allen's vast charities, later used him as a partial model for Squire Allworthy. [104]

Then in the immediately following mock heroic battle with the pack of hunting dogs, although Adams as usual is the focus for this kind of rough high jinks, Fielding has some fun with Joseph, too, describing in epic detail the provenance, career, and appearance of his staff with which he depletes the squire's kennel so terribly and narrating with ironic color his heroic actions in the fray. Even so, in the mock heroic frame Joseph acquits himself solidly and effectively without losing stature, and the squire retreats because of his performance. At the squire's dinner Joseph retires from the limelight for Adams, and we only see him upon their departure as he brandishes his illustrious staff menacingly at the servants. Next in the abduction of Fanny by the captain and his helpers, there is a *bona fide* fight in which he performs admirably, albeit with a touch of picaresque slapstick in some of the weapons he uses, and he is quelled only by a lucky blow which renders him unconscious, so that the captain escapes with Fanny.

After he has regained his consciousness in the next scene (III,

11), as he talks with Adams, he reveals a natural turmoil and anxiety about Fanny and despair at losing her, possibly forever, but Fielding does not joke with his disconsolation or make it ridiculous, except that in addition to the loss of his beloved he must listen to a long lecture by Adams on the use of reason to learn patience and submission in these circumstances. He is not comforted by Adams' dilation upon the beauties and virtues of the girl whom he has lost or upon the dangers to which she is now exposed, but he shows up well during the scene, endeavoring out of deference to Adams to overcome his despair. This scene looks forward to the later episode during which he is listening to another lecture on, among other things, submission to adversity, when the news is brought of the drowning of Adams' youngest child. A comparison of these two scenes shows Joseph's growth during the interim.

In the meantime Fanny is rescued and the captain apprehended, and they are brought to the inn, where Joseph exhibits proper manhood by beating up the captain. When all three resume their journey to Somersetshire, it is noteworthy that Joseph now has Fanny as his riding partner without any fuss, while Adams quietly gets into the coach with Pounce. [105]

III

DOWN in the country, Joseph shows further poise, balance, dignity, and good sense, which gain force in his now higher social status. Here he meets his severest pressures from experience, primarily in the most serious obstacles encountered yet to his marriage with Fanny and in the possible temptation in his new status to break with old acquaintances and submit to the Booby's plans for his social advancement. His behavior in all of these circumstances is admirable. In Book IV Fielding keeps the frame of the mock heroic and the ironic satire, still introduces scenes of picaresque hurly-burly, and returns to the burlesque of *Pamela* with some rare touches at the expense of Pamela and the Squire, but he almost entirely discards these techniques as regards Joseph and Fanny, except for the episode with Didapper's servant, and possibly Joseph's blow at Didapper in Adams' house. Nor is

Joseph so enmeshed in Adams' activities as before; consequently, the hurly-burly does not affect him much. Joseph and Fanny figure only slightly in the nocturnal rumpus involving Didapper, Slipslop and Adams, except that after Adams is found in Fanny's bed Joseph behaves toward him with a restraint and understanding which reflect his own balance and good sense. However, Fielding is not over-serious with Joseph in Book IV, occasionally presenting him in an amusing light to keep the fun going, but without using him to burlesque Richardson.

First, through Lady Booby's scheming, which Lawyer Scout carries to greater lengths than she had intended, Joseph and Fanny are both arrested, brought before the justice, and sentenced to Bridewell, with particularly dire prospects for Fanny as well as the possibility of separation for them both. Beyond the justice's attraction toward Fanny, Fielding makes no attempt to make fun of Joseph and Fanny, as he had done in previous scenes even when they were in trouble. The happy arrival of Squire Booby and Pamela in Somersetshire saves them, for the squire gets them released under his guardianship. Booby then brings his own clothes to dress Joseph, and although Joseph (unlike Pamela) is careful to select "the plainest dress he could find," he nevertheless "looked so genteel, that no person would have doubted its being adapted to his quality as his shape." Joseph has now become a gentleman outwardly as well as inwardly, and, without the snobbery of Pamela, [106] distinguishes himself by the bearing and dignity that a gentleman should have (he lapses from this dignity notably when he swats Didapper for making advances to Fanny!). He is so prepossessing in his new fashion that Lady Booby bursts into new flames so fierce that now she even considers him as a matrimonial possibility.

Next, in a significant interview, Mr. Booby and Pamela bring heavy pressure upon Joseph to give up Fanny for a match more suitable to his new station. But he refuses their demands, avowing his love, respect, and loyalty for Fanny and his determination to have her only. In this interview his manners are dignified and courteous; although firm, he is not clumsy or boorish in his refusal. This scene is a counterpart of the interview which Adams has held with Lady Booby about the banns, wherein with dignity and courtesy he refuses to deny the banns whatever his earthly jeopardy. When Joseph leaves the interview with the Boobys, he comes by accident upon Fanny in the evil grip of Didapper's servant, whom he routs after a fierce battle, in which he acquits himself nobly even if a few teeth are shaken.

The circumstances of the interview with the squire and Pamela and the ensuing perilous escape of Fanny give Joseph a deep concern about her, on the one hand from a fear of the interference of the Boobys and on the other a fear of future incidents like the attempt of Didapper's servant. His prophetic fears are justified soon after, too, by Didapper himself who undertakes a nocturnal excursion after Fanny, which, however, leads him instead into Slipslop's bed and concludes with the surprising discovery of Parson Adams in Fanny's bed the next morning. In his illuminating analysis of this episode, Professor McKillop, *Early Masters*, p. 114, has said that "Joseph and Fanny are as usual innocently passive." Professor McKillop's comment is in the main true as regards Fanny but it seems to me that Fielding gives Joseph increased force of personality and increased stature. He holds Joseph from participating in the hurly-burly to keep him from being ridiculous, because he wants to maintain Joseph's dignity—Joseph is definitely out of the frame of either the Pamelian burlesque or picaresque high jinks. When Joseph does come into the episode the next morning in Fanny's room where Adams is discovered slumbering peacefully, he is far from innocently passive but is quite positive and dominating. He [107] first strongly interrogates Adams how he came into Fanny's room, then "in a rage" he sharply questions Fanny "hath he offered any rudeness to you." Back in II, 13, Fanny was overwhelmed by Adams and shifted ground from her support to Joseph's desire for immediate matrimony to her agreement with Adams that this was a most improper request, and Joseph at this point was somewhat humbled by Adams and could not push her farther. But now when she sees Joseph holding a strong line toward Adams, she holds a mighty prim one herself. However, Joseph's old respect for Adams and his own balance and good sense which he has been displaying increasingly prevent him from any headlong conclusions, so that he allows Adams to give his own version of what has happened. But it is Joseph who comprehends what has actually happened and how Adams made his mistake, and he explains to Adams that "It was plain that he had mistaken, by turning to the right instead of the left." Adams, for once, agrees immediately without arguing, and the scene is over. When Joseph leads him away to his room, this action symbolizes Joseph's ascendency. Throughout this incident Joseph has held the upper hand, and Adams is on the down side and backing up.

After this incident, motivated now not just by his strong physical passion for Fanny but also by his genuine concern for her safety, Joseph asks Adams if he might obtain a license and have the marriage performed at once. Adams, of course, misses the point and, now recovered from his psychological dip of the early morning, begins a strong and lengthy lecture on the evils of carnality in marriage and of the necessity for curbing one's passions and for learning patience and submission to the divine will. At the height of his exhortations, the news that his youngest child has been drowned throws him into a tantrum of grief, from which his own teachings now warmly expounded by Joseph cannot relieve him. Upon the discovery that the child is alive, Adams immediately resumes, as if without interruption, his lecture to Joseph, whose patience is now exhausted so that he argues stoutly with Adams, protesting the propriety of his devotion to Fanny and of love between man and wife. Adams is setting off on another lecture on the evils of over-fondness for a wife, but Mrs. Adams comes to Joseph's aid by roundly berating her husband for preaching such doctrine and threatening to burn any such sermon that he has in the house. She strongly proclaims that Adams has loved her satis[108]factorily. This argument is going very much Joseph's way against Adams, but it is interrupted by a visit from Lady Booby.

The next unfortunate turn for Joseph comes when it appears that he and Fanny are brother and sister. This blow he bears with stoic dignity, although with the keenest pain, and again Fielding narrates this part straight without joking at him. But, as we know, all ends happily, and we get our last glance of him living in bliss with Fanny and refusing to publish any account of his new high life.

Thus it is clear that Fielding, however much fun he has at Joseph's expense, particularly in the early stages of the Pamelian burlesque, is treating him in a serious manner and with serious aims. He gives Joseph his share of the serious burden of the novel as well as the jocular, and in some instances Joseph is his spokesman as well as a counterbalance to Parson Adams, such as was lacking in *Don Quixote* for the Don. Whatever his original plan for Joseph was, in the actual fabric of the novel he describes in Joseph a noticeable and sympathetic change and development of character into maturity. From Joey, the beautiful singer, and from Joseph the footman who is a paragon of male chastity, Fielding has brought Joseph Andrews a long way. Even against the engrossing figure of Adams, he has given Joseph a personality of his own, a stature and force and meaning in the novel, which contribute to its thought and richness of characterization. [109]

from

THE MORAL BASIS of FIELDING'S ART: A STUDY of *JOSEPH ANDREWS*

Martin Battestin

BY now it should be clear that *Joseph Andrews* has from the start a surprisingly intricate design of its own—a pattern broadly allegorical, correlating theme and form and shaped by the Christian purpose of its author. But our analysis is not yet complete. Located at the heart of the book, the long biography of Mr. Wilson needs to be reckoned with.

Source: Martin Battestin, *The Moral Basis of Fielding's Art: A Study of Joseph Andrews* (Middletown, Conn.: Wesleyan University Press, 1959), pp. 118–29.

Fielding, of course, had ample precedent for the insertion of "irrelevant" tales into the midst of his narrative. The practice was common to every narrator from Homer [118] and Apuleius to Cervantes and Le Sage. In *Tom Jones* (V, 1), in fact, Fielding devised his own esthetic to defend the novelist's right to digress—"the art of contrast," he called it. Unlike their modern detractors, Fielding and his fellow writers did not *over*value unity of structure; to them the principles of variety and contrast were equally appealing.[1] Yet we do an injustice to the complex craftsmanship of a skillful artist if we let the case for the Wilson episode rest here. It can be defended as well on grounds more congenial to our own times.

Most critics, however, look upon Wilson's story as another flaw—the most serious and glaring of all—in the random architecture of *Joseph Andrews*. F. Homes Dudden's objection that Fielding's digressions, and particularly the Wilson episode, "can hardly be justified on artistic grounds" is typical: "Wilson's history, indeed, comprises some matter relevant to the plot," he allows, ". . . but it would have been definitely an advantage had the greater part of it been omitted."[2] Admittedly, though they do lend the spice of variety to the narrative and though their themes of vanity and false love and marriage are pertinent to the novel as a whole, it is questionable whether the stories of Leonora (II, 4, 6) and Leonard and Paul (IV, 10) are worth the telling. Far from being a needless or irrelevant interpolation,

[1] Cf. H. V. S. Ogden, "The Principles of Variety and Contrast in Seventeenth Century Aesthetics, and Milton's Poetry," *JHI*, X (1949), 159–182.

[2] Homes Dudden, *Henry Fielding: His Life, Works, and Times* (Oxford, 1952), I, 352. Several critics, of course, have made incidental attempts to justify the Wilson episode. In his recent monograph, John Butt briefly noticed one important function of the Wilson episode and its bearing on the novel as a whole: "Vanity of vanities is Mr. Wilson's theme." Since Fielding's action confines him to the highway, Professor Butt further observes, Wilson's story provides the opportunity to satirize the city. (*Fielding*, "Writers and Their Work," No. 57 [London, 1954], p. 18.) My own views of the function of the Wilson episode are in accord with Professor Butt's analysis, so far as it goes. The latest effort to explain the episodes in the novel is an article by I. B. Cauthen, Jr., "Fielding's Digressions in *Joseph Andrews*," *College English* 17 (April 1956), 379–82. Cauthen's observation that "these stories unmask the vices of hypocrisy and vanity in courtship, in marriage, and in the life of the rake" is, of course, true, but much too superficial.

however, the Wilson episode is essential. It stands as the philosophic, as well as structural, center of *Joseph Andrews*, comprising a kind of synecdochic epitome of the meaning and movement of the novel. Practically speaking as well, in a book whose satiric subject is vanity, provision had to be made for a long look at London, always for Fielding the symbol of *vanitas vanitatum*. Parson Adams, whose wayfaring is confined to the country, must be [119] exposed to and permitted to comment on the affectations of the Great City. Wilson's story thus serves, economically, as a narrative version of what is dramatically, and therefore more effectively, presented in the final third of *Tom Jones*. *Joseph Andrews* represents the moral pilgrimage of its hero, guided by the good counsel and example of his spiritual father, Abraham Adams, from the folly and vice of London toward reunion in the country with the chaste and loving Fanny Goodwill. The digression focuses and moralizes this movement by depicting Wilson's progress—nearly disastrous because "without a Guide"—through the corrupting vanities of the town to a life of wisdom, love, and contentment in a setting reminiscent of the Golden Age. Under proper tutelage, Joseph has escaped the moral contamination of Wilson's London period and may profit from his hard-earned wisdom. The meaning of both the digression and the novel as a whole is largely a variation on the themes of Ecclesiastes, Juvenal's *Third Satire*, and Virgil's *Second Georgic*, controlled throughout, of course, by the doctrine of charity.

As an alternative to the immorality of the great world, Fielding early establishes the ideals of chaste love and marriage and a simple, useful life of retirement. The first half of this antithesis relates to a recurring motif in his writings, what A. R. Towers has called "a literary programme designed to glorify the pleasures of conjugal love" [3] and culminating in *Amelia*. For Fielding, "the two principal Female Characters [are] that of Wife, and that of Mother," [4] and in the novels he embodies this ideal in Mrs. Wilson, Mrs. Heartfree, Amelia, and—by last-

[3] Towers, "*Amelia* and the State of Matrimony," *RES*, New Series, V (1954), 145.

[4] *The Covent-Garden Journal*, No. 57 (August 1, 1752); Jensen ed., II, 73.

page implication—in Fanny and Sophia. In the fugitive poem "To a Friend on the Choice of a Wife," he defines his [120] ideal at some length, and many of the features of this portrait reappear in the good women of the novels. A true wife, he feels, must attend to the useful domestic duties and must be a good-natured, sensible, and loving companion, yet willing to submit to the superior judgment of her husband. Speaking, perhaps, with the pattern of Charlotte Cradock in mind—"one from whom I draw all the solid comfort of my life"—Fielding conceives of marriage to such a woman as a necessary ingredient of earthly contentment: "If fortune gives thee such a wife to meet, / Earth cannot make thy blessing more complete." [5] This is more effusively borne out by Letter XLIV, which Fielding contributed to his sister's *Familiar Letters between the Principal Characters in David Simple:*

> "Now, in my eye, [writes Valentine to Cynthia] love appears alone capable of bestowing on us this highest degree of human felicity. I solemnly declare, when I am in passion of my wife . . . my happiness wants no addition. I think I may aver, it could receive none. I conceive myself then to be the happiest of mankind. I am sure I am as happy as it is possible for me to be." [6]

Fielding's conception of the highest earthly happiness thus combines the ideas of chaste conjugal love and, as we have seen, a simple country life dissociated from the luxury, avarice, and ambition of the great world. This ideal, depicted in the account of Wilson's mode of life (III, 4), is first represented in *The Champion* (February 26, 1739/40) as Fielding contrasts the vanities of existence in the house of "a certain person of great distinction" with the quiet, affectionate, self-sufficient life of a country clergyman. "I am convinced," Fielding comments, "that [121] happiness does not always sit on the pinnacle of power, or lie in a bed of state; but is rather to be found in that golden mean which Horace prescribes in the motto of my paper."

But let us have a closer look at the Wilson episode and its place in the novel. On one level, what Fielding is attempting

[5] Preface to the *Miscellanies;* Henley ed., XII, 247.
[6] Henley ed., XVI, 48.

in the history of Mr. Wilson is a prose version of Hogarth's "progress" pieces. Specifically, the analogy between *The Rake's Progress* and Wilson's account of his London days is inescapable.[7] The reason for this parallelism is not hard to find. In the Preface to *Joseph Andrews* Fielding virtually identifies Hogarth's conception of the comic art and his own. Even more to the point, however, is his great admiration for the moral utility of his friend's satiric prints, especially, "the Rake's and the Harlot's Progress":

> I esteem the ingenious Mr. Hogarth as one of the most useful satirists any age hath produced. In his excellent works you see the delusive scene exposed with all the force of humour, and, on casting your eyes on another picture, you behold the dreadful and fatal consequence. I almost dare affirm that those two works of his, which he calls the Rake's and the Harlot's Progress, are calculated more to serve the cause of virtue, and for the preservation of mankind, than all the folios of morality which have been ever written; and a sober family should no more be without them, than without the Whole Duty of Man in their house.[8]

Though the charity of Harriet Hearty saves him from Tom Rakewell's horrid end, the fictional tableau of Wilson's career as a beau and freethinker is a clear reflection of what Hogarth had done more graphically. [122]

The story of Mr. Wilson, however, is much more than an imitation of Hogarth. Its function within the novel gives it a direction and complexity of its own. As with *Joseph Andrews* as a whole, vanity of vanities is the message of Wilson's progress through London society, his hard-earned wisdom through adversity, and his retirement to a life according to the classical ideal. Although Fielding's talent is not well suited to the novel of analysis, in its personal application Wilson's story is essentially one of moral education and regeneration of the type Fielding undertook in treating the predicament of Captain Booth in *Amelia*. While the emphasis throughout is on the exposure of

[7] The similarities between the careers of Wilson and Tom Rakewell have been pointed out in some detail by Robert Etheridge Moore, *Hogarth's Literary Relationships* (Minneapolis, 1948), pp. 124–125.

[8] *The Champion*, June 10, 1740; Henley ed., XV, 331.

fashionable folly and vice, Fielding is careful to suggest the moral dimension, tracing Wilson's spiritual degradation to its source in irreligion and a faulty education. Unlike Joseph Andrews, Wilson has not had the benefit of Parson Adams' good counsel: to his "early Introduction into Life, without a Guide," he remarks, "I impute all my future Misfortunes" (III, 3). Bad standards of education, Fielding later declares in two numbers of *The Covent-Garden Journal*, Nos. 42 and 56 (May 26 and July 25, 1752), are responsible for the prevalence of modern vanity and affectation; they are the true source of the Ridiculous. In *The True Patriot*, No. 13 (January 21–28, 1746), Parson Adams and Mr. Wilson, after observing the profligacy, francophilism, and irreligion of a young "Bowe," agree upon its causes. Adams' remarks pertain as well to Wilson's biography:

> In discoursing upon this Subject, we imputed much of the present Profligacy to the notorious Want of Care in Parents in the Education of Youth, who, as my Friend informs me, with very little School Learning, and not at all instructed (*ne minime* [123] *quidem imbuti*) in any Principles of Religion, Virtue and Morality, are brought to the Great City, or sent to travel to other Great Cities abroad, before they are twenty Years of Age; where they become their own Masters, and enervate both their Bodies and Minds with all Sorts of Diseases and Vices, before they are adult.

Wilson's spiritual impasse is also placed in a Christian context recalling the arguments for free will and the operation of Providence as against Fortune in Boethius' *Consolation of Philosophy* and the homilies. His brief flirtation with the "Rule-of-Right" club of deists and Hobbesian atheists is indicative of his state of mind. By blinding himself to the "Principles of Religion" and the operation of Providence, Wilson becomes caught up in the machinery of Fortune. "Prosperity" changes to "Adversity," and he sinks to a nadir of despair. Wilson's description of the principles of the club of deists and political philosophers to which he subscribed illustrates the nature of his problem:

> These Gentlemen were engaged in a Search after Truth, in the Pursuit of which they threw aside all the Prejudices of Education, and governed themselves only by the infallible Guide of Hu-

> man Reason. This great Guide, after having shown them the Falsehood of that very antient but simple Tenet, that there is such a Being as a Deity in the Universe, helped them to establish in His stead a certain "Rule of Right," by adhering to which they all arrived at the utmost Purity of Morals. Reflection made me as much delighted with this Society as it had taught me to despise and detest the former [i.e., a club of carousers]. I began now to esteem myself a Being of a higher Order than I had ever before conceived; and was the more charmed with this Rule of Right, as I really found in my own [124] Nature nothing repugnant to it. I held in utter Contempt all Persons who wanted any other inducement to Virtue besides her intrinsick Beauty and Excellence. (III, 3)

Wilson's disillusionment with "this delightful Dream" is occasioned by the inability of his philosopher companions to translate their theories into practice without the compelling incentives of religion. For the Christian precept of charity, they substituted their own inadequate imperative, and their immoral "Practices, so inconsistent with our golden Rule, made me begin to suspect its Infallibility." Breaking with this company and its principles, however, Wilson as yet could find no spiritually sustaining substitute: the society of poets he then frequents only proves to him the general prevalence of vanity, "the worst of Passions, and more apt to contaminate the Mind than any other"; it does not relieve his "State of Solitude."

The change from Wilson's "prosperous Days" begins when he, symbolically, becomes a "Gamester" and, trusting to Fortune and Chance instead of Providence, loses the rest of his inheritance:

> This opened Scenes of Life hitherto unknown; Poverty and Distress, with their horrid Train of Duns, Attorneys, Bailiffs, haunted me Day and Night. My Clothes grew shabby, my Credit bad, my Friends and Acquaintance of all kinds cold. (III, 3)

After failing as playwright, hackney writer, and translator, Wilson, in a gesture significant of his spiritual blindness, "bought a Lottery-Ticket, resolving to throw myself into Fortune's Lap, and try if she would make me amends for the injuries she had done me at the Gaming-Table." [9] [125] The immediate result of his mistaken trust in Fortune is despair. Imprisoned for debt, he relates, "I had now neither Health . . . Liberty, Money, or Friends; and had abandoned all Hopes, and even the Desire, of Life." (Earlier in the narrative Adams had admonished him, "You should rather have thrown yourself on your knees . . . for despair is sinful.") Having disposed of his lottery ticket for a loaf of bread, he is plunged deeper into affliction by the news that he would have won three thousand pounds: "This was only a Trick of Fortune to sink me the deeper." And, like Job in his adversity, Wilson is deserted by his friends, one of whom, however, speaks with unconscious wisdom: "He said I was one whom Fortune could not save if she would." Languishing in prison like Boethius, and accusing Fortune of responsibility for his predicament, Wilson is rescued by the charity and love of his future wife and learns an important lesson. "Madam," he remarks to Harriet Hearty, "you mistake me if you imagine, as you seem, my Happiness is in the power of Fortune now." The moral is repeated as he smoothly corrects Parson Adams for an unfortunate figure of speech:

> "Sir," says Adams, "Fortune hath, I think, paid you all her Debts in this sweet Retirement." Sir, replied the Gentleman, I am thankful to the great Author of all things for the Blessings I here enjoy. (III, 3)

Thus, having missed the benefits of good advice and good example, Wilson must earn his wisdom through the harsh discipline of adversity. As spiritual biography, his story dramatizes Fielding's recurrent insistence upon the operation of Providence and the moral responsibility of the individual. It is the same Boethian argument developed [126] at greater length in *Amelia.*

[9] The identification of the government lottery with Dame Fortune would have been familiar to Fielding's contemporaries. Appearing in *The Craftsman*, No. 804 (November 28, 1741), and reprinted in *The London Magazine*, for example, an attack on the Westminster Bridge lottery notices the practice of one "cunning Shaver, who obliges his Customers *gratis* with *exceeding beautiful Schemes of the Lottery, and a Copper-Plate Picture, representing* Fortune *throwing a* Bag of Gold *amongst the Adventurers, who buy Tickets at his Office*." (*London Magazine*, X [December, 1741], 592.)

Fielding's introduction to the story of Captain Booth also has relevance to Mr. Wilson:

> I question much whether we may not, by natural means, account for the success of knaves, the calamities of fools, with all the miseries in which men of sense sometimes involve themselves, by quitting the directions of Prudence, and following the blind guidance of a predominant passion; in short, for all the ordinary phenomena which are imputed to fortune, whom perhaps, men accuse with no less absurdity in life than a bad player complains of ill luck at the game of chess.[10]

More important for the novel as a whole, however, is the apparent lesson to be drawn from Wilson's history: *vanitas vanitatum* and its solution in "a retired life" of love and simplicity.

> In short, [Wilson moralizes] I had sufficiently seen that the Pleasures of the World are chiefly Folly, and the Business of it mostly Knavery, and both nothing better than Vanity; the Men of Pleasure tearing one another to pieces from the Emulation of spending Money, and the Men of Business from Envy in getting it. My Happiness consisted entirely in my Wife, whom I loved with an inexpressible Fondness, which was perfectly returned; and my Prospects were no other than to provide for our growing Family; for she was now big of her second Child: I therefore took an Opportunity to ask her Opinion of entering into a retired life, which, after hearing my Reasons and perceiving my Affection for it, she readily embraced. We soon put our small Fortune, now reduced under three thousand Pounds, into Money, with part of

[10] Henley ed., VI, 13–14. The following remarks in *The True Patriot*, No. 8 (December 24, 1745), anticipate the opening chapter of *Amelia:*

> As the great Cardinal *Richlieu* maintain'd, Fortune or blind Chance doth not interfere so much in the great Affairs of this World, as her complaisant Votaries the Fools would persuade us. What we call ill Luck, is generally ill Conduct. Generals and Ministers, who destroy their own Armies and Countries, and then lay the Blame on Fortune, talk as absurdly as the passionate bad Player at Chess, who swore he had lost the Game by one d——n'd unlucky Move, which exposed the King to Cheque-mate.

Compare Tom Jones: "But why do I blame Fortune? I am myself the cause of all my misery" (XVIII.2).

> which we purchased this little place, whither we retired soon after her Delivery, from a World full of Bustle, Noise, Hatred, Envy, and Ingratitude, to Ease, Quiet, and Love. (III, 3) [127]

In depicting the Wilsons' life of retirement, simplicity, industry, and mutual love, Fielding presents as a wholesome alternative to the corruption of the Great City the familiar classical ideal of the happy husbandman—"Vanity had no Votary in this little spot" (III, 4). He is careful, however, to make that complete detachment and solitude that the latitudinarian ethic of practical benevolence required. Wilson is no misanthropist or hermit such as the Man of the Hill; he is hospitable to his guests and, what especially pleases Adams, charitable to his neighbors:

> These Instances pleased the well-disposed Mind of Adams equally with the Readiness which they exprest to oblige their Guests, and their Forwardness to offer them the best of everything in their House; and what delighted him still more was an Instance or two of their Charity; for whilst they were at Breakfast the good Woman was called for to assist her sick Neighbour, which she did with some Cordials made for the publick Use, and the good Man went into his Garden at the same time to supply another with something which he wanted thence, for they had nothing which, those who wanted it were not welcome to. (III, 4)

"This," declares Adams, "was the Manner in which the People had lived in the Golden Age." Indeed, there is a conscious flavor of a bucolic idyll to the Wilsons' course of life and to the chaste and innocent love of Fanny and Joseph (Joseph's song, we will remember, is that of a shepherd in an eclogue [II, 12]).[11]

"But no Blessings are pure in this World" (III, 3), observes Mr. Wilson with reference to the kidnapping of his son; and the cruel intrusion of the country squire upon [128] this scene of contentment (III, 4) makes it clear that, for Fielding, there is no earthly paradise even away from London. "From the expulsion from Eden down to this day," he asserts in *Tom Jones* (XII, 12), no such Golden Age "ever had any existence, unless in the warm imaginations of the poets." Barring uncontrollable

[11] Digeon (p. 70) has noticed this.

accidents from without, Wilson's solution is nevertheless as close as possible to Fielding's ideal of the happy life, and it serves as a model for Joseph and Fanny to follow (IV, 16).

Mr. Wilson's long history, then, is not really a "digression" at all, but rather an integral part of the plan and purpose of *Joseph Andrews*. The broad allegory of the novel represents the pilgrimage of Joseph Andrews and Abraham Adams—like their Scriptural namesakes, Christian heroes exemplifying the essential virtues of the good man—from the vanity of the town to the relative naturalness and simplicity of the country. While the main narrative exposes selfishness and hypocrisy along the highway, Wilson's rake's progress through the vanities of London completes the panoramic satire of English society. His own career depicts the nearly fatal consequences of immorality and irreligion, the twin results of a faulty education. It is what might have happened to Joseph Andrews himself had he lacked the good advice and good example of Parson Adams. With Wilson's wise adoption of the classical ideal of life his own pilgrimage is complete, symbolically reinforcing the movement of the novel as a whole, and a moral alternative is established in contrast to the ways of vanity. [129]

HENRY FIELDING'S COMIC ROMANCES

Sheridan Baker

HENRY FIELDING and "comic epic in prose" have become almost synonymous. But, though the words are undeniably Fielding's, is this really his own taxonomic term? As Ian Watt has recently pointed out, Fielding's remarks about the "comic prose epic," and perhaps his belief in his novels as epics, were

Source: Sheridan Baker, "Henry Fielding's Comic Romances," *Papers of the Michigan Academy of Science, Arts, and Letters*, XLV (1960), 411–419.

actually rather incidental and certainly brief.[1] Fielding's own name for his new genre is "comic romance," and, though he obviously liked the term no better than "comic epic," a reading of *Joseph Andrews* and *Tom Jones* as comic romances, I think, will somewhat correct our views of these two books.

Our critical error arises from Fielding's own uncertainty [2] and from his suspicion of the word "romance." Fielding opens his Preface to *Joseph Andrews* by stating: ". . . it is possible the mere *English* Reader may have a different Idea of Romance with the Author of these little Volumes. . . ." Let me repeat, it is with an "idea of romance" that he begins, not of a comic epic, setting the two little volumes of his kind of romance against the conventional one: the vast French romances in big gilt-edged folios. His models, which he thinks unfamiliar to "the mere English reader," are the Spanish and French works he enumerates in Book III: Cervantes, *Gil Blas,* "Scarron, the *Arabian Nights,* the History of *Marianne* and *Le Paisan Parvenu.*" Fielding's Preface then follows a practice common even to the French romances he scorns: he dignifies his work by claiming that it belongs under the "Epic" heading.[3] He then employs a rather common argument that poetry doesn't make the epic, that prose will do, and goes on to speak contemptuously of "those voluminous Works, *commonly* called Romances"—I italicize the antithesis, the one with which he began and which now continues on through his famous definition: "Now a comic Romance is a comic Epic-Poem in prose. . . . It differs from the serious Ro-

[1] *The Rise of the Novel* (Berkeley and Los Angeles, 1957), pp. 248–251.

[2] Ethel M. Thornbury, *Henry Fielding's Theory of the Comic Prose Epic* (Madison, 1931), p. 105: "He does not make a distinction between the comic romance and the comic epic." William R. Irwin adopts this idea and phrase from Thornbury, though he cites her page 50 instead: *The Making of Jonathan Wild* (New York, 1941), p. 96. F. Homes Dudden then plagiarizes from Irwin (*Henry Fielding: His Life, Works, and Times,* Oxford, 1952, p. 330, n. 4).

[3] Thornbury, pp. 38–45, 66–67; Arthur L. Cooke, "Henry Fielding and the Writers of Heroic Romance," *PMLA*, LXII (1947), 984–994; G.-E. Parfitt, *L'Influence française dans les Oeuvres de Fielding et dans le Théâtre anglais contemporain de ses Comédies* (Paris, 1928), p. 115.

mance in its Fable and Action . . . it differs in its Characters by introducing Persons of inferior Rank . . . whereas the grave Romance, sets the highest before us. . . ."

I have deliberately omitted the ruinous phrase: "differing from Comedy, as the serious Epic from Tragedy," in which we find "serious Epic" where the basic antithesis should lead us to expect "serious Romance." Fielding's own uncertainty, in other words, has allowed his predicate nominative momentarily to send his critics, from Dobson on, down the wrong road. But the subject of his defining paragraph is, nevertheless, "comic romance."

Unlike history with its unreal people, Fielding argues, in Book III, his fictive models are "true Histories." This is the term Fielding liked best and perpetuated in text and title—he even calls Hogarth a "Comic History-Painter" (Preface). And this is the phrase made much of by Cervantes,[4] the phrase also prominent in Scarron's *Comical Romance,* to use Tom Brown's translation, a work on Fielding's list that has been, I think, rather consistently underrated. I find it highly significant that Fielding begins *The Opposition* with a dream prompted by "the comical romance of Scarron."[5] *The Opposition* was published just two months before *Joseph Andrews*—while *Joseph Andrews,* in other words, was still in process. We find Scarron's "comical romance," like *Joseph Andrews,* talking about actual history and upholding *Don Quixote* against "imaginary Heroes," against "fabulous Stories, which have no Foundation in History," against *"Cassandra's, Cleopatra's* and *Cyrus's."*[6] Indeed, Tom Brown's [412] Scarron seems almost to speak from Fielding's own pages: "which I have told you somewhere before, in

[4] Bruce W. Wardropper, "The Pertinence of *El Curioso Impertinente,*" *PMLA,* LXXII (1957), 592–593; Sidney E. Glenn, "Some French Influences on Henry Fielding," *Abstracts of Theses . . . University of Illinois, 1931* (Urbana, 1932), p. 11.

[5] *The Complete Works of Henry Fielding, Esq.,* ed. William E. Henley (New York, 1902), XIV, 323; Wilbur L. Cross, *The History of Henry Fielding* (New Haven, 1918), I, 229; Parfitt, p. 114.

[6] *The Whole Comical Works of Mons. Scarron,* 4th ed. (London, 1727), I, 123.

this true History"—"as you may have read in the second Part of this true History"—"you might have perceived throughout the whole Comical Adventures of this Famous History." [7]

Cross credits Cervantes as the source for Fielding's book-and-chapter divisions, facetious headings and transitions, "drollery of style," the mock heroic diction, the ridiculous detail.[8] Granting this, granting Scarron's own debt to Cervantes, I am convinced that Fielding filtered some of his Cervantes through Brown's Scarron, whose first chapter begins:

> Bright *Phoebus* had already perform'd above half his Career; and his Chariot having past the Meridian. . . . To speak more like a Man, and in plainer Terms; it was betwixt five and six of the Clock. . . .

And ends:

> And whilst the hungry Beasts were feeding, the Author rested a while, and bethought himself what he should say in the next Chapter.[9]

Indeed, Fielding's narrative mannerisms are evident on a great many of Scarron's pages,[10] and he certainly seems to have suggested Fielding's term "comic romance." [413]

[7] *Scarron*, I, 244, 293, 317.

[8] Cross, I, 322. An anonymous reviewer of *Tom Jones* in *The Gentleman's Magazine*, XX (March, 1750), 117–118, notes that Fielding is "imitating the manner of *Cervantes, Scarron,* and *le Sage,* in the titles of his chapters," quoted by Frederick T. Blanchard, *Fielding the Novelist* (New Haven, 1927), p. 44.

[9] Tom Brown has slightly heightened Scarron's mock-heroic passage, which begins simply "Le soleil. . . ." Cf. the chapter beginnings of *Joseph Andrews*, I, viii; *Tom Jones*, VIII, ix; IX, ii; X, ii; XI, ix. Wayne C. Booth points out that Scarron's claim here of not knowing what is coming next, later underpinned by the admission that perhaps he has "a fix'd Design" (I, p. 48), is his unique contribution to self-conscious story-telling: "The Self-conscious Narrator in Comic Fiction before *Tristram Shandy*," *PMLA*, LXVII (1952), 169–170. Fielding always takes the opposite direction, the one more common to Scarron, the one initiated by Cervantes, which simply directs the reader on to "what will be found in the next chapter." But Scarron uses the formula oftener and elaborates it further than Cervantes' simple statement (used 9 times in 126 chapters as compared with Scarron's 14 in 60).

[10] Booth, attending to those passages in which the author intrudes "to comment on himself as writer" (p. 165), overlooks the frequent brief

Of Fielding's critics, only G.-E. Parfitt has done much more than to mention Scarron. Parfitt points to two battles royal at inns and their parallels in Fielding and asserts, correctly I think, that the climactic scene in *Joseph Andrews* (IV, xiv), in which Adams takes a wrong turn into Fanny's bed, is the most Scarronesque of all.[11] But Parfitt gives less than a page to Scarron, and, ignoring the strong stylistic similarities, insists more on differences than on resemblances. Indeed, Parfitt and Cross, and more recently Alan McKillop, in naming among Fielding's sources "the realistic fiction of France" (i.e., the works of Scarron, Le Sage, and Marivaux) have managed to conceal altogether the distinctly romantic cast of Fielding's two great novels.[12]

Scarron's central characters are a young man and woman of mysterious but undoubtedly noble background, disguised as actors, who are traveling chastely as brother and sister until the impediment to their marriage and to their rightful fortunes—they are, of course, hopelessly in love—is removed at last. This is hardly realistic, and it is suspiciously like the traveling companionship of Joseph and Fanny, perhaps even the source of their momentary brother-and-sister-hood. Within a boisterous context of picaresque adventures and prose fabliaux, in other words, Scarron accepts a great deal of pure romance. His main

phrases and asides which sound almost like Fielding himself. Sir Walter Scott believed that [413] Fielding's mock-heroic passages imitated Scarron rather than Cervantes (Blanchard, p. 327). Sidney E. Glenn thinks Fielding indebted to Scarron for no more than his chapter headings (p. 17).

[11] Parfitt, p. 114. See also Cross, I, 314–315, 322, 330. Parfitt does not give analogues in Scarron for Fielding's climactic scene; there are two, Part I, Chapter xii, and Part III, Chapter iv (*Scarron*, I, 47–48, 301–302). But Scarron does not give this ancient theme from fabliaux—the mistaken turn into the wrong bed (see Chaucer's "Reeve's Tale")—sexual complications. Fielding pretty clearly also has in mind Don Quixote's encounter with Maritornes (III, ii) and perhaps something of Chapter xlviii in Part II. For the thematic importance of this scene in Fielding, see Mark Spilka, "Comic Resolution in Fielding's 'Joseph Andrews,'" *CE*, XV (1953), 11–19.

[12] Cross, I, 321; Parfitt, p. 111; Alan McKillop, *The Early Masters of English Fiction* (University of Kansas, 1956), p. 110. E. M. W. Tillyard has recently redressed the balance (*The Epic Strain in the English Novel*, London, 1958).

story follows romance from mysterious origin to noble end, and all his inserted tales are straight cloak-and-dagger.

Almost precisely the same may be said of Fielding.[13] It is highly [414] significant that Fielding claims as universal truth, as the highest fictive realism, exactly those parts of Cervantes that would strike the modern reader as most romantic. Of "the Shepherd *Chrysostom,* who . . . died for Love of the fair *Marcella,*" Fielding asks: ". . . will any one doubt but that such a silly Fellow hath really existed? Is there in the World such a Sceptic as to disbelieve the Madness of *Cardinio,* the Perfidy of *Ferdinand,* the impertinent Curiosity of *Anselmo,* the Weakness of *Camilla,* the irresolute Friendship of *Lothario.* . . ."[14]

The romantic framework of Fielding's two principal novels is indeed stronger than we suspect and is by no means all burlesque. Andrews, like Havelock the Dane, begins his high life belowstairs; both he and Jones begin obscurely and mysteriously. Both must adventure for extended periods of time away from their unobtainable ladies, and their constancy is in no way basically comic like Quixote's. Quixote is a man of fifty who fancies himself a young knight dedicated to a beautiful young lady so unobtainable as to be, really, nonexistent. Andrews and Jones are young modern Englishmen of low degree, with no illusions, whose ideal young love is quite real, and both reveal unconscious traces of knighthood. When wounded in "battle," for instance, both disclose the knightly clue—a remarkably white

[13] In 1928 Oliver Elton pointed out the major flaw in the "comic-epic" view [414] of Fielding, noting that *Tom Jones* "is nearer drama than to epic, for an epic has no secret": *A Survey of English Literature 1730–1780* (New York, 1928), I, 195. But Elton overlooked the fact that the drama had derived the "secret" from the general stock of fairy tale and romance, and the epic theorists have overlooked Elton. W. Dibelius recognized the basic romance pattern in Fielding: "Englische Romankunst," *Palaestra,* XCII (1911), p. 92.

[14] *Joseph Andrews,* III, i. In 1752 Fielding objects to these same passages (after the epic *Amelia,* published December, 1751). Writing of Charlotte Lennox's *Female Quixote* in his *Covent-Garden Journal* (No. 24, March 24, 1752), Fielding remarks that Cervantes "in many Instances, approaches very near to the Romances which he ridicules. Such are the stories of Cardenio and Dorothea, Ferdinand and Lucinda, &c." Quoted in Thornbury, p. 126.

skin.[15] Andrews, for no functional purpose, is even an accomplished rider, able to bewitch money into the worldly pockets of Sir Thomas Booby with noble horsemanship. The framework of romance is more evident in *Joseph Andrews* than in *Tom Jones*: babies exchanged in the cradle, lovers taken as brother and sister, the gold amulet tied to [415] Joseph's arm, the strawberry mark, the gentle lineage. And the burlesquing of romance is more evident, too.

But Joseph must play Sancho to Adams's quixotic chivalry, and consequently Jones is much more the knightly hero, half comically, half ideally. He is the Quixote of his adventure, the benevolent idealist to Partridge's Sancho, though at times the roles reverse.[16] It is Jones who rescues the damsel in distress (Mrs. Waters, as Adams rescues Fanny and calls her, in fact, "damsel"), and who defends the aged Man of the Hill, with his own sword "stained with the blood of his enemies" (VIII, x). Jones's knightly magnanimity is not quite the wonderful quixotic thing that blesses Adams. Professor Crane has already noticed that Fielding "repeatedly depicts Tom, especially when he is talking to Sophia or thinking about her, in terms of the clichés of heroic romance." [17] And Fielding's intent seems serious. Jones's love is more romantic than Joseph's; his heroine is a "Sophia" not a "Fanny." Nevertheless, even Andrews, at least once, can speak the sublime diction of love: "O that I could but command my Hands to tear my Eyes out, and my Flesh off" (III, xi). Cerevantes's elaborate and delicate mockery of courtly love becomes in Fielding almost completely serious—comically counterpointed, to be sure, as in the Adams-Andrews dialogue from which I have just quoted, but never considered ludicrous in and of itself. Fielding's lovers, indeed, are at a center pretty much inviolate to the rough comedy outside. Fielding's comic romances, in other words, seem to deal with romance in two

[15] *Joseph Andrews,* I, xiv; *Tom Jones,* IV, xiv.

[16] Cross, II, 205; Gustav Becker, "Die Aufnahme der Don Quijote in die englische Literatur," *Palaestra,* XIII (1906), 152–153.

[17] R. S. Crane, "The Plot of *Tom Jones,*" *Journal of General Education,* IV (1950), 129.

opposite ways, often managing a synthesis: they accept courtly love and much of its romantic sublimity, and they mock heroic adventure with the picaresque scuffling of low life.

But it is the romantic structure that sustains the story. No matter how Fielding intended his offcast footman and his outcast foundling to mock the adventuring knight, they complete the romantic pattern in the end: their mysterious and natural nobility turns out to be sanctioned by birth, they step up into the elevated position so long deserved, they win the lady in the bower and live happily ever after. This is comic only in Dante's sense: the hero's travels end happy and [416] high. It is ludicrous, a burlesque of never-never land, only in a partial and almost cosmic sort of way—perhaps, one might say, only wistfully so.

In fact, throughout Fielding's work and career we can see a blend of the romantic attitude with the burlesque of romance, and we can see the serious wish deepening behind the conventional romantic ending. We can also observe the more interesting fact that Fielding is mixing his own self-portrait into that of his romantic hero, identifying himself in varying degrees with both his comic and romantic aspects. We will remember that Fielding at eighteen had attempted to carry from her uncle's clutches the fifteen-year-old heiress and mistress of his heart and that something of this seems to appear in the cloistered damsel of his first play.[18] In *The Author's Farce* (1730), written when Fielding was twenty-three, we find even more striking evidence. Cross pointed out some time ago (I, 81) that in "Harry Luckless," the protagonist, Harry Fielding was giving an obvious self-caricature of the playwright and his troubles. But no one has yet called attention to the fact that, in Harry Luckless, Fielding is also comically making himself the hero of a romance. In Luckless, he indeed acts out a complete little burlesque of romance, one which includes the very details of ro-

[18] Cross, I, 50–51, and 54: ". . . Fielding, by a mere change in the conclusion, adjusted his own romance to the exigencies of the stage"; and III, 268: "Such was the wild and headlong dash of the boy when spurred on by the romance and the animal within him."

mance that Fielding three years later was to omit from his translation of Molière's *L'Avare,* apparently as too romantic: boat wreck, an agate bracelet, rescue by an old servant.[19] Like the gold amulet which Joseph ties to his arm (I, xv) and which seems as if it might have once been intended to identify him to Adams (I, xiv), a jewel once tied to Luckless's arm uncovers his true identity as heir to the Kingdom of Bantam. Fielding even includes for himself as Harry Luckless a heroine of cognate name, using and burlesquing that siblingish amity and identity often found in the lovers in romance, as for instance in that flowery couple, Floris and Blancheflour: Harry's lady is Harriot, and when at the end her nobility is discovered along with his, the pair is proclaimed Henry and Henrietta, King and [417] Queen of Bantam,[20] and, of course, it is "Henry I." All this has been overlooked in the play's welter of social satire; all this is burlesque. But the point of highest interest is that Henry Fielding is identifying himself, in public, with the hero of his absurd little romance. He has, in other words, comically allowed himself to play the hero of romance and to fulfill the romantic wish: the play's penniless gentleman playwright has inherited his due of rank and riches and love. The self-pity of the temporarily unsuccessful young playwright and with his perennial human daydream of success and recognition has been buried and transmuted into comedy—indeed, into comic romance.

Fielding's portraits of Andrews and Jones include the chestnut locks, the fair skin, the nobility, the sweetness, and even the effeminacy of the conventional knight of romance,[21] and there

[19] I suspect that these romantic details in *The Author's Farce*—a jewel tied to the arm instead of the agate bracelet—indeed come from *L'Avare,* thus giving another clue to Fielding's reading. Cross (I, 63) sees suggestions from Molière in Fielding's first play, two years earlier.

[20] It is tempting to read "Bantam" as a variant of Lilliput, but the text touches only on outlandishness (cut from the 1734 version). I believe Fielding borrowed "Bantam" from Congreve's *Love for Love* (II, i), which play he parallels closely in phrase and situation in his opening scenes (cf. *Love for Love,* I, i).

[21] Arthur J. Tieje, *The Theory of Characterization in Prose Fiction Prior to 1740,* University of Minnesota Studies in Language and Literature, No. 5 (Minneapolis, 1916), p. 5.

is considerable evidence that in back of these conventional traits appear also the lineaments of Henry Fielding himself.[22] The boy who, we may infer from *Joseph Andrews* (I, i), had imagined himself Guy of Warwick and all the Champions of Christendom apparently was, in spite of himself, father of the man who railed against "immense" and "idle" romances "filled with monsters." [23] The evidence of *Amelia* only bears this out—though the structure of *Amelia* is consciously epic,[24] the devices of romance are more flagrantly evident than ever (Booth's entrance to his lady's house in a basket, for instance). I omit *Amelia* from my present discussion not because it lacks romance, but because Fielding's comic romance has changed, and the new kind of writing has grown prematurely old, has become interested in other things.

But the idea of comic romance pervades *Joseph Andrews* and *Tom Jones*, and the term, today more contradictory than when Fielding [418] used it, pretty well defines these two books. They are comic, and they are romantic. They contain Fielding's own romantic fancy along with his comic wisdom. The trueness and the durability come perhaps not so much from their realistic glimpses of eighteenth-century life or their realistic demonstrations of man's eternal self-deceptions and hypocrisies as from the even more essential realism that sees the comic impossibility of the ideal and romantic glories of life yet affirms their existence and their value. All of us, no less than Fielding, want to live happily ever after; we too like to fancy our innately noble selves rewarded at last by a climb from scullery to castle. And all of us—at least when we read Fielding and Cervantes and Scarron (who was actually shriveled and bent by pain when he wrote his comic work)—can appreciate the amusing impossibility and illusory nature of such a solution, and can see, for a moment, that the human condition itself, caught between fact and aspiration, is, after all, a kind of comic romance. [419]

[22] Cross, I, 168–169, 330, 348–350; II, 170–171, 328.

[23] *Joseph Andrews*, III, i; *Tom Jones*, IV, i.

[24] George Sherburn, "Fielding's *Amelia:* An Interpretation," *ELH*, III (1936), 1–14; Lyall H. Powers, "The Influence of the *Aeneid* on Fielding's *Amelia*," *MLN*, LXXI (1956), 330–336.

THE FRAMEWORK of *SHAMELA*

Eric Rothstein

FIELDING, in his prudence, did not let his ward Shamela go out to make her literary fortune alone. Her letters appeared with three epistolary chaperons, three addresses that are variants of her own correspondence. First, we have the letter of dedication from Conny Keyber to "Miss *Fanny, &c.*"; next, two letters to the Editor, "puffs" of the novel; finally, a pair of letters between Parsons Tickletext and Oliver, the one a praise of *Pamela* and the other an answer that denounces *Pamela* as a moral and literal fraud and that produces the genuine correspondence of Shamela. These three addresses seem to contain a puzzling contradiction. While Keyber styles himself Shamela's biographer, Parson Oliver claims that the work is an unintentional autobiography. One can dispose of the difficulty by assuming that Keyber, as putative author, has merely reproduced, or even written, the parsons' letters. Yet it would be quite out of character for him to have done so, even if we suppose, as a narrative justification, that he is using the parsons' letters to support the superiority of his own *Shamela* over *Pamela*, the rival product. In fact, any narrative explanation is unlikely, since Keyber dotes on Shamela, while the parsons' letters denounce her.

Fielding might have handled this seeming contradiction simply by having Oliver send Tickletext a copy of *Shamela* as edited by Keyber. As an alternative, he might have omitted one of the three addresses, since only the two "puffs" burlesque Richardson directly. Keyber's address in particular bears no relation to the form of *Pamela*. None the less, Fielding put it first, in a position of special prominence, an exposed position, where any sloppiness of conception would reveal itself even to a hasty

Source: Eric Rothstein, "The Framework of *Shamela*," *ELH*, Vol. 35 (1968), pp. 381–402.

author or a laughing reader. His craftsmanship, so rarely in doubt, ought to be sure-footed here: from his youth, Fielding had dealt with framework on multiple levels of fictional reality in plays like *The Author's Farce, The Tragedy of Tragedies, Pasquin*, and *The Historical Register*. [381] And just as "problems" in the framework of these plays cannot be disregarded, or the framework be plucked away from the burlesque without damaging a crucial relationship between literary parody and social reality, so in *Shamela*. The very presence of the framework in *Shamela* demands thought about the effect of framework and burlesque upon one another, and about the nature of the composite work that they make up. I should like to sketch in some detail what the results of such thought might be.

We may begin with the Dedication, which comes first; it is a ribald parody, setting the tone for *Shamela*'s sexual innuendos, of Conyers Middleton's dedication of his *Life of Cicero* to Lord Hervey. How thoroughly Middleton left himself open to this sort of parody is clear from a pamphlet approximately contemporary with *Shamela, The Death of M—l—n in the Life of Cicero*. Middleton, wrote "an Oxford Scholar," "creeps closer to his Patron, and begins to lay him on thicker and faster, 'till he has *bedaub'd* him all over . . . For shame, for shame Doctor. What talk to *my Lord Privy-Seal*, as if you was tattling to a *pretty Miss?* entertain a Peer of the Realm and a Privy-Counsellor with a *Lulla-by Baby-by!* Quite surfeiting!"[1] Fielding says the same thing through puns. Thus, when Middleton compares Hervey to Cicero, saying, "Your character would justify me in running some length into the parallel," Keyber slips into *double-entendre:* "your Character would enable me to run some Length into a Parallel."[2] "Intimately conversed" takes on overtones. And so on. The satire cuts because of Hervey's

[1] *The Death of M—l—n in the Life of Cicero* . . . By an Oxford Scholar (London, 1741), pp. 5–7. *The Gentleman's Magazine* lists this pamphlet for May, 1741, the month following the publication of *Shamela*. Whether Fielding was acquainted with its author, or he with *Shamela*, is unknown.

[2] Conyers Middleton, *The History of the Life of Marcus Tullius Cicero* (London, 1741), I, ii. Quotations from *Shamela* come from the revised edition of 1741, and are identified, where necessary, by Letter.

alleged hermaphroditism (a favorite charge of the Opposition's), which was made notorious by the nickname "Fanny," a slang term from at least the middle of the preceding century for the female sexual organs. Should anyone miss the joke on account of the commonness of calling Hervey "Fanny," Fielding not only prefaces the name with a "Miss," but also follows it with an "*&c.*" that makes no [382] syntactical sense, but that has the same slang meaning as does "fanny." [3]

He further embellishes the joke by mentioning Dr. John Woodward. At first, the choice of Woodward seems odd, even though a professional chair in his name had been held by Middleton. The Doctor had been dead thirteen years when *Shamela* was written, and one might have expected Fielding to hit upon a more current medical butt, like Dr. George Cheyne, whose *Essay on Regimen* he had recently satirized. Not only did Cheyne "mangle and maul" English, but he professed notions not too dissimilar from Woodward's, in a slightly less flamboyant rhetoric.[4] But Fielding was willing to give up the current for

[3] For the slang meanings of "fanny," see the entry in Eric Partridge, *A Dictionary of Slang and Unconventional English* (5th ed.: London, 1961); although he lists no date earlier than the nineteenth century, the term goes at least as far back as 1662, when Robert Nevil's play *The Poor Scholar* included the young lady Uperphania. For "&c.," see Eric Partridge, *Shakespeare's Bawdy* (London, 1947), and Shamela's last letter to her mother. Charges against Hervey, including his effeminacy, are discussed by Martin C. Battestin, "Hervey's Role in *Joseph Andrews,*" *PQ*, XLII (1963), 226–41.

[4] The *Champion* for May 17, 1740, given still wider circulation in *The Tryal of Colley Cibber, Comedian* (London, 1740), accuses Cheyne of having "so mangled and mauled" the English language that when a critic "came to examine the Body, as it lay in Sheets in a Bookseller's Shop, I found it an expiring heavy Lump, without the least Appearance of Sense" (p. 34). The two doctors had similar notions about diet, Woodward declaring that "The great Wisdom, and the Happiness of Man, consists in a due Care of the Stomach, and Digestion . . . ," with which Cheyne agreed: "It is *Diet* alone, proper and specific *Diet* . . . which is the sole *universal Remedy*, and the only Means known to Art, or that an animal Machin, without being otherwise made than it is, can use with certain Benefit and Success, which can give *Health, long Life* and Serenity." *The State of Physick and of Diseases* (London, 1718), p. 34; *An Essay on Regimen* (3rd ed.: London, 1753), p. x. Cheyne so obviously suggests himself for satire—he was even Hervey's physician—that Fielding's decision to use Woodward instead appears significant.

the perfectly appropriate. As early as 1710 the traveller Uffenbach was writing of Woodward: "In every respect he behaves like a female and an insolent fool. For a pedant he is much too gallant and elaborate. He is a man in the thirties, unmarried, but criminis non facile nominandi suspectus."[5] Englishmen found the suspicions easier to name. One, in 1719, refers to Woodward as a "great Lover of Boys"; and "Dr. Technicum," writing in the same year about a pretended autopsy on Woodward, is hardly less blunt: the ladies, he says, "will be inquisitive of *what Sex* he dyed: The Account of his Dissection will inform them in that Particular; and altho' [383] from the Softness of his Voice something may have been suggested to his Disadvantage in their Esteem, yet I know not whether that Constitution is not more eligible, that inclines one to the *Goût* of *Italy* and *Spain*, and gives a Man a stronger relish for the more *manly* Pleasures of those warmer Climates."[6] In the context of Keyber's remarks about "exciting the Brute . . . to rebel," these quiet allusions make excellent sense, helping Fielding establish a connection between the naturalistic and the perverse. He is to make use of the connection in dealing with Shamela's conduct, naturalistic as a corrective to *Pamela* and morally perverse as its analogue.

"Fanny," of course, meant more than an obscenity. "*Fanny* (my Lord)," wrote Pope to Hervey, "is the plain English of

[5] Zacharias Conrad von Uffenbach, *London in 1710*, tr. and ed. W. H. Quarrell and Margaret Mare (London, 1934), p. 178.

[6] *The Life and Adventures of Don Bilioso de L'Estomac* (London, 1719), p. 19. *An Account of the Sickness and Death of Dr. W—dw—rd* . . . By Dr. Technicum (London, 1719), p. 8. Once Fielding had Dr. Woodward on the hook, he used him as a blunt weapon against Richardson. Pamela's wedding-day snack of apple-pie and custard had already been made to sound aphrodisiac by having Shamela eat it—a hot buttered pie—to prepare for Booby's attack (Letter X). And Woodward had been teased for having called this dish, like the puddings and custards mentioned by Keyber, a stimulant—cf. *A Letter from the Facetious Dr. Andrew Tripe at Bath* (London, 1718), an anti-Woodward satire by Dr. Wagstaffe or Dr. Mead, which sneers: "the same Performance, contrary to the musty Rules of *Horace*, may contain a *State of Physick and Diseases*, and an History of *butter'd Applepye and Custard*," and warns that the "ancient custom of feeding School Boys with *Plumb-Cake* and *Applepye*, is certainly of the most pernicious Consequence . . ." (pp. 25, 29).

Fannius, a real person, who was a foolish Critic, and an enemy of *Horace:* perhaps a Noble one . . . This *Fannius* was, it seems, extremely fond both of his *Poetry* and his *Person* . . . He was moreover of a delicate or *effeminate complexion* . . ."[7] It is this Horatian reference that Pope thought of in contriving the name for Hervey, and that Fielding finds useful in *Shamela*. As Horace invokes him, Fannius emerges both a bad poet and a courtly sycophant. Satire 4 of Book I presents him as a vain and adored mediocrity. "Ce Fannius donc," Dacier commented, "quoique méchant Pöete, avoit tant fait par ses intrigues & par une espece de cabale qu'il avoit ménagée en lisant ses Poësies en tous lieux & à tous venants, que contre toute sorte d'apparence & de justice, on avoit permis qu'il se procurât cet honneur [of having his picture and works placed in Apollo's temple], & qu'il portât lui-même [384] ses Ecrits & son portrait dans la Bibliotheque." Dacier's note on Satire 10 of the same book fills out the picture further by telling us that Fannius was the parasite of a great man, one Hermogenes Tigellius.[8] Gazing on the picture, the Opposition to Walpole saw a perfect Fannius in Hervey. He had pretensions as a writer, as Middleton's and Keyber's dedications mention. He was deeply involved in Walpole's cabals, especially as a soothing confidant of Queen Caroline's, and had been rewarded with the post of Lord Privy-Seal just a year before the publication of *Shamela*. And finally, he was advertised as a puppet of Walpole's. Above the sexual innuendo, then, is a thematic layer in which false art and false politicking are bound together by the connotations of "Fanny."

Fielding develops this grouping throughout the Dedication. Hervey's politics, which according to Middleton measured the rival claims of royal prerogative and popular rights "both by the equal balance of the laws," descend into the artistic image of the debutante Fanny's dancing: "you was observed in Dancing to balance your Body exactly, and to weigh every Motion

[7] Alexander Pope, "A Letter to a Noble Lord" in *The Works*, ed. Warburton (London, 1751), VIII, 262–63. As Battestin suggests ("Hervey's Role in *Joseph Andrews*"), Fielding probably had not yet seen this letter of Pope's, but he did know Horace and the Horatian commentators.

[8] *Œuvres d'Horace en latin, traduites en françois par M. Dacier et le P. Sanadon* (Amsterdam, 1735), V, 191, 383.

with the exact and equal Measure of Time and Tune; and though you sometimes made a false Step, by leaning too much to one Side [i.e., royal prerogative]; yet every body said you would one time or other, dance perfectly well, and uprightly." In line with this imagery, the king before whom Fanny dances is not George II but the King of Bath, the master of the Pump Room's artifice, Beau Nash. Fielding is touching here upon the Augustan belief that government and humane culture have complex and unbreakable relations with each other, a belief that justifies his using Fanny's shaky dance as a metaphor for—as well as a reduction of—Hervey's politics. As *Shamela* moves on, the connections between the lack of artistic control in *Pamela* and the consequent lack of moral and familial control are to become a crucial issue in the letters of Parson Oliver. In the meanwhile, Fielding also works upon another theme central to *Pamela* and *Shamela* both, the expression of spiritual functions (like political judgment) in physical terms (dancing askew). In attuning the reader to this sort of transference, he offers several analogous processes, such as the *double-entendres* of which we have spoken and the religious metaphors of which we will speak. [385]

Hervey, tangentially and briefly addressed, could not by himself carry the broad moral and social implications of Fielding's satire. Therefore, Fielding mixed Middleton with Cibber and invented Conny Keyber. Keyber claims to have written *Shamela;* and Parson Oliver, reading the Cibberian puffs and Ciceronian eloquence of *Pamela,* suspects "him" of having written that book too. In introducing Cibber, Fielding continues from the *Champion* a series of attacks on his old adversary. Perhaps too, as has been suggested, he is enjoying revenge for Cibber's sneers at him in the *Apology.*[9] But more important, he is forwarding the themes brought up by alluding to Hervey. For the Opposition, Cibber the poet laureate mingled political and poetical baseness, best typified by his sycophantic birthday odes. Less notorious, but as much to the point, is the dedication be-

[9] For instance, by Martin C. Battestin, in his introduction to his edition of *Shamela* and *Joseph Andrews* (Boston, 1961), p. xiii; an edition to the notes of which this article is indebted.

fore his *Apology*. This fawning address "To A Certain Gentleman" ends with a comparison of the dedicatee to Cicero, which may well have suggested to Fielding the aptness of a conflated Conny Keyber: "This, Sir, is drawing you too near the Light, *Integrity* is too particular a Virtue to be cover'd with a general Application. Let me therefore only talk to you, as at *Tusculum* (for so I will call that sweet Retreat, which your own Hands have rais'd) where like the fam'd Orator of old, when publick Cares permit, you pass so many rational, unbending Hours . . . How many golden Evenings, in that Theatrical Paradise of water'd Lawns and hanging Groves, have I walk'd and prated down the Sun in social Happiness!"[10] We can see that Conny Keyber is a logical amalgam if we pose the adulation of Middleton's address to Hervey alongside this of Cibber's, and furthermore realize that one of the contemporary criticisms of Middleton's book was that it falsified the life of Cicero to flatter Walpole's and Hervey's politics. To fix the amalgam, Fielding hit upon a Christian name that drew on both "Conyers" and "Colley," and that in import related directly to "Fanny." Ian Watt remarks that the name "Conny" has the "appropriate suggestions of 'coney,' a dupe, and possibly of 'cunny,' latin 'cunnus.'" The obscene pun, I should think, is the more clearly appropriate of the two, and is certainly inescapable [386] given that "coney," "cony," and "conny" were all pronounced "cunny" in Fielding's time.[11]

Fielding had a reason for choosing Hervey, Middleton, and Cibber other than their appropriate names, biographical and dedicatory habits, and their support of Walpole. In these three men, he found representatives of the three cultural forms by which eighteenth-century society defined itself and its achievement: the state, the church, and the arts. Fielding had dealt with all three, admittedly with different emphases, in *Pasquin*. There he had made them aspects of the same kind of corruption. The

[10] *An Apology for the Life of Mr. Colley Cibber*, ed. Robert W. Lowe (London, 1889), I, lxx.

[11] Ian Watt, "Shamela," in *Fielding: a Collection of Critical Essays*, ed. Ronald Paulson (Englewood Cliffs, N.J., 1962), p. 46. For the word, see the entry in Partridge, *Dictionary of Slang*; for the pronunciation, see OED, under "cony."

political evils within the comedy that forms the first part of *Pasquin* appear as an equivalent of the artistic evils that are made clear through the use of the rehearsal technique. During the second part of *Pasquin*, the tragedy of Queen Common Sense, they re-appear along with the false religion of Firebrand as three congruent parts of Queen Ignorance's macabre reign. In *Shamela*, a similar reduction takes place. The political cleric and the political playwright blend into Conny Keyber, whose false worship and false art ape those of the sycophantic patron Fanny. Each has only the token of his integrity to offer, the "Vartue" symbolized by what Shamela happily calls "the dear *Monysyllable*." Whether we label that integrity a conny or a fanny, it has the same function: prostitution, selling oneself.

Lives of Cicero, Cibber, or Shamela turn out at this level to be mere merchandising devices, ways of deceiving society by using the fictional past of false history. It follows that a Cibber or a Shamela may be substituted for a false Cicero—exchanges that the conflation and the parody imply—without making much difference. Such reduction and analogy leads us to look for the themes familiar from the framework in the text of Shamela's letters later on. She becomes both the triumph and the *reductio ad absurdum* of the prostitute, the player, and the politician. So smoothly does the allusory world of Fielding's London melt into the fiction of her correspondence that we can see why John Puff, in the second of the commendatory letters that precede the burlesque, thinks that anyone who could write the life of Shamela could do just as well with Walpole's. Nor are we surprised to [387] find fiction melting back into reality at the end, as our heroine gets ready to have her life written by that expert clerical falsifier of biographies, Conyers Middleton, here lowered to the position of a mercenary through Fielding's generous hyperbole.[12] We are not quite sure whether that life is to be

[12] Sheridan Baker, in his edition of *Shamela* (Berkeley and Los Angeles, 1953) identifies "the Gentleman *who writes Lives*" with Middleton, supporting his argument from Parson Oliver's detecting "*Ciceronian* Eloquence" in *Pamela* (p. xxvi). I agree with him, finding myself unconvinced by the candidacy of Dr. Thomas Birch, which was first advanced by Charles Woods in "Fielding and the Authorship of *Shamela*," *PQ*, XXV (1946), 248–72, and repeated in his review of Baker's *Shamela*, *PQ*,

Pamela or *Shamela*—presumably the former, but it does not make much difference. The real world, made into self-serving fiction by the Herveys and their hirelings, turns into the fictional world that mirrors the real: art becomes a form of politicking. Once more Fielding offers a reduction, this one—so Parson Tickletext says—stamped for moral consumption by the Bishop of London, Edmund Gibson, Walpole's "lieutenant for Church affairs." [13] At every administrative level, the failures of art, church, and state show up as variants of a central failure in moral perception and in discrimination. Bishop Gibson's failure, like the others, is also to be sent forth in a letter, a pastoral letter.

The letter, as Fielding saw, is a composition both public and private, with claims to be true and possibilities of being a fiction, an advertisement for and a revelation of the self. It is a perfect vehicle for the themes that we have been discussing, for that complex traffic between a persona's aesthetic and moral follies which Lucian catches in tangles of sophistry, the Scriblerus group in projects and memoirs, and Fielding in various kinds of burlesque. [388] By writing an epistolary novel, Richardson played directly into Fielding's satiric interests and tested abilities. In fact, *Shamela* is formally so much a clever combination of gems that a Scriblerian might mine from the process of

XXXIII (1954), 273–74. Professor Woods argues that even allowing for exaggeration, the description of the busy venal biographer in *Shamela* does not fit the scholarly Middleton, biographer only of Cicero. Yet, aside from the "*Ciceronian* Eloquence," there are reasons for accepting Baker's reading. Birch has no advantages over Middleton as a satiric target, but Middleton has over Birch. Whereas Fielding would be unlikely to bring in a fresh and distracting allusion at the very end of his satire, a reference to Middleton makes sense: he has been satirizing Middleton as a biographer; he is ready at this point to return from the burlesque to the real world, and therefore to recur to the world set up at the beginning. Better yet, to read the biographer as Middleton, makes *Pamela*, puffed in the Cibberian vein and written in the Middletonian, the rival of Keyber's *Shamela*, an analogue and corrective by *Doppelgänger*. As to the exaggeration, it is quite in keeping with the rest of *Shamela*, particularly inasmuch as Middleton's *Life* was charged with inaccuracy and with dragging in contemporary overtones for Walpole's benefit.

[13] J. H. Plumb, *Sir Robert Walpole: the Making of a Statesman* (London, 1956), p. 69.

letter-writing, set with the analogical method that Fielding had used to unify his political plays, that one may wonder how different in intent it is from other Augustan burlesques. In very few of them is there much animus directed at any specific work; specific works, like the tragedies upon which *Tom Thumb* draws or like the parody of Middleton in *Shamela*, serve largely as convenient landmarks to localize the more general satire of the piece. Even at the cost of our losing the joys of much malice and gossip, I suspect that Fielding is using *Pamela* the same way. The satire on *Pamela* is much less his final cause than people, especially those who dislike Richardson, have been inclined to think. For one thing, the political motifs, which Fielding treats very much as he treats similar motifs in his plays, do not contribute to the attack on *Pamela*, not even as window-dressing. They say nothing about it that the burlesque omits, they distract the attention from the strict parody, and they also arouse expectations that the burlesque cannot fulfill, since *Pamela* is quite apolitical. One can, of course, insist that Fielding, on the hunt for Richardson, scatters some stray shot amid the miscellaneous foe; but Fielding is so rarely haphazard that this is neither a reasonable nor a flattering view. Furthermore, a second set of motifs, the religious, occupies a crucial position in *Shamela*, both in the burlesque and in the prefatory material, but is tangential to *Pamela*. Once again, Fielding seems to have his eye on something other than making sport of Richardson's gaucheries in telling a story or offering moral lessons; and once again, that something other is involved enough to require close analysis.

The most obvious religious satire in *Shamela* centers in the Methodistical Parson Williams, who preaches the convenient doctrine of the sufficiency of faith: "I purpose to give you [Shamela] a Sermon next *Sunday*, and shall spend the Evening with you, in Pleasures, which, tho' not strictly innocent, are however to be purged away by frequent and sincere Repentance" (Letter IX). In attacking the Methodists like this, Fielding was following the lead of his contemporaries, just as he did in his satire of Hervey and Cibber. These were fixed roots from which he could develop [389] and ramify his fiction. In the case of the Methodists, one might trace the lines of attack to Swift's portrayal of the Dissenters and their barely masked sexuality, but one need look no farther back than the two years or so before *Shamela* was published. In 1740, for instance, the Vicar of Dewsbury had asked his flock: "WHAT can we think of their *nocturnal Assemblies*, which, after their *Field* Matters are over, are held with the most profound Privacy, and into which none are permitted to enter, but such as are initiated into their Mysteries, and have received the Sign and Symbol of Admission?" And he had provided his own answer: "Associations of this Sort are seldom enter'd into merely upon a religious Account, but generally for contrary Ends and Purposes. When I reflect upon that monstrous Society of *Bacchanals* in the Grove of *Stimula*, which in the 567th Year of *Rome* was suppress'd by *Postumius Albinus*, I am apt to make ungrateful Comparisons . . ." His epigraph comes from Livy and refers to the grove.[14] A less learned work, "The Methodists" of 1739, has much the same burden, with London replacing Stimula:

> Cease ye Town Rakes old Ways t'explore,
> Or aim at Gaiety to Wh–re;
> Alter your *Rules*, new *Methods* try,
> To your Instructor *Wh–tf–d* fly;
> There learn to ogle, whine, and cant,
> For Love and for Religion pant . . .

In this way, "The *Spirit*, makes the *Flesh's Pimp*."[15]

Fielding's most immediately available source for such comments was "Richard Hooker's" *Weekly Miscellany*, a competitor of the *Champion*'s. In 1739, Hooker's paper suspected the New Birth "to be a Lure for all the Gossips in the Kingdom, who will be curious to experience these Throws and Stirrings within them, and may not be without them, if their nocturnal Assemblies go on much longer," and advised that Whitefield's interest in continuing his sect had led him to form a society of females who were to provide "a Supply of new Methodists for

[14] *The Imposture of Methodism Display'd: In A Letter To The Inhabitants Of The Parish of Dewsbury* . . . By William Bowman (London, 1740), p. 79.

[15] "The Methodists, An Humorous Burlesque Poem." (London, 1739), pp. 19–21.

future Generations." Its anti-Methodist campaign persisted until well after the publication of *Shamela*, running from direct denunciation and grave reservation to shocking historical anecdotes about the wicked [390] Anabaptists of Munster.[16] Such sexual allegations current about the Methodists perfectly suited Fielding's thematic treatment, and provided an easy bridge between the treatment of the Walpole men in the Dedication and that proper to *Pamela*'s "luscious" scenes in the burlesque.

This bridge, which makes explicit the analogy between the framework and the burlesque, is fixed in Tickletext's letter. Overtones of Methodism in the name and enthusiasm of Tickletext are supported by his praise for the Whitefieldian Parson Williams and for the doctrine of grace. On this basis, Fielding can let him go on to a nearly blasphemous paean to *Pamela:* "Thou alone art sufficient to teach us as much Morality as we want. Dost thou not teach us to pray, to sing Psalms, and to honour the Clergy? Are not these the whole Duty of Man? Forgive me, O Author of *Pamela*, mentioning the Name of a Book so unequal to thine: But, now I think of it, who is the Author, where is he, what is he, that hath hitherto been able to hide such an encircling, all-mastering Spirit?" Here Whitefield's much-resented attack on *The Whole Duty of Man*—"the whole Treatise is built on such a false Foundation, as proves the Author to be no real Christian at Heart" [17]—joins with his insistence on the sufficiency of Scripture and acts of faith. Within this conventional satire, Fielding proceeds to imply through Tickletext's language that *Pamela* is somehow a substitute for the Bible itself. This is a religious version of his earlier implication that a Shamela is worth a Cicero, and further ties the social to the aesthetic, and the truth (when in the wrong hands) to fiction.

He improves these connections by virtue of another common charge against the Methodists, that they misused English. For one thing, their enemies said, they were given to cant as a con-

[16] *Weekly Miscellany* for August 21, 1739. For other anti-Methodist attacks, see *Weekly Miscellany* for May 12, September 22, and December 15, 1739; August 30, and September 27 to November 29 *passim*, 1740.

[17] *A Letter from the Rev. Mr. Whitefield . . . shewing the Fundamental Error of a Book Entitled The Whole Duty of Man* (Charlestown, S. C., 1740), p. 4.

venient means of clouding their bare dogmas and shocking intentions; for another, they dealt in "the abuse and miserable Perversion of Scripture Sentences"; finally, they expressed spiritual relationships in carnal metaphors.[18] Fielding recognized these abuses [391] as cousins of Cibberian neologisms, perversions of the classics, and confusion between idealism and self-seeking. The language of Methodism, then, created yet another corrupt work of art; Whitefield was the Cibber of piety. With this in mind, one can better understand why Tickletext fills his letter with unintended puns about the casting off of ornament and the father of millions, and also why he quotes so freely from the Cibberian puffs to the second edition of *Pamela.* Fielding first alerts us to the puffs by placing two parodies of them just before Tickletext's letter. The one picks up the theme of egoism, the second of venality and politics. Tickletext then quotes from doctored versions of the real *Pamela* puffs, extending these themes from the anti-Walpole Dedication into the anti-Methodist satire to follow. He begins with his own complacent barbarism, telling Parson Oliver that the clergy's "common Business here [is] not only to cry it [*Pamela*] up, but to preach it up likewise." The jargon from the puffs follows, with "MEASURED FULLNESS . . THAT RESEMBLING LIFE, OUT-GLOWS IT," and a "Posterity, who will not HESITATE their Esteem with Restraint." Scripture becomes contorted by omission, as the puffs' bathetic use of Christ's parable of the mustard-seed recurs in a comparison of Pamela's "little, &c." to Heaven. And throughout the letter come carnal expressions, either metaphors or quotations from *Pamela*'s puffs, that balk at their intended function of symbolizing the spiritual, and thus turn a would-be advertisement into a tissue of self-revelations.

The reply to Tickletext is supplied by Parson Oliver. Cross theorized some years ago that Fielding had named his good

[18] The Reverend Mr. J. Tucker, Minister of All-Saints, Bristol, quoted in *The Life and Particular Proceedings of the Rev. Mr. George Whitefield* . . . By an Impartial Hand (London, 1739). The charge of misusing language was less common in Fielding's [391] time than it later became; "The New Bath Guide" and *The Spiritual Quixote* both use it directly, *Humphry Clinker* indirectly.

parson after a boyhood tutor, although the (slim) evidence rather points to the tutor's having been otherwise enshrined, as Trulliber in *Joseph Andrews*.[19] I should like to propose that the gentleman in *Shamela,* whose name seems genuine by contrast with the allegoric "Tickletext," is christened after Dr. William Oliver of Bath, a close friend of Fielding's patron Ralph Allen's, and a chief sponsor of the hospital in Bath.[20] Whether Dr. Oliver had [392] actually denounced *Pamela,* or whether Fielding was simply complimenting a friend and fellow-alumnus of Leyden, I do not know; but the choice was apt, for Oliver's public benefactions were well-known, enabling him to be set up as a spokesman for good works and charity. As doctor and practical moralist, he offered Fielding the chance of reversing the false ascent of the material to the spiritual which marks the parodies in the Dedication as well as Tickletext's metaphors, and which is carried out so thoroughly in the ethical structure of Shamela's adventures. Oliver as parson is a genuine spiritual extension of Oliver as doctor. In this double role, he can make real use of the first metaphor in his letter to Tickletext: the fad for *Pamela* is "an epidemical Phrenzy now raging in Town." For the healing of his brother parson, he sends the copies of Shamela's letters—i.e., he prepares the truth with his own hand, in direct contrast to the "editor" of *Pamela*—as "an Antidote to this Poison."

As the biographer transmits the facts and meaning of profane history, so the parson does of sacred history. The whole exegetical discussion about *Pamela* between Tickletext and Oliver, then, recalls glosses of Scripture as well as the biographer's care in shaping the past. The two themes are joined by the real parson-biographer, Conyers Middleton. In the early 1730's,

[19] Wilbur Cross, *The History of Henry Fielding* (New Haven, 1918), I, 22–23. Arthur Murphy is the authority for tracing Trulliber to Fielding's tutor.

[20] Unfortunately, we do not know when Fielding met Allen, and perhaps through him, Dr. Oliver. Battestin ("Hervey's Role in *Joseph Andrews,* p. 236) places [392] Fielding's invitation to Allen's Palladian house, referred to in *Joseph Andrews,* in the autumn of 1741. There is no reason to doubt that he had known Allen for six months or a year before that visit—he began riding the western circuit in 1740.

Middleton had engaged notoriously in controversy with the orthodox cleric Dr. Waterland about the best way to answer the Deists. Because Middleton had made a reputation as a polemicist, and because Waterland's original reply to the Deists was kept currently in print through the time when Fielding wrote *Shamela,* Middleton's name was indelibly stained with religious scepticism in 1741; or, as *The Death of M—l—n* put it, "the Name of *Divine* would make him *puke.*"[21] This religious scepticism had as a main tenet that it was proper to interpret Scripture by "desert[ing] the *outward letter,* and search[ing] for the *hidden allegorical* sense of the story." The way to handle men like Tindal was to confute them with reason and the principle of utility, Middleton told Waterland, and he denounced the notion that "*every single passage of the Scripture, we call Canonical, must needs be received,* [393] *as the very word and as the voice of God himself.*"[22] The controversy thereby aroused dragged its slow length along, with the unhappy Middleton making things worse for himself. *A Defence of the Letter to Dr. Waterland* presented Moses as an able legislator, whose expert sense of propaganda led him to pretend that his laws were inspired and so to compel a refractory people to accept them. Others in turn wrote an *Answer* and a *Reply* to Middleton's *Defence,* snaring him in such intricacies as the medical dangers of circumcision; but he held firm, despite the charges of infidelity, in his claim that "*the Scriptures are not of absolute and universal Inspiration.*"[23] It is this clerical supporter of Moses' expediency and fraud, of secular bases for the central spiritual document of Christendom, and of the individual's duty to pass judgment on Scripture with the aid of reason alone—it is this Conyers Middleton with whom Fielding begins *Shamela.*

The parallels between these attitudes of Middleton's and those with which the Methodists were charged become still

[21] *The Death of M—l—n,* p. 41.

[22] Conyers Middleton, *A Letter to Dr. Waterland; Containing some Remarks on his Vindication of Scripture* (London, 1731), pp. 21, 44–45.

[23] Conyers Middleton, *Some Remarks on a Reply to the Defence of the Letter to Dr. Waterland* (London, 1732), p. 79.

plainer in the light of Whitefield's famous sermon, "The Duty of Searching the Scriptures." There he says: "It is because the natural Veil is not taken off from their Hearts, that so many who pretend to search the Scriptures, yet go no farther than into the bare Letter of them, and continue entire Strangers to the hidden Sense, the Spiritual Meaning, couched under every Parable, and contain'd in almost all the Precepts of the Book of God."[24] Such tossing aside of authority was to lead to eclectic compilations of sound Anglican ideas like Ferdinand Warner's *A System of Divinity and Morality,* leveled against the deriders of the divine origin of Scripture and equally against the Methodists, who "recommend an amorous and enthusiastic sort of devotion," and who "by reasoning about the sense of [Scripture] from their own preconceived opinions . . . make any thing of any thing."[25] Fielding, artist rather than compiler, turned to analogy to illuminate such doffing of authority for personal assertion. He makes us perceive, through Parson Oliver's censure of *Pamela,* the social chaos inherent in [394] disrupting the established places of gentlemen, maids, and curates. He reminds us, through the Dedication, of government by sycophancy rather than by law and merit. And he shows the result, in Parson Williams, of an unrestrained personal interpretation of domestic, social, and religious modes of order.

The prefatory material to *Shamela,* in short, puts at our disposal two analogous spectacles, both satiric. One, which is predominantly political, lets us stare through a diminishing lens at representatives of the English court, clergy, and cultural life. Each turns out to be a prostitute, lowering himself for personal gain, which makes apt the diminution through sexual images and innuendos. Each too turns out to be a false artist, in the works of fact (biographies by Cibber and Middleton) and of imagination (literary efforts by Cibber and Hervey). The other satiric spectacle, the religious, presents us with Methodism on the one hand, rationalism on the other—a Tickletext and a Middleton. Like the objects of political satire, the religious follies

[24] George Whitefield, "The Duty of Searching the Scriptures" (London, 1739), p. 15.

[25] Ferdinand Warner, *A System of Divinity and Morality* (2nd ed.; London, 1756), I, vi.

are egoistic, materialistic, and corrupt both in reading (Whitefield's and Middleton's treatment of Scripture) and in writing (the abuse of words and metaphors). To these satiric views of the social and religious government of England—each containing its own warped version of the social, the religious, and the artistic—Fielding adds the artistic burlesque that is the center of *Shamela*. It—as it stands, and as the fraudulent *Pamela* —corresponds to, and is nominally the occasion for, the Dedication and Tickletext's letter. It therefore contains the same elements: thorough egoism, sexuality, and artistic falsehood (the existence of the cover-up biography called *Pamela*). And it presents a third spectacle that, like the other two, includes social, religious, and artistic spoilage. Fielding does not, of course, make all this so heavyhandedly regular as I am doing, for his genius consisted almost as much in his immense repertoire of relevant tones and emphases, rhetorical gesture and prestidigitation, as in his profound sense of moral correspondences. Those correspondences, however, are there and cannot be blinked.

Fielding's thoroughness in establishing them grows clearer if one looks not only at the analogous patterns, as we have been doing, but also at the parts of *Shamela* in their actual sequence. Viewed this way, the burlesque appears as the translation into action of the principles set forth by Keyber and Tickletext. The [395] way this is true in gross is plain; the way it is true in fine provides constant surprise and pleasure. The very first letter tells us that Shamela's mother solicits in the Drury Lane Theatre ("*the Old House*"), Cibber's stamping-ground; Hervey is paid tribute by the name of her lodging, the Fan and Pepper-Box, which picks up the sexual connotations of "fan(ny)" and adds the appropriate note of venereal disease. The Christian name of Shamela's mother, Henrietta Maria Honora, may mock the highfalutin tone of "Pamela," but probably also refers to the elaborately-named whore Teresia Constantia Phillips, for that lady's *double-entendre* of a nickname, "Con," recalls Fielding's own play on "Conny" in the Dedication.[26] The semi-liter-

[26] The anonymous author ("an Oxford Scholar") of *The Parallel; or Pilkington and Phillips Compared* (London, 1748) says, with some exaggeration, that Mrs. Phillips' "Actions have now employed the Trump of Fame almost thirty Years" (p. 30). Her name was distinctive enough to

acy of Shamela's letter, in this context, leads the mind back to the charges of ignorance and/or malapropism made against the three butts of the Dedication, whose false pretensions are thus tied to those of Richardson's servant girl with her preternatural literacy and learning. Finally, Fielding has Shamela end this first letter with an "*O! How I long to be in the Balconey at the Old House!*" which parodies Pamela's wish to come home "to my old Loft again" (*Pamela*, Letter XVIII). What Shamela has done, and what she does throughout the burlesque with her pious *sententiae*, is to interpret her prototype's cries so as to adapt them to her own circumstances; once more we are back, in an especially delightful way, to the serious belief of Middleton and Whitefield that (as Fielding saw it) the self should be the measure of moral truth.

Since Shamela is so thoroughly ignorant, Parson Williams, the Methodist exegete, takes over the theme of false learning. Her admiration for his scholarship (Letter IX) is betrayed when he describes Booby as having an "*Ingenium Versatile* to every Species of Vice." As Battestin says, "the [Latin] phrase acquires additional ironic point if we recall the original context, Livy's [396] praise of Cato: 'his genius was so equally suited to all things that you would say that whatever he was doing was the one thing for which he was born' (Livy, XXXIX, xl, 5)."[27] If one reads on in Livy, the joke becomes better yet, for the passage as a whole has to do with Cato's probity in the face of governmental corruption and power-seeking. As censor, Cato tried to restore the old morality, especially in purging the senate of one man who had abused his position out of favoritism to his male lover. Not only has Williams chosen a curious phrase to describe Booby, but he has chosen one that also bears rele-

have prompted Fielding's readers to recognize an allusion to it. Honora is close in sense and tone to Constantia; and as for the first names, Henrietta Maria and Theresia, the accession of Maria Theres[i]a in October, 1740, perhaps made Theresia sound regal, so that Fielding matched it six months later with the name of another Catholic Queen, and Englishwoman. Henrietta Maria fit his satire, since she had been involved with the theatre—Pryne had had his ears clipped for accusing her of whoredom after she had acted in private performances—as Fielding might well have known if the Licencing Act drove him to do any research into attacks upon the stage.

[27] Battestin, ed. of *Shamela* and *Joseph Andrews*, p. 369.

vance to the actions as well as the learning of Fanny and Keyber. His other Latin phrase, a claim of a clear conscience when Booby has him jailed for debt (Letter XII), is hardly more fortunate for in the original, Horace's first Epistle of the first book, the poet is telling his patron Maecenas that virtue is better than money. This is no more Williams' position than Horace's relationship with Maecenas, marked by benevolence and gratitude, is Williams' with Booby. Moreover, Horace prefaces the line that Williams quotes with a schoolboy rhyme, the burden of which is that if one is good one will be king. Since Williams' hold on his master has been his vote and its importance for Booby's parliamentary career, the quotation implies blackmail. Once more, the social breadth of the Horatian allusion, the reference to patronage, and the matter of venality tie this piece of false learning to the Dedication.

Sometimes, Fielding maintains continuity by repeating thematic groupings in new guises. For an example, we need go no farther than the references to Booby's Parliamentary ambitions, which have nothing to do with *Pamela* but tighten satiric unity here. Throughout the burlesque, Booby's politics are linked with Shamela's sexual intrigues: because of politics Williams enjoys some degree of impunity as her lover (Letters IX and X, and his poaching for hare—coney—in the last letter) and only Booby's lust for her can override his ambition. In the last letter from Shamela to her mother, this thematic grouping is fixed. Shamela first details her new domestic rule over the uxorious Booby, and then moves on to the analogous matter of "Pollitricks," where she complements the familiar pun on "*et cœtera*" with a fresh one of Booby's "Burrough" (and "burrow")—her *et cœtera* is, as we have grown to expect, a sort of political surrogate. A [397] political dinner follows, during which Williams takes over Booby's place at the head of the table and of the catch-singing borough corporation, just as he had earlier taken Booby's place in Shamela's *et cœtera* and affections. The analogy is insisted upon by Shamela's counter-pointing her description of the dinner by her statements of sexual desire. Finally, before going dissatisfied to bed, she says that the only thing she knows about politics, "that the Court-side are in the right on't," comes from Williams, who therefore usurps her husband's place as political advisor. Structurally, this reaffirmation of the analogy between politics and sex, and between domestic and national government, repeats—and prepares us for a return to—the "realer" world of the Dedication; and thus it is at the end of this letter that Parson Williams steps aside as biographer in favor of Parson Middleton. Or, for a simpler kind of thematic grouping, Shamela's library will do, for it contains, despite its seeming motley, only books about the domains of Middleton, Hervey, and Cibber—religion, politics and the playhouse. It includes a scandalous book about politics, the *New Atlantis;* a book about religious scandal, *Venus in the Cloyster;* and a play, Theobald's *Orpheus and Eurydice*, that Fielding had mentioned in the *Champion* for its varied views of Hell—this, in Shamela's library, directly follows *"God's Dealings with Mr. Whitefield."* [28]

If one accepts the sort of reading of *Shamela* which I have offered, he is left with at least two questions that the reading poses. First, given the wonderful formal skill that Fielding demonstrates, why do we find two seemingly incompatible means of introducing the letters? Second, what relationship does *Shamela* bear to *Pamela?* Both questions are related to the genre of *Shamela,* and also to the rhetorical balance between the framework and the burlesque. In beginning to deal with them, let me once more invoke the example of *Pasquin.* This play seems to draw on the tradition of *The Rehearsal,* but it is really quite different. In *The Rehearsal,* a silly author is mocked for his silly play. In *Pasquin,* though, dreary comedy and tragedy together constitute a social indictment that is both comic and tragic, and in the context of which the incompetence of the two would-be playwrights becomes a general social failure. Observers differing [398] in their wisdom look on at an absurd burlesque, and from both its form and its content draw their moral and artistic indictments. *Shamela,* which picks up the themes of *Pasquin,* also borrows its techniques, with one important change. Since the experiences of Shamela are supposed

[28] Fielding mentions the views of Hell in *Orpheus* in the *Champion* for May 24, 1740. The essay goes on to a Lucianic vision of the Styx which includes a mild censure of Whitefield for his self-righteousness.

to be true, the two outside observers, Keyber and Oliver, must see them independently as two historians. Fielding presents these historians to us in the order that he does, only for formal reasons: Keyber's letter, coming before we know quite what to expect, can be less deliberately germane than Oliver's, and therefore can set up the full range of themes more conveniently; the movement from Keyber to Tickletext to Oliver can follow the pattern of first false and then true ascent from the secular to the spiritual. One may protest the lack of narrative consistency, and the reader who thinks of Fielding as chiefly burlesquing *Pamela* may be nonplussed by it. There is much less problem if one thinks of *Pamela* as a means of localizing and focussing a wide-ranging satire. I do not mean, of course, that *Pamela* is a mere literary bystander struck down in someone else's fracas—Fielding obviously disliked it. But *Shamela* is rather an exploitation than an exposé of its older soberer sister.

Paradoxically, the exploitation may be more devastating to *Pamela* than any exposé. In it, Fielding felt free not only to imitate and exaggerate, as in a close burlesque, but also to depart cheerfully from his text, treating the Richardsonians' tawdry Scripture the way he accused the Methodists of treating the Bible. The theme of Methodism itself is such a departure from *Pamela,* such a false gloss. Another, more involved, has to do with motives. Richardson's fiction turns on the possibility of distinguishing, morally, between conscious and unconscious motives. Fielding's, except where one motive directly undercuts the other (as with rationalization), does not. The Preface to *Joseph Andrews,* for instance, assumes that affectation is a conscious act, or rather, that one can use the language of conscious act for an affectation at any level of consciousness. This is because, in the early 1740's at any rate, Fielding used the ethos of a character as his moral measure. In other words, Fielding calls for judgment in terms of the character's essential nature, from which all his actions, conscious or not, are deduced.[29] Therefore, the hypocrites of *Shamela,* [399] dealt with by Fielding, lack

[29] See John S. Coolidge, "Fielding and 'Conservation of Character'," in *Fielding,* ed. Paulson, p. 160: "the essential reality of a person [in Fielding] is a certain idea which is his nature and to which he has a kind of duty to conform."

that inner life that Richardson valued and cultivated in *Pamela.* We never know when or whether Shamela, or even Parson Williams, sees through Williams' cant, picks up his blunders with the classics, or enjoys the full scope of his ingratitude to Booby. We do not know the balance of loyalties in Mrs. Jewkes. And we do not know how far Conny Keyber is an absurd, and how far a cunning, hypocrite. Such questions are irrelevant, as they would hardly have been if Fielding had felt himself limited to a caricature of *Pamela* alone, with its insistent nagging at moment-by-moment scrutiny of motives. The result of this lack of awareness in *Shamela*'s characters is that, for all their vividness, they are flat and mechanical, like Popean Dunces or Swiftian Hacks. That very flatness offers Richardson an insult more stinging than does their coarseness, their inanity, or their abuse of his affectionate endowments.

Since Fielding did not alter his usual means of characterization to achieve this effect, I assume that its peculiar relevance to Richardson is serendipity, or a wise *laisser faire.* A related effect in *Shamela* is a trust in mechanical principles, and this sort of deadening of the will is carefully developed by Fielding, starting with the Dedication. We have already talked about some of its traces in discussing materialism there, but we can find more, beginning with the very act of parody, which entrusts set forms with the wrong content. In this conception of parody lies the logic of Keyber's final statement of indebtedness as he introduces his parody biography: "The Reader, I believe, easily guesses I mean *Euclid's Elements;* it was *Euclid* who taught me to write." The Editor's eagerness to have fashionable puffs before his book, which leads him to include those dubious ones written by himself and an obvious mercenary, and Tickletext's doting on *Pamela* as a sort of moral amulet, carry this theme through in different ways. So do the barren formulas of cant.

In developing such mechanism, Fielding hits at *Pamela* in two ways. First, he attacks the moral education of Pamela, who infuses the rules of duty with her rising knowledge of the world and its specific trials. For her, the possession of real virtue demands creative and maturing action, so that she grows with her fortunes and can move smoothly from individual concerns before her marriage to social ones after it. Shamela's rules, from her mother and Williams, remain constant and quotable throughout; [400] they are "methods," appropriate for a young Methodist; and until the last sentence of *Shamela,* her faith in cant and a quick hand under the sheets seems to suffice. Secondly, Fielding destroys the uniqueness of Pamela by showing Shamela acting according to formulas. Her analogy with her mother, early established within the burlesque, and with Keyber and Tickletext, reduce her from an exemplar to a type. This is one of the most significant satirical reciprocities that the framework and the text of *Shamela* have, as "the matchless *Shamela*" and the matchless dedicatee diminish each other cumulatively and in retrospect. By this means, the sort of empathy that Pamela had received was further stifled, for empathy depends upon individuality. Fielding makes much in two ways of Richardson's blunder in drawing, as Owen Jenkins has put it, "universal morals from the experience of characters the author has begun by portraying as types but concluded by revealing to be exceptional individuals." [30] By having Oliver object to the lessons of *Pamela,* he counters Richardson on Richardson's moral terms; by reducing Pamela—as Shamela—to a stereotype, working predictably according to the rules of others, he strikes a blow at Richardson's aesthetic achievement and personal affections.

Given Fielding's masterful use of continuity (through analogy) to expose the moral and aesthetic flabbiness of his satiric targets, it may seem especially witty of him to have created a striking effect through a sort of discontinuity within the framework and between the framework and the burlesque. I am thinking of a discontinuity of "realism," or of verisimilitude. The adventures of Shamela are both realistic and preposterous, the one as a corrective to *Pamela* and the other as an exaggeration of *Pamela.* To make us keep both in view, Fielding institutes a range of idioms which replaces the careful verisimilitude adjusted by Richardson. This variety of idioms works around the fixed character of Shamela just as the developing character of Pamela works in terms of a fixed idiom—if they did not, the

[30] Owen Jenkins, "Richardson's *Pamela* and Fielding's 'Vile Forgeries'," *PQ,* XLIV (1965), 203.

technical job of making us see Shamela's absurdity or Pamela's development would be very much complicated. Such a transfer of energies, as it were, makes the world of *Shamela* appear much less real (believable as a version of ours) than that of *Pamela,* although [401] it is crammed with another kind of "realism" (candor) and with *Realpolitik* in a way that Richardson would have thought tasteless. Once more, the framework performs a necessary task. Here the reader is attuned to the conflicting "realisms" in the exceptionally fatuous Dedication, puffs, and letter from Tickletext: as grotesque as they all are, they also demand to be, and can be, closely related to our own world and its realities of fame and power. Furthermore, the reader is attuned at this point to the difference between the framework, which he sees at first-hand, and the burlesque, which is retailed at second-hand; the incompatible perspectives of Keyber's and Oliver's introductions to Shamela's letters, too, not only erect moral watchtowers but also remind one that narrative realism is shaky in *Shamela* as a whole. When we add to this structure of allusions, of foolery, and of incompatibles the letter from Parson Oliver, with its contrasting good sense and genuine-sounding name, we can see that Fielding is inducing us to feel that corruption is somehow not quite real, however present and far from negligible it may be. This feeling is a traditional goal of moral comedy; almost incidentally in achieving it, Fielding splinters the created world of *Pamela.*

Shamela's vartue is at last rewarded: she loses her mother, then her husband, and with the publication of her letters, her reputation as Pamela. It is left up to us to reward the vartue of Middleton, Cibber, Hervey, and *Pamela* along the same lines. The analogical procedure, and the use of satiric targets so clearly exemplary, invite us to see every instance of selfish fraud as behavior less than human, than "real," than uniquely shrewd. To respond in these moral terms is to reward Fielding's virtue, for such a response takes implicitly into account the astonishing formal control with which he handles his matched lampoons, making his effects cumulative and universal. As a schooling for his later fiction, *Shamela* also succeeds impressively; and perhaps the greatest compliment that one can pay it is that one can see Fielding moving plausibly from it, hasty as it is, to the generous and delicate orchestration of *Joseph Andrews.* [402]

from

SOME REFLECTIONS on SATIRE

Patricia Meyer Spacks

It is dangerous to try to specify what a reader's reaction will be to any work of art. There are readers and readers; there are even readers who remain unaffected by Swift's manipulations, who read *A Tale of a Tub* without questioning their own sanity or the standards by which they judge sanity, read the fourth book of *Gulliver* without wondering about their own self-satisfactions. One can only try to specify the effects the work of art seems to demand; and the most important effect demanded by the *Modest Proposal* is profound disturbance, achieved by the development of various levels of uneasiness and complacency.

There is no critical disagreement about the fundamental satiric intent of the *Modest Proposal;* but the idea of uneasiness as a crucial satiric emotion is also useful in leading us to recognize satiric effects where the intent is less clear. A case in point is *Joseph Andrews,* which originated, we are told, in a desire to burlesque the assumptions of *Pamela* but unquestionably turned into more than burlesque. What, exactly, it turned into remains a vexed question. Most critics feel that it is comedy with touches of satire; I would argue that the satiric effect is more complex than is commonly supposed.

It is easy to make a case for this novel as comic—fundamentally sympathetic toward its characters, causing us to love life rather than to criticize it. Fielding's positive values are apparent: honesty, integrity, simplicity, charity. By these values Joseph

Source: Patricia Meyer Spacks, "Some Reflections on Satire," *Genre* 1 (1968), pp. 22–30. Reprinted by permission of the editors of *Genre.*

and Parson Adams are successful throughout. They are frequently ridiculous by ordinary social standards, but if we judge by such superficial standards we only demonstrate our own corruption. Their simplicity makes them seem foolish in a sophisticated and corrupt world, but their dignity survives, as in the episode where Adams is mauled by dogs and mocked by men, yet remains at all points the clear moral superior of his tormentors. Fielding recognizes the imperfectibility of human nature; he gives his characters flaws, causes them to demonstrate their weaknesses, but he loves their humanity. He responds to the comedy of pretension; as he says himself, his main concern here is "affectation" in all its forms. But although Beau Didapper or Parson Trulliber may suffer the full force of satiric condemnation, the enveloping tone of the novel is benign; human affairs work out at the end in a way which suggests that the universe itself is benign; like classic comedies, the novel ends with a marriage.

This description does not, however, account for the complicated feelings which the novel is likely to generate in its readers. In the first chapter of Book III, Fielding remarks, "I describe not men, but [22] manners; not an individual, but a species." As an example he uses the lawyer in the stage coach who argues for an act of charity on the grounds of self-interest. Such men, Fielding says, have always existed. This lawyer should not be taken as a portrait of any specific living person: It would do him "little honour to imagine he endeavours to mimic some little obscure fellow, because he happens to resemble him in one particular feature, or perhaps in his profession; whereas his appearance in the world is calculated for much more general and noble purposes; not to expose one pitiful wretch to the small and contemptible circle of his acquaintance; but to hold the glass to thousands in their closets, that they may contemplate their deformity, and endeavour to reduce it, and thus by suffering private mortification may avoid public shame. This places the boundary between, and distinguishes the satirist from the libeller: for the former privately corrects the fault for the benefit of the person, like a parent; the latter publicly exposes the person himself, as an example to others, like an executioner."

The distinction Fielding here makes between the private effect of satire and the public one of libel resembles that between uneasiness, the response to recognition of one's own flaws ("private mortification"), and complacency, the response to the evil of others. In fact, the characterization of the lawyer in the coach would seem more likely to produce the second response. It belongs to a group of characterizations in the novel which have been generally recognized as satiric in their broad strokes of caricature and their systematic presentation of social types. Such characterizations, although they are acute in their social observation, do not examine individual springs of action. Sometimes a sentence suffices to reveal a man. The famous coach scene provides abundant examples. First the postilion suggests that there is a "dead man" groaning in the ditch:

> "Go on, sirrah," says the coachman; "we are confounded late, and have no time to look after dead men." A lady, who heard what the postilion said, and likewise heard the groan, called eagerly to the coachman to stop and see what was the matter. Upon which he bid the postilion alight, and look into the ditch. He did so, and returned, "That there was a man sitting upright as naked as ever he was born." — "O J-sus!" cried the lady; "a naked man! Dear coachman, drive on and leave him." Upon this the gentlemen got out of the coach; and Joseph [23] begged them to have mercy upon him: for that he had been robbed, and almost beaten to death. "Robbed!" cries an old gentleman: "let us make all the haste imaginable, or we shall be robbed too."

The lawyer then points out that they might be in legal jeopardy if they fled after noticing the man's existence; they should rescue him for fear of what a jury might find. The lady remarks that "she had rather stay in that place to all eternity than ride with a naked man." The coachman wants to know who will pay a shilling for Joseph's carriage; the lawyer threatens him with an indictment for murder if he refuses to carry the young man; the old gentleman decides that "the naked man would afford him frequent opportunities of showing his wit to the lady," and the various arguments of self-interest finally combine to effect Joseph's rescue.

Fielding feels no need for direct authorial comment on these bits of action and dialogue; they are self-sufficiently revealing, their meaning depending on their conjunction as well as on the facts of each individual case. Only the lady seems controlled by that principle of affectation which Fielding has declared to be his central issue; the others, confronted with the Biblical situation of a naked man in a ditch, reveal without disguise their limited and selfish concerns; the satiric bite and focus are inescapable.

When Joseph begins to function in relation to this group, he is their clear moral superior, though the satirist's eye turns on him, too. "Joseph was now advancing to the coach, where, seeing the lady, who held the sticks of her fan before her eyes, he absolutely refused, miserable as he was, to enter, unless he was furnished with sufficient covering to prevent giving the least offence to decency. So perfectly modest was this young man; such mighty effects had the spotless example of the amiable Pamela, and the excellent sermons of Mr. Adams, wrought upon him." The riders in the coach act and speak by their conceptions of their social roles. The coachman worries about his fees and his schedule, the lady about her modesty, the lawyer thinks only of his profession. The old gentleman considers himself first as a man of wealth, later as a man of wit. Joseph, in contrast, governs himself by moral rather than social principles. He is manifestly less corrupt than his social superiors; he thinks about others rather than only about himself (although one may speculate that his ultimate concern is with his own "self-image"); yet his is hardly less ridiculous than the lady whose modesty he fears to offend. Perfect modesty is a virtue, by Fielding's standards and [24] even by ours. Yet to place its value before that of life itself seems misguided, and Fielding's invocation of "the spotless example of the amiable Pamela" at this point suggests his ironic awareness of the fact.

In another context such an episode might be taken as sheer comedy rather than satire, an amusing perception of the common weakness of mortals with no serious intent of criticism. But in this novel it functions as one of many episodes of the same kind, and the total structure makes a satiric network which involves the reader, forces him to self-examination in the privacy of his closet, however different he may be in all obvious respects from Joseph and Parson Adams at one extreme, from Beau Didapper at the other. Over and over *Joseph Andrews* calls our attention to people's deep conviction of their own rightness. Much of the comedy of the early scenes come from the tension between Lady Booby's unshakable self-confidence ("Have you the assurance to pretend, that when a lady demeans her self to throw aside the rules of decency, in order to honour you with the highest favour in her power, your virtue should resist her inclination?") and Joseph's equally unshakable confidence in the importance of his own virtue ("I can't see why her having no virtue should be a reason against my having any"; I.viii). The narrowest and pettiest of mortals believe that the laws by which they govern themselves are immutable principles: Parson Trulliber, Beau Didapper, Lawyer Scout, the practical jokers who set upon Adams and attack Fanny's virtue. Parson Adams, most large-spirited of men, has a similar conviction: so he alienates the generous host of the inn by stubbornly opposing theory to fact, insisting that "a skilful physiognomist will rarely be deceived" (II.xvii) in the face of his own deception by the owner of a kindly face. So he preaches fortitude under distress, but is quite unable to practise it. Joseph refusing Lady Booby or refusing to ride in the coach is similarly governed by theory rather than awareness of actuality. The difference between the "good" and the "bad" characters is that in the knaves, bad theory produces bad practice; when Joseph and Adams fill the satiric role of fools, it is because their good theories are inadequate to their complex experience. The good theory that men should be chaste makes Joseph insensitive, tactless and priggish in speech, but he refuses Lady Booby's advances; the related theory that modesty is vital makes him act foolishly in placing feminine sensibilities before survival. The good theory that Christians should be patient in distress makes Parson Adams talk rather than act when Fanny's virtue is endangered; it helps him not at all in his own brief bereavement. [25] But foolish or wise, practical or impractical, vicious or virtuous, every character in the novel retains an unalterable belief in the justice of his own principles, perceptions and actions. Lady Booby finds in herself a conflict of principles, her belief in the importance of rank and wealth clashing with her belief in her right to self-indulgence, but she really questions neither, although she pays lip-service to "virtue."

Lady Booby's talk of virtue ("How much more exquisite is the pleasure resulting from the reflection of virtue and prudence than the faint relish of what flows from vice and folly! Whither did I suffer this improper, this mad passion to hurry me, only by neglecting to summon the aids of reason to my assistance?" IV.xiii) exemplifies another theme and technique of the novel, closely related to its moral considerations. Fielding repeatedly calls attention to his own language or to that of his characters to dramatize the gap which may exist between language and substance, form and content. Lady Booby prating of virtue is thinking of lust; she adopts the language of the heroine of a sentimental novel or tragedy to disguise even to herself her true feelings and concerns. The dichotomy between tone and substance is yet more conspicuous in the mock-heroic sections where Fielding treats mundane affairs in epic vein; at the opposite extreme, he offers a commonplace explanation of his practice of dividing his work into books and chapters: "it becomes an author generally to divide a book, as it does a butcher to join his meat, for such assistance is of great help to both the reader and the carver" (II.i). Sometimes the two techniques co-exist: an elaborate satiric panegyric to Vanity precedes a down-to-earth disclaimer: "I know thou wilt think that, whilst I abuse thee, I court thee, and that thy love hath inspired me to write this sarcastical panegyric on thee; but thou are deceived: I value thee not of a farthing; nor will it give me any pain if thou shouldst prevail on the reader to censure this digression as arrant nonsense; for know, to thy confusion, that I have introduced thee for no other purpose than to lengthen out a short chapter; and so I return to my history" (I.xv). The effect is constantly to violate expectation—a comic effect but, in this case, a satiric one as well. If, as I believe, the satiric center of the novel is the human tendency to be sure of oneself in exactly the situations where one should doubt, Fielding's repeated demonstration that language is not a safe guide to meaning—but that men (and women) treat it as though they could impose meaning at will on their experience—participates in the satiric statement. "The question is, which is to be master," as Humpty Dumpty remarked in another satiric work [26] centrally concerned with language. On one level, Lawyer Scout manipulates language to make the law conform to the desires of his patroness; Lady Booby uses language to conceal reality; Mrs. Slipslop in her Malapropisms dramatizes the arbitrariness of linguistic impositions. On another level, the novelist himself plays with linguistic modes to demonstrate the lack of necessary relation between form and content. On a more profound level still, the reader finds himself involved in the problem of certainty. Like the characters, he wants to be sure of meanings; unlike them, he has had his attention called to the gulfs beneath his feet. The cavalier fashion in which comedy resolves its problems, creating infinite complications, unraveling them with scant regard to probability, becomes itself part of the satiric meaning. In a universe full of arbitrary events, where the most pious theory is inadequate to the demands of experience, where can sureness be found? Fielding's answer, of course, is that one can be sure of the value of virtue in action. Honesty, integrity, simplicity, charity, the positive values of this satire, provide the only security as they are exemplified in practice. But the human need to locate sureness in theory finds no answer in Fielding's universe. And one's uneasiness at being forced to recognize this fact, and to recognize one's own participation in the fruitless human attempt to assert more certainty than exists, is the satiric response.

It is not an intense or agonized response; uneasiness can be a gentle, almost a subliminal, emotion. Inasmuch as Fielding's satire involves Joseph and Parson Adams and finally the reader, it is gentle satire, close to the line of comedy. (Contrast the relative satiric intensity of the presentation of Mrs. Tow-wouse or Lawyer Scout.) But gentle satire is still satire, and mild uneasiness still uneasiness, as Pope pointed out in a letter concerned with *The Rape of the Lock,* most gentle of satires: "This whimsical piece of work, as I have now brought it up to my first design, is at once the most a satire and the most inoffensive, of anything of mine. People who would rather it were let alone laugh at it, and seem heartily merry, at the same time that they are uneasy. 'Tis a sort of writing very like tickling."[1]. . . [27]

[1] Letter to Mrs. or Miss Marriot, 28 February (1713/14), *The Correspondence of Alexander Pope*, ed. George Sherburn (Oxford, 1956), I.211.

RICHARDSON'S *PAMELA* and FIELDING'S *JOSEPH ANDREWS*

Douglas Brooks

WHY Fielding should have written two replies to *Pamela*—*Shamela* and *Joseph Andrews*—has puzzled critics ever since *Shamela* was proved to be by him. The chronology of literary events 1740–2 helps, however, to illuminate our understanding of the relationship between Fielding and *Pamela*. *I Pamela* was published in November, 1740; *Shamela* appeared in April, 1741; *II Pamela* was published in December, 1741 (though it was in the press as early as August),[1] and *Joseph Andrews* followed in February, 1742. *Shamela* parodies *I Pamela*, and *II Pamela*, in its turn, answers at length the objections raised in *Shamela*.[2] We have the beginning of a sequence here, and it seems logical to assume that *Joseph Andrews* completed the sequence. I hope to show in the rest of this essay that *Joseph Andrews* contains as much, if not more, of *Pamela*—*I* and *II*—as it does of its avowed model, *Don Quixote*. Fielding has virtually finished with parody (Joseph's two letters in Book I are not stylistic parodies like those in *Shamela*) and written his own

Source: Douglas Brooks, "Richardson's *Pamela* and Fielding's *Joseph Andrews*," *Essays in Criticism* 17 (1967), pp. 158–67. The Critical Forum, "*Pamela* and *Joseph Andrews*," objection by A. M. Kearney and rebuttal by Douglas Brooks, *Essays in Criticism* 18 (1968), 105–107, 348–349.

[1] See A. D. McKillop, *Samuel Richardson, Printer and Novelist* (Chapel Hill, 1936), pp. 51–54, 57.

[2] This has been shown conclusively by Owen Jenkins, "Richardson's *Pamela* and Fielding's 'Vile Forgeries,'" *Philological Quarterly*, 44 (1965), 200–210.

novel. It is a deliberate *imitation* of *Pamela,* though, because Fielding is showing Richardson how to write. The two novels—the bourgeois *Pamela* and its aristocratic 'imitation'—are structural and temperamental comments on each other.

The traditional view of *Joseph Andrews*'s indebtedness to *Pamela* has been conveniently summarised by Maynard Mack, in his introduction to the Rinehart *Joseph Andrews* (1948): Joseph, unlike Pamela, refuses to better himself by his virtue; Fanny, like Pamela, is often the object of sexual assault, and so on. But it goes much deeper than this. For one thing, the time-scheme of *Joseph Andrews* parallels that of *I Pamela* up to Pamela's marriage (in fact, it lags slightly behind it): in I, vi Joseph writes: ' "*Dear Sister,* SINCE I received your Letter of your good Lady's Death, we have had [158] a Misfortune of the same kind in our Family . . ." ' (quotations from first edition), and near the end (IV, iv), shortly before Joseph and Fanny are married, the marriage between Pamela and Mr. Booby is so recent that Lady Booby is surprised to hear of it. Finally, Joseph and Fanny are married in Mr. Booby's parish church, with Joseph 'drest . . . in a neat, but plain Suit of Mr. *Booby*'s which exactly fitted him,' and Fanny 'in nothing richer than a white Dimity Night-Gown' (IV, xvi). This is a manifest re-enactment of the wedding in *I Pamela,* for which Pamela had worn 'a rich white Satten Night-gown' (ii, 140 of Shakespeare Head edition, 1929, as all later references).

Joseph's role is thus a dual one: in his chastity, his retention of his virtue despite the onslaughts of Lady Booby and Slipslop, he reminds us of Pamela. But because he marries Fanny he is also (and more importantly) Fielding's version of Richardson's Mr. B.—that is why Booby's clothes fit him exactly. And it accounts too, I think, for the hint of irony we get in Fielding's treatment of Joseph in his resistance to Lady Booby: this is surely reminiscent of the bashful Mr. B. who, despite his stratagems, always fails, at the last moment, to take sexual advantage of Pamela. Fielding certainly seized on this in *Shamela*—Mrs. Jewkes remarks with surprise on Booby's 'parting so easily from the Blessing when [he] was so near it' (references to Augustan Reprint edition, 1956; p. 32).

It has already been noted that the wedding of Fanny and Joseph parallels that of Pamela and Mr. B. In fact, the latter couple are present at the wedding in *Joseph Andrews* IV, xvi and, significantly, they laugh and have to be rebuked by Adams. They laugh, surely, because they recognise in the ceremony going on before them a reflection, with a difference, of their own wedding: Joseph and Fanny embody values which (according to Fielding's reading of *Pamela*) Mr. B. and Pamela do not subscribe to. Their laughter is a rejection of the morality of Fielding's novel. So what we get, with Joseph writing to Pamela at the beginning and Pamela and her husband appearing in person at the end, is a framework effect akin to that in *The Taming of the Shrew* or Gay's *The What d'Ye Call It* (1715): *Pamela* [159] 'frames' *Joseph Andrews*, which mimes its action in turn. The appearance of Mr. Booby and Pamela so that, through their laughter, they can comment on the action they have been observing, is analogous to the comments of the 'frame' characters on the play going on before them in *The Taming of the Shrew*.

But just to what extent does *Joseph Andrews* reflect *Pamela*? I would suggest that the clothes imagery which permeates it is meant to remind the reader of Richardson's novel. As an analogue to the incident of Booby's clothes fitting Joseph—a symbolic equation of Joseph with Booby as a gentleman—there is the episode in *Pamela* where Mr. Andrews, Pamela's father, is dressed in one of Mr. B.'s suits, which 'fitted him very well' (ii, 99). The symbolism is identical. And *Joseph Andrews* IV, xvi, where the undressed Fanny appears in part as the traditional Naked Truth, again has its origins in *Pamela*. The Fielding passage reads:

> She was soon undrest; for she had no Jewels to deposite in their Caskets, nor fine Laces to fold with the nicest Exactness. Undressing to her was properly discovering, not putting off Ornaments: For as all her Charms were the Gifts of Nature, she could divest herself of none.

This recalls *Pamela* where Mr. B. says:

> . . . they will perceive you owe nothing to Dress, but make a much better Figure with your own native Stock of Loveliness,

> than the greatest Ladies, array'd in the most splendid Attire, and adorn'd with the most glittering Jewels. (ii, 42)

It also recalls the second prefatory letter: 'When modest Beauty seeks to hide itself by casting off the *Pride* of *Ornament*, it but displays itself without a *Covering* . . .' (i, p. xvi). This is quoted verbatim in *Shamela*, p. 2.

Lady Booby's psychomachy (I, ix, IV, i), her emotional conflict over Joseph, which Fielding treats at a distance through comic use of personification, originates in the ludicrous indecisiveness of Mr. B. over Pamela, e.g.:

> Mrs. *Jervis*, said he, take the little Witch from me; I [160] can neither *bear*, nor *forbear* her! (Strange Words these!)—But stay; you shan't go!—Yet begone!—No, come back again. (i, 71)

And even Mrs. Slipslop has her prototype in Mrs. Jewkes. The latter

> is a broad, squat, pursy, *fat Thing*, quite ugly, if anything human can be so call'd; about Forty Years old. She has a huge Hand, and an Arm as thick as my Waist, I believe. Her Nose is flat and crooked, and her Brows grow down over her Eyes; a dead, spiteful, grey, goggling Eye, to be sure she has. And her Face is flat and broad; and as to Colour, looks like as if it had been pickled a Month in Saltpetre . . . She has a hoarse, manlike Voice. . . . (i, 151)

Here is Fielding's description of Slipslop:

> She was an antient Maiden Gentlewoman of about Forty-five Years of Age. . . . She was not at this time remarkably handsome; being very short, and rather too corpulent in Body, and somewhat red, with the Addition of Pimples in the Face. Her Nose was likewise rather too large, and her Eyes too little; nor did she resemble a Cow so much in her Breath, as in two brown Globes which she carried before her. . . . (I, vi)

In little this is the difference between Richardson and Fielding that Dr. Johnson expressed so well. There is considerable power in the *Pamela* passage, but it is largely a psychological one: Pamela is afraid of the woman, and hence the excessive reliance on adjectives. There is little colour—'grey', 'pickled a Month in Saltpetre'—only an overriding impression of size ('broad', 'squat', 'huge') and malevolence ('spiteful'). In this context repetition ('Her Nose is flat. . . . And her Face is flat . . .') adds to the effect. The technique is cumulative and oblique: Mrs. Jewkes is not called an animal overtly. Instead we are told on several occasions that she 'waddles'.

The aristocratic temperament of Fielding was not one to cavil at calling a woman a cow, though, and Slipslop is essentially comic. She too is manlike—but we only discover [161] this when Adams, feeling her beard, mistakes her for a man in IV, xiv. The comedy is derived from perfect control of syntax, and a delicate use of periphrasis: contrast the effect of 'rather too corpulent in Body' with the two monosyllabic blows of '*fat Thing*'. And yet Fielding's use of personification and comic control—means of distancing, of avoiding the intense subjectivity of Richardson—does not mean that *Joseph Andrews* lacks the psychological depth of *Pamela.* On the contrary. It is interesting to note, for instance, that the function of some of the mock-epic similes is, in part, to fulfil for *Joseph Andrews* the role of the dream symbol passages in *Pamela*—e.g. that of the bulls (i, 205). (Ian Watt, *The Rise of the Novel,* ch. vii, is good on the symbolism of the unconscious in Richardson.) There is no need to quote Freud and Jung to confirm the sexual significance of

> . . . As when a hungry Tygress, who long had traversed the Woods in fruitless search, sees within the Reach of her Claws a Lamb, she prepares to leap on her Prey; or as a voracious Pike, of immense Size, surveys through the liquid Element a Roach or Gudgeon which cannot escape her Jaws, opens them wide to swallow the little Fish: so did Mrs. *Slipslop* prepare to lay her violent amorous Hands on the poor *Joseph.* . . . (I, vi)

Interestingly too, Joseph is a lamb here—traditional symbol of innocence. Fanny is also a lamb under similar circumstances in III, ix. I suspect that this was suggested by *I Pamela,* where Pamela is several times called 'lamb' or 'lambkin.' The following passage is particularly relevant: 'So, Mrs. *Jewkes,* said he, you are the Wolf, I the Vultur, and this the poor harmless Lamb, on her Trial before us . . .' (i, 251). As confirmation of a definite reminiscence of Richardson here, we have only to remember that Pamela calls Mrs. Jewkes a 'still more inhuman Tygress' (i, 240).

Fielding understood perfectly what Richardson was up to: it was his method and technique he disagreed with. Fielding, as a typical Augustan, was aware of, embarrassed by, the depths of the human psyche as Richardson was not. Even as late as the sentimental *Amelia* (1751) Fielding makes Atkinson's symbolic dream (IX, vi)—reminiscent of *Clarissa* [162] and ultimately of Shakespeare's *Rape of Lucrece*—dissolve in comedy: blood turns out to be cherry-brandy. It would probably be true to say that Fielding clowns most when he is nearest the complexities of human passions, emotions, and motives.

To Pamela in her period of persecution the world is predatory, peopled with animals: Mrs. Jewkes waddles, she imagines bulls, and Colbrand 'has great staring Eyes, like the Bull's that frighten'd me so . . .'. We note his implied lupine qualities: 'a monstrous wide Mouth; blubber Lips; long yellow Teeth . . .' (i, 225). All this occurs during Pamela's imprisonment which lasts, significantly, forty days and nights, and is a period of temptation (see M. Kinkead-Weekes's introduction to the Everyman *Pamela,* 1962). Pamela's temptations are mainly those of despair—thoughts of suicide, and so on—but her world is full of hostile animals because that is the world of the Christian saints. We recall the traditional embodiment of the Seven Deadly Sins in animal form, and that the last great allegory in the tradition, *The Pilgrim's Progress,* had been written not so very long before *Pamela.* Now this is also the world of *Joseph Andrews,* though seen in comic epic terms. The Biblical base is there—Joseph and Abraham travelling through strange countries to their homeland—and so, in comic (almost burlesque) form, are the hostile animals: Slipslop, Trulliber, Didapper, etc. We note, in passing, that in Book I Joseph encounters a 'lion' and a 'dragon'—both in the form of inns! While it is possible to regard *Pamela* and *Joseph Andrews* as independently drawing on this tradition, therefore, it seems more plausible to regard Fielding's novel in this respect (as in others) as an extrovert and comic version of Pamela's subjective vision, her projection of her fears into a 'real' world.

The climactic bedroom scene (IV, xiv) has been seen as deriving from *I Don Quixote* III, ii, and the style of the scene certainly supports this. It has not been noticed, though, that it is also a comic metamorphosis of the bedroom scene in *I Pamela* (i, 277 ff.): there Mr. B., disguised as a maid, gets into bed with Pamela, intending to rape her with Mrs. Jewkes' assistance. He abandons his intention when Pamela [163] faints. Two days later he tells her, in an interview: 'I know not, I declare, beyond this lovely Bosom, your Sex . . .' (282). In the *Joseph Andrews* episode Adams initially gets involved in bed with Slipslop and Didapper, mistaking her for a man and Didapper for a woman (recalling the disguise of Mr. B. as a woman, and the manlike Mrs. Jewkes). Mrs. Slipslop's roar, '"O thou Villain! who hast attacked my Chastity, and I believe ruined me in my Sleep . . ."', is an unequivocal comic reminder of Pamela's fears in the same situation. (But Slipslop really *wants* sexual intercourse, despite her protests to the contrary for appearance's sake. Fielding is hinting here at the supposed ambivalence in Pamela's attitude to Mr. B.) Then, his second big mistake of the night, Adams goes to bed with Fanny. This is discovered by Joseph in the morning, and Adams protests to him, recalling Mr. B.: '"As I am a Christian, I know not whether she is a Man or Woman"'. (Parodied in *Shamela*, p. 16). In addition, Joseph's question '"Hath he offered any Rudeness to you?"' seems to recall a moment in the *Pamela* scene when Mr. B. 'most solemnly, and with a bitter Imprecation, vow'd, that he had not offer'd the least Indecency . . .' (279).

Another echo is Mr. Booby's offer to Adams of a ride in his coach when he, Fanny, and Joseph see him crossing a field (IV, v). This recalls a similar situation concerning Mr. B., Pamela, and Parson Williams (ii, 87 ff.), but it has come via *Shamela*, where Williams is caught poaching hares, accepts a ride in Booby's coach, and discourses to Shamela on the difference between the flesh and the spirit (pp. 44–7). This recollection confirms the idea, held by Saintsbury and others, that Adams is Fielding's alternative to Williams. And the fact that Adams's chastity is 'tested' several times in *Joseph Andrews* is an additional reminder that Fielding always suspected Williams of having some directly sexual interest in Pamela. The hint found in Richardson's novel was fully developed in *Shamela,* to be transferred to Adams in *Joseph Andrews.* But it seems to me that the difference between Adams and Williams is to be explained not so much in moral terms (Richardson's Williams, before Fielding got to work on him in *Shamela,* was, after all, a respectable enough young man) as in literary terms. It is as a *literary* [164] creation that Fielding is offering us Adams; and as such the reader contrasts him with the Parson Williams of *Pamela.*

In *Joseph Andrews* IV, vii Mr. Booby tries to dissuade Joseph from marrying Fanny, and is seconded by Pamela:

> 'Brother,' said *Pamela,* 'Mr. *Booby* advises you as a Friend; and, no doubt, my Papa and Mamma will be of his Opinion, and will have great reason to be angry with you for destroying what his Goodness hath done, and throwing down our Family again, after he hath raised it.'

Fielding thus imputes snobbery to Pamela, and this passage, in conjunction with a later one when Fanny has been proved to be her real sister (IV, xvi), clearly recalls Lady Davers' initial hostility to Pamela, which expresses itself in a dislike of her low birth, its effect on her family, and a refusal to call her 'sister': 'Tell me, said my Lady. What, in the Name of Impudence, possesses thee, to *dare* to look upon thyself as *my* Sister?' (ii, 206). Lady Davers is not reconciled to Pamela until p. 279, and the sister theme continues well into vols. iii and iv. Indeed, Pamela's delight in being called 'sister' by Lady Davers ('I—HUMBLE *I*—who never had a Sister before,—To find one now in *Lady* DAVERS!' (iv, 34)) becomes quite monotonous, and is hardly likely to have escaped Fielding's sharp wit. So what he has done in *Joseph Andrews*—a superb comic twist—is to equate Pamela with the snobbish Lady Davers, leaving Fanny to stand as his unscheming and innocent alternative to Richardson's heroine.

So far examples have been taken only from *I Pamela* (and they have by no means exhausted the parallels). Fielding recalls it so extensively because he believed that Pamela's story really finished with her marriage to Mr. B.—this is why *Joseph Andrews* ends with a wedding, and why Fielding ends his novel with a jesting allusion to *Pamela*'s continuation. To Fielding *II Pamela* seemed an artistic failure: it might well justify the morality of Part I, but this was no artistic *raison d'être*. Structurally *II Pamela* falls very flat indeed, ending up as a series of essays on various topics with no real narrative thread. The reader's boredom is not helped [165] by Pamela's oft-repeated apologies—'I hope, Miss, you will forgive me for being so tedious . . .' (iii, 303).

It is as an alternative to this general flabbiness that *Joseph Andrews* appears to have been written. And since *II Pamela* was apparently completed by August, 1741 and Fielding's novel was not begun until the autumn of the same year, it is quite possible that Fielding could have been aware of the contents of Richardson's continuation. In *Joseph Andrews* Fielding therefore included, within the framework of the narrative of *I Pamela* (i.e., the events up to, and including, the marriage), virtually all the topics that occupy Richardson in *II Pamela*.

As A. D. McKillop suggested long ago (*Samuel Richardson*, p. 76), Fielding's Parson Adams could well have got his name from the Parson Adams in *II Pamela*. Pamela refers to a parson's being 'subject not seldom to the Jests of Buffoons and Rakes at a great Man's Table . . .' (iii, 289). Is this recalled by Fielding in Adams's disastrous meal with the 'roasting squire' (III, vii)? Pamela talks in detail about pluralism (iii, 270–96); is it coincidence that Fielding's Parson Adams is involved in the same problem at the end of *Joseph Andrews* (IV, xvi)?

It seems that Pamela's tedious discourse on the condition of the clergy, with which Fielding the moralist would have agreed, was too much for Fielding the novelist. He showed Richardson how this kind of thing should be done by including in *Joseph Andrews* at strategic points comments and incidents which, by the end of the novel, form for the reader a comprehensive picture of the condition of the mid-eighteenth-century clergy. Fielding is illustrating the art of the novelist as opposed to that of the moral essayist.

The beginning of vol. iv sees Pamela in London, and we are subjected to her detailed criticisms of plays and opera (pp. 58–93). *Joseph Andrews* I, iv shows us Joseph in London visiting play- and opera-houses. Even more to the point, III, x, which at first seems so irrelevant to the novel as a whole, is, we note, '*A Discourse between the Poet and Player*': this again, surely, refers in part to Pamela's lengthy excursions into the realms of literary criticism. The fact that the rest of the chapter-title reads '*of no other Use in this History, but to divert the Reader*' is all part of the jest. [166]

Much of vol. iv, however, is devoted to Pamela's comments on Locke's *Treatise on Education*. Pamela sees as practicable the method of teaching the young in a small school, where a master can look to the 'Morals and Breeding . . . as well as . . . Learning' of his pupils (317); she discusses corporal punishment (342 ff.), and agrees with Locke that ' ". . . Virtue, and a well-temper'd Soul, is to be preferr'd to any sort of *Learning* or *Language* . . ." ' (357). Fielding has reduced this discussion to manageable proportions in *Joseph Andrews* III, v, '*A Disputation on Schools* . . .'. Adams runs a small school like the one recommended by Pamela; he discusses corporal punishment; and he too asks: ' "What is all the Learning of the World compared to [a boy's] immortal Soul?" '

Finally, one wonders whether Mr. B.'s account of his reasons for marrying Pamela, which includes a survey of his 'rake's progress' and concludes with an acknowledgement of his reformation by Pamela (iii, 185–212), may not be reflected in the interpolated Wilson history, *Joseph Andrews* III, iii: Wilson's rakery admittedly goes much further than Mr. B.'s, but like Mr. B. he is reformed by marrying a beautiful woman, Harriet Hearty. And the similarity between Harriet, Fanny, and Pamela—in their beauty, their readiness to blush, etc.—is too obvious to rehearse here. (Is it worth mentioning, though, that a card-playing Colonel Wilson who 'passes his Time mostly in Town' appears in *II Pamela* (iv, 436)? Wilson is, after all, a common enough name.)

Joseph Andrews should not be read, or interpreted, in terms of *Pamela*—it has a meaning and structure of its own. But the aim of this essay (though without recounting all the similarities and ending up as a catalogue) has been to show that in writing *Joseph Andrews* Fielding was, in fact, rewriting *Pamela* in his own mode. In its structural symmetry, its comic approach to the psychological, its themes (the town/country antithesis is virtually absent from *Pamela* whereas it is central to *Joseph Andrews*)—indeed, in all respects—Fielding's novel stands as a symbol of Augustanism, opposed to *Pamela*, the real voice of the future. [167]

OBJECTIONS BY A. M. KEARNEY

IN his article on *Pamela* and *Joseph Andrews* (*Essays in Criticism*, April 1967), Mr. Brooks draws some very interesting parallels between the two novels, but surely some of them are a little too ingenious. When we are told, for example, that Joseph is Fielding's 'version of Richardson's Mr. B.' (159) on the evidence that Booby's clothes exactly fit him and because his resistance to Lady Booby's seductions is reminiscent of the 'bashful' (Mr. Brooks' word) Mr. B's failure to break down Pamela's defences, credulity is severely strained. Joseph is to be married and has to borrow a suit from Booby. Fielding is at pains at this point in the story to stress the happy solemnity of the occasion and to exclude that element of grotesquerie which has been the mainstay of the novel so far. Very well, Joseph must be dressed accordingly and in a fashion befitting his new-found gentlemanly status. As for the second point, the comparison between Joseph's behaviour and Mr. B's at the moment of seduction, I must confess I'm completely baffled. Joseph may be 'bashful', but Mr. B.? Surely not. Pamela owes her escape not to any shortcomings in the matter on Mr. B's part, but to her own quick-wittedness and 'happy knack' of falling into fits.

Mr. Brooks in search of further parallels, also calls attention to the basic similarity between Slipslop and Mrs. Jewkes. But is there really any evidence to suggest that Fielding had Mrs. Jewkes in mind when he drew Slipslop? As his other novels show, Fielding was perfectly capable of producing his own caricatures, and indeed had a predilection for grotesque predatory characters that obviously owed nothing to Richardson. To be sure, as Mr. Brooks points out both Fielding and Richardson use the word 'tygress' to describe their characteristics, but this seems to me neither here nor there. If we are bent on proving the point by equally flimsy evidence, why not insist on the parallel between Fielding's 'voracious pike' describing Slipslop, and the angling incident in *Pamela,* I, 115 (Everyman ed.) where Pamela thinks of herself as the baited carp about to be hooked? [105]

We are also told that the climactic bedroom scene in *Joseph Andrews,* while similar in form to the famous episode in *Don Quixote,* is also a 'comic metamorphosis' (163) of the scene in *Pamela* where Mr. B. disguises himself as a maid in order to slip into bed with Pamela. Mr. Brooks writes (164), 'Adams initially gets involved in bed with Slipslop and Didapper, mistaking her for a man and Didapper for a woman (recalling the disguise of Mr. B. as a woman, and the manlike Mrs. Jewkes)'. But Adams' muddling of the sexes of Slipslop and Didapper is simply a traditional comic device and in no way reminiscent of the incident in *Pamela.* Moreover, if we really wanted to make anything of the comparison, we would have to equate Didapper (who came to Slipslop's bed thinking it was Fanny's) with Mr. B., have Slipslop play the combined roles of Mrs. Jewkes and Pamela, and leave Adams out of it altogether.

No one would deny, of course, that Fielding had *Pamela* closely in mind whilst he was writing *Joseph Andrews;* the whole tenor of his argument is anti-Pamela. At the same time, it seems highly unlikely that he wrote with *Pamela* (so to speak) open at his side as Mr. Brooks seems to imply; his own interests took him in another direction. Indeed, Fielding's turn of mind made it almost inevitable that his fiction would produce contradictory echoes of Richardson's novels, but in a manner which does not necessarily imply that he had Richardson constantly in mind. For example, Honour's remark in *Tom Jones,* Bk. 7, Ch. 7, 'one's virtue is a dear thing, especially to us poor servants; for it is our livelihood, as a body may say', might well be interpreted as another crack at *Pamela;* but in the general context of Fielding's novels it can be seen as a piece of banter the validity of which has nothing to do with Richardson. The trouble is, once we start thinking of Richardson when we are reading Fielding, we find it difficult to resist the temptation to view the whole corpus of Fielding's work as a comment upon the *Pamela* morality.

Perhaps the most disturbing thing however about Mr. Brooks' essay is his thesis that Fielding was handing out some kind of lesson to Richardson. This emerges from remarks [106] like: 'Fielding is showing Richardson how to write' (158), 'Fielding understood perfectly what Richardson was up to' (162), and 'He (Fielding) showed Richardson how this kind of thing should be done . . .' (166). In fact, it seems fairly certain that Fielding did *not* understand what Richardson was up to; that Richardson was in reality attempting a different kind of fiction from himself—a fact which ultimately makes Fielding's parodies irrelevant. When Mr. Brooks subscribes to the view therefore that Fielding was 'illustrating the art of the novelist' (166) to his rival, I feel sure that he is on the wrong tack. I also doubt very much if Fielding would have seen it in this way. [107]

REBUTTAL BY DOUGLAS BROOKS

I found Mr. Kearney's remarks interesting but unconvincing.

1. It is generally agreed that Fanny's 'white Dimity Night-Gown' recalls Pamela's wedding dress, and marks Fanny out as being Fielding's version of Richardson's heroine. I fail to see how Mr. Kearney can logically object to my suggestion that Joseph's clothes work in the same way, especially when Fielding stresses the symbolism: they 'exactly fitted him'. (If you wear a man's clothes you identify yourself with him—Cloten and Posthumus in *Cymbeline;* Sue and Jude in *Jude the Obscure.*)

'Bashful', by the way, isn't my word; it is Fielding's, and comes from Shamela's letter (vi) containing the burlesque of the Mrs. Jewkes-Pamela-Mr. B. bedroom episode which is the subject of my remark (*'O what a silly Fellow is a bashful young Lover!'*).

2. Slipslop and Mrs. Jewkes still seem to me remarkably close, though of course I admit that Fielding wasn't solely indebted to Richardson 'for grotesque predatory characters'. However—and my memory may well be at fault—I don't recall such an extended portrait of this type in Fielding's other novels. For even Bridget and Mrs. Partridge (*Tom Jones* I, xi and II. iii) are described only by allusion to Hogarth, and the character who comes closest to Slipslop in the Fielding canon is Mrs. Tow-wouse (significantly, in *Joseph Andrews* again (I. xiv)). Which, if I am right, reinforces my original point.

As to the other matter, Mr. Kearney is surely aware that I am concerned with the close juxtaposition of both tigress *and* lamb in the two novels, and that the weight of my argument falls on the latter animal rather than the former. I am puzzled, therefore, by his concentration on the tigress.

3. I shouldn't have thought the readers of *E in C* needed reminding that the mixups in IV. xiv are 'a traditional comic device'. And I stand by my assertion that they are 'a comic metamorphosis' of the *Pamela* bedroom scene. Why else should Fielding have concluded his chapter with [348] two echoes of that same episode in Richardson's novel (p. 164 of my original article), echoes which Mr. Kearney presumably accepts, since he doesn't quibble over them in his reply?

4. I nowhere imply that Fielding 'wrote with *Pamela* (so to speak) open at his side'. What I *do* imply is that Fielding had read *Pamela* thoroughly, and that he had a retentive memory. This seems to be confirmed, for example, by his habit of profuse quotation from the classics. Does Mr. Kearney think that Pope wrote *The Rape of the Lock* with Homer, Virgil, and Milton 'open at his side'?

5. I remain unrepentant over my 'thesis that Fielding was handing out some kind of lesson to Richardson'. Obviously Fielding was aware 'that Richardson was . . . attempting a different kind of fiction from himself'—and he didn't like the result. So that he embodied *Pamela* in an Augustan structure (book divisions, symmetry, epic allusions, etc.) to show it up,

as it were, just as Pope embodied the dunces and their degradation in the Augustan edifice of *The Dunciad*. To the Augustan, Form symbolized Order; and I have a feeling that Fielding saw in Richardson a manifestation of some at least of the tendencies that provoked Pope's satire. In short, 'Fielding is showing Richardson how to write'.

DOUGLAS BROOKS [349]

A CHRONOLOGICAL OUTLINE

1707	April 22, Fielding born, probably at grandfather's estate, Sharpham Park, Somersetshire.
1709–19	Childhood in village of East Stour, Dorsetshire.
1719–24	Education at Eton.
1727	Probably comes up to London, in the fall.
1728	January 29, first publication: *The Masquerade,* a verse satire by "Lemuel Gulliver."
	February 16, first play produced: *Love in Several Masques.*
	March 16, matriculates at the University of Leyden.
1729	Returns to London in the fall.
1730–37	Becomes the leading playwright of the period, until the Theatrical Licensing Act, of June 21, shuts him from the stage.
1734	November 28, elopes with Charlotte Craddock of Salisbury.
1736	April 27, daughter Charlotte born.
1737	June 21, Licensing Act passed.
	Daughter Harriot born, day and month unrecorded.
	November 1, begins studying law at the Middle Temple.

1739 November 15, begins editing *The Champion* for the anti-Walpole party, three issues weekly.

1740 June 20, qualified to practice law, begins riding the Western Circuit.

November 6, Richardson's *Pamela* appears.

1741 April 2, *Shamela* published.

June, resigns from *The Champion.*

1742 February 22, *Joseph Andrews* published.

March 9, burial of his daughter Charlotte.

1743 April 12, publishes his *Miscellanies,* a gathering of unpublished poems and prose, including two plays and *Jonathan Wild,* with the intent of concluding his literary career.

1744 November 14, burial of his wife, Charlotte.

1745 November 5, edits *The True Patriot,* a newspaper directed against the Jacobite Rebellion of Prince Charles Edward Stuart.

1746 June 17, concludes *The True Patriot.*

1747 November 27, marries Mary Daniel, a servant of the first Mrs. Fielding, who was to bear him five children.

December 5, edits *The Jacobite's Journal,* his second anti-Jacobite newspaper.

1748 October 25, commissioned Justice of the Peace for Westminster, London, later to become magistrate also for the adjoining county of Middlesex, London.

November 5, concludes *The Jacobite's Journal.*

1749 February 28, *Tom Jones* published.

1751 December 19, *Amelia* published.

1752 January 4 to November 25, edits *The Covent-Garden Journal.*

1754 May, resigns his magistry because of illness.

June 26 to August 7, his voyage to Lisbon where, on his doctor's advice, he hoped to save his life by a change of climate. His *Journal* of this voyage appeared posthumously in 1755.

October 8, Fielding dies at Lisbon, where he is buried.

SELECTED BIBLIOGRAPHY

BASIC REFERENCES

Blanchard, Frederic T. *Fielding the Novelist: A Study in Historical Criticism*. New Haven: Yale University Press, 1926.

Butt, John. *Fielding*. Writers and Their Work, no. 57. London: Longmans, Green & Co., 1954.

Cross, Wilbur L. *The History of Henry Fielding*. 3 vols. New Haven: Yale University Press, 1918.

Digeon, Aurélien. *Les Romans de Fielding*. Paris: Libraire Hachette, 1923. Translated as *The Novels of Fielding*. London: George Routledge & Sons, Ltd., 1925.

OTHER CRITICISM

Alter, Robert. *Fielding and the Nature of the Novel*. Cambridge, Mass.: Harvard University Press, 1968.

Baker, Ernest A. *The History of the English Novel*. London: H. F. & G. Witherby, 1930; reprinted New York: Barnes & Noble, 1950. vol. IV, ch. 4.

Baker, Sheridan, ed. *An Apology for the Life of Mrs. Shamela Andrews*. Berkeley: University of California Press, 1953. Introduction.

Battestin, Martin, ed. *Joseph Andrews*. The Wesleyan Edition. Middletown: Wesleyan University Press, 1967. Introduction.

———, ed. *Joseph Andrews and Shamela*. Riverside Editions. Boston: Houghton Mifflin Co., 1961. Introduction.

———. *The Moral Basis of Fielding's Art: A Study of Joseph Andrews*. Middletown: Wesleyan University Press, 1959.

Boyce, Benjamin, Introduction, *The Comical Romance* by Paul Scarron, translated by Tom Brown. New York: Benjamin Blom, Inc., 1967.

Goldberg, Homer. *The Art of Joseph Andrews*. Chicago: University of Chicago Press, 1969. But see qualifying review by Sheridan Baker in *College English* 32 (1971): 817–22.

Golden, Morris. *Fielding's Moral Psychology*. Amherst: University of Massachusetts Press, 1966.

Hatfield, Glenn W. *Henry Fielding and the Language of Irony*. Chicago: University of Chicago Press, 1968.

Johnson, Maurice. *Fielding's Art of Fiction*. Philadelphia: University of Pennsylvania Press, 1961.

Kermode, Frank. "Richardson and Fielding." *Cambridge Journal* 4 (1950):106–14.

Kettle, Arnold. *An Introduction to the English Novel*. London: Hutchinson & Co., Ltd., 1951; reprinted New York: Harper & Row, 1960. vol. I, pt. II, sec. iv.

Mack, Maynard, ed. *Joseph Andrews*. Rinehart Editions. New York: Holt, Rinehart & Winston, 1948. Introduction.

McKillop, Alan D. *The Early Masters of English Fiction*. Lawrence, Kansas: University of Kansas Press, 1956. ch. 3.

Paulson, Ronald. *Satire in the Novel in Eighteenth-Century England*. New Haven: Yale University Press, 1967.

Price, Martin. *To the Palace of Wisdom*. Garden City: Doubleday & Co., 1964.

Sacks, Sheldon. *Fiction and the Shape of Belief*. Berkeley: University of California Press, 1964.

Woods, Charles B. "Fielding and the Authorship of *Shamela*." *Philological Quarterly* 25 (1946):248–72.

Wright, Andrew. *Henry Fielding, Mask and Feast*. Berkeley: University of California Press, 1965.